# What the critics have said about Veronica Sattler's *THE BARGAIN*

"Veronica Sattler . . . transports readers into a Cinderella story filled with Regency charm and sizzling sensuality . . . the best gothic-ending since *Ashes in the Wind* . . ."

—*Romantic Times*

"Veronica Sattler's *The Bargain* takes historical romance right back to the entertainment magic and excellence that generated a multimillion dollar industry."

—Anne Wassall, Hearst Cablevision

". . . an intricate love story, written exquisitely . . . Veronica Sattler has created a real winner. . . . It's superb!"

—*Affaire de Coeur*

Dear Reader,

Harlequin Historicals would like to introduce you to a new concept. Big books! Beginning with October, we will be publishing one longer title a month with books that will include everything from popular reprints to originals from your favorite authors.

Our first longer title, *The Bargain,* by Veronica Sattler is a sexy historical set during the Regency period. It's the story of Lord Brett Westmont and Ashleigh Sinclair, two people who are thrown together in a series of compromising positions, only to fall madly in love.

In *Tapestry,* by author Sally Cheney, heroine Dandre Collin discovers that the rough mill worker who rescues her from a runaway carriage is really her uncle's aristocratic neighbor.

An ex-masterspy grows bored with his forced retirement and winds up creating more mischief than he can handle by taking a wife in *The Gilded Lion,* a sensual tale from Kit Gardner.

Finally, author Louisa Rawlings returns to France as the setting for *Scarlet Woman,* an intriguing story of murder and revenge.

We hope you enjoy all four of this month's titles.

And next month, be on the lookout for the long awaited reissue of *Pieces of Sky* by Marianne Willman, the unforgettable story of a spinster who marries the cruel Abner Slade but finds true love in the arms of Roger Le Beau, her husband's sworn enemy.

Sincerely,

Tracy Farrell
Senior Editor

# Prologue

*Kent, England, 1795*

"Your parents are dead, boy, as is your brother, and you have yet to utter a word at their passing. Now I am asking you, what do you have to say for yourself in the matter?"

Ten-year-old Brett Westmont raised heavily lashed, startling turquoise eyes to meet the keen regard of his grandfather as he stood before him in the library at Ravensford Hall. The boy's small, square jaw was firmly set and gave no evidence of the quaking turmoil that had been threatening to break loose from a place deep within his small yet sturdy frame; he had been fighting to hold it in check for the past forty-eight hours, ever since he'd received news of the accident.

Leveling his gaze at the old man, Brett broke the silence in a clear, strong voice that did nothing to betray his chaotic feelings. "Only one parent, Grandfather, and the brother, a half brother, though I loved him well."

John Westmont, eighth duke of Ravensford, drew heavy, iron-gray brows over a pair of piercing blue eyes that endeavored to pin the boy to the carpet. Rising slowly from behind the carved-oak Georgian desk where he'd been seated, the duke drew himself up to his full six feet, three inches, and frowned disapprovingly at his grandson for several long seconds. "Boy, you are being impertinent! I requested your reaction to a senseless tragedy, not a nitpicking digression on the family tree!"

The turquoise gaze never faltered. "There was no impertinence intended, sir. I merely wished to point out that it was only one of my natural parents who was killed in the accident. My true mother—"

*"Silence!"* thundered the duke. "How *dare* you invoke the name of a person who ceased to exist for this household from the moment she left, over seven years ago? Have you forgotten my orders forbidding all mention of that female? A woman whose perfidy and betrayal could only result in her being branded and dismissed as the harlot she was? A woman who compounded the sin of her faithlessness to your father by then deserting both him and you—and you a child not yet out of the nursery? Well, boy, answer me!"

"No, sir," came the steady reply. "I've not forgotten." How could he forget, when every trace of the woman who was his mother had been removed from these halls, wiped away as if she'd never existed? When all his questions about her had been met by stony silence or the anguished look in his father's eyes? When the name, Mary, Viscountess Westmont, was forbidden from his lips while he went about yearning for some words that might put to rest his confusion, impart some sense to the tales he'd heard whispered. He had failed to reconcile those rumors with faint but persistent memories of warm, loving arms and—

"A terrible and senseless tragedy," the duke was saying, "and once again, a woman's fault. It was your stepmother, Lady Caroline, who brought them to this end. It was only after he married her that Edward began his profligate ways."

"John, can you not spare your censure at such a time? I—I cannot bear it. It is, moreover, not fitting to speak ill of the dead!"

It was only now that young Brett realized he and his grandfather were not alone. Looking toward the deepest of the shadows reaching across the far end of the richly appointed room in the fading autumn light, the boy perceived the tall, ramrod-straight form of his great-aunt, Lady Margaret, twin sister to the old duke, as she moved closer to the desk.

Her brother turned a disdainful profile to Brett as he coldly met the gaze of his twin. "I am not in the habit of being reminded of anything remiss in my behavior, Margaret. If you wish to continue to be privy to this interview—though why you would wish it is beyond me—you will refrain from interrupting. As for my castigation of the dead, let me simply say this—for the boy's benefit as well as your own: My son and his second wife were a pair of besotted fools!''

Ignoring the gasp of outrage that broke from his sister's throat, the duke continued. "It is no secret that they were blind drunk when they left the hunt party and appropriated the carriage that carried them and their young son to their deaths. Old Henry tells me it was Edward himself who wrested the reins away from the driver and insisted on driving the ill-fated vehicle at a breakneck speed; left the befuddled man in the dust on the drive as he whipped my finest pair of matched bays into a frenzy and took off for God-knows-where, with his still-tippling wife and their son in tow. Aye, and there's the real pity—that they had to drag young Linley with them! Who's to say if that faulty axle wouldn't have spared them a fatal end, if the carriage had been driven more sanely? Or at least have spared the life of that innocent child!''

The duke paused for a moment, and Brett thought he saw a flicker of pain cross his grandfather's face before the blue eyes shuttered and his anger returned in full force.

"Drunken fools, both of them, swilling and gambling their way from one drawing room to another, up to London and back again, in a continuing orgy of self-indulgence that made me ashamed to call Edward mine! And, say what you will, Margaret, you cannot deny that, on Edward's part at least, this unconscionable behavior began almost from the day he wed Caroline Hastings—a marriage, may I remind you, dear sister, that *you* arranged!''

"John, you cannot blame—''

"I can, and I *do*!'' spat the duke, glowering at his twin. "Caroline Hastings was a worthless piece of trash, no matter how fine her lineage and title. But, then—'' the duke smiled thinly ''—what else could one expect? She was—'' he returned his gaze to Brett ''—after all, a *female*. Remember that, boy. Your life will fare far better if you never let yourself forget—as

I shall take pains to see you are never *allowed* to forget—that *women* are the major source of evil in this world."

"Evil! Really, John," interrupted his sister, "I cannot allow—"

"Cannot allow? *Allow?* Woman, *I* shall decide what is allowed here! And I remind you for the final time that it is only through my sufferance that you are presently allowed in this chamber!"

The duke turned his attention back to Brett. Bracing his hands on the desk top before him, he bent forward and lowered his voice, the blue eyes piercing as they bored into the boy. "It was a woman every time, Brett. First, there was my mother, insisting on educating my twin sister here in much the same manner as I was educated, giving her unsuitable notions with regard to her place in life. Why, there were times in our childhood when I was hard put to remember Margaret was a girl!" He gave his sister a sneering half smile. "Isn't that so, Sister? And, being the elder twin by some fifteen minutes, didn't you chafe under the restrictions of the laws of primogeniture that gave the dukedom to me, the younger, simply because I was the firstborn *male*?"

Again a gasp broke from Margaret's lips, but this time it was followed by angry words. "I'll not listen to any more of this rubbish, John!" she snapped, striding toward the door. "Do with the child as you like. I wash my hands of the matter!" And with a swish of skirts, she was gone.

The duke stared momentarily at the door she had shut in her wake, then turned his attention back to his grandson. "You see, Brett? As I've said, *women*—they're a bad lot, always breeding strife and trouble. Latch onto this, boy—" the old man leaned forward almost conspiratorially "—women are good for only one thing, and that's breeding *sons*!"

He took a moment to search Brett's unwavering gaze, satisfying himself that he still had his undivided attention. "I particularly fault your grandmother, my own duchess. She managed to interfere in the rearing of your father, Edward, to such an extent and in such a manner, that he was a spoiled weakling from the outset. Coddled him, she did, despite my protests, and what were the results? First, he went off and wed that, that foreigner, and an unsuitable bluestocking to boot—a female whose subsequent behavior speaks for itself. A love match, they told me when the pair of them were found at Gretna Green after my weeks of searching!"

The duke pushed himself back from the desk and let his eyes roam carefully over the still figure of his grandson. "Believe me, boy, you were the only worthwhile thing to come out of that union," he said quietly.

Suddenly he turned his head sharply and focused on the door through which his twin had gone. "But *she* could not allow matters to rest there, could she? Oh, no, *she* had to interfere and arrange a second marriage, this time with one of her beloved Hastingses! 'Lady Caroline has the best of credentials,'" he mimicked. "'She will at last make a proper match for Edward.' *Bah!*" He took a backward step and fell into the chair behind the desk, suddenly looking, Brett thought, every minute of his fifty-nine years. "A proper enough match, that is, to lead him to an early grave!" he muttered. Then his voice grew faintly tremulous, and Brett caught a slight quivering of the old man's lower lip.

*Grandfather's hurting, just like me!* young Brett suddenly realized. *He merely pretends he is unaffected—also like me!*

"And," the duke was saying, "I find it difficult to forgive Edward for having the monstrous indecency to take the life of an innocent two year's child along with his own and that of his worthless wife!"

*In an unsafe carriage that was intended for me!* thought Brett, a shiver running through him as he recalled, not for the first time during the past two days, that the vehicle was to take him to Eton to begin his first term at the public school where he'd been registered since birth.

As if reading his thoughts, the duke's expression suddenly changed to one of speculative assessment. "I suggest you cease troubling yourself with the kind of debilitating guilt that comes of thinking your family died in your place, my boy. As one who has lived enough years to gain some wisdom, I tell you it is all a matter of accepting what was meant to be. Clearly, your death was not in the present scheme of things, while *theirs* was. Think no more on it. Do you understand me, Brett?"

The boy's turquoise eyes regarded the now tired-looking blue ones for several silent seconds before he responded in a voice that rang of stoical resignation. "Yes, Grandfather."

"Good. Then all that remains is for me to tell you of the changes these unfortunate events have wrought in my future plans for you."

Watching a flicker of interest enter the boy's eyes, John paused for a moment. *He's sharp as a whip,* he mused, *and mature beyond his years...and almost too beautiful for a boy, with that sculpted face, and thick chestnut hair... Well, all the more reason to arm him well against...them!*

"Brett, I have decided not to send you away to school after all." Pausing again to make sure the statement had sunk in, and perceiving no reaction beyond alert interest on the boy's part, John continued. "Public schools like Eton and Harrow do well enough in turning boys into men, I suppose, but after watching the muddle your father made of his life despite such an education, I've decided to modify yours somewhat. You have, of course, the advantage of the absence of meddling females, your Great-Aunt Margaret aside. She's never liked you much, has she, boy? Ah, well, more to the better! No loss there, believe me!

"Now, as I was saying, I've changed my plans. You see, I wish to take no chances on preparing you, my only heir... now...to take your place at the helm of the powerful dukedom you will one day inherit. My priority in this is to make a formidable man of you, Brett—a man whom no one will dare take charge of, least of all, a *woman*!

"The education you are about to receive will afford you every advantage in a world where advantage is everything. And, by advantage, I do not merely mean that of birth or wealth. These things you already have, and although they will serve you well, *you must be carefully armed against the pitfalls and weaknesses that can attend them!*

"It has long been my belief that a man is off to a good start if he is brought up on a regime of Spartan living and strenuous raining in the manly arts, enhanced by an assiduously followed academic program that tests the limits of his intelligence. If this is coupled with unrelenting instruction in the almost forgotten art of being a gentleman of high moral fiber, and accompanied by an inquiring mind never given to swallowing things whole simply because others put them forth as true, then a man cannot help but succeed in this life. . . ." Here the duke leaned forward in his chair, his blue eyes keen as they searched his grandson's face. "At least," he continued, "given the high native intelligence and inherent nobility of character I have already observed in you, Brett.

"Therefore I have decided to begin you on this course by sending you to sea for the next two years."

The duke noticed Brett's eyes widen slightly at this news, but, seeing no further reaction, he hurried on. "You will serve as cabin boy on one of my friends' oceangoing vessels, under the guidance of Captain Joshua Stockton, a fair but exacting master. In that position you'll be given no privilege or special treatment because of your title. Indeed, other than Captain Stockton, no one on board will have any inkling of your status, and you will be known simply as Brett Westmont, cabin boy. You will be expected to work hard and to earn your keep by that labor. Over the course of your two-year stint, I shall be receiving regular reports from Captain Stockton as to your progress, and I expect them to be excellent. Is that clear?"

Brett's young voice answered without wavering. "Yes, Grandfather."

"The only exception to what would be the normal routine for a cabin boy is that a private tutor will accompany you on board, and any free time you have will be taken up with an intensified program of studies such as you might have encountered at Eton. To put the crew and officers off the scent, Captain Stockton has agreed to hire another cabin boy from hereabouts, and it will be given out that *he* is the younger son of some nobleman, or perhaps a wealthy merchant, who wishes his son's experience at sea to be enhanced by academic studies, and that *you* are merely being included because you will be sharing quarters with him. We wish no hint of special privilege to attend *you*!

"When you return from sea, your education will continue here at Ravensford Hall. You will receive further academic tutoring as well as training in the things with which you already have experience—riding, shooting, fencing and the like—but you will also receive intensive instruction in estate management, commerce and the law.

"Eventually you will attend university—Cambridge, surely—and by the time you come down, I shall expect you will have read both history and law, for your present tutor seems to think you have a genuine natural aptitude for those, and having sat in on some of your sessions with him, I'm inclined to agree."

There was a moment's pause, and then the duke added, "Finally, I wish to reiterate the main goal of this plan. It will free you temporarily from one of the most contaminating aspects of our society, that weight on man's shoulders—*woman*!"

At last the duke fell silent, and for the first time since he had begun this discourse, Brett saw him relax his posture; his face softened, bearing that hint of a smile.

He continued speaking in a somewhat subdued tone. "I fear I have come across rather harshly, boy, and that has not been my intent. Rather, it is precisely because I have inordinately high hopes for you, and because I—" the duke's voice faltered and grew yet softer, and Brett beheld a rare infusion of warmth fill the blue eyes "—because I love you, dear Brett. Can you comprehend that, and will you accept what I have planned, courageously and with good grace?"

The boy's eyes met those of his grandfather with a look of understanding that went far beyond his years. Whether he did indeed at that moment comprehend the entirety of what was in store for him, he would many times ponder it in the years to come. But what he did understand was that this gruff, severe old man had always *loved him*—deeply and without reserve.

Brett reached deep within himself for the strength he knew he would need and resolved to put grief aside. His beloved yet weak father was gone; weeping would not bring him back. The mother he had yearned for was equally lost and apparently not orth seeking out, for he would no longer dare to question his randfather's words about her; to do so would risk losing him s well—the last person on earth who truly cared about him.

And so, with a resolute forward thrust of his chin and a shake f his chestnut curls, he answered the duke. "Yes, Grandfaher...I understand, and I accept."

# Chapter One

*London, April 26, 1814*

Wiping the perspiration from her brow with her forearm Ashleigh Sinclair bent again to her task. Sweeping out the cinders from the hearth in the drawing room was one of her earliest chores—one that had to be done at dawn, even before she'd be allowed to have breakfast; Madame detested the lingering scent of a dead fire, one that could soon permeate the room in this kind of damp weather. But the task always made her feel so dirty! Straightening for a moment over her char broom, Ashleigh moved her slim, delicate hand unthinkingly to the small of her back before she whisked it away at the last moment, thankful she'd remembered in time to avoid soiling her plain gray servant's dress, patched though it was. Then, heaving a brief sigh, she reached for the dustpan and prepared to scoop the last of the cinders and ashes into the dustbin at her feet.

Suddenly she heard a shuffling sound out in the hallway and whirled around to see what it might be. She knew it was rare to encounter any of Madame's girls about at this hour, but the nastiest among them, Monica, occasionally prowled about in the early morning, usually in search of a powder for one of her fearsome headaches, especially if she'd been drinking too much wine with one of her "gentlemen" the night before.

But then the appearance of a great shaggy head in the doorway prompted Ashleigh's sigh of relief as she recognized Finn, "the huge wolf dog of Ireland," as Megan termed him, and whom Ashleigh loved perhaps better than any creature on earth.

"Finn! What are you doing out here?" she gently chided as the great beast made his way toward her with a glad wagging of his long, slightly curved tail. "Don't you know they'll have both our hides if they catch you?"

But as Ashleigh spoke to the dog, her deep sapphire-blue eyes shone with delight, giving the lie to her scolding, and she accepted a loving lick of the dog's tongue on her cheek. Dropping her broom on the hearth, she encircled the big beast's neck with a pair of slender arms and gave him a fond hug. The embrace required little bending on her part, owing not only to Finn's majestic size but to Ashleigh's own diminutive stature. She was nearly nineteen years of age and had long ago given up hope of adding any height to her present five feet and *almost* two inches.

Now, as she fondly scratched the shaggy gray head of the dog she had rescued from the cruelties of a gang of street toughs almost a year ago, Ashleigh smiled as she considered how Finn had grown since that rainy night. Her thoughts flew back to the scene she'd encountered in the alleyway behind Madame's town house, where she'd surreptitiously set out a pan of milk for some of the stray, starveling neighborhood cats.

A series of half-muffled guffaws and then a burst of malicious laughter had drawn her attention to the far end of the alley where she spotted four shabbily clothed youths bent over a dark form on the ground, busily attending to it in some manner. As it had been dark in the alley, with only the dim light of some upper windows from an adjacent building affording any visibility, she had cautiously stepped closer to try to see what was afoot. She hadn't liked the nasty sound of that laughter!

Then she had spied a fifth youth, as ill-kempt and ragged as the rest, endeavoring to loop a length of rope over the support for a rainspout several feet above his head. She had just seen him accomplish this end when her eyes had caught sight of a similar rope hanging from the side of the opposite building that abutted the alleyway. And, there, dangling from the end of it, its poor neck broken, hung one of the stray cats she'd intended the pan of milk for!

Fighting the raw bile that rose in her throat at the ghastly sight, Ashleigh had forced herself to take a few more tentative steps forward when she heard the boy with the rope snigger and say to the others, "Truss 'im up neatly, blokes. 'E'll swing a might better'n 'at scruffy cat!" It was then that she had seen what the dark form lying on the ground was. As the four accomplices stepped away from it, apparently satisfied they'd accomplished their task, she had made out the shape of a bony, wet and miserably bedraggled pup, its feet and muzzle securely bound with additional pieces of rope. It lay in a puddle of water at their feet, abject in its misery, helplessly writhing against its bonds. Then, as she'd heard a pathetic, muffled whimper from its throat, Ashleigh had known what she must do.

Throwing caution to the wind, she reached into the deep pocket of her serving apron where she'd stashed the kitchen knife she'd been using prior to escaping to the alleyway with her gift of milk. Thrusting it out before her as a weapon, just as Megan had taught her, she advanced upon the young hangmen with a dangerous gleam in her blue eyes. "The first one to lay a hand on that pup is dead!" she'd heard herself say. Five pairs of surprised eyes had suddenly focused on her as she advanced in their direction with all the fury of an avenging angel.

Spying the glint of metal in her hand and the professional manner in which she wielded the knife, slowly arcing it before her in a no-nonsense fashion, three of the youths had begun to back away from the object of their cruelty, but a fourth had apparently decided to stand his ground, while the one with the rope gave her a menacing sneer. "Blimey, an' wot 'ave we 'ere? It's a meddlin' kitchen wench fancies 'erself a reg'lar member o' the King's Guard, she does!" Suddenly he'd reached forward and given a shove to the shoulder of the youth who remained near the pup, a mean-faced beggar of about twelve or thirteen, with dirty red hair. "Take care of 'er, Jake!"

A sinister smile had crossed the redhead's face, and he'd taken a bold stride in Ashleigh's direction. Assessing the situation in a split second, Ashleigh had become aware of several things at once. The three who seemed to be less bold, had retreated to a spot a good dozen feet from the others and had seemed content to wait to see what might happen; the one with the rope had bent over the dog and begun fashioning a noose about its neck; and the one named Jake was advancing toward her with a confident swagger. Remembering Megan's admonitions to try to remain on the offensive, even in self-defense, and realizing she had not a moment to waste, Ashleigh had concentrated on the plight of the poor animal lying in the puddle nearby, using the image as a rallying point to summon all her fury and its attendant courage. Suddenly she'd felt an enormous surge of strength flow through her slender form, and with it, the conviction that she was invincible. With a feline snarl, she'd lunged at the redhead, her knife a blur of movement in the shadows. The small weapon made contact with the youth's hand, which had been extended, apparently with the intent of disarming her, and Ashleigh had seen a look of surprise cross his features before he'd snatched his bleeding appendage toward his chest and given forth with a howl of pain.

But Ashleigh hadn't stopped at that. Capitalizing on her advantage, she'd wielded her blade a second time, bringing it perilously close to Jake's face. It was enough for the boy; pivoting on his heel, he had stumbled and then begun to run toward the cronies who had backed away, muttering a series of choice expletives as he ran.

Then Ashleigh had whirled to face the youth with the rope. Seeing he still held onto the noose, which was now around the unfortunate dog's neck, she had lunged forward with the idea of severing the rope before it could do its dirty work. But the young tough, believing she meant to slice the hands that held it, had dropped the rope instantly, a disbelieving look on his face. "Bloody 'ell!" he'd exclaimed as he'd felt the blade stirring the air when it passed close to his hand. Then, leaping away from both dog and furious female with a fearful look, he'd turned toward his fellows and bolted, shouting, "Run for it, blokes! She's a bloodthirsty bitch, she is, an' balmy as Bedlam, too!"

But his comrades were already out of sight by then, and in seconds, Ashleigh had seen the last of him as well. She saw to the poor creature on the ground, untying its bonds, running her fingers carefully over its emaciated frame to ascertain whether it had suffered further harm and, finding none, gently scooped it up into her arms, all the while crooning to the pup in soothing tones to assure it of her kind intentions.

Later, when she'd carried him inside to be warmed and fed by the fire, Dorcas, the cook, had admonished her, saying, "Ye foolish gel, did ye not consider yer own welfare? An injured 'r frightened beast could've turned on ye out o' sheer terror o' bein' hurt further. 'Tis a wonder the poor thing did ye no harm!"

But Ashleigh had merely smiled, remembering Finn's intelligent, soulful eyes on her as she'd released his bonds and carried him inside, wrapped in her apron. If gratitude and instantaneous love had a name, it would be Finn, from the moment his eyes had met hers out there in that alley.

Now, as all these things ran through her head, she gazed lovingly at her canine friend while giving the shaggy head a few strokes. The dog hardly resembled the starved and frightened pup she'd rescued last spring. Well fed from all the scraps that found their way through Dorcas's kitchen, and tall—over thirty inches at the shoulder—he had a clean, healthy coat and an air of robust power about him, always carrying himself like some proud king of Ireland. In fact, Megan had suggested she name him Cormac, after a particular favorite of hers from history, an Irish king from the fourth century, but when Megan had told Ashleigh some of the tales of early Celtic literature in which Cormac figured, it was always the parts about Cormac's legendary master of hounds, Finn, that had captured her imagination.

Suddenly a noise at the doorway drew Ashleigh's attention back to the present. She looked up to see Monica standing there in her night rail, an angry, accusing expression on her face. At the same moment she felt the hackles rise on Finn's coat, a low, warning growl rumbling from his throat.

"So, you've brought that disgusting creature into the house again!" Monica hissed. "You wretched, ungrateful child! How dare you disobey Madame's orders!"

Ashleigh straightened, clutching her fingers about Finn's collar as she watched the tall blonde approach. "I—I didn't disobey, Monica," she attempted. "Finn just followed—"

"Shut up, you little beggar!" the blond woman snapped. Then, as if the sound of her own voice were too much to bear, she stopped and brought both hands to her temples. "Oh, now look what you've gone and done! *Oh*, my head!"

Seizing her opportunity, Ashleigh released her hold on Finn's collar and silently signaled him back to the kitchen. The dog looked for a split second as if he were about to resist, but then quickly obeyed his mistress, albeit not without a low, parting growl for Monica's benefit.

"Now, Monica," said Ashleigh quickly, "why don't you let me fetch you something for that headache? Dorcas was just telling me she received a packet of some new type of powder that works wonders in no time at all—got it from that seaman friend of hers when he came calling last week." She reached out and placed a comforting hand on Monica's arm, steering her out of the chamber.

"Hmm, yes, that does sound promising," said the tall woman, much soothed by the prospect of being rid of the hammering in her head. "Perhaps I shall try—"

Just then, Monica chanced to look down at Ashleigh as they walked toward the door, and she suddenly spied the sooty imprint of the younger woman's hand on the snowy white cambric sleeve of her best night rail. "Oh! Look what you've done to my new— Oh, you clumsy bitch!" And with an angry shriek, she raised her arm and struck Ashleigh smartly across the face.

Ashleigh reeled from the unexpected blow, although later she was to tell herself that she had been careless not to anticipate something of the sort from the blonde. Monica's behavior, especially when she had one of her headaches, was at best unpredictable, but beyond this, Madame's most popular whore, queen bee of the fashionable stable on St. James's, had always been less than kindly toward Ashleigh. Recently, she had been positively hostile, although Ashleigh was at a loss to figure out why. Even now, as she felt the sting of tears assault her eyes and bit her lip to keep from crying, she asked herself what she had ever done to earn the beautiful courtesan's enmity. What she could not know was that, like all persons who measure their entire personal worth by their looks, Monica felt deeply threatened by those around her who might provide competition in that arena, and she regarded Ashleigh as just such a threat.

It hadn't mattered that, at the time they'd met, some three-and-a-half years ago, Ashleigh had been a stick-thin, under-developed fifteen-year-old kitchen menial who worked solely below stairs to earn her keep. Even then, the fragile, almost ethereal beauty of the youngster's heart-shaped face had been apparent. With its perfect, exquisitely proportioned features, porcelain-smooth creamy complexion (the tiny mole high on her right cheek in no way marring it), and a pair of huge sapphire-blue eyes, clear and wide set, framed by the thickest of long, silky jet lashes that matched a natural abundance of shiny black hair, it was a face that caused anyone to look twice, and then again, in total wonder at its perfection.

And now, with the advent of womanhood providing a softly curving, blossoming body, evident even beneath the dowdy servant's clothes the girl wore, she was becoming a more formidable threat every day in the blond woman's eyes. Moreover, Madame had not allowed these changes in Ashleigh's appearance to escape her watchful eye. Monica had overheard her commenting on the girl's growing potential to Drake, her sometime butler, sometime procurer, just the other day. And it did not signify that Dorcas, when she had been informed by Drake of Madame's interest, had hotly defended her young charge's right to remain an innocent and angrily sent the man from her kitchen with a fiercely wielded rolling pin. Monica knew Madame well; when she set her sights on the acquisition of something that would increase her profits, nothing could stand in her way. It was only a matter of time, she knew, before Ashleigh Sinclair would find herself working *above stairs* at the brothel—on her back!

Ashleigh entered the kitchen a couple of steps ahead of Monica. She was grateful to find no sign of Finn there, and seeing Dorcas busily involved with extracting something from the bake oven that was built into the side of the huge cooking hearth, she assumed the cook had sent him outside. Grateful that the old woman's face was averted, Ashleigh did her best to arrange a bland expression on her features, for it would not do to let Dorcas know she was upset over Monica's treatment of her. Dorcas, old dear that she was, would once again storm upstairs to Madame's chambers and complain in outraged fashion over the incident (as only Dorcas might—Madame's almost obsessive desire for well-prepared food and her inordinate pride in the skills of her cook of some twenty years made her forgive Dorcas anything, so long as it did not interfere with the delights that consistently graced Madame's table). But Ashleigh knew that once Dorcas had spoken to Madame, and Madame had reprimanded Monica (though never in words harsh enough to satisfy Dorcas), Monica would then proceed to do everything in her power to make life miserable for Ashleigh in the ensuing days and weeks. Like the time she'd "accidentally" bumped into Ashleigh on the stairs, sending her and the full chamber pot she was carrying careening backward in an unbelievable mélange of filth and confusion—not to mention a wrenched ankle that had Ashleigh hobbling about for weeks afterward. Or the time she'd forced Ashleigh to come upstairs to her chamber and help her out of her gown while Monica's "gentleman" of the evening stood by and *watched*.... No, it would not help matters at all to let Dorcas know anything of what had transpired a few moments ago.

"I believe we put the new powder over here, Monica," Ashleigh said as she walked toward a narrow, step-back cupboard displaying a number of various-sized apothecary jars.

"Ashleigh, lass, I've been wonderin' where ye've been!" exclaimed the cook as she turned around with a pan of steaming muffins in her hand. "The great beastie wanted out, so I— Oh, hello, Monica." Dorcas's usually cheery voice had suddenly lost some of its exuberance. "'Tis a mite early t'be seein' *ye* about.

Another headache, I suppose,'' added Dorcas, a sly look on her normally open, cherubic features.

But then the stout little cook drew herself up short, and a glowering scowl darkened her face as her eyes fell on the bright-red imprint of a hand on Ashleigh's left cheek. Her sharp blue eyes darted quickly over to Monica and then back to Ashleigh, and the scowl deepened. Setting the muffin pan down on a nearby worktable with a sharp *thunk*, Dorcas set both hands on her ample hips, narrowed her eyes and spoke menacingly to the tall blonde. "So... ye've been after the wee one again!"

Monica's first reaction to the restrained fury in the old woman's voice was surprise. "How did—"

"Are ye stupid as well as vicious?" questioned the cook between clenched jaws. "'Tis there upon the child's cheek—the mark o' yer cruel hand fer all the world t'see!" Dorcas stepped toward Ashleigh and put a comforting arm about the young woman's shoulders. "There, there, now, lass. Ye'll be all right now, with Dorcas t' take care o' things. Just come over here t' the table and have a breakfast muffin and a cup o' tea whilst I fix a poultice fer that poor, wee face," she said soothingly.

Ashleigh was torn between allowing herself to be comforted and staving off any forthcoming abuse from Monica, who was standing near the cupboard glaring at her with ill-concealed hatred. "It—it's all right, Dorcas, really, it is. I—I merely slipped near the hearth and—my head struck the side of the mantel. Clumsy of me, I'll admit, but no real harm done. Monica here was just coming by and was about to help me fetch a headache powder. I'm afraid my head does ache a bit from—from the fall, you know.'

Dorcas fixed a disbelieving gaze on her young charge, then looked askance at Monica who was suddenly busy with the apothecary jars in the cupboard. She didn't believe Ashleigh's story for a second, but she well realized the reasons for it. What to do? She loved the wee one as much as if she had been her own, and had since she'd first set eyes on her that cold winter's night more than twelve years ago when her sister, poor Maud, rest her soul, had brought the lass to her—a skinny, bewildered little thing, frightened out of her wits at being burned out of her home and left an orphan, with none but her beloved nursemaid Maud to see after her, to care if she lived or died.

A gentleman's daughter she'd been, raised in the lap of luxury from the moment she'd been born ... only all that was suddenly gone for her the night the fire claimed the lives of her doting parents and all they owned.

And that was the thing Dorcas had never really been able to understand. Why had no protection been set up for the child? It was as if all traces of the Sinclair family had vanished from the face of the earth.

And then there had been Maud's semicoherent ramblings before she passed on, a victim of the deadly inhalation of smoke from that terrible fire. She'd cautioned Dorcas *not* to try to investigate, pleaded with her to let well enough alone, lest there be—what was it she had said?—"more skulduggery afoot"; yes, that was it. And what was Dorcas, a simple cook in the employ of one of the most lavish and notorious brothels in London, to make of that?

But after Maud's death, when the child had been taken in and given a place as a kitchen helper by Madame, Dorcas had enlisted the aid of her seaman friend Roger in looking into that matter. Roger found the family's solicitor, and the word came back that the Sinclair family had been living on the margin. Ashleigh's parents had been fond and loving, but not very wise with money. There had been debts, some of which stemmed from stretching their wealth beyond their means. Ashleigh and her brother had once had the best in clothes, servants, tutors, horses and the like.

This older brother, Maud herself had once explained to Dorcas years earlier, had been trained at sea, then sent to make the family a fortune in trade (on a ship they had again overextended themselves to purchase) to the West Indies whence he never returned. Lost at sea, he was, when his ship went down, and he was never heard from again. The Sinclair lands were sold off to satisfy creditors after the fire, and no one, the solicitor included, took any interest in the fate of the Sinclair daughter. Roger had offered to make further inquiries, but then poor Maud had breathed her last, and new demands had claimed Dorcas's attention.

So here little Ashleigh had remained, lovely little sprite of a thing that she was, toiling away in the kitchens of a notorious house of wicked doings, when she'd been born to a life of leisure and was clearly a lady, from the top of her luxuriant black tresses to the tips of her dainty pink toes. And nary a whimper of complaint out of her, either.

Dorcas allowed herself a small swelling of pride for what she believed to be her own part in this; she had instantly taken to the wee child, happily tucking her under her wing in an outpouring of maternal affection that seemed to have been stored inside her until then for the children she'd never had.

Now, as her observant blue eyes took in the lovely profile of her charge while Ashleigh stood near the cupboard measuring out a dram of headache powder into a cup, a worried frown crossed the old woman's brow. And it was the overwhelming sight of Ashleigh's growing beauty that caused this, for it reminded Dorcas of Sunday's encounter with Drake and what the lout had hinted of Madame's interest in the girl.

Something had to be done, and done soon, or the lass would find herself an unwilling and helpless addition to the business up *there*!

Just then, there was a noise at the door to the hallway, and with a rustling of skirts, a tall, strikingly beautiful woman with flaming-red hair appeared.

"'Tis a might early t' be gatherin' fer tea, isn't it?" questioned the woman, the distinct crispness of an Irish brogue lacing her speech.

"Megan!" chirped Ashleigh with a quick look of surprise and then a grin. "What are *you* doing up and about at this hour?"

"'Twould be servin' the truth better if ye were t' ask me if I've been t' sleep yet," replied the redhead with a slow, mildly wicked smile that was belied by a merry twinkle in her large green eyes.

"Oh-h," replied Ashleigh with a blush. Try as she might, even for all her years of living and working in this house, she was still not blasé about the nature of the "entertainment" it offered. Part of this accrued from the heavy wall of protection built about her by Dorcas and her well-trained, loyal band of kitchen help, part of it by her own natural reticence. Although she had learned the function of the place well enough after coming here a dozen years ago, most of Ashleigh's knowledge was gained secondhand, in carefully couched phrases from Dorcas, or Tillie, the pantrygirl. And for Ashleigh this was sufficient; she was still an innocent in every sense of the word, and she was content to be so.

Oh, it wasn't that she lacked a lively curiosity about life and the world. She had this in abundance, but wise old Dorcas had seen to channeling this in the healthiest way; thrice a week, hired by Dorcas out of her own carefully stored savings, a tutor had come from the other side of town and given Ashleigh an ongoing challenge to her quick intelligence. Ever since she'd turned seven, Monsieur Laforte, a French emigré from the Reign of Terror, had engaged her in lively repartee, both in English and French, feeding and filling her hunger for knowledge. Laforte had formerly been a tutor to the House of Bourbon itself, and his qualifications were the best. But of this Ashleigh had cared little; what had delighted her had been the little man's enthusiasm for his work. In recent years Ashleigh suspected there was also an appeal to his Frenchman's sense of the ironic that he should have been called to instill the teachings of everyone from Plato to Shakespeare in a house such as this.

"Daydreamin' again, little one?" questioned Megan, her humor-rich voice rousing Ashleigh from her reverie.

"What—? Oh, yes, I suppose I was," answered Ashleigh with yet another blush. "I'm sorry, Megan."

"Think nary another thought on it, me lass. 'Tis best ye be closin' yer mind t' the doin's o' the likes o' *our* ilk, t' be sure!" Megan peered down at the blonde who stood between them, for although Monica was tall, the top of her head reached barely to the perfectly chiseled nose of the six-feet-tall Irishwoman. "Isn't that the truth, Monica, *darlin'*?"

The sarcastic intonation was not lost on Monica, who seethed with barely pent-up hatred for her chief rival at the brothel. She looked up at Megan now, taking in the proud Celtic beauty of her competitor: the perfect oval face with its high cheekbones and finely sculptured features, the knowing green eyes, heavily lashed and upward slanted at the corners, the fine, straight nose and wide, sensual mouth that smiled to reveal pearly white, even teeth—and that *hair*!

Monica clenched her jaw and ground her teeth as she surveyed that mass of fiery glory, clutching her hands into fists as well, as she forestalled an urge to wrap her fingers around those cascading curls and tear them out of Megan's head by the roots.

"I'd say it is about time your little friend did learn some specifics about the likes of us and our—ah—profession!" she said with a sly smile in Ashleigh's direction. "It would better prepare her for what Madame has in mind." Her eyes darted carefully over Ashleigh's slender form, and there was cruelty in her voice as she added, "She's fully grown now, and, I daresay, eats more these days than she did as the waif she was. I'd say it was high time she began to really *earn* her keep!" With a quick motion, she snatched the cup of prepared headache remedy from Ashleigh's grasp and downed it in several gulps; and after thrusting the empty cup back into Ashleigh's hands, she whirled about and strutted haughtily out of the room.

"What a strange thing to say!" Ashleigh exclaimed, looking first at Megan, then at Dorcas and finally back at Megan again. "Megan . . . ?"

"Ah, 'tis only more o' her wicked blatherin', Ashleigh, darlin'. Pay her no mind—no mind at all!" Megan threw a meaningful look at Dorcas over Ashleigh's head. "Ah, didn't I hear ye sayin' ye had an errand t' be sendin' the lass after, Dorcas?"

Nodding, Dorcas jumped in quickly. "Ah, yes, lass, 'tis some bones and scraps ye're t' fetch from Mister Tidley, the butcher." She glanced at the kitchen clock on the mantel. "He's been savin' them fer that beastie o' yers. 'Tis a good time t' run t' his shop and fetch them. Run along, now! There's a good lass!" And with the asperity of a mother hen shooing her chicks out of the path of danger, she urged Ashleigh out the back door.

When Ashleigh had gone, Dorcas gave Megan a brief, knowing glance and then spoke, her voice barely above a whisper. "I knew it wasn't a social visit that brought ye down here this early, Megan. What's afoot?"

The redhead's green eyes darted swiftly about the large kitchen. As it was early yet, none of the other help were about, but it paid not to be careless. Although Dorcas's staff were a good lot, and mostly loyal, it was also true that Madame was known to pay well to be kept abreast of what was going on under her roof, as well as about town and beyond, and Megan didn't care to have their conversation bandied about where her employer could catch wind of it. At last satisfying herself that no extra pairs of ears were about to pick up her words, Megan spoke, her own voice subdued to a near whisper. "Ah, Dorcas, 'tis just as we feared after yer encounter with Drake. Me gentleman last night was a young toff who patronizes these quarters rather regularly, a harmless enough lad, youngest son o' the earl o' Dunvale . . . kept me up the entire night with the need t' be stroked and petted, he did; nothin' more, if ye can fancy that. . . ."

"Megan!" Dorcas fixed her with a frown of disapproval.

"Ah, yes . . . well . . . sorry, Dorcas." Megan sent the cook a contrite smile. "Well, t' get on with it, the toff told me before he left that Madame promised him, the next time he's in town, that he might have a *virgin* she's got comin' aboard—a raven-haired beauty with a pair o' deep blue eyes the size o' saucers and a natural beauty mark high on her cheek!"

"Ah, Megan, *no*!" Dorcas exclaimed, her ruddy complexion suddenly gone ashen.

"Aye, 'tis what he said," Megan nodded somberly. "The worst has happened—or soon will—unless we speed the poor lass away from here."

"Away? But how? Where would she go? And how would she get on, once she got there?" Dorcas's aged face reflected earnest worry in every line.

"Calm yourself, Dorcas. I think I have an idea. . . ."

* * *

"Allow me to ascertain whether I understand you precisely," said the woman they all called Madame. She sat facing Megan and Dorcas in a small, handsome antechamber adjoining her boudoir, a room unofficially designated as her office. Decorated in varying shades of soft green and rose with cream accents, it was tasteful and discreet, as were all the rooms of the well-proportioned town house Madame had purchased twenty-five years ago in the best part of town, with what she called "conscience money" from her last lover when he had sought to rid himself of his notorious mistress.

A cozy fire crackled in the grate, throwing softly undulating waves of light and shadow across the rose and green florals of the Aubusson carpet on the floor, and a Louis XV gold ormolu mantel clock ticked its way toward the hour, which was nearly four, the time at which Madame had indicated she would be taking tea and their interview would be at an end.

Dressed in a soft rose dressing gown of watered silk and cream-colored Alençon lace, Madame was holding court from her seat on a George II green damask-covered armchair. A handsome woman of fifty-eight years, she had once been the foremost beauty of her time, a courtesan who, it was whispered, had enjoyed the favors of kings and dukes on both sides of the Channel before settling at last on English soil during the time of the French Revolution. She was of medium height, but appeared taller, owing to a pair of exceptionally long legs that, even now, as she crossed them under the parting folds of her dressing gown, displayed a youthful shape. Her hair had once been a deep honey-gold, though now it bore more silvery tones, but it was still abundant and shiny, something Madame fervently believed she achieved with the warm olive-oil treatments she'd been giving it since the day she'd learned of this beauty secret from an Italian *principessa* who used it to barter for her husband's release from the young Madame's amorous clutches. In her youth, when she was the toast of London, as she had been in Paris before that, it was said she owed her delicate coloring with its fair, porcelainlike skin, to an aristocratic English father, while her angular, Gallic features were the

legacy of a long line of French courtesans, of which her mother
had been the last.

Now, as she arched one delicate red-gold eyebrow while sur-
veying the two women who sat across from her, those still-
handsome Gallic features spoke of a keen shrewdness.

"If I understand you correctly," Madame was saying, "you
want me to find the girl some sort of honest employment elsewhere or the pair of you will leave my employ immediately and
take Ashleigh with you." Madame's pale gray-green eyes were
riveted on Dorcas as she spoke. "Is that the gist of it?"

Dorcas's clasped hands twisted nervously in her lap, but
thoughts of what might happen to Ashleigh if she failed her
now, forced her to return Madame's look and, after swallowing hard, answer, "Yes . . . yes, it is."

The shrewd eyes shifted and focused on Megan. "Megan,
this business bears your signature more than anyone's, I'll
warrant, so I'll put my question to you. Do you have any idea
what has happened to girls who have endeavored to leave my
employ without my assent?"

Until now Megan O'Brien's emerald eyes had been cool and
watchful during the interview, revealing little as she and Dorcas had laid out their terms, but now Madame detected an ever-
so-faint glimmer of heightened interest in their cool green
depths.

"My dear," Madame continued, "surely you cannot tell me
you've forgotten the tale of Liza Fairchild, who was going off
to become that young earl's mistress and was found by Drake,
months later, lying in the gutter, drunken senseless with a babe
in her belly and rags on her back?" She uncrossed her legs and
leaned forward in her chair. "Or what about that headstrong
brunette from Dorset—what was her name?—ah, yes . . .
Marion. What of her and her grandiose scheme of setting up
her own house with that young seaman lover of hers who
claimed he could supply her with no end of Oriental beauties
fresh from ports like Shanghai and Hong Kong?"

Suppressing a shudder, Megan suddenly rose to her feet. She
had no wish to recall the details of how the foolish Marion had
been found, brutally raped and abused, with her throat cut,

near one of the docks of Liverpool only a month after she'd left Madame's house. Rumors had flown that she was only one of almost a dozen such victims of the devil who'd pretended to be a sailor going into business with an unsuspecting whore. "I'll not pretend we relish the idea o' moving out on ye, Madame," she said, carefully watching the older woman's eyes as she spoke. "Dorcas and I have been treated well here, and we've come t' regard Hampton House as our home." She cast a brief glance at Dorcas, who nodded solemnly. "But as ye know, we've both become fond o' the wee mavourneen downstairs, and we've sworn not t' allow her t' be sucked up in a life here, Madame—we've *sworn* it!" Finding that her voice had gained more inflection than she'd intended with this last statement, Megan collected herself, softening it somewhat, to resume speaking. "Therefore, Madame, we have prepared ourselves ... t' go t' considerable ... lengths t' protect the lass."

Madame caught something in Megan's eyes as she spoke these last words, and whatever it was—she wasn't certain, but her instincts told her to pay attention to it—she picked up on the signal with keen interest. "Threatening to leave Hampton House and rob me of my prized cook and one of the best girls I've had in years ... those aren't the only clubs the two of you have to hold over my head, are they, Megan?" She watched the tall redhead's face with avid interest.

Megan smiled and gave her a look that acknowledged her respect for the older woman's ability to perceive things quickly. She'd always admired Madame's astute mind. "Ah, no, they aren't, Madame. Ye see, Dorcas and I, we've made it our business over the years t' become acquainted, shall we say, with some o' the quieter doin's at Hampton House...doin's ye'd be wishin' we weren't privy t'...like—" she cast a brief appraising glance at Madame's anxious expression and then hurried quickly onward "—like what goes on in the stables on certain nights when 'tis extra dark because there's no moon...or things that have t' do with a certain king's minister who frequents these chambers fer reasons other than us lovelies—although we're well aware that his lordship isn't above liftin' a skirt or two while he awaits the true business he's after."

"There's an ugly word for what you're up to," said Madame. "It's called blackmail."

"There are uglier words I can think of," snapped Megan. "They're called smugglin' and spyin'."

"Touché," acknowledged Madame with a small smile. Whatever her misgivings about having trusted the girl with too much carelessly dropped information, she had always admired Megan for her spunk and the wit behind that amazing beauty. She heaved a small sigh. In fact, if she were to admit it, she had always known Megan O'Brien to be a cut above the rest of the clever and not-so-clever beauties she'd seen come and go over the years, and she listened to the voice inside her now that told her the beauteous redhead would probably find a way to take herself beyond the walls of Hampton House one of these days; it was inevitable, really. "Very well, Megan, Dorcas—" she nodded at each in turn "—it seems you two have me over the proverbial barrel. Ashleigh may go." She watched as Megan smiled and Dorcas heaved an obvious sigh of relief.

"Now, the problem remains as to how. Hmm...." She tapped two long, well-manicured nails on the arm of her chair, deep in thought. At length she brightened with a smile of accomplishment. "I have it! Baron Mumford was complaining to me only last Saturday night of the loss of a governess he'd engaged for his young twin daughters. As the two of you may not know—" she gave them a quick look of appraisal "—then again, perhaps you do.... Well, at any rate, I have had the chore, from time to time, of placing some of my girls, those who haven't worked out for one reason or another, in various positions in the houses of some of the gentry with whom I've—ah—had the pleasure of becoming acquainted. With Ashleigh's background in academics—yes, Dorcas, I know all about Monsieur Laforte and his able tutoring—it shouldn't be too difficult to place her in the good baron's household. I'll write the dear fellow today, and if he agrees—and I have no doubt of it—his written reply will, I shall inform him, constitute a formal promise of employment for our dear Ashleigh.... Well, what do you say?"

Dorcas was quick to respond with a question of her own. "Madame, this Baron Mumford, is he a decent sort? I mean . . . he won't be one t' compromise the dear gel, will he?" Dorcas was hardly able to believe they'd won their case so quickly with Madame, and her skepticism showed.

Madame laughed and glanced at Megan. "Tell her, Megan, dear."

Megan's low, throaty laughter joined Madame's. "Baron Mumford is completely under the thumb of his dowager mother, his wife and his five daughters, all of whom live with him in a henpecking order in which *he* is at the *bottom*! It's the chief reason the poor man escapes and comes here whenever he can. No, rest your fears on that one, Dorcas. Our gentle lass will be safe in such a household."

"Well, then, Madame, I guess 'tis settled," said Dorcas, rising. She gave her employer a sheepish look. "Beg pardon fer our—our. . ."

"Tactics?" questioned Madame as she escorted them to the door. She laughed. "Never mind, Dorcas, I have every intention of allowing the two of you to make it up to me—in spades! And you can begin by preparing me a dinner of roast swan with truffles for tomorrow evening. I'm expecting none other than His Royal Highness, the prince regent, for dinner."

"Prinny? Here?" questioned Megan with a show of mild surprise. "But I thought he was in Brighton."

"He was supposed to be," replied Madame, "but some recent antics of his despicable German wife have sent him into a major depression, and I, as a dear old friend, have offered to help him shake it off. Dinner will be served at nine, Dorcas. Do not fail me."

"No, Madame," murmured the cook. She disappeared down the hallway muttering about where on earth she was to come by decent truffles on such short notice.

When both women had gone, Madame rang for her tea before settling back into the chair she had recently vacated, her thoughts filled with visions of Ashleigh Sinclair's perfect features.

*A pity*, thought Madame as she rearranged the skirts of her dressing gown. *She would have made such a lovely whore.*

# Chapter Two

*Ravensford Hall, Kent, May 27th, 1814*

John Westmont sat in a sunny patch of light that warmed a bench beside a eucalyptus tree in the conservatory of his country house, vainly trying to absorb enough of the heat from the sun's rays to warm his withered frame. It had been a long time since he had felt truly warm inside his aging bones, and he realized that he would never feel warm again. He was dying, and he had known it for some time now, despite the empty words of consolation offered by his physicians.

*Well, no matter,* he thought to himself in what was becoming a familiar attitude of philosophical reflection. *I have done what was necessary to ensure the safety and continued health of the dukedom. Brett is all I could hoped for, I can go to my grave in peace, and—*

The opening of the conservatory door interrupted the duke's ruminations, and he looked up to see Lady Margaret approaching; spying her tall, spare frame, he could not help admiring the manner in which his twin carried the weight of her years. They'd both turned seventy-eight last November, yet where time had left John's body shrunken and racked with pain, it had done little to denote the same passage of years in his sister. She walked toward him now, as lean and straight-backed as she'd ever been, with a mildly lined face that could have belonged to a woman twenty years younger.

Annoyed with himself that he should be feeling a twinge of envy at this, he made an effort at clearing his throat, as if by the action he could clear his mind, and glanced up at his sister. "Well, what news?"

"He's home," replied Margaret. "His carriage just came up the drive, and I've instructed James to have him come to the library once he's settled in his chambers, in about half an hour." She waited a moment, giving her brother's face a careful scrutiny. "Those *were* your instructions, were they not?"

"Yes, yes," answered her twin with an impatient gesture. "Now, help me up and to the library. I want to be behind my desk when he arrives."

As Margaret did his bidding, handing him his cane and offering her arm as well, John asked himself whether he was being foolish in attempting to disguise his state of health from Brett. It wouldn't be long before the lad found out anyway. He allowed a small smile to crease his withered lips. *He's hardly a lad anymore. Though I haven't laid eyes on him in over ten months, I can picture him as well as if he'd stood by my side yesterday... tall and strapping, with a healthy bronze color to his skin from all that seafaring.... Ah, Brett, I've missed you, boy!*

Margaret led him to the library with slow, measured steps, stopping frequently to allow him to catch his breath and recoup his strength, but even so, he arrived at his desk exhausted and paler than before, and they barely had enough time to secure a lap robe about his lower torso when a firm knock at the door signaled Brett's arrival.

"Come in!" called the duke, trying to sound heartier than he'd felt in months.

The door swung open and in strode the tall, dashing figure of his grandson. Broad shouldered, with curling chestnut hair that just reached the high collar of his impeccably tailored riding jacket, he evinced a healthy male vitality that more than equaled the old duke's memory of him from ten months before.

*It's damned near indecent for a man to be so handsome,* thought John. *And those eyes!*

The very eyes the duke was regarding now lit up from within their turquoise depths as they met his grandfather's across the desk.

"Your Grace! How good it is to see you again!" Brett exclaimed. His eyes ran quickly over the old, familiar and beloved visage, and then a small frown creased the handsome brow. "I trust you have been well, sir?"

"Well enough for my eight-and-seventy," lied the duke. "But you, m'boy, you're looking wonderful! The sea continues to agree with you, eh? Here, no need to stand on formalities with me, Brett." He gestured toward a nearby armchair. "Sit down, sit down!"

"Ah . . . yes, Grandfather," replied Brett, "but first," he added, turning to his great-aunt who stood silently off to one side of the desk, "allow me to correct my manners. Lady Margaret," he said as he nodded politely in his great-aunt's direction. He had dispensed with the term "Aunt" years ago when addressing his grandfather's sister. There had never been any degree of affection between them, and if anything, the relationship had cooled even further over the years. "I trust you are well?" he added perfunctorily.

"I am, thank you." Margaret's reply was as routinely cool and distant as ever. "John," she said, turning toward her twin, "shall I send for tea?"

"No, time enough for that sort of thing later," answered the duke, ". . . ah, that is, unless *you're* in need of some refreshment, Brett. Are you? Should I offer some brandy, perhaps! Or—"

"Nothing, nothing!" laughed Brett, holding up his hands in mock protest. "You're out of character, you know, Grandfather. Remember your strictures of the past? Business first; pleasure later—*if* time and inclination allow!"

The duke smiled. "Ah, yes, I was a bit of a martinet then, I suppose." He shook a bony finger at his grandson. "But it was all done for a good and noble purpose!"

"True enough," agreed Brett as he took a seat after a brief, questioning gesture at his great aunt and the chair near her. But the barest shake of the old woman's head had told him she wished to remain standing. "Now, then, Grandfather, what is it you wish to hear of first? Shall I recount the latest turn in profits from your mercantile investments, or would you be more interested in hearing the details of my recent interviews with your estate managers in Sussex and Surrey? Or my chat with George Jenkins here in Kent? I saw them en route here, you know. The *Ravenscrest* docked well nigh a fortnight ago. You might say I took the long way home."

John nodded his approval of his heir's diligence, and they launched into an hour's discussion of the duke's vast business interests and holdings, with Brett doing most of the talking, the duke merely interrupting on occasion to ask a pertinent question or two and otherwise listening attentively, the old head with its snowy mane of hair nodding sagely from time to time. And during it all, Margaret said not a word, though her steely blue eyes registered comprehension as she seemed to follow all the details of their conversation with ease.

"...So that about sums it up, sir. Even with the crop failure, it looks to be a profitable year." Brett finished with a look of genuine satisfaction on his face, a look that was mirrored by his grandfather's features.

"Well done, m'boy!" said the old man. He was more than gratified by what he'd heard. Brett had told him far more than the state of his financial empire during the interview; he had confirmed in the old man's mind what had been apparent for some time: Brett had become everything he had trained and raised him to be—a highly competent manager of his vast estates and their agrarian holdings; sometime captain/commander of an ever-growing merchant fleet that it had been the boy's idea to invest in, despite the disapproving rumblings of disdainful fellow members of the aristocracy who eschewed the idea of a member of the peerage soiling his hands with trade; a well-educated and honorable person in his own right—fair with his friends and ruthless with his enemies; in short, everything the duke himself held worthwhile and valued highly.... Of course, there was one more arena in which he'd consistently instructed his grandson, and he was about to embark upon that subject now.

"Tell me, Brett," said the old man, with a brief glance at Margaret. "What of your personal life these days. Are there any...steady friends I'm to learn of? Some I haven't met yet, perhaps?"

Brett laughed. "Well, sir, there's a giant of an Irishman you may not have heard me speak of yet...well, half Irish in blood, but Irish to the bone, to look at...knew him from the days we were cabin boys at sea together, but then I lost track of him for years—until a few months ago, that is, when we ran into each other at Almack's. You can imagine my surprise when Lady Jersey introduced us and she called him Sir Patrick! It seems he'd inherited a title in the interim!"

"Yes, yes," murmured the duke, "seems like a remarkable fellow, but what I meant was—ah—that is—are there any *friendships*—"

"Good Lord!" exclaimed Brett, nearly rising out of his seat. "Come now, sir! You cannot mean what I *think* you mean!" He gave the duke's visage a careful scrutiny. "You mean *women*?" Brett threw back his head and laughed as if he'd just heard the best joke of his life.

When at last he had calmed down enough to resume speaking, he threw his grandfather an amused look, saying, "Oh, that's ripe, it is, and coming from *you*, of all people!"

Finally he added in a more subdued tone, "Forgive me, Grandfather, but wasn't it you yourself who taught me all there is to know about that treacherous sex? They're nothing but trouble of the worst sort, and a man would do well to remember it. 'A major source of evil in this world,' if I remember your words correctly, sir. Wasn't that what you told me?"

The duke nodded slowly, not even bothering to look at his twin, although he was acutely aware of her presence while this was going on, as well as of what was on her mind right now. "Yes, well, I'm gratified to see you've taken my words to heart, Brett," he said thoughtfully, "but—ah—the fact remains that there is one area in which their presence cannot be avoided in our lives. Do you recall it?"

"As well as I recall my own name," said Brett with a wry smile. "They are necessary for the begetting of sons...heirs, if you will."

"Precisely," nodded the duke with a meaningful glance.

Brett caught the look and suddenly rose forward even farther in his chair. "Here, now! Oh, come, you *cannot* be thinking... You *are*! You are actually asking me to consider... *marriage*! But *why*?"

"For the begetting of heirs, naturally." The words came from Lady Margaret. They were the first she'd spoken in more than an hour, and both men looked at her as if surprised she should be there at all.

But then the duke recalled exactly why he'd included her in the interview and rushed to explain. "You are nearly thirty years old now, Brett. It is an age at which it is not unusual for a man to consider marriage and the begetting of sons."

"Rubbish!" replied Brett. "And if this was a part of your plan for me, why wasn't I informed of it until now?" He peered closely at the duke. "Is there something you haven't told me?"

John hesitated under his grandson's careful examination, wondering whether now was the time to tell him of his failing health. It was the chief reason he had allowed Margaret to make certain inquiries, after all. He was not long for this world, and it was a world he could leave far more easily if he knew his only heir was well settled, with perhaps an heir on the way—or even, if he were lucky and God were truly merciful—an heir already born and thriving before John met his reward.

Seeing his hesitation, Margaret decided to save him the trouble of deciding what to tell Brett. "John, I know how you feel about this, but it is clear the boy needs the point driven home to him." She turned toward Brett. "His Grace's health is in jeopardy. He is failing by the day, as should have been apparent—"

"Margaret!" thundered the duke. "How *dare* you break our confidence!"

"It was not a confidence; it is common knowledge. One has only to look at you to learn the truth." Having silenced her brother, she turned again to Brett. "It is your duty to provide an heir—and soon."

Brett cast his grandfather a questioning glance. "Is it true?"

The old man nodded. "I'm afraid it is. And so you see the reason for the timing of my suggestion ... or perhaps you can call it a request."

A frown of annoyance crossed Brett's brow. "And who, pray tell, is the fair lady I am to wed? I assume you've worked that out as well?"

The duke threw him a sheepish look and glanced at his twin, who rose to the occasion.

"You are well acquainted with the lady already," she replied with the first evidence of a smile Brett had seen since his return. "Lady Elizabeth Hastings is in every way a suitable—"

*"Elizabeth Hastings!"* roared Brett, bolting from his chair. "I might have known! It's always been the Hastingses with you, hasn't it, Lady Margaret? You've cared more about all of them over the years than you have about any of us. So much so, that you not only arranged that ruinous liaison between Lady Caroline Hastings and my poor, besotted father, but now you would compound that error by having me wed her bitch niece!"

He ignored the gasp of indignation from Margaret and turned to his grandfather. "And you, sir, how *could* you allow her to set her plotting claws into us once again? Lady Elizabeth Hastings! My God! I'd rather choke on the bile the thought of wedding her brings to my throat!"

"Brett," said the duke, reaching toward him with a gesture meant to placate. "It was my health. I *had* to let Margaret do the arranging!"

"Save your breath, Grandfather," said Brett, striding toward the door. "I have no intention of marrying for a long while. You've said it yourself. Women are a scourge, and the actions of the present company prove it." He turned at the door and scowled darkly at his great-aunt. "As far as I'm concerned, Lady Margaret, you are of a piece with women like the mother who deserted me and all the rest—ever treacherous. And as for Lady Elizabeth Hastings—" he sneered "—disabuse your mind of the notion that I shall ever align myself with that simpering niece of the stepmother who led my father astray!'' He then turned sharply on his heel and left.

As they heard his footsteps echo down the hall, Margaret turned toward her twin. ''Well?'' she asked. ''What now?''

The duke allowed himself a sigh. ''It was to be expected, of course. Never mind, Margaret, leave him to me,'' he added tiredly. The interview with his grandson had taxed his strength considerably, and he was feeling exhausted. ''Go ahead and arrange the marriage with the Hastingses. Brett will come around.''

But after Margaret had gone, promising to send one of the footmen to help him to his chamber, John had second thoughts about what he'd told her. He thought he understood his grandson well. After all, he'd been the principal influence in his upbringing all these years. But what if he'd been assuming something that was missing here? In urging the lad to beware of women and never to trust them, had he perhaps done his job too well? He remembered the look on Brett's face as he'd raged against the so-called fairer sex. It had been full of utter disdain, even hatred. Was it possible that the lad had never even *had* a woman? He pondered the question for a moment. It was highly unlikely, wasn't it? That was to say, given the boy's arresting good looks.... Suddenly a horrifying thought raised its ugly head. What if, by some errant twist of fate, some mischief perpetrated by the gods, the boy weren't . . . normal? But as quickly as the thought came, it dissipated. The duke had traveled in sophisticated circles in his day, and had met his share of gentleman of that ilk, and he knew in his bones that Brett could never, by any stretch of the imagination, be one of them.

Well, what then? And once again the improbable notion arose that the lad might somehow have survived all those years of his youth, owing to the hard and relentless schedule of his rearing and training, as a *virgin*! Impossible though it sounded, that would explain it . . . would it not?

Suddenly he pulled open the top drawer of his desk and withdrew a piece of the fine ivory vellum that bore an imprint of his family coat of arms at the top. Dipping a nearby quill into the Limoges inkwell that sat on the desk, he hastily penned a note. A few moments later, when it had been sealed and sanded, the seal also bearing the Ravensford family crest of a raven atop a battlement, he was handing it to the footman who had come to assist him to his chambers. "See that this is delivered to my solicitor, Merton, one Mister Robert Adams. The gentleman is down from London, by my request. You will find him staying at the Red Dog Inn in Folkstone. No need to wait for a reply."

Early the following morning the duke was once again seated behind his desk in the library. It had always been his chosen spot for conducting business, but lately it was the only place from which he would expedite matters of importance with others. He was acutely aware of his ever-increasing physical frailty, and he was grateful for the vantage point he felt the impressive piece of massive furniture afforded him.

Across from him, seated in the Chippendale armchair Brett had occupied yesterday, sat a distinguished-looking man of about fifty. Robert Adams had been his personal solicitor for over twenty years, having followed his father, Raymond, in that position when the older Adams died in a fall from his horse in 1792. He regarded Robert as a bit of an aging dandy, his attire always bearing the unquestioned stamp of the influence of Beau Brummell in every aspect, but this in no way affected the duke's regard for the man's competence. Over the years he had come to rely on Robert Adams in a great many matters, some of them highly personal, and the man's professional diligence as well as his trustworthiness in matters requiring the utmost discretion had long ago earned the duke's respect. Not the least of such matters had been the business of assigning him to be his eyes and ears where the progress of his grandson was concerned, and it was in this regard he'd decided to call upon his services this morning.

"So you see, Robert, it is important to me that the boy be persuaded to marry—the sooner the better," said the duke. "Yet, for the reasons I've just suggested to you, it would appear that Brett's attitude is the only real obstacle to such an event."

Adams took a moment to respond, pensively gazing at the carved ivory head of his fashionable walking stick as he mulled over the duke's words. Finally he raised a pair of intelligent gray eyes to his old friend and client. "Your Grace, allow me to see if I understand you clearly. You feel young Brett may have so taken to heart your enjoinders to eschew the company of women, that he has, er, abstained totally from association with—with the opposite sex, and therefore perhaps even *fears* involvement with them—albeit even for the respectable and necessary pursuit of wedlock?"

"That is my fear precisely," replied the duke. "Oh, I know it sounds preposterous at first consideration, Robert, but, believe me, if you had seen and heard his reactions to my suggestion that he take a wife . . . well, sir, it would, perhaps, have begun not to sound so farfetched after all."

"I see," said Adams, again with a greatly pensive air about him. "Very well, Your Grace, then what is it you have in mind that might require my services?"

"Your *discreet* services, as ever, Robert."

"As ever, Your Grace," Adams nodded, smiling.

A conspiratorial look entered the old man's eyes as he leaned forward over his desktop. "A very simple thing, really," he said, his voice dropping to a lower pitch. "I want you to inquire about and locate a high-quality house of—ah—illicit pleasures—"

At Adams's raised eyebrows, the duke continued with even greater emphasis. "That is correct. You heard me right, Robert. Locate a brothel—but only one of the finest sort. We both know they exist, even down here, away from London, but travel as far as you require. Your sources should provide you with the proper information soon enough."

Adams nodded, awaiting more.

"Once contacted, inquire after the hire of a professional there who is young and *guaranteeably free from disease*. In short, Robert, you are to hire me a clean whore."

Adams looked slightly uncomfortable. "Hire *you*, Your Grace . . . ?"

"Dammit, man, I mean for my grandson!" exploded the duke. "It's clear to me now the boy lacks experience! I intend to rectify that, through the use of the woman you will procure, and through doing so, demolish the only barrier to seeing my grandson wed and on his way to producing *heirs*! *Now* have I made myself clear?" In his excitement, the duke had become flushed in the face, and by the time he had finished, he'd nearly collapsed over his desk in a fit of helpless coughing.

Alarmed by what he easily recognized as the old man's failing state, Adams rose and worriedly peered over the duke's bent form. "Your Grace, you must not tax yourself so! May I fetch someone? Are—are you all right?"

With some effort, the duke pushed himself to an upright position and waved him off. "I'm fine, Robert, or I shall be, just as soon as this business is taken care of. Now, man, do I have your promise to do my bidding?"

Still shaken by the evidence of greatly increased infirmity he'd just witnessed, and unwilling to excite him further, Adams nodded anxiously. "At once, Your Grace. You may depend on it."

Minutes later, as Adams sat in the hired carriage that had taken him to Ravensford Hall, he was deep in thought. What a muddle! If he hadn't been before, he was now deeply convinced that his old friend and client was on his way out. It was the only reason he could ascribe to the duke's succumbing to this preposterous notion of his; not only was he physically failing, his mind must be weakening as well. . . . Brett Westmont a *virgin*? Suddenly Adams began to laugh, the source of the laughter so outrageous it soon reduced him to helpless tears and prompted his driver to halt the carriage and inquire within as to whether anything was amiss.

"Oh, no, no, thank you, my good fellow," answered Adams between still only half-controlled outbursts of merriment. He gestured to the driver's seat, visible through a small window inside the passenger compartment. "You may proceed."

When they were once again under way, Adams sobered enough to consider his predicament. Over the years it had been his job to keep an eye on young Brett's activities and periodically report to the duke on his findings. He had never actually considered it spying, although he knew some would call it that. Rather, he'd regarded it as a gladly assumed duty to put at ease the concerns of an old friend, not to mention the foremost client of his firm. And since almost all of his reports had been positively and for the most part truthfully glowing, it had been a duty that was easily borne by him. Of course there was one area in which he'd not been truthful with his client, but as it had been what he'd always regarded as such a minor one, his bending of the facts in that regard had never really troubled his conscience a whit.

*Face it, Robert,* he now told himself, *in seeking to spare the old man's doting heart, you were too cowardly to tell him that, in addition to being every inch the golden boy his grandfather dreamed of raising, Brett Westmont has become one of the worst rakes in England—at least where women are concerned!*

Adams sat farther back into his upholstered carriage seat and pondered the facts. Brett Westmont had left a trail of broken hearts and pining females from one end of London to the other, and God knew how many other places besides. He was widely known in sophisticated circles as one who used women ruthlessly, attracting them immediately like flies to honey through his astounding good looks and outwardly charming manner, then dropping them just as quickly when his fancy strayed to another. All of London whispered about it. Why, he was becoming almost as notorious as Lord Byron, who was frequently seen in his company.

And the only reason his grandfather, the duke, had never found out about this one, less-than-savory, side of the young heir's nature, was because the duke of Ravensford lived like a virtual recluse, buried away in the family estate here in Kent—that, and Adams's prudent discretion and his decision that it would be harmless to spare the old man's feelings.

But now Adams wondered if it had been as harmless as he'd always imagined. What should he do? If he procured the woman—a simple enough task—and unblinkingly allowed the duke to offer her to Brett, the young man was likely to explode—with anger or amusement, he wasn't certain which—and give away the entire game he'd taken such pains to cover all these years. No, owing to the old man's poor state of health, that way could result in disaster. There was only one answer: sometime between now and the presentation of the woman, he would have to corner Lord Brett Westmont and confess all to him. Yes, that was it. The man had always impressed him as being possessed of more than a modicum of good sense and understanding, and Adams now felt he could be relied upon to help protect his grandfather and keep up the game.

With a final sigh of satisfaction, Adams relaxed in the briskly moving carriage. Tomorrow he would travel to London. He knew just the place—what was it called?—Hampton House, that was it. Tomorrow he would make inquiries at Hampton House.

# Chapter Three

Monica Chatworth's almond-shaped eyes narrowed to chocolate slits of ill-concealed hatred as she observed Ashleigh through the half-open doorway of her chamber. The younger woman was down the hallway, bending over a narrow stand just outside Madame's suite, where she was preparing to lift an ornate silver tray that held the remains of Madame's breakfast and carry it down to the kitchen, a task she accomplished promptly every morning at eleven. From where she stood Monica missed neither the feminine, curved outline of Ashleigh's hips and derriere beneath the simple servant's frock she wore, nor the lilting melody of the tune the young woman hummed gaily to herself as she went about her work; and the observed combination rankled.

The increased shapeliness and other obvious charms of Ashleigh Sinclair were becoming a constant reminder to Monica that she herself was not getting any younger in a profession where youth and its accompanying beauty were everything, and that there would always be newer, younger flesh waiting in the wings to replace her when her own allure began to fade. The happy tune emanating from Ashleigh's lovely throat was even more disconcerting; word was out in the house that Madame had been prevailed upon to find the chit a "decent" position of employment elsewhere: *Ashleigh* was going *free*! It was surely this that was prompting the carefree and joyful demeanor, and why shouldn't it? Any day now Ashleigh would leave this place to become settled into some nice, safe situation where she would be spared the social ostracism and insecure future that had never sat well with Monica after she'd been forced to choose this way of life.

Oh, it wasn't that she'd been completely unhappy with her life at Hampton House. It was far better than anything she might have expected before Drake found her walking the streets, frightened and hungry, and deserted by a young lord. First he'd compromised her honor when she'd been a companion to his sister during the Christmas holiday season several years ago, then run off with her, promising marriage, but leaving her alone and penniless in their rented chamber in an inn not too far from here, never to return.

Monica shut her eyes and gave a toss of her blond mane of hair as if in an attempt to shake off the unpleasant memories of that time. She rarely allowed herself to think of the weeks she'd been forced to take to the streets to eke out a living before Drake found her, just as she kept at bay all thoughts of the home in which she'd grown up. *Home!* It had been a veritable prison! Her stern-faced father, the vicar, with his ever-present admonitions to her to deny herself any form of pleasure lest she "fall into the ways of sin," the tight-lipped mother she loathed, a holier-than-thou creature bent on keeping Monica from enjoying life in even the smallest ways... No, she certainly had no desire to go back to their way of life, even if it were possible.

But what wouldn't she give to have the chance that Ashleigh Sinclair now had! To be privately employed in the fine house of some wealthy lord, where who-only-knows what sorts of possibilities might lie in store for a woman who was enterprising and clever—it was a chance Monica longed for with every nerve and fiber of her being, and to see such an opportunity thrust haphazardly in the lap of that little bitch, Sinclair! Yes, it rankled....

Suddenly the door to Madame's chambers opened, just as Monica saw Ashleigh disappear down the servants' stairwell at the end of the hall, and Madame appeared, dressed in a superb apricot silk traveling dress and matching pelisse. Missing nothing, as usual, she spied Monica standing beside her partially ajar door and smiled knowingly.

"Prying about for useful information, Monica?" she purred in the blonde's direction. "I cannot think there is much you will come upon at this early hour. We both know most of the working women of this household are yet asleep, and so, I think, should you be, if you wish to retain your looks!"

Monica stifled the gasp that rose to her throat at the pointed mention of her need for beauty rest and assumed an air of nonchalance. "Just looking about to see if I might be of some service to anyone, Madame. I've had all the sleep I require today."

"Just so," nodded Madame in patently disbelieving fashion. "Yes, well, since you seem to wish to be of such . . . use, perhaps there is something you might do for me. I am leaving London to spend several days with old friends once I've done some shopping, and I fear I am rather in a hurry. Do be so kind as to run down to the kitchen with a message for Dorcas, would you?"

At Monica's nod she walked briskly toward the main stairway, continuing rapidly over her shoulder, "Tell her that letter we've been awaiting at last arrived by this morning's post and she will find it on my writing table in there." Madame gestured behind her as she reached the top of the stairs. "Tell her that when I return, I shall expect Ashleigh Sinclair to be gone." She paused and gave one last look at Monica over her shoulder. "That should make you quite happy, I daresay, should it not, Monica?" And with a low, throaty peal of satisfied laughter, Madame disappeared down the stairs.

Monica clenched her fists, attempting to control her rancor over Madame's amusement at her expense. Then she took a deep breath and was about to head for the kitchen to do Madame's bidding when an idea hit, its possibilities so overwhelming she held her breath for a moment to make certain she was sure of it and not just daydreaming some impossible foolishness.

Seconds passed. No, it was real enough, she realized as she heard the downstairs door close and knew that Madame was truly gone—and for several days!

Glancing stealthily over one shoulder and then the other as she stepped farther out into the hallway, she confirmed that she was alone and unobserved. She paused and listened for any approaching footsteps, but the only sounds she heard were those of the horses and wheels of the departing carriage that was taking Madame from London. A slow, sly smile stole across Monica's face as she headed for the doorway to her employer's chamber. She couldn't believe her luck!

Quickly Monica opened Madame's unlocked door, taking care that she made absolutely no noise. Then she stepped inside the antechamber and soundlessly closed the door behind her.

Moving rapidly, Monica headed for the delicate Louis XV escritoire that stood near the room's double windows at the far end. There she looked down and spied a pile of correspondence, some of it as yet unopened. Madame, she thought, must indeed have been in a hurry to leave her mail in such a state. Finally she spotted what she sought. It was a sheet of heavy white vellum that had been stood up on its edge against the back of the writing desk, propped there by a beautiful Clichy lily-of-the-valley paperweight.

Monica could barely contain her excitement as she perused its brief contents:

To Whom It May Concern:
This missive constitutes, to the young lady who bears it, a promise of employment in the household of his lordship, Baron Mumford, as governess to his youngest daughters, the Honorable Misses Mumford, Diana and Daphne. The terms of employment are as herein follows...

Monica's elation was complete. Not only did the letter speak for itself, it contained the name of *no specific* "young lady" anywhere in its body! In short, it was completely usable by whoever bore it! Suddenly she began to laugh, then quickly took care to stifle the sound. Here was the answer to all her worries! All she had to do was appropriate the letter for herself and no one would be the wiser—at least not for several

days, and by then—she shrugged—if she were not able to par-
lay this venture into something both lucrative and stable for
herself in a short time, then her name wasn't Monica Chatworth. She knew the baron well. He was an old fuddy-duddy
she had "entertained" herself on numerous occasions, and she
knew just what his preferences were, knew just what to do to
make him putty in her slim white hands. Oh, but imagine his
surprise when he found out who his daughters' new governess
was!

Just then Monica's glance caught the unbroken seal bearing
the arms of the duke of Ravensford, on a fold of ivory parchment atop the stack of Madame's unopened mail. The duke of
Ravensford! Everyone knew of that distinguished lord's wealth
and power! Monica's palms began to perspire as a new wave of
anticipation hit her. What if there was something in this unopened missive that she could also put to her own use? Suddenly a wealth of possibilities began to unfold, crowding her
avaricious, plotting brain.

But first she picked up the entire stack of unopened mail and
hastily thumbed through its contents. No, not much else that
looked promising. Again her eyes fell on the letter bearing the
duke of Ravensford's seal. Should she chance it? If, when Madame returned, she recalled she hadn't yet opened the letter
before she left, what of it? Monica would be long gone by then,
whether by way of the good graces of old Baron Mumford or...

With fingers that shook with anticipatory eagerness, she took
hold of the ducal letter, tore open the seal and read:

Madame:
As a supplement to my personal inquiry of last week on
behalf of His Grace, The Duke of Ravensford, I would
remind you that the manner of professional we seek from
among your employees be, at all costs, in good health and
*young*—under twenty, let us say. She is to remain with the
duke's grandson at Ravensford Hall until she has instructed the young man in the ways of her expertise, to the
best of her ability. If she performs her task well, both you

and she will, under the terms stated last week, be many pounds the richer for it.

I shall be arriving by carriage at precisely five o'clock on the evening of the third, expecting to wait discreetly in the street outside your residence for no more than five minutes, for the young woman to join me.

Moreover, as discretion is ever of foremost consideration in these matters, I would ask you to return this missive to me by way of your young employee. She is to hand it to me when she enters the carriage; it will thus further serve as her identification on that occasion.

Thanking you in advance on behalf of His Grace, I remain

Your Obedient Servant,
Robert Adams, Solicitor
on Behalf of His Grace,
The Duke of Ravensford

The gleam in Monica's eyes dulled with disappointment as she finished perusing the letter. There was no help here. She was thoroughly familiar with the practice among certain members of the aristocracy in hiring those of her profession to tutor their sons—and grandsons, it would seem—in the ways of Eros. She herself had even performed this function a few times. But the duke and his solicitor were specifically requesting a *young* woman—"under twenty," the letter said. (Why, Monica couldn't imagine; she herself would have thought that the more experienced the instructress, the better the outcome of the "lessons.") But Monica was twenty-eight years old—twenty-nine on her next birthday, and no matter how well preserved her beauty might be, no matter how much rest she took the night before, there was no way on earth she was going to pass for a girl of less than twenty.

Ever the practical opportunist, Monica shrugged, preparing to set aside the solicitor's letter as she reached for Baron Mumford's, when suddenly an idea took hold, and her resigned expression gave way to a feline smile. Of course! Here was the perfect opportunity to both cover her tracks in the theft of Mumford's letter and hand that little bitch, Ashleigh Sinclair, her comeuppance at the same time!

Chortles of glee emanated from Monica's throat as she scanned the solicitor's letter one more time. Ah, it was perfect! There was nothing in the contents to specify the nature of the "task" the woman was to perform. Now, all she had to do was fabricate a suitable explanation for Dorcas as to the reason for the offer of employment to be coming from the duke of Ravensford instead of Baron Mumford. Moreover, she had to devise a way of seeing the letter fell directly into Ashleigh's hands on the evening of the third, and not allow it to be seen by the cook or—God forbid—Megan O'Brien! Ashleigh was naive enough to assume the letter spoke of a governess's position, but Dorcas and Megan had been around and were nobody's fools.... Ah! She had it! She would concoct the tale that Madame had instructed her to tell Dorcas to have Ashleigh await the arrival of her new employer's solicitor on the third, just as the letter stipulated, but omitting the business about delivering the letter by hand. She would say that Madame had herself been delighted by the duke's superior offer (his position alone would attest to that) and had accepted it over Mumford's on behalf of the girl, that it was clearly in Ashleigh's best interests to take the duke's offer of employment. Then, only at the last minute on the evening of the third, she would personally press the letter into Ashleigh's hand as she prepared to go out to meet the carriage....

Again and again, Monica went over these plans in her mind as she stood in Madame's antechamber holding the two letters. Oh, it was going to *work*—it *was*! In just a few days' time, she would be delightfully installed within the household of old Mumford as an upstanding employee while Ashleigh Sinclair... Monica nearly choked on her own suppressed laughter. She could just picture Ashleigh's face when she at last discovered what sort of instruction His Grace's grandson desired! Oh, it was rich, it was!

A sudden recognition of the need to be away from Madame's chambers spurred Monica to action. Grasping both letters, she secured them carefully out of sight in the folds of her dressing gown and turned toward the door. She opened it and peered carefully down the hallway in both directions and, finding no one about, exited, a look of triumph on her face. She felt she was at last on her way as she entered the haven of her own chamber. "Ashleigh Sinclair," she whispered as she closed her door behind her, "your days of sweet innocence are numbered!"

Ashleigh sat beside the distinguished-looking gentleman who had identified himself briefly as Mr. Adams while the richly appointed carriage carried her steadily away from Hampton House and all she had known there for the past twelve years. In view of the obvious dignity and businesslike mien of her escort, she tried valiantly to hold back the tears that threatened to spill from her eyes at any moment. She knew she should be happy to be where she was—on her way to a brand-new way of life, one that would relieve her of the uncertain future that had awaited her in the house where she'd spent the major portion of her formative years—but she felt only sadness instead. Hampton House had been her home for so long! And if she wasn't pained at the thought of leaving behind the place itself, or what it stood for, she was more than miserable at bidding farewell to some of the friends she had made within its walls.

There was Dorcas, dear old thing that she was, who had functioned almost like a mother to her all these years. Oh, how the two of them had wept in each other's arms late this afternoon when the moment of parting had become imminent!

And Megan, wonderful, wildly beautiful Megan, who had a heart of gold and the soul of a poet, no matter what she did to earn a living! Megan O'Brien, for all her worldly ways, had become her friend and her foremost protectress at Hampton House, teaching her how to defend herself from bodily harm and just as deftly teaching her the words to many a Gaelic song once she'd learned Ashleigh was half Irish, insisting it was her right as well as her duty to awaken and keep burning the flames of that noble heritage. Megan had spent half last night sitting up with her and talking of the good times they'd shared together under Madame's roof, and then, too, the tears had flown freely....

And then there was Finn. In some ways leaving the great wolfhound had been the hardest of all, for the big dog somehow seemed to sense she was going without any need for parting words or gestures, and the sad, soulful look in his eyes had told its own story.

Now, as she sat beside the immaculately groomed gentleman on her right, blinking back her tears, Ashleigh wondered if she hadn't made a mistake. Who was this duke of Ravensford, after all, or the grandson he seemed eager for her to instruct? Oh, she'd heard Megan's account of the rumors about the man—his fabulous wealth, the importance attributed to his particular title and its power, and she'd seen the looks of envy in the eyes of several of the women when word got around as to who her new employer would be. Then, too, Dorcas's friend, Roger, had told them that the duke of Ravensford had a reputation for being morally upstanding—straitlaced, even—so Dorcas and Megan had given their blessings to the arrangement when they'd heard, and here she was....

She glanced surreptitiously at the silver-haired man beside her. He hadn't said very much to her after she'd handed him the letter Monica had given her on her way out to meet the carriage, though he'd taken a good, long moment to look her over from head to toe when she'd appeared. This open perusal of her person brought the suggestion of a blush to her cheeks even now as she thought about it; it had been a more thorough examination than any she'd ever received, with the exception of a few unwelcome looks she'd gotten from some of Hampton House's visiting "guests" on the few occasions when she'd inadvertently been seen by such gentlemen. Her thoughts fastened with distaste on the look she'd seen on the young lord Monica had been entertaining the evening she'd forced her to help her out of her gown; the look had not been intended entirely for Monica, she knew, and what bothered her now was something—she wasn't sure what, exactly—but there was a flicker of similarity in the expression of Mister Adams when he'd studied her out there in the street before turning away with a nod and bidding her enter, apparently satisfied.

Now, as she again glanced at the man's distinguished profile, she wondered if she ought to say something to him, question him, perhaps, about the nature of the household he was taking her to, or the daily routine her duties would involve. But suddenly Adams himself turned toward her, and while she blushed at having him catch her looking at him, he saved her the trouble by addressing her instead.

"I wonder…Miss Sinclair, isn't it?" At her shy nod he smiled and continued. "I wonder if I might ask how old you are, Miss Sinclair?"

Surprised by the question, but beginning to relax somewhat under his benign gaze, Ashleigh smiled back. "Nineteen, sir, or I shall be, at the end of the month."

A nod, coupled with another smile. "Very good. Now, I should like to ask you only a couple more questions, Miss Sinclair, and then perhaps I can be of some service if you should have questions of your own."

At her smile he continued. "Although my letter stipulated it, I cannot underscore enough the necessity that you meet His Grace's foremost request. Are you *certain* that you—ah—enjoy excellent health?" He watched her face carefully as he awaited Ashleigh's response.

"Oh, yes, sir!" she replied eagerly. "I am, as they say, in the very pink and can assure you, I've never been sick enough to lose a day's work—um—since I've been old enough to do work, that is, sir."

"Ah, yes, well, I'm glad to hear it," replied Adams, perplexed by the nature of her reply. He wasn't sure why, but he was beginning to feel slightly uncomfortable in the role he was playing. He wondered if it had anything to do with the girl's youth. Of course, he had been expecting someone young after the letter he'd sent, but Ashleigh Sinclair somehow did not fit the picture he'd had in mind. To begin with, she looked not only young, but actually *innocent*! He supposed it had something to do perhaps with a kind of studied allure she affected. There must be some call in these brothels for women who gave off the *appearance* of innocence, and so, he assumed, any shrewd madame who knew what she was about would cater to such tastes, as well as to heaven only knew what others among her clientele. Yes, that must be it: it was a pose.

But moreover, the girl was a stunning beauty. Oh, he'd long come to expect physical attractiveness among women of her ilk; hadn't some of the greatest beauties of the past been courtesans? Du Barry? De Pompadour? Or on England's own soil, Castlemaine in Charles II's time, not to mention Nell Gwyn? But the beauty of the girl sitting beside him now had almost robbed him of breath when he'd first seen her: hair of a midnight hue, so thick and lustrous it almost begged to be touched; delicate, chiseled features of perfect proportions, covered by creamy, flawless skin; and those eyes! Incredibly large and deep blue in color, they truly resembled sapphires—only there was far more warmth in their depths, and when they turned on a man, as they were regarding him now, they affected such a perfect image of unblemished innocence, of allure without guile....

And then there was the *rest* of her! She wore a high-waisted cornflower-blue walking dress, well displayed when she'd loosened her pelisse in the warmth of the carriage's snug interior; it was in no way immodest or overly revealing, but he could easily discern, through its soft, gauzelike folds, the outlines of a high, rounded and well-endowed bosom as well as other lithe curves and lissome lines of feminine loveliness on her diminutive, almost fragile-looking young body.

And that brought him to the final aspect of Ashleigh Sinclair that was so disconcerting: she appeared for all the world like a delicate, fragile flower, all freshness and youth, coupled with a look in the eyes that said, "Be gentle with me...handle me with tender care, lest I snap and break like some poor faerie creature's child." Even now, as she sat looking at him with those wide, lovely eyes, he thought he saw the brightness of unshed tears in their depths....

*My God!* he almost exclaimed aloud. *She makes me feel all at once tender and protective, as though she could be my own daughter! What am I doing, procuring her for—*

Quickly Adams cleared his throat and addressed Ashleigh with sudden haste. "Your employer has assured us you come with all the necessary—ah—skills and qualifications for the position, Miss Sinclair. Do you feel she is correct in this assessment?"

Ashleigh's face lit up. Madame had been generous, indeed, to make such a recommendation! "Oh, yes, sir! I've been fortunate enough, you see, to have the ablest of tutors to prepare me—"

"A tutor, you say!" exclaimed Adams. The girl had been taking lessons!

"Oh, yes," replied Ashleigh. "I was tutored for twelve years."

*"Twelve years!"* Adams choked. "You had a tutor for *twelve years?"*

"Yes," responded Ashleigh, a little puzzled at Adams's surprise. "He was a Frenchman, you know—"

"Ah! A Frenchman!" exclaimed Adams with a nod of comprehension.

"Yes," smiled Ashleigh, "fresh from the court of Louis himself, poor man." She shook her head sadly, suddenly filled with compassion at the recollection of all she'd heard of the terrible Reign of Terror from Monsieur Laforte.

Adams nodded and smiled weakly, uncomfortable again. Here it was once more; just as he'd begun to think he knew and understood what she was, she presented him with a look of tenderness and compassion so sincere, so believably filled with concern for others less fortunate, that he was hard put to think of her as anything less than good—wholesome and pure in a manner that totally conflicted with his knowledge of what she was.

*Dammit!* he swore to himself. *She's only a whore—nothing more! And you'd better not let yourself forget it, old man!* He took another deep breath and addressed Ashleigh again. "Well, then, Miss Sinclair, now it is your turn to ask questions. Is there anything you would care to know of the—ah, arrangements that await you?"

Ashleigh thought for a moment. Questions! She had dozens of them! How old was the duke's grandson, for example; she hoped he was about six or seven—an age at which she could instruct him most comfortably. And what was the duke, his grandfather, like? Would she be seeing much of him as well? And what of the boy's parents, and the rest of the household? Yes, she had all too many questions, and she suddenly felt as if, perhaps, it might be rude or seem too forward of her to bombard this poor man with all that weighed on her mind. It wouldn't do to make a nuisance of herself before she'd actually begun her stay or assumed the governess's position. So in the end she settled for merely one query, and a rather innocuous one at that. "What is His Grace's grandson's name, sir? I'd like to know that."

Adams's eyebrows lifted mildly at the question. For some reason he hadn't thought such a female would be interested in the identities of her clients, and certainly not to the extent that it would be her first question regarding the task she was to perform. He'd rather expected questions about money, for example, or the nature of the amenities she would enjoy while staying at Ravensford Hall—the size of her chamber, perhaps, or the number of servants at her disposal. Well, she had surprised him again, and with a shrug to try to dispel the aura of perplexing intrigue she'd begun to weave, he answered her. "His lordship's name is Brett Westmont—Lord Westmont to you, Miss Sinclair. He currently holds one of His Grace's lesser titles. That is, he is officially known as Viscount Westmont. Of course, on the day his grandfather passes away, he will become His Grace, duke of Ravensford. He is the heir, you see."

"I see," said Ashleigh, somberly nodding her head. She was recalling the now faraway world of her own early upbringing, where the daily use of such titles was automatic and taken for granted. Her own father had been a peer with the lesser hereditary title of baronet, but his line had been an old one, reaching back to the days of William the Conqueror, and their small but closely knit family had enjoyed many of the privileges she felt she could expect to witness under the roof of her new employer. Suddenly a lump formed in her throat and she felt the sharp sting of tears threaten her eyes as, for the first time in years, she allowed herself a keen sense of longing for the life and family she had once had.

*Oh, Mother, Father!* her heart cried out. *Why did you have to die so young? I can barely recall your faces, yet sometimes, like now, I miss you terribly! And Patrick...how could fate be so unkind as to rob me of you as well? Sweet brother with the devil's own mischief in your eyes! What I wouldn't give to be going into this new adventure with you by my side!*

But as the hoofbeats of the carriage horses and the turning of the wheels moved steadily onward, Ashleigh's longings faded and she knew she must face her future alone. Closing her eyes, she forced herself into a state of calm acceptance, laced with just the barest hint of a plea. *Oh, let them be kind,* she prayed. *If they will just be kind and decent, I shall surely manage the rest!*

# Chapter Four

Robert Adams looked down at the drawn, pale face on the pillows and felt a rush of pity overwhelm him. *So this is how it all ends,* he mused darkly. *Here is this man who in his time represented the best his era had to offer—intelligence, strength, power, wealth, all of it, and yet, being so richly endowed, he managed to use all of his gifts well, making the most of what he'd been given. How we used to envy him, we common folk who had the privilege of knowing and serving the man—and did so happily, yet always with a twinge of regret that we were not in his place....*

Adams closed his eyes for a moment, anxious to ward off the tears that threatened, and which he, for all the world, would not have his old friend awaken and see. There came to mind the time, in the past century, that the duke had made a speech in the House of Lords, defending the rights of the American colonials to fair representation in parliament, considering the taxes they were being asked to pay their mother country. Adams smiled to himself. *You were so very astute, old friend. You were among those who warned of dire consequences if no one took heed of what was happening in America, and time bore out the truth of those prophetic warnings. Sir Edmund Burke's speeches notwithstanding, yours were the best and wisest of that time. Would that the nation had listened to you!*

*Ah, yes,* Adams continued, *the best his era had to offer...and yet, now here he lies, taking his final breaths and looking for all the world like any common grandfather on his*

*deathbed.... Well, John Westmont, duke of Ravensford, I shall
be saddened to see you go, and I shall miss your undeniable
presence in—*

"Robert!" came the thin rasp of a voice from the bedclothes. "You can just stop your looking at me like that! I'm
not dead yet, you know...though it won't be long...." The
duke paused a moment, seeking to catch his breath, but he held
Adams's eyes as he did so, daring him to comment on his
weakened condition.

At last feeling he had gathered enough strength, he continued. "I have no illusions about my own future, old friend, so
spare me your pity, but what I am anxious about is Brett's! Tell
me, did you bring her? Is the woman here?"

Adams nodded. "Lady Margaret has seen to her installation in the proper chamber, Your Grace."

The duke nodded weakly, even this small exertion costing
him strength. "Good, good," he rasped, then beckoned with
a finger for Adams to draw closer. "I hope," he added with an
amused smile, "my sister's withering glare did not scorch you
when you presented the woman to her, Robert! Owing to my
poor health, I've been forced to include Margaret in my
scheme, and she's consented to go along with it because she's
so hot to set up the alliance with her dear Hastingses again, but
if you could have seen her face the day I stated my plans! Ah,
Robert, it was a vision I'll carry to my grave." He chuckled.
"To see that haughty visage of hers wrinkled up in distaste at
my—"

Here the chuckle gave way to a paroxysm of coughing; Adams leaned over him with concern, then turned and reached for
a goblet of water that stood on a nearby stand; he quickly held
it to the old man's lips, propping up his head at the same time
with a hand beneath the pillows. At length the coughing subsided, and the duke fell weakly back upon the bed.

"Ah, yes...best conserve my strength, I suppose." John
Westmont's voice was a mere shred of a whisper. "Especially
since I'll need it in dealing with my grandson! Now, Robert, will
you do me one favor?"

"Anything, Your Grace," Adams said quickly.

"Give me a few minutes' rest," said the duke, "and then send Brett to me. It's time I forged the final link in his education regarding women!"

Half an hour later Brett Westmont was striding from the stables toward the rear garden entrance to the house, it being the closest to the wing where the duke's private quarters lay. He was still full of the exhilarating effects of the ride he'd just taken across the lush countryside of his grandfather's estate. *Ah, Kent in springtime!* he thought as he paused before the massive chestnut tree in the garden where he used to play as a young child. *I'd forgotten how lovely it can be!* His eyes roamed over the slowly darkening meadows and shadowy trees in the distance, beginning to purple now in the fading light. From the corners of the garden walls came the steady chirrup of crickets, and not too far away, the mellow sound of cattle lowing, but all else was silent, with not even the faintest stirring of a breeze to mar the still, evening air.

He stopped for a moment longer, running his hand over the tree's rough bark and was all at once filled with a sense of melancholy so deep, it seemed to pierce his soul. *What am I doing with my life these days,* he asked himself, *that is so all-consuming, so terribly important, that I have failed to take the time to pause and drink of beauty and tranquillity such as this? How long it's been since I even realized such moments still exist!*

He shook his head sadly then, at what he suddenly perceived as his own folly and followed this with a bark of mirthless laughter. All at once his head filled with scenes of his life as it had been for the past several years—the long, empty days at sea where, more frequently than not, his official mission was so boring, he would doff his gentleman's garb and throw himself headlong into common seaman's labor, just to make the time pass faster . . . the wild, senseless nights in London, the incessant rounds of parties, routs and balls, crowded with people who spoke much, yet said little . . . the boredom of frivolous gossip, high-stakes card games and beautiful, yet dull, mistresses who with predictable regularity dropped from sight as quickly as they appeared . . . Where was it all taking him?

He thought, then, of the old man lying amid the bedcovers in his upstairs chamber, awaiting his end. *Ah, Grandfather! Is this what it's all been for? You bade me work hard and apply myself while you trained and groomed me for the life I was to lead one day, to follow in your footsteps, and I have done so, willingly, unflinchingly, for it was important to earn your respect...your love.... But now that I've done so, where do I go from here? How do I apportion some sense and meaning to an existence that, by virtue of those very skills and achievements you exhorted me to attain, runs along so smoothly, I cannot fail but to look about me now and ask, what now? What are my challenges? Shall I too end up a sick and failing old man, lying alone in an upstairs chamber, waiting for the lights to dim?*

At last Brett sighed and dropped his hand from the tree's trunk. He glanced upward and saw the dimly lit windows he knew to grace the south side of his grandfather's corner room. *Well,* he thought with more than a trace of stoical resignation, *enough of me and my world-weariness right now. Up there lies the only person in the world who gives a damn whether I live or die, and he's waiting for me. I'd better see what I can do to make his last moments count.* And with a resolute squaring of his shoulders, Brett went into the house.

The duke was asleep when Brett entered the chamber, but woke readily to the soft click of the latch as his grandson closed the door behind him. "Ah, Brett, boy, you're here!" He gestured toward the bedside chair where Robert Adams had been sitting earlier. "Come, sit down beside me and we can talk without your having to strain to hear." The duke gave a weak chuckle. "Ah, this damnable failure of the body! I tell you, Brett, I'd have ended it all long ago if I'd known it was to be like this!"

Brett threw the old man a sharp look of concern as he lowered his tall frame into the chair. "You cannot mean that, sir. It's not like you to talk of—"

"It's not like the me I *used* to be, you mean!" interrupted the duke. "The man you see before you is a different kettle of fish,

I assure you, but I've not called you here to discuss me and my frailties. I've asked you to come because I want to talk about *you*."

"About me," said Brett, interest showing in his turquoise eyes. "With regard to—?"

The duke was silent for a moment as the question hung in the air. He was at a loss to know how to approach the subject agreeably. Finally he decided to plunge in headlong, for he was acutely aware that time was running out for him. "Brett, it's about this attitude you have toward women and marriage. It's been troubling me."

The look on Brett's face couldn't have been plainer, accompanied as it was by a snort of obvious disdain. "*Troubling* you! I fail to see why, since it was an attitude bred wholly *by* you! 'Women are a canker,'" he quoted, "'a blight on—'"

"Yes, yes," rasped the duke impatiently. "I know all that and need no reminders of my speeches. And the fact remains, dear Brett, that all I've cautioned you about, regarding the so-called delicate sex, is lamentably true, believe me!"

"So—?" Brett questioned. "Where is the problem?"

"The problem," snapped the duke with a surprising spurt of vigor that reminded Brett of the grandfather of his youth, "is that you seem to have forgotten that I nevertheless also taught you that females are, in one unavoidable regard, totally necessary: in the breeding process, to produce heirs!" He fell back upon the pillows from which he had arisen, again looking weak and tired.

Brett watched the old man's face for a second and was momentarily moved to pity, but, seeing which turn their conversation was taking, forced himself to deal with his irritation. "I see," he said at last. "So you would have me wed...to the Hastings cow...and see her quickly breeding!"

The duke's eyebrows lowered in a darkening scowl that again reminded Brett of earlier times. "You can save the stings of your acid tongue for your friends at Almack's, m' boy! I'll have none of it!" Here a sudden spasm of coughing seized the duke's wasted frame, but as Brett reached for the bedside water goblet, he waved him away, and soon the coughing ceased. "'Cow,' indeed!'' sniffed the duke. ''Heavens, man, she's one of the most sought-after heiresses of the season, I'm told!''

Brett's sneering smile preceded a voice laced with disgust. ''It would seem you've allowed the Lady Margaret your ear. Can it be you no longer find her company tedious or repulsive?''

At this the Duke shook his head in a gesture of sad dismay. ''Dammit, boy, I had hoped to get through this session with a modicum of intelligent discussion and civility, not to mention *sensitivity*, but I now see I must take the bull by the horns, and sensitivity be damned!''

Brett looked at the resolute will now resting in the blue eyes and waited, knowing something important was forthcoming.

''It has occurred to me,'' continued the duke, ''that there may be a major underlying cause for this unreasonable resistance of yours toward taking a wife—a cause that I have taken immediate steps to counteract.''

Watching the turquoise eyes that met his gaze, the duke knew he had his grandson's complete attention now, and so, plunged ruthlessly on. ''I speak of your singular omission in the education that has been lavished on you, Brett—your *inexperience with women*! No, it's no use to deny it, so don't even bother. Uncomfortable as it renders me to admit it to you, I've had careful and close tabs kept on you over the years, and not once has any word come back to me about your fraternization with females. It *must* mean you are yet a virgin, or close to it. What else would explain it? Adams has a remarkable penchant for thoroughness, as you can well attest, and—'' Suddenly a fit of coughing overtook the old man again, and this time it was so violent, it seemed it would tear his withered frame in half.

Brett's look of incredulity at the words he'd just heard gave way to one of deep concern as he witnessed the attack. Compassion etched his features as he reached for the water goblet that, this time, was gratefully accepted. When the fit had at last subsided, he saw before him the specter of his grandfather as he'd known him—a strong man who was now dying—and the acute realization of this robbed him of any speech of denial he

had been prepared to make. Softly, he queried, "Are you too
ill to continue, Grandfather? Shall I leave you to rest until—"

"No...no," came the much weakened response. "No...
time...let me finish...." There was a long pause as the duke
appeared to be mustering his remaining energy. Then he began
again, though Brett had to lean forward to catch all the words.

"You need to learn the ways of bedding a woman, lad, and
I've arranged, through Adams, to take care of that for you."
He smiled weakly. "After all, your ignorance is actually my
own doing, my...fault...so it is only fitting that I see that it
comes to an end.

"Listen carefully. Installed at this very moment, in your
chamber, is a tasty little morsel...a woman of...pleasure,
handpicked by Adams for me, for the sole purpose of—of instructing you along the lines I've been discussing."

The duke suddenly made an enormous effort to rise, bracing himself shakily on his elbows, a look of eager concern on
his face. "Promise me now, lad, that you'll go to her...now—
at once! It's the last thing I may ever ask of you. Spend whatever time you feel you require to feel comfortable in bed with a
woman, and then make plans, posthaste, to wed.... *Promise
me!*"

These last words were uttered in the weakest of whispers, and
with them, the old man fell back on the pillows, silent and exhausted.

Brett stood looking at the still figure, not knowing whether
to laugh or cry. It was almost on his lips to set his grandfather
straight, but the grayish-purple hue about the duke's lips prevented him. Sadly, he chose what he hoped would be a wiser
course. After all, he mused, what harm would come of satisfying an old man's dying illusion?

And so, with a weary sigh, he took the duke's hand and answered, "Very well, Grandfather, I promise."

# Chapter Five

Ashleigh looked about her in the spacious, lavishly appointed bedchamber, her eyes feasting on its richness, its symbols of taste and obvious wealth. Against the interior wall to her left stood the room's focal point, a high tester bed, its heavy, deep blue velvet hangings not obscuring the massive grace of Chippendale's design. It was a style from an earlier era, she knew—not like the furniture in the majority of the rooms at Hampton House, which were done in the latest Regency mode; its quiet elegance as well as that of the other pieces in the chamber, spoke of a place furnished with care, in a manner that would tastefully withstand the fleeting dictates of fashion's whims.

She glanced down at the thick Eastern carpet under her feet, its intricate designs drawing the eye into a splendid maze of deep wine reds, jewel-like blues and delicate creams, and she resisted the urge to kick off her slippers and dig her toes into its silky softness.

There had been a carpet like it in a room she now recalled with vivid clarity—Patrick's bedchamber at Sinclair House. Suddenly her gaze drifted to the two windows with their velvet draperies that matched the blue of the bedhangings. She knew why she was thinking of her childhood home so much right now, and it had little to do with Turkey carpets or fine English furniture.

Quickly, she walked over to stand before one of the twin windows and, pulling aside the blue velvet, looked out. It was quite dark now, but a nearly full moon had appeared over the horizon as she accompanied the man named Adams to this place, its pale shape casting enough light over the changing landscape to enable her to view most of the scenery in some detail through her carriage window. Now, as she surveyed the lovely bucolic countryside, she was again caught up in the aching sense of familiarity that had first hit her during the journey. Yes, incredible though it seemed, she was sure: this was the countryside of her childhood!

Although she'd been not quite seven the last time she'd seen Kent, there were memories of her early years here that would always remain with her. Looking south, she fancied she could still see the gentle banks of the Medway River, which, Adams had confirmed, was the one they'd spied as they were passing over the Downs en route. Not too much farther south lay the town of Tunbridge Wells, where Patrick and her father had taken her to a wonderful country fair when she was five. And that way lay Knole, home of friends she and her parents used to visit, while Penshurst Place, another vast country house she'd once visited, lay in yet another direction, but not too far from here either.

Even the air had seemed familiar when she alighted from the carriage after it pulled to a halt on the large circular drive below, and she remembered Adams giving her a queer sort of look after she'd paused for a moment, closing her eyes and breathing deeply, just to drink in the sweet nostalgic scent of it. *How very odd*, she thought, *to be returning here after all these years.... It's almost as if life were circular, in a way.... I wonder what other surprises this new turn in my life has in store for me....*

She turned from the window and took another long, slow look about the room. The only inelegant object in it was the small, worn leather valise Megan had lent her to hold the few meager belongings she owned. Her friend had apologized profusely for the shabbiness of its appearance, explaining with a wry laugh that she owned no other, owing to the fact that she traveled very little these days, her "profession" being a stationary one. But Ashleigh had protested the apology, saying it was hardly necessary. Hadn't Megan already outdone herself by digging into her hard-won savings to present her with a parting gift—a beautiful walking dress with matching pelisse and bonnet?

She paused a moment in front of a handsome walnut chest of drawers with a serpentine front and peered into the graceful little Queen Anne looking glass above it. The bonnet, like her dress, was a beautiful cornflower blue, with a double row of paler blue ruche about the brim, echoing the dozen rows of similar ruche at the hem of her skirt. She smiled into the mirror, revealing a single dimple in her left cheek as well as a row of perfect white teeth. *Why,* she thought with some surprise, *I actually look...pretty!* Then she frowned, glancing away from the glass in confusion. Were governesses supposed to look pretty? Would the duke find her so, and if he did, would it suit?

But Ashleigh had no more time to contemplate her doubts over her appearance, for just then there came a firm knocking at the door. Without thinking, she responded with a form commonly used at Hampton House when bidding someone enter; instilled among its inhabitants by Madame, it was always uttered in French. *"Entrez,"* she called.

The door swung open and there, before her, stood the handsomest man she'd ever seen! He was easily six feet tall, with a head of deep chestnut hair worn in a casually tousled version of the à la Titus so in mode at the moment. His clothes, consisting of fawn-colored riding breeches that fit him like his own skin and a well-tailored deep green riding jacket, were also cut in the latest fashion, and he wore them with an air of casual grace, neither detracting from, nor adding overly to, their quiet, understated elegance.

But it was his face that captured and held Ashleigh's astonished attention: masculine perfection met her eyes in a symmetrical blending of features that could have been the model for classical statues of old—a wide, handsome brow, fringed by those chestnut curls; a straight, chiseled nose that harmonized with the wide, sensual mouth that just then was faintly turned up at one corner, hinting of a lazy smile; high, angular cheekbones; a firm, square chin that bespoke strength and perhaps a hint of stubbornness; and then there were his *eyes*! She'd not known such a color to *exist* in eyes before! Of a rich, sea-foam turquoise, they were heavily lashed and ever so slightly deep-set; but beyond this, they were far more than a summation of their color and shape. There was something disturbing and yet equally compelling about them, and Ashleigh found herself curious over the complex mysteries she sensed in their depths; they were the eyes of a man who had seen and tasted much, yet yearned for something more, and with this longing came a tinge of...sadness, yes, that was it, she decided, although if anyone had asked her how she knew these things, she'd have been at a loss to tell him.

Then, just as she was about to tear her riveted gaze away and form the courage to say something, the look in his eyes changed, and she thought she saw something else—a hard-ness, perhaps, coupled with a hint of arrogance, maybe even cruelty. But before she could analyze any of this, he spoke, his rich, masculine voice filling the chamber.

"It appears I may have been done a service after all. I sud-denly find myself sequestered with as fetching a vision of Aphrodite as I've yet to encounter!" He grinned down at her as he closed the door behind him, and the combined action, together with his words, suddenly made Ashleigh feel afraid. Sequestered? What did he mean by that? And shouldn't the door have been left open during this interview?

Quickly swallowing to moisten a mouth suddenly gone dry, Ashleigh endeavored to steer the conversation into safe and sensible waters. "I—that is—ah—I'm pleased to meet you, Your Grace. I—I am Ashleigh Sinclair." She finished with a brief little curtsy.

A mirthless chuckle met her ears. "Do not elevate me to the dukedom yet, my pretty. My grandfather still lives."

"Your—your *grandfather*?" Ashleigh questioned. "B-But aren't *you*...I mean, I'd assumed..."

Her words trailed off into a bewildered silence, for the handsome stranger was obviously no longer listening to her. He had begun to peruse her person instead, slowly walking around her frozen form as she stood—perplexed and now even a bit alarmed—rooted to the carpet under her feet. Slowly, languidly, he circled, studying her body from every angle, thoroughly, expertly—totally, until she began to feel like some leg of mutton at the butcher's; indeed, she could scarcely remember ever selecting the choicest items on a shopping list for Madame's table, on market day, with more care than the infinite thoroughness this man brought to bear on this examination.

Brett, meanwhile, was amazed at his luck. What he'd expected when he arrived to do his grandfather's bidding he couldn't quite say, as he'd been intent on humoring the old man, but he was quite sure it hadn't been anything like the vision that now greeted his eyes. The creature was dazzling! As tempting and perfect a little bit of muslin as any he'd ever seen!

His gaze moved wonderingly over her slight, delicately curving form that appeared all at once fragile and slender, yet ripe and alluring. Although the high-waisted dress she wore fell in straight lines, the soft sheerness of its folds served more to emphasize her slender curves than to hide them, and the round, tempting fullness of the breasts above the waistline was more than accentuated by the Empire cut. His eyes traveled again down the flowing lines of her skirt, and he knew that despite her tiny, almost elfin frame, she possessed graceful legs that were long in proportion to the rest of her.

Soon his gaze moved upward again, until it found her face. *And what a face it was!* He sucked in his breath for a moment at its beauty, then slowly let it out, at the same time drinking in the perfection of those features and the heart-shaped elegance they graced: the delicate prominence of her cheekbones, her straight little nose and sweetly shaped mouth; the huge sapphire-blue eyes with their generous fringe of sooty black lashes matching the pile of shiny, raven-colored curls that peeked from beneath the ridiculous looking bonnet she wore.... Here he paused and pondered what he saw for a moment.... Yes, she was a rare beauty, flawless in every respect, but ... something was wrong somewhere....

Quickly Brett's eyes went back to hers and lingered there, carefully assessing, until suddenly it came to him. Her eyes...he would *swear* they were *guileless*, *innocent* somehow; and yet he knew that *couldn't be*! This girl—for girl was what she was; she had to be very young, scarcely out of her teens, if that old—was a *whore*! How, then, did she come by such a look of purity and unsullied innocence? It would bear finding out, and so he decided to pursue a different tack.

Straightening, Brett gave her an engaging grin—one he'd known to charm the ladies at court and anywhere else he cared to bestow it—and followed this with the briefest of bows. "It would appear my *manners* need tutoring as well as ... *other things*, ah—Miss Sinclair, isn't it? Forgive my rudeness at not inquiring after your comfort. Tell me, have you dined?" This was asked casually over one shoulder as he ambled over to a small secretary and, lowering its drop leaf, revealed a silver tray bearing several crystal decanters; these were filled with liquids ranging in color from pale amber to the deepest honey brown. From the tray he also produced a pair of finely cut crystal wineglasses, which he held as he looked at her questioningly.

Realizing belatedly that she had yet to answer his question, Ashleigh hurriedly cleared her throat and replied, "No, Your Gr—ah, my lord, I've not dined this evening, but I had a late-afternoon repast ... with tea, that is, and I—ah—find I'm not all that hungry." The truth was that, up until the moment this man had entered the chamber, she had felt she was near starving, for "tea" at Hampton House had consisted of just that, a single cup, for she'd been too apprehensive over her forthcoming journey to avail herself of even a single crumb of any of the cakes and tarts Dorcas had pressed upon her.

At this moment, however, she found herself caring little about food and a great deal about the circumstances of her imminent employment. Who *was* this man? If not the duke, as he'd indicated, but his grandson, then just what was his relationship to the child, Brett, whom she was to have as her charge? Had the duke remarried at an advanced age, producing a second set of children much younger than the father or mother of this man, thus producing a later and much younger grandson as well? Or were the two grandsons simply born many years apart as occasionally happened in families?

She must have appeared puzzled while she pondered all this, for her companion chuckled as he handed her a half-filled glass of a pale-colored liquid saying, "You needn't look so perplexed, my dear. It's only sherry. I thought we might share a glass while we discuss your—ah—situation." This last was spoken with a decided inflection of amusement while at the same time his eyes roamed freely over her, and again Ashleigh experienced a sense of discomfort under his perusal.

When his eyes met hers, her discomfort grew so great, she quickly dropped her gaze, hearing him laugh softly as she did so. Then, remembering her manners, she accepted the glass he held out to her, made a murmur of thanks and took a sip.

When she at last dared to raise her eyes to him, she found him once again looking intently at her, those turquoise eyes piercing in their intensity. Slowly, he raised his glass to his mouth, his eyes never leaving hers as he drank. Then the glass was lowered and a slow, lazy smile curled his lips.

"Tell me, Miss Sinclair," he murmured languidly (for there was nothing rushed in his manner), "you're new at your profession, are you not?"

*Ah, here it is,* thought Ashleigh. *He thinks me too young and inexperienced to be a governess for his brother...or half brother, or whatever. Well, I'll just have to show him otherwise!* Drawing herself up as tall as she could, she fixed him with a bold look, saying, "I may be young for my chosen profession, my lord, but I believe you will find me well qualified. I have studied many years to attain my present level of proficiency."

Brett's eyebrows flew sharply upward at her proud response, and a broad grin spread across his features. With a rapid movement, he freed her wineglass from her hand and took both it and his own and set them down on the tray. Then, before she knew what was happening, Ashleigh found herself drawn up into his arms in a tight embrace as his mouth descended on hers.

Her first sensation was of a warm mouth covering her own, of a hard, well-muscled male body pressed ever so tightly against her softer, more pliant form. Dimly, in some nether part of her brain, she knew she must stop what was happening, but at the same time she felt herself being swept away by a host of new and incredible sensations. There was still his mouth meeting hers, but it was moving now, his lips gliding sensuously, his tongue sliding between, to tease and play until it had parted her lips, and then the feel of his tongue actually *entering her mouth*! A giddy weakness spread itself throughout her body, turning her knees to jelly, her limbs to water, and she wondered if it was the sherry she'd swallowed. She was faintly aware of his hands, which had begun to wander up and down her back, gliding over her quaking shoulders, then moving sensuously downward until they clasped her rounded buttocks and drew her impossibly closer...*unthinkably, dangerously closer!*

It was this last action that finally roused her from her benumbed and passive state. With a sharp gasp of outrage, she pulled her tingling lips from his and began to push at his chest with her hands, which, until now, had been gently imprisoned there.

"Sir! Your—your lordship—whoever you are, you *must* not—you must *stop* this *at once*!" she cried, even as his mouth searched hers again.

A low rumble of laughter met her ears as his hands easily caught hers and drew them behind her back while turquoise eyes bored into her own. "The name is Brett, my lovely, Brett Westmont, and I fail to see the problem. We're simply beginning my first—ah—lesson!"

*Brett Westmont!* her disbelieving mind cried out. *This was her charge!* Her brain reeled against this new piece of information, trying frantically to come to terms with its import, but then she suddenly had no time to think any further, for his mouth was against hers again, sucking the very breath from her body. She tried to free her hands, but he captured them easily with one of his while the other one worked at the ribbons of her bonnet, quickly untying them, sending it tumbling to the floor. Then she felt his lips at her throat where they nibbled and played with the tender flesh there, and seconds later his free hand slid to her breast where it cupped, then stroked, then lightly pinched the tip.

Now Ashleigh was assaulted by an even wilder sensation. It was as if a direct line existed between the peak of her breast and some place deep within her core, in the region of the juncture of her thighs. All was sensation—a rushing, then eddying, then spiraling sensation that hovered somewhere between need and longing. With a sharp cry, she twisted to one side, thinking to break this latest contact, but she only succeeded in rubbing her throbbing nipple more intensely against those caressing fingers, and the result was a white-hot heat assaulting her loins.

A whimper escaped her lips as she felt her knees buckle, but Brett was ready for her; with a quick movement he bent to swoop her up in his arms and then turned toward the bed. With a couple of easy strides he carried her there and deposited her gently on the coverlet.

Ashleigh thought to take this respite to try to reason with him, stop him, tell him that somehow there'd been a terrible mistake, but he allowed her not a moment to do so. All at once he was beside her on the bed, his big body stretching alongside hers, then covering it as he again pulled her to him.

Now Ashleigh fought with all her might, twisting, biting, kicking, doing whatever she could to fend him off. This met with some success, for no one could have been more surprised than Brett when he finally realized she was protesting in earnest, and he loosened his hold on her to murmur, "What the devil . . . ?"

Ashleigh seized the reprieve, rolling quickly off the bed and onto her feet. She stood beside the bed, her black hair loosened from its pins, tumbling wildly about her shoulders, her chest heaving, fire shooting from her sapphire eyes. "Now, see here, Lord Westmont—Brett—whoever you are, I demand to know—"

But she got no further. Leaping from the bed, Brett was beside her in an instant, and the look in his eyes stilled her tongue. "No, *you* look here, Miss Sinclair! I don't know what game it is you play in that bawdy house you come from, but I do happen to know my grandfather, the duke, paid good money for your services, and I intend to see he receives full value for the pound!" He jerked her to him, his mouth cruelly claiming hers while his fingers worked at the fastenings of her dress. In spite of her struggles he held her close for several long moments, then suddenly released her, but as he did so, her dress fell from her shoulders and then, with brief assistance from him, landed softly at her feet in a heap.

Ashleigh's face went white with shock, and she stared at him in open disbelief, but Brett, anxious now to get on with it, his lust whetted by the tempting curves he saw revealed through the semitransparent fabric of her shift, drew her roughly to him and again plundered her mouth with his.

Still Ashleigh was determined to thwart him, her furiously racing brain all the while trying to impart some sense to what was happening. She was just coming to terms with the notion that she must have come up against a madman when she heard a loud ripping sound and a second later, felt her shift fall from her body.

With a shriek, she stepped away from him a pace, shock and fear registering in her eyes as they met his. But only soft masculine laughter met her eyes as Brett returned her look. Then she saw his eyes travel downward, coursing slowly over the exposed flesh, looking for all the world as if he would devour everything he saw.

Ashleigh felt her face grow hot with shame, for no one, not even Dorcas, had ever seen her woman's body naked, and she tried vainly to cover herself with her hands, the pitifully useless movements making her feel all the more ashamed and embarrassed beyond telling.

Then, as she stood there gaping at him in astonished horror, he began to remove his own clothing. His jacket hit the carpet, quickly followed by his cravat and shirt. When his hands went to the fastening at his breeches, Ashleigh turned her head, but this merely met with more soft laughter.

Screwing up her courage, she fixed her eyes on a spot on the carpet and addressed him, her words tumbling out in a breathy whisper. "My name is Ashleigh Sinclair. I've been hired as a governess for the duke of Ravensford's grandson. It's true, I resided in a—a house of light virtue for the past dozen years, but my lord, you *must* believe me, I made an honest living there—as a servant maid. My lord, I beg you, I—I am not what you think!''

"A pretty tale," Brett replied. "I commend you on your dramatic abilities, m'dear. You play your part with consummate skill, but now I fear you must leave center stage to *me*! *I* shall be the master of revels tonight!''

Ashleigh saw his breeches fall to the carpet, atop the boots he'd already removed, and reluctantly raised her eyes to meet his. When she did, she was instantly sorry, for she beheld a turquoise gaze burning with smoldering passion. Without realizing what she was doing, she dropped her eyes, only to recoil in horrified shock: it was her first sight of a man naked.

Instantly she turned to flee, her cheeks burning with shame, but he reached out and captured her easily, again swinging her up in his arms until she was nestled against his bare chest.

"My lord!" she gasped. *"Please!* I tell you, *you must not do this!* It's all been some kind of horrible mistake!''

But Brett was beyond listening or giving credence to what he had made up his mind, was a fantastic tale concocted by a highly experienced young whore for the sole purpose of whetting a man's appetite. Tossing her lightly on the large fourposter, he quickly joined her there, pinning her struggling body beneath his. With a rapid movement, he drew her frantically waving arms above her head and then secured them there by holding both her wrists with one hand. Then, with the other, he began to explore her writhing, naked body.

Ashleigh shut her eyes tight, wishing she could close out what was happening to her as easily as she could the sight of it, but there was no dismissing the devastating, intimate things he was doing to her body. His mouth covered hers while his tongue probed between her lips, gained entrance, and slipped seductively inside; his free hand found her breasts, softly stroking their roundness, then lightly brushing their peaks. These actions, meanwhile, resulted in the same strangely devastating reactions within her body as before. Deep inside her center she felt as if a liquid fire were building, its wet warmth stealing outward in ever increasing spirals until the very tips of her fingers and toes felt deliciously weak.

She lay in helpless, bewildered confusion as Brett's lips moved from her mouth to her chin and on to the graceful arch of her throat, placing soft, nibbling kisses where they went; and all the while the fire raged....

Then his mouth trailed over her bare shoulder, moving steadily downward until it reached one breast and closed over the aching peak. He curled his tongue around and played and sucked and nibbled, and still the unbearable sensation in her loins grew.

Somewhere she thought she heard a moan, and when it came again, she realized it emanated from her own throat! She at last opened her eyes, and then uttered a sharp, helpless cry, for Brett's gaze was bent intently on hers, and he smiled, a look of triumph on his face.

Then she felt his knee between her thighs, forcing them apart, and before she could think to protest, his body lowered on hers, and she felt the proof of his manhood at the place where they joined. The shock of this intimate contact brought her sharply to her senses; all languor fled, and she was about to cry out for him to cease when a sharp, tearing pain shot up between her thighs, deep inside her.

Her cry of pain came directly on the heels of Brett's astonishment; he'd felt the obstruction briefly before driving home his desire, and a look of stunned surprise registered on his face. But he was far beyond stopping at this point, himself a captive of his lust, and he began to move in her, rhythmically, expertly, in and out, again and again, until finally his body convulsed in a mighty heave, and it was done.

When at last Brett was able to gather his wits and analyze what had just occurred, he rolled off the still form beneath him, sat on the edge of the bed and turned to look at her.

Ashleigh felt his weight leave her body, and immediately turned on her side, away from him. She curled herself into a tight little mass as the sobs began to rack her body.

Brett continued to stare at her, bewildered and amazed at what the past several moments had revealed. His eyes traveled from the sobbing, huddled form on the bed to the telltale smears of blood on the coverlet beside her. *"Christ!"* he muttered, running his fingers roughly through his hair. "How in hell—" He broke off as the sobbing continued, now sounding to him even more pitiful in the otherwise still chamber. He made an awkward gesture in the direction of the girl, then thought better of it and turned instead to the foot of the bed where an additional coverlet lay folded. This he quickly snatched, giving it an impatient shake to unfold it, and placed it hurriedly over the weeping girl.

Then, with a muttered curse, Brett turned, strode to the secretary across the room and quickly poured himself a glass of brandy; he downed its contents in one gulp, welcoming the fiery sensation as it went down. As he poured himself another and sipped it slowly, he began to sift through his turbulent thoughts, trying to piece together something that made sense of what had occurred.

The girl had been a *virgin*, yet she was a *whore*! *It didn't make sense!* Slowly his mind sorted out what he knew of womankind's oldest profession. There were, he knew, certain well-operated houses where those who ran them saw to it that they were able to cater to every kind of taste and preference. Some of these even found an occasional virgin to satisfy men with a preference for them, though he himself had never been so inclined. Indeed, he'd rarely availed himself of the talents of any kind of professional woman, finding he had a more-than-willing assortment of females to pick and choose from among the well-bred ladies of the *ton*. And in fact until tonight, he'd never actually bedded a virgin—though he recognized well enough the signs of a woman's having been one from boastful stories he'd heard over the years. Was this Ashleigh Sinclair one of those professionally trained virgins? His thoughts flew back to the brief time they'd spent together prior to her deflowering. There'd certainly been little in her behavior to indicate she'd been trained to please a man! In fact—what was that tale she'd tried to pass off? *Had* it, indeed, been just a story, or... And why would Adams—or his grandfather—have selected a virgin, even a trained one, if their objective—misguided as it was—had been to see *him* tutored?

Finishing the contents of his glass, he turned toward the bed. All was quiet there now, and from the slight but steady rise and fall of the form beneath the coverlet, he knew she'd fallen asleep.

Suddenly Brett's lips curled into a grin. She had been the most tempting little piece of baggage he'd seen in some time, and a true beauty. How was he to be blamed for what had happened when all the circumstances were considered? He sighed. The point was, now that he'd deflowered the chit, what was to be done next? And if she wasn't what they'd thought, and there had been some sort of mistake or mix-up as she'd claimed, would there be any nasty repercussions? An irate father to be dealt with? A family honor to be righted? His mind was just fastening on this last possibility—for he suddenly realized the girl had spoken with the polished accent and correctness of the upper classes—when suddenly there came a knock at the door.

"Yes?" he called, reaching for his breeches.

"The Lady Margaret wishes to know if you will be joining her at table this evening, your lordship." It was the voice of Higgins, his manservant.

Brett tossed the breeches onto a side chair as a new notion struck him. Glancing briefly at the sleeping form on the bed, he answered his man. "No, Higgins. My—ah—guest and I shall dine from a tray in this chamber. See to it, will you? In about a half hour or so."

"Very good, your lordship," replied the voice on the other side of the door, and then there were soft footsteps going down the hallway.

Brett walked over to the large bed and peered down at the sleeping girl on the far side of it. There was little he could see of her face, for the dark, tumbled mass of her hair hid it from his view, but merely the sight of those silken, shiny tresses renewed the heat of his blood, and in seconds he was remembering in detail how she'd felt in his arms. *Very well, little nymph,* he thought as a wry grin worked across his features, *perhaps there has been a terrible mistake, or even two,* he corrected, remembering the mistaken assumption about him, on his grandfather's part, that had brought her here in the first place. *But one thing is certain: One of us in this chamber could benefit from a few "lessons," and I've just made up my mind to enjoy that challenge!*

With a quick movement he was lying beside her on the bed, pressing his face into her fragrant hair and running his hand lightly over her draped form.

Ashleigh awoke slowly, a pleasant warmth infusing her body as she gradually moved into consciousness. Then, as the last vestiges of slumber left her, she began to remember where she was and what had happened to her here.

"You!" she breathed as she turned to look at the man who hovered over her, entirely too near.

"The name's Brett," he answered with a lazy grin, just as his hand reached to tuck an errant tendril of hair behind her ear.

The movement, especially the touch of his fingers on her delicate flesh, sent a shiver through her, and Ashleigh tried to pull away but found she was trapped, for part of her long hair was caught under his arm as he leaned on the mattress. "Wh-what are you doing, my lord?" she managed to whisper as she felt his finger trace the delicate line of her jaw, then move to brush her lips.

"Brett. The name is Brett," he said as his finger again grazed her bottom lip. "Say it, beautiful Ashleigh. Say my name."

"I . . . Brett . . ."

"That's better," he murmured, and his head slowly lowered until his mouth reached then lightly tasted where his finger had touched.

The kiss was soft and light at first, but then, as his lips lingered, it grew firmer, with a sensuous plying of her lips beneath his, until, before she knew it, her own were parting as the tip of his tongue slipped lightly between. Then she felt him pull softly at her bottom lip with his teeth while at the same time his hand caressed her shoulder, pushing the coverlet aside.

She was all at once reminded of the circumstances that had brought her here in the first place and drew breath to protest, but his mouth closed firmly over hers while his hand went lower to cup her bare breast. Alarmed now, and suddenly mindful of the shame and pain of their recent union, Ashleigh twisted her head to the side and pushed at his chest with her hands.

"No, little one, don't fight me," he murmured against her cheek. "I mean to give you pleasure this time."

"Pleasure!" she gasped, drawing back within the circle of his embrace to look at him. "Surely, my lord, you—you toy with me! You—oh, please—please don't hurt me again, I beg—"

Brett's soft laughter interrupted her plea as his turquoise eyes met her wide, fearful blue ones. "It doesn't hurt after the first time, little Ashleigh. Didn't they tell you that in your instructions?" Again his hand found her breast, and this time the thumb brushed expertly across the nipple, causing it to peak and harden instantly.

Ashleigh tried to ignore the answering response in her loins, concentrating on what he had just said. "In—instructions? I've had no instructions in—in *this*!" she insisted, and suddenly she felt the urge to weep, and the sharp sting of tears assailed her eyes. "Please, I—I beg of you, my l—Brett—let me go! I—I'll just return to—to where I came from. You—you needn't p-pay me. I—oh, just let me go...*please*!"

Brett watched her eyes fill up with tears as she spoke and almost relented, but then the echo of a refrain he'd heard a thousand times entered his head: *Women are duplicitous and evil, bringing no man aught but ill...good for only one thing...*

Suddenly Brett's embrace tightened, and he rolled until she was completely beneath him. "Hush!" he ordered, and his eyes bored into hers with a look of command. "This isn't going to hurt you, so be still. You might even come to enjoy it." All the while he spoke, his fingers played with her breasts, lightly stroking them, teasing their tips into hardened peaks. Then his head bent to follow where his fingers had been, his tongue working expertly until she began to writhe beneath him, soft little cries breaking from her throat as she succumbed.

Soon his hands were traveling lower, across the expanse of her soft, flat abdomen, then lower yet, his fingers tangling gently in the raven curls of the dark triangle below.

Ashleigh gave a gasp of surprise as one of them found the wet warmth of the crevice between her thighs, and before she could do more, his mouth closed over hers, and at the very moment his tongue entered her mouth, she felt his finger follow a similar course below. Slowly, and ever so gently, tongue and finger slipped in, then out again, then in, and then his thumb brushed the tiny bud above her opening, and all at once a shock of pleasure assaulted her. Again, his thumb did its work, and now Ashleigh's entire body responded with a quivering shudder of pure pleasure.

Brett raised his head and recognized the glazed look in her eyes. He made yet one more pass with his thumb, and at her answering moan, he smiled with knowing satisfaction. "Now, my lovely one," he whispered. "Now I'll prove that pain is no longer a part of this for you."

With a quick shifting of his weight, he positioned her beneath him, parted her trembling thighs and thrust into the waiting warmth between.

Ashleigh's mind fled her body, and all that was left was pure sensation. From the throbbing core at the center of this, and where she now felt an incredibly satisfying pressure building, she sensed a spiraling outward, as ring after ring of sweet pleasure pulsed through her. Vaguely she realized the man who possessed her body was moving on it in a steady rhythm, and she had begun to move with him, caught up in the heady throes of it. And all the while a longing was building, growing steadily stronger, robbing her of her senses.

Brett's mouth found hers again and, without even a protest, she found herself accepting the sensual thrusting of his expert tongue, even as her body accepted the demanding thrusts below, and in the next instant, she felt his body tense and then convulse on hers.

Then there was a muted male groan and a final thrust before he released her lips, and all was suddenly still, except for their ragged breathing; she felt him bury his face in her hair, and knew another part of him still lay buried within her. They lay together this way for several long minutes, neither speaking, while their breathing returned to normal.

At last, when he was sure he could speak intelligibly, Brett rolled to one side, pulling her with him in an embrace. "You—you either learn very fast, little one, or you finally remembered what they taught you," he said.

To Ashleigh, who was barely recovering from the shock of this latest experience—not to mention her surprise at how it had differed from the first—his words were like a splash of ice water on her senses. She wrenched herself away from his arms and jerked herself into a sitting position on the bed. "You—you *bastard!*" she snarled, using a word she'd only heard till now, and had never uttered herself. "How *dare* you cling to that fabrication—or misconception—or—or whatever it was, that I—that I'm—that I was *trained* for something like this! I was trained as an academic, I tell you! As a governess! Or, at least, that's what I was hired for. *Why* won't you believe me?"

Brett watched her blue eyes sparkle in anger and was momentarily captivated. She was, by far, the loveliest creature he'd ever taken to bed, and right now she resembled a small, spitting kitten, caught up as she was, somewhere between sexual arousal and irate femininity. He doubted she even realized the fetching picture she made, either in those moments before, when she'd enticed him beyond telling with her lush, perfect little body, or now, as she sat with her shiny black hair charmingly tangled, her eyes huge and blue, her ripe lips bruised by the passion of his kisses. And suddenly Brett made up his mind as to what he would do about the situation. The girl, whatever her background, was a natural and superb bedmate. He currently had a mistress in London—Lady Pamela Marlowe—but she was beginning to tire him, and who could be a more perfectly timed replacement than this tempting little piece of baggage? That was it! Of course, she required further training. . . .

With a devilish grin, Brett suddenly hopped off the bed and bent to pick up Ashleigh's discarded shift and traveling dress. He gave the shift a quick glance, eyeing its shredded fabric, and immediately discarded it, but the dress he tossed to her on the bed.

"Dress," he told her. "I'm sorry about the chemise, but don't fret. We'll order you a dozen new ones tomorrow."

Ashleigh looked at him warily as she drew the dress toward her; then, realizing what he'd said, responded angrily. "I have no intention of remaining here long enough to—"

"Dress!" he commanded.

His tone brooked no argument, and so she hastily began to comply, doing her best to clothe herself in the single garment under such awkward circumstances.

When at last she had succeeded in the difficult business (made doubly so by having to do it all under his relenting gaze), she slipped off the bed and bent to retrieve her discarded stockings, garters and slippers from where he'd somehow removed and thrown them earlier.

At last she stood before him totally clothed, and she was about to head for her valise where she knew she'd packed a hairbrush and some extra pins, when she heard him say, "Now remove your clothes."

Thinking she hadn't heard correctly, Ashleigh turned to him with a puzzled look. "I beg your pardon?"

Brett's voice was firm with command as he looked her straight in the eyes. "Strip," he said.

Ashleigh's eyes widened in disbelief. "But, I—you just told me—"

"I know what I told you, my dear," came the response, "but now I am telling you something else. It is time for a broadening of your...education. *Strip!*"

Ashleigh quaked at the tone in his voice and knew she had no choice but to comply. With shaking fingers and a face gone red with embarrassment, she reached for the fastenings of her dress.

After some time, during which the room remained deadly silent, her dress once again fell to the floor. Without looking at the man next to her, she then dutifully bent to remove her slippers, but a sharp command from Brett stopped her.

"Stop!" he ordered. "We shall leave your slippers and stockings on this time."

Ashleigh straightened, but kept her eyes focused on the floor.
She began, automatically, to cross her arms in another vain attempt at covering herself, but once more Brett's voice rang out
to forestall her movements.

"No! Leave your arms at your sides. You have a beautiful
body, and I would see all of it—unencumbered."

Ashleigh did as she was told, but the act cost her greatly. She
felt her cheeks go hot with shame as she stood rigidly facing
him.

"That's better," he murmured. "Now go to the bed and lie
down."

*Oh, God, he's some kind of cruel madman, I just know he
is!* she thought, but she turned and climbed onto the large bed,
even as a pair of silent tears traced their way down her burning
cheeks.

"No, not that way," came the strong voice behind her. "On
your belly. It's not too soon to learn of a little variety."

Ashleigh detected a note of amusement in his tone, and the
thought that her humiliation should so humor him sent a stab
of white-hot anger through her. With a furious toss of her curls,
she glanced at him over one shoulder and spat a sarcastic retort. "I'm so *glad* this sport amuses you, my lord!"

A low ripple of laughter met her ears, nothing more, and she
had to satisfy herself with a withering glare as her answer. Then
she turned on the bed, squirming to place herself in the position he'd demanded, little realizing that each wriggling movement of her small, curving derriere rendered her all the more
appealing to the man who watched and waited.

When at last she lay face down in the prone position, Ashleigh felt her tears subside; in their place her anger returned,
this time without any attendant words, but in full force. Duke's
son, or no, she vowed, some day this man would be made to
regret his behavior tonight. Just who did he think he was, anyway, to take her maidenhood from her so? Even the king or
prince regent wouldn't treat a young woman of good family this
way, she was sure of it. But then the thought came to her that
she had no way of proving to him that she was such a one—a

baronet's daughter. Why, he hadn't even believed her when she'd told him she was a virtuous servant girl!

But suddenly Ashleigh had no more time to contemplate her anger or the vagaries of Brett's treatment of her, for there was a soft footstep and then the feeling of a man's hands on her body. She sucked in her breath as they ran over her back and buttocks, then gasped as his fingers traced the crevice there before finally finding their way into the opening between her thighs. She moaned then, with humiliated resignation and abject shame, as she felt one strong finger enter her, and momentarily raised herself up on her elbows and tried to pull away.

"Be still!" he commanded, even as his finger probed deeper.

But Ashleigh's misery was so complete by now, she no longer cared what happened. With a sharp twist of her hips, she wrenched away from the devastating touch of those fingers, only to cry out in pain as his hand came smartly down with a sharp, spanking slap on her buttocks.

"Be still, I said!" he ordered.

Then, just as she was wondering what he would do next, Ashleigh felt the bed sag and the weight of him on her back as he mounted her from behind. She tried to struggle, but only succeeded in pushing her squirming buttocks into a position of utmost vulnerability, and with a gasp of dismay, she felt him drive his shaft into the place he'd already violated.

"Oh!" cried Ashleigh, partly in surprise, mostly in shock, for never, in all her years at Hampton House, had any piece of information slipped down to her that this was a way a man could take a woman.

"Hush!" Brett rasped, even as he gave forth with another hard thrust. Then the thrusts came even harder and faster, and Ashleigh felt herself caught up in the same incredible whirlwind of longing as before. His arms wrapped around her from behind and his hands found her breasts, cupping them while the thrusting rhythm continued. Then Brett's face was buried in the mass of heavy hair at her neck and she felt him tense momentarily before one final assault of his body told her it was over.

Moments passed while the room echoed with Brett's ragged breathing, and then, finally, he rolled to his side, pulling her with him.

"An admirable pupil, my sweet," she thought she heard him whisper, as she was drifting off to sleep, exhausted and ashamed.

# Chapter Six

Robert Adams was annoyed. Had he been the kind of man given to excessive emotions, he might even have been said to be furious, but such was not Adams's manner. Nevertheless, it took him a great deal of control to assume the well-modulated voice and external appearance of calm he had always assumed—indeed, prided himself on assuming, when dealing with others—as he stuck his head out the door of his hired carriage to address the driver.

"Well, my good fellow, what progress?"

The driver, a short, burly man with auburn hair and side whiskers, answered in a Scottish burr. "She's nae ready yet, sir, for a' the time it's cost, bu' gie us anither fi' minutes an'—ah, there ye hae it, Davey! Well done, laddie, well done!"

The "laddie" was the driver's son, a brawny youngster of about fourteen or fifteen; the pair of them had just spent the past two hours—and six minutes, Adams calculated as he dared to peer at his pocket watch again—removing a massive oak tree that had fallen across the only road that led from Cloverhill Manor to Ravensford Hall. It had apparently been uprooted in an early-summer thunderstorm that hit the area the night before last, and since the only ones to use this road were members of the Hastings and Westmont households and those who had business with them, Adams assumed it had not been cleared because he was the first to travel this route since the storm, curse the luck!

He had spent the afternoon at Cloverhill Manor at the request of Lady Margaret Westmont, meeting with the Hastingses on behalf of the duke to set the wheels in motion for an alliance between the two families. Adams smiled briefly at how easy it had been. More than twenty years ago his father, Raymond Adams, had had the task of setting up a similar arrangement between the Hastings family and the Westmonts, and most of that paperwork had survived—the firm of Adams and Adams kept meticulous records—forever. This had served him adequately as guidance in what would prove to be a detailed and intricately wrought contract.

As Adams felt the carriage lurch forward and heard its wheels grind beneath him, however, his thoughts turned fretful again. Normally he exhibited the patience of Job when encountering obstacles in the routine of his day-to-day affairs. This was because Adams rarely left anything to chance. If he estimated a meeting would take an hour to be completed, he always allowed an hour and a half; if the distance between two points of business required a two-hour journey, Adams allowed three. Punctuality was at the top of his list of virtues in all his dealings, business and personal, and he rarely fell short of it.

This morning, when he had arrived at Ravensford Hall at the behest of Lady Margaret, he'd heard her request that he begin arrangements with the Hastingses and planned his day accordingly. After a footman had been sent ahead to announce his visit, he'd traveled back to the inn at noonday to gather his papers. He dined well, though sparingly—Adams was vain enough to resist the gastronomical temptations that would force him to wear the corset donned by many men of fashion, the Prince of Wales included. He allowed what he thought would be more than adequate time to conclude his business and be back at the duke's home in time to intercept Brett before he arrived. At least, he'd *thought* he'd allowed enough time.

But during his visit with the Hastingses he'd learned that Brett was already home—Lady Elizabeth had heard it from servants' gossip after his horse had been spotted by a groom. The lady had also, Adams recalled, been highly miffed that neither his lordship nor anyone in his family had taken pains to send her word that he was returning home at this time, and it had taken a great deal of diplomatic skill on Adams's part to smooth her ruffled feathers. This news, however, had alarmed him greatly, for Lady Margaret had totally neglected to inform him of Brett's arrival when she spoke this morning, and he'd feared his plans to confess his sin of having kept Brett's grandfather in the dark regarding his social life all these years, might already have been thwarted.

But Lady Margaret's silence had also indicated to Adams that any disturbing encounter between Brett and the duke had probably not occurred; surely, if Brett had raged, or worse, laughed in the old duke's face, over their scheme to present him with a whore's tutoring, he would have heard about it! Indeed, he would probably have been called on the carpet by either the duke or his heir, or both, once his well-intentioned duplicity was uncovered.

Strange, Adams thought as he felt the carriage make the turn that would take it up the main drive of Ravensford Hall. Why wouldn't that old witch have mentioned her grandnephew's return?

Adams smiled grimly as he pictured the face of Lady Margaret Westmont, with its elongated contours, long, straight nose and icy blue eyes. He had no illusions about that woman. She was as formidable a personage as any he'd ever met in breeches or pantaloons, and he'd spent the years in which he'd served the Westmont family assiduously avoiding any confrontations with the one he knew the servants called Iron Skirts. It was better, he'd long ago resolved—having learned it from his father before him—to deal with the no-quarter-given, yet open and forthright demands of His Grace than to become enmeshed in the underhanded machinations of his sister.

Again Adams smiled as he settled, with this last notion, on the probable reason for her omission over Brett's arrival. She had been completely in her element this morning, he thought, so wrapped up in her plans to see her matchmaking scheme come to fruition, she could hardly be bothered with the arrival of the grandnephew she'd always hated.

Adams drew himself up rigidly. *Hated?* Had he actually used that word to describe the woman's attitude toward her grand-nephew? After a moment's pause, Adams settled back in the carriage, nodding slowly to himself. Yes, it was appropriate, all right, though he was damned if he'd ever figured out why she'd harbored such deep feelings of enmity against the boy, feelings that went back to Brett's *childhood*! Perhaps that was it, Adams concluded as he glanced out the window and saw the magnificent brick facade of Ravensford Hall come into view. She's never married and had any offspring of her own—although, if his father were to be believed, she'd been quite an attractive woman in her youth and had not lacked for suitors. She probably harbored an old maid's resentment of those who had wed and produced progeny. There certainly had been no love lost between her and her twin over the years, and the woman's sourness and perversity had simply extended to the duke's progeny as well.

Well, thought Adams as the carriage pulled into the great circular drive fronting the Hall, enough time spent on figuring out the character and motives of that old crone. Right now he had to be concerned with making some explanations to her grandnephew.

But as Adams alighted from the carriage and beheld the faces of several servants who rushed out to meet him, he quickly realized those explanations would have to wait.

Ashleigh sat, brooding and stony faced, at the dressing table in the chamber where she'd spent the past twenty-four hours. She succumbed to the careful brushing of her long, heavy tresses by a young maid who'd arrived an hour before to help her bathe and dress. Behind them, busily fluffing up the pillows on the huge tester bed Ashleigh had come to hate the sight of, was an older woman who'd arrived with the maid, cheerfully introducing herself as Mrs. Busby, the housekeeper.

Catching sight of Mrs. Busby in the mirror gathering up the soiled linens she'd recently replaced with fresh ones, Ashleigh quickly averted her glance. The linens reminded her all too painfully of the look of abashed amazement on the older woman's face when she'd begun stripping the bed a while ago and noticed the bloodstains that bore silent witness to Ashleigh's loss of virginity.

*I won't cry in front of them, I won't!* she vowed as she forced her eyes to look at her reflection in the glass. Not that it mattered. Any fool could see, by looking at her, that she'd been weeping.

And why? Because some insane mix-up had convinced Lord Brett Westmont that she'd been a professional woman of pleasure, and despite her protestations, the blackguard had arrogantly set about using her, ruthlessly, for hours.

She resisted the temptation to part her dressing gown and glance down at her lower limbs to see if there were any marks to testify to the soreness she felt about her thighs and buttocks. She ached in several places at once, but it was not the physical damage that threatened to overwhelm her; it was the shame . . . and the anger.

Reluctantly, her thoughts turned to the handsome fiend who had caused her—and cost her—so much pain. He had spent the entire night here in the chamber with her, forcing her, again and again—dear God, the *shame* of it!—to submit to all manner of intimacies. He had taken her so often during the night, she'd lost count; it seemed he was insatiable. Several times he'd allowed her to fall asleep, exhausted, in his damnable arms, only to reawaken her a short time later, eager to have his way again.

Then, sometime late in the morning, he'd told her to get some sleep and left—without another word. She'd waited until she was reasonably sure he wasn't going to return right away and hurriedly dressed to leave. But when she'd grabbed her valise and tried the door, she found he'd locked her in!

The rest of the day she'd spent alternately weeping and shouting for someone to release her, but whether anyone heard, she couldn't tell; no one came. Sometime late in the afternoon she'd at last fallen asleep in an armchair near the fireplace. (She'd resolved never to go near that bed again!)

Finally she'd awakened to the sound of the door being unlocked, and Mrs. Busby and the young maid had appeared, cheerful and solicitous, looking for all the world as if a strange young woman's disheveled appearance in the guest chamber were an everyday occurrence.

*Perhaps it was,* reflected Ashleigh as her sapphire eyes narrowed and she thought of her tormentor. A man like that's probably had no end of women, probably in this very chamber!

*Oh,* she seethed, *Brett Westmont, lord or no lord, someday I'll see you pay for what you've done to me! Just you wait and see if I don't!*

Just then the door opened, and the object of her anger entered, looking as if he too had recently bathed and changed. He was immaculate, from head to foot, dressed in a dark blue evening coat and crisp white waistcoat, his cravat as expertly tied as Brummell's.

Her perusal of him stopped just short of examining the powerful thighs that were encased in pale, skintight pantaloons; they were a reminder of parts of his anatomy she had no wish to recall, but the effort of ignoring them cost her: in the mirror she saw her cheeks flame.

Brett saw this too—an observation prompting low laughter as his eyes found hers in the mirror. But then he turned and bestowed the most gracious of smiles on the housekeeper.

"Thank you, Mrs. Busby. Your expert assistance is appreciated. That will be all for now, I think."

Mrs. Busby's cheerful countenance lit up like a chandelier at his praise. "Very good, your lordship," she chirped. "Come along, now, Annie." She addressed the maid who was busy giving Ashleigh's freshly washed hair a final stroke. "The lady's hair looks just lovely."

Annie giggled at the compliment and hurried to follow Mrs. Busby. Then the door closed behind them, leaving Ashleigh alone again with Brett.

Ashleigh eyed the closed door warily, then turned to her captor. "Why am I being kept prisoner here?" she asked in her most demanding tone—although if the truth were told, the inflection came with difficulty; she had never been accustomed to demanding anything in all her years at Hampton House; it was not an attitude that sat easily with her.

Brett strolled casually toward her until he stood immediately behind her chair at the dressing table. Giving no evidence he'd heard her question, he absently fingered the plain cotton collar of her dressing gown for several long moments. "Where on earth did you come by such an unattractive garment?" Then he glanced at the worn valise lying on the floor nearby. "In fact, all your meager belongings are beggarly. We'll order some new ones at once."

*"Order some—"* Ashleigh almost choked. "I—whatever are you talking about? You have no cause to—"

"What I am talking about, my beautiful little spitfire, is the outfitting of your person at a level that's suitable. All of my mistresses have been exquisite dressers."

"All of your..." Ashleigh's mouth gaped as she was hit by the impact of his implication. A moment passed while her stunned silence filled the room.

Then, suddenly, she was all action as the message cleared her brain and made way for the mounting storm that replaced her initial shock. With an angry outthrusting of hands, she pushed her chair away from the dressing table and jerked herself to her feet. She turned at once to face him, eyes blazing. "It will be a cold day in hell before I ever consent to being your mistress, Lord Westmont! There is only one thing I desire right now, and that's to get out of here and go home. I demand you release me—at once!" This time the tone of her voice demonstrated no unfamiliarity with a capacity to demand.

Brett's eyebrows rose slightly at her unexpected reaction. He'd been well aware of her resistance to his advances until now, but he'd succeeded in convincing himself it was still part of some game she was playing, most likely to hold out for more money than she'd originally been offered. Now he wasn't so sure.

Dozens of women he knew would have jumped at the chance to become his mistress, for he was well known to be a generous lover. And this even extended to his parting with a woman. Why, just this morning, as he'd begun his day riding over the estates, he'd made a mental note to pay off Pamela Marlowe with what some would term a staggering figure.

But here was this near child telling him quite unequivocally she was refusing his offer! It made him recall the doubts he'd momentarily entertained last night after she'd protested with that tale of hers about a mix-up.

He decided to put it to a final test. "Ashleigh," he said softly, "perhaps you haven't understood what my offer implies. A position as my mistress would mean a sizable increase in...income for you. I am known not to be ungenerous. Depending on the length of time we remain together, you could, I'm sure, many times triple or quadruple whatever it is Adams has offered you, and you wouldn't have to split it with your—"

"*Not ungenerous!* Hah!" Ashleigh's outrage was almost palpable. "Was it generous to ignore my innocent pleas and take my—my honor, on th-that piece of furniture there?" She gestured hysterically at the bed across the room. "Was it generous to hear my explanations of how I came to be here and then ignore them and proceed to—to rape me, sir, and not just once, but again and again?" Her voice had been rising with the rhetoric of each angry question, and she really began to get into the emotion of it now, her hands on her slim hips as she paced back and forth before him. "And what sort of generosity was it, pray tell, that induced you to leave me incarcerated in this chamber for the duration of the entire day?" She glared up at him with this final query, her small, pointed chin outthrust, her lips in a straight angry line.

Brett sighed as he looked down at this small figure of righteous, indignant fury. At last he was forced to admit the chit might have been telling the truth, for no woman in his ken would have dismissed an openly generous offer from the heir of the wealthiest duke in England, and she had just thrown it in his face!

He frowned. If Ashleigh was the innocent she had said she was—and now it seemed this was possible—just who and what else was she? No serving menial had the speech and manners she used—not to mention a level of education that would have prepared her to take the governess's position she claimed she'd been hired for. Some answers to these and a host of other questions he had about the girl were suddenly necessary, and he knew just the person to put them to. He'd seen Adams's carriage moving toward the Hall in the distance as he glanced out the window when he finished dressing a short while ago.

"Ashleigh . . . ah, Miss Sinclair," he said quietly, "it seems we just might have been operating under—ah—some kind of a misunderstanding after all. If that is so, you'll soon have my apologies, I can assure you; but for now, I want you to wait here a little while longer while I get to the bottom of this. Have a seat. I shan't be long." He whirled and headed for the door.

"Apologies!" Ashleigh cried. "I don't want your apologies! I only want to get away from here!"

But she found herself finishing this to the closed door Brett had shut behind him. Too late, she heard his key turn in the lock. He might be talking of apologies, but it was clear he didn't trust her a whit!

Brett hurried down the long hallway until he reached the grand staircase that led to the house's huge entrance hall and descended two steps at a time. As he neared the bottom, he saw Adams speaking to Mrs. Busby, and Mrs. Busby was crying.

"Adams, I need to speak with you—now, if you don't mind. Let's go to the library." Brett turned as if to go there.

"Lord Westmont, I beg of you, hold a moment," said Adams.

Brett turned to him, impatiently ignoring the softly weeping housekeeper. He was astonished to see tears in the older man's eyes as well.

"Lord Westmont," Adams repeated, "or perhaps I should say 'Your Grace.' Tragic news. The duke, your grandfather, is dead."

# Chapter Seven

"It's a disgrace, that's what it is, Henry. His Grace, not yet cold in the grave, and Young Brett running up to London like he did, and while that poor girl sits here under lock and key! It's inhuman, too, if you ask me!"

Hettie Busby sat on a stool, in the butler's pantry at Ravensford Hall, addressing her husband. The couple had been employed in the duke's household for over thirty years—all of their adult lives—with Hettie beginning as a scullery maid, then rising to housekeeper, and Henry progressing from stable boy to trusted head groom through their tenure. During that time their loyalty to John, duke of Ravensford, and his family had been unquestioning. But now, as Hettie faced old Henry there was an unmistakably disloyal gleam in her eye.

Her husband saw it and sought to soothe her. "Now, 'Ettie, ye oughtn't t' be carryin' on so about th' young duke. 'E's 'ad a rough time of it 'imself, what wi' th' old duke dyin' and th' funeral and what all. Surely ye can understand th' man's grief?"

Hettie shook her head adamantly. "He has no right to keep that wee young thing prisoner here, Henry! Just as he had no right to—to do what he did to her before he left!"

"Now, 'Ettie—"

"And her a *virgin*, too, Henry! Ah, it's like to tear my heart out, listening to her pitiful crying when I pass that chamber door. I'm a woman, too, you know! And I ain't made of wood!"

"There, there, now, lovie." Henry offered her a comforting pat on the shoulder. "P'r'aps ye might take it up wi' Iron Skirts?"

*"That one!"* Hettie's look left little doubt as to what she thought of his suggestion. Over the years there had been times when the duke's twin had strained the limits of Hettie's patience. "All she's concerned about these days is arranging a date for Lord West—for His Grace's wedding. A wedding, mind you, and her brother just five days buried! It's all she talks about to any of us. And this morning she told Jameson and me she's invited Lady Elizabeth over to stay for a fortnight, 'to make the planning easier,' she says. Of course, that was before His Grace up and decided to take off to London without a moment's notice! Now, I suppose, we'll be hearing how the visit will have to wait until His Grace decides to return."

Henry gave her a gap-toothed grin. "Don't suppose 'at'll sit too well wi' th' Lady 'Liz'beth! She's a nasty temper, 'at un!"

Hettie nodded knowingly. "For the life of me, Henry, I never could figure out what it is that draws Iron Skirts to them Hastingses. Lady Elizabeth's a beauty, all right, and clever enough, but a peevish shrew, and that Lord Hastings is the dullest soul going, even when he's not in his cups—which ain't very often! And the old mum, well, I take pity on her, I do, but a half-wit's a half-wit, and that's the best can be said of her!"

Henry nodded sympathetically. "Odd, though, 'Ettie. Old Loomis told me 'bout 'er afore 'e died. Swore she warn't al'ays 'at way. Said she 'ad a good 'ead on 'er shoulders in th' long ago."

Hettie nodded. "I heard something like that, too, from old Mavis Towler, the midwife in the village before the war. Said it was the birth of them twins that changed her. Of course, Mavis wasn't the one called in to help with the birthing. Said the family called in some 'secret persons' to deliver Lady Caroline and Lord David. It was an odd way of putting it, don't you think? Of course, Mavis could have been jealous."

It was Henry's turn to nod. "Mmm, Mavis was a jealous one, she was. Recall 'ow she went green when th' Lady Mary 'ad me fetch th' doctor th' night Lord—'Is Grace was on 'is way?'' Henry lowered his voice when he came to the name Mary, looking guiltily over his shoulder as he did so.

Hettie chuckled. "No more need to be worrying about mentioning *her*, Henry . . . unless it's a ghost you were expecting to come up behind you!"

Henry cleared his throat and gave his wife a frown of disapproval. "Well, time I was gettin' back t' th' stables. 'Is *Young* Grace 'spects as good care of 'is 'orses as 'Is *Old* Grace did!"

Hettie took his look as fair warning. Rising from her stool, she sighed, saying, "Guess I'll go upstairs and see if the child ate anything on her tray. She never touched her breakfast, or dinner last night, either. See you at supper, lovie."

But it was much sooner than suppertime that Henry saw his wife again. Less than ten minutes later he beheld Hettie hastening down the path to the stable yard, out of breath and looking distraught.

"Henry! Henry!" she cried. "She's gone! Escaped out the side window by tying some sheets together!"

"Who?" came her husband's bemused reply.

"Who? Why, who but just one that was here would have had the need to do any escaping?" Hettie answered with some vexation. "The little miss, of course!"

Brett gave his stallion a pat on the neck before handing the reins over to the one stable boy he trusted with his prized personal mount when in London. "See that he gets a good rubdown and a double ration of oats tonight, Tim. I'm afraid I pushed him a bit to get here at this hour."

Tim took the black horse's reins with the same look of reverence he always had when given the honor of caring for the Westmont bloods.

"I'll treat 'im like th' prince 'e is, your lordship. Raven's me fav'rit, 'e is!"

Hearing the boy refer to him as "your lordship," Brett resisted the urge to correct his form of address as a means of informing him of the duke's death. Higgins was probably in the kitchen right now, telling the small staff he maintained here on

King Street that the duke had passed on. The lad would learn the facts soon enough through the servants' grapevine.

Brett sighed wearily with this thought as he turned and headed for the house. Responding to mournful inquiries and condolences was the last thing he wanted to do right now, yet there was little chance of avoiding them when he entered the fashionable town house that now belonged to him. During the past week, he'd dutifully participated in all the trappings and rites of mourning society demanded, and he was tired to the bone with it. Now, all he wanted was to be alone with his grief. Indeed, it was the very reason he had left Ravensford Hall so soon after the funeral and interment. Here, he hoped, his real mourning might begin.

Still, it was with good grace and all the instincts of fine breeding bequeathed him by the grandfather he sorely missed, that he patiently endured the softly spoken sympathies of Bradshaw, the butler, and Mrs. Martin, the housekeeper, before climbing the stairs to his chamber a short while later. Murmuring a dismissive thanks to the footman who had lighted his way, he saw the door shut before sinking tiredly into a huge wing chair next to the fireplace. Then, stretching his long legs out toward the newly built fire crackling in the grate, he ran his hands absently through his hair and allowed his thoughts free rein.

He was gone... the one human being on earth he'd cared for... and who'd cared about him... now a part of the dust all would inherit some day. He shut his eyes, trying to make the notion of this absence feel real, for it was a problem that he'd been wrestling with since he'd gotten the news. Somehow, although his head and body had functioned with the rational behavior of one who has learned of the death of a loved one, he'd been keenly aware that his heart had yet to deal with the loss. For years his grandfather had been a persistent and monumental presence in his life; had, indeed, shaped it into the thing it was today... and now he was gone. Yet why couldn't he feel anything beyond this dull weariness?

Death was something he'd dealt with before. Slowly, his mind turned back to the time when he was ten and he'd heard the news of his father's passing. He remembered the sharp stab of pain he'd felt then, but also the almost simultaneous and insistent need to subdue it. Yes, he thought, nodding at the memory. It had been necessary—important somehow—that he will away his grief and remain strong in the face of those around him. Part of this had to do with not succumbing to any sort of emotional weakness—"womanish behavior," the duke would have called it—but another part came as a result of forces he little understood at the time and, in fact, still failed to comprehend. There had been sinister undercurrents surrounding the time of his father's death, undercurrents he'd felt with the sharply honed instincts of the child he was, a child allowed to see much, yet express little.... Such was the order of things in his grandfather's house.

Did he want to pull out all those long-buried questions now and hold them up to the light of day, examining the crosscurrents that, as a child, he'd not dared to pursue? Or was he merely being maudlin, the victim of ghosts and phantoms of fancy, perhaps as a means of getting in better touch with the emotions that now threatened to elude him? If he forced himself to go back in time and release the pent-up grief over his other losses, would this allow him to open this latest dam that seemed to have been erected in his heart? Did he dare exhume what he, perhaps with a child's unusual wisdom, had buried?

Suddenly an image of an even earlier time in his childhood came to mind. In it he stood in the shadows at the end of the hallway that led to his parents' bedchamber and watched as two footmen came through the door carrying a portrait in a heavy, gilded frame. It was a portrait of a woman with chestnut hair and soft eyes ... of *her*.... He saw himself standing there, unnoticed, as a pair of silent, bewildered tears coursed down his cheeks.... *Damn!*

With a jerk, Brett raised his head and gave it a shake of impatience. What in hell was the matter with him? He'd never, in recent memory anyway, allowed himself any groping in such sentimental sludge! It was time he took hold of himself. Rising, he was about to reach for the decanter of fine French brandy he kept on hand—fine *smuggled* French brandy, he thought with a wry smile—when there came an urgent knocking at his door.

"Yes?"

"Begging yer pardon fer th' late hour, Yer Grace," came the reply, "but I must 'ave a word wi' ye!" The voice was old Henry's. What was *he* doing here?

"Come in then, man," Brett answered as he poured the brandy.

The door opened, revealing the disheveled figure of his head groom. He looked half dead on his feet, and Brett lowered the snifter he'd raised to his mouth. "Good grief, man, what is it?"

Gasping, Henry stumbled into the room. "I...be—be sorry t' be troublin' ye, Yer Grace, but th' news—I—th' wee miss—she's run away!"

"The wee—?"

"Th' wee Miss Ashleigh, Yer Grace, she's *escaped*!"

Brett held the old man's eyes for one glaring moment, then downed the contents of his snifter before setting it on a nearby table.

"When?" he asked.

"Not an hour after ye left, Yer Grace. Me missus—ah, Mrs. Busby and me—we thought ye'd want t' know and—"

"Yes, of course," Brett replied, not sure he wanted to know at all. He'd all but forgotten the girl in the whirl of events surrounding his grandfather's death, and now he wondered why he hadn't released her as she'd wished. It would have been simple enough. With his grandfather dead, there was no longer anyone to appease by making use of her. Yet, for some reason, when the question had come from Higgins—instigated, he supposed by Hettie—as to what was to be done with the girl, he'd given orders to detain her at Ravensford Hall.

Why had he done that? And, more to the point now that he'd learned she'd escaped, why was he troubled by it? Surely she meant less than nothing to him. And yet, as this thought crossed his mind, he was seized immediately by an inexplicable desire to find her and bring her back.

Briefly his thoughts flickered to the morose sentiments that had been gripping him just before Henry's appearance. No, he

clearly wasn't ready to indulge in *that* again. Perhaps what he really needed was a diversion. A lovely little raven-haired diversion with deep blue eyes as big as saucers and a body that—
"Henry, can you tell me any more particulars about Miss Sinclair's—ah—escape?"

"Aye, Yer Grace. She stole th' black filly ye brought over from Ireland last year."

"Irish Night?"

"Aye," said Henry with a tired grin. "Either she's crazy as a lune 'r she knows a 'ell of a lot about 'orseflesh!"

"But that filly's not completely broken to saddle!"

Henry's grin grew wider. "She didn't steal a *saddle*, Yer Grace."

Brett groaned. "Are you telling me she took off on a half-green horse, riding bareback?"

"Aye, Yer Grace, an' th' missus be worried sick fer th' wee mite—ah—th' young miss, I mean."

Suddenly Brett's considerations took a new turn. Until now, he'd only concerned himself with the return of a plaything—a term he had no trouble ascribing to the girl. But now, quite unexpectedly, he began to imagine additional problems, problems that had to do with the chit's safety. It was one thing to think abstractly of her running away from him; it was quite another to imagine her lying bloody and broken in a ditch somewhere as a result of being thrown from a half-wild horse she'd been stupid enough to steal and chance riding!

Immediately Brett was propelled into action. "Henry," he said, "do me one small service before you go to take a well-deserved rest."

"Aye, Yer Grace?"

"Send Higgins to me, if you will, and tell him to hurry!"

As Henry left to do his bidding, Brett laid out his course of action. From what he'd been able to piece together, Ashleigh had been found in a first-class brothel here in London. That piece of information would narrow down his search somewhat, but not completely. Although he was reasonably sure she would have headed back to where she'd come from, its location could be one of perhaps four or five in the city. If he was to find her, he had to learn more. That is, he added darkly, if she'd made it back at all.

Less than an hour later Brett was in possession of a hastily written note from Robert Adams, whom Higgins had caught at his apartments on St. James's. Noting that the solicitor's directions to Hampton House required but a short drive, he ordered his barouche brought around and took the reins himself.

Ashleigh summoned what felt like the last remaining strength in her body and slid wearily off the lathered back of the filly. Then she managed a rueful grin while delivering a pat to the game little horse's withers.

"I'm sorry I pushed you so hard, sweetheart. But I didn't do it to pay you back for those two times you threw me, honestly, I didn't."

She began walking the final hundred yards along St. James's toward Hampton House, using this distance both to cool the filly down and to collect her thoughts before she arrived. It had been a gruelling, yet satisfying, day. First, she'd succeeded in escaping from Ravensford Hall without being detected—no small feat. From the moment she'd lowered herself to the ground via some knotted bedsheets, it had felt as if there were obstacles everywhere, from the gardeners pruning hedges near the house, to the footmen and grooms lurking near the paddock where she'd spied the lovely little black filly she'd borrowed.

Of course, the filly had been pure luck. Never would she have dreamed of stumbling upon such an animal, one that had clearly been bred for stamina and speed. It had shown in every sleek, muscular line of her. Again a rueful grin worked its way across Ashleigh's tired features. Of course, while her early childhood acquaintance with horses had stood her in good stead for gauging the potential the black horse had for making a speedy escape, it had fallen somewhat short in preparing her to assess the extent of the filly's training.

"Leave it to me to pick a half-green youngster!" she said aloud. At the sound, the little horse's ears pricked forward and Ashleigh chuckled. "But we're fast friends now, aren't we, sweetheart?'' She smiled to herself as she recalled the two spills she'd suffered at the outset of their ride. The first had been entirely her own fault, for she'd failed to take proper stock of her mount before settling down for some serious riding. ''Always get to know your animal before asking anything significant of it,'' Patrick had often told her, but she'd been far too involved in fleeing to remember that basic equestrian rule. Then, to make matters worse, after she'd climbed right back on the filly with an I've-got-to-show-you-who's-in-charge attitude, she'd ridden the horse about a mile farther before trying to take a low hedge—again, without thinking! The animal had balked at the last instant and sent Ashleigh careening over the hedge *sans* mount!

''It was just lucky for me there was nice, soft, boggy ground where I landed,'' she said as her free hand reached back to rub the spot on her posterior that had suffered the most from the fall.

Suddenly Ashleigh's thoughts took a darker turn as she considered the word *lucky*. *Hardly!* Here she was, returning to an uncertain future in the only place she could call home, jobless, ravished and bedraggled. What would she tell them when she got inside? That she had come upon a demonic madman who had used her brutally without cause? That someone had made a horrible mistake that had cost her her virginity and a great deal of additional misery? That she'd been hired by a duke who was now dead and the one who had taken his place sought to make her do a different kind of service?

As her thoughts spun along these lines, she wondered if it wasn't she who had gone mad. She knew little of men and their ways. Had she, unwittingly, done something to provoke the outrageous behavior of Brett Westmont—now the ninth duke of Ravensford? Suddenly she wasn't sure any longer of what to think about all that had happened, or how to deal with it—much less explain it to those who lived here at Hampton House. With great effort she choked back the sob that threatened to break and raised her chin a resolute notch, thinking Megan would approve of her courage, if not her experiences. . . . Megan . . . Yes, she was the one to seek out. Megan would know what to do, tell her what to make of all that had happened. Taking a deep breath, Ashleigh clucked to the little filly and quickened her pace.

They were a dozen yards from their destination now, and Ashleigh guided the horse into the shadows of a nearby building as she saw a large, handsome carriage pull to a stop before Madame's establishment. Placing her hand over the filly's velvet nose to forestall any nickered greetings to the team of horses ahead of them, she waited while a pair of elegantly attired bucks descended from the carriage and were greeted by a liveried footman who quickly led them within. She held her breath as the carriage then proceeded to pass within a few feet of her and the filly before continuing down St. James's and out of sight.

Eyeing the brightly lit windows of Hampton House, she decided, without wasting another moment, to make for the narrow side drive that led to the stables. It was Wednesday evening, and she'd hoped to arrive here undetected, owing to the fact that since it was Almack's night, traffic would be slow—most of Madame's patrons being among the hallowed few who were favored with access to that lofty establishment—but it appeared not to be the case. Judging from the number of lighted chambers, business tonight appeared brisk, and as if to confirm this, another expensive-looking carriage drew to a halt before the house just as Ashleigh succeeded in disappearing from view down the drive.

The stables were immersed in shadows, and there appeared to be no one about, yet Ashleigh gritted her teeth at the resounding clip-clop the filly's hooves made on the cobblestones; to her ears it sounded like booming thunder, and she imagined the whole house coming out to investigate the source.

Then, suddenly, she heard a yelp and saw a flash of gray, and she was besieged by Finn's wet and eager tongue as it covered every inch of her face in happy welcome.

"Finn! Oh, Finn, it's *you*! Oh, I've missed you so!" All at once the joy she felt at seeing her beloved canine gave way to a wellspring of emotion, and the floodgates broke. Great sobs racked Ashleigh's small frame as she threw her arms around the shaggy neck and wept. How long she remained thus, she didn't know, but it seemed as if every drop of emotion had been wrung from her body when, an uncertain time later, she felt comforting arms surround her and looked up to see a familiar face.

"Father in Heaven, it's Ashleigh!" cried Megan. "Now, darlin', don't say a word. It's Megan who's found ye, and everythin's goin' t' be all right, colleen. Ye're home."

# Chapter Eight

Brett looked at the woman sitting across from him and smiled, but it was a cynical smile. No warmth shone in his eyes. "Then, if I am to understand you correctly, Madame, you not only intend to keep the handsome sum my grandfather's solicitor paid you for a totally inexperienced woman—indeed, you admit, a total nonprofessional who was sent by mistake—but you are now asking an even greater sum for her return."

Madame's gray-green eyes leveled with his for a moment before their lids half closed and she answered him with bored indifference in her tone. "It would appear to me, Your Grace, that the mistake you speak of was entirely in your favor. Ashleigh Sinclair was a virgin when she left these premises several days ago. Now she sits upstairs sobbing that she is one no longer. Do you have any notion of the price commanded by young virgins these days? And this is not to mention one as beautiful as our lovely Ashleigh. Let's be honest, Your Grace, you have already received a bargain."

"It was a bargain we did not request."

"Ah! Just so," nodded Madame. "And so now you feel you have every right to come here and demand *further* use of this 'unrequested bargain'?" It was Madame's turn to smile cynically.

"Touché," Brett returned. "But the fact remains, if what you have told me of the girl's background is true, the mistake you were responsible for has caused a great deal of embarrassment on both sides and—"

A sharp trill of laughter cut him off. "Come, come, Your Grace, surely you can do better than that! What you really mean is that it is *you* and your *family's* lofty reputation that stand to suffer a great deal of embarrassment—ah, that is, should word get out as to how you used the poor child." One red-gold eyebrow arched in shrewd assessment. "I'm told she has several bruises on her person—one, in fact, on her sweetly rounded little—"

"Enough!" snapped Brett with a look of disgust. "I realize it's pointless to assure you I could not have been responsible for such physical damage to her person, so I suggest we come to the heart of the matter. What if I were to walk out of here without accepting your terms? What would happen to the girl then?"

Madame's eyes widened in a look of arranged surprise. "Why, I'd assumed that was obvious, Your Grace. She'd be put to work here, of course. I have a soft enough heart, but I cannot afford to run a house of charity, sir—ah, Your Grace."

"And I suppose that by 'work' you don't mean to signify her previous position as a menial?"

"Really, Your Grace." Madame smiled. "What kind of a businesswoman do you take me for? The girl is young, beautiful and orphaned. When she was still untouched I allowed myself to be persuaded to send her away from here to secure—ah—*honest employment* of a common sort. But now..." She shrugged. "As I have said, she is a bargain."

"To *you*, you mean."

"To me, to you, to whoever can afford her, Your Grace."

Brett sighed. He knew when he'd been bested. He wanted the girl, and this woman knew it, although what she did not know was that it was not the exorbitant price she was asking that made him hesitate; no, nor was it the threat of scandal she'd implied that drove him to accept her terms. What caused him his dilemma was the astounding story she'd told of how Ashleigh Sinclair came to be a ward of this house and the reaction this engendered in him. The girl had been a true innocent, and he had run roughshod over her; violated her, despite her protests. This did not sit well with him, to say the least. Indeed, when he had first come here this evening, it had been for the sole purpose of resecuring the "diversion" he'd felt he needed. That, and perhaps a restoration of his pride that had been slighted somewhat by the girl's running away from him after he'd made her a handsome offer.

But now something more was at work. He'd always been abrupt in his treatment of women, knowing what they were like by their very nature, but he felt it had always been with a sense of utmost fairness. Never had he trifled with a female who hadn't asked to be trifled with; indeed, to a woman, they had all sought *him* out first.

But this Ashleigh was another story. True, she was a woman, and therefore someone to be taken not altogether seriously, but still.... If he were to sleep with a clear conscience, he would have to make some amends, even if it meant meeting this creature on her own terms!

Sighing a second time, Brett rose from his seat. "Very well, Madame, I'll meet your demands. Do you require my promissory note now or—"

"That will hardly be necessary, Your Grace." Madame was smiling as she too rose from her chair. "You can have your solicitor come around in the morning." She gave him a sidewise glance. "I suppose you realize your reputation for prompt payment in this city is without blemish? Quite a recommendation, I assure you! There are not many of your set that can boast—"

"Yes, yes. Now, where is the girl, and how soon can I have her?"

Now Madame sighed. "I'm afraid it isn't going to be that easy. I'm informed she arrived rather badly shaken, and she's upstairs now in the care of one of my other employees who refuses to leave her side." She cocked her head to one side, looking up at him. "There may be some—ah—problem in prying her loose from this self-appointed watchdog, Your Grace. And...I'm afraid I'm going to leave the business of getting her to go with you, up to you."

Brett gave a grimace of displeasure. He hadn't thought of how to get the chit to come with him! He was silent for several seconds while he pondered this dilemma. At last he met the gaze of Madame, who waited with the patience that could only be ascribed to one who is wholly satisfied with her bargain.

"Very well, Madame," he told her. "Lead the way."

Upstairs in Megan's private chamber Ashleigh sat before a satinwood dressing table as she allowed Megan to towel-dry her hair. "Really, Megan, you needn't put yourself to all this fuss," she scolded good-naturedly. "You've been wonderful enough to me already."

"Sure, and I'd be doin' far more than the meager business o' helpin' ye bathe and the like, darlin' girl, if I thought it might help ye forget the ordeal ye've been through," said Megan as their eyes met in the mirror above the dressing table. Then the redhead's eyes narrowed to slanting green slits. "Faith, I don't know which I'd like t' get me hands on first, yer wicked duke or that stinkin' piece o' blond slime, Monica!"

Ashleigh shuddered, as much from the venom in her friend's voice as her mention of the two people who had recently done her so much injury. Then she shook her head while her eyes held the green ones in the mirror. "Oh, Megan, never think I consider him *my* duke!"

"Softly, darlin'," Megan replied. "'Twas merely an expression." She cast aside the towel she'd been using and reached for a mother-of-pearl-backed hairbrush, then carefully began pulling it through Ashleigh's long hair. "'Tis odd," she continued, "but with all I've heard o' the former Viscount Westmont, I've never actually laid eyes on him. He certainly avoided showin' his fancy face around here!"

Growing increasingly uncomfortable with the subject under discussion, Ashleigh was about to try changing the topic when a frantic onslaught of scrambling and shuffling sounds drew both women's attention. Suddenly the door swung open, and three figures burst into the chamber.

"No, ye don't, ye hairy beast!" Dorcas's voice rang through the room as she wielded a stout broom in the direction of a gray blur that was heading straight for Ashleigh. "'Tis bad enough ye found yer way up here where ye're not supposed t' be, but I'll not have ye herdin' yer little beastie as well!"

Ashleigh's arms were encircling Finn's muscular neck as she heard this, and she was just puzzling over what Dorcas had meant by "yer little beastie" when a loud, high-pitched squeal answered her question.

There, trying frantically to burrow under the velvet skirt of the dressing gown Megan had lent her, squirmed a small pink pig!

"Saints preserve us, 'tis the pesty porker!" cried Megan. She bent forward to thrust a wagging finger in Finn's direction. "Don't ye know better than t' be bringin' yer friend up here?"

Ashleigh watched in amazement as Finn withdrew from her embrace and bent to give the piglet a swipe with his long tongue. And her amazement grew when she saw the small, plump animal immediately begin to calm at the gesture, settling down with a series of contented grunting sounds onto the carpet. "Megan, Dorcas, what on earth—?"

"Ah, lass!" Dorcas exclaimed as she slowly lowered the broom she'd been brandishing. "I'm so sorry t' be troublin' ye with this interruption at such a difficult time, but ye know how quick Finn can be when he—"

"Yes, but—" Ashleigh's glance shifted from Dorcas to the softly grunting form at her feet *"—the pig?"*

"'Tis a long tale," Megan offered, "but I'll try t' make it brief. Shortly after ye left, himself here—" she cast a disapproving glance at Finn "—took up with makin' his own trips t' Mr. Tidley, the butcher, fer handouts. Well, all went smoothly enough the first few trips. Mr. Tidley seemed well-disposed t' be sendin' Finn back with all kinds o' scraps, and Finn seemed pleased as a leprechaun with his gold over the whole business. But *then*—" Megan's eyes returned to the wolfhound who was in the process of bestowing yet another lick on the contented pig.

"But then, *what*?" encouraged Ashleigh.

"But then the most outlandish thing happened." It was Dorcas's voice that had taken up the story. "I might as well tell it, as I was there!" she added with a glare at the tail-wagging Finn. "It was the day Mr. Tidley asked me t' come by and approve the choice he'd made fer the main course fer Madame's special spring banquet—a main course o' *roast sucklin' pig*! Well, Mr. Tidley had just gone out back t' fetch the little bugger, when all of a sudden, we customers in the shop heard the most ferocious growlin' comin' from the back o' Mr. Tidley's shop, and a moment later, the poor butcher's frightened voice. 'Dorcas,' cries he, 'Dorcas Ainsley, come here and help—*please*!'

"Well," said Dorcas, her blue eyes bright in her rosy face, "ye could have knocked me over with a feather, I was that surprised t' be hearin' him callin' *me*! But still, I wasted no time answerin' the poor man's request, and in a minute I was runnin' t' see what the trouble was. And I did." Again a damning glare in Finn's direction. "What I saw was yer beastie there, standin', with all his hackles raised, squarely over this pork chop! And he was barin' his fangs and growlin' in a menacin' way at Mr. Tidley, who was shakin' and backed against the wall!

"Well, it took me only a moment t' size up the situation, I can tell ye!" 'Finn,' says I, 'ye leave this place at once! That pig is Madame's dinner!'" Dorcas gave an exasperated sigh. "And what do ye think that outrageous beast did next?" She paused to bestow a disgusted look upon the object under discussion. "Oh, he left the premises, all right. But only after lookin' me square in the eye and then proceedin' t' pick that four-footed piece o' pork up carefully in his great jaws and take it with him!"

Ashleigh's jaw hung open for a moment as she digested Dorcas's words. "Finn *kidnapped a pig*?"

"Aye," nodded Megan, "and there's been no separatin' them since. Kidnapped him and adopted him, all in the same minute."

There was a moment of astonished silence as all three women looked at Finn. As for the wolfhound, he was looking mighty pleased with himself; indeed, Ashleigh would have sworn he was grinning as he sat there with his mouth widely agape, his great tail thumping and his eyes bright and happy.

It was Megan who broke the silence. "Ye needn't look so pleased with yerself, me boy! 'Tis bad enough we've had a problem keepin' *one* beast out from under Madame's skirts. With *two* o' ye, 'tis well nigh *impossible*! And then there's poor Mr. Tidley! How, in the name o' the saints are we t' continue traffickin' with him when ye're daft enough t' keep goin' *back* there fer more handouts—and after what ye did?'' She turned to Ashleigh. ''Why, last evenin' it nearly scared the life out o' me t' be glancin' out the back window and seein' Finn makin' a beeline straight fer home, with the butcher hot on his heels, wavin' a meat cleaver like he meant business!''

'''Tis true,'' echoed Dorcas. ''I saw it too, and *heard* it! 'Keep that thievin' animal out o' my shop!' says Tidley, 'or ye'll be buyin' yer meat across town!' ''

''Oh, dear!'' exclaimed Ashleigh. She bent her gaze on Finn. ''You certainly have made a hash of things, haven't you?'' Then, to the two women across from her, ''Er—what does Madame have to say of all this?''

''Those animals have until tomorrow morning to be gone from this house,'' said the adamant voice that came through the partially ajar door.

All three women's heads turned sharply toward the sound, and at the same moment the door swung open to reveal an angry looking Madame and the tall, striking figure of the duke of Ravensford.

Ignoring Ashleigh's gasp of shocked surprise and the low canine growl that followed, Madame snapped, ''Dorcas, remove those two animals at once!''

As Dorcas hurried to obey, Madame fixed her gaze on the tall redhead. ''Megan, I allowed you a free evening to tend to your friend, but I'm afraid I must now ask you to take over for me as hostess downstairs.'' She glanced briefly at the man on her left. ''His Grace and I have business with Ashleigh.''

Megan's focus shifted from the begowned figure of Madame to the man beside her. Slowly, and with a composure that went far beyond anything Ashleigh had ever seen her affect before, she allowed her gaze to traverse the tall man in impeccably tailored evening dress. When her perusal had run its course, she turned back to Ashleigh. ''Are ye up t' seein' this . . . visitor, darlin'?" she queried softly, though loudly enough for the two in the doorway to hear.

Ashleigh had also been taking in the figure of Brett Westmont, and from the instant he'd appeared in the doorway, she'd been fighting to ignore the feelings that welled up inside her. Her clenched hands had gone white at the knuckles and her heart seemed to be beating so furiously, she fancied they all could hear it. The last thing on earth she wanted just now was to be subjected to his presence and its shameful reminders, but as she took in the poised stance of her employer and the set features of her face, she felt she had little choice but to capitulate to the older woman's wishes.

Forcing her words out over a tongue suddenly gone dry, she answered Megan in halting tones. "I—I'll be all right, Megan. You . . . you run along."

Hearing the uncertainty in her voice, Megan hesitated for a second and gave the pair in the doorway one more glance. Then, looking as if she'd made her mind up to something, she nodded to Ashleigh, saying, "Very well, *mavourneen*, I'll be goin', but if ye should change yer mind, ye've but t' call." Then, with a swish of emerald-green skirts, she left, parting the two figures in the doorway as she did so.

Madame swept into the room, saying, "Do come in, Your Grace."

As Brett followed her invitation, Ashleigh's eyes followed him. Dressed immaculately in perfect Corinthian fashion, he appeared every inch the duke he now was. The chestnut curls that closely hugged his finely shaped head were clean and shining; the snowy cravat under his strong, chiseled jaw would have done Brummell proud; a dark blue evening coat fit him to perfection as it covered those wide, muscular shoulders and tapered without a wrinkle down to his lean, masculine waist and hips; a white waistcoat and skintight pantaloons completed the picture of sartorial splendor, echoing both the modish dictates of the day and his long, lean and decidedly virile shape.

But Ashleigh had only a split second to note all of this; she quickly found herself under the well-remembered scrutiny of that turquoise gaze, its intensity forcing her to shift her eyes hurriedly away while she felt the heat creep into her face.

"Ashleigh, my dear, where are your manners?" Madame was asking. "You are hardly to remain seated when a duke of England enters the room!"

"It's really not necessary," Brett replied, but Ashleigh was already rising from the delicately curving X-frame Regency stool she'd occupied in front of Megan's dressing table; being of such diminutive stature, she felt herself at enough of a disadvantage beside the towering Brett and had no wish to compound this by remaining seated while His Grace stood!

With a flickering glance at Madame, Ashleigh made a brief curtsy in Brett's direction, hating herself for feeling so intimidated. Where were her manners! What she'd like to be doing this very minute was to hurl every object within reach at her arrogantly smiling tormentor, and then be darting from the room, never to lay eyes on the man again!

As for Brett, the slow smile that had dawned on his handsome features may not have been exactly arrogant, but it was prompted by the look of ill-concealed rebellion he caught in Ashleigh's sapphire eyes. Then, too, he'd been absorbing the delicate beauty of the girl; it was, for some reason, almost as if he'd never seen her before—the finely sculpted, heart-shaped face that was framed by a cascade of blue-black hair, softly curling now that it had begun to dry, over her back and shoulders; the perfect, straight little nose that complemented a beautifully shaped mouth that seemed to tilt upward at the corners, despite her glum expression; the creamy complexion, offset by a tiny mole high on her right cheek; and, of course, those incredibly blue eyes with the barest hint of violet in their depths when she grew angry, as now. Somehow it all seemed fresh and new to him, as if he hadn't really looked at her before—and yet, of course, he knew he had....

"You...spoke of having business with me, Madame?" Ashleigh purposefully kept her eyes on her employer as she spoke, for Brett's presence in the chamber was intensely unnerving. The way he had looked at her! Why, if her hands weren't nervously fiddling with the deep periwinkle folds of the borrowed dressing gown she wore, she'd have sworn she'd been undressed!

"Ah, yes, child," said Madame. "That is, both His Grace and I, to some extent, do." She threw a glance at Brett. "I shall state the nature of our business, so far as it involves me, as succinctly and briefly as possible, Your Grace. From then on, you are on your own."

Catching Brett's nod through the veil of her downswept lashes, Ashleigh felt a frisson of apprehension course through her as she pondered Madame's words. What did she mean by "on your own"?

"As you might have guessed," Madame was saying, "by virtue of your return to Hampton House this evening, you have again come under the aegis of my protection, or my employ."

Ashleigh nodded uncertainly, unsure of what she was leading up to.

"But you must know, Ashleigh dear, that under the circumstances, I can no longer afford to keep you in the position you enjoyed while you were growing up. You are a lovely young woman now, with far more—ah—assets than a menial's position might make use of. However, it has been made more than clear to me by certain other members of my staff that you would be opposed, if not ill suited, to a—um—position such as that occupied by the majority of the women in my employ. Is that not so?"

Again, Ashleigh nodded, but her eyes locked with Madame's as she awaited further elucidation.

"Moreover, His Grace informs me that he sorely misses your company, that you left his employ without his leave, therefore—"

"His 'employ'!" cried Ashleigh aghast. "I arrived at his home to assume a *governess*'s position, only to find myself *violated* and—and held *prisoner*! How can you—"

"My dear Ashleigh," Madame cut in, "it is neither here nor there to me, what the nature of your employment at Ravensford Hall was! The fact remains that you are once again in my hands and His Grace has—ah—need of you. Since you are unwilling or unable to perform the only acceptable function I have need of here, I have been forced to conclude a bargain with His Grace, regarding your services—services, my dear, which His Grace has already purchased."

There was a shallow gasp from Ashleigh before the room fell deadly silent for several seconds. Then Ashleigh raised tear-flooded eyes to meet the gray-green gaze of the older woman. "How much?" she asked in a voice that quavered somewhere above a whisper. *"How much did you sell me for?"*

"That," answered Madame, turning toward the half-open door, "is privileged information—unless, of course, His Grace should decide to inform you. I suggest," she added as she moved through the door with a careless wave of a bejeweled hand, "you take it up with him." And with a swish of rustling taffeta, she was gone.

Staring into the wake of her departure, Ashleigh was silent for one tension-filled moment, then whirled to face Brett. "How very clever of you, Your Grace!" she sneered through the tears that threatened to choke her speech. "Having found you couldn't *buy me outright*, by a direct offer, you made straight for the one person from whom you *could*!"

Brett watched the lovely face streaked with tears and cursed inwardly. *Damn!* He'd known this wouldn't be *easy!* "Miss Sinclair," he murmured softly, taking a step toward her.

"'Miss Sinclair'!" Ashleigh cried. "Oh, that's wonderfully proper, that is! Tell me, Your Grace, do you always use such unstintingly fine manners to sugarcoat your debauchery?"

Stung, yet feeling somehow he'd earned it, Brett moved a step closer. "Now, see here, Ashleigh, I—"

"No, *you* see here!" came the harshly bitter retort. "There is nothing on God's good earth that will make me become your mistress! Your *bought-and-paid-for* mistress! Do you hear? *Nothing!* I'm leaving here and somehow I'm going to find *honest* employment. I don't care what it is—scrubbing floors, selling flowers, whatever—so long as it is clean and honest work! And you had better tell me what it is you paid that—that—woman—" she gestured half hysterically toward the open doorway "—so that I can *repay* it. And I will! Every rotten shilling!"

Brett heard all this with as much patience as he could muster. No one had ever berated him in this fashion, and least of all, a female! Nevertheless, there was a certain amount of uneasiness residing within him where this female was concerned, and besides, he'd already made up his mind what to do here, and he was anxious to make it clear to her.

"Ashleigh," he said calmly, trying not to let the note of chagrin he felt creep into his voice as he viewed her tearstained face, "suppose I were to tell you that I have no intention of installing you in my home as a mistress. Suppose it was *I* who was offering you a chance at this 'honest employment' you speak of. What then?"

He was standing very close to her right now, and, even before she was able to digest the full import of his words, Ashleigh thought she caught a look of sincerity in the turquoise eyes, shimmeringly visible through her tears. "You—you mean...?" Her eyes scanned his face, hovering on the brink between doubt and hope. "Wh-what kind of employment?" she asked tentatively.

"Aye, Yer Grace," came a bold female voice from the doorway. *"What kind, indeed?"*

Both Ashleigh and Brett turned to see Megan's tall, emerald-clad form leaning against the doorjamb. She was toying desultorily with a long lock of red hair that had fallen over one shoulder, but the look in her eyes was canny and intense.

"Ye'll pardon me, Yer Grace, but I don't think we've been properly introduced. Me name's Megan O'Brien, and me line o' work—" she shrugged "—has just altered. I am newly appointed Miss Sinclair's—ah—business agent, and I'd be interested in hearin' what it is ye're proposin' t' her."

"Newly appointed...? Megan, what on earth are you *talking* about?" Ashleigh exclaimed.

"Well, newly self-appointed ye might say, Ashleigh, darlin'. Ye see, I just caught wind o' what Madame's done t' ye, and I've up and quit me post. No, none o' yer protests, me lass. 'Tis time I did it! Now," she added, turning her eyes on Brett, "as I was sayin', Yer Grace, what kind o' work did ye have in mind fer the wee colleen, and, by the way, while we're at it, ye'd better know that wherever she goes, *I* go too!'' Megan's perfect white teeth flashed in a smug, satisfied smile.

With an inward groan, Brett appraised the situation as he glanced from Megan to Ashleigh, and then back to Megan again, and for the first time in his life he cursed the sense of honor his grandfather had raised him with. Now he'd be forced to deal with *two* useless women, one of them a childlike near virgin, the other, a newly retired whore! He fixed Megan with a look of reproach. ''Am I to take it you don't trust my honorable intentions, Miss O'Brien?''

''Ye may, if ye wish, Yer Grace. But far more than that, I'm after seein' that the little colleen here has a friend beside her this time, when she goes off t' this new work ye mentioned. And again, Yer Grace, if ye don't mind . . . the *type* o' work . . . ?''

Hearing the adamant tone in her deceptively lilting voice, and suspecting it was restrained fury he caught in the green eyes, Brett sighed, deciding he'd probably have to go along with her. ''Miss Sinclair,'' he then began slowly, ''would be installed in my household as a hostess of sorts—or assistant hostess, if you will. My great-aunt has performed that function for years, inasmuch as my grandfather was a widower, but she is getting on in years and would, I'm sure, appreciate the help.'' Brett paused for a moment with this lie; if there were anyone in the world who could be counted on *not* to appreciate such unsolicited assistance, it was Lady Margaret, but since this in no way fit in with his plans, he decided to go right past it. Time enough to deal with Margaret later!

''Your duties would be simple and clear-cut. I shall be entertaining friends both in Kent and in London on occasion, and at such times, I shall require a hostess. From what I have seen, and learned of your breeding and background, you should be able to carry out such responsibilities admirably, Miss Sinclair.''

Ashleigh's mind whirled with this proposal, for it caught her completely unprepared. Did he really mean what he was saying? Could he be trusted? After all, duke or not, he'd been no gentleman before, and once she was back in his clutches, what was to prevent him from ... Her mind balked at the horrible possibilities, and she felt the blood rising to her cheeks.

Of course, she would not be alone this time—Megan would be there, bless her heart. And then, too, what other choices did she have? To remain here and become one of Madame's stable of fallen women? To go into the streets, seeking God-knows-what? She cast a brief sidelong glance at Brett who stood, waiting patiently for her response, but his expression was shuttered and gave her no further clues. Finally she looked at Megan.

"Well, Ashleigh, darlin', what do ye think?"

"I was about to ask *you* that question, Megan."

"Hmm," said her friend as her glance darted from Ashleigh to Brett. "And ye'd be havin' no objections t' Ashleigh havin' a couple o' friends along in the bargain, Yer Grace?"

"A *couple*?" Brett queried.

"Ah, well, yes," said Megan, the green eyes suddenly hinting at merriment. "There's meself, as I've already plainly stated, and then there's Finn...."

"Finn?" Brett's eyebrows rose suspiciously.

"The fine Irish wolfhound ye laid eyes on but a short while ago. Ye see, Yer Grace," she added with a smile that indicated she was now enjoying herself tremendously, "he's the only *male* Ashleigh trusts these days."

Brett made a sound that was somewhere between a snort and a protest, but then glanced at the small porcelain clock on the mantel and, seeing the hour, said hurriedly, "Yes, yes, I'll find a place for you all"—although a momentary consideration of what Margaret's reaction would be when she learned of the redhead's background caused a small inward shudder. He shifted his gaze to Ashleigh. "Well, Miss Sinclair?"

Ashleigh's indecision registered in her eyes. "I...I'd have to have some sort of—of income. That is, I meant it when I said I intend to repay what you spent to—to have me, and I don't see how I'm to do it unless ... unless ..."

"I'll have my solicitor deposit five hundred pounds with the Bank of England in your name, first thing in the morning. We'll consider this your yearly stipend. In addition—"

"Ah, I was after thinkin' a *thousand* pounds a year would be more like it, Yer Grace," came the interruption from the doorway.

Brett's frown of displeasure was blatant. "A thousand pounds is a lot of money, Miss O'Brien."

"Aye." Megan nodded. "But since 'tis the very amount ye paid Madame fer Ashleigh's—ah—services..." She shrugged. "After all, Yer Grace, ye'd wish her t' be able t' repay ye, wouldn't ye?"

Brett's sigh was nearly a groan. He nodded. "A thousand yearly."

Megan returned the nod. "Now, Yer Grace, as ye were sayin'...?"

"As I was saying, in addition, there will be fifty pounds for each specific occasion—a dinner party, whatever, wherein you perform the duties of hostess. And of course, all of your expenses will be borne by me. Does that suit?"

"Ex-expenses?"

Brett made an impatient gesture. "Food, clothing—living expenses."

Wide-eyed, Ashleigh nodded. She hadn't dreamed the offer would be so generous. But then her eyes went to Megan who remained in the doorway, taking all of this in with a look of total satisfaction on her face. Returning her eyes to Brett, she ventured one more request. "There—there would have to be some—some compensation for my companion, too," she managed to tell him.

Brett let out an exasperated rush of breath. "Three hundred pounds a year and she doubles as your abigail." He cast an appraising glance at Megan, then at the hairbrush on the dressing table. "She *was* helping you with your toilette earlier this evening, was she not?"

Ashleigh looked uncertain and glanced at Megan. "I'm not sure—"

"It'll be fine fer me, darlin'," Megan put in. "Companion and abigail...aye, I like the sound o' that!"

Brett was glancing at the clock again. It was after ten, and if he was to make Almack's before they closed the doors at eleven ... His eyes focused on Ashleigh's. "Well, Miss Sinclair? Are we agreed?"

As Ashleigh met his gaze she was still far from deciding. It seemed like such a risk-ridden thing to do! But then a sharp burst of drunken laughter from a chamber down the hall and the sound of a door slamming reminded her of her alternatives. With a brief glance at Megan, she took a deep breath and answered him. "Very well, Your Grace, we'll go."

# Chapter Nine

The following morning Ashleigh sat across from Brett and Megan in a carriage bearing them across town. It was a grand vehicle, far larger than the light, open barouche into which their motley group had been squeezed when leaving Hampton House the evening before. And as Brett had given her and Megan a hand up into the present vehicle, she had glimpsed the handsome black, gold and crimson Ravensford coat of arms emblazoned on the door and been properly awed. Now, as she sat comfortably ensconced in the rich, soft leather interior as they were whisked around Hyde Park, Ashleigh felt that awe growing.

What, she at last dared ask herself, was she doing here, riding in a duke's carriage in the midst of London's most fashionable district? She, Ashleigh Sinclair, who only one short week ago had been unquestioningly discharging her duties as a scullery and serving maid. Somehow, despite the cementing presence of the cool-visaged man across from her, the reality of the bargain she had entered into last evening hadn't seemed quite real—until now. Now, with London's late-spring sunshine filtering through the carriage's clean, shiny windows, the enormity of what she was presently involved in became apparent to her, almost as if in the bright sunlight there could be absolutely no pretense. Now she had to admit her life had suddenly changed, and in ways unalterable and all *too* real.

She allowed herself a covert glance at the man sitting across from her. He seemed totally impervious to the presence of the two women with whom he shared the carriage. Immaculately groomed, as always, he wore a morning coat of deep blue superfine, a perfectly tied cravat above his tan waistcoat, and buff-colored breeches that snugly covered the muscular lower reaches of his tall frame until they met a pair of blue and gold Hessians. The profile he presented to her as she chanced a second glance from beneath lowered lashes might have been carved of stone as he fixed his turquoise gaze on the scenery outside the window; the wide, handsome forehead fringed by a chestnut brush of curls, the straight, well-chiseled nose, the arrogant mouth that perfectly complemented a square, strongly carved jaw—all could have been made of granite.

Ashleigh sighed inwardly. She had no need, actually, to be glimpsing those handsome, formidable features. Their every line had been unwillingly committed to memory during that awful twenty-four hours when she had been his plaything, etched and re-etched there during those hours when he had used her so cavalierly and then again, later, when he had held her prisoner. Even now, when she dared allow herself to think of it, her body burned with shame, her cheeks feeling as if they were on fire.

Despite this recollection, she found herself stealing yet another glance at Brett's profile, this time with the hope of assessing his mood and guessing at his thoughts. He seemed not to have moved an inch over the past minutes and appeared to her cool and distant, even brooding. There was no hint of the lazy smile she knew could transform his entire aspect; with that smile his face took on inestimable charm, with its flashing white teeth and a pair of deeply grooved dimples. No, this morning she saw a different man altogether from the rakish captor who had dishonored her; different even from the brisk, efficient man of business of last evening.

Recalling a scene from the evening before, Ashleigh suddenly found herself biting her lower lip to keep from giggling, for there had been one instant when His Grace had lost his businesslike aplomb. It had been the moment when they were about to enter his barouche. Actually, Brett had already handed her up and was turning to assist Megan in similar fashion when the redhead had suddenly whirled about, crying, "Wait! We've forgotten a couple o' things, Yer Grace!" And Ashleigh had watched the duke's face change from a look of annoyed impatience to one of horrified disgust as Megan had emerged from Hampton House a few moments later with a tail-wagging Finn behind her, and, bringing up the rear, a happily grunting pig! Oh, but it had been difficult to keep from laughing aloud as His Grace's "What in hell do you take me for, Miss O'Brien, a Gypsy circus master?" had cut across the warm night air! Nor, she merrily reflected now, was it any easier to stifle her giggles when she saw the look on his face as Megan had peremptorily marched her little ensemble straight past him and into the waiting carriage with a look of smug disdain on her beautiful Gaelic features.

Ashleigh's gaze shifted to Megan, and as their eyes met, she could tell from the answering twinkle in the green eyes that Megan must have read her thoughts, for after a quick glance at Brett's averted profile, the corners of the redhead's mouth began to twitch with amusement.

"I've been givin' it a great deal o' thought, Ashleigh, darlin', and I've at last come up with a solution," Megan suddenly said aloud. At Ashleigh's look of puzzlement she hastened on. "'Tis over what name t' give the wee lady piglet, o' course! Ye recall, we were after findin' one last night?"

Ashleigh nodded, but couldn't help darting a glance in Brett's direction. His Grace hadn't moved a jot during this exchange, but Ashleigh thought she detected a slight tightening of the muscles about his mouth and perhaps the barest flaring of those arrogant nostrils as well.

"The wee porker, ye may have noted," Megan was saying, "has the loveliest pair o' dimples gracin' her sweet little rump, and bein' she's a lady pig, what would ye think about callin' her Lady Dimples?" It was Megan's turn to glance at the rigid profile of their carriage companion, but unlike Ashleigh's, her glance was bold and saucy, and when she returned it to Ashleigh, it was accompanied by a wickedly wide grin.

Again Ashleigh had to stifle a giggle, for the grin reminded her of yet another episode from the evening before. Once their unlikely ensemble had been crowded into the barouche and Brett began driving them to his town house, he had plied Ashleigh with a host of questions about her background. He'd learned from Madame that her father had been a minor nobleman of some sort; what was his title? Did she have any living relatives? Where had her family home been located? But each time he had set forth one of these inquiries, it had been Megan who'd answered or, rather, parried a response. Giving Ashleigh's hand a surreptitious squeeze to indicate she should be still, the Irishwoman's replies had been deftly evasive: "Well, now, 'tis a long time since the poor colleen's tragedy, and herself bein' such a wee lass when it all happened, I'm sure she only recalls callin' her da 'Papa' or 'Father,' Yer Grace.... Sure and ye'd not be wishin' t' dredge up all those tragic memories fer the poor lass by askin' her t' recall a home that is no more!"...and, finally, "Ah, 'tis a poor, homeless orphan she was, ladylike down t' her bones, and the *soul of virtue! Anyone* with *half an eye* could've seen that!" And this last had been accompanied by, first, the most accusing of looks aimed directly at His Grace and then a wide, devilish grin.

Of course, Ashleigh now recalled with a shiver, His Grace's expression had grown darkly ominous at this last impertinence, and she had been forced to deliver a well-placed nudge to Megan's ribs with her elbow when she'd seen it; it was one thing to enjoy a joke at the duke's expense as a means of getting some small recompense for what he'd done to her; it was quite another to provoke the carefully leashed anger she now realized lurked just beneath the surface of that cool, seldom ruffled exterior, especially since he was now to be her employer for at least a year.

Later, when she and Megan had been shown to their chamber in the town house and were at last alone, Ashleigh had questioned her friend about the entire business. "Aren't you afraid of pushing him too far, Megan? And what was it you meant to accomplish by avoiding his questions that way?"

Megan had smiled before taking Ashleigh's hand and giving it a warm squeeze. "Ah, Ashleigh," she'd said, shaking her head, "have ye no faith in me judgment? 'Tis me, Megan

O'Brien, ye're talkin' t', and I've made me way fer the better part o' five years by makin' it *me business* t' *know men*, remember? Don't ye fret, me lass, I'll not push him too far—although, I must admit,'' she'd added a bit softly, and more to herself, ''that one does appear t' be a bit more complicated than most. I wonder what divil it is that irks him so...'' Then, her tone immediately lightening, she'd looked Ashleigh in the eye, saying, ''As fer the other, I can only tell ye that it never pays t' tell a man too much about yerself. Take me word fer it, me lass, a woman can go ever so much further in dealin' with her men when there's a wee touch o' the mysterious about her.''

''Oh...'' Ashleigh had said, bemused. Then, picking up on one phrase, she'd hastened to protest, ''But Megan, His Grace is not one of *my men*, as you seem to put it! Why, he's merely my employer, and—''

''Hush now, Ashleigh, darlin', 'twas merely an expression... a way o' puttin' things, ye might say.'' Their discussion ended with this last pronouncement, but as Megan finished, Ashleigh wondered at the flicker of craftiness she could have sworn she'd glimpsed in those green Irish eyes.

''Well, we're here.'' Brett's voice swept aside the curtain Ashleigh had drawn about herself with her ruminations, and she looked at him with a start, thrown back into the present.

''Madame Gautier is the foremost dressmaker in London at the moment, or so I am told.'' He eyed the plain black cotton pelisse Ashleigh wore over an even plainer gray dress. Then his gaze traveled to the emerald-green silk evening cloak that covered most of Megan's statuesque form, and he bit back a grimace of distaste. He hadn't been able to get them here fast enough to suit his liking this morning, his new charge with her elfin beauty all but marred by the drab attire she'd been forced to wear as a menial, and her companion, outrageously accoutered in overdone finery that fairly shouted what her profession had been.

Seeing their wardrobes suitably altered had, in fact, been a primary motive in his making it to Almack's last night— something he'd hardly have done under ordinary circumstances so soon after his grandfather's death. But he'd gone under the pretext of accepting condolences from friends who'd not been able to extend them personally, owing to the fact that his grandfather's had been a small, private funeral. At least, this is the story he'd offered Lady Jersey when she'd approached him with raised eyebrows and questioned the propriety of his appearing there at such a time. Of course, she'd looked at first as if she weren't about to believe him, but when he managed to go the entire evening without a single dance, not to mention spending most of it in conversation with *her*, she'd finally relented with a twinkle in her eye. Brett after all, along with his friend Lord Byron, was one of her favorites, and although her standards were strict, she was ready to forgive him much.

It was during his talk with the formidable patroness of Almack's that he'd been able to ferret out that Madame Gautier was still the only *modiste* used by the fashionable ladies of the *ton*; Pamela, his recent mistress, had left by the time he'd arrived, a close five minutes before eleven, and, he now decided, he'd actually been relieved at not having to ply such information from her; she might have taken it into her head that he was suggesting he buy her some new additions to her wardrobe, and this was the last thing he intended to do. Pamela Marlowe was quickly growing tiresome to him, and if anything, he intended to deluge her with hints that their association was drawing to an end. Perhaps this had even already been accomplished; if what Lady Jersey had hinted at were true, Lady Marlowe had spent most of the evening searching him out and finally left in a huff of annoyance a quarter hour before he'd arrived. "Tell His Grace when you see him," she told the patroness, "that I find my patience at last at an end this evening."

Brett smiled with this thought as he helped Ashleigh and Megan down from the coach, but the smile was short-lived, for whom did he spy exiting Madame Gautier's exalted establishment but Lady Jersey, followed close at hand by Lady Bessborough and Lady Castlereagh! Groaning inwardly, he quickly pasted a facsimile of a smile in place of the vanished genuine article and strode forward to greet the three.

"Ravensford! Fancy meeting you here, Your Grace!" Lady Jersey's look was artful, and Brett saw her glance dart immediately to the pair of women beside him.

"M'lady," Brett murmured as he bowed over her extended hand. Repeating the gesture with Lady Bessborough and Lady Castlereagh, he turned toward the two beside him. "Ladies, allow me to introduce my—ah—my new ward, Miss Sinclair, and her companion, Miss O'Brien."

"Indeed?" intoned Lady Castlereagh. She was easily known as the grande dame among the patronesses at Almack's, and her "indeed" implied much as she peered down her haughty nose at Ashleigh.

Guessing from the looks on the faces of the three women, Brett knew he would need to move quickly if the appearance of the other two in his life were to be accepted. "Miss Sinclair is the daughter of an old family friend who died years ago. My grandfather, just before he died, learned she'd been raised in an orphanage all these years and took steps to bring her to live with us. We were just about to see Madame Gautier about exchanging her—ah—institutional garb for something more... suitable." He stared boldly back at Lady Castlereagh's questioning gaze, as if daring her to doubt him, inwardly cursing the constraints society sometimes forced him into. An image of the unfurled sails of his ship, the *Ravenscrest*, flashed into his mind, and he sincerely wished he were on it, the salt breeze blowing through his hair and society be damned!

"Sinclair... hmm..." murmured Lady Castlereagh. "And just how do you spell your surname, Miss Sinclair? Is it S-I-N-C-L-A-I-R or S-T.-C-L-A-I-R or S-T.-C-L-A-R-E? One never knows with spellings of common names, you know. Dr. Johnson did a great deal to fix the spellings of the common nouns with his *Dictionary of the English Language* but with proper nouns one can never be sure. And occasionally the variations can even lead to the most execrable mispronunciations. Why, in America, I'm told, they've actually begun to call the latter two spellings I've cited by the atrocious pronunciation of *Saint Clare*! As a matter of fact," she added with a pointed look in

Lady Jersey's direction, "there is a young lord who has just recently been admitted to Almack's who uses such an abomination. Had it been up to me, the upstart would never have been allowed access!"

The censure in her gaze as it fell upon Lady Jersey left no doubt as to *who* had admitted the "upstart," but a second later her attention was focused once more on Ashleigh. "And which so.....  ....urs, my dear?"

......... ..icked her lips nervously before replying in a small voice, "The first, m'lady."

"Ah," nodded the grande dame, "then in your case there can be no corruption.... Hmm...I knew a Sinclair family once. Tell me, did your parents—"

"Ah, I don't believe I've expressed my appreciation over the kind letter of condolence you sent at my grandfather's passing, Lady Castlereagh," Brett hastily interrupted. *Anything to get her off the scent of Ashleigh's background!* "Allow me to do so now."

"How pretty you are, my dear," Lady Jersey was saying to Ashleigh, and Brett was grateful for the change of subject. "I agree it is high time you were attired to show off such beauty. You will find Madame Gautier up to snuff in that arena, I daresay."

Ashleigh blushed under the compliment and felt more than a little relieved when the scrutiny of all three ladies passed from her to Megan.

"Miss O'Brien, is it?" Lady Bessborough was asking Brett.

"Ah, yes. Miss Sinclair's companion is also in need of a new wardrobe," Brett said quickly, at the same time throwing Megan a look of warning. "It seems hers was lost in a fire at the inn where she was staying, and the only clothes the poor woman was left with were the evening attire she was wearing while dining with some friends."

"How perfectly awful for you, Miss O'Brien," Lady Bessborough murmured sympathetically.

"Yes," added Lady Jersey with an appraising glance at the tall redhead, "but on the other hand, how perfectly fortunate that you were not *with* your wardrobe when the fire broke out."

She turned toward Brett. "Don't you agree, Your Grace? I mean, life does have a way of balancing ill fortune with good, does it not? Take the situation of your new ward, here." She inclined her head briefly in Ashleigh's direction but kept her shrewd gaze focused on him. "Finding oneself an orphan at a tender age must indeed be a terrible blow, but being—ah—*rescued* by none other than the duke of Ravensford himself! Well, that, I should say, is an inestimable stroke of good fortune!"

Just then a second grand coach pulled up behind Brett's, and Lady Jersey noted it with a scowl. "Ah, well, it seems my coach has arrived." She turned to Ashleigh. "So good to have met you, my dear. You must come to call someday soon for tea. We shall find a great deal to chat about, I'm sure."

With briefly murmured farewells the three were soon ensconced within the handsome blue and gold coach and off down St. James's. The silence that fell in the wake of their departure was broken by an audible sigh of relief from Megan.

"Sure and 'twas the color o' me shift they'd have been after knowin' next," she declared. "Faith, Yer Grace, are they always that pryin'? I've seen hounds on the scent give up more easily!"

Brett chuckled as he led the two women to the door of the dressmaker's. "Never underestimate the investigative capabilities of those women or the *power* they wield, especially Jersey and Castlereagh! As patronesses of Almack's, their social influence is unlimited. For some years now, vouchers of admission to Almack's have been the yardstick of social acceptance in this country. Without it—and by that I mean without the nod of those half-dozen or so dear ladies who function as Almack's patronesses—no one who aspires to be included among the *ton* can really say he has arrived."

Brett was holding open the handsome green and gilt door of the shop for them, and as they passed through, Ashleigh commented, "But surely such social assets as birth and position have more to do with this selectivity than—"

An explosive chuckle met her ears as Brett closed the door behind them. "Don't you believe it!" he told her. "As of this year's standing, for example, I'm told that out of some three hundred officers of the Guards, only a half dozen have been honored with vouchers of admission.''

"No!" exclaimed Megan. "But the Guards are considered the cream—"

"Exactly," countered Brett. "And not only are the standards for admission high; once admitted, there are still the very strict and somewhat arbitrary rules that can exclude. Take the sacrosanct edict that forbids anyone entry after eleven in the evening. Guess what happened to none other than the duke of Wellington himself when the poor man had the misfortune to arrive at seven minutes *past* that prescribed hour.''

"But of course, 'e was excluded!" said a French-accented female voice from across the room.

Ashleigh turned and saw a small, birdlike woman of about forty advancing toward them. She was modishly, but not elegantly, attired in a simple day frock of gauzy black cotton. It matched the black hair she wore severely pulled back from her angular face in a chignon and the black eyes that darted over the two younger women in quick, assessing fashion.

*"Bonjour, monsieur le duc."* She nodded at Brett with a smile.

"News travels fast in London," Brett returned.

"And nowhere faster than in ze places where ze favored go to decorate zemselves," said the Frenchwoman. "And while we are about eet, allow me to convey my deepest sympathy to you on your *grand-père*'s passing. All of London ees shocked by ze news."

Brett nodded his appreciation and watched the woman's attention shift to the somberly clad figure of Ashleigh beside him. "Madame Gautier, allow me to present my new ward, Miss Sinclair."

As Ashleigh smiled shyly in greeting, Madame Gautier's glance shifted briefly back to Brett. There was a knowing, contemplative look in the dark eyes before they returned to Ashleigh. "Hmm," she murmured. "Eet would seem not *all* ze news 'as made eet zrough my doors. I congratulate you on your... ward, *monsieur le duc*. She ees exquisite." She looked back at Brett. "But of course, what ees needed ees to transform *exquisite* into *superbe*, by way of ze appropriate costume, eh? And for zat, you 'ave come to me, *n'est-ce pas?*''

Assuring her they would have used no one else, Brett launched into a brief recapitulation of the story he'd given Lady Jersey, thus assuring its rapid installation into the channels of gossip that London thrived on. As he finished, he watched Madame Gautier's eyes dart to the figure of Megan who, until now, had been standing behind him, taking everything in.

The Frenchwoman took only a moment to assess the appearance of the tall redhead, then exclaimed, ''*Mon Dieu!* I c? 'ardly *believe* eet! Suzanne! Suzanne, come 'ere at once!'' She turned toward the rear of the shop as she called, and as all four of them looked in that direction, a tall figure emerged from a doorway there.

Ashleigh gasped as they all beheld the source of Madame Gautier's excitement. Walking toward them was a tall, redheaded young woman who resembled Megan so closely, they might have been sisters. Lovely, slanted green eyes lit up the young woman's strikingly beautiful features as she too saw the reason she had been so enthusiastically summoned.

''Saints preserve us!'' breathed Megan.

''My daughter, Suzanne Gautier O'Sullivan,'' Madame Gautier said proudly. She gave a small apologetic smile in their direction. ''I use my maiden name because eet ees much better beesness to be a *French modiste* wiz a *French* surname. But my poor dead 'usband was as Irish as you are, Mademoise' O'Brien,'' she added.

''Yes, well, Miss O'Brien will be needing a new wardrobe as well,'' said Brett with a brief glance at his pocket watch. ''I was—''

''Say no more about eet, *monsieur le duc*,'' Madame Gautier told him with Gallic assuredness. ''Suzanne ees my ablest assistant. I myself 'ave been training 'er for years. And oo better to understand ze needs of zis tall beauty wiz ze exotic coloring, eh? *Alors!* Take Mademoiselle O'Brien to your fitting room, Suzanne. You can begin showing 'er some fashion sketches while I attend to ze little one 'ere.''

As a bemused Suzanne showed an equally bemused Megan to the rear chambers of the shop, her mother turned toward Ashleigh. "Now, Mademoiselle Sinclair, tell me, what ees eet you are in need of, eh? A couple of new ball gowns? A walking dress or two? Some morning gowns, per'aps?"

"Oh," murmured Ashleigh, at a loss. She was hardly accustomed to ordering anything in the way of elaborate, specifically designated attire. In all the years at Hampton House, she'd had only two frocks at any one time—the one she was wearing and a spare when that was being laundered—and these she had always stitched herself, with Dorcas's help. She could vaguely recall some fittings she'd had as a child, upstairs in the sewing chamber as Mother had watched while a local seamstress had draped and pinned fabric about her, but these recollections were clouded by time. Moreover, she had no idea what gowns and the like cost these days, and inasmuch as Brett would be paying for whatever was ordered today, she felt awkward over making any decisions in that regard.

But as the silence grew and Madame Gautier continued to look at her questioningly, she forced a response.

"I...that is..." She glanced apprehensively up at Brett who appeared absorbed in the myriad bolts of cloth and pieces of ribbon and lace that were scattered haphazardly about. No help there. "W-would one of each be too much to expect?" she asked timidly.

"One of each? One of each what, *chérie*?" Madame Gautier asked as she gestured about her. "One of each color? One of each fabric? One of each—"

"I—I meant one of each kind," murmured Ashleigh. "You know, one morning gown, one—"

"She'll need at least a dozen of each sort, Madame Gautier," Brett interrupted. "I plan to do quite a bit of entertaining, and Miss Sinclair will be acting as my hostess."

Ashleigh's head swung around as he spoke, her mouth forming an O of surprise. *A dozen of each! She'd had no idea . . .*

"But of course you are right, *monsieur le duc*." Madame Gautier was beaming as she began to move toward the rear of the shop. "Excuse me for just one moment, please. I must collect my sketchbooks.... Hmm...a dozen ball gowns...a dozen day gowns...a dozen carriage dresses...a dozen walking dresses..." They heard her murmuring to herself as she disappeared through the door through which Megan and Suzanne had gone earlier.

When the door had shut behind her, Ashleigh turned and glanced at Brett. This was the first they had been alone together since he had charged back into her life—was it only last evening? And she wasn't exactly comfortable with this sudden realization. Standing beside her, looking ever so tall and broadshouldered and spectacularly handsome, was the man who had arrogantly invaded the privacy of her body not so long ago, who had forced intimacies she had not even guessed could exist between male and female; and now, all at once, she was expected to appear beside him as if none of this had happened, to be escorted about like a lady and introduced as his ward! This last thought brought with it a sharp gust of anger at the story he'd concocted. His ward, indeed!

At the small but unmistakable frown of annoyance she exhibited, Brett arched one eyebrow speculatively. "Something concerns you, Ashleigh?"

Oh, so now it was *Ashleigh*, was it? She gritted her teeth in an effort to control her mounting anger, which, she vaguely realized, was really prompted by a subtle undercurrent of fear at being alone in his presence and without the protective benefits of Megan's chaperonage. Swallowing twice and then taking a deep breath, she managed to answer him in a voice she could only hope did not betray her fears. "That tale you gave out about my being your ward, Your Grace: it does not sit well with me, I must tell you."

"Really, my dear?" Brett replied, a hint of a sneer implicit in his tone. The turquoise eyes bored into her. "And why is that?"

Ashleigh fidgeted with the plain black piping on her pelisse and attempted to draw the garment more tightly about her, as if to use it to block his gaze. "It—it is simply that—that I am quite unaccustomed to...dissembling, Your Grace. Even as a small child, my—"

"Disabuse yourself of the notion that you are being asked to do anything immoral, miss!" Brett's eyes flashed with the statement, then shuttered, and she was left with the well-remembered lazy, mocking grin. "All immoral acts," he softly added, leaning down toward her to be sure they would not be overheard, "that you might have been induced to participate in, are well behind you. You and your companion had, I'd believed, my assurances last night. You have my word on it now."

Later, Ashleigh was to ask herself where she came by the boldness to say it, but whatever the cause or impulse, she suddenly found herself remarking flippantly, "You are contrite, then."

Again there was a flash of turquoise as his eyes locked with hers. Ashleigh forced her gaze downward, damning her impudent tongue, and she chanced to see his hand made into a fist, clenching and unclenching while he sought to control himself.

At last he spoke, his voice ominously low. "My dear Ashleigh, not only am I contrite, as you put it, I am doing *penance*! Damn my soul for the code of honor I must live by! Why else do you think I would invite two such...*females* into my life? For the sheer pleasure of it?"

Ashleigh felt the blood drain from her face at the onslaught, for, though his words were softly uttered, there was no mistaking the anger that fed them. Taking a backward step, she swallowed past the lump of fear that had lodged in her throat and answered him with eyes gone huge with fright. "N-no, Your Grace. I—I only meant—"

"Well, you can put such concerns out of your head—at once!" he snapped. "From now on, you are my ward. A letter went out to Adams, my solicitor, early this morning, instructing him to take the necessary steps to make that situation a reality. As for the tale I gave out regarding your past, I suggest you begin to memorize it until you know it as well as your own name—and begin *believing* it as well! Our only hope in having you received by those who matter lies in its total acceptance, and there's an end to it." He took a step toward her, and the turquoise eyes held hers. "Is that understood?"

Speechless, Ashleigh nodded, her own eyes wide and unblinking.

Brett nodded, but his gaze continued to bore into hers. "See that it is. As for your other concerns, know this: I deeply rue the day I mistook your innocent protests for manifestations of other motives, for it has begun to cost me in all kinds of ways. Suffice it to say, therefore, that I have no further designs on your person—" his eyes travelled briefly down the length of her, then back to her face "—lovely as it may be. Having once been burned by its temptations, I'd be a fool to be lured in that direction a second time." He paused and withdrew the gold pocket watch Ashleigh had seen him consult earlier, then turned his eyes back to hers. "And I," he added with a snap of the timepiece's hunter-case cover, "am not a fool!" He turned and headed for the door.

"Wh-where are you going, Your Grace?"

Brett turned at the half-opened door and regarded her. "My dear Ashleigh," he said in a tone that was better suited for speaking to a child, "the fitting session you are about to embark upon should take a good two, perhaps three, hours. I assure you, I have better things to do with my time than stand about and wait until you are through. My carriage driver has instructions to wait and collect you and your companion when you are ready. I shall find my own way home and see you this evening at dinner. Good day." With the briefest of nods he passed through the door and was gone.

# Chapter Ten

Brett relaxed in his chair at White's and regarded the man across the table from him. There was an amused sparkle in the turquoise eyes as he appraised his companion.

"And what in hell is it you find so damned amusing?" demanded the huge man who was the object of his crinkled gaze. "Is it my cravat that's askew, perhaps? I'll admit, I certainly didn't spend the entire morning with my valet, like that fellow there obviously has," he added with an inclination of his head in the direction of the man sitting stiffly in the bay window a few tables away, "but then, I've better things to do with my life than emulate Brummell."

The upturned corners of Brett's mouth widened into a grin with the remark. "And I thank God you do, Patrick! I've had enough of dandies lately, to choke on! And, no, my friend, your cravat appears to be disgustingly perfect."

Patrick St. Clare grinned, displaying a set of white, even teeth in his deeply tanned face. It was an intelligent face; big, handsome and square-jawed—well suited to the gigantic proportions of the man. Bright blue eyes shone keenly from beneath heavy black brows that matched the inky curls covering his huge, well-shaped head. His nose, proportionately large but straight and even, bore a small scar on its bridge, but this in no way marred his rugged good looks. Completing the picture was a wide, pleasant-looking mouth that seemed easily disposed toward laughter, and as if to bear this out, Patrick now began to chuckle merrily as he looked at his friend.

"It's through no fault of my own, if it is, Brett! But, see, you haven't yet told me what it was that amused you so a moment ago. Out with it! Have I sprouted horns or the like?"

It was Brett's turn to chuckle. "The only horns you'd be associated with, you rogue, are the ones on the husbands cuckolded through your indiscretions!"

"Ha!" came the retort. "There's an example of the pot calling the kettle black, if I ever heard one! But, come to think on it, we might both be accused of sprouting the devil's horns, were the fair ladies of this land asked for an opinion."

"True enough." Brett grinned. "But lucky for us, just now they're too busy pinning that label on George Gordon. Thanks to Caro Lamb, it's he who has the public's eye and ear at the moment."

"Poor Byron—lionized and bait for scandal, all in a season! But come, back to the source of your merriment a few moments ago, sir! And I warn you, no further digressions!"

"Ah, yes," nodded Brett. "Well, it had to do with an encounter I had with Jersey and Castlereagh this morning...."

"Egad!" Patrick shrank back in mock horror. "Two from Olympus itself!"

Grinning, Brett continued. "Castlereagh, it seems, takes exception to Jersey's giving you a voucher for, ah, Olympus."

"Does she now? And what seems to be the problem? No, don't tell me. Let me guess.... Ah! I have it! My hair's too black ... or perhaps it's my height. They've decided to exclude those over six-and-a-quarter feet! Poor Jersey must be redfaced, for she'll be having to carry her yardstick from now on." Patrick finished by making an exaggerated mime of a haughty patroness measuring a would-be applicant for admission to Almack's.

"You've missed your calling, Patrick," Brett chuckled. "You'd have made a fortune on the stage. Edmond Kean is no match for you!"

Patrick nodded with mock regret. "Ah, yes, and here I've wasted all those years being shipwrecked and carving out my fortune from scratch in America." He shook his head in mock solemnity. "Sad ... so sad."

"Especially the American business," Brett told him with a wagging finger that matched his mocking tone. "For it was your years there that account for your pronunciation of your surname, *Saint Clare*, and it just won't do for Castlereagh. For the grande dame it's *Sin Clare* or nothing!"

"Ah! So that's the way of it, is it? She'd have me publicly voice the *sin* in my life! There may be hope for the old girl yet."

"She's certainly having nothing of the *saint* you're parading about!" Brett quipped, and they both joined in a merry chuckle at their wit.

But then Brett's expression changed, and he regarded his friend with a serious look. "But, speaking of your family name, tell me—any news on your search?"

Patrick sobered instantly with the question; he shook his head, all trace of humor gone. "None. It seems there was a fire in the offices of the family solicitors several years back, and that, on top of the news I received a while ago that the senior partner we dealt with had died in 'oh-two, leaves me at a complete loss as to my next step."

"I'm sorry, my friend," said Brett as he placed his hand on Patrick's. "What will you do now?"

Patrick sighed. "Oh, I'm not sure, exactly. Go back to Kent, perhaps. After all, I went there in the first place to learn the news of the tragedy."

Brett nodded. "It was a hell of a homecoming. Tell me, though, didn't you suspect something amiss after your letters went unanswered for so long?"

Again a sigh. "You're forgetting that I spent most of those years abroad not knowing who I really was. For a dozen years of my life I was Patrick Saint, with not a trace of a recollection of my past before the shipwreck. The only reason I retained the bulk of my name was that the shirt I was wearing had part of a label left on it, inside my collar where I'd sewn it myself: *Patrick St.*—"

"No, I'm not forgetting, Patrick. But I was referring to the letters you began to write a little over a year ago when that fall from your horse brought everything back. After all, that's still a good while before you made it back to England."

"I know," Patrick nodded. He paused a moment to sip at the cup of coffee he held. "It took me a while to settle things on my estate in Virginia. You might recall the Americans and the British have been having a bit of a time of it lately. The end of 1812 was a hell of a time for me to get my memory back and discover I had strong ties on both sides!"

"Agreed. It must have been even more disconcerting to discover, after you arrived here, that you were a Virginia planter who was now also an English baronet!" A note of compassion entered Brett's voice. "But the worst had to be the way you learned of your family's end."

"I've had the time to digest it now, and I've done my mourning for my mother and father."

"But not for your young sister," Brett said pointedly.

"No, not for my sister." Patrick's eyes deepened to the color of sapphire, and for a moment Brett had a twinge of something vaguely familiar, but it was fleeting, and he proceeded to give his friend his full attention.

"Dammit, man," Patrick continued, "why should I? The one piece of information I was able to glean from those left in the area who were able to tell me anything, was that there was no body of a child found in the ruins of the fire. My parents', yes, and those of several servants, all of whose graves I've seen, for they're plainly marked, but of the little one there's no trace! That's why I've got to keep searching. I must! Until I know for certain one way or the other, I cannot give up hope. Can you understand that, Brett?"

Brett glanced away, not wanting Patrick to read his thoughts. He, too, had buried family over the years—his beloved grandfather just last week. But because of the circumstances affecting the earlier losses—those of his childhood—he'd come to a method of dealing with such tragedy that tended to make him cut his losses and put them behind him, forcing himself to concentrate on the future. Being of such a mind, he wasn't at all sure he could sympathize with Patrick's obsession with finding out what had happened to his sister. He was inclined to think the girl was dead and put it into the past. After all, if she were alive, where was she? Why wasn't she coming forth to claim the rightful place in society she was entitled to? The St. Clares, if Patrick was to be believed—and Brett had no reason to doubt him—might have wound up impoverished, but theirs was an old and honorable name, going back to the time of the Conqueror. Surely a surviving daughter with that kind of legacy wouldn't simply have disappeared into the woodwork!

Still, Brett thought as he turned back to his companion, Patrick was his friend—their relationship going back to their days as cabin boys, even if it was interrupted by the big man's hiatus in America—and as such, he deserved his full-hearted support. Smiling, he reached forward to clap him warmly on the shoulder. "Patrick, if there's anything I can do to aid you in your search, you know you need only ask."

Patrick returned his smile. "Thanks, my friend. And perhaps there is. When we've done with this business at Carlton House, I think I'll make that run to Kent again. Can you put me up while I'm down there?"

"I wouldn't think of your staying anywhere else." Brett looked thoughtful for a moment as he took a sip of his coffee. "I have my own notions of why our prince regent might be interested in each of our views on what's been happening since the allies made their triumphant entrance into Paris at the end of March, but you haven't told me yours." He glanced around the room, which had begun to fill up since the two had met there a half hour before. "I think we'll have more privacy if we stretch our legs a bit, don't you?"

Nodding, Patrick rose while Brett signaled their waiter, and a few minutes later, both were strolling casually along the street outside.

"It's clear I was overheard that night a few weeks ago when we shared a few draughts together," said Patrick. He looked only mildly abashed as he added, "I usually hold my liquor better than that, but I hadn't eaten a bite all day, and—"

"You said nothing that could be constituted as loose-tongued. After all, what harm is there in wondering about the wisdom of sending Napoleon to a Mediterranean island? Elba *is* a bit too close to France, if you ask me!"

"Yes, and not only that," Patrick added, "but they called it an unconditional surrender and then proceeded to give him an income of *two million francs a year*! And his wife, Marie-Louise, receives the duchies of Parma, Piacenza and Guastalla, and *they both retain their imperial titles!* It's lunacy! The man almost succeeded in swallowing up all of Europe, and they treat him with—with kid gloves!"

"Of course, I agree with you, Patrick—as I did then. We've not seen the last of the Little Corsican yet, mark my words."

Patrick chuckled. "Evidently somebody did exactly that, that night at the Red Lion. They marked *both* our words!"

Brett grinned. "You're right, of course. So now, with the entire city in a flurry over welcoming the heroes of the allied victory, I suppose the prince regent and his ministers don't wish to take any chances. They'll sound us out on our recently, and—ah—publicly, expressed views over the wisdom with which Boney was handled."

"Well, I can't blame them," Patrick told him. "It could be awfully embarrassing if, in the midst of a victory celebration, Napoleon were to somehow make it off that island and begin to gather troops about him again."

"Don't tell me you're going to tell that to Prinny!" Brett stopped and gazed at his friend in mock horror.

"Oh," answered Patrick with a grin, "I might...I just might.... You know, Brett, they really don't know what to make of me. I've functioned as an American citizen for years, but suddenly, one day I turn up here in England and we all discover I'm a blue-blooded, full-fledged member of the peerage. Add to that my Irish good looks inherited from my sainted mother, and you know what you've got?"

"The kind of man who keeps political ministers lying awake at night."

"It's the truth!" Patrick's voice rang out cheerfully with the comment, causing the heads of several passersby to turn. He immediately lowered his voice. "It's a good thing I have a bona fide intelligence man as a friend to vouch for my harmlessness."

"Softly, man, softly," Brett warned him in a whisper. "Because you saved my life that night in the alley, and, of course, because of so much more I've learned about you since we've resumed our friendship, you know I'd trust you with my life. But there are times when I wish your rescuing me from the knives of those French assassin-spies hadn't made you privy to the nature of my undercover occupation. You haven't had the training in watching your tongue, and—"

"But all that's over and done with now, isn't it?"

Brett smiled, but the look in his eyes was cynical. "With Napoleon only as far as Elba? I wouldn't bet on it, my friend. I wouldn't bet on it."

# Chapter Eleven

Ashleigh and Megan sat in the smaller, front drawing room of Ravensford Hall and sipped the tea Brett had asked the butler to serve them. To an observer they might have appeared to be two genteel English ladies stopping for a visit on their round of afternoon calls.

Ashleigh wore a frothy pink voile concoction newly cut by Madame Gautier in lines that were the last word in feminine fashion, its high waist tied with a deeper pink satin ribbon that matched the ties of her bonnet and the slashes in her full sleeves. Its floor-length, slightly flared skirt was edged in delicate lace that echoed the lace at her wrists and the yoked neckline. On her feet were matching pink kid slippers, and the spirals of glossy black curls that peeped from beneath the fashionable bonnet were appropriately chic and feminine at the same time.

Megan's outfit, while cut along the same lines, was more sedate. Understanding the need to play down the use of ribbons and frills when designing for a woman with Megan's statuesque proportions, Suzanne O'Sullivan had put together a dress of soft, sage-green silk with only the narrowest piping for trim where it was needed—this cut from the same sage-green fabric. Her bonnet, in a straw that had been dyed to match, was wide-brimmed, yet simple, and served perfectly to set off the understated elegance of the whole ensemble. To anyone's eye, Megan O'Brien was as far removed from her former profession as any well-dressed lady of the *ton*.

"Another spot of tea, m'lady?" Megan queried in a perfect imitation of an aristocratic London accent. It was a game they had been playing ever since their lavish new wardrobes had arrived from the dressmaker's, and Ashleigh responded in kind.

"Don't mind if I do, m'dear," she said, giving a good approximation of the inflections they'd heard Lady Castlereagh use. But with her next remark she slipped back into her own soft mode of speaking. "What do you think is taking so long, Megan?" She glanced at the ornate porcelain clock on the mantel across from them. "It's been nearly a half hour since he deposited us here."

"Hmm," said Megan, setting down a heavy silver teapot and following Ashleigh's glance. "His Nibs niver said what it was he'd be checkin' into whilst we waited, but I've a good idea. I saw a narrow-faced old crone peerin' down at us from one o' the upper windows when our carriage pulled up. That'd be the great-aunt, now, wouldn't it?"

"An austere face with snow-white hair piled high atop—?"

"That's the one! What's she called again?"

"Lady Margaret . . . Westmont, I believe. The housekeeper here told me she never married. I only met her briefly, when I— Megan! Where are you going?"

Megan had set down her teacup and risen while Ashleigh was talking and now tiptoed carefully toward the closed double doors through which they'd been shown earlier. Her face wore a determined expression. "I've niver been one t' sit still and wonder when I was curious t' find somethin' out, darlin'." She had reached the doors and began, very carefully, to open them. Then, just as carefully, she peered around a partially ajar door into the hallway. A moment passed, and then she looked back over her shoulder at Ashleigh, a wide grin on her face. Silently, she motioned for Ashleigh to join her.

As Ashleigh neared, she began to hear the sounds of voices coming from somewhere across the hallway. Though they were muted, nevertheless she could perceive they were strident and angry.

"Megan," she began in a hushed tone, "should we—?"

"Shh!" Megan put a forefinger to her lips. "We've got to get closer," she whispered, pushing the doors farther apart. She tiptoed into the entry hall, toward a partially ajar door about a dozen feet away. The tall redhead moved directly toward it, motioning for Ashleigh to follow.

Glancing left and right to be sure no servants were about, Ashleigh complied, and a few seconds later they were both standing beside the door. Through it, Brett Westmont's voice came, loud and clear.

"You think to hold me to this alliance because it was my grandfather's last wish?"

"I more than think it," came the confident reply. "I *know* it! Brett, there are many things, I am well aware, that no one can force you to do if you do not wish to do them, but on this, I cannot imagine your refusing. My brother's dying wish was that you wed. He told you as much in your last interview—I was there, remember? And, after you left, he gave me leave to make arrangements with—"

"Yes, of course!" Brett's voice spat out. "The Hastingses! Who else? You know, Lady Margaret, I, as well as a great many others hereabouts, I'll warrant, have long wondered at your most singular attachment to that family. And someday I'll get to the root of it!"

"Wh-what are you referring to?" came the uneasy response.

"Don't play the guileless innocent with me, dear Aunt! I am speaking of your almost unnatural obsession with the Hastings family over the years, or, more particularly, with forming alliances between them and the Westmonts—through marriage—not to mention your constant attention to that clan in myriad other ways. Do you think, because I was away so much during my formative years, I was unaware of your constant visits to Cloverhill Manor? Did you think me deaf, dumb and blind that I did not see your hand in the unfortunate alliance between my father and Lady Caroline? And now, in recent years, it's been that bitch, Elizabeth, who's been the focus of all your unending attentions. 'Lady Elizabeth is, I daresay, an extremely accomplished young lady,'" he mimicked.

"'Lady Elizabeth was the foremost young woman presented this season. She is a true beauty, is she not? Lady Elizabeth would make the perfect wife. Lady Eliz—'"

"Stop it!" cried his great-aunt. "You've no cause to carry on so! It is merely that—that I am the child's godmother, as I was Caroline's before her, and never having had a husband and children of my own, why, I just naturally feel drawn to her.... And, besides, she *is* all of those things I've said of her!"

"I wonder..." Brett murmured. "I wonder..." There was a long silence, and Ashleigh was about to motion to Megan that they hasten back to their tea table when Brett resumed speaking.

"But there are some things in which I'll give you your due, Lady Margaret. In the matter of my taking to heart my grandfather's final wishes, for example. It carries a powerful weight with me. Well, I suppose I should have married sometime, sooner or later. I suppose, as well, that Elizabeth Hastings will do as well as any other well-bred brood bitch."

"*Brett!*" The word was almost a gasp.

"For God's sake, Lady Margaret, spare me your outraged sensibilities! We all know why a man of our class takes a wife. It's to ensure a continuation of his line. Do you think I've not seen all the careful parading of young, blue-blooded feminine flesh about London's ballrooms and drawing rooms during 'the season,' with the carefully arranged machinations between their parents and those of the slavering young—and sometimes not so young—prospective bridegrooms that goes on behind the scenes? Why, my finest-blooded mares are not given as much consideration with regard to bloodlines and breeding ability when it's time to choose which studs will service them!"

"Brett, I forbid you to speak in so base a fashion in front of me! I find it highly offensive, and—"

"Yes, yes," Brett replied wearily. "Well, we're straying from our subject, and in the interest of sparing you a further wasting of breath and energy, allow me to congratulate you, Lady Margaret. No, don't look so dumbfounded. I'm telling you, you've won. Go ahead and make what arrangements you will with the Hastingses. You were right. I cannot easily neglect grandfather's last wishes, but—''

''I knew you'd listen to reason!'' Lady Margaret crowed triumphantly. ''Now, when—?''

''Not so fast, dear Great-Aunt,'' Brett interrupted. ''There is one condition, I'm afraid, and it has to do with the matter I called you in here to discuss initially.''

There was a second's silence, followed by an audible intake of breath by Lady Margaret. ''You—you mean—?''

''Precisely. The girl, Ashleigh.''

''Brett, do not toy with me! You cannot mean to—''

''I can, and I do. The girl stays—as my official hostess, although you're free to share such duties with her if you care to.''

''You are mad! I thought I told you—''

''And I, in turn, have told *you*! I have an obligation to the chit, and I will not see it compromised. Besides, I have need of a youthful, energetic hostess.''

''And what of your obligations to your betrothed?''

Brett sounded bored. ''I care not in the slightest about that. If Elizabeth Hastings is so eager to become the next duchess of Ravensford, I hardly think she's in a position to interfere. Certainly, with our family in mourning, the wedding cannot take place for some time . . . perhaps not for a year, and during that time I shall need—''

''Brett, I will not have that girl in this house! It is unthinkable that you should ask it—that you should seek to install her here, at Ravensford Hall, the home of—I won't have it Brett! I demand—''

''My dear Lady Margaret,'' came the cold reply, ''you are in no position to demand *anything*! I am the master of Ravensford Hall now, and what I decide to do here, I shall do! Ashleigh Sinclair is—''

''Is a common *tart*! A whore, a creature who—''

''She is actually none of those things, as I believe I've already explained, though what she is and how she came to be here are really none of your concern.''

''*None* of my—!'' Margaret's tone was incredulous. ''Brett, I have stood aside and said little over the years as I watched my

brother bend and mold you into the person you are, though
there has been much I've disapproved of. But this time you have
gone too far. I find it hard to believe what I've just heard! *None
of my concern!* I have been mistress of Ravensford Hall for
twenty years! If the identities of persons lodging under this roof
are none of my concern, then whose should they be?''

The voice that answered her was dangerously soft. ''Mine,
Lady Margaret. Only mine.''

''Brett, I warn you—''

''I suggest you reconsider that remark. You are in no position to warn me of anything. You yourself continue living under this roof merely through my indulgence. I could easily have
you removed to the old dowager's cottage near the lake. . . .''

Margaret's gasp cut the air. ''You would not *dare*!''

''I would, and I just might. The girl stays. See that you make
her feel at home. And now, if you don't mind, I must leave. I
merely came down to escort Ashleigh and her—ah—entourage. I have business in London that will keep me away for
some time. When I return, I shall probably be bringing guests
and shall send word ahead—to both you *and* my new ward, so
that you may be prepared to perform the duties of hostess—either jointly or alternately, take your pick. Good day, madam.''

As the sound of Brett's voice indicated he was nearing the
door, Ashleigh and Megan had just enough time to scamper
back to the drawing room where they'd been having tea.
Quickly reseating themselves, they both managed to arrange
blank expressions on their faces before Brett pulled open the
double doors and entered.

As Brett stepped into the room his eyes quickly took in the
tableau of the two young women on the sofa. The sight gave
him more than one reason to halt abruptly in his tracks, and
there was a long pause as he slowly contemplated what he saw.

Not only were the two of them the total picture of graceful
English gentility, sitting there before the Queen Anne tea table
in their fine new frocks, but the image of Ashleigh Sinclair as
she held a fragile Sèvres cup and saucer nearly took his breath
away. Dear God, but she was lovely! She looked for all the

world like a fragile Dresden doll, her creamy skin faintly flushed with color, her huge, deep blue eyes clear and bright, meeting his in what appeared to be a look of open expectation. Was there, had there ever been, a face more beautiful, a countenance more serene or full of grace?

All at once he found himself recalling some lines his friend Byron had let him see a few days ago when they'd met in London.

> She walks in beauty, like the night
> Of cloudless climes and starry skies;
> And all that's best of dark and bright
> Meet in her aspect and her eyes;
> Thus mellow'd to that tender light
> Which heaven to gaudy day denies.

Abruptly, Brett stopped, catching himself in a frame of mind he wasn't sure he was prepared to deal with. Ever since they'd left London he had intentionally avoided any close scrutiny of his new ward. Somehow, he had known, if he hadn't, there would have been the very sort of disturbing fascination he found himself experiencing now. He'd known she was a unique beauty from the start, but in their earlier encounters her beauty had been somewhat subdued by the drab clothing she'd been wearing. Now, however... *Damn!*

A sudden scowl marred the young duke's handsome face, and he quickly stepped forward and addressed Ashleigh and Megan.

"Everything has been arranged for your stay, ladies. I'm leaving word with the butler and housekeeper that they are to see to your comforts, for I shall be returning to London for a time. While I am gone, Ashleigh, I trust you will make yourself familiar with the estate and its inhabitants, so that your duties as hostess may be assumed when I return. Have you any questions before I leave?"

Ashleigh looked at Megan for a moment, but the redhead's features were carefully schooled into a look of blank innocence. Slowly, she returned her gaze to Brett. Did she have any questions! Only a hundred or so! What was she to do in a situation where the mistress of the household had just made it clear Ashleigh was unwanted? How was she to conduct herself in this strange place when the man who was responsible for her being here was to be absent? How, when she met her—and she had no doubt that she would—would she react to his new fiancée, Lady Elizabeth Hastings? How was she going to manage anything at all?

But Ashleigh could never put any of these questions to him. Besides having to admit to eavesdropping, she would have to overcome her feelings of being intimidated whenever she was in his presence, and this she was not ready to do—perhaps would never be ready to do. So, swallowing past the lump that had formed in her throat, she put forth the most innocuous question she could think of.

"Am—that is—are we—" She glanced at Megan briefly. "Are we to be allowed to ride, Your Grace?"

A derisive snort met her ears. "What? Do you mean you are actually asking my permission this time? How very thoughtful of you!"

Immediately recalling her theft of the little filly the day she'd escaped, Ashleigh felt the heat rise to her cheeks; she looked down in embarrassed silence and nodded.

"How very prettily you blush, my dear," Brett sneered. Then, seeing her discomfort and choosing to ignore Megan's glare, he softened his tone. "As it happens, my head groom informs me that Irish Night is none the worse for your escapade on her back. In fact, he marvels over the filly's increased tractability since she's returned. It seems, my dear, that you know how to manage fine horseflesh. We shall have to discuss, sometime, how you came about it. The stable help will be alerted to make suitable mounts available to the two of you. Ah—I assume you also ride, Miss O'Brien?"

"Me da was the finest horse trainer in all Ireland," came Megan's response. "I was *weaned* in a saddle, Yer Grace."

Brett chuckled as he dismissed the coarse response he might have made. Despite her former profession, there was something about the tall Irishwoman that made him behave as a gentleman. "Very well," he said, giving them both a nod of satisfaction. "Then, if there are no further questions, I'll be taking my leave. Try to stay out of trouble while I am gone."

"Trouble?" Ashleigh exclaimed, and then mentally kicked herself for her hasty remark. The last thing she wanted was to antagonize Brett Westmont!

Brett's eyebrows lifted briefly with her response, and then a cynical smile spread itself across his handsome features. "Yes . . . trouble," he replied. "After all, you will be two *females* left largely to your own devices, will you not?" And before they could reply, he made them an elaborate, courtly bow and left.

There was a brief silence as the two women stared at the doors through which he'd gone. Then Megan clucked her tongue and began to shake her head with exaggerated slowness. "'Tis as I've said before—I wonder what divil's botherin' the man . . . I do, indeed. . . ."

# Chapter Twelve

Lady Elizabeth Hastings stepped from her family's carriage onto the crushed white stones lining the circular drive before Ravensford Hall. Tilting her elegant, bonneted head slightly, she surveyed the towering brick facade of the structure that had been the family seat of the Westmonts for more than a dozen generations. There was a cool look of satisfaction on her classically beautiful features.

Soon, soon, she thought, all the waiting will have been worth it. Sometime within the coming year she would be the new duchess of Ravensford and mistress of all this—and more! She would be the wife of Brett Westmont, and clearly the envy of every marriageable woman of her set—not to mention their ambitious mamas and, no doubt, any number of married women as well. "Her Grace, the duchess of Ravensford"—how often she had dreamed of the sound of it! Yes, she thought smugly, it had just the right ring to it, a title in every way appropriate and in keeping with what a woman of her worth deserved. Lowering her gaze, she nodded haughtily to the waiting footman, and with a swish of her blue silk skirts, swept boldly toward the front door.

Upstairs, looking down from where she was standing at the front window of the chamber she'd been assigned by Mrs. Busby, Ashleigh bit her lip in consternation. She'd been dreading this moment for two days, ever since Brett had left and a brief and highly uncomfortable meeting with Lady Margaret soon thereafter had left her with the knowledge that

Brett's fiancée would be arriving soon. Yesterday Lady Margaret had had herself driven over to the Hastings estate, which, Ashleigh now knew, bordered the western acreage of Ravensford Hall and was called Cloverhill Manor. There the duke's great-aunt had spent the better part of the afternoon, returning shortly after teatime to announce to the staff that they might expect Lady Elizabeth in the late morning.

There had been no direct contact between Ashleigh and Lady Margaret herself at this time. Instead, Brett's great-aunt had seen fit to inform her through a written message delivered by one of the footmen to Ashleigh's chamber:

His Grace's fiancée, the Lady Elizabeth Hastings, will be arriving tomorrow shortly before noon. Please do not consider it necessary to act the hostess on this occasion, for I shall be seeing to this duty myself, as I have always done in the past. You may present yourself in the blue drawing room shortly after Lady Elizabeth arrives, however, for an introduction, as I have already told her of your presence and she had expressed a desire to meet you. I shall send a footman up to collect you at the appropriate time. Please be prompt.

Lady Margaret Westmont

Ashleigh shivered, despite the pleasant warmth of the day, as she recalled the contents of the coldly worded message. She could just imagine Lady Margaret informing the young woman of her "presence," and all that that had entailed! After all, why else had the older woman taken it upon herself to visit Cloverhill Manor personally to arrange this visit? And she had stayed for hours! It didn't take too much imagination to reconstruct what had transpired during the exchange between the two women—"My dear, I know you must find it difficult to bear, but the truth had to be told.... Yes, he found her in a house of ill fame.... She was employed there.... No, my dear, I have tried my best to dissuade Brett from entering into this piece of folly, but to no avail.... He insists upon having the tart installed at the Hall.... Be brave, my dear—we all have our crosses to bear, and surely, once you are duchess and mistress of Ravensford Hall, you will be in a position to dismiss the little beggar at the first opportunity...."

Ashleigh turned from the window and sighed. From what she had just seen, Elizabeth Hastings appeared every inch a lady, the epitome of the best the English aristocracy had to offer. Tall and willowy, she wore her pale, flaxen beauty with an assurance that proclaimed to all who viewed it that she was a pampered darling of her class. From the top of her fashionable blue bonnet to the tips of her elegantly shod, satin-slippered feet, she had stood before the entrance to Ravensford Hall as if she already owned it; the regal air of her posture, the aristocratic manner in which she held her head, her very walk as she moved toward the house—all bespoke an attitude of assumed acceptance of grace and privilege that had been bred into her lineage long before she was born, and been taken as her due from the time she had been in the cradle.

How could she, Ashleigh Sinclair, an orphan who had worked as a menial in a brothel, even begin to deal with the day-to-day presence of such a creature? And especially with the lady knowing how she had come to be employed here! Oh, it was almost too much to contemplate, let alone act on!

She glanced down at the buttercup-yellow, sprigged muslin day gown she wore and thought briefly of the smile of pleasure it had brought when she viewed it in the cheval glass this morning after Megan had helped her dress. With matching yellow primroses woven into her carefully braided coronet with a cascade of curls tumbling out of it and down her back, she had thought herself more than passably pretty and ever so chic. But now, with the image of the elegantly gowned noblewoman who waited downstairs firmly entrenched in her mind, she felt, by comparison, like a callow schoolgirl about to brave her first grown-up tea.

Oh, if only Megan were here! But, for some reason, Lady Margaret had arranged for her presence elsewhere at this time, having sent word through Mrs. Busby that Megan was to meet Mr. Busby at the stables for the purpose of assisting him in the selection of a pair of suitable mounts for her and Ashleigh to use while they lived here. Ashleigh had thought little of the message at the time, but Megan, quick to sense something in the directive, had laughed, saying, "Ah, 'tis a clever old crone she is, t' be herdin' me out o' sight when the favored princess comes t' call. 'Twill be difficult enough havin' t' explain *yer* presence t' the likes o' Lady Blueblood, but how d' ye think she'd explain *me*? Aye, Her High-and-Mightiness knows what I be, darlin', make no mistake about that," Megan had continued. "I have it on the authority o' the household's highly efficient servants' grapevine that the Lady Margaret sent a footman t' Hampton House the day we arrived with some questions about me and me illustrious past. *Wirra*, but I'd love t' have seen the expression on her face when she received all her answers!"

Ashleigh gave a small, rueful smile at the recollection of Megan's words. Her friend's easygoing manner and witty sense of humor had been the mainstay and saving grace behind much that she'd had to deal with in recent years, and had taught her a great deal about meeting life's difficulties and making the best of them. But there was certainly nothing of this Megan, the one she knew and called her friend, that Lady Margaret could have learned of, or guessed at, from the inquiries she'd made. Indeed, it would have been difficult even for Ashleigh herself to have told a stranger what the tall redhead was really like. How could anyone, in a few short words, paint a picture of a woman whose unfortunate choice of profession was the least of what she was?

And even where Megan's career at Hampton House was concerned, there was so much that *ought* to be told—and wouldn't be—of how she'd come to be there. How did one explain to an inquiring stranger what it was like to be the terrified daughter of an impoverished Irish widow with many young mouths to feed? How did one express the half-told stories Megan had allowed to come to light over the years, of what it had been like to be sixteen when your adored father died and you found yourself the eldest of ten children, and going to bed at night to the sounds of the younger ones crying themselves to sleep because they were hungry? Would a stranger care that most of Megan's hard-earned coins had been sent back to Ireland to keep alive the loved ones she had left behind? And even if someone had taken the trouble to try to find out such things, there was no likelihood that anyone at Hampton House could have told him, for Megan rarely spoke to its inhabitants of her past. The little that Ashleigh knew had only slipped out here and there during their friendship, until, by bits and pieces, Ashleigh had at last begun to understand.

Ashleigh shook her head, and her lips twisted into a wry shadow of a smile as she thought of the two women downstairs and the impossibility of their ever understanding the likes of Megan O'Brien. And with her next thought, the smile disappeared. Indeed, what was the likelihood of their ever understanding *her*? Brett had explained to Lady Margaret how it was she had come to be in this situation; but had it mattered or even been believed? And if Lady Margaret was so far from being inclined to accept her presence here, wasn't the possibility of Lady Elizabeth's doing so even more remote? " . . . She has expressed a desire to meet you," the note had said. Why? Was she curious about a creature foolish enough to allow herself to be so compromised? Would she gawk at Ashleigh, would she—?

Suddenly Ashleigh stopped and considered where her thoughts were leading her. *Grab hold of yourself, Ashleigh Sinclair!* she scolded. *All this worrying will certainly not help the matter, and perhaps it's even unnecessary. It could be that Elizabeth Hastings is a warm, compassionate person, ready to meet and accept you on friendly terms. After all, truly, why else would she express an interest in meeting you? Yes, fix your thoughts on that. Her wanting to meet you is a positive sign. All you need do is behave graciously and everything will be just fine. You'll—*

At that moment there came a knock at the door, and Ashleigh took just a second to paste a smile of what she hoped looked like confidence on her face before she opened it. "Yes?"

A liveried footman whom she recognized as the older son of the Busbys made a small bow. "You are expected in the Blue

Room, Miss Sinclair," he said in words spoken so carefully Ashleigh suspected they'd been rehearsed.

She smiled at the young man's earnestness, knowing he'd been promoted to this position only a short while ago and was trying his best to look and sound like a footman and not the stable boy he'd been. He looked so uncomfortable in his new clothes, Ashleigh felt sorry for him, but she fought to keep this from showing. "Thank you, Jonathan," was all she said, and then followed him downstairs.

The blue drawing room of Ravensford Hall was a large, magnificently furnished chamber more than forty feet wide and half again as long. Undoubtedly receiving its name from the blue-damask-covered walls and perhaps the predominance of blue in the Savonnerie carpet that was an elegant feast for the eye, with its cool colors and soft, exotically shaped patterns, the vast chamber successfully blended the splendors of Renaissance treasures with native English elegance and charm. Complementing its generous scale was the grandeur of its focal point: an enormous marble and gilt rococo fireplace, complete with overmantel mirror and elaborate frieze above, and an Italian tapestry fire screen below. Flanking this was a pair of massive ebony and gold ormolu cabinets. Paintings by Tintoretto, Van Dyck and Canaletto rested comfortably on the walls beside others by Lely, Reynolds and Turner. The ceiling was a study in the classical arabesque mode, its ivory and gilt-toned decoration echoing the colors of the cut-velvet patterned draperies hanging at the floor-to-ceiling windows.

But despite this impressive, formal ornamentation, the room had a warm, inviting look to it, and Ashleigh decided it must be because of the small, random groupings of the Adam furniture that filled much of its space. These clusters of chairs and tables seemed to invite intimate conversation, and she began to breathe in a more relaxed fashion when she stepped forward into the room and beheld Lady Margaret and Lady Elizabeth in such a setting.

Jonathan Busby had been replaced at the doorway by Jameson, the austere-looking butler who announced, "Miss Sinclair, my lady," and then backed out of the room, pulling the double doors shut after him.

"Thank you for coming, Miss Sinclair," said Lady Margaret from the chair where she remained seated. "Please come forward."

As Ashleigh approached the two women, she had a moment to observe them. Lady Margaret wore the black of mourning in the form of a plain cotton day gown with narrow, tight-fitting sleeves and a high neckline. Unrelieved by ornamentation of any kind, it served to call attention to her face and hair. Indeed, the latter, which was snow-white and piled atop her head in thick, natural waves, seemed an ornament of sorts in itself. Her long, narrow face retained something of what once must have been an arresting beauty, for the features were even and well balanced over a bone structure that was strong and better able than most to withstand the ravaging effects of age. But it was a pale face, almost ghostly in its lack of color, except for the piercing blue eyes that were its focal point and were presently fixed on Ashleigh in an acute, assessing gaze.

To Lady Margaret's right, in a matching armchair sat Elizabeth Hastings. If Ashleigh had thought Brett's fiancée beautiful from her glimpse at the window, now she was positively overwhelmed. Lady Elizabeth had to be the finest specimen of female perfection she'd ever seen. Hair so pale in its flaxen silkiness that it appeared almost silver under her ice-blue bonnet, curled charmingly about a perfect oval face. Widely spaced, silvery-gray eyes gazed coolly at Ashleigh from beneath delicate, silvery arched brows in a porcelain-smooth complexion. Her small nose, slightly aquiline and finely boned, formed a perfect counterpoint to her soft, delicately curved mouth, which was the cupid's bow fashion loved. Like Lady Margaret, she held her tall, willowy frame regally erect in her seat, never allowing her back to touch that of the chair. Her ice-blue, softly flowing Empire day gown clung to her slender figure in graceful folds, and it was smartly accented with rows of delicate lace at the square, low neckline and at the edges of its soft little puffed sleeves. Finally, making the definitive statement as to her wealth and class, there was her jewelry. A pair of large, perfectly matched, diamond-encircled sapphires studded her earlobes, echoed by the sapphire pendant she wore about her neck on a fine silver chain. Wealth, elegance, breeding—they were all there, and with this fact staring her blatantly in the face, Ashleigh's impulse was to turn and run—not only out of the room and away from these two women so obviously far above her on the social scale, but out of Ravensford Hall and all they represented—never to return.

But, of course, fleeing was not possible, and so she merely drew to a halt before the two, bent her knee in a brief curtsy and softly murmured, "You wished to speak with me, Lady Margaret?"

"Actually, no," Lady Margaret replied abruptly.

Ashleigh's downcast eyes, which had been studying the carpet patterns in her nervousness, flew upward to meet the old woman's. "I—I beg your pardon, my lady?" she asked with some surprise.

Lady Margaret's pale lips curved into a line that was more a sneer than a smile. "My intent," she intoned loftily, "from the moment you first set foot in this house, Miss Sinclair, has been never to exchange more words with you than I absolutely must . . . or none, actually, if I were to have my way. But my godchild here, Lady Elizabeth Hastings, persuaded me to arrange a meeting. I believe I explained as much in my little missive earlier." Ignoring Ashleigh's disbelieving gasp, she turned to Elizabeth. "Well, pet, what do you think?"

Elizabeth Hastings had been carefully scrutinizing Ashleigh from the moment she entered the drawing room, and she was far from happy with what she saw. Instead of some overdone, cheaply dressed little tart, the young woman who stood before her was a raving, elegantly accoutered beauty! She'd instantly recognized the stamp of Madame Gautier's handiwork in the graceful design of the yellow day gown. That miserable wretch, Brett, had obviously seen to the chit's wardrobe! And the eye-catching loveliness of the girl was almost more than she could bear! This was no worn-out trollop fetched from some back-street brothel. Anyone could see the creature radiated freshness and, yes, innocence from every pore. Those shiny raven

tresses played spellbinding counterpoint to the delicate peaches-
and-cream expanse of her flawless skin; that perfect, straight
little nose was just the nose *she'd* always coveted; and those
*eyes*! Their deep blue depths put all Elizabeth's sapphires to
shame!

As she continued to eye Ashleigh's face with its fragile, elfin
beauty, a deep-seated pool of jealousy began to bubble and
seethe within Elizabeth; as she glanced at Ashleigh's petite,
perfectly proportioned body with its generously swelling breasts
and long, lissome limbs, a cancerous envy filled her being; as
she beheld the sweet openness of Ashleigh's expression, she
knew she hated her and would not rest until the little bitch was
out of her life—*and Brett's*—forever.

Tearing her eyes away from Ashleigh, she turned to Lady
Margaret. "How much of a wardrobe has he bought her?"

Margaret shrugged. "There were several trunks with her
when she arrived, and she had almost nothing during her first
stay."

"Just as I thought," Elizabeth seethed, "and Madame
Gautier does not come cheap!"

"No," Margaret replied, "but I suggest you cease troubling
yourself on that account, pet. His Grace can easily afford it. It
is the girl's presence here that we are about. How are we to deal
with it?"

Ashleigh stood in stunned silence as she listened to their exchange. They were discussing her like . . . like some object—a
stick of furniture or the like! It was as if she weren't even present in the room! Why, they hadn't even asked her to sit down,
but instead, kept her standing here before them while they
scrutinized every inch of her and picked her apart with their
eyes! Was this what fine ladies of the English aristocracy were
all about? If so, she was glad she'd lost her title and its so-called
advantages years ago. Oh, dear God! What was she to do?

"I never actually thought Brett favored brunettes," Elizabeth was saying, "and she seems a bit small for his tastes, don't
you think?"

Margaret smiled thinly and arched one white eyebrow.
"Surely, my dear, you know of his rakish reputation by now!

Tall or short, blond or brunette, young or not-so-young, His Grace has had them all, and quite indiscriminately, I'm told. Only his grandfather failed to learn of my grandnephew's reputation with women, and sometimes now I wonder if it wasn't a mistake on my part, not to correct his ignorance." She shrugged. "Of course, in recent years his health was failing, and the physicians warned that any great shock—well, that's water beneath the bridge. Tell me, have you seen enough? Shall I dismiss her?"

Ashleigh wanted to scream. She'd never encountered such base rudeness in all her life! Even at Hampton House, where there was jealousy and competition aplenty, the rivalries had been forthright and fairly open. Why, even Monica had addressed her as a *person*! But *this*! This was a cold and brutal cruelty, calculated, she was sure, to put her in her place—which was nowhere, but certainly out of this house, if these two women had anything to say about it!

"There's just one little thing..." Elizabeth was saying. She leaned forward in her chair and reached for the skirt of Ashleigh's gown. "Hmm, the sprigged muslin is of a superior quality, but there's something about the way the skirt hangs that isn't—" she was fingering the gown's material now, as Ashleigh watched in silent apprehension "—quite as it should be," Elizabeth continued. "Perhaps...*there*!" With a jerk of her wrist, she yanked at a fold in Ashleigh's skirt and a sharp ripping sound cut the air.

Horrified, Ashleigh looked down to see half of the front skirt of the lovely yellow gown torn from its high waistline and sagging to the carpet. Instantly she looked up and met the snidely smiling, cold-eyed visage of Elizabeth Hastings. The look in the silvery eyes was pure hatred.

"Ah, well, what a pity," Margaret said. "It was such a lovely gown. Perhaps you can have your, ah, abigail repair it. Good day, Miss Sinclair."

Hot tears stung Ashleigh's eyes as she gazed for a moment in stunned horror at the two women before her. Then, a sob tearing at her throat, she picked up the damaged folds of her skirt, whirled and ran from the room.

## Chapter Thirteen

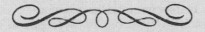

Brett relaxed in his saddle, allowing Raven to find his own way on the path that followed the lake along the western edge of Ravensford Hall's vast acreage. It wasn't the most direct route back to the Hall, but the midsummer air was cooler here in the afternoons, and the lake a lovely, refreshing sight. It was especially reviving to one who'd had a surfeit of the hot, stifling air of London's drawing rooms and the humid confines of its paved streets and narrow alleyways.

A frown of annoyance creased Brett's brow as he thought of the difficulty he'd had getting away this visit. After all, it was the height of the warm season when most of London's inhabitants with the ability to do so headed out of the city to their country estates or to resorts such as Bath, or Brighton, by the seaside. Brett smiled to himself, thinking of Brighton, for it had been the lure of that favored pleasure resort of the prince regent that had at last freed him from the relentless rounds of meetings at Carlton House and Whitehall during the past several weeks. Count on the attraction of luxury to lure Prinny away from the boring demands of rulership!

The frown settled back in place as Brett reviewed the reasons the prince and his ministers had been reluctant to allow him to return to Kent. He could be more forgiving if the endless meetings and conferences had demanded the type of national security work he'd been involved with in recent years. But what was it that had all the government agencies and most of the peerage jumping and feverishly bustling about? A major treaty? No. A battle campaign? Hardly, for the fighting in Europe was over. No, it was the unbelievably frivolous business of a round of celebrations to honor the national and international heroes of the victory over Bonaparte. There had been party after party, ball after ball, speeches, fireworks, parades and banquets, and Brett's presence had been required at all of them. Damn, he swore to himself, it would be a cold day in hell before he welcomed the sight of cheering crowds again, no matter how bloody patriotic the occasion!

A smile found its way across his face again as he pictured poor von Blücher at a recent celebration; he had little doubt that the Prussian field marshal who was one of the Allies' foremost heroes had suffered the recent round of toasting and speechmaking with as little enthusiasm as he. It was a shame that the world couldn't allow military men to remain where they were largely most comfortable—with their men. But of course, he mused, the populace must welcome its heroes, and perhaps it was just as well; for most Englishmen at home, as well as the civilians in the allied countries of Europe, the conflict had been going on for so long, they needed to cheer and touch the hems of the returning victors to feel it had at last come to an end and peace was truly here....

At least, he *hoped* it was here.... Brett's thoughts turned momentarily dark as he contemplated the likelihood of a comeback by Napoleon. A lot depended on the stability of the new French government that was in the throes of being formed, on whether de Talleyrand could marshall the necessary strength to support the Bourbons and—

Raven nickered, drawing Brett's attention away from such pessimistic musings; looking up, his gaze swept the placid surface of the lake, but could detect little to draw the stallion's attention. But for his grandfather's beloved swans serenely skimming its waters, all seemed quiet and devoid of movement.

Then, off to his left, he heard an answering nicker; it appeared to come from the area beyond a small copse of trees that abutted the path. He knew a wide meadow lay in that direction, just out of sight from where he rode. Curious, he turned

Raven's head toward the trees and began to thread his way through them.

Ashleigh had been working with the filly she now knew as Irish Night since midday, and she'd begun to despair of ever making any headway with her plan. The problem was the little horse's skittishness, and in particular, the way it had become an obstacle when it came to taking her over fences.

When Megan had implored Old Henry, as Mr. Busby was now known to them, to allow Ashleigh to ride Irish Night while at Ravensford Hall, the head groom had insisted he could not allow it until the filly was better schooled. Instead, he'd assigned Ashleigh a placid gelding by the name of Major who was safe enough for a baby to ride and ever so dull. But Megan had not allowed the matter to rest there. Pleading and cajoling, begging and wheedling, she'd at last gained Old Henry's consent to allow Ashleigh a few hours a day to work with the filly to try to correct her bad habits, providing Ashleigh promised to adhere to some very exacting safety standards the old man set forth.

The most vexing of these was that she *never mount* Irish Night for the training; all effort must be accomplished with Ashleigh on foot and the filly at the other end of a lunge line, as the long training tether was called.

Now, as she eyed the uprooted tree two of the grooms had located and set up for her in the meadow as a jumping barrier, Ashleigh heaved a sigh of disgust. She'd coaxed Irish Night over the barrier several dozen times this afternoon without any problems—as long as the scene remained tranquil and serene, with nothing interfering to alarm the little black. But during the intervening attempts when, at a signal from Ashleigh, Finn had darted out from a nearby clump of wildflowers, barking, the filly had consistently shied and refused the hurdle. The same was true when Ashleigh herself issued disturbance from her end of the lunge line, accomplished by banging together a pair of tin pie pans she'd "borrowed" from the kitchens, pierced with a nail and tied to her waist with a bit of string.

"All right, Finn," she called, "back to your post. We'll try it again." Ashleigh watched as the big dog happily padded over to the gently waving clump of tall daisies and lay down behind them. To Finn this was all some kind of exciting game, and he eagerly pursued it, no matter how often the repetitions. As Ashleigh faced the filly, out of the corner of her eye she caught a flash of pink and knew that Lady Dimples had ceased her investigation of a rabbit hole and was falling in beside Finn. Ashleigh grinned. The two animals were inseparable, and even during the tedious horse training, the pert little piglet had been stoutly behind the wolfhound on every venture. It hadn't taken the pig long to learn the routine; she only wished Irish Night were schooled as quickly!

"Very well, Irish," she said to the filly. "Here we go!" Ashleigh gave a small yank on the lunge line and began to run toward the barrier. Understanding this much of what she was supposed to do, the filly pricked her ears forward and began to move, parallel with Ashleigh. Ashleigh kept her eye on the horse, and when she saw Irish Night's muscles begin to bunch to take the hurdle, she waved her free arm at Finn.

The big dog pounced from the flowery thicket with an excited bark, Lady Dimples squealing behind him, and at the same moment, the filly, her eyes rolling in fright, swerved to her left and avoided the jump.

Ashleigh groaned. Even the penetrating squeals of Lady Dimples sounded humdrum to her ears by now; why couldn't that skittish filly learn to ignore them? And if she still shied at familiar disruptions, what would she do at *un*familiar ones? Of course, she smiled to herself, she doubted that Irish Night would ever be likely to run into something as noisy and distracting as a giant barking dog followed by a squealing pig!

Suddenly Ashleigh stopped and pondered. Maybe the problem was that there was *too much* of a distraction. "Finn!" she called. "That pig has got to go! She's enough to wake the dead. March her over here right now and see if you can't get her to stay. I want you working alone." She gestured for the dog to approach.

As if he understood every word, Finn came to stand by his mistress with Lady Dimples in tow.

Ashleigh patted the piglet, urging her to lie down in the grass. "Lady Dimples, stay!" she ordered, then signaled Finn to return to his post. She led the filly back to the starting point and prepared to repeat the procedure.

Ashleigh gave Irish Night the signal to advance and began to run with her. At the appropriate moment, she raised her arm to communicate to Finn. She steeled herself for disappointment as she began to read the familiar signs of balking in the filly as Finn emerged from his hiding place when, all of a sudden, a shrill squealing and a blur of pink to her left told her Lady Dimples was on the move!

What happened next occurred so fast, Ashleigh wasn't sure she was seeing right. Darting toward the filly's heels from either side, like a perfectly coordinated team, Finn and the pig urged the horse forward with a din of barking and squealing that rivaled the sounds of Bedlam. The filly, looking like all the demons of hell were after her, took the barrier with feet to spare!

It was all over in seconds, and when she had time to slow down and realize what had happened, Ashleigh gave a howl of delight, plopped herself on the soft grass and burst into laughter. The filly, who had come to a stop at the other end of the lunge line, eyed her curiously, but Finn bounced to her side and began to lick her laughing face while Lady Dimples grunted contentedly at his side.

"Oh, heavens! Who would have thought it?" Ashleigh chortled. "A horse-training pig!" And she launched into another peal of merriment.

Brett sat quietly in his saddle and watched the strange little group. He had witnessed the entire scene, and he couldn't help the wide grin that spread across his features as he listened to the sounds of Ashleigh Sinclair's delight. His eyes took in the charming sight she made, blue eyes merry, cheeks flushed with laughter, raven hair tousled and spilling wildly over her shoulders.... He couldn't help thinking she resembled some wood sprite as she leaned back in the fragrant grasses and took such simple pleasure in her unexpected success with the horse.

Suddenly Brett was doubly grateful to Brighton and its princely attractions for allowing him this visit home. Gone were his chafings at the restrictions imposed on him during recent weeks, his concerns over Napoleon, his boredom with life. Right now Kent, with its meadows and streams and the charm of midsummer, seemed to bid him stay, and at the center of that attraction, though he didn't stop to ponder it, lay an elfin beauty with midnight curls.

Just then, Finn lifted his head and held it very still while he sniffed the air; his eyes focused on the stand of trees across the meadow. With a sharp bark he suddenly bounded in Brett's direction.

Knowing he'd been discovered, Brett didn't wait for the wolfhound to reach him, but urged Raven forward. "Hello, there, Finn," he said, recalling what Ashleigh had called the dog. "So you're to become a master of horses, rather than hounds. Not very true to your namesake, though."

Ashleigh sat erect in the grass, her eyes wide with surprise at their intruder. Since no one at Ravensford Hall had been aware of when its master was expected back, Brett's appearance came as a shock; he'd been gone for many weeks, and she'd grown accustomed to a daily routine in which thoughts of him rarely entered her mind. Indeed, ever since the day he'd left, she'd been preoccupied with staying clear of Lady Margaret and her houseguest, Elizabeth Hastings. Since this had been accomplished through activities such as the horse training, she'd spent most of her waking hours with the animals and stable help and occasionally with Hettie Busby in the kitchens. Hettie and Old Henry had become fond of her and Megan, and, owing to the hostility of the gentry in the house, the two young women found what social life they had around the elderly couple and their friends.

Now, as she beheld him sitting astride his big black stallion, just a few yards away from her, she was assailed by a host of unpleasant, confusing feelings. Here was the man responsible for the most harrowing experience of her life, but also the one responsible for her welfare and, she could only hope, an upward swing in her fortunes. He was arrogant, a callous rogue;

he was also devastatingly handsome, rich, titled and powerful. And he held her future in his hands. Worst of all, appearing so suddenly on the scene, as now, he had the power to make her heart race and moisture gather on the palms of her hands. She was afraid of Brett Westmont; of that there was no doubt. It mattered little that he'd faded from her daily thoughts, when here, all at once, at his sudden appearance, he had the power to reduce her to a trembling weakling. Also, there was no Megan nearby to lend her courage. It was one thing to deal with him under the watchful eye of others, including her strong and supportive friend; it was another to face him in the middle of an open meadow, a good distance from the nearest place where cries for help might be heard and heeded.

Wishing at all costs to hide the effect he had on her, Ashleigh sought to deflect his scrutinizing gaze by commenting on what he'd said to Finn. "I wasn't aware you knew Irish history, Your Grace."

Brett laughed, white teeth flashing in a bronze face. "Not as well as the history I read at Cambridge, but I've a friend with an Irish heritage who drinks deeply of the heady stuff and never lets an evening's companionship go by without regaling me with a tale or two. Cormac's Finn is one of his favorites."

Ashleigh nodded. "I should like to meet your friend sometime, then, though 'Ashleigh's Finn' is *my* favorite!" She reached out and gave a pat to the dog who had returned to her side as soon as Brett began speaking. The gesture was meant to appear casual, but at the back of Ashleigh's mind was the sudden notion that she was not truly alone with Brett, after all. Finn was here and, if need be, would protect her with his life. The knowledge was immensely comforting, and she began to relax.

"Perhaps you will," Brett told her as he began to dismount. "And soon. He's promised to follow me down from London shortly." He took Raven's reins and looped them over his head so they trailed on the ground; it was a signal to stay, and the big horse obeyed. Then Brett walked the few remaining paces that separated him from Ashleigh and offered his hand to help her up.

Hesitating but a second, Ashleigh placed her small hand in his, then felt his strength as he pulled her upright.

Turquoise eyes met hers as he asked, "How are you, little one? Have things gone smoothly for you since I left?"

He continued to hold on to her hand as he spoke, and Ashleigh felt her heart thudding in her chest. "Well enough, Your Grace," she murmured softly.

"No tedious country days? No nasty run-ins with the Lady Margaret?"

At the mention of Brett's great-aunt, Ashleigh's eyes grew dark, but she quickly averted her gaze. It would hardly do to complain to her employer about his nearest relative, she reasoned; what if he thought her peevish and decided to sack her? She shook her head.

Brett caught the look in her eyes before she turned away, thought momentarily to pursue it, then decided he could better do so later, perhaps after he'd encountered Margaret and saw how the wind was blowing there.

Releasing her hand, he gestured toward Irish Night. "So you've been working with my prized import. I ought to take Old Henry to task for that. I told him to see to your safety in assigning you a mount."

Ashleigh's eyes widened with apprehension. "Oh, he did, Your Grace! I'm only allowed a few hours a day with Irish, and I'm not allowed to mount her! Major's the one I ride. Oh, please, Your Grace, don't be blaming Old Henry. He merely—"

Brett's laughter cut in. "Major! My God! He's twenty-two years old! No wonder you needed time with this spirited little devil! Old Henry must have taken my admonitions seriously, indeed!" He smiled, looking down at her anxious face. "No, little one, I'm not about to blame anyone."

"Ohh," Ashleigh murmured, relieved. "Thank Heaven, Your Grace, I—"

Brett raised his hand to cup her chin, gently forcing her to look at him. "It's Brett, remember?"

The thudding in Ashleigh's chest grew so, she was afraid he could hear it. "I—" Her lashes fluttered under the directness of his gaze. "Brett," she said at last.

He smiled, releasing her chin, but his fingers stretched and lightly brushed the mole that rested high on her cheekbone. "Women have been known to paste patches on their faces to enhance their beauty. Yours is God-given," he told her, "along with a beauty that needs no enhancing."

Ashleigh blushed, then dimpled as she recollected the morning they'd left for the dressmaker's. "I seem to recall, Your Gr—Brett . . . a time you were eager to see it helped along with finer clothes." She watched him with her head cocked slightly to one side to gauge his reaction, but knowing somehow he would not anger with her retort. She sensed his lighter mood, different from those she'd seen him in before, and it both pleased and intrigued her. What a complicated man he was! And whereas before she'd found this realization intimidating, now she was drawn by it and not at all frightened.

Brett smiled. "There was, in my actions that morning, not even the slightest sense of 'helping' your beauty along. If a man has an exquisite gem, a sapphire, let us say—" he was looking directly into her blue, blue eyes as he spoke "—and he takes it to a goldsmith to have it mounted into a ring, perhaps, or worked into a pendant, is the value of the stone diminished or enhanced by the setting? The answer is no, for the stone will always be the stone it is, beautiful in its own right. The setting merely makes it possible for others to admire it, something which would not happen if it were locked away in a box or drawer somewhere, where it could not catch the light and dazzle the onlooker with its loveliness." His eyes flickered wonderingly over her upturned face. "No, Ashleigh, I was helping nothing along that day, but merely playing humble goldsmith to your beauty's jewels."

She stood, rapt, looking up at him. This was a different Brett Westmont indeed! It wasn't that he hadn't remarked upon her appearance before—their first encounter, she knew, though the specifics were hazy, had been full of his comments on the attractions of her . . . flesh. . . .

But right now something quite different was at work. There was nothing passionate or lustful in his words. Rather, it was as if he uttered them with the emotional detachment of an artist—a painter, or a writer, perhaps.... At last Ashleigh broke the lengthening silence. "You... are a poet, I think... and perhaps a philosopher?"

Brett laughed, shaking his head. "Hardly! Though I know a few—*real* poets, that is—and, yes, they are philosophers, too. As a matter of fact, you'll be meeting one or two of them soon. They're among some friends I've invited down from London." He paused for a moment, as if considering something he'd just said. "I doubt that Byron will be with them, however. He's too busy brooding about some private devils, as usual, to want to socialize down here in the country. A pity, too. I'd thought he and Percy Shelley would get on well together."

Ashleigh's delicate eyebrows lifted with her recognition of a name she'd often heard. "Did you say Byron, Your Gr—Brett? *Lord* Byron?"

"The same." Brett's grin went roguish. "I take it you've heard of him."

Ashleigh's cheeks pinkened. Who in England hadn't heard of the dashing, romantic poet who'd taken the country by storm with the publication of his *Childe Harold* a couple of years before and then gone on to cap it by having a notorious affair with Lady Caroline Lamb?

But the real reason behind Ashleigh's blush was Brett's remark that the poet was brooding about "some private devils." It was the very phrase Megan had used about Brett, and the irony of this struck her at once. To cover the cause of her reaction, however, she seized on the public image of Lord Byron. "His lordship enjoys a... remarkable reputation."

Brett chuckled as he reached to pet Finn's shaggy coat. "Indeed, he does, though I suspect it's not knowledge of the one he gained by his pen that tints your cheeks!"

Realizing her ploy had worked, Ashleigh's hue deepened. She was not accustomed to using such tactics, and it made her uncomfortable, but it would never do to let him suspect the nature of her private conversations with Megan wherein *he* was the primary topic!

Brett's chuckle deepened into a low rumble of laughter. "Poor Byron! He awoke one morning to find himself famous for his literary genius, and that was well enough; then, along came Caroline Lamb, and the famous became *infamous*!"

Ashleigh's confusion registered in a mild frown. "*Poor* Byron?"

Brett nodded. "It may surprise you, but the entire business with Lady Caroline is anathema to him. From its very inception, he was the pursued, not the pursuer, and to this day, he regrets the whole involvement. He'd give anything to free himself of the lady's, ah, affections."

"Oh," said Ashleigh, "I see. . . ."

Brett saw her eyes darken before she glanced away and knew she'd been reminded of another unwanted pursuit. *Damn!* He hadn't wanted to resurrect that!

Looking about, he searched for a change of subject; a few yards away he spied Irish Night prancing nervously before his stallion who, though still obediently rooted to the spot where he'd been commanded to stay, was tossing his head and eyeing the filly with obvious interest.

"Ashleigh," said Brett, "how would you like some help following up on the lesson you've just taught Irish Night? I might be able to assist a bit."

Grateful for the change of topic, Ashleigh answered him enthusiastically. "Oh, Brett! Would you? I've just been bungling along here, not knowing if I'm on the right track or not."

Brett grinned. "I would hardly call it bungling! Especially when I consider your brilliant use of these two able assistants here." He glanced down at Finn who, tail thumping, sat happily at his feet, and then at the grunting pink mass beside him.

Ashleigh smiled happily back at him. "I'll take full credit for Finn, but Lady Dimples is on her own!"

Brett arched an eyebrow. "So I've noticed. You know, I've heard it said pigs are among the most intelligent of the four-footed beasts. In France they use them to harvest truffles." He glanced down then, and his eyes fastened on the conspicuous leather belt she had tied over the yellow day gown she and Megan had stitched together following the humiliating incident with Elizabeth and Margaret. "What on earth is that?" he questioned, amusement apparent in the turquoise eyes.

Thinking he referred to the obvious repair in the costly gown he'd bought, Ashleigh tensed. While she'd made up her mind not to complain to him of the incident—her pride, if nothing else, wouldn't let her—she hardly wanted him to think she'd been careless with something he'd purchased for her, either. "Th-there was an accident, I'm afraid," she began.

"Accident?" Brett looked puzzled as he reached for the pair of pie plates hanging at her side. "An *accident* made you tie this—this paraphernalia about you?"

"Oh!" exclaimed Ashleigh, obviously relieved. "Oh, *that*!" She took the tins from his hand and rapped them together. "That's just a homespun device for training a skittish filly to grow accustomed to unexpected noise."

And as if on cue, Irish Night danced nervously away from where she'd been calmly cropping grass moments before.

"Hmm," said Brett with a nod. He eyed the filly who'd backed as far away from them as the lunge line would permit and stood watching them with apprehension in her large, liquid brown eyes. "I think it's time we resumed her lessons, don't you?"

Ashleigh grinned. "High time indeed, Your Grace!"

Brett gave her an overdone frown. *"Miss Sinclair!"* he admonished.

Ashleigh grinned. "I mean, *Brett*!"

The next few hours flew by for Ashleigh as Brett fell in beside her to work with Irish Night. First they used Finn and Lady Dimples, repeating the procedure Brett had witnessed from the stand of trees. Then, when that became familiar, the little horse all but yawning at the animals chasing at her heels, they switched tactics. For the next half hour or so, Ashleigh deployed her pie pans from one side while Brett rushed at the filly from the other, brandishing a leafy limb he'd broken from a tree and shouting, "Hyah! Hyah!" This they followed with a combination of Brett wildly waving his riding jacket as he emerged from behind Raven, and Ashleigh pelting the ground on the horse's other side with a barrage of pinecones. In the final hour they finished with various combinations of all these methods, relentlessly forcing the little horse to jump and jump again, refusing to let her balk, repeating and repeating, until at last she, and they as well, stood exhausted in the fading afternoon light.

Brett stood with his jacket slung over one shoulder and watched Ashleigh feed Irish Night a lump of sugar as a reward for her performance. "You'll spoil her rotten, you know," he said, but as Ashleigh glanced up at him, his smile told her the criticism was not to be taken seriously.

Ashleigh returned his smile. "Reward, I think, goes so much further than punishment in driving a lesson home. And that's the reason I refused to take along the training whip Old Henry offered me when I started to work with Irish. Your head groom was highly indignant, I'm afraid. 'Yer not t' *use* it on 'er!' he cried. 'Merely t' take it *wi'* ye t' show 'er ye mean business!' "

Brett laughed at her excellent imitation of Old Henry's humble country accent. "So, off you stalked, whipless and armed with sugar lumps and your faithful little menagerie!"

Ashleigh watched him come forward and run a firm but gentle hand over the filly's withers. "She's far too fine and spirited a horse to risk breaking harshly, Brett. When I was a little girl I saw a horse that had been thus broken, and—and it was *horrible*!" The blue eyes turned dark with pain as she recounted the incident. "You see, I'd seen the horse before it happened...such a fine young colt. He was being sold at a country fair I attended with my my father and brother. I remember staring at his shiny, blood-bay coat and wishing I might have such a horse someday, when I outgrew my pony. Father laughed and said I'd have to wait several years for *that*.

"Well, the day at the fair ended, and we returned home, all thoughts of the blood-bay colt forgotten...until a winter's day several months later..." Ashleigh stared off into the distance and was silent for several long seconds before shaking her head sadly and resuming her tale.

"He—he'd been purchased by the drunken son of an earl who was one of our neighbors . . . a huge brute of a man who liked to boast of his taking a 'personal interest' in his father's stables." She raised her face to Brett and he saw the shimmering tears in her eyes. "Oh, Brett, it was pitiful! That beautiful young animal, reduced to a bro—" a sob caught in her throat "—a broken thing . . . a piece of dull meat on four legs with all the spirit beaten out of it! Dear God! I wish I could forget that sight!"

Tears were streaming down her cheeks now, and Brett found himself somehow immeasurably moved by this evidence of her compassion, and surprised that he felt so. He'd always disdained weeping and other displays of conspicuous emotion by women, regarding them as just so much additional evidence that females were weak and frivolously sentimental—if not devious—using tears as a means of manipulating men to their own selfish ends. But the pain and selfless sincerity he saw in Ashleigh's face was far removed from the maudlin hysterics he'd witnessed in the women he'd known, and he felt himself drawn by it in ways he wasn't sure he was prepared to deal with.

Slowly, as if feeling his way through uncharted waters, he placed a hand on her shoulder while, with the fingers of the other, he gently wiped the tears from her upturned face. "Sometimes things happen for a reason, little one," he said softly. "Perhaps you were meant to have seen and recall that brutality."

Ashleigh looked at him questioningly.

"From what I've seen today, you have a delicate way with animals. Your every action speaks of a finely honed sensitivity, not to mention endless patience. And the proof is in how they respond to you. Perhaps your bitter memory has served you well."

Ashleigh beheld his gaze with wonder in her own. Was this gentle man the same who had so ruthlessly taken her and stripped her of her honor not two months earlier? Where was the mocking laughter, the cynical gleam in his eyes? Nothing about the man who stood before her now, or who had laughed with her in this meadow moments before at their successes with the little filly, reminded her of the one she'd sworn would pay for his callousness of an earlier day!

Dizzily she tried to fit the two images together, her head swimming with scenes of Brett forcing her onto the bed, of him standing beside Madame with an immovable expression on his face, and then—*this*! She closed her eyes, to shut out the confusion, telling herself now was not the time to sort out what was happening. She only knew she was immeasurably grateful for the apparent transformation and resolved, for the moment, to deal with it as she found it. Opening her eyes, she looked again at his, which were still focused on her face as if trying to read what they saw there, and she slowly nodded her head and smiled.

When he beheld her smile, at once so open and full of joy, Brett felt a wrenching in his gut the likes of which he'd never known before. Suddenly he was overwhelmed by a desire to take her in his arms and never let her go, to hold her to him and protect her from ever again facing anything that could frighten her or give her pain. What in hell was happening to him? *It was only a smile, for God's sake!* But even as he attempted to dismiss it, he knew it was far, far more than that. With it her whole face lit up, lovely beyond telling, and the beautiful spirit within Ashleigh Sinclair shone like the sun in the heavens.

Abruptly, awkwardly, for he knew he was out of his element here, Brett turned and glanced about them. "It's getting late, little one. I don't know when you told Old Henry to expect you back, but I think we'd better be going before they send someone to search for you."

Wondering at his sudden uneasiness, Ashleigh merely nodded, then followed him as he strode toward the horses. When they reached Irish Night, she looped the lunge line several times, shortening it until she had a coil that ended just beneath the filly's halter and prepared to begin the long trek back to the stables. She looked up at Brett who was now astride his stallion. "I—I thank you for your help this afternoon," she told him. "If you should find them worrying about me at the stables, please tell them I'm fine and will be along shortly."

She was unprepared for the frown that crossed the duke's brow. "And just where do you think you might be going?" he queried.

"Why, I—er, to the stables, Your Grace," she stammered.

*"Afoot?"* he demanded incredulously.

"Well, y-yes," she replied. "I promised not to mount—"

"I'm well aware of what you promised, young lady, but if you think I'm going to allow you to *walk* back while *I ride*, think again! You're riding with me!"

With a quick, muscular movement, he reached down, and before Ashleigh realized what was happening, she found herself swung upward by two iron-strong hands and seated sideways before him in the saddle, her lunge line left in the grass. Brett grasped for the filly's tether, let it play out behind them, and urged his stallion forward. "That's better," she heard him murmur just behind her right ear.

His strong arms came about her as they began to move, and Ashleigh found herself shivering, though the air was warm. She could smell the scent of him with this nearness, a scent that was a combination of some masculine soap he used, clean sweat, tobacco and horses, and for some reason, inhaling it made her giddy. Once again she found her heart hammering in her chest, dampness gathering on the palms of her hands. She tried to tell herself this was all because she had reasons to fear this man's nearness, but in her heart she knew these sensations were born more of pleasure than fear.

"Of course," Brett was saying, "I suppose I could have overridden Old Henry's order forbidding you to mount Irish Night. She's perfectly safe on the flats." He glanced down at Ashleigh's yellow gown, then eyed the filly as she trotted beside them. "But neither you nor she seems to be accoutered for riding...." Suddenly he chuckled. "Not that that seems to have stopped you before! Where did you ever learn to ride, little one? And bareback, at that!"

Ashleigh giggled, then arched a delicate eyebrow as she glanced up at him. "I assure you, Your Grace, the bareback riding was a first for me that day. As for the other—" Brett saw her eyes darken, and she looked away "—I had a brother once.... He...taught me how to ride."

Seeing she found discussion of her dead family difficult, Brett decided not to pursue it, though he found himself increasingly curious about her early past. Perhaps, now that he was back in Kent, and would be likely to spend more time with her in the days to come, he might soon find a chance to broach the subject again, especially if they got to know each other better.

Suddenly Brett found himself looking forward to the coming weeks, in a way that far exceeded the anticipations of a few hours before, and a light ripple of laughter broke from him with the realization.

Ashleigh heard it and smiled. How different he was when he laughed! Guessing at the reason, she asked, "You're glad to be back, then?"

"Yes, little one—" he grinned "—I am most glad to be back!"

# Chapter Fourteen

Chauncey Jameson had been the butler at Ravensford Hall for fourteen years, and during that time he had always discharged his duties with a remarkable degree of efficiency and aplomb. Nevertheless, on this particular morning in mid-July 1814, Jameson was conspicuously lacking in the air of unruffled confidence he normally commanded when seeing to the well-oiled running of the Westmont household. He stood in the butler's pantry that adjoined the kitchens and carefully blotted his perspiring brow with a white linen handkerchief before resuming his speech to the staff he'd hastily assembled there not five minutes earlier.

"Merton," he said to the tall footman who stood at attention in front of him, "are you sure there were *three*?"

"Aye, sir, three coaches, all of 'em 'eaded straight fer the 'All."

If Jameson had been the type to groan aloud with the announcement of distressing news, he would have done so now, but as it was, he merely raised the white linen and blotted again. "Three coaches filled with guests.... I see." He turned to face Hettie Busby who stood waiting expectantly, next to Merton. "Mrs. Busby, you're sure the Lady Margaret had no prior knowledge of this?"

Hettie shook her head. "She was as much in the dark as the rest of us when I questioned her a moment ago. Said to ask His Grace whilst she hurried and dressed. But His Grace—"

"I know, Mrs. Busby. We have already covered that ground. His Grace is out riding with the Misses Sinclair and O'Brien." Jameson's angular head snapped to his right, and he regarded a young woman in chambermaid's apparel who looked as if she were about to burst into tears at any moment. "Betty, ah, is Lady Elizabeth still . . . ?"

"Aye, sir," sniffed Betty. "'Er ladyship's still 'avin' a fit in 'er chamber! Broke two vases, she did, an' one of 'em just missed me 'ead! Fairly screamin', she was, carryin' on t'—"

"That will be all, Betty, thank you," said Jameson. He had no wish to be reminded of the tale that had already been carried throughout the Hall, that Lady Elizabeth Hastings, upon awakening in her guest chamber and learning that her betrothed had gone riding without her—and with whom—had flown into a rage at the news, bruising the cheek of her own ladies' maid, Dorothea, who had followed her here from Cloverhill Manor, and wreaking havoc on her room's furnishings for the better part of an hour. Moreover, as head of staff, it was Jameson's responsibility to quell unseemly gossip among his subordinates, especially when it had to do with the gentry it was their duty to serve.

On the other hand, it now became his problem as to how to deal with the existence of a shrieking harpy in one of the upstairs chambers in the face of a virtual caravan of unexpected guests. Oh, thought Jameson, if only His Grace, the old duke were still alive! *He* would never have countenanced such irregularity!

Turning his gaze toward Old Henry, who stood a couple of paces behind his wife, the harried butler asked his next question. "Will the stables be ready to receive the overflow on this short notice, Mr. Busby?"

Old Henry grinned. At last Jameson would receive a promising answer. "No problem there, sir. The lads're already on it!"

"Good, good," murmured Jameson. "Very well, then. It seems there's no help for it but to do our duty as best we may." He began issuing orders. "Mrs. Busby, take Cook into the kitchen and begin planning a menu list. . . . Mr. Busby, back to the stables, if you please.... Betty, take Flora and Emily and begin airing out the guest chambers in the north wing...."

Ashleigh's face was flushed with exhilaration, her eyes bright with pleasure as she bent over Irish Night's neck and felt the power of the young horse beneath her. The filly might be small, but she had long, muscular legs and a deep chest, the result of a breeding program that coupled heavy Arabian lines with excellent Irish racing stock, and the results were proving spectacular.

Up ahead, she caught sight of Brett and Megan waving at her from where they sat on their mounts. "Rein her in now, Ashleigh!" Brett called. "We've got to be heading back."

Nodding, Ashleigh eased the pressure she'd been applying to the filly's sides with her knees and shifted her weight to signal the change in pace.

A few moments later, she approached the other two riders at a subdued canter, a wide grin etched on her face.

"Well?" asked Brett, grinning back at her. "How was she?"

"Oh, Brett! Couldn't you tell? She was *magnificent*!" Ashleigh's joy bubbled over into her speech. "I've never *had* such a ride!"

Megan's laughter blended with Brett's. "Ah, darlin', ye were a grand sight t' behold! The two o' ye, I'm meanin', ridin' across those flats like ye were part o' each other, and born on the wind!"

Ashleigh's grin grew wider. "You two didn't do too badly yourselves, you know. From where I stood, it looked like a dead heat. Was it?"

Brett chuckled. "Not quite. I owe Megan two guineas or a new bonnet, her choice, but that's the last time I'll let her talk me into surrendering Raven for a race. *Bad cess*, indeed!" he added, giving Megan a glare.

Megan grinned and shrugged, then bent over Raven's lathered neck and gave it a pat. "Can I help it if I'm subject t' superstitions, Yer Grace?"

"A superstition, I suspect," Brett returned, "conveniently resurrected at moments like the onset of a wager!"

They were talking about the moment when, after challenging the duke to a short race, Megan had suddenly looked down at the beautiful gray colt she was riding and exclaimed, "Oh! I'm so sorry, Yer Grace, but I'm afraid I'll have to withdraw from the wager. Gray Mist, I fergot, is, after all, a *gray* colt, and gray horses are *bad cess*, er, that is, bad luck, fer me family. Now . . . if we were t' be switchin' mounts—fer the duration o' the race only, mind ye—well then . . ."

Reluctantly, Brett had agreed, for while Raven was the finest blood in his stables, the gray colt was coming up fast and held a great deal of promise, and he was curious to try his mettle. Of course, now it seemed that that promise hadn't yet been quite enough. . . .

"Well, small matter," Brett was saying. "The real reason we flagged you in, Ashleigh, is that we saw some coaches winding their way along the post road when we reached that bluff a few minutes ago. It looks as though those guests I told you about are arriving. You *did* tell Lady Margaret we could be expecting them?"

They had turned their horses' heads toward the Hall and were moving along at an even pace. In the distance Ashleigh could see smoke rising from what she surmised was the chimney of the kitchen at Ravensford Hall.

"Lady Margaret had already retired when I went to inform her last night, Brett. But Lady Elizabeth overheard me speaking to her maid and said she would see to it that your great-aunt received the message." A frown of dismay crossed Ashleigh's brow as she recalled the viciousness of Elizabeth Hastings's response to her query about whether Lady Margaret could be disturbed. "She certainly has no business being disturbed by the likes of *you*, you cheap little flit! *I* shall see she gets His Grace's message in the morning!" Even now, as she recalled the hurtful words, Ashleigh's eyes clouded with humiliation.

Brett saw her look and could well guess its source. Yesterday, when he and Ashleigh had entered the Hall following their afternoon of horse training, they were met at the entrance by Margaret and Elizabeth Hastings. He'd been astounded to find his ill-remembered betrothed not only waiting for him, but firmly ensconced at his home as a semipermanent guest! He'd vaguely recollected a letter from Margaret while he was in London, telling him she'd proceeded with the planning of his nuptials, "with circumspection, owing to the fact that the family is in mourning," but he was positive she'd written nothing of Elizabeth's encampment in his domicile! Then, after he'd barely had time to digest this fact, he watched as Elizabeth proceeded to snub Ashleigh Sinclair in the most blatant manner. Moreover, he'd have had to be blind not to see the look of absolute hatred in his betrothed's eyes each time they fell on Ashleigh, which was mainly during a tedious and uncomfortable dinner. Ashleigh, he'd noticed, had carried herself graciously through the whole affair, making polite conversation when it was required of her and appearing to quite overlook the fact that neither Elizabeth nor Margaret deigned to speak directly to her at all, and carried on much as if she were invisible at the table.

But Brett had noticed the two spots of color staining Ashleigh's cheeks as the evening progressed, and had readily acquiesced when she asked to be excused early to look in on Megan, who'd taken to her chamber with a headache. The truth here, although Brett was unaware of it, was that Megan's eyes had glittered with a blood lust any time they looked upon Elizabeth and Margaret, prompting Ashleigh to make her promise to avoid encounters with them at all costs; the result was that Megan had "headaches" whenever household routine required that she spend any time with them.

"And just who is it ye're expectin', Yer Grace?" Megan asked now. "From the fine look o' those coaches, 'twould appear t' be a pretty fancy group o' visitors, I'd be thinkin'."

"Oh, no one that daunting," said Brett. "Just some friends from London. I do wonder how it is they all seem to be arriving at once, though. I expected various people to be trickling in over a period of days. I thought I recognized Lord Edwards's team of bays, though. Ah, that would be Lord Christopher Edwards, the earl of Ranleagh."

Ashleigh's head suddenly went up with a start at this news. "Lord Edwards, the earl of— Oh, dear! I just *realized* . . . I'm supposed to be acting as a hostess in just a few minutes!"

"That would seem to be an accurate assessment of matters, yes," Brett replied with some amusement. "Is there a problem with—"

"Oh, but—but, Your Grace! . . . Brett! Just *look* at me!" She glanced down at the hem of her blue and cream riding habit, which was soaked with the dew that had lain on the grass when they began their outing several hours earlier.

*I am looking at you, lovely little witch,* Brett thought, seizing on a term that had occurred to him late last night as he lay in his bed. While visions of his afternoon with her danced through his mind, he had been hard put to explain such a preoccupation. What was it about the girl that so entrapped his thoughts? Surely not her beauty, for he'd known scores of beautiful women before. . . .

What, then? Was it the host of surprises that had consistently sprung up about her as he'd gotten to know her? It was as if she'd bewitched him, he'd finally decided, and the thought had not sat particularly well with him. He'd even told himself, as he was drifting off to sleep, that he'd do well to create some distance between them in the future—after all, she was a female. . . .

And yet, when morning had dawned and the day promised to be a rare one, breezy and blue-skied, with the sun brightly shining, he found himself quickly dressed and sending a maid to inquire if Miss Sinclair would like to join him for a ride! Of course, the note that had come back, penned by Megan in coarse block letters—she had been illiterate until Ashleigh began to teach her how to read and write some months earlier, he'd learned—had informed him Miss Sinclair would indeed care to join him, provided she might be accompanied by Miss O'Brien and also that she might be allowed to ride the filly, Irish Night, which she would do with care, and only on the flats.

Brett smiled wryly as he recalled the tall redhead's audaciousness. But then he frowned as his mind returned to his own impromptu behavior. He was at a total loss to explain it. . . . Finally his helpless thoughts had seized on that first fanciful explanation of his midnight musings. . . . She was a witch, a beautiful, fascinating, blue-eyed witch. . . .

But now he found himself grinning as Ashleigh ran a slender hand through her charmingly windblown curls and lamented her disheveled appearance.

"I cannot greet your guests looking like this, Brett! I simply cannot!" Her blue eyes pleaded with his.

Brett chuckled. "Very well," he told her, "you and Megan take the path that leads to the kitchens and use the rear entrance. I'll hold them off while you change. Come and join us in the front drawing room when you're ready."

"Oh, *may I?* Oh, Brett, thank you!" she chirped. "Oh, I can never thank you enough for understanding! I won't take too long—"

Brett's laughter intervened. "Yes, well, if you take any more time thanking me, you *will* be late. Off with you, now! I'll see you at the Hall."

The two women cantered off in the direction he'd indicated, and Brett sat and watched them go. His turquoise eyes fastened on the gleaming mass of raven curls the wind whipped about Ashleigh's slender back and shoulders, even as he reminded himself that this was the second decade of the nineteenth century, and rational men no longer believed in witchcraft.

Margaret Westmont's face was livid as she confronted her goddaughter amid the shambles the latter had made of her guest chamber at Ravensford Hall. Her blue eyes bored into those of the younger woman, who stood with outthrust, quivering lower lip beside a broken looking glass, but still Margaret did not speak; it was imperative that she assume control over the emotions that raged inside her, for if she did not, if she succumbed even one iota, like the creature who stood before her, all could be lost, and Margaret had no intention of losing . . . not ever, ever again.

"Well, you needn't look at me like that," Elizabeth told her in a querulous voice. "I—I had my reasons for—for this." She made a small gesture to indicate the broken bits of china, overturned chairs and other debris that gave mute testimony to the temper tantrum she'd indulged in during the past hour or so. She stepped forward a pace and began to wring her hands, adding. "Oh, for God's sake, *say* something, will you? You remind me of—of *him*, your—your brother. He used to gaze at me that way, even when I was a child and it was clear he didn't like me, and—*stop it*, I tell you! I am no child to be peered at in such a forbidding manner!"

"Then I suggest you cease behaving like one," came the barely controlled reply. Finding she could deal with the situation now, Margaret advanced farther into the room from the position she'd been maintaining near the door. She eyed the perfume-stained, disheveled pink satin dressing gown Elizabeth wore and made a grimace of distaste. "You look a sight. Where is your abigail?"

Elizabeth pouted. "I sent her away."

"Well, summon her back. We've work to do, and there isn't much time. Any moment now, a virtual horde of guests will be pulling up in—"

"Guests! Auntie Meg, how can you be talking of guests when I have been so sorely put upon? You just don't *know* what's happened! Your grandnephew—oh, I could *kill* him! You cannot realize—"

"Of course, I realize!" snapped Margaret, her anger threatening to return in full force. "The *whole house realizes*, you little idiot! And if you and I don't take steps to amend the damage, in a few moments all of London will begin to be privy to your indiscretion. Think on that, why don't you, but think on it while you complete your toilette and prepare to make a presentable appearance downstairs as the future duchess of Ravensford!"

Elizabeth appeared to shrink at the force of her words. "Auntie, surely you can't expect me to—"

With irate strides, Margaret closed the distance between them and seized her arm. "I can and I *do*!" She leaned forward until her face was just a few inches from Elizabeth's. "Now, you listen to me, you little fool! In just a few moments some of the most prestigious members of society will be filling the drawing room downstairs. How will it look if that little guttersnipe is the one to greet them at the door while their host's betrothed sits cowering in an upstairs chamber? Hadn't we agreed that the only way to demolish the effect of Brett's demented whim regarding that girl was to install you here at the Hall, so that your presence would overwhelm hers and perhaps even send her packing? Pull yourself together! In fifteen minutes I expect to see you dressed and downstairs."

"Fifteen minutes! Oh, Auntie, how *can* you be so hateful? I don't *want* to go downstairs! Have you seen the way he looks at her? Why, last night at dinner, he hardly took his eyes off her! How will *that* appear when others view it in—in my presence? I'd be humiliated beyond—"

"*Silence!* Sit down at that dressing table and begin repairing your face," ordered Margaret. "I shall call for your abigail." She hastened to the door and Elizabeth could hear her murmuring a few words to the footman who stood in the hallway. Then Margaret returned to her goddaughter, who had reluctantly seated herself at the dressing table.

"As for your worries about Brett's attentions to that little whore," Margaret told her quietly, "I have only one thing to say to you, and then I shall have to leave and play interim hostess myself, no matter what Brett and his bit of muslin say."

She was standing behind Elizabeth now and addressed her in the looking glass that hung wildly askew on the wall above the dressing table. "Most marriages, including those of most of the people soon to be arriving here, are never expected to be love matches. It has always been thus among our class, and I expect you to know this and remember it. It therefore follows that when a nobleman's eye wanders, it is accepted as quite the done thing. He did not marry for love, so he must be expected to have his *little things* on the side from time to time.

"To the guests downstairs, this Ashleigh Sinclair will, if you are capable of carrying off your part as I think you are, appear to be just one of those *little things*, no more. And no one will think twice on it. So His Grace's eye roams...so what? Was it not always so? Would a betrothal make any difference with a man like him? They'll hardly think so.

"Moreover, I think you'll find there are advantages to having a husband who slakes his lustful appetites elsewhere. Aside from the times your duty will necessitate your sharing the marriage bed to produce heirs, you will be largely freed from that obligation. That should, in the long run, be a welcome relief."

Margaret paused and tilted her head, sending a shrewd, assessing glance at the reflection in the mirror. "I have observed you closely in the years since you matured to womanhood, Elizabeth. You do not strike me as the sort who hungers for the pleasures of the flesh. Tell me . . . am I wrong in this?"

Elizabeth gazed at the blue eyes that were riveted to hers in the glass. Then her mind flitted briefly over the few times she'd been alone with someone of the opposite sex. She remembered the horrid, sweaty hands of Sir Peter Halifax, who tried to embrace her at a garden party last spring; she recalled the disgusting wetness of George Mowbry's lips as he stole a kiss at her last birthday ball; she thought of the nasty male scents of snuff and horses that she'd encountered on dozens of men she'd chatted or danced with in recent months, and her flesh began to feel as if it were suddenly crawling with vermin.

Resolutely returning her godmother's gaze, Elizabeth answered, "No, you are not wrong."

Margaret's smile oozed satisfaction, and she nodded knowingly. "I thought so. So, why the alarm over a husband-to-be and his wandering eye? Certainly, after what I've told you of our set, it cannot be from pride?

"You're young, Elizabeth, and perhaps, despite your successful season, you've lived in the country too long. Look around you today. See if you can't find evidence among our guests that what I speak is the truth. And go downstairs and hold your head proudly erect and act the aristocrat you are. You *must*!" Here Margaret's voice lowered and she peered more intently at the reflection in the mirror. "Need I remind you that everything we've planned depends on it?"

Elizabeth heard the hard edge of steel in her voice and shivered, then solemnly nodded.

"Good. Ah, that must be your abigail. I'll let her in and wait for you downstairs." She walked toward the door, then turned.

"And Elizabeth?"

"Yes?"

"Do not fail me."

# Chapter Fifteen

With a glass of sherry in his hand, Brett stood at the huge mantel in the drawing room and smiled wryly, his turquoise eyes roaming casually over the two-dozen guests who sat or stood in clusters here and there about the room. "Darnley," he said to the blond, heavyset young man standing near him, "the next time I'm fool enough to mention publicly I've a birthday coming up, stifle me with my own cravat, will you?"

Bruce Darnley chuckled. "Surprised you, did we, old chap? But, see here, surely you're not turned out over this? I mean, what are birthdays for, if not to have a few friends pop in to celebrate... you know, bend an elbow a bit, that sort of thing... nothing too elaborate."

Brett suppressed a guffaw. "Oh, no, nothing elaborate! Only a couple dozen men and women, dressed to the hilt and bent on several days' worth of mischief, I'll warrant. Nothing elaborate at all!"

"Now, Brett, dear," said a striking brunette with dark, almond-shaped eyes as she overheard their conversation. "You must know Pamela wasn't going to allow your birthday to pass without making some kind of a to-do! Why, it was just the other day when she said, 'I'll wager His Grace is going slinking off down to the country without allowing us to give him a proper send-off, and it's his birthday on the sixteenth, too! Why, we simply mustn't allow him to celebrate it alone!' And before you knew it, half of us at Lord Edgemont's dinner party recalled your leaving an open invitation to come down and visit you here in Kent, and everyone began to make plans to go. After all, Your Grace," she simpered, "being in mourning shouldn't signify that one stops living himself, should it?"

"Hmm," replied Brett absently. He was eyeing the graceful, elegant form of an amber-eyed, honey-haired woman in green as she nodded and laughed at some remarks made by her two gentlemen companions on the sofa across the room. So, this was Pamela's idea after all. He might have known she wouldn't give up that easily. *Damn!* Now he'd have to spend the next several days being polite to her while not allowing one jot of encouragement to shade his behavior! How in hell was he going to manage *that*?

Just then, he saw several heads turn, and following their gaze, beheld Ashleigh Sinclair entering the room with a footman at her heels bearing a tray of light refreshments. She was an absolute vision in a filmy aquamarine cotton day gown with matching ribbons woven into the lustrous curls that were arranged atop her head. She paused for a moment and caught his eye; at the same time her face broke into an enchanting smile, revealing the single dimple in her left cheek, and suddenly Brett knew exactly how he was going to manage the difficult business of curbing Lady Pamela Marlowe!

"Egad!" exclaimed Bruce Darnley, his eyes fixed on Ashleigh. "Where, in all of Heaven, did you find *that*? Brett, old man, who *is* she?"

But Brett didn't reply, for he was busy making his way across the room to connect with his hired hostess, a smile of anticipation curving his mouth.

"Why, haven't you heard?" the almond-eyed brunette asked young Lord Darnley. "Brett has a new . . . ward. All of London's abuzz over it. Surely the gossip cannot have gotten past you?"

"New . . . ward?" Darnley looked bemused for a moment. "Egad, Vanessa, you don't mean to say—"

"Oh, no, no! Nothing like that," Vanessa quickly assured him. It was possible, the brunette surmised, that the situation could, after all, be innocent—the girl could indeed be his ward and nothing more—and if this were so, she had no wish to be the one on whom blame was cast, should His Grace learn of unsavory gossip; Brett Westmont was known for his fierce temper, and Vanessa had no wish to incur his wrath!

"But you must agree," she continued to Lord Darnley, "the girl is a beauty, and, well, you know how His Grace attracts beautiful women."

Suddenly Vanessa's eyes searched the room for Pamela Marlowe. Finding her intensely absorbed in the scene of greeting that was taking place between the duke and his ward, Vanessa allowed a catty smile to curve her lips. "Oh, this is going to be too good," she purred, remembering all too well a series of insults she'd suffered at Lady Pamela's hands over the years. "Pamela is about to meet her comeuppance, Bruce dear, and we have a front-row seat!"

Ashleigh had watched Brett approach with a tremor of anticipation; he was being so kind to her since his return, she could scarcely believe it. Indeed, the man who now bent over her hand in courteous greeting was so far removed from the demon she'd first encountered, she half expected him to revert to his old form at any moment, and each time he smiled and spoke gently to her, as now, she found herself both relieved and warmed by the encounter.

"You're lovelier each time I see you, sweet," Brett was saying.

Ashleigh dimpled. "I'm sure it's just because my...'setting' has been changed."

Brett shook his head. "There is a roomful of beautiful women here today, and not one of them can hold a candle to you, no matter what you might be wearing."

Feeling the heat rise to her cheeks, Ashleigh sought to change the subject. "I hope I wasn't overly late. I tried to hurry as much as I could, but Megan was ever so stubborn about making me sit still for a 'proper coiffure,' and—"

Brett's chuckle cut her off. "Think nothing of it, sweet. Your delayed entrance merely served to attract the notice of everyone in this room, judging by the looks you're getting, and if I know that Irishwoman, she probably calculated it just about right."

Glancing about to indeed find all eyes in her direction, Ashleigh blushed, then hastened to exclaim, "Oh, but Megan wouldn't—"

"There you are, darling," a purring female voice broke in. "I should have known you would have gone straight to your guests without changing from your riding clothes, but I fear I'm late because I searched ever so long for you upstairs."

Brett and Ashleigh turned to find Elizabeth Hastings walking toward them, a confident smile on her aristocratic face. Beside her, looking every inch the grande dame, strode Lady Margaret.

"Yes," added Margaret. "Your poor betrothed was hoping the two of you could greet your guests together, Brett, dear, rather as an informal means of making your engagement known."

"Really?" Brett replied, his mouth turned up in a mocking smile. "I would have thought Lady Elizabeth was too busy, ah, rearranging her chamber, to even notice we had guests."

Ashleigh suppressed a giggle as she caught the look of outrage in Elizabeth's eyes. She and Megan had heard the news of her ladyship's temper tantrum when they returned from their ride; and so, she now realized, had Brett.

"Suppose," said Margaret, her tone steely and disapproving, "you take you fiancée about the room and introduce her as such, Your Grace. It is, I think, high time we were making the news public."

"As you wish, *Grand-tante*," Brett murmured with an overly polite, exacting bow to Margaret. Then, as he took Elizabeth's hand and placed it on his bent arm, he whispered to Ashleigh, "Have no fear of being deserted, my dear. Half the gentlemen in the room are on their way to the rescue."

And as Ashleigh looked up, she found he was right. Several gentlemen she'd spied earlier seemed, with Brett's departure, to be making a beeline in her direction. Out of the corner of her eye she saw Lady Margaret retreat with a satisfied smile on her face, but then she had no time to think about anything else, for a crush of well-groomed male bodies surrounded her.

"Allow me to introduce myself," said a tall, slender young man with light brown hair. "I'm William Rhodes, marquis of Wright. And you are—?"

"Come, come, Will, where have you been?" said a shorter man with straight blond hair and a mischievous twinkle in his blue eyes. "This young woman is the buzz of the *ton* without having met most of it—yet. Miss Sinclair, isn't it?"

For the second time in as many minutes, Ashleigh had her response snatched from her before she could begin.

"By Jove, yes! Ashleigh Sinclair, Jersey told me! Lovely name, Ashleigh, but not as lovely as its owner, eh?" This commentary was being put forth by an older man, perhaps in his forties, who introduced himself as Lord Selkirk.

Ashleigh smiled politely at all of them and was just beginning to think her head would spin off her shoulders if she had to remember one more name when a tall, incredibly handsome, dark-haired man bent over her ear and murmured, "If you've had enough of this crush, I think I can arrange a graceful escape."

Looking up to meet a pair of green eyes smiling down at her, Ashleigh smiled back and gave a tentative nod.

"Lady Margaret has announced luncheon being served on the terrace, gentlemen, so, if you don't mind..." He offered Ashleigh his arm and proceeded to lead her away.

Amid several grumbles from her band of admirers, Ashleigh heard him say, "I hope you don't mind, but I thought you looked rather overwhelmed just then."

"I think I was," Ashleigh nodded, then looked up at him. "But, sir, I believe you have the advantage...."

A warm chuckle met her ears. "I guess that makes me just as bad as the rest of them. The name's Edwards... Christopher Edwards. And I hear you're Ashleigh Sinclair."

"Oh, you're the earl of Ranleagh!" she exclaimed.

Another chuckle. "I see my reputation preceded me. Nothing too terrible, I hope."

"Oh, no, not at all! It's just that I heard His Grace mention you when we were riding earlier and he thought he recognized your team."

Christopher grinned. "He ought to recognize them! They used to be his. I won them from him at whist last year."

Ashleigh's eyes went huge. "You *won* them . . . ?" She had heard that high-stakes gambling was common among the rich and titled, but the actual specifics of such a wager amazed her. From the looks of that team of bays, they must be worth a small fortune!

"But just to be honest about it," the earl was saying, "I must confess he won at least as much back from me the next night— probably more, come to think on it."

They were walking through the conservatory now, following the lead of their host who, with Lady Elizabeth firmly attached to his arm, was ushering them toward the open French doors that led to a wide brick terrace with a slope of immaculately tended gardens beyond. Hedges of box yew curved symmetrically about well-clipped green lawns, and everywhere the eye chanced to glance, flowers bloomed, competing with one another in a riot of color, some in well-tended beds, others in large clay pots and urns, still more against strategically placed trellises and stone walls.

On the terrace itself, several tables had been set up, each covered with snowy damask cloths and bearing tableware of paper-thin porcelain and heavy, ornate silver. Among these, footmen rushed to and fro, bearing trays of food and drink.

Suddenly Ashleigh wondered who had put all of this together on such short notice, and with a guilty start, realized that perhaps *she* ought to have been involved. But just then, as she looked toward an open door leading into a wing of the house that abutted the terrace at one end, she spied Jameson, the butler, conversing animatedly with a tall, redheaded female figure. *Megan, of course. What would I do without her?* she thought for what seemed like the hundredth time since she'd come here.

Lady Margaret, however, seemed to have taken charge of the seating arrangements, for Ashleigh saw her directing the footmen toward various people who were led to specific tables. One of the footmen now approached her and the earl.

"Begging your pardons, Miss Sinclair, your lordship, but her ladyship and His Grace would have you sit at the table with the blue floral arrangement. If you will kindly follow me . . . ?"

Ashleigh saw Christopher glance at the table where yet another footman was in the process of seating the marquis of Wright and a honey-haired woman in green whom Ashleigh hadn't met yet.

"We'll find our own way to the table in just a moment, thank you," said Christopher, dismissing the footman with a nod. Then he turned to Ashleigh. "I might as well warn you, my dear. Judging by the look on Pamela's face, we're not likely to have a pleasant time of it over luncheon. She's in a snit over the news of Brett's engagement."

Ashleigh glanced toward their table and, in particular, at the beauty in green and saw that Ranleagh spoke the truth. If looks could kill, anyone in the honey blonde's line of vision would have been fodder for the graveyard right then. "Pamela . . . ?" she questioned tentatively.

"Why, yes, my dear," Christopher replied as he took her arm, "Lady Pamela Marlowe, Brett Westmont's mistress."

Ashleigh summoned all her resources to keep from gaping as she digested Christopher's words and allowed him to lead her to their table. *His mistress!* At that instant all of the warming thoughts about her employer that had been building during the past twenty-four hours fled, and she was filled with an abhorrence of the man, nearly as keen as that felt with her original assessment. What kind of a man was he, she fumed, to be capable of entertaining his mistress in his home on the very day he made his betrothal known? *Rake* and *blackguard* came to mind, but neither seemed to do adequate justice to Brett Westmont.

As she was being helped to her seat, she had a moment to glance at the table where a politely smiling Brett bent his chestnut head in Elizabeth's direction and nodded at something she said. He looked totally at his ease, cool and unruffled, as if such a situation were daily routine, and Ashleigh had to glance away quickly, lest her face reveal the repugnance she felt. Oh, the conceit, the arrogance of the man!

But then she had little time left to contemplate this latest revelation, for Christopher was introducing her to Lady Pamela.

"Ah, yes, so you're the mysterious ward we heard of in London." Lady Pamela smiled, but the smile never reached her eyes, which were cold and brittle, like the amber they resembled. "I must say I'm taken aback by you, Miss Sinclair. From Lady Jersey's remarks, I had thought you to be a young miss not yet out of the schoolroom."

"But Pamela," the marquis broke in, "I hardly see where Jersey's words can be faulted. She *is* 'a beautiful child, too exquisite to be ignored,' if you ask me." He smiled at Ashleigh. "Delighted to be seated at table with you m'dear."

Ashleigh blushed and smiled shyly at the marquis, none of which was missed by Christopher Edwards. The handsome earl was thinking he'd never seen beauty such as hers before, perfect in every delicate line and curve, yet awash in fresh, young innocence. Moreover, there was just the barest hint of mystery about her accruing not only from the as-yet-vague circumstances of her becoming Ravensford's ward, but from some quiet aura about the girl as well. One saw it in the depths of her eyes at times, or in the subtle tilt of her head as she listened, and at moments, in her smile, which would then bear the fleeting suggestion of sadness in its curve.

Christopher Edwards was a connoisseur of many things, including fine food and wines, blooded horseflesh, good music and art, but, most of all, he was an appreciator of beautiful and unusual women. Along with Ravensford, Byron, and one or two others, he was known among the members of the *ton* as a man who sent female pulses racing, and he lived up to this reputation with a flair that kept the gossips busy. Moreover, Ranleagh enjoyed the role he played, and play it he did—to the hilt.

And just now it was Ashleigh Sinclair he sought to play it with. She was the most refreshing piece of femininity he'd come across in many a day, and he couldn't believe his luck at the opportunity presented to him. He'd seen the way Ravensford's eyes had fastened on the girl when she appeared earlier; it was almost as if he caressed her with the slightest glance. But the duke had other commitments to keep, and Christopher was not above moving into the breach. If Brett Westmont chose to overload his barge, that was *his* problem!

Ashleigh had noticed the attention the earl was paying her from the outset and found herself instantly charmed, but also a bit wary; that he was a handsome, sophisticated gentleman, she was well aware, and it was these very qualities that caused her to maintain her reserve, for she had already learned the hard way that, where the rich and titled were concerned, things were not always what they seemed and one could get trampled in the process of dealing too openly with them.

But now, as she once again caught sight of Brett Westmont and his fiancée out of the corner of her eye and at the same time noticed Lady Pamela glaring at them, Ashleigh had a notion to toss her reserve to the wind. So he thought he was the one to play games, did he? Well, she could play a game or two of her own, and Brett Westmont could go to the devil!

With her brightest smile, Ashleigh turned to the man beside her. "Tell me something of yourself and the life you lead, my lord. I am most anxious to learn all about it...."

As Brett listened politely to yet another boring snippet of gossip from Elizabeth, his eyes traveled beyond the white floral centerpiece atop their table until they came to rest on a table where the flowers were blue. He ignored the damning glance of Pamela Marlowe as his gaze swept swiftly past her, and he focused on the obvious display that was taking place nearby. Christopher Edwards was leaning closely, even intimately, Brett thought, toward Ashleigh and favoring her with his most charming smile. In the next instant he saw him whisper something briefly in Ashleigh's ear, to which, a few seconds later, she responded with a delighted peal of laughter. And in yet the next moment he saw the two of them looking into each other's eyes and smiling as if they shared some delicious secret.

Suddenly Brett found himself seized by a wave of anger so fierce, he scarcely recognized it as such. What was the matter with him? He'd seen Ranleagh flirt with women of his acquaintance before; why, in the case of a ball a fortnight ago, where it had involved Pamela, he'd even welcomed it! *Yes,* a small voice told him, *but you are anxious to be quit of Pamela, whereas with Ashleigh*...

Whereas with Ashleigh, what? Just exactly what *were* his feelings in that regard? Briefly Brett reviewed his acquaintance with Ashleigh Sinclair, finishing with a close mental scrutiny of the past twenty-four hours. Slowly—for he was loathe to probe too deeply—he found himself admitting that a change had begun to take place in his regard for the girl. But what did that mean? That he was attracted to her physically? This he had no trouble accepting; lust was a familiar companion in his life by now. But his lustful pursuits had never demanded exclusivity in the women he used before now. And besides, he himself had put Ashleigh off-limits; she was not to be touched by him again. So why was it that he suddenly felt himself gripped by— *Good God in Heaven!* he thought; I cannot possibly be *jealous*!

But even as he denied it, a peal of merriment from Ashleigh Sinclair, in response to something Christopher was sharing with her, sent a hot flush of rage through Brett's body. Knowing he'd never before experienced such emotions, he chose to give them a form he did recognize. Ashleigh Sinclair was a female, wasn't she? And all females practiced to deceive, regardless of the innocence they presented on the surface. Well, this was one female that wouldn't get to *him*!

Brett relaxed in his chair. There, he'd found the problem and neatly handled it. Now he could be himself again and enjoy his guests, even enjoy his birthday.

But as he glanced again across the terrace and saw Ashleigh bestow her dazzling smile on Ranleagh, a small voice mocked, *Can you?*

# Chapter Sixteen

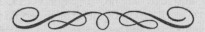

Once luncheon was concluded, Brett, with Elizabeth clinging to his arm, moved among the guests to make suggestions as
to how they might wish to spend their time until the formal
dinner, which would be served at eight and be followed by
dancing in the Hall's ballroom upstairs. Some of the guests
merely opted to retire to their chambers—which by now had
been aired and made ready, to Chauncey Jameson's utter relief—some chose to avail themselves of the duke's excellent
choice of mounts in the stables and go riding, while yet others
decided to remain downstairs and chat in one of the drawing
rooms or to wander casually through the gardens leading down
from the terrace.

It was this last that Christopher Edwards suggested to Ashleigh as a means of passing the time, and as it was such a perfect day for being out of doors, she agreed. They strolled along
a pebbled path flanked by hedgerows of boxwood and yew,
chatting about subjects ranging from the unusual spell of fair
weather Kent was enjoying to the beauty of the gardens, but all
the while Ashleigh had the distinct impression it was not the
weather or the gardens that piqued the handsome nobleman's
interest, but she herself. Frequently she would look up to find
Christopher's eyes on her, their green depths lit by a glimmer
she could by no stretch of her wits attribute to the mundane
topics on which they conversed.

As for Ashleigh, she found this attention flattering and the
earl a comfortable companion, but that was the extent of it; no

pulses fluttered in her breast and no sighs escaped her lips. The earl was obviously a man many considered a charmer, but he left her feeling singularly uncharmed. Still, he was good company in a social setting where she knew almost no one, and for that she was grateful.

They were approaching a place where the path widened and then gave way to a cleared, grassy space where a few garden benches rested, and here they heard several voices. Looking up, Ashleigh spied a small group of unfamiliar people who sat and conversed while two she did recognize stood nearby.

The latter were Lady Pamela Marlowe and the marquis of Wright—who, halfway through luncheon had insisted she call him Will—and as she and the earl approached, the marquis merely smiled a greeting to them.

The reason for the marquis's silence seemed to be his reluctance to interrupt the discourse of a serious-looking young man who was seated near them and talking in animated fashion to an equally serious-looking young woman on the opposite bench.

"And so you see, Mary," the young man was saying, "in the end we may view history as nothing more than the ongoing struggle between liberty and tyranny, with sometimes one in the ascendency, and sometimes the other. In the periods of democratic ascendency—for example, the Golden Age of ancient Greece—culture and literature flourish, while in the ages of tyranny—for instance, during the decline and fall of Rome— they stagnate and die."

The young woman addressed as Mary nodded. "History is cyclical, then? Oh, Percy, how depressing! If that were true, we might now merely view the great advances of liberty in the American and French revolutions as being subject to a decline with the first strong countermovement—"

"No, no, my dear—not cyclical, but spiral!" her companion exclaimed. "The forces of freedom and progress, I feel certain, are now in so secure a position that no oppression, however bitter, can detain them from a relentless and inevitable climb to a higher social order."

Mary smiled. "An egalitarian social order such as my father envisioned in his *Political Justice*, of course."

Christopher bent to whisper in Ashleigh's ear, very softly, so as not to interrupt the serious discussion they were witnessing. "That would be the 1793 publication of the social philosopher, William Godwin. Mary Godwin is his daughter."

"I see," Ashleigh returned as she nodded.

"Not completely," Christopher told her with a glint of amusement in his eyes. "For while Miss Godwin is aptly known as the daughter of two famous—or perhaps I should say infamous?—people—Mary Wollstonecraft, the bluestocking is her mother—she is more readily identified at the moment as the love interest of young Percy Shelley here, and, unless I miss my guess, one of the major figures of a scandal in the making."

"Ohh." Ashleigh nodded, remembering Brett's mention of the name Shelley . . . what had been the reference . . . ? Ah, yes, he was a poet or philosopher of some sort . . . but what did the earl mean by "a scandal in the making"? She glanced up at Christopher and was about to question him on this when the raised voice of Percy Shelley intervened.

"Brett! I was wondering where you'd gone to!"

All heads turned to see their host walking toward them on the path, Lady Elizabeth possessively holding his arm.

"Shelley, you scamp!" accused Brett with no small hint of amusement in his turquoise eyes. "I might have known you'd slip in unannounced. When did you arrive?"

"Oh," replied Shelley, "in the midst of the decadent luncheon you and your millions were setting forth. But, truth to tell, Mary and I had dined en route, so we begged your majordomo's leave to take a stroll in your well-manicured gardens and await your pleasure here until the feasting was done."

Ashleigh had no doubt that by his intonation of "well-manicured gardens" Percy Shelley was being as critical as he'd been with the term "decadent luncheon." The man was obviously a reformer, if not a political radical, and she wondered at the strangeness of his obvious friendship with one of England's foremost members of the aristocratic peerage.

"Really, though, Percy," Brett was saying, "knowing you as I do, I should have thought the natural beauty of the greenery would count for something in your aesthetic ideal. But, come now, we can pursue that argument later. For now, there are acquaintances to be made. Have you met my fiancée? Allow me to introduce..."

Brett proceeded to make introductions all around, although, in the case of the earl of Ranleagh, it was only Mary Wollstonecraft Godwin he presented, as Christopher and Percy were already acquainted. Ashleigh smiled politely at the poet and his lady friend when it was her turn, then found herself blushing under young Shelley's appreciative gaze, which seemed to linger a few seconds more than might be deemed proper before he bowed over her outstretched hand and murmured, "Enchanting... and lovely... yes, so lovely...."

The final introductions involved the marquis of Wright and Lady Pamela Marlowe, and no sooner had Shelley released Pamela's hand than the honey-haired beauty turned from the poet and fixed her cold amber gaze on Elizabeth Hastings.

"Lady Elizabeth," she drawled, "when we met earlier, in the drawing room, I hadn't the opportunity to tell you how beautiful I find your dress." Her glance filled a pause in her speech and coolly traversed the length of the powder-blue silk afternoon gown Elizabeth wore with a matching shawl trimmed in white lace. "Of course," she continued, "it is a pity, isn't it, that it's a bit overdone for afternoon wear?" A brittle laugh punctuated her speech here. "But of course, how silly of me! You're probably far more clever than the rest of us. This way you won't have to bother changing for tonight's festivities. You're already dressed for the evening."

Elizabeth Hastings's eyes flashed silver fire, and she visibly stiffened on Brett's arm. "But of course I shall change for dinner, Lady Pamela," she countered. "After all, I have an abundant selection in my private chamber upstairs. You see," she intoned as her eyes narrowed on the honey blonde, "I've already been in residence here for some weeks—it makes planning our wedding so much easier, you know." She finished with a sugary smile at Brett as she gazed up at him with a possessive look in her eyes.

As Ashleigh felt the sparks fly between these two, she wondered, as official hostess, what she might say to halt the conflagration that was surely coming. Notwithstanding Christopher's anticipation of difficulties, Lady Pamela had been surprisingly quiet during the luncheon, although her glares in the affianced couple's direction had told their story; but now it seemed she'd merely been biding her time until a direct confrontation might allow her the proper opportunity to vent her spleen, and judging by the look in those amber eyes, she had only begun!

But it was Percy Shelley who saved Ashleigh the necessity of a prudent interruption, although later Ashleigh was to wonder at exactly how prudent it had been.

"So, you are to succumb to matrimony at last!" He grinned at Brett. "Well, I suppose, for one with such extensive holdings as yours, it was inevitable. Your kind will affix its stamp of ownership where it can."

"Why, whatever do you mean, sir?" inquired Elizabeth with an air of growing indignation.

"Yes, Percy, do elucidate," added Brett, his grin matching Shelley's.

"Why, Your Grace, simply this: From its earliest inception, marriage has been an institution set forth by men to signify their ownership of women. Women, in ruder ages and countries, were considered the property of men because they were the materials of usefulness or pleasure. They were valuable to them in the same manner as their flocks and herds were valuable, and it was important to men's interests that they should retain undisturbed possession. The same dread of insecurity that gave birth to those laws or opinions that defend the security of property suggested also the institution of marriage; that is, a contrivance for keeping property that others might try to take away.

"Now, of course, we are all aware that much has occurred to modify the nature of this institution between then and now, but I wonder... Has the basic premise, that is, of male ownership, really altered?'' He finished this speech with a questioning smile as he looked at the engaged couple.

If Elizabeth was indignant before his lengthy explanation, she was fairly bristling now. "I suppose you are entitled to your opinions, sir, but I can assure you, your pretty speech was spoken only as one who has never entered the bonds of wedlock himself."

"Ah! But you are mistaken, my lady!" It was Mary Godwin who spoke now. "Percy *is* married and has been for three years!"

"What?" exclaimed Elizabeth. "But I thought that—that is, didn't I hear your name to be Godwin?"

Mary laughed. "And truly, it is! Percy is wed, but not to *me*! Mrs. Shelley's name is Harriet. I am Percy's mistress!"

Elizabeth blanched, and there was a moment of uncomfortable silence as all looked on, watching her digest this news. At last she straightened and said, quite woodenly, to the poet and his companion, "Yes...I see...I do, indeed." Margaret's lecture in her chamber had gone home.

But Elizabeth wasn't the only one to be shocked by Mary's admission. Ashleigh found herself in quite a quandary over what she was witnessing. Despite her reservations about the revolutionary thinking of Shelley and his companion, she had found herself liking them somehow. Not only were their views given forth with a great deal of idealistic enthusiasm, but it was clear they were committed to being honest and forthright about who and what they were and what they believed in. And they both seemed utterly pleasant and likable besides, each with a ready smile and open countenance. What a world of difference between these two and the hidden snipes and barbs that had flown between the ladies Elizabeth and Pamela!

But at the same time Ashleigh was uncomfortably aware that Percy and Mary struck at the heart of the moral code with which she'd been raised. It mattered not that the locale of her upbringing had been Hampton House; through all the years she'd lived there, she'd been more a product of Dorcas's strongly held traditional views than anything else—views that were strongly aligned with those of her parents and the household of her youth. Now, all at once, she discovered herself exposed to people whose behavior and thinking were in some ways more shocking than all the doings of Hampton House—more shocking because they were being set forth here in open and polite society, at the home of one of the most prestigious families in the nation. What was she to think? She'd have to ponder on this a long while.

"I read your *Queen Mab* last year," Christopher was saying, "and I must say, your vitriolic verse trounced us all soundly. Not only did the institution of marriage come under the lashing of your bitter pen, but so did, if I recall correctly, the monarchy, the aristocracy, religion, and war."

"And don't forget his barbs against economic exploitation," Brett added with a good-natured grin. "Sir, that piece, I fear, has irrevocably launched you in English intellectual society as a rabidly dangerous radical."

"Ah, but he was well on his way to that with his visit to Ireland the year before," said Christopher, his grin matching Brett's. "Did you really think, Percy, that you could make any headway in the movement for Catholic emancipation and freedom from English control?"

Percy grinned back at both of them. "I produced two pamphlets and spoke at a huge meeting of the Irish nationalist leaders in Dublin, didn't I?"

"My dear fellow," said Brett, "it's not your activities in Ireland that we question and marvel at. It's that you have subsequently returned to England and lived to tell about it!"

There was shared laughter by all three men at this jest, with even the marquis of Wright joining in at the end, although Ashleigh could tell the poor man was having a difficult time reconciling the presence of Shelley with the aristocratic gathering in the duke's gardens. As for Ashleigh herself, here she'd found the contradictions the poet presented even more confounding. Her mother had been an Irish Catholic, and although, after much soul-searching, her parents had decided to raise her and her brother in their father's Anglican faith, she had always had strong feelings about the Irish Cause.

And now here was Percy Shelley, a man she had been on the verge of dismissing as too dangerous to pay attention to, espousing the very cause she would champion if she could!

"Tell me, sir," she advanced cautiously to the poet, "do you really think the Irish have a chance?"

"A better one than the French, though perhaps not as good as the Americans," said Shelley, apparently not at all surprised that a woman was posing questions of a political nature.

"And why is that, sir?" Ashleigh asked, and then, as if struck by an idea, she attempted to answer her own question. "Would it have anything to do, perhaps, with how much physical distance separates the oppressed from their oppressors?"

"My God, we have a thinking woman here!" cried Shelley with an expression of delight. "Quickly, Mary, do not let her get away without an invitation to come and visit. The two of you would add intellectual spice, as well as beauty, to our drawing room."

But Elizabeth at this juncture had had about all she could take of Shelley and his shocking ideas—not to mention the overbearing burden of having to suffer the presence of both Ashleigh Sinclair and Pamela Marlowe at once.

Her eyes narrowing until they resembled silver slits, she fixed her gaze on Ashleigh. "Miss Sinclair, I hardly think your views on politics, no matter how they charm Mr. Shelley here, are appropriate for a hostess at Ravensford Hall. And, speaking of your duties, I rather think it's time you withdrew to see to them, don't you?"

There was a brief gasp from Mary Godwin at the overt rudeness of her tone, while condemning glances from the others said as much, but Ashleigh was beyond reacting with anything but a desire to take the escape Elizabeth's words afforded. Feeling utterly foolish at having thought she might be at ease in the company of these worldly aristocrats, and feeling the sting of yet another snipe from Elizabeth Hastings, she bit her lower lip to stem the flow of tears that threatened, made a brief curtsy in the direction of the betrothed couple, and murmured, "Of course, my lady." Then she whirled and moved rapidly toward the path.

Christopher took a moment to send Elizabeth a scathing look, then strode quickly after Ashleigh's departing figure. "Ashleigh, wait!" he called. "I'll escort you back."

When he had gone, several pairs of accusing eyes fell on Elizabeth, but it was Pamela Marlowe who broke the silence.

"Oh, well done, my dear," she crooned. "A perfect preview of how the well-bred duchess should behave. How very *superior* of you!" After a low, exaggerated curtsy in Elizabeth's direction, Pamela picked up her skirts, turned, and she, too, headed for the path.

Brett's gaze followed Pamela's green skirts as they disappeared from view. There was little in his stance to indicate his emotions at the moment, but anyone looking more closely would have noted a tightening about the muscles of his jaw and mouth and the glacial quality of the turquoise eyes.

There were several things working at once in his mind, and each had to do with a female. To begin with, of course, there was the despicable behavior of the creature at his side, confirming all he'd envisioned he might expect from the inbred hothouse plant he was taking as his wife; then there were the less predictable but equally irksome actions of his mistress. Oh, he'd been well enough prepared for her snide and catty remarks earlier in the conversation, but it was her retreating thrust that really rubbed. He wished *he'd* been the one to have said them! And the fact that his position hadn't left him the liberty to do so while that of Pamela, of all people, *had*—it almost didn't bear thinking on!

And finally there was Ashleigh Sinclair. Or, to put it more specifically, Ashleigh and Christopher. How it galled him to stand helplessly by and watch that rake of an earl ply her with his green-eyed looks and solicitous words! *He* should have been the one to escort her back to the Hall and lend comfort where it was needed—*not* Christopher Edwards!

But did Ashleigh, as his legal ward, send him one look that would have encouraged such help? Did she, even once, during all of Ranleagh's fawning attentions, seek *him* out with a glance or throw a smile *his* way? No! Instead, he had to stand aside and play the virtuous guardian, driven by his own damnable sense of honor not to touch her, never again to—*Damn!* Was he to play the fool in his own house? He'd never before been caught in such a coil by a female, and, by God, he wasn't about to endure it now!

Suddenly Brett turned and threw a quick glance at those left with him in the clearing, his eyes finally resting on Elizabeth.

"Well, my dear," Brett said ever so softly, "it seems you are indeed bent on playing the duchess, therefore I leave you to carry on. Shelley... Wright," he murmured, ignoring Elizabeth's gasp and bowing slightly to the two remaining men in the group, "see Mary and Her Grace-to-be back to the Hall, won't you?"

And with a courteous bow to Mary Godwin and a barely perceptible nod to Elizabeth, the duke of Ravensford became the fourth person to retreat up the path in as many minutes.

# Chapter Seventeen

"I tell you, I shall be perfectly fine, Christopher, though I do thank you for your solicitations. This is not the first time I have had to deal with the, ah, high-handed behavior of...certain people, and—"

"High-handed!" exclaimed Christopher. "Ashleigh, it was positively rude and vicious, and all of us there in that garden knew it!"

"Nevertheless," Ashleigh sighed, "I am in no position to do anything about it, nor do I plan to, other than seek out a few quiet moments by myself. Please, your lordship, allow me to be excused and avail myself of some privacy?"

It was the earl's turn to sigh. They were standing in a little-used hallway that connected the servants' passageway to the terrace, with the formal rooms of the first floor. At the opposite end from where they stood there was also a door that led to the kitchens, and this was where Ashleigh was headed, hoping she'd made it clear to Christopher that he should go back to join some of the other guests in the drawing room or elsewhere.

"Very well, princess," said Christopher. "I'll withdraw if you're sure you'll be—"

"At the risk of sounding tedious, my lord, I tell you I shall be fine." Ashleigh smiled. "And I really should look in on what's happening in the kitchens—my duties as hostess, you know...." She finished with a wide-eyed, imploring look she hoped would convince him.

Christopher smiled, more taken than ever with the guileless sincerity he read in her face, then took her hand and bowed gracefully while bestowing a soft kiss on it. "Until later, princess," he murmured, then turned and headed for the sounds of low laughter and voices drifting from the formal rooms at the front of the Hall.

When he had gone, Ashleigh hurried toward the door to the kitchens, opened it and slipped inside.

It wasn't the main cooking room itself she entered, but the creamery, a chamber roughly twelve feet square and lined with floor-to-ceiling shelves that held a multitude of crocks and jars of varying sizes. In one corner stood an ancient wooden butter churn and beside it, a small worktable bearing an assortment of ladles, skimmers, funnels and the like, all of them in gleaming, highly polished brass. The room was immaculate, and Ashleigh smiled as she thought of the high standards of Hettie Busby.

But suddenly Ashleigh's attention was drawn to another corner of the dimly lit chamber. There a rustle of silk and a quick, furtive movement indicated she was not alone.

"Oh . . . oh, dear!" exclaimed a soft, tremulous voice. "I suppose I've been caught out this time."

Peering toward the voice, Ashleigh made out the slightly plump, rounded figure of a small, elderly woman dressed in a dove-gray gown that appeared costly and well made, but of a design that belonged to an earlier era, for though it lacked hoops or panniers, it was sashed at the natural waistline, and the modest neckline was supplemented by a snowy-white fichu. The wearer's head was covered by a soft mass of gray curls bobbing about a face that would have appeared benign, were it not for the look of apprehension in the hazel eyes that now met Ashleigh's.

"Hello," said Ashleigh. "I'm sorry if I frightened you. I didn't mean to."

"It—it's the cream, you see," said the woman. "I just love it so. They . . . they almost never let me have any at home." Here the hazel eyes blinked a moment, then stole a furtive glance toward the partially ajar door leading to the kitchen.

"Will...will... You won't tell on me, will you?" the woman added at last as her gaze returned to Ashleigh.

Ashleigh glanced down and saw that the woman's hands held a small saucer filled with cream, and they were trembling. A closer inspection of the small, plump face revealed a creamy white "mustache" lining her upper lip.

With a smile Ashleigh shook her head. "Not if you don't wish me to." She stepped forward a pace and held out her hand. "I'm Ashleigh Sinclair. I'm His Grace's official hostess and, also, his ward."

The gray curls bobbed again, but their owner made no move to release the saucer of cream. "Yes...yes, Sinclair... *Oh, yes*, I've heard all about *you*! David told me." Suddenly the hazel eyes widened. "Oh, but my dear! You must get yourself away from here—at once! They'll never allow you to stay, you know." Another furtive glance at the door to the kitchen. "Once they're crossed, there's only trouble, you know...yes...I know all about the trouble *she* can cause...."

"Trouble? But who...?"

"Elizabeth doesn't like you at all, you see. Oh, but you must *know* that. And *she*..." The hazel eyes flickered and then seemed to go blank.

"Elizabeth!" Ashleigh exclaimed. "I...see. Oh, but look here, madam, I hardly think—oh, I don't even know your name."

"My name...oh, yes, I have a name, of course. How silly of me! I'm Lady Hastings. But you may call me Jane. Everyone does."

"Lady Hastings! Why, you must be Lady Elizabeth's grandmother!"

A ghost of a smile broke over the old woman's face. "So they tell me," she murmured.

Her words had a faintly cryptic ring to them, and Ashleigh was just about to question her when the door to the kitchen flew open, and a tall figure in black stepped into the chamber.

"So there you are, Jane!" exclaimed Lady Margaret. "I might have known you'd be into the cream again. For shame! Now, come along with me or I shall be forced to—" The steely blue gaze fell on Ashleigh. "And what are *you* doing here, miss?"

"Well, I was just—"

"Your abigail's been searching for you for some time. I suggest you go to her." Margaret turned toward Lady Hastings. "And, as for you, little Jane, I think it is high time you were taking your nap. You know you cannot go about all afternoon without it. It worsens your behavior. And your theft of this cream proves it!"

With a swift movement, Margaret reached for the saucer in Jane's hands, but the small woman saw the action coming and sought to forestall it by backing away, at the same time raising the saucer toward her mouth with a half frightened, half willful look in her eyes.

"Oh, no, my dear!" Margaret's words bit into the air as she closed the gap between them, causing Lady Hastings to start. In a split second the saucer fell to the floor, sending cream and shards of porcelain in all directions across its stony surface.

"Now look what you've done, you foolish creature!" snapped Margaret. "Haven't you learned yet not to defy those who know better?"

Jane Hastings hung her head, totally cowed by the sharp tones—not to mention, thought Ashleigh, the condemning look in Margaret's eyes. Then, blubbering softly, she raised her head a fraction and murmured, "Y-yes, Margaret."

"Very well, and see that you don't forget it so easily. Now come along." Margaret sidestepped the mess on the floor and fastened a bony hand about Jane's wrist, then, as if remembering a detail at the last second, glanced at Ashleigh. "You will call someone to clean up this accident, please, Miss Sinclair."

Ashleigh watched as Margaret then proceeded to lead Lady Hastings from the chamber. She felt a sharp twinge of sympathy as she saw the small woman in the dove-gray dress cast a last, longing look at the cream on the floor before she was whisked briskly out of sight.

* * *

Patrick St. Clare sat in the humble caretaker's cottage on the grounds of what used to be his family's estate and held the yellowed pages of the letter he'd just read with trembling fingers. Then he glanced up at the old man sitting across from him.

"Jemmy," he said, "why, in heaven's name, when I was down here a few months ago, didn't Martha tell me there was a letter?"

The old man glanced at his wife who sat near the window beside a huge wheel, spinning. "'Cause she didn't know of it, sir," he replied matter-of-factly. "Th' lady only give it t' *me* t' keep fer ye, said I was t' trust no one else wi' it." Jemmy nodded, as if that settled the matter.

Patrick smiled, for he well remembered the literal single-mindedness with which Jemmy Stokes would keep anything entrusted to his care. It was one of the chief reasons his parents had relied on him and only one or two others to help them carry out their clandestine involvement in the free-trading operation they'd engaged in during Patrick's youth.

Of course, in this instance, it had almost backfired where he was concerned. When he'd at last returned to Kent, back in May, Jemmy had been absent, visiting a sick brother who lived many miles away, and it was only Martha he'd spoken to in his search for details of his family. If fortune hadn't decided to smile on him by allowing him this second chance visit, he'd never have come across the contessa's letter.

Patrick scraped back his chair from the table that stood between him and the old man and rose to his feet. Reaching into his waistcoat pocket, he withdrew a sheaf of five-pound notes and placed them on the table. "I'm deeply grateful, Jemmy," he said.

"Now, then, sir, ye needn't be doin' that. Ye were gen'rous enough th' last time ye come down. Me Martha—"

"Please accept it," said Patrick. "It's little enough, considering how you helped our family years ago, and the information in this—" Patrick indicated the letter he was still holding "—is more valuable than gold to me, old friend. Please, take the money, and all I'll ask is that you drink a draught or two to me when you spend a bit of it at the pub in the village to-night.''

Jemmy smiled a gap-toothed smile before glancing briefly at his wife and then back at Patrick. "Aye, that I will, young sir, but th' rest goes fer boots fer th' lads and a new Sunday dress fer Martha.''

For the first time since Patrick's arrival at the cottage, the old woman by the window stopped her spinning and focused on the men. A wide smile graced her plain features as she nodded at the two, then she bent back over her wheel and continued spinning.

"Well, I'll be on my way, then,'' said Patrick as he moved toward the cottage's single door. "I'll be staying at Ravensford Hall for a few days if anyone needs to find me. After that, well, that piece of paper I gave you has my London address as well as that of my home in America . . . er, do any of your lads read?''

Jemmy shook his head. "No, sir, but th' vicar can do us th' service if we've a need fer some'n wi' letters.''

"Good,'' said Patrick. "Well, I'm off—no need to see me out. Farewell, my friends, and again, my thanks.''

When he had gone from the cottage and mounted his horse, Patrick took a final look about the place where he'd spent many happy hours as a boy and then turned his horse's head in the direction of Ravensford Hall. Only then did he allow the flood of elated tears to wash his rugged face as he let the full import of what he'd learned move him.

*Ashleigh was alive!* Somehow he'd felt all along she hadn't perished in the fire, and now he had proof of it. He refused to consider the fact that it had been twelve long years since then and that death, or God only knew what else, could still have befallen her in that time. The little one lived, he was sure of it, and now all he had to do was *find her*!

Slowing his horse to a walk, he brushed the moisture from his cheeks with an impatient hand and reached for the letter in the pocket where he'd stashed it. Quickly, he unfolded the sheets of yellowed parchment and scanned their contents again.

My Dear Patrick,

I have no idea when this letter will reach you, or if indeed it will at all. It is over two months since the fire, and my husband's people tell me your ship is long overdue from its western voyage, and there are rumors it went down in a storm with all hands lost. Of course, the mere fact that I am taking this chance to return to England one more time to personally deliver this missive into our good friend's keeping, says all that is necessary about my hopes that it did not perish or, at least, that you were not among those who were lost if it did. I say 'one more time' because this is the last time I shall return to the country where I grew up. It has become entirely too dangerous for me to do so, and by this I do not mean to indicate the hazards of wartime Europe or even of the free trading I was happy to assist your family with in exchange for your many kindnesses toward me, for how should I have had those cheering glimpses and other heartening news of my son without your help? The danger I speak of has to do with something far more pernicious than threats from governments abroad or at home; it has to do with an evil I feel to be close at hand, although if you ask me how I know this, I could not tell you—but I *feel* it, Patrick, and I am as certain as I am of my breathing that it is *real*.

The fire that took your parents' lives was, I am sure, deliberately set, and the fact that it began in my chamber leads me to believe it was intended to destroy me, and not the innocents it took. The only reason I escaped, along with your sister and her nursemaid, Maud, was that I was in the nursery that night. Little Ashleigh had had one of her nightmares about that poor horse she'd seen mistreated and I was singing her to sleep with one of my little Italian *canti*. The nursery being a distance away from the other sleeping quarters, as you know, it was a good while before the fire reached us, and even then, we three barely escaped with our lives. Alas, by then, too, the rest of the house was a blazing torch, with no hope of rescuing those inside.

The grooms and stable men and others who slept apart from the main house spoke of first seeing the flames shooting from the windows of *my guestchamber*, and when I heard this, I determined that evil work was afoot and the chance could not be taken that further harm might come to those who were lucky enough to survive. In the confusion and noise that ensued from those vain attempts to put out the fire, I removed some rings from my hands and pressed them into Maud's while urging her to the stables with Ashleigh. Once there, I told her of my fears and made her promise to take your sister to a place of safety—a sister's she'd spoken of in London—and not to tell anyone until she heard from your family's solicitors, whom I would contact, and whom she must also contact after a reasonably safe amount of time had passed.

Alas, dear Patrick—and this brings me to the primary objective of this letter—I regret that now, even after all these weeks, your solicitors have received no word from Maud, and I fear for her whereabouts, not to mention the little one's. The only vehicle I was able to manage for them that terrible night was little Ashleigh's pony cart, for Maud was no driver, and it was only through Ashleigh's pluck and bravery that we were able to use that. *The child drove it!* I had no wish to endanger them further by going with them, you see, for I could not be certain that whoever had set the fire was not yet watching...and waiting. So the last I saw of Maud and her charge was the little cloud of dust they left by moonlight as I turned my horse's head and made for the road to the Dover coast.

So if this letter should reach you, Patrick, and I pray it does, I beg of you, if you have not done so already, go to London and begin the search for your sister. She *must* be found!

As for the rest, you know where to reach me, and I pray you do, in person, with your dear little sister by your side. My husband, as you know, is a wealthy man, and if this tragedy has left your family without means—as I have reasons to suspect it has—you must know that you and the little one can always find a home with us—Gregorio has said as much, and it is the least we can do for all your family's kindnesses over the years.

Praying this will come to pass, I am

Your dear friend,
Maria,
Contessa di Montefiori

Patrick's hands went limp as he finished rereading the letter. Maria... Mary... formerly Viscountess Westmont... since then, many years happily remarried to the son of a family friend in the country where she'd been born. He knew her story well. The daughter of an Italian prince and an English opera singer, she'd accompanied her homesick mother back to England to live when but a child, and had been raised there with the best that wealth could buy, for her father had died and left his fortune to his wife and daughter. Then she'd met Lord Edward Westmont, Brett Westmont's father, and, against the wishes of John Westmont, the duke, married him in a runaway love match. All had gone well for a time, and she'd borne him an heir—Brett. But a few years later, something had gone very wrong, according to the tale Mary had given his parents and which they'd told Patrick later.

Someone had deliberately set about planting false evidence to make it appear that Mary had taken a lover, and when John, the duke, heard about it, things happened very swiftly. Within a week, in which she was given no chance to explain or vindicate herself, she was dismissed from Ravensford Hall, put aboard a ship and sent to her father's family in Italy with notice that a divorce would ensue. Her son, of course, remained with his father, and no amount of pleading or reasoning was able to prevail against the old duke's mind.

The rest, Patrick knew from firsthand experience. Before too much more time passed, Edward remarried. Several years later, he and his second wife and son were killed in a carriage accident. Then Brett was sent to sea, and Patrick along with him, as a companion cabin boy.

When they returned, Patrick and his parents had a surprise visit from the woman they had known as Mary Westmont, Brett's mother. It had been a shock more than a surprise, for one night, her face blackened with soot, and dressed in the clothes of an Italian seaman, she had turned up quite unannounced in the company of Jemmy Stokes, already a participant in the business many enterprising Englishmen engaged in: smuggling items that were outrageously taxed into a country that would have had its people financially crippled if they were to pay the tariffs on goods that were a necessary part of their life-styles. In a network that ran the length of the English coastline, and from there inland, thousands of otherwise fine upstanding subjects of the king had, for decades, been risking their freedom and their lives to bring to the rest of his subjects items such as tea, soap, spices, tobacco, brandy, and linens at prices that were affordable, thanks to the bypassing of customs.

The smuggling had become an entire industry and England, particularly in wartime, depended on it. Indeed, as Patrick had been told by his parents as soon as he was old enough and could participate himself, if it weren't for the free traders, many a legitimate industry or business could not have survived. Without smuggled madder for the dyers, for example, how could the textile industry have continued? Without the gin, wines and brandies, what inn or public house would not have perished? And the purveyors of fashion! How would their businesses have fared without the silks and laces from abroad?

So, largely because they were having trouble keeping their own financial heads above water, Patrick's parents had sought out a couple of local people they'd had good reason to suspect were involved in free trading, and had joined in, and Patrick, once he returned from his stint at sea, went along with them.

But he could still remember the look of astonishment on all their faces the night Mary Westmont had appeared on the arm of Jemmy Stokes, ready to take their contraband to its hiding place in the cellar beneath the stables. Of course, what had been more astonishing was her reason for doing so, in lieu of any monies she might have accepted for her part. She had prevailed upon her adoring Italian husband to set up this liaison for her through one of his many shipping connections so that she might smuggle *herself* into the country where her desperately missed son still resided, so that she might occasionally have firsthand word of the lad and even, when she was lucky, a fleeting, distant glimpse.

After hearing her story, Patrick's parents, always ready to help a friend, had readily agreed to let her stay with them during these brief visits. They had been inordinately fond of Mary Westmont as a neighbor during the time she'd lived at Ravensford Hall—and just as *un*enamored of the cold duke, her father-in-law, and his even colder sister; to hear what had befallen the woman at those uncaring hands had stirred their outraged sympathies. Mary had found a means of watching over her son.

Of course, Patrick himself had been sworn to secrecy, especially where Brett Westmont was concerned. Fearing reprisals should word of these doings reach the elder Westmonts, Mary had decided it best not to involve her son. Moreover, from what she learned of the lad's tutored attitude toward her and women in general, she was not very sanguine about reestablishing any kind of personal relationship with Brett during those years. She sometimes hinted of dreams that she might one day meet with him and heal the breach, but for the time, she was content with the knowledge that he was well.

Patrick made a gesture of impatience as he thought of the tragedy of Mary—Maria, now, he amended—and the Westmonts. Such a waste of years...such a terrible schism...to separate a loving mother from her son. And who, he wondered, not for the first time in all these years, had been responsible for it? Who was it who had blackened Maria's name all those long years ago?

But suddenly Patrick's thoughts had no more room for ancient mysteries. A far more personal mystery had been cleared up, thanks to the contessa. Ashleigh was *alive*, and now, for the first time in months, he could truly go about a search for her! Tonight he would take advantage of Brett's invitation to stay at the Hall. Then, tomorrow, he would begin his search in earnest—and this time, by God, he would find her!

## Chapter Eighteen

Ashleigh threaded her way through the clusters of conversing guests in the drawing room, stopping for a moment here and there to listen or smile politely as a remark was thrown her way. From time to time she gave quiet directions to efficiently moving footmen when she saw the need for a gentleman's glass to be refilled or a tray of refreshments that required replenishing. This, she thought, was the easy part of being a hostess. All one had to do was imagine oneself as one of the guests, and the rest followed as a matter of course.

What Ashleigh didn't realize was that she was a natural candidate for the role. She may have spent only the first seven years of her life in such genteel surroundings, but the foundation she had received then, coupled with her own native intelligence and an inborn capacity to consider others, was more than adequate to see her through a role that some might spend a lifetime trying to assume. There was an art to making others feel at ease and welcome in one's home, and without realizing it consciously, in this regard, Ashleigh Sinclair was an artist.

But as she moved about the room, Ashleigh's serenely smiling countenance failed to reveal a number of thoughts that had to do with what she regarded as the more difficult aspects of her role as the duke of Ravensford's hostess. As she saw it, her chief shortcoming in being able to carry out her duties was that she was not only unsophisticated but also naive when it came to the mores of the *ton*. Why, she could still remember her shock as the earl of Ranleagh had informed her, ever so casually and much as if he were discussing the weather, that Lady Pamela was the duke's mistress! And she'd had a similar reaction when she'd learned of the liaison between Mr. Shelley and Miss Wollstonecraft. Surely, she thought to herself, her callow sensibilities had been obvious to all. She reflected for a moment on the polished air of someone like Lady Jersey, who was renowned for her abilities as a hostess, and tried to imagine how she would have handled such incidents. One thing was sure; she certainly wouldn't have acted like a schoolgirl about to recite her first piece!

Ashleigh was just chastising herself along these lines when she saw Christopher Edwards making his way toward her from where he'd been standing in conversation with Pamela Marlowe.

"Ah, there you are, princess," said the earl. "I told Pamela I was hoping we wouldn't have to search you out."

"Search me out? Why, Christopher, I've been readily available for whoever needs me for the past—"

"Oh, yes, of course—" he smiled "—and a more perfectly charming hostess Brett couldn't wish for, though I'm convinced he hardly deserves you. But, no, what I was referring to was our desire—Lady Pamela's and mine, that is—to be as inconspicuous as possible in making our farewells."

"You're leaving?"

"I'm afraid so, princess, though the charming look of disappointment on your beautiful face almost persuades me to stay."

"Oh, but then, why don't you? The dinner we've planned for this evening promises—"

"Ah, yes, I'm sure it's to be a gastronomical delight, but the fact is, you see, that it's Pamela who needs to withdraw, and I have promised to see her home."

Ashleigh glanced past his shoulder and saw Pamela Marlowe looking at them, an unhappy glimmer in her eyes. "I see," she said quietly. "Well, I'm not sure where Brett is right now, but—"

"Good God, Ashleigh," Christopher interrupted, "Brett is the *last* person we'd wish to summon up now! That's why I've sought *you* out. Pamela has no wish to see His Grace, ah, 'before Hell freezes over,' I believe is the wording she used.''

"Oh," said Ashleigh, nodding. "Very well, then, your lordship, allow me to see you and the lady to your carriage.'' She threw an encouraging smile at Pamela as she said this and was gratified to see the blonde nod stiffly and attempt a smile in return.

A few minutes later, as Ashleigh turned in the entry hall, having seen Pamela and the earl off, she was approached by a footman coming from the far end of the hallway.

"What is it, Robert?'' she asked with a smile. She congratulated herself on remembering his name, even though Robert was new to the Hall. In fact, she now knew the names of all those who served on the vast staff at Ravensford Hall—no mean feat in itself, but it had been one of the first duties she had taken upon herself when she came to work here, and the servants noticed and appreciated it. Why, there were some who, even after years of service, were still hailed by Iron Skirts as "boy," or "you, there, miss," but the little miss knew and seemed to care about each one of them, and they were not apt to forget it.

"A message for you, Miss Sinclair,'' said Robert. "Your presence is requested upstairs, in your chamber.''

"In my chamber? But who would want...? Whom is the message from, Robert?''

"Ah, that I couldn't say, miss. It was transmitted to me by Mr. Jameson.'' The look on Robert's face seemed to indicate he was genuinely sorry he couldn't give her more information.

"Very well, Robert.'' Ashleigh smiled reassuringly. "Thank you.''

Robert bowed respectfully and retreated down the hallway.

Now, who could be summoning her up to her chamber just when she was sorely needed down here? Ashleigh wondered as she headed for the stairway. Margaret and Elizabeth seemed to have disappeared, and she hadn't seen Brett in over an hour, so it was imperative that she remain below with the guests. *Someone* had to see to their needs!

A few minutes later she turned the ornate brass handle on her chamber door and pushed it open. When she entered, she found herself staring into the stern turquoise gaze of Brett Westmont.

Not sure how she should react to his presence in her chamber, Ashleigh glanced at the still-open door she'd been about to shut behind her, and then back at Brett.

"Go ahead, leave it ajar if you wish," he told her. "I wouldn't want any...confusion to attend the purpose of this interview." There was a faint hint of mockery in his tone.

Ashleigh decided to ignore it. "You sent for me, Your Grace?"

"Ah, ever the polite, ever the proper, ever the perfect, formal Miss Sinclair," he mocked. "You were to call me *Brett*, remember? *Say it*, lovely Ashleigh, say my name, or has the name of another replaced it in your lexicon?"

This last was delivered with a vehemence that was so far beyond his usual range of cool reserve that Ashleigh took a moment to study him before replying. He was standing near one of the windows that faced the front drive of the Hall, looking every inch the noble lord of the manor in his well-cut riding clothes, but he'd removed the jacket and hung it over the back of a nearby chair, and his stock as well. This left him in shirt sleeves, and the shirt was half undone at the top, displaying more than a glimpse of the whorls of deep mahogany hair that covered his chest. The result was not so much an image of dishevelment as of roguish indifference to propriety, and Ashleigh felt herself shiver at this effect.

Then she noticed he held a glass in his hand, and on the floor, near the chair that bore his jacket and stock, stood a half-empty bottle of brandy. Remembering another time she'd seen him drinking in a similar chamber down the hall, she swallowed past the lump that formed in her throat and answered, "...Brett."

"Ah," he nodded, "so you can yet recall the syllable, but still, that does not signify that you would not prefer to be uttering another name, one...shall I say, of greater length?" He took a step toward her, and Ashleigh, who had not moved from beyond the doorway since entering the chamber, had to force herself not to retreat into the hall.

"I—I do not take your meaning, Your Gr— Brett."

"Do you not?" he inquired sharply as he closed the distance between them. "Well, then, allow me to spell it out for you. The name you would prefer to speak—" he held out his glass in the pose of an actor delivering a soliloquy "—'trippingly on the tongue,' is it not . . . Christopher?" There was a brief, bitter twist of his lips as he finished the question, and his eyes looked cold and cruel as they held hers.

The insinuation was so far from anything Ashleigh might have expected, she drew in a quick, sharp breath before giving her reply. "Why—why, no, I—what would make you ask such a thing?"

Brett turned, set his glass on a stand near the bed and walked back toward the window, acting much as if he hadn't heard her. "You just saw Christopher Edwards to his carriage. Why?"

Beginning to feel annoyance at his incessant questioning, Ashleigh took a few steps into the room and placed her hands at her hips as her gaze followed his out the window. "I was seeing *both* his lordship *and* Lady Pamela Marlowe to his carriage, to be precise. The lady, it seems, had had enough of your insouciant bad manners and asked to be taken back to London."

Brett whirled on her, his gaze a menacing turquoise glare. "So, the little kitten has claws, has she? Well, perhaps you'd care to enlighten me, pretty cat, as to just what I have done to bring such words of condemnation down upon my head?"

He was standing very close to her now, near enough for Ashleigh to notice the thick sweep of mahogany lashes that framed eyes that were almost too beautiful for a man's, and at the corners of those eyes, faint little lines that were pale in contrast to the bronze of his tanned face and came from squinting against the sun.

But, as if making up her mind not to let his nearness intimidate her, Ashleigh stood her ground as she spat up at him, "What sort of man are you, that you would invite your mistress to your home on the day of the announcement of your betrothal to another woman?''

"Hah!" exclaimed Brett, glaring down at her. "And what sort of woman are you, that you would flirt and play the coquette to one of the most profligate rakes in England when you are an official hostess and recipient of another man's largesse?''

"'Coquette!' 'F-flirt!' '' Ashleigh sputtered.

"Those are, I believe, the words I used. You needn't repeat them like a pet parrot! And as for your accusations regarding my poor, injured mistress, disabuse your mind of such, here and now! It was Pamela Marlowe's own idea to show up here at Ravensford Hall with half of bloody London in tow—*not mine*! If anything, I'd more than made it clear to her when I saw her last in the city, that it was over—done—and she was free to seek...other liaisons. But could the bitch have done with it? Oh, no, she had to drag an entire caravan of people down here to celebrate my birthday, of all idiocies, and Christopher Edwards among them!''

Taken aback by this hotly delivered revelation, Ashleigh felt the wind go out of her sails for a moment. Then, picking up on what else he'd told her, she felt it rise again and billow forth. "I did *not* flirt with Christopher Edwards!''

"Didn't you?''

"No, and what if I had?" she added, feeling the anger of righteous indignation begin to well up. What business of his was it *whom* she flirted with? He was merely her employer, nothing more. They both knew his trumped-up guardianship was a sham. "I'll thank you to allow me to flirt or—or talk to whom I wish! You have no right—''

"*No right?* You bloody little fool! I have the clearest right of all—the right of someone who took your honor—to see to it that it is somehow restored. I have told you, Christopher Edwards is—''

He stopped as he noticed the sudden drain of all color from her face, the anguished look in her eyes at his reference to her humiliating deflowering at his hands. It was his undoing. He looked into those eyes for several silent seconds and felt his anger crumbling. Then, with a groan, he bent and drew her to him.

Ashleigh felt his arms envelop her even as his lips buried themselves in her hair. It was a sensation of strength and softness all at once. There was the very size of him, huge and muscular as he held her against his length, but at the same moment the feel of his mouth at her temple, her ear, the delicate, sensitive place beneath, sent shivers of longing through her, and she responded with a rush of feelings that had nothing to do with rational thought.

With a cry, she threw her arms about his neck, even as his mouth came down to claim hers in a fierce, demanding kiss. With it, the room began to spin and disappear from her ken, for in seconds there was nothing but the sensation of his mouth on hers, moving, tasting, seeking entry. She felt her lips open under his, felt the hot thrust of his tongue as it grazed her teeth and slipped between.

Then his hands began to move, slowly at first, then in more demanding fashion, coursing over her back and shoulders, then down again, lower, until they clasped her hips and drew them close to his.

"Ashleigh...sweet, beautiful Ashleigh," he murmured against her mouth, "God, how I've wanted to do this.... You're far too lovely to resist, do you know that? You're a witch...a sweet, unbearably, enticing witch...."

A hand came around and moved to her breast, and with this Ashleigh suddenly realized the danger of what was happening. "Brett," she breathed, "Brett, no..."

But then he found her nipple, and as he fingered its budding hardness, a jolt of pleasure shot through her, straight to her very core. Suddenly there was a melting sensation in her loins and her knees threatened to buckle under her. Again, his fingers moved, and the feeling seemed to build, dragging her will with it. She heard herself moan, found her arms tightening about his neck as she reached upward to accept the renewed onslaught of his mouth, and all the while the feeling below was building...building....

Suddenly there was a sharp bark from the doorway, and the door sprung wide, the crashing sound driving them apart. Finn stood there with his hackles raised, the feral gleam of his fangs transmitting an unmistakable message.

Ashleigh felt as if a bucket of cold water had been thrown over her as she instantly recovered her senses. "Finn!" she cried, "Finn, it's all right. Stay back. It's all right."

The dog ceased his snarling and gazed at his mistress with puzzled eyes. He heard her words and was moved to obey, but there was something wrong somewhere....

"Finn, down!" came the command, and this time the message was so powerful, the big dog complied at once.

Then there came, from out in the hallway, the excited snuffling and grunting sound that could only belong to one creature.

"Lady Dimples!" Ashleigh exclaimed.

"Damn!" swore Brett before glaring turquoise daggers at, first the pig, then Finn, then Ashleigh. "My dear, I take back all I said or implied about the dangers of Christopher Edward's presence—or any other's, for that matter. It would seem you are more than adequately... chaperoned. But," he added with a hint of a twist to his handsome mouth as he made for the door, "if I were you, I would see that your protectors are kept more firmly about you—at all times!"

And with nary another glance, he was through the door and gone.

Brett made his way down the hallway until, at the head of the stairs, he turned toward the opposite wing of the house, the wing that held the library. If he'd been less than clearheaded when Ashleigh had entered her chamber, he was stone-cold sober now. What insanity had taken hold of him? Not only had he found himself in the throes of some unnameable emotion that had led him to send for her there in the first place, but he'd then gone on to toss all reasonable behavior to the wind when in her presence, and— *Damn! Bloody damn!*

As he made his way toward the sanctuary of the library—his grandfather's favorite sanctuary, he reminded himself, but now his, as if it were a legacy—his mind ran over the events of the day that might account for his unusual state.

First, there'd been that delightful morning outing with Ashleigh and Megan—delightful, yes, but that didn't alter the fact that he'd found himself instigating it against all his earlier determinations....

Then there'd been the unexpected crush of guests, with the distasteful business of having to parade about with Elizabeth on his arm...cool, beautiful Elizabeth, the perfect English lady who could hardly bear the touch of a man on her person. It was something he'd always suspected before, but when, before arriving upon the little scene with Shelley, he'd attempted a brief embrace in the gardens, Elizabeth Hastings had frozen under his touch with a look of revulsion in her eyes that confirmed his suspicions. And to think that he must spend his life tied to that frigid creature! Damn Margaret and her interference, anyway!

But, as if that weren't enough, he'd had to endure the feline exchange of barbs between a fiancée he couldn't abide and a mistress he no longer wanted. *There'd* been a fine kettle of birthday fish!

But was that sufficient for the gods that seemed determined to mock him today? Oh, no! For, beyond all endurance, he'd had to sit idly by and watch his ward, whom he'd foolishly just come to deciding he was growing to like, fall under the spell of that rogue, Ranleagh! Didn't the chit realize that all he'd worked for—to carefully build her reputation before the eyes of those like Lady Jersey and her ilk—

Suddenly, as he stood before the door of the library, a door he'd faced countless times in his youth before gathering the strength to brave the stern visage on the other side, the obvious occurred to Brett. In his mind he let the names, the identities slip by...Ashleigh...Elizabeth...Margaret...Lady Jersey...*women*, all of them—*women*! And each of them a bloody thorn in his side!

With a vengeance, Brett shoved at the library door and stalked inside. He was surprised to find the candle burning in the heavy silver candlestick on his grandfather's desk, and then there came the pungent aroma of tobacco.... His eyes flickered from the empty chair behind the desk to the smoky haze coming from the armchair to the right of it....

"Patrick!"

"I was wondering when you'd show up, old man. Another quarter hour and I'd have been forced to let your majordomo announce me formally, just when I'd thought myself prudent in convincing him to let me wait for you here. Didn't want to intrude on your house party dressed as I am." Patrick gestured at the dusty riding boots on the feet he'd crossed casually before him as he sat in the chair.

"The devil with formalities," said Brett, crossing to clasp his hand. "You're a sight for sore eyes, and I'm glad you're here. Can I get you anything? A glass of wine, perhaps, or—"

"In a moment, maybe, if you'll join me, but first, I'm hot to tell you my news."

"Which is...?" said Brett as he pulled up a nearby chair.

"It's about my search," said Patrick, a look of absolute joy lighting his rugged features. "Brett, my sister is alive!"

Brett flashed him a delighted smile. "I thought you looked rather pleased with the world just now when I walked in. How do you know?"

Patrick drew on the clay pipe he held between giant, tanned fingers, then let out the smoke slowly before answering, "It's a long story, but if you're prepared to listen..."

He proceeded to tell Brett of the letter he'd discovered, carefully editing out the details of who Maria was, other than a friend who'd aided his family in their free trading years ago. While it was his fervent wish that Brett might come to know his mother's story and that a reconciliation be effected, especially now that the old duke was dead, he and his parents had sworn an oath to Maria that they'd never reveal her secret; and where Patrick was concerned, his word was sacred.

Brett listened carefully to the tale, and when Patrick had finished, he rose to pour them each a sherry to toast his friend's good fortune.

"So," he said, after lowering his glass, "I suppose you're off to London to try to track down this sister of the child's old nurse?"

"I am, although I think I'll stay and make a few more inquiries here in Kent first. You never know when someone might recall something about what went on back then. Look at what happened with Jemmy Stokes."

Brett nodded and was silent a moment. Then he raised his eyes to meet his friend's, a somber expression on his face. "Patrick, far be it from me to spout gloom and doom, but—" he twisted in his chair and looked uncomfortable for a moment "—but it's been twelve years since—"

"The fire, yes I know, but if you think that's going to daunt my enthusiasm, you can forget it. I've had faith that the little one is alive for some time now, even before my trip to Kent, as you well know, so all the gloom and doom in the world isn't going to faze me at this point." Patrick leaned forward in his chair, his elbows on his knees as he gazed at his friend with earnest intent. "What I would like to ask about, however, is what it is of gloom and doom that's troubling you, old man. No, don't deny it. I saw the scowl on your handsome puss when you came through that door. What's amiss, and can I help?"

Brett sighed, then met Patrick's compassionate gaze. "You're right, of course. And since you've just finished telling me your fantastic tale, perhaps you won't consider mine too incredible."

"I'm all ears, Your Grace," Patrick told him with a dramatic flourish of his arm.

"To begin with, I'm engaged to be wed—"

"Brett, that's wonderful!"

"Save your congratulations. The lady is a cold, passionless bitch, chosen by my grandfather, with a bit of urging from the Lady Margaret, before he died."

"I see." Patrick's tone was sympathetic.

"Not yet, you don't. We announced our betrothal today, and Pamela Marlowe showed up at the party."

"Oh," murmured Patrick. "I see."

"Still not yet. There is a third complication. I have under my roof just now a new responsibility. A female ward . . . a very young and beautiful female ward . . ."

"God, Brett, you don't mean to tell me—"

"Wait! You haven't heard the worst of it. Sit back in your chair, Patrick, and have another sherry while I regale you with a tale of the most dramatic coil a man ever found himself involved in...."

In as few words as possible, but omitting none of the facts that pointed a guilty finger his way, the duke told his friend of the appearance of the new ward and "hostess" in his life, beginning with the well-meaning intentions of his dying grandfather and ending with his frustrated attraction to "the chit."

"And so you see before you, my friend, a man who is promised to a woman he cannot abide, sought by a woman he no longer desires, and desirous of a woman he has wronged and dares not touch again. A pretty picture, is it not? And, if you've listened carefully, you've heard the common thread: *woman*! I tell you, Patrick, I'm beginning to think my grandfather was the wisest of all men alive.... Well, and just what is it you find yourself able to grin about?"

Patrick's grin grew even broader. He had long known of Brett's well-tutored antipathy toward women, but he'd also made it clear he'd never share his view. Women, to Patrick St. Clare, were the most wonderful, beguiling, fascinating creatures alive. Beginning with the mother and sister he'd adored, he'd always relished their company, frequently finding them far more intelligent, wise and talented than their male-dominated society would admit. And women seemed to recognize this affinity in Patrick, for they frequently sought out his friendship as well as his sexual favors, for his good looks and blatant virility were hard to pass by. But where Brett used women and then discarded them with nary a backward glance, Patrick frequently found his loves of yesterday becoming his friends of today.

Moreover, Patrick was not about to tell Brett something else he recognized right now, though he was sorely tempted: Brett Westmont's current dilemma, which he attributed to women, was of his own making; it was he who subscribed to taking a wife to be nothing more to him than a brood mare; it was he who ensnared and then dumped the Pamela Marlowes in his world; and it was he who'd abused this poor little ward he'd spoken of, through his own arrogance—misunderstandings or no.

Well, it would be a deucedly interesting time he'd have while here at Ravensford Hall, watching to see how his friend worked his way through this one. He wouldn't miss it for the world!

"I was wondering what was so amusing," Brett was saying.

"Oh, nothing I'm capable of explaining to you, old man," said Patrick. "But I am looking forward, ever so much, to being invited to stay for dinner!"

## Chapter Nineteen

"But Megan, I cannot see why you won't come downstairs and join the guests for dinner. Your position in this respect is perfectly clear: you participate as my companion, not my abigail! Those people down there haven't the faintest idea you've that status!" Suddenly Ashleigh grew thoughtful. "Oh, dear! I've just realized something.... Megan..." She turned to look at her friend who'd been helping her complete her toilette for the dinner party that was soon to commence downstairs. "Is it because you're fearful that if you join the guests from London, someone might recognize you...?" She continued awkwardly. "You know... from Hampton House, and—"

"Ah, no," Megan chuckled, "'tis not that, darlin'. Ye might not have noticed, but I did plenty o' checkin' on the duke's guests durin' the luncheon, ah, from afar, ye understand. No, it turns out the only one here who knows what I was before I, ah, retired, is Mr. Shelley—No, don't fash yerself—Percy, whom I met later this afternoon on the terrace, is the last person who'd give me away. He even told me so! Said he was delighted that a poor Irish lass had worked her way through the insufferable English class barriers. No, Ashleigh, ye've naught t' fear on that score."

"But then, why?" Ashleigh questioned. "If no one who matters recognizes you, and they're only acquainted with you as my companion, what could be keeping you from joining us?"

Megan looked at Ashleigh's reflection in the cheval mirror as she worked at the row of tiny buttons at the back of her dinner gown. "Faith, darlin', what ye say may be true—*now*—they don't know I work as yer abigail—but they could *find out*—just as soon as Iron Skirts or Lady High-and-Mighty decided t' inform them!"

"Oh, piffle!" Ashleigh exclaimed as she stamped a delicate foot on the carpet. "And shock their guests that someone so lowly could have found her way to their precious dinner table? I cannot think it likely they would risk such a scandal."

"Hmm," murmured Megan. "Perhaps, but that's not the whole o' the problem. Are ye fergettin' me own difficulties in dealin' with the miserable company o' those two *oinseach*? 'Tis hard put I'd be t' keep from settin' me *skean* t' their bloody throats the first time either o' them looked at ye crosswise!" She slipped the final button through its delicate loop and stepped back to join Ashleigh in viewing the finished product they saw in the mirror.

Tonight Ashleigh wore a beautifully cut Empire gown of flowing white silk, its diaphanous folds of a texture so fine, Madame Gautier had been begged by Ashleigh, when she first saw it, to employ double, and even triple, layers of the fabric in several places for the sake of modesty, if not warmth.

White, especially for evening, the *modiste* had assured her, would be all the rage this season. When the first English ladies had flocked over to Paris following Napoleon's abdication and exile, they were astonished to find the French still wearing the classical white instead of the myriad colors that had permeated the Englishwoman's wardrobe in recent years. On the other hand, the Frenchwoman's skirt, instead of falling straight to the ankles like her counterpart's across the channel, now flared out slightly at the hem. The impact of this news on the fashionable world of the *haute ton*, Madame Gautier had declared, would be an instantaneous flood of orders for "*blanc wiz ze flare.*"

Of course, there was still much about the gown to proclaim it far advanced beyond the white Grecian mode of a dozen years earlier. Its tiny puffed sleeves were still more substantial than the almost nonexistent sleeves Ashleigh recalled her mother wearing in an era when feminine gowns more often resembled nightdresses in their scantiness of cut and fabric. And they were almost met on her upper arms by the tops of long silk gloves that hugged like a second skin. Also, while it was true that a wide band of exquisite lace, set across the daring décolletage, barely kept her generously curving breasts from spilling free, at least there was no attempt at draping these charms with a swath of fabric so sheer it had encouraged, at least among the more daring in that earlier age, an application of rouge to the nipples beneath!

Nevertheless, as Ashleigh eyed the curving mounds of flesh that rose above this gown's square-cut décolletage, she felt a blush invade her cheeks. "Megan!" she gasped. "I don't know how I could have allowed Madame Gautier to—to cut this so!" She took tense fingers and attempted to tug the band of lace upward. "How could it have escaped our notice?"

"Ah, colleen, don't ye recall ye donned it at the final fittin' minus its lace, which hadn't yet arrived from Paris? Suzanne told us 'twould be added later, just before 'twas delivered."

Ashleigh's blush deepened as she recalled the moment, realizing at last that she'd deliberately put out of her mind the image of her standing before the dressmaker's looking glass with the twin peaks of her breasts peeping over the edge of her neckline. "Ohh, Megan, yes—yes, now I do, but—but the *lace*! I thought it would be ever so much more . . . *generous*!"

Megan chuckled. "And here I'd begun t' think ye were becomin' a newly sophisticated woman o' the *ton*!"

Megan's choice of words hit Ashleigh like a blast of cold air. *Sophisticated!* Why it was the very facet—or the lack of it— she'd bemoaned earlier today that kept her feeling inadequate in dealing with the polished ladies and gentlemen of the duke's set!

Thoughts of her employer intruding on her reflection sent an additional surge of emotion through her slender frame. After the disturbing scene earlier in this chamber, she'd found herself more than a little shaken by what had transpired between them. She had not enjoyed recalling her inexplicable capitulation in his embrace, had not wanted to examine too closely what this implied about her own inclinations, and so, in the hours since then, she'd kept all introspection at bay, attributing her puzzling behavior to just one more aspect of a severe lack of sophistication on her part when it came to dealing with the experienced members of the *ton*, and especially its *men*!

Now, as the sounds of Megan's remark echoed in her ear, she made up her mind to something: if she was to measure up to what was expected of her as the duke of Ravensford's hostess—and she had no illusions that she had any alternatives—she must begin to develop the degree of worldliness she'd witnessed in those about her, downstairs and in the gardens this afternoon; she must outgrow the naiveté of her sheltered upbringing; and she would begin this very night—*by wearing this gown*!

Ashleigh gave an assertive nod, causing the mass of shining ringlets Megan had fashioned atop her head to bounce and shimmer in the room's flickering candlelight. "Megan, you're absolutely right. I *am* sophisticated enough to wear this gown . . . or at least I shall begin to be . . . more so, that is, once I go downstairs in it." She cast one final appraising glance at the mirror, then turned to face her friend. "Well, what is it you find so amusing?" she demanded, seeing the redhead's mouth begin to work as a twinkle enlivened the green of her eyes.

"Ah, *mavourneen*!" exclaimed Megan, allowing a grin to break free at last. "'Tis just the determinin' look in yer eye as ye made yer momentous decision. So 'tis sophistication ye crave, is it?" She eyed the much-discussed neckline, then glanced at the blue-enameled clock on the mantelpiece. "I'm thinkin' 'twould not be a bad idea t' be wearin' this gown t' give yerself a confident feelin' o' increased worldliness when ye venture forth downstairs this evenin', but I tell ye what—'tis early yet! Why don't ye relax here for a wee bit while I run t' me chamber and fetch that shawl Suzanne made me? 'Tis made o' the same fine lace as—" her eyes fell on Ashleigh's neckline again "—as that. Then, at any moment that ye might be findin' yerself . . . chilly, why ye could just . . . cover up a wee bit!"

She finished with a broadening of her grin and one arched, questioning red eyebrow.

Ashleigh returned the grin. Shawls were highly in vogue now, and she accepted the perfection of Megan's solution with not a little of the ever-growing admiration she'd come to have for the redhead's quickness of wit. "Megan," she said, "I shudder to think what the men who run this country would do if they realized just how narrowly they escaped their fate by the accident of birth that made you female . . . and Irish. If you'd been born an Englishman, you'd be running this country by now, I'm sure of it. Yes, of course I'll wait while you run to your chamber, but while you're there, I wish you'd change into that gold silk ensemble for evening. It has a matching shawl, too, if I recall."

Megan was halfway to the door, but she turned to give her friend a rueful smile. "I'm thinkin' 'twould take nothin' short o' some earthshakin' event t' make me change me mind on *that* score, lass. Now sit and relax. I'll be back in a wink." And with a wink of her eye, she left the chamber.

Patrick had finished bathing and changing into evening attire with the help of Brett's man, Higgins, and was ready to seek out the duke before venturing downstairs. Glancing briefly at his reflection in a wall mirror he had to stoop to peer into, he gave a small smile of satisfaction at his reflection. The stock that rose above the high points of his starched collar was immaculate and perfectly tied. Brett's man was a veritable genius, he decided, and he began to realize why it was that certain members of the set of dandies of the *ton* vied with each other almost to the point of bloodletting over the services of a good valet, often resorting to stealing these talented fellows away from one another with enormous briberies and the like. Higgins had accomplished the tying of this particular stock in only a single try, and the results were far handsomer than anything Patrick himself might have aimed for. And the deep blue cutaway he wore over his silver-embroidered white satin waistcoat had arrived from its pressing immaculate.

"Well, Patrick, old boy," he grinned as he saluted himself in the mirror, "you look to be a fine enough specimen of a man to tempt the ladies tonight, I'll wager. Let's see, then, what's afoot." Opening the door to his guestchamber, he stepped into the hallway and crashed, head-on, into a quickly moving figure.

"Here, now, I beg your pardon, but—" Patrick gazed down at the apparition that sat in indignant shock on the polished marble floor amidst a swirl of jade-green skirts and found himself tongue-tied for the first time in his life. There, shaking a head sporting a wealth of fiery-red curls, as if to clear it after being knocked silly, was the most ravishing creature he'd ever laid eyes on!

"Well," demanded the beauty. "Are ye goin' t' stand there all evenin' or is it a gentleman ye're callin' yerself?" Megan continued to glare at the lengthy pair of strong, muscular legs encased in deep gray pantaloons and matching Hessians with silver tassels as she reached out a hand in an attitude of expecting to be helped up.

Patrick stared in awe for a moment at the beautifully shaped hand with its long, slender white fingers, then reached to clasp it and draw the redhead to her feet. But in the next instant he found himself awestruck once again as he gazed into the most incredible pair of slanting green eyes set in a face that could have been a symbol for the beauty of woman incarnate.

Finding herself again on her feet, Megan had a moment to blink before looking up into the bluest eyes she'd ever seen on a man. Moreover, the fact that she actually had to gaze *upward* to meet their stare was no small thing in her experience, and she found herself curiously arrested by it. Then, as the seconds ticked by, with neither of them moving a muscle as they stood there, gazing at each other, she began to realize it was not only the eyes or the size of the man that was so compelling; from the top of his curly black hair to the tips of his well-polished Hessians, this was a man *any* woman would look twice at and then some! When she'd at last taken all this in, a slow, wide smile etched itself across her wondering face.

Seeing the smile, Patrick found himself in danger of choking on his own bated breath until, letting it out with a whoosh, he quickly met it with his own, saying, "Irish...you're as Irish as a shamrock!"

"Aye," Megan responded, "that I am, and proud t' be, I can tell ye, Mr.... ?"

"St. Clare... Patrick St. Clare, *ma geersha*, and who might *you* be?"

"Faith, ye speak the tongue yerself!" Megan exclaimed. Faintly she realized that this dashingly handsome and virile stranger still held her hand clasped in his own giant one, but she made no move to disengage it. "Me name's Megan."

"Megan," murmured Patrick, sounding much as if the sound of it were a prayer ushering in a miracle.

Megan, too, remained transfixed as she continued to look into his eyes. "O'Brien," she whispered at last.

"Megan O'Brien... a beautiful name, *macushla*, and who might you—"

"Patrick!" exclaimed a deep male voice from down the hallway. "I was wondering if you were ready."

They both turned to see Brett heading toward them.

Broken from his dazed trance, Patrick released the hand he'd been holding and wondered if the heat he felt about his ears meant he was blushing—something he couldn't recall doing in years.

"Ah, I see the two of you have met," Brett told them as he drew near. Then, at their silence, he glanced quickly at the face of each before adding, "Um... need I further the introductions or—?"

"Oh, no, no," assured Patrick. "Miss O'Brien's just told me her name...though perhaps, on second thought, it might help to learn how you've come by her acquaintance."

Here Patrick gazed inquiringly at his friend. It had just occurred to him that Brett was no slouch when it came to inviting beautiful women into his circle and, more important, into his bed, and the notion did not sit happily with him that the beauty standing beside them could very well be a candidate for Lady Pamela's replacement in the duke's affections.

"Well," said Brett, "it happens that Miss O'Brien is a companion to the ward I've recently acquired. You do recall, don't you, Patrick—"

"Oh, yes, of course," said Patrick enthusiastically. The ward... how could he have forgotten the poor girl and the duke's awkward entanglement there! Well, all the better—at least it was not Megan O'Brien who occupied that unfortunate young lady's shoes.

"But Megan," Brett was saying, "you're not dressed for dinner. Surely you weren't thinking of abstaining? I thought I'd made it clear, after missing you at the luncheon, that you were to feel free to join the guests."

"What?" said a startled Megan, for she'd gone back to gazing in rapt fashion at the rugged, virile appearance of the huge man beside her... the one with the startling blue eyes... Irish blue eyes... "Oh, forgive me, Yer Grace," she murmured. "Yes, o' course I'm goin' down t' dinner...." *Nothin' short o' some earthshakin' event*... "So," Megan added, looking at each of them in turn, "if ye'll both excuse me, I must be off t' change me attire or I'll be late!" And with a nod at the duke and a warm smile at Patrick, she hastened down the hallway toward her chamber.

Ashleigh eyed Megan's willowy form with a speculative glance as they entered the drawing room. Her friend looked as beautiful as she'd ever seen her in the tissue-fine, cloth-of-gold Empire gown she wore with perfect grace, and Ashleigh was delighted Megan had changed her mind and decided to join the dinner guests. But what was foremost in Ashleigh's thoughts at the moment was *why* this change had occurred.

Megan had offered little in the way of explanation when she'd returned to Ashleigh's chamber wearing the most spectacular of the creations Suzanne had designed for her new wardrobe. When Ashleigh questioned her about her abrupt about-face, the redhead had merely smiled enigmatically and said, "'Tis time we were makin' our way downstairs, darlin', but I promise, once we get there, ye'll be havin' yer answer soon enough—that is, if ye're able t' put two and two t'gither, which 'tis sure ye are.''

Now, as they made their way into the throng of beautifully dressed ladies and gentlemen in the huge room, Ashleigh saw her friend casting about, as if in search of something, but just as she was about to ask her what she sought, a familiar voice broke in.

''Well, if I ever had any doubts about the value I'd receive for the outrageous fees that French seamstress charged for her services, they've been handily squashed this evening,'' said Brett as he came up to them. ''The two of you look absolutely ravishing, and while I hope I'm the first to tell you so, judging by the heads you're turning with your entrance, I know I shall not be the last.''

Smiling her appreciation at his words, Ashleigh glanced about the room and found he spoke the truth. Underscoring the sudden lull in the buzz of conversation that had filled the room when she and Megan first entered, there was the unmistakably appreciative gaze of every male in the drawing room as it focused on the two women, coupled with the assessing stares of most of the women as well.

''Unless I'm mistaken,'' Brett continued, ''we'll soon be besieged by a press of gentlemen begging for introductions, Megan. Are you prepared for the crush?''

Megan gave the room another cursory glance, then looked at the duke. ''I've no problem with admirin' males, if that's yer meanin', Yer Grace, but I was rather lookin' forward t' makin' an introduction meself.'' She glanced down at Ashleigh. ''Ah, ye see, there's someone I think the colleen here has yet t' meet, and, ah . . .''

Brett noticed the sudden flush of color that heightened the pink of Megan's cheeks. Hmm, so that was the way of things, was it? He'd had his suspicions after coming upon Megan and Patrick earlier in the hallway upstairs, but Patrick had grown uncharacteristically closemouthed about his meeting with the tall beauty when he'd questioned him about it.

Brett chuckled as he placed his hand lightly on Megan's shoulder and leaned to whisper in her ear. ''I think you'll find what you're looking for in the small drawing room across the hall. A few of the guests have gotten involved in a discussion there with Percy Shelley and his thoughts on the Irish Question."

"Ah," said Megan, a delicious smile turning up the corners of her mouth, "a subject after me own heart.... Ashleigh, Yer Grace—" she nodded "—I'll be askin' ye t' excuse me presence fer a wee while, but I'll be back before ye know I've been gone." And with the soft rustle of her cloth-of-gold skirts, she turned and left the room.

"Megan, what—?" Ashleigh turned puzzled eyes toward Brett. "What was that all about? I—I've never seen Megan acting so oddly!"

Brett chuckled softly. "I think she means to answer you with a surprise she has in mind, and far be it from me to spoil a lady's surprises! I'm afraid you'll just have to wait *'a wee while,'* my dear. I think—"

"Brett!" a male voice interrupted. "Egad, but it's been a while, eh?"

Brett and Ashleigh turned to find a medium-tall, middle-aged man with pale blond hair approaching them. By his side was Elizabeth Hastings.

Brett's tone was cool—even a bit bored, Ashleigh thought— as he answered the older man with a curt nod. "M'lord. I see you've finally made it over here."

"The deuce, I swear! You know I'd have come about a bit earlier, but the girls'd have none of it." The man shot Elizabeth an accusing glance.

"Now, father," said Elizabeth, "you know you aren't able to abide these lengthy house parties. Lady Margaret and I had only your best interests at heart."

"Miss Ashleigh Sinclair," Brett intervened, "allow me to introduce Lord David Hastings, Lady Elizabeth's father and my nearest neighbor."

As Ashleigh curtseyed, Lord David took a moment to look her over before bending over her hand with an exaggerated bow. "Charmed, m'dear," he murmured. As he spoke, Ashleigh smelled the scent of brandy on his breath.

Then Lord David turned toward Brett. "Egad, Your Grace, she's a real beauty, she is." Then, to Elizabeth, "Small wonder she's got you hopping, eh, m'dear?" This was accompanied by a small, sly grin.

Elizabeth's silver eyes narrowed as they fell on Ashleigh, but just as she was about to say something, her father turned abruptly and hailed a passing footman bearing a tray.

"I say, my good fellow," said his lordship, "I'll be having one of those." He moved rapidly toward the footman with one arm reaching toward the tray.

The expression on Elizabeth's face changed to one of annoyance. "Father, really, *must* you?" She turned and followed Lord David, adding, "Oh, where *is* Auntie Meg, anyway?"

Brett glanced at Ashleigh who was watching David Hastings down a glass of amber liquid in one gulp. "My erstwhile neighbor and future father-in-law," he mocked with a grimace of distaste, "present-day scion and crest bearer of the infamous Hastingses!"

Ashleigh watched Lord David reach for a second glass of liquor and raise it to his lips before turning her eyes toward Brett. "I . . . take it you're not overly fond of the man."

Brett gave a bitter laugh. "An understatement, if you've ever made one, my dear, for what is there to be fond of in a man who spends all his waking hours drinking himself into a stupor?—unless, of course, he's intercepted by his daughter or my great-aunt, if she's around. And then, if he manages sobriety long enough, what is there to be fond of in what's left? For without drink, he's the dullest nonentity you could imagine, a man singularly without opinions, passions or convictions of any sort. God, what a waste of human flesh and blood."

As they spoke, Ashleigh watched Elizabeth return from where she'd disappeared at the far end of the room, Lady Margaret by her side. Together, the two women seemed to swoop down on Lord David with hugely disapproving expressions on their faces and, a few seconds later, escort him toward a door at the opposite end of the drawing room.

Brett followed her glance, then met it as she turned back to face him. "The reason you've only just now met his lordship is that those two ladies—" he nodded in the direction of Elizabeth's and Margaret's disappearing skirts "—haven't allowed him to join this gathering until now. If he'd put in an appearance any earlier, he'd most likely be under the table somewhere by now—or sleeping it off in an upstairs chamber. But my fiancée and her godmother usually forestall such behavior by keeping a pretty tight rein on him—thank God! I suppose there's something to be said for Margaret's high-handedness at times, after all."

At the mention of Margaret's name in conjunction with the Hastingses, Ashleigh's thoughts flew back to her encounter with Lady Jane Hastings, and she was just about to comment on this when Brett looked up, past her shoulder, and a wide grin creased his face.

"Ah, here you two are!" he exclaimed.

Ashleigh whirled about to see Megan coming through the doorway through which she'd disappeared earlier. But it was the tall, dashing figure at her side that made her gasp and then freeze where she stood.

Brett caught her reaction and glanced down to find her staring straight ahead as all the blood drained from her face. "Ashleigh?" he questioned softly. "Are you all right?"

Ashleigh stared at the beloved face that had haunted her thoughts and dreams for twelve long years and wondered if she wasn't dreaming now. *"Patrick?"* she at last managed to whisper. Then, finding her voice over the lump of emotion that had formed in her throat, she shouted, "Patrick! Oh, my God... *Patrick*!"

Patrick St. Clare gazed, bewildered, for a moment at the exquisitely beautiful young woman standing beside Brett, wondering at the stricken look on her face. Then, as he heard her speak, he noticed the tiny mole high on her left cheek, and a shock of recognition rocked him.

*"Ashleigh!"* he shouted, even as he rushed forward to sweep her into his arms. "Ashleigh, darling, *is it really you?*"

Ashleigh couldn't speak as the old familiar arms enveloped her. Mutely, she nodded into her brother's chest as sobs began to shake her slender frame.

"Ah, God in Heaven, *I cannot believe it!*" cried Patrick, his own voice threatened with tears. "Little one... oh, little one, I knew I'd find you.... Oh, thank God!"

Brett and Megan stood beside them wordlessly, although, by the expression on their faces, it was difficult to tell which was more thunderstruck by the events of the past several seconds.

At last Patrick broke his hold on Ashleigh, but only long enough to place her at arm's length while he perused her tear-streaked, laughing face. Then, his laughter joining hers as a roomful of guests looked on, he drew her boldly to him again, lifting her off the floor as he swung her about in a joyful embrace.

Ashleigh was alternately laughing and crying as she cried, "Oh, Patrick, I thought you were dead! Oh, I love you so *much!*"

"I love you, too, sweet, darling sister!" Patrick's big voice boomed, tears running unashamedly down his rugged cheeks. "I never gave up hope, did you know that?"

At last he set her down in front of him, taking a moment to let his gaze wander completely over her fragile form. "You've become a beauty, little one," he said softly at last. "Every bit the beauty that was the promise of your youth."

Suddenly Patrick's gaze flickered to Brett, and when it returned to Ashleigh, he questioned, "But how is it you've come to be here, at Ravensford Hall? I was just a few days' short of tearing London apart, looking for you."

Ashleigh stared into her brother's deep blue eyes—eyes so much like her own. How could she begin to explain how it was she'd come to be here? In her childhood there'd never been anything but total honesty and truth between them, but the circumstances of her coming to Ravensford Hall were far more complicated than the childish fears and confidences she'd shared with Patrick all those years ago. Time... she needed time to think on this, but, seeing the expectant expression on Patrick's face, she knew she couldn't dodge his question entirely at this point, and so she decided to give him the safest part of the truth for the moment.

After a glance in Brett's direction, she returned her eyes to her brother's. "Patrick," she smiled, "you'll be happy to know I am currently Brett Westmont's ward."

Patrick heard her words and remained stone still for several seconds as he digested their import. Then his features went rigid, and a moment later he turned a cold blue gaze on the man who'd been his lifelong friend.

"Your Grace," Patrick said quietly, an undercurrent of steel lacing his softly spoken words, "I think I shall have to kill you."

# Chapter Twenty

Ashleigh sat in the blue velvet armchair in her chamber and thought. She was very still. As it had for a good while now, her mind tripped desperately over the facts that had been lodged there, one by one, since the fateful moment, the night before, when her beloved Patrick had come back from the dead.

First, there was the excitement that had erupted among the amazed dinner guests when they witnessed the emotional scene of recognition between Patrick and her. But it was an excitement that gave way to puzzled, sidelong glances and hushed whispers after Megan suddenly coaxed Patrick and Brett out of the drawing room following a few low-spoken words between the two men, for it left only Ashleigh and a grim-faced Lady Margaret to see everyone through the rest of the evening.

That dinner party had been one of the most difficult events of Ashleigh's adult life. Hour after hour, she had somehow managed to play the perfect hostess, making small talk, seeing to the efficiency of the serving staff, forcing a smile she did not feel, while the minutes ticked by with her heart racing and her brain in a turmoil, wondering what was happening in another part of the Hall, expecting at any moment to hear the sounds of a violent quarrel, or worse, a duel taking place.

Adroitly, she had sidestepped and parried the barrage of questions directed her way. How long had she been an orphan? How had she come to believe her brother dead? Could she account for the variation in the spellings of their surname that had, perhaps, made it difficult for Patrick to locate her?

How did it feel to realize she was now the *Honourable* Miss Sinclair, and how was it she had not taken the title earlier, even in her years in the orphanage?

On and on, the questions had come, but somehow, Ashleigh had managed, until at last the hour had grown late and the dancing began. Then the dancing had ended, and there had still been no word from upstairs; still no Patrick, still no Megan, still no Brett, duke of Ravensford. Finally, when it became apparent that His Grace had inexplicably deserted them—for the one question their rearing and manners forbade their asking had to do with this apparent rudeness on the part of their host—one by one, these polite members of the *ton* had taken their leave, this accompanied by sympathetic looks directed at Ashleigh, Lady Margaret and Lady Elizabeth, until at last, the three women had found themselves alone.

Of course, that had set the stage for the following scenes: Elizabeth's tirade over her "insufferable humiliation" as she raced upstairs to seek Brett out; Margaret's tight-lipped anger as she followed; and finally, the discovery, by all three women, of Brett and Patrick in the library with Megan, where the duke, white with suppressed anger, had just completed the signing of a document of betrothal—to wed, as a somber-faced Patrick put it, "the girl he has wronged, my sister, Ashleigh St. Clare!"

Now, as she sat in the chair, Ashleigh felt herself wince as she relived that mind-wrenching moment. She remembered feeling the blood drain from her face as she gazed at her brother in disbelief, even as Elizabeth Hastings's shriek of denial rent the air, followed quickly by Margaret Westmont's gasp of outrage; and then the older woman had actually *smiled* when Elizabeth resolutely marched forward and struck Brett across the face!

Immediately afterward, Ashleigh now realized, much that happened became a blur. She vaguely recalled Brett ordering Margaret to remove herself "and that screeching harpy" from the chamber, faintly recalled Megan and Patrick rushing to her side as the room began to spin, and then, suddenly, all had gone black.

That had been late last night, when she had fainted and been carried to her chamber—here, where she'd chosen to remain, even after Megan and Patrick had summoned Hettie Busby and they'd revived her with salts and cold compresses. Pleading shock and weariness, she'd succeeded in sending Megan and her brother away, saying she needed time by herself...time in which to rest...and to think....

But, of course, the morning had come, and with it a solicitous inquiry from Patrick, saying he was concerned for her health and thought they ought to talk. And talk they did, with Patrick giving her a quick summary of his time away, the amnesia that kept him from locating his past, the prosperous years in America where he now made his home, and his use of an earlier spelling of their family's name when beginning his seafaring venture, in a youthful effort to be his own man, to avoid capitalizing on the fact that he was a baronet's son and scion of a family that, although no longer wealthy, had one of the oldest and most respected names in the peerage.

Then it was her turn, and Ashleigh haltingly went over the significant details of her life during the past twelve years, culminating in the awkward series of events that had led to her final arrival and position at Ravensford Hall.

Then had come her heartfelt pleading with him to cease this madness to have her wed to Brett Westmont. She had seen the anger in Brett's face, read the fury in those turquoise eyes as they'd briefly fallen on her when her brother broke the news; Brett Westmont was as opposed to this marriage as others in the household, and they both knew the severity of *those* forces of opposition! Why couldn't he see that this would constitute a grave mistake?

But Patrick, for all his loving, gentle looks, had been adamant, and no amount of pleading could persuade him to change his mind; Brett Westmont might be his closest friend in England, but either he would do the proper thing by Patrick's beloved sister, or Patrick would see him dead.

Seeing the resolution in her brother's eyes, and recalling all too well the mind-set that had always made him a determined man once he set his will to something, Ashleigh had at last relented. She felt she had no choice; she certainly didn't want a man's death on her conscience, nor did she relish the thoughts of the consequences to Patrick, should this occur. Of course, neither did she wish a marriage to a man who, given the temperament she'd witnessed from time to time, would probably come to despise her for it . . . but she wished for the alternatives even less.

So now, as she sat here trying to piece together the incidents that had led to this unhappy state of affairs and make some sense out of them, she also awaited the arrival of Megan. She'd sent word to her friend that she would be happy to see her sometime after the dinner hour, although Ashleigh had taken her meal in her chamber, on a tray, and then had only picked at the food, pushing it about her plate as she'd mulled everything over in her mind.

As if her thoughts of the tall redhead had summoned her, at that moment there came a soft tapping at the door, followed by an Irish brogue saying, "Ashleigh, are ye there?"

"Yes, Megan, please come in."

The door opened and her friend entered, a gentle, questioning smile on her face. She moved quickly toward the chair from which Ashleigh rose, and bent to give her a fierce hug.

"Ah, *macushla*, it breaks me heart t' see ye lookin' so sad! There, there, it cannot be as bad as ye think . . . ye'll see! We'll see a way yet t' make lemonade out o' the lemon we've been handed!"

At the sounds of her friend's words and the feel of her comforting arms about her, Ashleigh at last gave way to the tears that had hovered all day. Suddenly, great wrenching sobs began to shake her small frame, ushering in a torrent that seemed as if it would never cease.

And all the while Megan held her, letting her cry out her heartbreak, her doubts, her confusion. Megan had a long acquaintance with those things; she'd been there before . . . many times.

After some time the weeping ceased, dwindling down to small, hiccoughing sobs that finally ebbed as well, fading into a long, shuddering sigh. Here Ashleigh raised her swollen, tear-streaked face to her friend, saying, "Oh, Megan, help me, please. What am I to do? How am I going to make it through all of this?"

Megan gently smoothed back from her forehead some of the strands of hair that had fallen over her face and gave Ashleigh a small, promising smile. "Ye'll make it, just as ye've managed t' make it through the last dozen years or so, darlin' girl— by the pluck o' yer heart and the grit o' that fine spirit ye were born with. Ye'll see." Suddenly Megan's eyes narrowed and grew hard as the emeralds they favored. "There be some in this house that think His Grace has found himself saddled with a guttersnipe fer a duchess. But ye, me lass, are about t' prove them wrong. Unless I miss me guess, they're shortly t' discover His Grace has found himself a queen!"

"You're . . . resigned to this match for me, then, Megan?" Ashleigh kept her eyes raised to her friend's face as she allowed her to lead her toward the bed.

Megan sighed as she turned down the coverlet and began to help Ashleigh undress. "'Tis what yer brother wishes fer ye, darlin', and I'm after thinkin' 'tis not the time t' be doubtin' him. Ye've been without family fer so long, 'twould be a mistake, I fear, t' be disregardin' the blessed miracle that brought the protection and guidance o' one back into yer life." She removed the gown she'd finished unbuttoning and turned toward the chest of drawers where Ashleigh's nightclothes were kept. "I'm thinkin' 'tis time t' turn yer cares over t' someone who has yer own best welfare at heart.

"Lean on yer brother, Ashleigh," she said as she returned with a delicate pink-and-white dimity night rail. "He's lived far more than either o' us, and t' me way o' thinkin', the man knows what he's about. Ye could do far worse than heedin' Patrick St. Clare!"

A small smile found its way to Ashleigh's lips as she viewed Megan's face in the growing darkness. "You're . . . impressed with my brother, aren't you, Megan?" she queried.

An unusual glimmer of emerald light danced in Megan's eyes before the tall woman hurriedly turned and began making an extraordinary fuss over tidying up the clothes Ashleigh had discarded. "Well-l-l," she said at last, after a too-long silence, "he *is* a fine, upstandin' figure o' the best his sex has t' offer, and he certainly handled that rogue, Ravensford, in short order, and he obviously loves ye more than his own life and limb... aye, I find all that impressive...."

Ashleigh eyed her carefully for a moment. She had the feeling Megan was not dealing directly with her question, but as the redhead had suddenly turned away to adjust the wick of a nearby lamp and avoided her gaze, she shrugged and decided to let the matter drop.

Yawning as she stepped up to the high tester bed and slipped between its silken sheets, Ashleigh forced herself to ask the question that had been nagging all day; the rest could wait until tomorrow. "Megan, does anyone know... That is, what— what has—has Brett been saying or—or doing through all this?"

Megan gave her a long, thoughtful look. "He's not been up here t' see ye, has he? Or made any attempts t' talk with ye?"

A solemn shake of the head.

Megan sighed, then reached to place her hand over Ashleigh's, which were folded over her chest atop the coverlet in a posture that was curiously childlike... and forlorn. "Ye must know that the two o' them had fierce words over the matter last night. Oh, 'twasn't about the business o' how His Grace came t' do ye wrong. Ye must have guessed Patrick had already heard about that—minus yer identity, until he put two and two t'gither there in the drawin' room.... No, it had more t' do with Patrick tryin' t' fathom the nature o' His Grace's attitude toward the incident and toward *ye*, or, more particularly, toward *women* in his life.

"Ah, Ashleigh, I fear the man's all twisted apart inside when it comes t' females! I suspected somethin' o' the like before, but..." Sadly, Megan shook her head. "It has somethin' t' do with the way he was raised by that grandfather o' his, the old duke... and with betrayals and losses goin' way back t' his childhood."

Here Ashleigh interrupted with a question that had been plaguing her for some time. "What happened to—to Brett's mother? Did she die a long time ago?"

Megan shook her head. "That's just it—she didn't die. There was some trouble with the Westmonts and she...she left, when His Grace was but a wee lad. I think—"

*"She deserted her own child?"* Ashleigh sat up, wide-awake now, with a look of horror imprinted on her face.

"I'm not sure. The duke's words seemed t' imply it, but Patrick..." Megan's expression grew speculative, then suddenly, the green eyes met Ashleigh's. "Ashleigh, how much do ye know about the friendship between yer Patrick and the duke? How far back does it go?"

"I—I'm not sure. Since they're about the same age, and my family's home was located not too far from here, I guess I just assumed they knew each other back then, when I was just a baby and too young to be aware of it. I know I never met any Westmonts as a child, but that never puzzled me after coming here to Ravensford Hall as an adult. My father was only a minor nobleman, you see, and the lofty Westmonts—"

"Didn't Patrick talk about it, or about what happened t' him durin'—"

"Oh, wait! I think he did say something...it was when he spoke of his seafaring venture and changing the spelling of our name to the old one...he didn't want any special privilege, just as—as *Brett* hadn't when they were cabin boys together, years earlier! I'd almost forgotten that because I was so distraught over..." She stopped and made a helpless gesture with her hands.

"Hmm," murmured Megan. "I think perhaps we'd better be havin' a talk with Patrick. The saints only know, we can use all the information we can get t' shed some light on the nature o' that puzzle ye're about t' wed!"

At the mention of the man who was to become her husband, a look of panic flooded Ashleigh's face. "Megan," she whispered, "I know he—he hates this! I saw his face in the library. We all did."

"Hush, darlin'. Don't fash yerself so... and, besides ... I'm not so sure.... Oh, I know the man's full o' more than his share o' hatin'—but I doubt that what ye saw in the library had as much t' do with weddin' ye as it had t' do with bein' forced t' somethin' that wasn't his own doin'. He's full o' more than his share o' pride, too, I can tell ye!"

"B-but, Megan, it amounts to the same thing! He resents Patrick for forcing it, and me for—for the part I play in it."

Megan gave her a sly look. "Would ye be wagerin' on the prospect he'd rather have the Lady Elizabeth?"

Ashleigh's thoughts flew back to the day before, to images of Brett and his fiancée walking together... talking together, and for some strange reason, she felt a lump form in her throat.

Megan saw her look and laughed. "Ye can stop fashin' yerself where her High-and-Mightiness is concerned. Take me word fer it, *macushla*, he's gladly rid o' her, 'screechin' harpy' that she be!"

They shared a small laugh over this, but soon Ashleigh's face grew somber again. "But Megan, that still doesn't mean he wants marriage to *me*, any... any more than I do," she finished lamely.

"Aye," said Megan, the word coming out in a sigh as she reached to tuck the coverlet gently about Ashleigh's shoulders. "But the deed's been set in motion, Yer Grace-t'-Be, and that's the fact o' the matter. Now all we can do is work t' find a way t' make it better." She leaned toward the nightstand to extinguish the lamp. "Trust me, darlin'," she whispered as she bent to place a kiss on Ashleigh's brow in the darkness. "I've found a way out o' worse fixes than this before, and I'll find a way t' help us do it again."

With quiet footsteps, Megan left the chamber as Ashleigh's even breathing told her she slept.

Minutes passed, and then, noiselessly, the door to the chamber opened and a tall figure stepped into the darkness. Without a sound, Brett walked toward the bed until he stood beside it and gazed down at the shadowy form of its sleeping occupant.

He wasn't entirely sure why he'd chosen to come here at this time, when he was sure she was asleep. He only knew that, ever since early this morning, when he'd ridden purposefully away from the Hall with the idea of separating himself from the sources of his anger, he'd been hard put to keep thoughts of her at bay. Even when he'd thrown himself into the work of the estate, ceaselessly pushing himself for hours, to attend to things that, under more ordinary circumstances, would have taken him days to accomplish, he'd been unable to dismiss her from his mind.

But the anger had won in the end, refusing to yield even when, after only a light supper of bread and cheese, he'd closed himself in his chamber and attempted to blot it out with a bottle of brandy, ruthlessly downed. Well, the brandy had almost accomplished what the hours of work had not . . . *almost*. He was no longer furious with Patrick, of that he was sure. Indeed, he'd come to view the actions of his friend with a rational eye, seeing them as nothing untoward—nothing, in fact, too different from the way *he* would have reacted, had their positions been reversed. Patrick's motivations had sprung from a sense of upholding his family's honor; Brett could readily relate to that.

And even his fury with that hysterical bitch, Elizabeth, had been reduced once again to the level of disdainful contempt with which he'd always regarded her. He'd even had a moment of faintly amused pity for Elizabeth, thinking that now she'd be forced to market her coldly chaste body in exchange for a title beneath that of duchess. There just weren't that many eligible dukes around!

But where Ashleigh Sinclair was concerned . . . or was it now St. Clare? The corners of his mouth twisted into a smile of grim self-deprecation as he thought upon the ironic little quirk of fate that had caused him to separate the two spellings of his friend's surname in his mind, or, rather, the two *pronunciations*! What dullness of wit had it been that had led him to think of Patrick only in the Americanized version of his name? *He*, who'd been surviving by his wits for years when it came to making a success of his work for the crown! Surely if he'd been on his toes, when he'd heard the chit's name was Sinclair and, already having an awareness of Patrick's search for his sister, he'd have given pause. . . .

Brett's smile grew even grimmer as he stopped himself— suddenly bitterly aware he was wasting productive energy with such self-flagellation. It was keeping him from focusing on the real source of his concern: the young woman lying in the bed before him and the state of confusion she brought to his mind.

Why was he still so angry with *her*? And why were his angry images of Ashleigh equally riddled with relentless memories of the night he'd taken her body, of overwhelming longings to taste that sweet flesh again? Even now, as he stood here above her in the darkness, it was all he could do not to slip in beside her and take her into his arms, to make delicious, prolonged and passionate love to her until she yielded to him, erasing the irrational anger from his mind.

A rational, practical part of him told him it might be guilt that played the demon, but he was not convinced. If guilt were the culprit, why then should he not welcome the chance to make amends, assuaging it by "making an honest woman out of her"? After all, she was far sweeter by nature, and therefore infinitely preferable, to Elizabeth. Since he must eventually wed anyway, why not this beautiful baronet's daughter who pleased his flesh as well? Marrying her would serve several purposes at once, even mending and solidifying his friendship with Patrick, one of the few men he respected and admired. What, then, was his problem?

Suddenly his gaze shifted to the window, which, as it was a warm night, had been left open and the drapes undrawn to encourage the breeze that was gently wafting through. At that moment the moon, which was nearly full, appeared from behind a high, passing cloud, throwing a shaft of silvery light across the coverlet and onto Ashleigh's still face.

*God, she's lovely!* thought Brett as he watched the moonlight wash those delicately shaped features, imparting them with an ethereal glow that made them seem as if they were not of this world. Slowly, he let his eyes follow the fragile contours . . . the slightly flaring brows, the sooty fringe of midnight lashes, the small, straight nose and finely drawn mouth, its ripe lips barely parted in slumber. His glance sought the dark mass of her hair, separating it from the inky shadows on her pillow, tracing the richness of its luxuriant silk as the moonlight caught the shine of a curling lock here and there. It was a silent poem to all that was beautiful in the human form—lovely not only for the physical perfection residing there, but from something far more ephemeral.

Here was beauty from an inner light—the loveliness of child-just-become-woman, of the spring of life in its freshness and goodness and, yes, innocence, in the best sense of the term. Here was a female who, even in her waking hours lost none of the qualities he viewed now. Here was no trick of features temporarily released in slumber, only to revert to the artful poses of the real world when she awakened, as he'd had occasion to witness countless times in the women he'd bedded. Ashleigh Sinclair was totally different from all the other women he'd known, and it was this, he realized at last, that troubled him.

When would it begin? When would the cankerous poison that he knew to be a portion of her sex begin to insinuate itself, as it surely must, destroying all he saw here, changing it before his very eyes as he lived with her day by day? The very notion sent a sharp twist of pain to his center, causing him to turn his head and look away.

Oh damn! At this very moment she could be visited with dreams that turned her guileless thoughts to ones of bitterness and revenge for what was being forced upon her. He'd seen her face when her brother broke the news. The only thing that matched it was his memory of her reaction that night at Hampton House when she'd learned he'd come for her. But then, at least, he'd been able to view her with some detachment. Such was not the case now.

Now he must shortly bind himself to this enchanting creature he'd just begun to come to know and proceed to watch helplessly as she slowly turned evil.... From deep within the recesses of memory Brett felt the ghost of an old pain: it had happened before, and it would happen again. *Oh, Christ! It did not bear thinking on!*

With a convulsive swallowing of the bitter bile that rose in his throat, Brett shut his eyes for a moment in a vain attempt to blot out the pain, then whirled and stumbled blindly from the room.

# Chapter Twenty-One

A fortnight later Ashleigh stood in the mauve-and-cream-decorated bedchamber upstairs in the dowager's cottage near the lake and looked about her with a sigh. In a few more hours it would be done; she would be wed to Brett Westmont, ninth duke of Ravensford, and spend her wedding night here. Yet, why did it all seem unreal to her? Why did it feel as if it were someone else standing here in an exquisite cream silk gown lavished with old lace, waiting to become a duchess?

Once again, her eyes traversed the expanse of the chamber that had been hurriedly refurbished for this occasion. A wry smile broke out as Ashleigh considered the way this had come about. She had seen almost nothing of Brett since the awkward night of their betrothal, but one morning soon thereafter, he had sent Hettie Busby to her with a note saying it had been a tradition for the Westmont brides to take up residence in the dowager's cottage in the weeks prior to their nuptials; that in earlier times it had often been with a Westmont dowager in residence as well, but as the nearest thing to a dowager Ravensford Hall had was the Lady Margaret, he was sending instead his housekeeper with instructions to take Ashleigh to the cottage with a crew of workmen and others from the Hall to see it was made ready to receive a bride.

That had been more than ten days ago, and in the ensuing time, no amount of industry or expense had been spared in seeing the Tudor-style cottage redecorated. In record time dozens of painters, plasterers, carpenters and footmen had swarmed over the structure's ten rooms—five below, including a kitchen and accommodations for a small staff, and five above: this spacious bedchamber; a sitting room; a dressing room; one maid's room; and a small drawing room that, like the bedchamber, had had a small wooden balcony added during Queen Anne's time, when the dowager had been a former French *comtesse* who thought the lake too lovely a sight to be viewed only from indoors on a warm evening.

Thoughts of the balconies prompted Ashleigh to wander toward the French doors that had remained closed for most of the day, owing to a soft rainfall that had been with them since last night. But now she saw a shaft of sunlight breaking through the receding clouds of an afternoon that was growing brighter, turning the droplets of water that clung to the newly replaced balcony railing and the leaves of a nearby chestnut tree into tiny prisms of light.

With a quick movement, she pulled the doors open and was instantly greeted by a rush of cool, sweet air. It bore all the freshness of an English summer's day washed clean by the kind of soft rains she would always remember as the sweetest part of Kent. Drifting up to her from the lovely flower garden that had not been neglected during the years the cottage remained vacant came the faint but heady scent of damask roses, while her glance met with a riot of color she soon perceived in the more definitive shapes of geraniums, lupines and lamb's ears, and then climbing hydrangeas on a small stone wall near the front gate.

Her eyes lifted to the near distance where the waters of the lake lay tranquil and smooth. A pair of elegant white swans rounded a small island in the center, then seemed to check themselves, pause and swing back in the direction from which they'd come.

Then Ashleigh saw what prompted their behavior. Cutting swiftly across the lake from the other side was a small skiff, or rowboat. It bore two people; the one that rowed looked like a liveried footman, judging by the vermilion color of his coat; the other appeared to be a woman, for she wore a bright, flower-bedecked bonnet that seemed to be slightly askew on her head. The boat was moving unusually fast.

Carefully raising her silk skirts to avoid tripping on them, Ashleigh turned and headed for the door. There was no one else with her at the cottage right now, as Hettie and Megan had gone to tell Patrick she was ready to be escorted to the church in the village—where a special license obtained by Brett, with Patrick's urging, had made it possible for the vicar to marry them in such short order—and, Ashleigh realized, since whoever occupied that rowboat was heading for the cottage, she would have to see what they wanted.

Moments later she was out the front door and walking toward the gate, just in time to see the skiff touch the shoreline. As the red-coated man jumped out and began to haul it further onto dry grass, she got a closer view of the bonneted passenger. It was Lady Jane Hastings.

"Oh, Miss Sinclair, Miss Sinclair!" cried the little rotund figure as the liveried servant helped her from the boat. "I'm ever so glad to have found you still at the cottage!"

Holding her skirts carefully aside to avoid catching the droplets of rain that still clung to the hollyhocks nearby, Ashleigh released the latch on the gate and passed through, then walked down the cobblestoned path toward her approaching visitor.

"Why, Lady Jane, what a pleasant surprise! It's nice to see you again," Ashleigh told her with sincerity. She'd become genuinely fond of the little woman during their brief encounter the day of the party. It came from nothing she could put her finger on, but there was something about her that invited instant sympathy and kindness. All the more reason, Ashleigh thought with a brief inner grimace as she extended her hand in welcome, to deplore the insensitive behavior of Margaret Westmont toward this sweet little woman that day.

"Oh, Miss Sinclair, I hope you'll forgive this intrusion, on this, of all days," said Lady Jane as she panted from the exertion of having climbed out of the skiff and then fairly run up the path. "It—it was my only chance to come away, you see." She glanced briefly over her shoulder to scan the lake, then back at Ashleigh. "They'd be terribly upset with me if they knew. That's why I had to wait this late, until Blye here came off duty to do the rowing. Blye and I go back a long way, don't we, Blye?"

The old man's crumpled lips rounded into a yellow-toothed smile. "Yes, m'lady."

"Well, Lady Jane," said Ashleigh, "won't you come inside? My brother is coming with the carriage soon to take me to the village, but perhaps I can fix a quick cup of tea before—"

"Oh, dear me, no," smiled Lady Jane, "and, please, *do* call me Jane. It's all I'm accustomed to. But, no, my dear. It's awfully kind of you to invite me, but I wouldn't dream of it. I only came to—to wish you well—on your wedding day, you see...and to—" She turned again to the patiently waiting Blye. "Blye, dear, I've forgotten them in the boat. Would you be so kind...?"

"Of course, m'lady." With a polite nod, the old retainer turned and headed for the skiff.

Jane returned her attention to Ashleigh. "My, my, how lovely you look, all dressed up in your bridal finery...." Suddenly a faraway look crept into the old woman's eyes. "I was a bride once, too...a very...beautiful bride, or so they said. Everyone came...it was all so lovely, with the church all decked in roses and the children's choir singing...."

All at once Jane's eyes went from misty to dark. "I was a mother once, too," she said, but her voice was so low, Ashleigh had to bend to catch the words. "But it all turned wrong...all wrong...and empty...yes, an empty cradle.... But they filled it up again soon enough, oh yes they did. Made me a mother, double, they did! But—" she raised forlorn eyes to Ashleigh "—but I wasn't really a mother. I tried to tell them, but they wouldn't listen! Can you understand? She forbade them to listen!"

Ashleigh grew uncomfortable, not so much from the strangely disjointed words Jane Hastings uttered, although in themselves they were perplexing enough, but from the chill, hollow sound of her voice as she spoke—not to mention the look of anguish that shone from her hazel eyes.

"Jane," she said softly, "perhaps you've overtaxed yourself coming across the lake. If you like, we can sit—"

"Oh, here they are, fresh as when I picked them!" interrupted Jane as she whirled to meet Blye. "Thank you, Blye." Turning back to Ashleigh, she handed her a bouquet of gorgeous tea roses. "For you on your wedding day, my dear. I grew them myself, in my own garden, and while I may not be allowed to see you at the church, I do hope you'll let them take my good wishes with you when you go." The gentle smile that accompanied this was filled with warmth, bearing not a hint of the dark looks that had haunted her eyes a moment before.

*"Ohh,"* said Ashleigh, smiling and pulling the bouquet toward her to inhale its scent. *"How beautiful!"* She breathed in the soft, heady fragrance, then looked at Jane with a smile. "Jane Hastings," she said with a small tremor, "you've just given me the loveliest wedding gift a bride could wish for. Thank you. Thank you so much."

"Not at all, my dear. I knew you would love them, and so I determined that you should have them, didn't I, Blye? Well, we must be off, now. So sorry to run, but they'll be missing me before long if I don't." She turned and placed her hand on Blye's proffered arm, then paused a moment and turned back to Ashleigh. "Be happy, my dear. I wish it for you with all my heart. There are too many about who wish you ill, and—" she glanced at the bouquet "—well, my tea roses have always been lucky flowers, and I dearly hope they'll bring you luck, too."

She turned toward the lake again, but as the two started back down the path, Ashleigh cried out, "Wait! Please, I'll only be a moment!" and then darted toward the cottage.

A few moments later Ashleigh had what she wanted. Taken from the tiny springhouse behind the kitchen, it was a small bottle of fresh cream. She handed it to Jane.

The old woman's eyes grew wide, then bore the shimmer of instant tears. With a quick movement, she reached out and gave Ashleigh a hug about the shoulders. "How very kind you are, my dear. I shall never forget this. God keep you!'' Then she turned, took Blye's arm, and walked to the skiff.

Ashleigh watched them row out until they disappeared into the mist that was forming on the far side of the lake. She was still standing on the path holding the bouquet of tea roses and pondering the significance of some of the things she'd heard Jane Hastings say when the sounds of an approaching carriage drew her attention.

"There you are, sweetheart!" Patrick called out over the barking of a joyful Finn who bounded down the drive ahead of the brougham.

Laughingly ordering the wolfhound to "stay" before he could cover her gown with mud from his huge paws, Ashleigh patted his head and then turned her attention toward the carriage. There, being helped out by the liveried driver, she suddenly beheld the most striking couple she'd ever seen.

Patrick had followed Megan down from the brougham and the two of them stood together facing her. Tall and majestic, each of them wore attire befitting a guest at a duke's wedding. Patrick, in his black coat over a white satin waistcoat embroidered with gold thread, and black pantaloons with black and gold tasseled Hessians, was the image of the perfect Corinthian in heroic proportions; Megan, wearing a simply cut, yet utterly elegant, pale misty violet voile gown with a deep violet silk pelisse over it, played the perfect female counterpart to his masculine grandeur. With her glorious hair bound up with violet and gold bands into a high version of a Grecian coiffure, she appeared nearly as tall as he, and as they stood there, side by side, Ashleigh had to fight the notion that they had somehow always been together, having been wrought together to form a pair from the outset.

"Well, you two," she finally managed to say as they began to walk toward her, "Don't you look grand!"

"Not half so grand as the colleen we're lookin' at now," smiled Megan as she came to Ashleigh with an embrace. "Faith, but she's grown lovelier since I left t' fetch ye, Patrick.''

"Indeed, a beauty," murmured Patrick with a soft, tender look at his sister. "How are you, little one?"

"Well enough, I suppose," Ashleigh told him honestly. She and Patrick had spent many hours together, daily, since the morning of their initial talk, and she knew he entertained no illusions regarding her feelings toward this marriage. He knew she was reconciled to it as a means of honoring his wishes—for she loved him to distraction and told him so, often—but where her groom was concerned, her attitude was more one of resignation than reconciliation.

"But still not all that excited about becoming a duchess, I see," Patrick was saying.

"Oh, Patrick, surely you know me well enough by now, despite our years of separation! I really—"

"Cannot place all that much value on the importance of a title. Yes, yes, I know," said Patrick with a smile. "You know, Ashleigh, with sentiments like yours, you really ought to try living in America. You'd feel right at home there."

"And 'tis not surprisin' that that poet, Shelley, had sent an invitation t' Ashleigh t' visit him in London," Megan added. "Apparently he and his lady friend found her ideas t' their likin', too."

Patrick raised an eyebrow at his sister. "So now you're taking up with radicals, are you?" There was a teasing light in his blue eyes.

"Mr. Shelley and Miss Wollstonecraft? Why, I hardly spoke with them!" Ashleigh protested.

Patrick broke into easy laughter as he led her toward the brougham. "Bristles easily, doesn't she, Megan?"

Megan was also laughing. "Well now, Patrick, d' ye suppose 'tis against the rules fer a duchess t' bristle? Why, I'd have thought they were *twice* entitled t' do so!" She winked at Ashleigh. "All that upper crust makin' them so stiff in their skirts, ye know!"

"All right, all right, you two!" said Ashleigh, joining in their laughter. She recognized what they were doing, falling into this easy banter and cajolery. They were trying to ease her apprehension in the face of what was about to take place in the church, trying to lighten her mood as the time for the wedding drew near, and she loved them for it; therefore, she was determined not to let them down by showing just how fearful she actually did feel inside and readily matched them in their lighthearted tone. "Just remember, after today when you're out with me in public, I expect to be 'Your Graced' to the utmost."

"Oh, aye!" giggled Megan as they reached the carriage and she withdrew a cloth-of-gold, floor-length cape to place over Ashleigh's shoulders. "We'll 'Yer Grace' ye t' death, won't we, Patrick?"

"Of course," nodded her brother in mock solemnity as he and the driver helped them into the vehicle, "and bow low before her so much, she'll soon forget what our faces look like and begin to recognize us by the tops of our heads."

"Well, just see that you don't forget it!" said Ashleigh with all the imperiousness she could muster, even as the corners of her mouth twitched with humor.

The brougham's door shut, muffling the sounds of mingled laughter from its passengers, the driver took his seat at the reins, and, with a bark from Finn—unaccompanied, for a change, by Lady Dimples, for Hettie Busby, much to Patrick's relief, had heartily insisted Finn's porcine companion be left behind on so momentous an occasion—the carriage departed for the village.

# Chapter Twenty-Two

Despite all the banter about the pomp and ceremony that would come with being wed to a duke, the wedding was a simple one. Among other things, the Westmonts were in mourning, and while a small, quiet wedding during this period might have raised some of the staunchest eyebrows, a grander affair, to the *ton*, would have been considered beyond the pale. Therefore, when the brougham arrived at the small, early Norman church in the village, it was met there by only three people: the vicar, his wife and the groom.

Brett awaited them outside, beside a shiny black phaeton he'd driven himself. He looked, to Ashleigh, as handsome as he ever had, clad in black coat and breeches that contrasted with the snowy-white stock that he wore against his tanned, masculine face and a white waistcoat decorated with gold thread; like Patrick, he'd forgone the formality of silk hose and dress pumps, for the mud left behind by the recent rain rendered such footwear impractical, but instead of Hessians, he sported high black riding boots polished to a mirror shine.

Yet there was something beyond simple attire and good looks that struck the bride as she looked at the man she was about to marry. As he stood there with his booted feet planted well apart, his arms folded across his broad chest, she had the sense that something very male and primitive rested beneath that civilized facade. Raw, barely leashed power emanated from his every pore, giving her the feeling she was looking at something dangerous and invincible, and suddenly Ashleigh was afraid.

She was a fool to think Patrick hadn't underestimated the lengths to which he could push Brett Westmont, a double fool to think she had only to acquiesce and all might somehow be well, as Megan had implied. One look at those hard turquoise eyes, the angular planes of his face formed by those cheekbones, that implacable slash that was now his mouth, made her throat suddenly run dry, her chest go tight with fear. What was she doing here? How had she forgotten the dark, brooding side of this man who was still a stranger to her, and beyond that, an enigma? And what's more, now that she did remember, how was she going to escape?

But, even as she thought of it, the avenues of escape quickly closed to Ashleigh. She felt herself being handed down from the carriage, saw Mr. Smythe, the vicar, come forward to greet her tiny party, felt her feet moving inexorably closer to the man who gave her a last, unfathomable look before nodding to her, and following the vicar and Mrs. Smythe into the church.

As she walked with leaden feet toward the simple altar, she thought she heard Megan whisper a phrase of encouragement, but couldn't be sure. She felt the strength of Patrick's arm under her hand and clung to it as a solitary rock in a sinking world. Finally she heard only the centuries-old words being read from the Book of Common Prayer: "Dearly beloved..."

As the vicar intoned the words originally penned by Sir Thomas Cranmer, Brett gazed straight ahead at the altar, but in his mind's eye he saw Ashleigh. He wondered if she would ever look more beautiful . . . or more frightened. He'd watched her alight from the carriage with far more than the casual interest he'd schooled his features to display. That first glimpse had been enough to take his breath away as she seemed to float down to the ground, a vision in creamy ivory and rich gold, her black hair contrasting vividly with the light, translucent loveliness of her skin, softened only by the hint of a blush that spread across her cheeks as she paused to raise those huge blue eyes to him.

But then he'd seen her grow suddenly pale, her eyes become even larger in her face as her gaze fused for an instant with his. A moment later he witnessed a blank look replace the one of panic he knew he had not imagined in those eyes. It was then he realized how frightened she was, and he felt a moment's urge to rush forward and fold her into his arms, to murmur words of comfort and reassurance in those delicate, shell-like ears and to tell her she needn't be afraid.

But the moment had passed, and now he concentrated on not allowing it to repeat itself. That way lurked weakness, and where weakness resided, disaster followed. Besides, she had, rationally speaking, nothing to fear from him. Apart from the appalling circumstances of their first meeting, hadn't he treated her with utmost courtesy and respect? Hadn't he gone out of his way to be kind to her, bending over backward to see she was cared for, even going so far as to swear off intimate contact with her person? And this had by no means been easy, for the bald truth was, he wanted her . . . *Oh, yes, he wanted her. . . .*

And tonight he would at last again be able to have her. In that instant Brett glanced down at Ashleigh. As he heard her repeat the words " . . . for better for worse, for richer for poorer. . ." he suddenly wondered if he'd hit upon what had her quaking with fear. Was she frightened of the marriage bed? Mentally, Brett ticked off the events of their disastrous first encounter. God knew, he hadn't been gentle with her. Yes, that was quite likely the problem, then.

Suddenly Brett smiled inwardly to himself. This was a problem he could deal with! If he had prowess in any arena, it was in pleasing a woman in bed—if he chose to do so. All he need do, then, was to make sure he satisfied her tonight. Once she'd learned the pleasures that awaited her between his sheets, she'd come to lose her fears; then he could get his heir from her and all would be well. It was what marriage was all about, wasn't it?

With these last thoughts in mind, Brett allowed himself a small, victorious smile as he joined Ashleigh in kneeling to receive the vicar's blessing.

Following a wedding toast of champagne, which Brett had had sent ahead to the vicar, a benumbed Ashleigh stood beside the brougham that was to take her and Brett back to the dowager's cottage while Patrick drove Megan and himself to the Hall in the duke's phaeton. As she readied herself to be handed up into the carriage, Megan grasped her hands and bent down to give her a warm kiss on the cheek.

Ashleigh smiled her thanks with grateful eyes, then turned toward Patrick. Her brother gave her a long, tender look, then reached down to swoop her into his arms in a familiar bear hug.

"Be happy, my darling," he murmured with emotional fervor. "It's all I wish for you."

Ashleigh hugged him fiercely about the neck, much as she remembered doing as a child. "Oh, Patrick!" she murmured in a quaking voice. "I love you so!"

Then Brett was shaking Patrick's hand with assurances of no bitter feelings passing between them, and Ashleigh was clinging tightly to Jane Hastings's tea roses as Brett helped her into the brougham and climbed in beside her. And then, amid a murmur of good wishes, the driver signaled to his team and they were off.

After they were deposited at the cottage, Brett remained below to give instructions to the driver to have Old Henry send Raven and Irish Night to them the following morning, while Ashleigh went on upstairs. Walking past the open door to the drawing room, she saw someone had left ajar the French doors to the little balcony outside. Without thinking, she entered and walked to the balcony. It was growing dark and she could barely see the lake, which was melting into the deep purple shadows of dusk. Late-summer evening sounds of nightjars and crickets punctuated the silence, and these familiar noises should have given her comfort, but for whatever reasons, tonight they did not. Staring into the fading landscape, Ashleigh felt herself shiver, though the air was still warm. Then the tread of booted feet sounded on the stairs, causing her to whirl about and drop her bouquet of roses as Brett's voice broke the silence.

"Ashleigh? Ah, there you are!" He stood by the open door to the drawing room. "Ashleigh? Is something wrong?"

Determined to override the fears that had been plaguing her, Ashleigh forced a smile and crossed the room to meet him, saying, "No, not at all. I was merely enjoying the view."

"Ah, yes." He smiled. "Lovely, isn't it? But I fear I must persuade you to ignore it for now and join me in the sitting room." He gave her a small, enigmatic smile. "I've been given, ah, orders."

"Oh?" questioned Ashleigh as she allowed him to escort her down the short hallway. "What kind of orders?"

"I'm afraid your brother was being terribly mysterious. He merely told me that once we arrived here, we were to go directly to the sitting room without delay. Ah, here we are."

In the sitting room they came upon a small table set for two, with yet another bottle of champagne chilling beside a tea table laden with various silver-covered dishes and platters. A single red rose in a narrow vase sat in the middle of the small dinner table and, leaning against it, a folded piece of white vellum, which Brett quickly took and read aloud:

"'My luve is like a red, red rose....'
—May the two of you hear the words
—and come to hear the music!

Love,
Megan and Patrick"

"Why, those two silly romantics!" exclaimed Ashleigh, at a loss for what else to say. But she and Brett had endured a near-silent ride in the brougham, punctuated only by a few strained remarks about the improved weather and the excellent job the staff had done in restoring the cottage, and she felt she had to say something to bring about a thaw between them.

Brett regarded her with a small half smile. "Is that how you view things romantic, then?" he asked as he came forward to help her off with her cape. "Are they merely silly?"

"Oh, why...no!" exclaimed Ashleigh as she raised her eyes to his with a start. And her protest was genuine. For as far back as she could remember, she'd always been a romantic, from the time she was a little girl in her parents' house, when she would look for the first star in the sky at night and dream of the man she'd one day marry—and imbue him with Patrick's strengths and admirable qualities—right up through the long years at

Hampton House, when she'd believed in her heart that someday, somehow, someone would come to rescue her from those sordid surroundings, whisking her off into the night with wonderful words of love.

Only, now, as she stood uncertainly before this man she would actually be sharing her life with, it seemed none of that was to be. Now it seemed that dreams were only ashes, and romance was nothing more than a distant star for fools to wish upon....

Suddenly, and to her complete mortification, Ashleigh's eyes welled up with tears as she looked at him, and she had to fight a constriction in her throat. Embarrassed, she looked away, saying, "It...it's just that...I mean I—" But the dam broke, and she heard herself choke on a sob as twin tears traced their way down her face.

"Ashleigh...little one, what is it?" asked Brett as he turned her back toward him and drew her into his arms.

"Oh, Brett! This isn't at all the way I—the way it's supposed to be.... *It just isn't!*"

"Oh?" he questioned, an amused but tender smile on his face. "And just how is it ... supposed to be?"

Very conscious of his strong arms about her, his broad muscular chest against her cheek, Ashleigh pulled her head away as she made an effort to check the flow of her tears. "R-romantic," she managed as she gazed up into his gently inquiring eyes.

"Ah," said Brett, keeping one arm about her as he reached to wipe a tear from her cheek. The sight of her face wet with tears, its blue eyes huge and bright as they gazed at him, was almost more than he could bear. He wanted very much right now to pull her even closer to him, tight against his body, which had begun to throb with awareness of hers. God, she was lovely...beautiful beyond telling, and sweet and fresh...and *all his*.

But he sensed her need to talk more than anything else right now, and so he smiled, saying, "So my new wife is a romantic, is she? Well, Your Grace—" he turned her gently toward the table set for two with candles flickering in the darkening room.

"—I don't see how one can get more romantic than this. And I'll tell you a secret theory of mine," he added as he led her to her chair. "Romance is all well and good, but I doubt anyone ever really reaps the benefit of it on an empty stomach." This last was spoken with a brief tap of his finger on her straight little nose.

Warming as much to his tone as to the words, Ashleigh giggled and gave him a sudden quick smile that sent Brett's senses spinning, almost making him regret he'd not followed his inclinations of moments before. But instead, he seated her at the intimate little table, reached for the champagne, and they began to dine.

During their dinner they began to relax together as they talked of many things. Ashleigh told him of her early years with Patrick and her parents, falling readily into accounts of tomboy exploits that were aimed at emulating the big brother she adored, anecdotes of winters spent skating on ponds and riding in a horse-drawn sleigh, of summers filled with swims in cooling streams and horseback rides to country fairs.

Through the telling she became again the child she'd been, excited with her recollections, animated in recreating her memories, and through it all, Brett never took his eyes off her, watching with growing fascination, enthralled by her winsome charm.

Then it was his turn, Ashleigh told him, and he began, carefully at first, then with increasing openness, to talk of his past. He told her what it was like to be a boy in his grandfather's domain, utterly committed to following a carefully prescribed regime in an effort to please the one person he truly cared about in the world... and who, he felt, cared for him. He included tales from his time at sea, with bits and pieces about the friendship that developed between him and her brother; he spoke of his years at the university, of his fascination with history and the law; and he told her of the time when he returned home once more, of coming before his grandfather with his training and education behind him, ready at last to receive the old man's approval.

Ashleigh listened, wide-eyed, to these accounts of his boy-hood, feeling she was beginning at last to get glimpses of what went into the building of Brett the man. She had never heard of anyone who'd grown up according to such a carefully laid-out plan, and she wondered at the effect it must have had on him. Had he ever had the chance merely to be a boy at play? Had he ever known a child's wonder at Christmastime, or what it was like to toss a snowball, or catch a firefly and then let it go? When had there ever been room in his young life for aught but duty... and measuring up? And what had he felt when it happened, as occasionally it must have, that he didn't? Whom had he turned to then?

It was then she sensed something else that was missing from these stories, something she faintly recalled Megan having touched on once, but which, perhaps because of her eagerness to learn about him—and perhaps because she was on her sec-ond glass of champagne—she now could not recall.

"Tell me about your parents," she asked as she took a sip from her glass. "Do you remember them at all?"

All at once she saw Brett's face go rigid and his eyes shutter. "They're gone," he said.

"Oh," murmured Ashleigh, "I'm sorry. I—"

"It's grown somewhat close in here, Ashleigh." Brett rose abruptly from the table. "Why don't we finish our cham-pagne out on that balcony? It's cleared up quite nicely and promises to be a lovely night. We might even see some stars."

Perhaps it was the champagne, and perhaps it was because her guard was down from the warmth they'd shared, but as Ashleigh walked back into the drawing room and toward its balcony, she ignored the warnings she might otherwise have sensed from his abruptness of tone and curt manner and per-sisted in asking, "But surely you have some recollection of them? I mean, you said you were ten when your father—"

"I've no wish to discuss it!" Brett said sharply.

Ashleigh had gone through the open French doors and now whirled around to face him. "But why?"

"I said to *leave it alone, Ashleigh*!" This time his tone was unmistakably harsh, the look in his eyes cold and forbidding.

Ashleigh fell backward as if from a physical blow. Needing to focus her eyes elsewhere—anywhere to avoid the ice in his— she glanced down at the now wilting bouquet of tea roses she'd dropped earlier, biting her bottom lip to keep it from trembling.

Brett saw the gesture and felt instant remorse. He'd meant to charm and calm her into their bed tonight, not to send her into bewildered tears. "Ashleigh, I—"

"No! Don't come near me," she warned, taking another step backward.

It was then she felt the balcony's railing at her back, but as she continued to gaze at the forlorn little bouquet of roses, she decided she must pick them up, for somehow they reminded her of herself just now.

It was this that saved her. Just as she began to bend forward to reach for them, she heard a splintering sound and felt the railing give way at her back. All at once she felt herself falling, her arms flailing out in front of her as her champagne glass crashed to the ground.

She screamed, just as Brett charged forward, shouting her name. There was a flash of movement before her as she felt herself going over the edge where, seconds before, a stout new railing had rested.

The moment was a blur of terror, filled simultaneously by the sound of her own scream in her ears, the realization that she was about to die, and the syllables of her name splitting the air.

Then, a second later, she felt a strong hand grasping her arm, sensed her horrible loss of balance being restored, and then warm, masculine arms were holding her, pulling her back from the edge.

"*Ashleigh!* My God, Ashleigh, you almost—" Brett crushed her fiercely to him, his mind at a momentary loss for words from the horror of what had nearly happened.

Ashleigh was silent in his arms for several long seconds as her initial shock passed. Then she gasped and fell into hysterical weeping, her small body heaving and shuddering against his chest as she released the pent-up terror of seconds before.

Brett let her cry it out, giving what comfort he could as he held her close, all the while murmuring soft, calming words into her hair, her ear. "That's it, sweetheart, cry... It's all right...you're safe now. Shh, you're fine, little one, it's over...."

After some time her sobs gave way to soft little watery sounds murmured between hesitant, uneven breaths, and finally she was quiet.

Slowly, Brett released his hold and brought the curled fingers of his hand gently under her chin to tilt her face up toward his. "Better now?" he questioned softly.

Still feeling too choked up to trust her voice, Ashleigh merely nodded, her eyes, sparkling with tears, bigger and brighter than ever in her small face.

A dozen thoughts were assailing Brett's brain just then, not the least of which was the question of how a brand-new railing could fail to support her insignificant weight and give way as it had. But foremost in his mind was the need to see Ashleigh restored to mental comfort, to allay any emotional damage she might be suffering, for he had caught the look of barely subdued terror in her eyes just now, even after the tears had subsided.

Without another moment's hesitation, he caught her under the backs of her thighs and swept her into his arms, then proceeded to carry her to the bedchamber. Once there, he stood her beside the lovely old canopied Queen Anne bed and, continuing to murmur soft words of comfort, began to remove her gown.

Ashleigh stood quietly, submitting to the disrobing like someone in a dreamlike trance, and Brett attributed this to a continuing state of shock from what had transpired. Soon her gown and simple petticoat lay about her feet in a heap on the floor, and she stood before him wearing only her daintily embroidered shift.

Brett took one look at her slender body with its ripe charms barely concealed by the semitransparent material and forced himself to look away as he turned down the coverlet on the bed. The sight of those sweet, lush curves could, he knew, prove a sore temptation, but he also knew it would never do to set his mind in that direction right now. Only a monster would take advantage of a woman under the present circumstances, and Brett had a hundred reasons for proving, to himself, if no one else, that he was in no way deserving of such an epithet, especially where Ashleigh was concerned.

When the bed was ready, he lifted her gently onto the mattress, swiftly removed his boots and climbed in beside her. Then he again wrapped her in his arms, coaxing her head onto his shoulder with soft, soothing words.

"Sleep, little one. It's the best balm to heal the fear you've just suffered. You're safe now, here with me. Nothing's going to harm you.... Sleep...."

She seemed to acquiesce to his words, closing her eyes and nestling in closer to his soothing warmth, but as she did so, Brett found he was not as immune to the soft curves she pressed against him as he would have preferred to be. As the silk of her hair touched the underside of his chin and the soft, sweet scent of her perfume drifted about his senses, he found himself gritting his teeth in an effort to steel himself against the heady onslaught.

Curse him for a fool, but he hadn't imagined it would be this difficult! Desperately, he tried to focus his brain on other things—anything to avoid thinking about the ripe, feminine nearness that even now was causing beads of sweat to appear on his forehead and a bulge in his breeches beneath the coverlet.

*Damn,* he thought, but what a coil this was! Here he lay beside his own bride on their wedding night, and he dared not touch her! Here was this bewitching creature who was now totally his, whose body he had craved for weeks, whose flesh he was *meant* to get an heir upon, and she was beyond touching. Ah, he thought bitterly, how the capricious gods must be laughing at him with this!

Ashleigh closed her eyes as she'd been bidden and tried to sleep, but sleep wouldn't come. She had succeeded in calming her inner turmoil from the terrible scare she'd suffered; Brett had helped with that, but now, as she lay in his arms, something else was at work.

*It was their wedding night!* And, though he'd been wonderfully tender and considerate in the aftermath of her scare, he now seemed content to merely lie beside her and urge her to sleep. *And it was their wedding night!* True, it might not be the romantic union she had dreamed of, but he was her wedded husband now and...

Could it be he didn't desire her? Had the injury to his pride from Patrick's ultimatum been so great that he couldn't bring himself to follow through with his husbandly rights? Was she, perhaps, not sufficiently attractive to him?

All of these questions and more assailed Ashleigh's spinning brain as she lay there in the darkness beside him, as the silent minutes ticked by.

Finally after some length of time had passed and she still found herself wide-awake, Ashleigh decided she could bear it no more. It didn't even matter to her that she would risk encountering that wrath that she had seen so often and which she knew lurked beneath the surface. She had to know.

Shifting slightly to raise herself up on one elbow, she looked at him in the light given off by the beams of the full moon that slanted in through a window opposite the bed.

"Brett?"

Surprised to see she was not close to sleep, as he'd suspected—and fervently hoped—Brett withdrew the arm he'd thrown across his brow in an effort to shut out the softly insinuating effects of her movements. "Yes, what is it?" he questioned as he opened his eyes.

Then he wished he hadn't. The picture she presented, above him in the moonlight with her hair all silvered and curling about her arms and shoulders, her face breathtakingly beautiful as she faced him, caused a tight knot of desire to form in his loins, blotting out almost everything but his hunger for her.

Almost put off by the look on his face—a look she didn't understand—Ashleigh forced herself to continue. "I was wondering... That is, I—" Now that she was into it, the right words just wouldn't come!

"Ashleigh, for God's sake, what's the matter?" he asked, sitting up beside her now.

There was no help for it, but to simply blurt it out. "Brett... I— Don't...? *Don't you want me?*"

Her words hit him like a sledgehammer blow to his middle, and there was a passing second of silence while he digested their import. Then he shut his eyes and reached for her with a groan.

"*Want* you? Oh, sweet, merciful God, *I cannot think for wanting you!*" And with a strong, masterful movement, he drew her beneath him on the bed.

Ashleigh's senses danced at his words. He *did* want her! He... But then the time for thinking was torn from her as she felt him begin to show her what he meant. She saw him looking down at her for a moment, his eyes a flaming message of desire. Then he lowered his head as his hands caught hers gently on either side, and she felt the hard warmth of his mouth covering her own.

The kiss seemed to go on forever; it began as a strong, insistent demand, plying her lips apart as it sought their inner softness, forcing her to yield what he sought.

Then she felt his tongue seeking entrance; it lightly touched the tips of her teeth, then began to explore the sweet inner recesses of her mouth, languorously teasing, then withdrawing, then seeking entrance again. And all the while his lips moved softly over hers, tasting, plying the sweetness from them again and again.

Then she felt his hand begin to move, sliding gently through the hair at the sides of her head, moving down to her shoulders and caressing them while his mouth traced a slowly moving trail of scorching kisses across her ear and down the side of her delicate neck and throat.

"Ashleigh," he murmured, "was ever a woman more beautiful than you? So lovely... so very... very... lovely..."

As he spoke, his hands drifted lower, seeking softer flesh, until at last he had her breasts beneath his palms and felt their budded peaks under the thin material of her chemise.

He raised his head and looked into her eyes. "I want to see you, Ashleigh, all of you," he told her, and with a quick movement, he slipped the straps of the chemise down her arms, baring her breasts to his gaze.

Ashleigh gasped, shocked by the moment of intimacy, but as she began to turn her head to avoid his eyes, he whispered, "No, don't turn from me, sweetheart. I want you to see me looking at you...oh, God, but you're beautiful...*so damned beautiful*!"

Ashleigh did as he asked, forcing herself to hold his gaze as his hands returned to her breasts. Slowly, ever so slowly, he stroked their lush roundness, until at last his thumbs found their peaks. These he began to tease with tantalizing strokes, once...twice...and again....

Suddenly Ashleigh was assaulted by an acute, twisting sensation in the pit of her stomach, and then lower, at the juncture of her thighs. It came again, and she moaned aloud with the sensation.

She saw Brett smile at her reaction, his eyes fixed on hers as his thumbs worked their sorcery.

"Do you like this, love?" he asked softly. "Does it give you pleasure?"

Ashleigh managed to nod before closing her eyes in an effort to contain the ever-building sensation within. "Ohh, Brett," she whispered as she felt his lips at her ear, then her throat, and the tender place where her neck met her shoulder. A hot furnace seemed to be burning somewhere in the lower part of her body, and she began to writhe and move with its heat.

Then she felt his mouth descend farther and, an instant later, close over the peak where his thumb had played. Gently, he pulled at the aching bud with his lips while his hands began to slip her chemise down past her thighs.

There were multiple sensations gripping Ashleigh from several places at once. She felt the cool flow of air on her naked thighs as he bared them, felt the rush of candent heat to her body as his mouth moved to the rosy crest of her other breast, felt her belly tighten with need as his hands moved across its flat softness.

Then she saw him rise above her, his breath coming hard and fast as he began to shed his own clothes. She watched in mute fascination as he bared the hard, muscular expanse of his chest and massive shoulders, saw his eyes glitter with desire as his breeches followed his shirt to the floor. She had a weak, distant memory of having seen him naked before, but she also knew it had never been like this. His huge body looked, to her in the moonlight, like that of some pagan god, all silvery and intoxicatingly male, and rigid with his need of her.

Then he lowered himself beside her again, and his hands and lips resumed their quest. Soul-drugging kisses captured her mouth again and again, and she felt herself returning them with an ardor she never knew she possessed. In a great wellspring of passion, she threw her arms about his neck, drawing him closer... closer....

As for Brett, he couldn't get enough of her and had all he could do to force himself to take his time. Her body was so perfect, so sweetly perfect, and the innocent passion of her responses was nearly driving him insane.

Carefully, ever so gently, he traced his hand down her silken hips and across her thighs. Then, with the softest of movements, he let it come to rest in the dark, silken triangle between.

Again, Ashleigh gasped, bringing her thighs tightly together with a startled movement, but Brett's voice was at her ear, murmuring, "Easy, now, love... No, don't close to me... I mean to give you pleasure, little one... sweet... unthinkable... pleasure...."

Then his knowing fingers began their final assault on her senses. Moving them lower still, he gently pried her thighs apart, noticing they were trembling now. With a deft movement, his thumb stroked the hard little protrusion above her nether lips, his mouth at the same moment covering hers in a sweet, pliant kiss.

At this latest touch, Ashleigh went into a frenzy, opening her mouth to his while arching her back and spreading her aching thighs to his seeking caress. Then she felt his fingers gain entry below, while at the same time his tongue probed her mouth, but gently... oh, ever so gently....

Brett heard her moan deep in her throat, felt the wet, slippery femininity below flex and tighten as she pushed herself against his questing hand. At the same time he felt his own hardness throb, its swollen contours near to bursting. And he knew they were ready.

Carefully shifting his weight, he braced his hands on either side of her shoulders on the mattress and poised above her arching body. Then he drove himself deep into her waiting warmth.

As she felt his hardness fill her, Ashleigh cried out softly with the relief it brought, but this was only for a moment. Soon she felt an ever greater need burning her loins, sending a sweet, aching pain to the core of her. Then Brett began to move on her, slowly at first, then, as he felt her hands at his back, felt their nails digging into his skin, he moved faster, harder, giving her what she sought.

The throbbing vortex at her center drew Ashleigh spiraling upward until she felt herself teetering at the brink of something wonderful and unknown, and then she found it. Great, searing spasms of pleasure began to rock her very being, binding her mind and body in a cataclysm of sensation. Upward, far into the heavens she soared with it, giving herself to it completely, giving herself up to the man who took her there.

Brett felt her pleasure break just as he felt he could no longer contain his own. He felt her coming again and again, and his head reeled with the knowledge. Then, with her yielding, throbbing flesh beneath him, he found his own shuddering release as he joined in the rapture.

For a long, long time afterward, neither of them moved. Neither could they speak, so complete was the repletion they felt. Then, after a long while—a *very* long while—Brett raised his head to look at her.

Ashleigh felt him move and opened her eyes to find his, turquoise-silver in the moonlight, gazing directly at her. And then he smiled, his deeply grooved male dimples causing her breath to catch and hold for a moment before she released it in a long, shivery sigh.

"Sweet wife," he breathed as he continued to smile at her with those incredible eyes, "I think you've just given me—" he bent to place a soft kiss on her love-swollen lips "—the greatest treasure—" he kissed her softly again "—a man could wish for...." Then he buried his face in her hair, whispering, "Ashleigh, darling, how very perfect I find you."

And Ashleigh felt herself expand, as if there were a great, buoyant bubble of delight inside her, lifting her upward in ecstasy, giving her soul flight... singing with joy. *She'd pleased him!* This sometimes dark, often brooding near-stranger she'd wed under the most doubtful of circumstances had found her *pleasing....*

And oh, *what he had given her*! A "treasure," he said she'd given him? Dear God, but he had given her as much! More... Tonight, in his arms, surely she'd touched Heaven....

"Brett," she whispered, "Oh, Brett, I never knew...."

But even as she tried to tell him how she felt, he was pressing further kisses to her temples, her brow, her eyes, and, incredible though it seemed to her, Ashleigh felt renewed longing seep into her limbs. She realized with a start that his manhood was still buried deep within her when she felt it stir again and she moaned softly with this awareness.

"Ah, Ashleigh, I cannot have enough of you," she heard him say, and then she knew it was the same with her as she welcomed his hands at her breasts, cried out with the latest wash of pleasure they brought.

He made love to her again and again through the long night, pausing between times to let her sleep, holding her close as she did, but for Brett there was no sleeping, no desire to do so. As many times as he took her, he only found himself wanting her more, and so he merely held her while she dozed, and after a time found himself waking her again with sweet, languid kisses that seemed to touch her very soul. During these times he let his senses fill with her sweet presence, making himself content to find joy in the moment, forcing, to the nether reaches of his mind, by sheer dint of his will, a small voice that threatened, telling him to take his joy while he might, for never could it last.

Finally, as the dawn began to break, extending its rosy fingers into their chamber, he feared he would never stop unless he removed himself from their bed. But as he rose to leave, he heard her cry out softly, "Brett, no...please, I...want you again...."

And with a groan of renewed longing, he bent and pulled her into his arms, and the magic began anew....

# Chapter Twenty-Three

Ashleigh awakened to a flood of golden sunlight pouring into the chamber like melted butter. It reached her even before she opened her eyes, penetrating her closed lids with its lemony color and warmth. She kept her eyes shut for a moment, savoring what her other senses brought her: the sound of birds chirping outside the open window, the scent of roses carried on the breeze from the gardens below, the feel of silken sheets on her naked skin....

Suddenly her eyes snapped open as she fully savored this last impression. She was *naked* in this huge bed with the silken canopy overhead! Naked because... Hastily Ashleigh shut her eyes again, feeling a blush invade her cheeks as she recalled her wedding night. Oh, dear, Heaven, had she really...had they really—

"Good morning, slugabed," drawled a lazy male voice from across the room.

Ashleigh opened her eyes a second time to see Brett grinning at her as he leaned casually against the side of the chamber's marble fireplace. He was fully dressed.

"G-good morning," she stammered, hating the blush she knew was deepening under that direct, turquoise gaze.

Laughing softly, her husband bent to a nearby table and removed a tea cozy from a small silver teapot on a matching tray, then brought the tray, which also bore a cup and saucer, to a stand beside the bed.

"Your breakfast tea, Your Grace," he said, an amused tone in his voice as he set it down with a flourish. "You take your tea plain, as I recall."

"*You* fixed me tea?" marveled Ashleigh as she rose to a sitting position, her embarrassment forgotten with this surprise.

"Of course," he said offhandedly as he looked down at her from his height beside the bed. "Did you think I wouldn't know how? You must realize that, as a cabin boy, it was required that I know." He poured the tea into the cup and handed it to her on its saucer.

As Ashleigh reached for the tea, she suddenly stopped and glanced downward. Her movement had caused the sheet to fall away from her, revealing a pair of rosy-tipped breasts. "Ohh," she moaned, blushing furiously, and reached for the sheet.

But Brett's free hand shot out and forestalled the action. "Don't," he said, covering lightly the knuckles of her two hands as they clutched the edge of the sheet. "I love looking at you. Your breasts—" he brought the teacup forward again, but his eyes were on her pinkening face "—are beautiful."

Ashleigh lowered her eyes as the blush deepened, but managed to take the teacup. "Th-thank you," she murmured before taking a quick swallow of the excellent brew, mainly to silence the sound of the cup rattling against its saucer as she held it.

Brett chuckled and helped her set both cup and saucer back on the tray at the bedside. He was enjoying himself immensely this morning, and he knew the reason for it was sitting before him now. Ashleigh had given him the most satisfying bedding of his life last night, and she was his *wife*! He recalled with distaste his feelings about husbandly marital duty just a short time ago when he'd gritted his teeth against a future with Elizabeth, and then he recalled the fury with which he'd greeted Patrick's ultimatum. But here he stood, flaunting fate in the face of both those recollections; here was the very opposite of those earlier expectations, in the person of this tiny, fragile beauty who sat blushing before him, to his total delight and not a little amazement.

"Ashleigh," he said quietly. "Look at me."

There was a flutter of the dusky eyelashes for several seconds before she raised eyes that were pools of deep blue water.

But in the next instant, when Brett lowered himself to sit on the bed, she closed them while her hands again grabbed for the sheet.

"Ah-ah." He grinned, shaking his head. Then, before she realized what was happening, he reached for her, and she found herself sitting in his lap.

"Mmm, that's better," he murmured against her hair.

"Oh, but, Brett—" she protested.

"'But, Brett,' what?" he questioned as his knuckles tipped her chin, forcing her to look at him.

The blush would not go away. It had been one thing, Ashleigh thought, to be caught up in the throes of passion from his lovemaking last night, when it was dark, but having to endure his physical contact with her nude body now, in full daylight... well, it seemed even more intimate somehow, more invasive of her person... especially since he was fully clothed. Also, she began to perceive an unmistakable scent emanating from the bed where they had made love—and, yes, from her own body.

"B-Brett, I—well, it's just that I—you see, I've not yet bathed and—and there's a scent about—"

She broke off to the sound of her husband's delighted laughter.

Ashleigh's flaring brows drew together in a frown. "I see nothing humorous in it! I smell like—"

"Us?" he questioned with a roguish grin. At her increasing blush, he laughed again, softly. "Oh, sweetheart, you are a joy, I swear!" His eyes found hers and he lowered his voice to a whisper. "Tell me, what is the source of this latest blush? Does it come from remembering my touch on your pretty nipples?"

"Brett!" Ashleigh's face deepened to a beet red.

He grinned at her with shameless delight. "Or does it come from recalling the way your lovely thighs parted for my—"

"Brett!" she choked. "I *beg* you...*please*!"

He laughed softly while he reached to kiss the tip of her nose. "Please, what?" He grinned, and he began to touch the parts of her flesh he'd named; then Ashleigh moaned helplessly, and succumbed once again to the passion.…

Later, a very long time later, Ashleigh lay beside her husband in a tangle of sheets on the large bed, thinking. It was a lazy process, a product of the repletion she felt in the aftermath of their lovemaking.

She wondered if she looked as different this morning as she felt inside, for she knew there had been a change. It was a change in the way she conceived of herself; heretofore, at least in her adult life, she'd always assumed she was a self-reliant person where her emotions were concerned; she took total responsibility for her feelings, be they joy, anger, fear—whatever. But now she realized something new was at work, and it had as much to do with the man lying beside her as with herself.

In the past twenty-four hours, Brett had played the chords of pleasure that controlled her body, much as a master musician plies the strings of an instrument to evoke sweet music. She'd had moments of soaring joy and rapture she'd not have imagined herself capable of. What did it signify? What was it about this discovery that now, as she thought about it, unnerved her and sent her scurrying for solace?

She was afraid she had the answer. By surrendering herself to him so completely, by allowing him such total control over her body and then, more importantly, her emotions, she feared she had surrendered her heart and soul as well: she feared she loved him.

And why was it fear that accompanied this devastating realization? Ah, that part was very simple: She had every reason to doubt her love was returned. Oh, he'd relished the way their bodies meshed, the hours of blinding passion they'd shared; that much was clear. But never once, through the long night and into this morning, had she had the sense that his deeper emotions were involved. He'd made love again and again to her gladly awakened flesh, murmuring fond words and endearments in the process, but never once had he spoken of love, not once had his eyes conveyed aught but desire… or repletion.

No... she was sure of it: Brett Westmont's body had been completely hers last night; but his heart, he held to himself.

What, then, was she to do with her own newly budding emotions? How was she to live with them, knowing they were not returned? Well, one thing was certain: She would die before she let him see how she felt! She could well imagine the path that would take; at best, he would come to pity her for her youthful foolishness; at worst, he would come to despise her for it. Hadn't she seen the way he'd treated Pamela Marlowe? And for her, it would go worse than for the hapless Pamela; she was his wife and would not be free to seek a new love elsewhere.

"A penny for your thoughts, sweet," she heard Brett say as he turned on the bed to look at her. He was holding her very close to him, but had raised his head as he spoke, giving her the full benefit of that devastating turquoise gaze.

Broken from her reverie, Ashleigh flushed at his words.... *Oh, no... never... not for a million pennies!* she vowed silently. Casting about for a safe response, her eyes fastened on a heavy gold chain he wore about his neck, and, dangling from it, a small, oval, gold locket. The two pieces looked incongruous together, with the chain so obviously a masculine adornment, the locket a small, almost dainty piece beside it, and she realized it was something he'd donned this morning, under his clothes; he hadn't worn it last night.

"I was wondering..." she said, tentatively. "What is this locket and chain you wear about your neck?"

Raising himself up on one elbow, Brett was silent for a moment as he gave her an inscrutable look. At last he heaved a sigh, saying, "I'd forgotten I'd put it back in place." He reached for the chain and slid his fingers along it until he was fingering the locket.

"I've worn this piece for more than a dozen years." Flipping the locket over, he revealed a miniature of a handsome man who looked much like Brett himself, except that his eyes were more blue than turquoise, and his hair was black. "My father, Edward Westmont," he said simply. "And, actually, if you look closely, you'll note that this is really half a locket." He indicated the tiny gold hinge to the left of the miniature. "The missing half, I've never seen."

Ashleigh nodded, but he saw her eyes were curious.

"I came by it in an unusual way," he continued. "One night, not long after I'd returned from a long sea voyage, I made ready to retire in my chamber at the Hall and found the locket lying on my pillow. Of course, I recognized at once whose picture it contained, but I had no idea who'd put it there—or why. I thought of going to my grandfather with it, thinking perhaps, in a sentimental moment, he'd decided to surprise me with it, but when I approached him the next morning, he was in a fine fettle of rage over some parliamentary speech he'd read about in the papers, calling the speaker a driveling sentimentalist. At that instant I decided my grandfather could never have succumbed to an emotion that would lead him to place this locket on my pillow."

Ashleigh nodded. "So you said nothing to him of it."

"Correct," said Brett, "but for some reason I decided to indulge in one little act of sentimentality myself: I bought a chain to hang it about my neck the very next day, and have worn it ever since."

Ashleigh gave him a rueful smile. "Except for last night."

Brett's smile echoed hers. "Except for any night I thought...I might not be alone." He was again silent for a moment, appearing to ponder what he'd said. Then he looked at her with a tender smile. "Ashleigh, I know there have been moments when...when I've not been easy with you, and I would have you understand why this might sometimes be. Take last evening, for example, when I cut you so readily with my damnable bad temper. You'll recall it was after you'd questioned me, rather persistently, I might add—" he gave her a wry smile "—on some things about my past, my...family."

"Brett...I didn't mean to pry."

"No, and I realize that now, Ashleigh. Besides, I don't think it could be called prying for a wife to want to know about such things. And you *are* my wife now, Ashleigh Westmont, as well as my duchess." He tapped a playful forefinger on her nose.

"Therefore," he continued, "I deem you have a right to be privy to certain . . . information.

"Ashleigh, there are certain things in my past that are not easy for me to dwell upon. Foremost among these is the story of how I came to lose one of my parents at a very tender age. . . ."

He told her then, of the painful and largely mysterious disappearance of his mother when he was but a small boy, of the vagueness of the story he'd been given to explain her disappearance and then of the total removal of evidence of her existence from the Hall, and from his life. He spoke, too, of the unhappiness he'd witnessed in his father during the years that followed, of his father's second marriage and tragic death when he was ten.

Through it all, Ashleigh listened, wide eyes filled with compassion as she imagined what it must have been like to have been that boy, and the pain he must have suffered. At the end she had to swallow past the lump that had formed in her throat with the telling of his story. "Oh, Brett, I had no *idea*. . . . Oh, how *awful* for you!"

Brett's eyes gazed past her, as if he were looking off into the distance, into another time and place. "No, not awful, really . . . just . . . instructive."

At her silence, he explained. "It taught me, among other things, to keep silent about what I might be feeling, especially if the feelings involved pain. It's evolved into a lifetime habit, and has stood me in good stead in many of my dealings with men . . . and women." He reached out to run the front of his crooked forefinger softly along her cheekbone and jaw.

"But with you it must be different. Because you are my wife, because even now you might be carrying our child. . . ." His hand moved to lightly touch her bare, flat belly, then back to cup her cheek. "Be patient with me, Ashleigh. God knows, I'm not a patient man myself, but if you will try to show me some forbearance, I might just be able to . . . to overcome this ingrained tendency to want to shut you out. . . . Well, sweet, what do you say?"

Seeing the momentary, naked look of pleading in his eyes, and knowing it to be foreign to his nature, Ashleigh's heart swelled with a surge of joy...and hope. He might not love her...now, but he had taken a very important step to drawing closer to her by sharing with her this intimacy, and she would not abuse his trust.

"Oh, Brett!" she cried, throwing her arms about his neck. "I'm going to try! I'm going to try so very hard!"

Brett let out a gust of shaky laughter. "Well done, Your Grace. Well done, indeed, for that is all I ask."

As he held her in his arms, Brett's turbulent thoughts spun erratically. Perhaps he'd been wrong. Perhaps she would prove to be a woman he could place his faith in. Perhaps....

But deep inside, a skeptical voice warned, *Beware. Nothing lasts forever.... Life is, at best, a tenuous gamble...and woman is the ever-changing, wildest card of all....*

A SHORT WHILE LATER, when Ashleigh had just finished her bath and toilette and stood before a large cheval glass wearing a new, sky-blue riding ensemble, she heard the sound of horses on the drive outside.

"That's probably Old Henry with our mounts," called Brett from the top of the stairs where he held a pair of buckets containing her now cool bathwater—to Ashleigh's astonished delight, he'd actually drawn, and heated and carried this bathwater upstairs for her, enough to fill a lovely rose-and-cream enameled hip bath in the dressing room! "Join us down below when you're ready."

A few moments later he met her at the bottom of the stairs. "There's a small problem. It seems Irish Night's thrown a shoe. The farrier's with her now, but it will take another half hour or so until she's ready to ride."

"Oh," said Ashleigh. "Well, then, I can wait here for them to bring her over."

"Would you mind, sweet?" asked Brett as his eyes roamed appreciatively over her slim, fashionably attired figure. Then he reached out impulsively to place a soft kiss at her ear. "You're lovely," he whispered.

Ashleigh felt a thrill ripple the length of her spine, and it took her a moment to respond to his initial comment. "No, of course I wouldn't mind. You'll be riding back now, then?"

"I'm afraid I must," he replied, indicating a folded sheet of paper he held at his side. "I've just been handed a letter from Whitehall. I'm being summoned back to London and I'll need to speak with Higgins about preparing for the trip."

Privately Brett was thinking of something else he must do; it concerned the accident of last night. This morning, while she slept, he'd gone to the balcony and scrutinized the broken railing. Not being a carpenter, he couldn't be sure, but he thought there was something peculiar about the break. Hardly wanting to consider the possibilities, he nevertheless had determined to summon the carpenters who'd worked on the renovations, bringing them out here when Ashleigh had gone. She had endured enough of a shock with the incident, and although she'd recovered remarkably afterward, he had no wish to upset her further today. He fervently hoped his fears would prove unnecessary; he'd enjoy taking her to London for a few days without such a concern on his mind.

"A bit of official business," he was saying, as he turned to go. "I'll see you back at the Hall for luncheon, and, remember, keep to the flats on that filly. We've not completed her schooling on the jumps yet."

As Ashleigh watched him leave, she wondered about his summons to London. He'd said nothing of her accompanying him. How could he desert a new bride in the face of business? He wouldn't . . . would he? After all, she was familiar with the London town house, and there were things in the city she could find to do to occupy her time while he was at Whitehall. . . .

Suddenly the warm sunlight streaming through the windows of the vestibule didn't seem so glorious anymore, and Ashleigh found herself biting her lower lip as she heard the sounds of horses leaving the drive.

A SHORT TIME LATER, AS SHE sat in a Chippendale wing chair in the sitting room, trying to read a book of poetry she'd discovered, she heard the sound of the downstairs door opening.

Thinking it must be one of the stable lads with word that Irish Night was ready—probably a new, untutored one, she guessed, for no properly trained servant would enter without knocking—she wondered as she headed for the stairs why she hadn't heard them approach.

As she reached the top landing, a familiar female voice met her ears.

"Why aren't there any servants about to take my wrap? I—Oh, there you are, Miss Sinclair." Elizabeth Hastings's pronunciation of the name echoed with a sibilant hiss.

Ashleigh bristled as she beheld the lavender-garbed figure advancing up the stairs. "It's Ashleigh Westmont now, Lady Elizabeth." A prick of mischief twitched in the blue eyes. "Or, to put it properly, it's now 'Your Grace.'"

Elizabeth's eyes held no warmth as they fell on the woman she regarded as an opportunistic usurper. "Well, *Your Grace*," she sneered, "let's see how well you fulfill the obligations of your title. A duchess is a lady, and a lady knows how to invite a guest in." She walked directly past Ashleigh and toward the first door on her right. "Shall we make it the drawing room, *Your Grace*?"

Wondering whether a duchess had ever thrown a caller out, Ashleigh gritted her teeth and followed her into the drawing room.

Once they were both inside, Elizabeth turned to face her. "I shan't sit down. What I have to say won't take long."

Wondering whether Brett knew Elizabeth was here—whether he'd passed her as he left—Ashleigh questioned, "How did you arrive here? I heard no horses on the drive, but—"

"I rowed myself across the lake," Elizabeth snapped. "I'm actually very good at rowing," she added, "and so is Lady Margaret. She taught me."

"Why have you come here, Elizabeth?"

"Ah, so it's merely 'Elizabeth' now, is it? How the lowly have risen!" She fastened her silver-slitted gaze on Ashleigh's face. *"You little usurper!"* She paused to glance rapidly about the room, then focused again on Ashleigh. "All this was supposed to have been *mine*!"

"If you've come here merely to rail at me for—"

"Actually, I have not, though you deserve it, I can assure you. No, my dear little duchess, actually what I've come here for is to do you a service . . . or perhaps you could consider it a warning."

"Go on," Ashleigh told her. There was a deadly calm in the blue eyes, and had anyone who knew her well seen it, as Patrick had at times in their youth, on those few but memorable occasions when he'd seen his sister truly angry, he would have given pause before going any further.

But Elizabeth Hastings was oblivious to anything about Ashleigh but her immediate purpose, and so she hurriedly continued. "You think you're the cat who's got the cream, don't you? You stand here in all your stolen finery and assume you've arrived at your place in life at last."

"Elizabeth, I don't—"

"Well, let me tell you something, you little guttersnipe! You don't *begin* to comprehend what it means to be Brett Westmont's wife!

"But that's where *I* come in, for, believe me, *I can tell you!*" A slow, ugly smile spread Elizabeth's lips. "How practiced are you, little Ashleigh, at pretending to be blind? For that is what you must do—and often! Every time your randy, philandering husband decides to roam away from your bed!

"Why, I do believe I've shocked you, my dear! What a pity. Didn't you know your new husband enjoys a reputation as one of the greatest rakes in London? Probably in all of England, now I think on it, but—" here she punctuated her speech with a brittle little laugh "—but it's in London, I hear, where he's found most of his mistresses. I mean, really, my dear, did you think that, by wearing his ring, you would see the last of the Pamela Marlowes in his life? Not so, I can assure you. Why, even now, he's likely planning a little side trip into the city to amuse himself. A man with Brett's hot blood doesn't wait very long to afford himself, ah, varied outlets."

Until now, Ashleigh's face had merely displayed angry shock—and doubt—at Elizabeth's words. But her visitor's chance hitting on the one factor related to what had just been on Ashleigh's mind—trips to London without her—had the effect of turning her face deathly pale.

"Ah, I see I've hit a mark!" crowed Elizabeth triumphantly. "Tell me, is our lusty duke already making plans to leave for the city of his amorous pursuits? On the very morn following his wedding night?

"*You little fool!* You don't know how to *begin* to deal with his faithlessness, do you? You thought all you need do was turn those big blue kitten's eyes on him and he would remain by your side!

"Well, let me tell you something, you little bitch! *I* would have known how to deal with it! *I* would have been able to do what any well-bred wife with a roving husband must! I'd have suffered my wifely duty in his bed often enough to beget the heirs he must have, and then, quite happily, I assure you, become deaf and blind while he satisfied his lust elsewhere.

"That's the only reason he's wed at all, you know. It's the only reason any gentleman of the *ton* with such appetites marries: to beget his precious heirs!

"So, you see? I've done you a service, after all. Perhaps, now you've learned the truth, you can begin to school yourself to accept it...*but I doubt it!*" Elizabeth began moving toward the door. Once there, she gave Ashleigh a twisted parting smile. "And if you can't, well, there are ways to extricate yourself. Divorce, among those who can afford it, is not unheard of. And when you do decide to cut him loose, Your Grace, depend upon it, *I shall be waiting!*"

She left the room, her ugly laughter following her down the hall.

Ashleigh remained where she'd stood through Elizabeth's harangue and thought she was going to be sick. Her throat felt dry and choked, a sickening lump lodged at its base.

*Oh, God, what shall I do?* she asked herself. *It was bad enough to think of enduring the day-to-day as his wife and strive to hide my love for him, knowing he doesn't love me...but to do it in the face of his pursuit of other women? No! Never! I'd die inside...slowly die....*

The sickening feeling increased, and she forced herself to walk to the French doors and open them. As fresh air met her lungs, she gazed at the scene of last night's mishap. Dimly she realized that all she had felt during that scare was nothing compared to the anguish and fear she felt now.

Glancing downward, she saw the little bouquet of Lady Jane's tea roses, wilted and fading now, in the morning sunshine. She thought about how she had begun to reach for it before the railing had given away, how this had probably saved her life.

"Lucky flowers," Lady Jane had said. . . .

Stooping to pick them up, Ashleigh felt hot tears choke her throat. Blindly, she clutched the dying flowers to her breast. *Lucky!* her mind cried out brokenly. *Oh, poor roses, your luck may have come to me last night, when you were yet fresh and new . . . but now . . . now I think it's as faded as you.*

Suddenly Ashleigh straightened, catching herself. What was she allowing to happen here? Since when, through all she had endured in the past, had she ever succumbed to self-pity? Well, she was not going to succumb to it now! She was made of sterner stuff than that! What was it Megan had said? She'd spoken of grit and pluck, and a fine spirit!

She whirled about and left the balcony, her tears forgotten. Now she knew what she must do. It was just a matter of timing it right.

The sounds of horses on the drive broke her thoughts. Without a moment's hesitation, she dashed for the stairs, eager to enact her plan.

"Ashleigh, are you there?" Patrick's big voice boomed as she came through the front door.

"Patrick! And Megan! Oh, God, it's good to see you!"

Patrick alighted from the stallion he rode and came to help Megan from her mare. Behind them, on a long tether, stood a prancing Irish Night.

The two rushed forward to greet Ashleigh.

"When we heard what kept ye, we decided t' bring ye yer filly ourselves." Megan grinned. "How are ye, darlin'?"

Ashleigh had thought her tears were stoutly behind her a few moments ago, but now, seeing their dear, loving faces, she found she'd been wrong. Suddenly a great, choking sob welled up in her throat and hung on the air.

"Oh, Megan! Patrick!" she cried, and threw herself into their arms.

## Chapter Twenty-Four

Brett stood on the balcony beside Tom Blecker, the master carpenter at Ravensford Hall, a man he'd known since he was a boy. He watched as the old man kneeled and peered worriedly at the underside of the piece of broken railing.

"So you think it's been tampered with, Tom?" he asked grimly.

"I don't *think*, Yer Grace...I *know*! Pried loose at this joint," he said, pointing to a place on the railing. "'Ere, see fer yerself...'ere's th' marks wot th' crowbar left...neatly 'idden t' view, unless ye creep way under it, like this."

Brett knelt down beside him and looked, but the act was mostly a courtesy. He knew the old man well, and one thing he'd learned over the years was that, in matters of his trade, Tom's word was unimpeachable.

With an uneasy sigh, Brett stood and ran a hand through his hair. What in hell was going on? Who would be trying to kill Ashleigh...or him? Images drifted into his mind...images of another accident—only that one had been fatal.

Shaking his head as if to clear it, Brett looked at Tom. "Thank you for coming out for this," he said.

Tom nodded respectfully, a worried look in his eyes.

"But now, Tom, I must ask you one more thing."

"Aye, Yer Grace?"

"Please say nothing of this to anyone. I wish to do some careful thinking on what this discovery implies before I decide what we're to do about it. Can you give me your promise?"

Tom's eyes met the turquoise gaze openly. He'd known the lad almost all his life, and he was heartily fond of this present duke of Ravensford. His Grace was a fair-minded man, and a smart one, to boot. If he'd determined the matter needed studying and closed lips in the process, there was likely good reason for it.

"Ye hae me word on't, Yer Grace."

"Good man," said Brett, clapping him on the shoulder. "And now I'll be heading back to the Hall while you remain to make your repairs. Shall I send one of the other men to help you?"

Tom gave him a gap-toothed smile. "Nay, 'tis easily mended by one. But, if ye d' nae mind, Yer Grace, I'll be checkin' on t' other balcony as well." He gave his employer a pointed look.

"You're one step ahead of me, Tom. I was just about to ask that." Brett headed for the stairs. "Take your time with it. I'll water the pony and move him and your dray into the shade before I leave."

As Brett rode toward the hall, his thoughts were grim. What was he to do with this discovery, now that fact had replaced mere suspicion? He knew most men would immediately call the constable, but for him, it wasn't so simple. Most men weren't involved in clandestine government service. He'd suffered attacks on his life before, the most recent being the one in which Patrick had saved his life. But all those had occurred while there'd been a war raging, and now England was at peace—except for a little matter of her former colonies in America, he corrected, but that had never been in his sphere of operation.

And what if the foul play had been aimed at Ashleigh? It had been generally known that it was she who'd be spending most of the time here once the cottage was restored.

Still, he couldn't think why anyone would wish her dead. Or could he? Briefly his thoughts focused on an image of Elizabeth Hastings's furious face when she'd learned of his new betrothal, but he dismissed it as quickly as it came. Elizabeth might be a shrew, but he hardly thought her capable of murder. No, Elizabeth was a female more likely to use words to inflict harm.

As the thought came to him, he realized he'd better warn Ashleigh to be prepared for that, if nothing else. After all, Elizabeth lived close by, and it was hardly likely that his marriage would keep her from continuing to visit the Hall and her beloved godmother.

Well, all the more reason to take Ashleigh away for a while. The summons to London couldn't have come at a more opportune time. And, among other things, the time away would afford him a chance to mull things over . . . to think what to do to ensure there would be no more accidents.

His thoughts shifted to his bride, bringing a soft smile to his lips. He was going to enjoy showing her around London. She was such a wide-eyed innocent, so ingenuously appreciative of all she saw in this new life-style that was such a contrast to her years of ignominious drudgery in that brothel!

And he could hardly wait to see her face when he presented her with his wedding gift this evening. His smile broadened as he patted the papers he carried in his waistcoat pocket while reining Raven in, for they were approaching the entrance to the stable block. The papers were a transfer of ownership of one black filly named Irish Night to Her Grace, the duchess of Ravensford, otherwise known as Ashleigh Sinclair Westmont. *He couldn't wait!*

A half-dozen anxious faces met their duke's heated gaze as he stood before them in the entrance hall.

"Do you expect me to believe that none of you saw them leave, *in broad daylight*?" Brett thundered.

Chauncey Jameson exchanged a worried glance with Hettie Busby, then exerted all his powers of self-control to avoid reaching for a handkerchief to wipe his perspiring brow before his duke, and replied, "Her Grace never returned to the Hall from the dowager's cottage, Your Grace, and as for Sir Patrick and Miss O'Brien, we thought they were taking Her Grace's mount to her when they left, and that was late morning."

"Aye, Yer Grace," added Old Henry. "I 'anded Sir Patrick Irish Night's tether meself, I did."

Brett was frantic with worry. It was now early evening, and they'd searched the house and grounds for hours after the three of them had failed to return for luncheon, as scheduled. Where could she be? How could all three of them have disappeared as they had? As he thought, a cold chill of apprehension seized him. Was this the ultimate foul play, a final piece of dirty work to correct the failure of last night's accident? And if so, there had to be someone with might, as well as cunning, involved, for Patrick was powerfully built and a mean fighter, especially when defense was concerned.

Suddenly, as he stood there wondering what to do, he heard footsteps running up the drive, then a furious knocking at the door.

Jameson went to the door, opening it to reveal the anxious faces of Jonathan Busby and the young footman named Robert.

"B-beggin' yer pardon, Mr. Jameson, sir, but w-we wish t' see 'Is Grace, if ye please," stammered Jonathan.

"Aye, sir, ye see, we've found somethin'," Robert added.

"Send them in," Brett called out.

The two young men approached, Jonathan with a quick glance at his parents, Robert with his eyes on the floor.

When they stood side by side in front of the duke, Jonathan gave Robert an elbow in the ribs. "Show 'im," he muttered.

Darting a glance at his duke's stern visage, Robert withdrew a sheet of parchment from his sleeve and handed it forward while Jonathan proceeded to explain.

"Ye said t' keep searchin', Yer Grace, so Robby 'n me, we decided t' give th' cottage a good goin' over, onct we was done wi' th' garden." He looked slightly apologetic. "Th' door was open after ye left, ye see."

"An' we found that paper under a table in th' upstairs drawin' room, near th' window. Th' wind must hae blown it t' th' floor, ye see, an' so everyone missed it earlier."

"I see," said Brett, quickly unfolding the parchment. "Good work, lads."

Beaming, both footmen retired beside Hettie and Old Henry while Brett scanned the letter.

Dear Brett,

I don't know how to say this, except to tell you I am leaving. I know now our wedding was a mistake, and I am correcting it the only way I know how. I would like to explain further, but my feelings are too raw right now, and I find I lack the words.

Please do not try to find me. I convinced Megan and Patrick to accompany me, so I shall be safe enough.

Finally, suffice it to say that I hope you are able to obtain a quick annulment or divorce and marry Elizabeth Hastings as you had planned. She will be infinitely more suitable, I am sure.

Ashleigh

Brett's face was as expressionless as stone as he finished reading the letter, but the turquoise eyes glittered dangerously as he raised them to Henry Busby. "Have Raven saddled at once," he bit out.

Recognizing the chilling look in those eyes, Henry knew not to question the command and moved instantly for the door with an "Aye, Yer Grace."

"Higgins," came the order to Brett's valet, "finish packing and go on ahead to London when you're ready. I leave now!"

And with a quick stride, he was out the door after Henry.

As he strode toward the stables, Brett's mind was a seething sea of fury. So she'd proved true to form, after all. Like all womankind, she was as false as a lie. Well, more the fool he, for not anticipating it coming this quickly! Leave him on the day after their wedding, would she? Well, he'd see about that! He'd find her, and when he did, she'd regret the moment she ever laid eyes on him. No woman was ever again going to play him false and get away with it—*no woman*!

With a grim set to his chin, Brett quickened his pace to the stables.

* * *

Ashleigh stood uncertainly beside Irish Night's stall in the stable of the White Horse Inn just outside of London where they'd taken lodgings for the night. In her hand she still held the note the innkeeper's wife had delivered to her chamber as she was preparing to undress for bed. "Ashleigh," it read, in the crude block letters her friend still labored to produce, "Patrick's gone to fech sum linamint fer his stalyonz leg, but I need yer help. Meet me in the stabel. —Megan."

They had made this unplanned stop on their way to another inn near the docks in London where Patrick knew he'd find the first mate of his sloop, the *Ashleigh Anne*. The sloop was their ultimate destination, but, inasmuch as she carried an American flag, he'd had to hide her in one of the many secret coves along the Devon coast that he'd known from his free-trading years, and because his trusted first mate stayed in London during their layover, Patrick had taken them on this round-about route before he planned to sail them all to his home in America—for good. But then, shortly after dark, Saint, Patrick's beloved chestnut stallion, had gone lame from a particularly rough spot in the unpaved road they'd been traveling—for Patrick had kept them to back roads and away from main highways in an effort to avoid being seen in their flight—and they'd had to stop here for the night.

After a supper in the inn's common room, Ashleigh had left Megan and Patrick to retire early. It had been a long, exhausting day for her, both physically and emotionally, and she was bone weary. But then she'd received Megan's note, and now, here she stood in the stable, and there was no sign of Megan or Patrick, or anyone else for that matter.

Thinking it odd that not even the old stable man was about—the one she'd spoken to earlier with special instructions for rubbing Irish Night down—she walked the few steps to the next stall, expecting to see poor Saint, but when she got there, Saint was gone!

At the same instant, she heard a rustling behind her, and as she turned to see what it was, a pair of strong hands grabbed her from behind, one quickly clamping across her mouth as she opened it to scream, the other pulling her roughly against a large male frame. She felt herself yanked upward, her feet dangling in the air as an arm clasped her in an iron band of muscle that held her immobile against her captor's chest.

Frantically, Ashleigh sought to loose herself, twisting her head from left to right to free her mouth and kicking backward with her legs, for her arms were held firmly against her sides, but it was no use. Although it was dark in the stable, she had no need of light to know the man was almost twice her size and many times stronger. A growing terror seized her as she realized she was entirely at his mercy.

Then a familiar scent met her half-covered nostrils over the equine smells of the stable, and a roughly whispered voice she recognized cut the air.

"I'm going to release your mouth as soon as you nod your head to indicate you won't scream, but I promise you—one sound, and I'll knock you unconscious, so help me, I will!"

*Brett's voice!* And she'd recognized the male scent of his, too, with its combination of sandalwood soap, tobacco and leather meeting her nose. Terror giving way to dread, she nodded.

He removed his hands and set her down on the hay-strewn floor, then grabbed her none too gently by the shoulders and spun her about to face him. She raised her eyes to meet his in the dim light given off by a single lantern at the end of the row of stalls, and what she saw then caused a cold lump of fear to settle in her midsection.

Eyes that had been chilling often enough in the past, now bored into hers with an icy regard that made all previous looks seem like nothing by comparison. Even in the near dark, their turquoise shards telegraphed an anger so monumental, she drew in her breath with an audible gasp.

"Get your tack and saddle the filly," he ground out at her from between clenched teeth, "and, *dear wife*, make not one errant move, for it would still be very easy for me to render you unconscious."

When Irish Night was saddled and bridled, he forced her to mount, then took a length of rope and bound her wrists together before handing her the reins. Her eyes widened as she saw him lead Raven forth from a stall farther down the row and take, from where it was draped over his saddle, a long cloak she'd kept at the stables at Ravensford Hall to use on chilly mornings when she'd worked with the filly. This he promptly threw over her shoulders, fastening and draping it so that it concealed her bound wrists. Then he extracted an old silk scarf she'd also kept in the stables to tie back her hair on occasion, when it got in the way of her work. She watched in silence while he mounted Raven, moved the stallion alongside the filly and reached out with the scarf in such a way as to indicate he would gag her.

"Oh, Brett, no!" she cried out softly. "Please don't—"

"One more word, and you'll find yourself bound hand *and foot*, as well as gagged, and slung over your saddle like a sack of meal!" he bit out with fury, and proceeded to tie the gag in place.

They rode for what seemed like hours, though in her weariness, Ashleigh couldn't tell for sure. The only words Brett imparted came at the beginning of the journey when, as he saw her casting about the inn yard, he told her not to bother looking for help. He'd sent the stable man out to exercise Saint's stiff leg after the liniment had been applied. As for Megan and her brother, he said, they were soundly tucked away in their beds at the inn. The note she'd received had been forged—by him. Did she realize, he mockingly inquired, that some of his wartime government service had involved learning to pen forgeries? Megan's simple letters had been child's play for him!

Sometime well after midnight, judging by how high the moon rode in the sky, Ashleigh saw the cobbled streets and narrow buildings they'd been passing give way to the familiar breadth of St. James's, and then King Street, and she knew he was taking her to his London residence.

Dismounting and throwing his reins to a sleepy-eyed stable boy he called Tim, he lifted Ashleigh from the black filly's back, gave her gag a tug to pull it free and, with a menacing look that said he would brook no attempts at fleeing or calling for help, ushered her to the rear door of the town house.

A wide-eyed Higgins met them at the door, but, aside from a brief response to a curtly phrased question from the duke as to how soon ahead of them he'd arrived, remained wisely silent as Brett bade him good-night and marched Ashleigh firmly upstairs.

Once there, he did not take her to the chamber she'd shared with Megan when they were in London in late spring, but instead, led her into a large, well-furnished bedchamber done in a masculine style, with its colors in varying hues of brown and dark blue. Shutting the door behind them, to Ashleigh's dismay he then locked it and pocketed the key; then he turned to her with eyes that glittered with impending menace.

Now that they were away from where other ears might hear, Ashleigh felt she dared risking speech. She *had* to know his intent. Swallowing past the growing lump in her throat, she turned apprehensive blue eyes upward. "Brett, I know you must be ang—"

"Shut your lying little mouth, you false bitch!" he snarled, roughly undoing her cloak. "Your charming little note said all I need to hear from you—ever!" He began to untie her bonds, the grim line of his mouth offset not a whit by the white lines that formed around it and the faint tick in his jaw muscles as he strove to hold his temper in check.

Then, as she rubbed at her sore wrists where the rope had been tied, he reached for the buttons of her smart little riding jacket.

Ashleigh took a step backward in alarm, her wide eyes flying to his face. Did he mean to undress her? Was he going to force intimacies upon her while in this forbidding mood? For it would be force he would have to use; she couldn't begin to think of giving him willing access to her body with things as they were between them now.

But Brett avoided her eyes and merely jerked her toward him and removed the jacket; then he spun her around and started on the buttons at the back of her habit.

"Brett, I—"

"One more word—just one—and I'll make you wish you'd never been given speech," he spat. Then he was pushing the habit down around her waist, her hips, her thighs, until it fell at last in a heap about her ankles.

This done, he began to divest her of her undergarments, finishing the shameful disrobing by throwing her heedlessly on the bed where he pulled off her boots and rolled down her stockings.

While he accomplished this, Ashleigh remained carefully silent, but had all she could do to push back the tears of fright and despair that choked. Unbidden, her thoughts flew back to an earlier time of humiliation and fear at his hands.

Finally, when she lay cowering and nude on the large tester bed, he stood looking down at her from his great height, his turquoise eyes gleaming with naked anger.

"I don't think you'll be going anywhere without your clothes," he sneered, "but just to make sure..." He retrieved the discarded scarf and began to bind her wrists again with it instead of the rope, oblivious to Ashleigh's moan of distress at the act. Then, almost as an afterthought, he pulled the bed's coverlet over her trembling form; this done, he blew out the lamp and headed for the door.

After he had unlocked it, she saw him turn toward her in the light given off by a pair of candles in a sconce in the hallway. "Sleep well, Your Grace," he mocked, then shut the door, and a moment later, a soft click told her it was locked.

Exhausted as she was, Ashleigh lay awake for a long time, unable to sleep. Myriad questions kept assaulting her brain, tumbling her thoughts about. What did he intend to do with her? Surely he couldn't keep her locked up like this indefinitely? Didn't he realize Patrick and Megan would tear London apart to find her? But would they know she was here? What if Brett kept her whereabouts hidden when they came to his house? And how long would Brett keep her from speaking, from trying to explain to him what had prompted her to leave? For she felt she could thereby perhaps gain enough of his understanding, if not his sympathy, to convince him to let her go.

She realized now she'd been wrong to leave the way she had, that she ought to have found the courage to face him and give him a fuller explanation. But her newly found awareness of how she felt about him, of her love, hadn't allowed her to think very clearly; she'd been too frightened of the vulnerability caused by her own feelings to consider his.

Well, now he would make her pay for it, and in spades! She had few illusions about what he was capable of; she'd sensed those barely leashed, flammable emotions smoldering just beneath his surface. No, he would not easily come around to feeling sympathy for her!

But somehow, she convinced herself as she at last felt her eyelids begin to grow heavy, she must find a way to convince him—that, or thwart him and find a means of escape.

*Oh, Patrick,* she cried silently to the darkness.... *Megan...someone, please find me...I'm frightened....* She drifted off into an uneasy slumber.


ASHLEIGH AWOKE THE NEXT MORNING to the sound of her door being unlocked. She had been sleeping fitfully, especially in the hours after dawn when her half-awake state was fraught with unsettling dreams of a man wearing an executioner's hood standing over her unclothed body, holding an ax.

She had little trouble, therefore, owing to the lightness of her slumber, in coming fully alert when Higgins entered the chamber. Recalling instantly where she was, she brought her bound hands before her to jerk up the coverlet that had slipped below her shoulders during the night. Willing the blush to leave her cheeks, she then turned her eyes to the manservant carrying a tray toward a stand beside the bed.

Smelling the aroma of hot chocolate and freshly baked scones, Ashleigh realized she was famished. "Oh, Higgins, how very kind of you," she said. "That smells delicious!"

The narrow-faced valet flushed with apparent pleasure at the compliment, but kept his eyes doggedly on the tray as he set it down and said, "Merely following orders, Your Grace." He turned about and headed for the door before pausing and adding, "I'm also to prepare you a bath—" he gestured to an adjoining dressing alcove partially hidden by a blue-and-gold coromandel screen "—over there."

"*You* are to prepare my bath?" Ashleigh asked in astonishment. When she and Megan had been here in the spring, a bevy of kitchen help had performed that service, for it involved the menial task of hauling heated water up a steep flight of stairs, something a servant with the status of Higgins should not need to do.

Higgins turned; his face flushed pink, and instead of looking at her, he proceeded to stare at a point somewhere on the wall above her head as he responded. "I'm the only one here, Your Grace. The London staff have been given several days' holiday."

"Oh," murmured Ashleigh, unwilling to examine what that implied.

"So, if you'll excuse me, Your Grace, I'll be going downstairs to fetch your bathwater while you enjoy your breakfast."

Ashleigh watched as he unlocked the door, exited, then shut it behind him; a second later she heard the click of the lock. Now it was her turn to flush as she imagined what the manservant must be thinking, being as involved as he obviously was in her incarceration. Then she realized he probably didn't know about her wrist bonds or her nakedness under the coverlet and would wonder why she hadn't begun to consume her breakfast when he returned. Her flush increased as she realized she'd be forced to tell him!

Determining not to allow such a humiliating situation to come to pass, Ashleigh thrust her bound wrists up before her and began to work furiously at untying the knotted blue scarf with her teeth. She only managed to tighten it further, and as the seconds ticked by, she cursed the quality of silk that allowed it to shred so easily while stubbornly refusing to become unknotted. At last she felt herself making some headway, however, and she forced herself to remain calm so that her small white teeth could operate efficiently.

Finally the knot loosened, and she tore her hands free at the same moment that she heard footsteps outside the door. Then as she reached for the tray at the bedside, a second panic set in;

if she extracted her arms from the coverlet, Higgins would re-alize she wore nothing underneath!

Several seconds later, as Higgins walked into the chamber carrying a pair of steaming buckets of water, he came upon the new duchess of Ravensford wearing a blue silk shawl over her shoulders as she nibbled daintily on a scone.

Ashleigh finished her breakfast while Higgins made three more trips for water. Then, when he informed her the bath was ready and she was expecting him to withdraw, she was sur-prised when he went to a large armoire across the room and proceeded to empty it of the dozens of pieces of male attire it contained.

"Wh—what are you doing, Higgins?" she stammered.

Higgins had the grace to flush deeply as he replied, "I'm terribly sorry, Your Grace, but I've orders from His Grace to remove every article of clothing from this chamber before I leave."

Now it was Ashleigh's turn to flush deeply. *Higgins knew!* He knew not only that she was being held here against her will, but that she was being kept stark naked in the process, not even al-lowed to wrap herself in her husband's shirts for modesty's sake!

Higgins left a few minutes later, laden with a huge pile of the duke's clothing, and as she heard the key turn in the lock, Ashleigh began to seethe with frustration and fury. So that was the way of things, was it? Not satisfied with kidnapping her and frightening her half out of her wits, her husband intended to humiliate her beyond decency in front of a high-ranking ser-vant! Oh, he was *despicable!* He was an *unfeeling brute*, a worse husband than—

Suddenly she broke off her mental tirade, focusing on one word she'd used . . . *husband*.

She glanced down at her left hand, seeing for the first time in twenty-four hours the ornate gold wedding ring he'd placed on her third finger two days before. Hands trembling with rage, she wrenched the glittering band from her finger and hurled it across the room, where it landed with a metallic clink against one of the brass andirons in the fireplace, then rolled some-where out of sight.

"So much for past mistakes!" she muttered to the empty room before throwing back the coverlet, sliding off the bed and marching straight for the dressing alcove.

Moments later she was soaking lazily in a steamy, rose-scented bath, her heavy mass of hair tied high on her crown by the blue silk scarf. She was just deciding to let the warmth of the water soak away her tension before beginning to scrub with the large bath sponge that had been provided on a short stool nearby, when she heard the door to the bedchamber open. Thinking Higgins had misjudged the time a woman might need to complete her bath, she called out anxiously, "Oh, please, Higgins, I'm not finished yet!"

"It isn't Higgins," said a biting male voice that was all too familiar.

With a groan, Ashleigh sank deeper into the perfumed wa-ter, just as Brett's impeccably attired profile came into view beside the screen.

"Wh-what are you doing h-here?" she stammered as she eyed his tall, booted form over the high rim of the brass tub. In addition to shiny mahogany riding boots, he wore a hunter-green riding jacket over a white shirt whose snowy stock ap-peared dazzling beside the bronze of his summer tan; an un-adorned white waistcoat and snug, thigh-hugging, buff-colored breeches completed the image. Unprepared as she was for the sight of him, his stunning virility nearly took her breath away. He was oh-so-unspeakably handsome with his dark chestnut hair curling negligently just above his collar and a lock of it falling rakishly over his forehead!

Then, as the turquoise gaze met hers, Ashleigh realized he'd caught her staring and hastily looked away.

An unpleasant, sardonic burst of laughter broke from his throat. "Did you really think I'd ask your permission to visit you in your bath?" As he uttered the final word, his eyes roamed freely, quite slowly, and, yes, deliberately—insult-ingly, Ashleigh thought—over her naked form beneath the water, for he was very close to the tub now, and could command such a view from his towering height.

Crossing her hands self-consciously over her breasts in embarrassed anger, Ashleigh felt heat rise to her face and knew it had nothing to do with the water's warmth. "If it has been your wish to shame me, Your Grace, then know that you have done so, and please leave." Eyes that had gone violet with emotion met his for a brief second, then lowered beneath a sweep of sooty lashes.

Observing the incomparable beauty of the tiny woman before him, Brett knew a moment of regret. She was so exquisitely lovely sitting there, her cheeks tinted with a rosy flush, ebony hair framing her beautiful face so enchantingly with ringlets that had escaped the thin twist of blue silk. And her eyes, when she'd raised them to his briefly, were the same hue they'd assumed when she lay beneath him in passion....

With a muttered curse, Brett brought himself back to the present. She was a lying, deceitful bitch who'd barely warmed his marriage bed before playing him false! She might be beautiful, but beyond that, she was a deserting wife... a cheat... a betrayer...a...*woman*! And here she spoke of her shame with an order for him to *leave* in the same breath! *Shame!*

A shriveling sneer twisted his lips as he gave her his softly spoken retort. "Your Grace, I haven't *begun* to teach you the meaning of shame."

Ashleigh's lashes fluttered open as she raised anxious eyes to his, all anger gone at the impact of his words. In its place came a hard, cold knot of fear that settled in the region of her stomach. "Oh, Brett," she pleaded, as frightened tears stung her eyes, "won't you please listen to me? I can explain if you'll just—"

An ugly bark of mocking laughter cut her off. "*Explain! Explain, Ashleigh?* I fail to see the need for any explaining! Indeed, your actions have been quite clear. Having lived up to the letter of your brother's enforced bargain with me, you promptly sought to rid yourself of a slight encumbrance you found yourself saddled with: the small matter of a *husband*!"

Tears streamed down Ashleigh's cheeks as she shook her head in denial of his words. "Brett, no!" she cried. "It wasn't that way at all!"

"Oh it wasn't, was it?" he mocked viciously, and the bite of his tone cut Ashleigh to the quick.

"No!" she shouted through her tears, a thread of anger returning to her voice. "You're making it sound all wrong, ugly, somehow, and I cannot bear to think you would believe I—"

"Oh, I can believe it, all right," he sneered, "of you ... of them," he added, pointing to an ivory carving of several dancing female figures resting on a low table nearby, "*of every female alive! You are perfidy itself!*"

He was bending forward now, the heels of both hands braced on the rim of the tub while he excoriated her sex. As he spoke, his fierce gaze was riveted on her face, his eyes scorching her with turquoise heat.

But Ashleigh thought she caught something else in his eyes, hiding behind the rage. Recalling some things Megan had told her about the way his grandfather had raised him, she had, at the same moment, a vision of a small boy trying desperately to hold back his tears as his mother's portraits were being stripped from the walls. And suddenly she understood what was happening. Suddenly she understood why, no matter what her own feelings were, she had been wrong—cruelly wrong—to leave him.

Leaning forward until her face was only inches from his, she cried in urgent tones, "Brett, have done with this hatred! I am *not* your enemy!"

Brett's voice was dangerously soft. "Oh, aren't you?" he questioned.

"No!" she spat, her compassion forgotten at the loathing she read in his response.

"And I say you are!" he thundered, "You, and your kind, more than any!"

"My kind!"

"Yes, you with your surface look of honesty and innocence! You are the most dangerous of all as with your guileless eyes and sweet words you lull a man into believing he might finally trust, might finally—*ah, hell*!''

White with rage, he took her shoulders and jerked her forward, his fingers biting cruelly into her flesh. Then his hands fell to her waist, and he hauled her roughly out of the tub.

Ashleigh's eyes widened with shock as she found herself lowered to the marble floor, water sluicing off her while she met his anguished gaze. ''Oh, Brett,'' she whispered brokenly, ''I never meant to—''

But she never completed her sentence. His mouth came slashing down across hers with a harsh cry. Stunned for a moment by the abrupt reversal in his actions, she didn't move a muscle as his arms came about her unclad form and drew her tightly to him.

But then she felt another change in him. The mouth that had swooped over hers like a hard, punishing thing began to work more slowly, his lips becoming softer, more pliant, as they molded hers in warm, sensual movements. Under this gentler onslaught, Ashleigh found her mouth opening to him, admitting the light thrust of his questing tongue.

When his tongue touched the tip of hers, she felt a fire ignite into a now familiar coil of pleasure at the base of her belly, and she shuddered, quickly reaching wet, slender arms about his neck.

This brought a groan from Brett, and he lowered one hand to span her buttocks, pulling her more closely against his hips where she felt the rigid proof of his desire through the skin-tight breeches. His mouth shifted to her ear, then to her hair where he muttered hoarsely, ''Damn you, Ashleigh! I've never wanted anyone this way before!''

Ashleigh's own passion was soaring and before it grew out of control, she wanted to reach him, to try one more time to make him understand. ''Brett,'' she murmured as he buried his lips in her hair, ''Brett, you must understand. I left you because I was afraid—''

Her voice reached Brett through the haze of passion that was building to a fever pitch, and so it was that he only heard the words ''I left you,'' but to him, it was more than enough.

"Damn your cheating soul, you bitch!" he shouted, all traces of passion gone as he thrust her violently from him. "Get yourself out of my sight!"

Ashleigh staggered backward from the force of his shove, and she lost her footing on the now slippery marble floor. Bending her knees and twisting with outthrust hands to break her fall, she landed on the back side of her thigh; this cushioned her fall but was nonetheless painful, yet, when she raised the back of her wrist to her open mouth, it was not the physical pain she stifled.

Brett stood over her, making no move to help her up or in any way come to her aid. Instead, an expression of contempt crossed his features as he snarled at her with ill-concealed loathing. "How appropriate! Stay there, you bitch, for that's where you belong—on the floor with the other dogs!" And with a parting look of pure hatred, he pivoted and quit the alcove.

# Chapter Twenty-Five

A slim ray of morning sunlight found its way through the drapes that had been drawn over the single window of Megan's chamber at the White Horse Inn. It slanted across the narrow, empty rope bed and onto the wide-planked oak floor where there was a tangle of blankets, sheets and pillows.

From this mass of bedding Patrick cocked one eye open to see what it was that had dared disturb his blissful state. Noting the culprit was nothing more than an errant sunbeam, he grunted, closed the eye again and reached for the long-limbed woman who lay sleeping beside him.

Megan stirred, then snuggled contentedly into the comforting warmth of his big body. A moment later a smile curved her lips when she felt his beard-stubbled chin nuzzle her ear.

"Faith, but ye be needin' a shave, ye big *aulaun*," she murmured as the smile widened to a grin.

This time Patrick opened both eyes and raised his head to see a pair of slanting green eyes meeting his gaze. "Ah, so 'tis complainin' ye are, *ma dilse*, and so soon after our first night t'gither!" he grinned while responding in a fair imitation of the brogue he'd come to love.

Megan's eyes became two limpid pools of sea-green water while she shook her head and whispered, "No, *macushla*, no complaints."

Patrick's blue eyes held a twinkle as he bent to kiss the tip of her nose. "I should hope not!" he growled. Then his blue gaze softened with infinite warmth. "I love you," he told her.

Megan's eyes shut with the sweet pain this wrought; she reached for him with trembling arms, burying her face in his shoulder in an effort to contain the emotions coursing through her. *He loved her,* and she returned that love with a fierceness she hadn't thought possible. Indeed, when he'd seen her up to her chamber after supper last night and taken her in his arms just outside her door to give her that first intoxicating kiss, she'd been totally unprepared for the emotions that rocked her. Oh, she'd been expecting the kiss for some time, considering her awareness of their incipient attraction to each other. But Patrick had curbed his appetite and bided his time, wanting, as he'd confided last night, to be sure their emotions were of the kind that endure, something more than just a passing infatuation.

And she had not rushed things, either; but on her part the lingering had had more to do with fear. She'd been grossly afraid that she'd be unable to respond to him physically, for she had been like stone to every man she'd taken to her bed in the years at Hampton House. Well aware that she'd always had to fake all the ardor she displayed in her former profession, she had feared that she was, by nature, cold and unresponsive in the physical sense.

So Patrick's kiss caught her by surprise, awakening a passion she'd been convinced did not exist, and Megan had soared on wings of rapture last night, eagerly greeting his whispered suggestion that they spend the night in her chamber. And the joy they'd found together! That the chamber's single narrow bed was inadequate to hold a pair their size had not daunted them. They'd gaily torn the bedding away and thrown it on the floor, and themselves after it, giving themselves up gladly to their passion.

Yes, it had been wonderful, but during the course of the night, when she'd come to realize she was falling in love with him, and now in the wake of his own declaration, a deeper fear had seized her. How, in the name of all the saints, was she going to tell him what she was, or rather, what she'd been?

Oh, it was true that, as he'd begun to undress her there on the floor last night, she'd stopped him briefly to give him a solemn look and said, "Patrick, I'm no virgin." And it was also true that he'd taken in her words silently for several agonizing seconds before he'd responded, "Neither am I," and then gone on to kiss her with such sweet, tender warmth, she'd found her gladdened senses spinning.

But admitting to a loss of maidenhood was a far cry from confessing to five years of whoredom! And yet now she knew, no matter if it cost her everything, she must tell him. It was part and parcel of the underlying honesty that formed her character. He loved her, and she could no more deceive this man who'd confessed it and come to mean so much to her than she could deceive herself. He had to know.

Slowly, agonizingly, knowing the risk she was taking, Megan drew back within the circle of their embrace and raised tremulous eyes to his. "Patrick," she said, her voice barely above a husky whisper, "I must tell ye somethin'."

"Yes, *ma dílse*?" he inquired softly, arrested by the pain he suddenly saw in the green eyes.

Megan swallowed, almost convulsively, then continued in a hesitant voice. "D-d'ye recall me tellin' ye last night I was no virgin?"

Patrick nodded and smiled, then reached to hold her head gently between his huge hands. "Yes, I recall it, but you were wrong," he told her.

At her puzzled expression, he continued. "You may have been without a physical maidenhead, my darling, but I knew, from the moment I caught the surprise in your eyes at your own passion, that your body was responding for the first time."

Startled that he'd perceived so much, Megan's eyes grew wide; then she nodded. "Ye read me well, Patrick. But ye see, there's more to it than—than that." *Oh, Holy Mother Mary, this is so hard!* she cried inwardly, then forced another swallow to dislodge the lump forming in her throat. Lowering her eyes, afraid to see the disgust in his face when he learned the truth, she made herself continue. "Ye see, Patrick, before I knew ye—"

"You were accustomed to faking your passion," he finished for her, a queer and tender expression in his eyes when hers flew up to meet them. "But, Megan, *macushla*, I'm hardly surprised, for what else could a sensitive soul like yourself have done at Hampton House?"

Megan's eyes widened and her hand flew to her mouth, but still, a gasp of shock escaped. "You *knew*?"

Patrick's eyes held only tenderness and warmth as he raised one hand and caressed her cheek in a soft, loving gesture. "I knew," he nodded.

Megan's face was an incredulous mask of shock, then dawning joy, before she threw herself into his arms with a sharp cry. "And ye can still say *ye love me*?" she questioned, her words breaking through a sob.

The rumble of Patrick's joyous laughter met her ears. "I can still say I love ye and hope ye'll not have as much trouble believin' I'm askin' ye t' wed me as well, colleen, *asthore*!"

Megan's deliriously happy cry reached him through her tears. "Oh, Patrick, *I love ye*!"

"And . . . ?" he questioned, stretching her at arm's length to grin into her laughing face.

"And I'll wed ye!" she grinned.

Patrick pulled her to him again, his glad laughter joining hers. "Ah, colleen, I'm going to enjoy doing all I can to make you happy!"

A long time later, after they had made slow, languorous love that transcended even the rapture of last night, Megan turned to look at him as he lay, smiling his repletion, beside her on the floor.

"Patrick?"

"Mmm?"

"How is it ye came t' learn o'—o' me past?"

"Oh, that." He smiled, then raised himself up on one elbow to look at her. "Do you remember when I disappeared for a couple of days last week while we were awaiting the wedding?"

Megan nodded. "Ye said ye had some affairs t' take care o' in London. I assumed ye were referrin' t' the purchasin' o' yer weddin' gift fer Ashleigh and Brett." She smiled, remembering the beautiful set of Belleek china with its four hundred exquisite pieces, each bearing the initials AWB, and the Ravensford coat of arms.

"Well, yes," said Patrick, "I did purchase that in London, but I also went there to look into what kind of a place it was that my sister had resided in for so many years."

*"Ye didn't know?"* Megan questioned incredulously.

Patrick chuckled. "That it was such a house? Oh, yes, Ashleigh told me as much, although I'd already learned the basics from Brett. But I wanted to know more of the specifics. I wanted to learn just how it was that she'd been able to retain her innocence for so long, despite her surroundings."

"So ye spoke t' Madame." Megan's tone was flat.

"Yes, I did, but more important, I spoke to Dorcas," he said with a meaningful look. "It was from that dear woman I learned of a multitude of kindnesses extended to my sister, not the least of which involved consistent protection by a tall, beautiful redhead with a heart bigger than she is."

Megan shrugged, then offered him a small, self-effacing smile. "'Twas nothin' much. I love the wee lass, Patrick."

"I know, *macushla*, but never underestimate what you did for her—you and Dorcas, bless her."

Megan's eyes grew dark. "But 'tis what I was finally unable t' do fer her that fashes me now. Oh, Patrick, what are we goin' t' do fer the poor lass? 'Tis the present I'm concerned about!"

Patrick nodded, his eyes equally troubled. "I cannot help thinking her running away is a mistake. But I have my own guilt to deal with for forcing the marriage. Megan, when she met us looking so heartbroken, so much in pain, what else could I do but promise to help her get away?"

It was Megan's turn to nod. "Aye, 'twas a difficult situation fer ye. I wonder what he said t' her, t' convince her he'd be an unfaithful husband. I mean, I couldn't help feelin' there was more t' her tale than she told."

"I know," Patrick agreed. "I felt it too." His eyes drifted to a point somewhere across the room. "I cannot help thinking it would have been an unlikely thing for Brett to tell her on their wedding night, no matter how angry he'd been. After all, he told me earlier he held no grudges.'' Patrick ran a hand carelessly through his rumpled hair. ''And I also cannot shake the notion that Brett has some feelings for Ashleigh. I've seen the way he's looked at her—when he thought no one was watching.''

His gaze found Megan's again. ''Well, we've not left England yet, and it will be several days before we can. Perhaps we'll be able to bring her to open up to us more, maybe even persuade her to reconsider . . . in time.''

''Oh!'' said Megan, sitting up suddenly. ''Speakin' o' time, what o'clock is it? I'd forgotten the beasties are locked in yer chamber, and although that porker's housebroken, I wouldn't care t' test her too far.''

''True,'' Patrick grinned, reaching for his breeches, ''and if I know my little sister, she might already be seeking me out in my chamber. She's an early riser, and if she fails to find me there, she's apt to come here. Then she'd put two and two together quickly enough!''

Megan laughed as she reached for her shift.

A half hour later, Megan raised worried eyes to Patrick's as they stood outside Irish Night's stall at the inn. ''What could have prompted her t' leave, d' ye think, and without any word t' us?''

Patrick shook his head, bewildered. ''And beyond that, where has she gone?''

''Somethin' isn't right about this, Patrick. The innkeeper said he didn't see her leave this mornin', but he also said Mrs. Quimby's the early riser. I'm goin' back inside t' see if she's returned from her trip t' the hen house. Perhaps she saw Ashleigh leave.'' Megan turned and headed for the inn.

''I'll search around here a bit,'' Patrick called after her. ''Perhaps I'll turn up a clue.''

As Patrick entered the empty stall, Finn joined him, his shaggy head bent to the ground. Behind them, a softly grunting Lady Dimples imitated the wolfhound's posture.

Suddenly Patrick heard Finn begin to sniff, and rather loudly. He glanced down to find the big dog pushing his nose into the straw—or was it straw? The light in the stable was poor, but he caught sight of something white beneath Finn's paw as the hound suddenly raised his head and barked.

"What's that, boy? Found something?"

A moment later Megan came running through the door. A puffing Mrs. Quimby, the innkeeper's wife, was right behind her.

"Patrick!" Megan called. "Someone sent her a note last night. Mrs. Quimby says—"

"I know," said Patrick, looking at her oddly. He handed her a piece of wrinkled parchment. "Finn just found this on the floor there."

Megan took the parchment and rapidly scanned its surface, then raised her eyes to Patrick's. "'Tis my writin' form, but, Patrick, I niver wrote this!"

"Oh, no," asserted a breathless Mrs. Quimby as she craned her neck about Megan's shoulder to view the parchment. "'Twas a gentlemun gave me that. Th' lady 'ere, she'd already gone abed."

Patrick's eyes went from the innkeeper's wife to Megan, then returned to the parchment. "I didn't think you could have written it, Megan. You were with me from the time Ashleigh left us until—" he glanced briefly at Mrs. Quimby, then threw Megan a half smile "—until you retired. But," he added with a tap on the parchment with the backs of his fingers, "someone with a knowledge of your penmanship went to a great deal of trouble to make Ashleigh believe you'd written it."

"Someone rather skilled in the art o' forgery," Megan added grimly.

Patrick turned to the stout, middle-aged matron. "Mrs. Quimby, you said a gentleman handed you the note. Can you tell us what he looked like?"

"Oh, that I can, sir," said Mrs. Quimby, suddenly brightening and no longer twisting her apron nervously with her hands. "'E was tall—oh, not as tall as you be, sir, but tall enough, just th' same—and 'e 'ad 'air th' color o' ripe chestnuts—'andsome 'e was, too, with eyes neither blue nor green, but a startlin' color somewheres in betwixt—beautiful eyes, if I may say so.''

"Oh, no," groaned Megan.

"Brett," groaned Patrick.

"Is aught amiss?" questioned Mrs. Quimby, her hands again wringing her apron.

"Nothing you need trouble yourself about, Mrs. Quimby," Patrick sighed. "Thank you for your help." He glanced over at the stall that held Saint. "I may have to ask your help in one more matter, however, or Mr. Quimby, perhaps. My horse requires at least another couple of days' rest before he can travel. I'll pay well for someone to tend him, as well as for a mount to hire until he's fully mended. If you'll assist me . . ."

Ashleigh sat wrapped in a monogrammed silk sheet and gazed about the chamber she'd come to regard as her silken prison. For three lonely, frightening days and three miserable nights, he had kept her imprisoned here. Beyond the lack of clothes and someone to talk to, she hadn't wanted for anything. Well-prepared meals were served to her three times a day by a taciturn Higgins; Higgins also lit a fire for her in the beautiful Georgian marble fireplace if the evenings became chilly; daily baths were prepared; candles were provided for the numerous silver candlesticks in the chamber, and even lighted for her following the manservant's trip with the evening supper tray. . . . She had everything she required—except her freedom.

She had no doubt as to why he'd brought her here, of course. It was to punish her for leaving him; that much was clear. But what she hadn't learned was what his plans for the future entailed—or if he indeed had any.

A carriage rumbled by in the street outside the open front courtyard, but Ashleigh paid it no heed. It wasn't that those passing by couldn't hear her if she chose to open the front window and yell for help; it was that she was completely helpless to do so. How could she yell publicly through a window in a fashionable part of the city when she wore no clothes? Even if she dared risk it, what could she say to an answering stranger, wrapped as she was, only in a sheet? Considering the incredible details of her story, and whose house she was in, she suspected such passersby would think her a shameless prankster, or worse, stark raving mad; and this was to say nothing of the scandal it would create!

Her thoughts swung back to her husband and his unmitigated anger, as well as his relentless determination to keep her in the dark as to what he planned to do with her. Oh, it wasn't as if she had no access to him! On the contrary, he entered the locked chamber nightly, always arriving well after midnight in the blackest of moods.

He rarely spoke two words to her then, but would cast dark and forbidding looks her way before staggering to the bed and throwing himself, fully clothed, upon the mattress beside her. And always, on these occasions, she would smell the scent of liquor and some strange perfume he brought with him, before flinging herself to the far side of the bed in fear and disgust.

But he never made any further moves to touch her. In the mornings, when she awoke later than was her custom—for she usually had trouble falling back to sleep once he joined her—she'd find him gone, with nothing to show he'd even been there, except a lingering scent of brandy and perfume. And if she'd had doubts about leaving him and the fears that had prompted it, this present behavior erased them from her mind. Not only was he spending his evenings with other women; he was deliberately coming to her with evidence of it—flaunting it before her with obvious intent.

So, as the gray light of dawn crept through the windows, Ashleigh's thoughts would focus on one thing: escape. Desperately, she willed Patrick and Megan to find her, clung to the hope that they would—and soon—for she wasn't sure how much more of her present wretchedness she could endure.

While Ashleigh sat upstairs contemplating her fate, Brett was facing a problem of his own on the floor below.

"Really, Lady Margaret, I cannot see why you've come," he said with cool annoyance. "You hardly ever come up to London, and I especially don't see why you should be here in the warm season."

"Well, then, Brett," said Margaret as she stepped farther into the entry foyer, "you will simply have to allow me to explain myself." Glancing about, she added, "Where are your servants? I'm aware that you occasionally stoop to answering your own door, but—"

"I've given all but Higgins a week's holiday."

"Holiday? But whatever for? Surely you realize—"

Impatient, Brett cut her off a second time. "Lady Margaret, kindly state your visit's purpose and then leave. As you can see, without a staff, I am hardly in a position to entertain guests."

Ignoring him, Margaret walked toward the double doors on their right. "In the drawing room, if you please, Your Grace. You can hardly expect me to discuss anything standing in your foyer. Your manners are disgraceful! And ring for Higgins to fetch some tea," she added while pulling open the double doors. "I've had a long ride."

Sighing with dislike and frustration, Brett did as she said, and a few minutes later, found himself sitting across from her in an upholstered chair in the drawing room. "Now," he said, "what is of such monumental importance that it would bring you all the way up to London in the heat?"

"To begin with, *this*," she told him, handing over a sheet of paper she'd extracted from her reticule.

Brett's jaws clenched as he recognized the flowing script of his wife, spelling out her parting words.

"You dropped this in your haste the evening you left," said his great-aunt. "One of the maids found it and brought it to me, and I thank Heaven she did. Imagine the scandal if it were found by one of the servants who can read!"

Crumpling the note with a look that denoted weary disgust, Brett met her icy blue eyes. "So you've come about the content of…this," he said, gazing at the crumpled mass for a long moment before letting it drop to the thick carpet. His gaze returned to Margaret. "Well, what of it?"

A soft knock at the door indicated Higgins had arrived with the tea. Brett endured the interruption with a growing impatience that was mollified somewhat by the sight of a brandy snifter and a bottle of his best contraband on the tray bearing the tea service. He quirked an eyebrow at the sober-faced manservant as he set the tray before them, but Higgins's only response was a knowing look, coupled with a quick glance at Lady Margaret before he withdrew.

Pouring himself a liberal helping of brandy, Brett again faced his great-aunt. "As you were about to say, Lady Margaret?"

Margaret finished stirring a lump of sugar into the tea in a delicate porcelain cup, set aside the silver spoon she'd used, and gave him a prolonged look before saying, "I've come to help ease the way for your divorce."

Brett's brows drew together menacingly. "And just what makes you think I'm going to obtain one?"

Margaret stopped in the midst of taking a sip of tea and lowered her cup to its saucer. "Well, isn't it patently obvious? The chit's left you. And good riddance to bad rubbish, too, I say! Now, I realize there may be a scandal. Divorce isn't easily overlooked, even for those of our class, but there's where I may help. I know enough of the old guard of the *ton*, and all it takes is a few carefully chosen words placed in the right ears—of certain gossipy sorts, I mean—and I'm sure I can make it appear you were totally blameless in the entire affair. Why, all I need mention of that girl is that she—"

"You will do nothing of the sort!" Brett ground out from between clenched jaws.

Margaret gave no evidence she'd heard the menace in his tone. "Really, Brett, it's the only way. Face facts. The baggage is gone. What else can you mean to do? Run after her and cart her back? Why, she's likely halfway to America by now with that brother of hers. Divorce her, I say! You have no alternative!"

The turquoise eyes narrowed as he gave her a contemplative look. "But I do have an alternative."

Margaret arched her eyebrows over the rim of her teacup. "Which is . . . ?"

"To remain wed."

"To a woman who is not here?"

"To a woman who *is* here!"

The teacup rattled against its saucer as Margaret's jaw dropped. *"Where?"* she breathed.

"Upstairs in my chamber, where she's been since the day she left."

The blue eyes narrowed. "Willingly?"

There was a second's hesitation. "No."

"Oh, for God's sake, Brett! What's the point?"

Brett drained the contents of the snifter, set it down on the tea table, and rose abruptly from his chair. "The point is," he said, walking toward one of the tall front windows, "that I've prevented her from deserting me, and that I *want* her here. At least, until I decide what to do with her."

"And when will that be? Brett, don't you realize that every day that passes may make things more difficult? What happens when her brother comes looking for her? Or have you detained him, too?"

Brett shook his head as he gazed abstractedly out the window.

"There, you see? The man is bound to come around, asking questions. Think of the scandal if he chooses not to be discreet!"

"Enough!" Brett whirled from the window to face her; his eyes held a mixture of rage and frustration. "I don't wish to discuss it further. Perhaps I shall divorce her. I won't say it hasn't crossed my mind. But, until I decide what's to be done, I'll brook no more arguments from you. Is that clear?"

Margaret rose from the velvet settee and gave him a long look. "Perfectly. Now, if you do not mind, Your Grace, I've had a long, tiring afternoon, and I am no longer a young woman. I fear you will have to endure my presence in your house, like it or not. I shall take the green room. Please ring for Higgins to make it ready for me."

"You intend to stay, then?"

"Is it not what I have just said? Fortunately, I've brought my abigail. She's waiting with my baggage in the coach without.

You will please have her—and it—sent to me." She headed for the double doors.

Brett watched her cross the room, angry frustration evident in his rigid stance. "Wait," he snapped as she reached the doors. When Margaret turned to him, he continued. "Since you appear determined to stay here, you may as well make yourself useful. Higgins hasn't had as much as an afternoon off in weeks. I've business at Carlton House of the like that takes me away during the day and frequently, far into the night. As long as you plan to be here, I'll want you to... keep an eye on things while I give Higgins the time off that he has earned."

Margaret's face registered mild shock. "You wish *me* to be your wife's jailer?" she questioned snidely.

Brett made a gesture of impatience as he, too, headed for the doors. "Call it what you like. Between you and your abigail, you ought to be able to manage for a few hours at a clip."

Having opened the doors and passed through them, he headed for the front entrance before pausing a moment and turning back to her. "Oh, Lady Margaret—" his tone was deceptively soft "—I wouldn't be entertaining any enterprising notions if I were you. If my wife is allowed to escape while in your charge, you will pay dearly for it, I promise you. Remember the dowager's cottage. Even with its refurbishing, I shouldn't think you'd enjoy inhabiting it permanently. Moreover, if Ashleigh disappears while under your... care, I shall *never* seek the divorce you so devoutly crave—*never*! Tell that to yourself and your darling Elizabeth!"

This said, he whirled and made for the door.

Oliver Higgens was feeling quite pleased with himself as he lurched through the side door of the Three Coachmen pub, which was located at the edge of London's West End. He'd more than doubled the five quid he'd brought with him tonight, having bested Will Barker at four out of five rounds of draughts and then trounced Geordie MacNeil at the dart board—and with six pints of ale in him, too!

Now he needed relief from all that ale he'd consumed, hence a trip to the narrow alleyway before walking home. Positioning himself to face a wall that, judging by the stench, had endured countless visits by the customers of the Three Coachmen over the years, Higgins reached for the front closure of his breeches when he suddenly felt a hard object jam against his ribs.

"Make not a move," said a deep voice behind him.

Higgins froze, a lump of fear closing his throat. *Oh, hell!* he thought. *Now some bloody Dick's going to lighten my pockets of my winnings!*

"Answer my questions satisfactorily," came the voice from somewhere above, as well as behind, him, "and you'll have nothing to fear, understand?"

"Y-yes," stammered Higgins, wondering why a thief should wish to question him.

"Is your name Higgins?" asked the voice.

Beginning to wonder at the cultured tones articulated by a man who ought to sound like a street tough, Higgins nodded.

"The same Higgins who is employed as valet to the duke of Ravensford?"

Again, Higgins nodded. Damn, if the voice didn't sound familiar! It had just the barest hint of a drawl to it. Where had he heard it before?

"Very well, Higgins, answer my next question correctly and you may soon be on your way and safely home. Where is His Grace detaining Her Grace, the duchess?"

It was the brother, the one who'd lived in America! Oh, he was a big one, he was! But His Grace would have his hide if he—

"Answer quickly or you'll wish you had!" The object at his rib cage jabbed harder.

Well, he'd been feeling awfully sorry for the little miss anyway.... "She—she's here in London, sir."

"At the house on King Street?"

"Yes, sir," Higgins paused, then thought, *Ah, well, in for a pence, in for a pound.* "She's locked up in His Grace's chamber there."

"Thank you, Higgins," said Patrick. "You may turn around, now."

"Um, ah, sir?" Higgins squirmed.

"Yes?"

"Before you came, I was just about to, ah, that is—"

A snort of amusement met his ears. "Of course. But don't try anything foolish. I've no wish to harm you, and I've a few more things to discuss with you."

When he'd relieved himself, Higgins turned about to see Patrick standing before him with nothing more than a fashionable walking stick in his hand. *Bloody hell!* he thought, but then, upon considering the size of the hand, not to mention the man, who held it, he meekly followed Patrick's gesture to accompany him out of the alleyway.

Twenty minutes later Higgins was sitting opposite Patrick and Megan in their large, hired carriage as it sat outside Patrick's lodgings.

"You understand what you must do, then?" Patrick questioned him.

Higgins glanced nervously one final time at the ferocious-looking wolfhound who sat on the floor between them and answered, "It—it doesn't seem too difficult, sir. I'm to be sure the Lady Margaret is sufficiently distracted after you've made off with the little—with Her Grace in the carriage, to give you time to get completely away before her absence is discovered."

"Good man," said Patrick. "Before that, you need only admit me to see Old Iron Skirts."

Higgins smiled for the first time since encountering Patrick this evening. He had little love for Iron Skirts, and it pleased him to be putting one over on her. He was beginning to think he might enjoy this after all! It might even compensate for the guilt he'd feel at betraying his employer. Besides, he'd already been feeling guilty for keeping Her Grace confined. And helping the brother and the Irishwoman rescue her was a damned sight preferable to being at the mercy of the big man, or worse, this hellish hound of theirs.

"The critical thing," Megan was saying, "is to take advantage of any distractions available. You say she insisted you be home tomorrow afternoon because she's expecting someone for tea?"

"Lady Bunbury, yes," nodded Higgins.

"Perfect," said Patrick. "We'll time it so that I arrive just as Bunbury is leaving. That way Iron Skirts will already be in the drawing room and I can prevail upon her to offer me a cup of tea. It will give Megan more time."

"You must listen at the door," instructed Megan, "and when Lady Bunbury rises to depart, go to the other front room—the library, isn't it?—and twitch the draperies at the window two times. We'll be in our carriage outside the courtyard, waiting for your signal . . . and, Higgins?"

"Yes, miss?"

"The beasties will be with us."

Higgins's eyes flickered to the pig at her feet, and then grew wider as they swung to the great shaggy animal beside her. He swallowed and nodded.

"Good. We're all set, then," said Patrick. "I'll let you off a bit of a distance from King Street, just to take no chances of anyone seeing you with us, and then, love," he added, looking at Megan, "you and I must make a stop at the dressmaker's."

# Chapter Twenty-Six

While Patrick and Megan were en route to Madame Gautier's a few blocks away, Brett stood pondering the locked door of Ashleigh's chamber. It had been a hellish three days for him, with the nights the worst of all, and tonight didn't promise to be any better. When he'd first decided to kidnap her and bring her here, there'd been little in his mind but the need to lash out and punish her for what she'd done—for revenge. But now that he had her under his roof and totally at his mercy, he found little satisfaction in it; if anything, he'd learned revenge is a double-edged sword, quite capable of cutting the one who wields it, as well as the one at whom it is aimed.

He should be enjoying the humiliation of this woman who had attempted to desert him! Why wasn't he? Why, after his government business was done each day, did he find it necessary to inundate himself with brandy and a string of faceless women, before he could bring himself back here at night? Upon awakening each morning, why did he almost run from the sight of her sweetly sleeping face, eager to throw himself into an endless series of meetings and the like, those boring yet time-consuming rounds of duty that he hoped would drain his thoughts of unwanted things, but that never quite managed to do so?

He'd thought to take his revenge, making her suffer for a few days, then release her and seek the divorce she'd suggested, wiping her out of his mind and his life in the process. But his mind would not be quit of her...nor the yearnings of his body, he reminded himself sardonically. And now, here was Margaret, arriving with her urgings to seek the severance he himself should have instigated by now, reminding him of what he knew only too well: he'd been putting it off because he wasn't sure he really wanted it. Divorcing a woman he'd erased from his mind would have been easy; divorcing one who hovered in his thoughts every waking moment, her presence stronger than ever, was impossible.

Well, tonight he'd forgone the trips to clubs and gambling halls following his last session at Carlton House. Tonight he'd taken a light supper in his chamber—God forbid he should join Lady Margaret in the dining room! He'd bathed, changed his clothes, and then waited until he heard Higgins depart from Ashleigh's chamber with her bathwater before stepping across the hall to stand here before her door. It was time he made a decision.

Ashleigh sat in a chair before one of the open windows in her chamber; it had turned hot earlier in the day, and nightfall had brought no promise of cooling the city of its closely held heat, so she had come here to catch what breeze she could, to dry her hair after washing it in the bath. Wrapped around her body, from armpit to ankle, was the ever-present sheet she'd clothed herself in for the past three days. She was beginning to grow accustomed to it!

She smiled, recalling Patrick's descriptions of islands he'd visited in his seafaring days, where he said the women wore little more than this as their daily garb. But her smile quickly vanished as thoughts of her brother reminded her of how much she missed him and of her dwindling hope that she might see him again soon.

A sound at the door plunged her into the present. Setting down the hairbrush Higgins had found for her, she straightened in the chair just as the lock turned and Brett stepped into the chamber.

He was dressed informally, in pale gray breeches with black and gold Hessians and a white shirt that was open at the throat, minus stock, waistcoat or jacket. His hair was still damp, indicating he'd recently bathed; it curled casually about his ears and over his forehead, adding to the informality of his appearance, but more than this, it gave him the effect of being more youthful, even boyish. He was oh-so-handsome, and Ashleigh's stomach did a little flip-flop when she saw him.

Aware she was looking at him, Brett took a moment to observe her in return. She sat very still in the chair before the window, and a soft breeze caught her long, midnight curls, ruffling them about her face and bare, silken shoulders. The chair was upholstered in deep blue velvet; against it, her small, slender body, wrapped as it was in the white sheet, stood out in relief, accentuating her lithe curves. Her eyes as they met his had never seemed bluer, and they sparkled, catching the candlelight that also bathed her skin in a warm, mellow glow, making it appear sensuous beyond reckoning. He felt an instant's urge to rush to her and pull her against him, that he might feel that powder-soft skin and the countless other textures of the ripe body he'd come to know so well: the whisper softness of her eyelids; those silken strands of hair; the satin curve of her lips when she smiled...

Gritting his teeth, he put aside this inclination, knowing they must talk if he was to reach any decision at all.

"I see you've adapted to your surroundings quite well," he said, indicating her placement of the chair before the open window.

"To my prison, you mean," she corrected.

"As you wish." His reply was noncommittal.

"But you must know I do *not* wish it! Brett, can you not tell me what you intend to do with me? I—I must tell you, it has been very difficult for me. If such was your intent—to make me suffer—it has been successful, but—oh, please! Won't you let me go?"

Brett took a few steps toward her. "And to what end, Your Grace? If I should release you—now, this very night—where would you go? Would you run to your brother, to the very man who, only last week, threatened to kill me if I did not make you my wife? Would you merely pick up where you left off three days ago, and go blithely on your way to some solicitor's offices to seek your freedom? Is that all these three days have bought me? By God, I'll not have it! Not until I have some an-swers at least!''

Ashleigh heard the growing anger in his voice and was dis-mayed. She had, upon seeing him at first, hoped he'd come to discuss the situation without rancor. It was the first time since their encounter the evening he'd come upon her in her bath, that he'd seemed willing to talk, and she'd been hopeful they might come to an understanding, that he might even be ready to release her. But now she saw that the bitterness was still there, feeding the anger, and she realized she'd better try to head it off; she might never have this opportunity again.

Rising from the chair, she met his gaze, saying in as calm a voice as she could summon, ''I agree, Brett. We must both have some answers.''

''Then we'll begin with the only real question I have.'' As he said this his face held no expression, but his eyes telegraphed a host of emotions—rage, bewilderment, pain, they were all there. ''*Why?* Why did you run from me, Ashleigh? Was one night in my lawful bed so repugnant to you that you could not bear the thought of repeating it? Did you find marriage to me so distasteful, you could not wait to set it aside?''

Ashleigh began shaking her head at this questioning, slowly at first, then ever more wildly as tears started to spill down her cheeks. Oh, she loved him! She was sure of it now, especially when she saw the raw emotion that was choking him inside, releasing itself in anger instead of some terrible pain he couldn't seem to acknowledge.

''Brett, no! It wasn't any of that, I swear to you! *Please!* You *must* believe me! Oh, I know now I was wrong to leave with-out talking to you first, but I—''

''So the only thing you'd have done differently was that you'd have *talked to me first*? 'Oh, Brett, I'm terribly sorry,''' he mimicked, '' 'but I've just had a change of heart.' *Is that it?* No further explanations? *Nothing?* Did that brief time to-gether mean so little to you?''

Ashleigh had opened her mouth to try to tell him he was wrong, that she wished to give him some sort of explanation—having to do at least with Elizabeth's words to her, if not her own fears that came of the vulnerability she felt at loving him—but then his last question hit her with an impact that wiped all else from her mind.

"No, Brett," she said, her words barely a whisper. *"It meant everything to me."*

Brett stopped and stared at her for a moment, stunned by her words. Then, with a hoarse, animal cry, he reached out and pulled her to him in a fierce embrace, bending to bury his face in her hair as he held her.

Locked in his arms, Ashleigh felt the powerful trembling of his body; she moved her own arms upward about his neck without thinking, for she was beyond thought now, answering only to a compulsion deep within her. It said: *This is the man you want, the man you need, the man you love. This is Brett, your husband. Love him, love him, just love him!*

Brett's lips found her temple, her brow, her eyes, wet with the salt of tears. Again and again, they passed over her face while he held her tightly to him. "Ashleigh," he murmured. "Ah, Ashleigh, I can't ever let you go! You've become some kind of desperate fire inside me . . . consuming me. . . ."

His arms loosened and he began to move his hands over her slender frame as he spoke in hoarse, hushed whispers, his voice shaking with emotion. "I've never needed a woman before, love . . . not in the way I've found I need you . . . not like this, *never like this . . ."*

Gently, he loosened the sheet about her body until it drifted in soft folds to the floor. Then he withdrew a pace, holding her at arm's length, and his eyes swept hungrily over her body before coming to rest on her face.

"Ashleigh . . . ?" he questioned.

She raised her eyes to meet his, then gasped at what she saw there. Of course, she had expected desire, and it was clearly evident, a raw hunger so powerful her knees threatened to buckle with its impact; but going far beyond this was something that touched her to the core: his eyes held a look so vulnerable, she thought at first she might be imagining it, but then she knew it was real. Here, for the first time, was Brett with his defenses stripped away. Gone was the taunting mockery, the anger, the worldly sophistication, all the things she'd felt were a barrier between them; in their place was a naked plea that said: *I am showing you my soul. I am baring my pain. Take it, and do not throw it away. It is all I know how to give you right now, but it is everything I have. . . .*

Ashleigh's breath caught as she understood. He might not love her—at least, not yet—but he was giving her far more than he had ever given before. For now, it was enough. Her breath came out in a rush as she threw herself into his arms with a small cry. "Oh, Brett, *I'm so sorry!* Forgive me, darling, forgive me! I—"

"No need now, love," he rasped. "Just stay with me . . . be with me. . . ."

Then his mouth swooped down to capture hers in a kiss that was fraught with longing and urgent need. Hungrily, his lips crossed hers, then crossed again, tasting, taking, giving everything his eyes had promised.

Then he was bending to sweep her into his arms, carrying her to the bed they'd shared in celibate loneliness the nights before. Once there, he eased her gently onto the mattress, stood, and quickly undressed before he joined her.

Ashleigh watched with greedy eyes as he shed his clothes, realizing she was finally as ready for the sight of his naked flesh as he had been for hers. Silently, her face full of wonder, she drank in the sight of the broad, massive shoulders, the muscular chest covered with whorls of dark chestnut hair, the powerful thighs, the hard, flat abdomen and lean hips, and— oh yes—the very bold and evident proof of his arousal!

Brett caught her stare, and when he had stretched beside her on the bed, his eyes held gentle amusement as they found hers. "I take it I meet with Her Grace's approval?"

"Oh, Brett," she cried, "I find you so—*so beautiful*!"

His laugh was shaky as he drew her to him. "Sweetheart," he breathed, "beauty didn't exist until God made you!"

He began to make love to her then, with a gentle tenderness at first, his hands and caressing lips repeating the message of his words; with kisses light as down, he found her eyes, her ears, the sensitive corners of her mouth; with a touch lighter than a butterfly's wing, his fingers traced the slim, white column of her throat, the satiny curve of her shoulder, the lush fullness of her breasts. But when they grazed the rosy peaks of her nipples and Ashleigh's eyes flew open, meeting his and telling him instantly of the potent response he'd wrought, his touch became more insistent, urging her passion forward to meet the growing hunger of his own.

And Ashleigh responded wildly, arching her hips upward to meet his, pulling his head to hers as her mouth opened for his kiss. Eagerly, she met his questing tongue as her slender hands moved down the back of his head, his neck, and across the broad shoulders that, in her mind's eye, she could still see as he'd stood before her moments before. And when Brett's hands were slow to descend to her waist and lower, to her undulating hips and thighs, she reached for one hand and drew it to the dark triangle between.

A hoarse, surprised gasp from him was followed by a warm murmur of approval as his lips moved to her ear. "So eager, little one?" he laughed softly. Then, "Oh, sweetheart, how it pleases me when you show me what you want!" Knowing fingers found the wet, delicious warmth of her woman's place... then caressed... and caressed....

A maelstrom of yearning built in Ashleigh, blossoming beneath his touch, and she cried out with her need. "Brett! Oh, Brett, I want... I... oh, please!"

"I know, love," he murmured, "I want it too... want you... only you...." With a quick movement, his hips met hers, his mouth at the same time hovering over her parted lips. "Open to me, love," he whispered, "... now..."

And gladly, Ashleigh gave him what he asked. Thrusting her hips upward, she eagerly parted her trembling thighs and a moment later was rewarded by the bold, turgid heat of him filling her.

A cry of rapture broke from her lips, and she reveled in the feel of his weight on her body, of his pulsing manhood inside her; meeting his thrust with her own, she took what it promised, crying out for more with every glad muscle of her body.

And Brett exulted in the pleasure he gave her, taking it and making it a part of his own. Again he thrust, and again, until their candent movements built to a crescendo of driving passion.

Then, in a high, soaring moment of pure joy, Ashleigh cried out his name, her pleasure breaking over them, through them, melding them as one.

And Brett answered her cry with a harsh note of his own as his body convulsed with hers, shuddering its release while they clung together, aware only of each other.

After a long time following, when their spinning senses had stilled to the point where they could at last begin to think again, he moved his lips in her hair, murmuring, "Ashleigh...never before, love, I swear...nothing I ever felt was like this."

Ashleigh closed her eyes, savoring his words. What did it matter that there'd been other women, if this were so? If the ecstasy she'd felt were any measure of what he, too, had shared, surely he would no longer need to seek others...surely he'd find all he needed in her bed, just as she knew, for her, there'd never be another man. It was all she required right now. Love, if she was patient, might come in time, and as long as she had his body for her own, she felt she could wait. It would not be easy, and she would need to be strong, but she would do it; she must. And he *would* be faithful...wouldn't he?

"Brett," she whispered, just as she felt him slipping from inside her. She paused for a moment, regretting the loss.

"Yes, sweet?" he murmured, turning on his side to pull her close again.

"Will—will you stay with me?" she ventured, not knowing how to voice her lingering doubts more clearly.

Misreading her question, Brett laughed softly, saying, "All night long, sweetheart. Wild horses couldn't pull me away!"

Dismayed that she hadn't gotten through, she lost the courage to question him further. With a sigh, she snuggled against his warmth, promising herself to approach him again...soon.

They slept then, with Brett's arm wrapped possessively about her as their sated, naked bodies took a respite from their passion.

It was many hours later, during the time they call false dawn, that Ashleigh awoke to find Brett thrashing about on the bed beside her. His voice split the air with an anguished cry.

"But what did she look like? Won't you tell me . . . ? Please! Tell me why she would leave without even saying goodbye. . . . I beg you . . . please, I need to understand. . . ."

"Brett!" Ashleigh reached for his shoulder to give him a shake. "Brett, wake up! You're dreaming!"

"Mother, don't go! I—" Suddenly Brett sat upright, his face an anguished mask, beads of perspiration along his brow.

"Brett, it's all right," Ashleigh soothed. "It was just a bad dream."

Picking up on the crooning note in her voice, he stiffened, fully alert to his surroundings now, and yet deeply suspicious of what, in his sleep, he'd revealed. "What did I say?" he asked sharply.

Bewildered by his tone, Ashleigh withdrew her hand from his shoulder. "It was nothing," she told him. "You were merely having a—"

"For Christ's sake, Ashleigh! *What did I say?*"

Not comprehending the fear that fed his anger—fear of his own vulnerability, that he might have exposed to her some deeper part of himself without knowing it—she reacted only to the sting of his tone. "You spoke of someone leaving you . . . a— a woman . . . of her going without any farewell, I believe."

"And . . . ?" Brett's lips were drawn into a hard, straight line and his eyes scrutinized her face with unwavering coldness.

Hurt that he should behave toward her in this manner, especially after what they'd shared just hours before, Ashleigh reacted with an anger of her own. "For God's sake, Brett! You question me as if I have been privy to a confession of murder! Leave it alone! What is it to me that in your dreams, you cry out for your mo—"

"Damn you!" he shouted, grabbing her by the shoulders. "Damn you to hell, Ashleigh!"

"Me? Damn *me*?" she responded incredulously, shaking free of his grasp. "What have I done? I only sought to wake you, that you would cease to be tormented by—by childhood pain at your mother's desertion. Damn *you*, I say! Yes, *you*! Brett, *I am not your mother!*''

Brett's face turned white with emotion for several long seconds. Then, without saying a word, he left the bed and quickly donned his breeches; pausing only a moment to gather up the rest of his clothes, he went to the door without a single glance in her direction, opened it, and left, slamming it behind him. A second later Ashleigh heard the sound of the lock turning, and, choked with disbelief, she crumpled to the mattress with a sob.

From her position at one of the tall drawing-room windows, Margaret watched Brett's phaeton leave the drive. She'd risen early, awakened by the sound of a door crashing shut, down the hall from her chamber. Aware neither of their servants would have dared to slam a door, she'd guessed it was her grandnephew departing, and from his wife's chamber—in a fury!

Smiling slyly to herself, she turned from the window. It was a perfect time to effect a plan that had been growing in her mind since her discussion with Brett yesterday. She could not chance waiting until he—*perhaps*—came around to her way of thinking on what to do about his disastrous marriage. The situation warranted action.

Hastening toward the stairs, Margaret thoughtfully fingered the key she'd taken from the ring the housekeeper had left in the pantry: the key to Ashleigh Sinclair's chamber—she would never refer to her as anything but Sinclair; just the thought of the creature as a Westmont was anathema to her. Margaret's smile reappeared as she reached the upstairs hallway. If she hurried, she might still find the girl immersed in the tears she'd heard her shedding earlier when she'd listened outside her door, and that would help; she wanted Ashleigh Sinclair at her most vulnerable.

Ashleigh raised her tear-stained face from the rumpled bedclothes as she heard someone approach. Thinking it might be Higgins with her breakfast tray, she hurriedly slid off the bed and retrieved the sheet she'd been wearing, barely managing to stave off a new flood of weeping when she recalled how the sheet had come to be on the floor. She had just finished wrapping it about her when she heard a key turning in the lock, and wondered at this, for Higgins always knocked before entering. With a quick swipe at her wet cheeks with the back of her hand, she tried to assume a dignified stance as the door opened, but when she recognized the black-clad figure who entered, her attempt at composure fell apart.

"Lady Margaret! What are— I mean, I—I beg your pardon, but I didn't know you were here."

"I've just arrived . . . a few moments ago," Margaret added mendaciously. It was important to her plan to have the girl think she'd been summoned *after* the scene that had prompted her weeping. "I—ah—had been staying with a dear friend in town . . . she's been ill, bedridden, that is, and therefore I remained in her home rather than here, for I wished to be available to read to her, to cheer her up, you see, while she was recovering." The door closed behind her, Margaret stepped closer to Ashleigh.

"I see," said Ashleigh, wondering what any of this had to do with her.

*Not yet, my dear . . . but you will,* thought Margaret. She continued speaking, eyeing Ashleigh's tear-ravaged face as she did so. "Brett was aware of where I was, so it was quite easy for him to ask me to come by this morning. . . ." Margaret allowed her words to trail off suggestively while she watched Ashleigh's face for a reaction.

"Brett sent for you just now? But, why?"

"Well, I suppose it was because he couldn't attend to . . . *things* himself, my dear. When he dropped by, he was in a frightful hurry . . . something about a riding engagement with Lady Pamela Marlowe, I believe."

Ashleigh gave a short, involuntary gasp of dismay at the mention of her husband's mistress. *Oh, dear God, no! How could he?* she cried inwardly. *The bed we shared last night still bears the imprint of his body while he—* Hastily taking a breath in an attempt to regain her composure, she made a deliberate effort to focus on what else Margaret had told her. "*Things*, Lady Margaret? What things? I'm afraid I don't—"

"You look a bit pale, my dear," said Margaret. "I understand you've only Higgins to wait on you, and he's presently busy in the stable. Shall I send my abigail for something in the kitchen? Would you care for some tea or—"

"Oh, no, no, thank you," Ashleigh replied hastily, for she was anxious now to learn why her husband had sent for his great-aunt with such apparent urgency this morning; she had an uneasy feeling it had something to do with her, for why else would this woman, who had clearly never cared for her, have come to seek her out? "But Lady Margaret," she continued, "you mentioned some 'things' Brett wished attended to...?"

"Ah, yes," said Margaret, turning deliberately toward the fireplace so Ashleigh couldn't catch the look of satisfaction she feared her face might reveal. Appearing to study the Turner landscape that hung over the mantelpiece, she added, "Well, I was speaking of the immediate arrangements Brett wishes to make—for the divorce, that is."

There was a deadly silence in the room, punctuated only by the steady ticking of the mantel clock beneath the painting, while Ashleigh closed her eyes in a futile attempt to blot out what she'd heard. So he was seeking the divorce at last.... Well, it was what she'd wanted, wasn't it? But then, why did she feel as if she'd been cut to the heart? *Because, after what he shared with you last night, you'd assumed there was a chance for this marriage!* a small voice answered. *Yes, but that was before that insane quarrel this morning,* another voice countered. *That was before he showed you he carries some demons inside that will never allow him the peace to be happy with a woman, to love a woman! Face it, you foolish girl! He wants to be rid of you. Margaret's being summoned is the final proof.*

Opening her eyes, Ashleigh met the older woman's cool blue gaze. "I understand," she said softly. She hoped Margaret couldn't see the absolute act of will it took to keep her voice from revealing anything more than a tone of quiet resignation. It was all too obvious she'd been crying before the older woman came to her chamber, but she'd die rather than allow her to see her succumb to such emotion now.

Forcing her face to remain blank, Ashleigh asked, "Am I to be allowed to leave, then?"

"Oh, His Grace did not say," replied Margaret as she turned toward the door, "but I'm sure you will be shortly, my dear. Just as soon as our solicitors...well, you know how these things are...preparations need to be exact—to avoid any hint of a scandal, you see." She turned back to Ashleigh when she reached the door. "That is where you can be of some help, I should think. Perhaps the next time you see the duke, you can quietly insist he reach your brother. Ah, he does maintain a residence in London, does he not? It shouldn't be too difficult to convince Brett that the best way to avoid unpleasant talk would be to have you accompany your sibling back to America. Out of sight, out of mind, you know." Margaret turned and opened the door.

"Well, my dear, I can see this hasn't been easy for you but I'm sure, in the end, you'll realize it was the wisest thing. In the meantime, have a spot of tea. It does wonders for an upset. I'll send someone up with a tray. Good day."

She stepped through the door, closed it, and after turning the lock, left Ashleigh alone.

# Chapter Twenty-Seven

The large brougham turned into the paved courtyard of the Georgian town house on King Street, then pulled up behind a barouche that was already standing there, its calash lowered in obvious deference to the warm weather, a liveried driver nodding sleepily in the sun while he loosely held the reins.

"That would be Lady Bunbury's carriage," whispered a male voice inside the second vehicle, "just where Higgins said it would be."

Megan looked up at Patrick from where she sat, dressed in seaman's clothing, on the floor of the closed carriage. "How clever or alert does the driver look?" she asked in a low voice.

Patrick chuckled. "He looks neither, and might even be snoring. That old windbag's probably kept him out here for an hour. But even so, not to worry, love. Thornton's ready to distract him if we need it." He gestured in the direction of the driver's seat where Abner Thornton, the *Ashleigh Anne's* first mate, posed as their driver. "Now, the important thing for you to remember is not to run for the side of the house until I've been inside for at least five minutes. That way—"

"Patrick St. Clare! D' ye take me fer a *bosthoon*?" Megan fumed in a rough whisper. "We rehearsed this half the night! I can surely remember t' give ye time t' distract the old crone so she doesn't see me makin' fer the bushes outside o' the chamber where they've incarcerated the wee one!"

Realizing Megan had deliberately included a detailed description of where she was to go, just to show him she recalled everything they'd rehearsed, Patrick grinned. "No, love, I'd never think *you* a child." He gave her trousers an arch look. "Not even in those, do you appear anything but a full-grown woman."

Megan flushed, then glanced at the seat opposite Patrick where Suzanne Gautier sat wearing one of Megan's carriage dresses. "'Twas never meant t' fool anyone," she muttered, "merely t' make it easier fer me t' climb that tree and throw Ashleigh the— Patrick! Where's the rope?"

"I believe ze peeg 'as eet," whispered Suzanne while gesturing at the pink wiggling mass on the floor beside Megan.

Megan clamped an arm over Lady Dimples, who was pushing her snout above the seat where Suzanne sat and appeared to be of a mind to join the well-dressed redhead.

"Megan, for God's sake, keep that pig out of sight!" Patrick muttered.

"I'm tryin', Patrick, but she's atop the rope, ye see, and I've got t' get it—out! Ah, here we be!" she exclaimed, holding aloft the piece of ship's rigging they'd brought along as a rescue ladder.

"I see," said Patrick, trying his best to keep his voice down, "but the damned pig—"

"'Tis churlish o' ye t' be swearin', Patrick St. Clare," Megan sniffed, "and besides—" Suddenly her attention veered to Lady Dimples, who, grown to a goodly size by now, had managed to wriggle her way out of the Irishwoman's grasp, thrust her bulk onto her lap and, from there, plop both forelegs on the seat beside Suzanne.

All at once the floor of the carriage became a tangled mass of arms, legs, rope and squirming pig.

"Lady Dimples, no!" Megan hissed. Then, "*Dammit, Finn!* Can't ye keep yer porker in line?" She glared at the wolfhound who was stuffed into the floor space on the other side of her, looking miserable about the whole business.

"Tsk, tsk, Megan O'Brien," muttered Patrick, "it must be that seaman's outfit leadin' ye on t' such *churlish* behavior!"

It was his turn to be the recipient of Megan's glare, but in the next instant he dropped his mimicking accent, saying, "Oh, no! She's sitting on the seat!"

And Lady Dimples was, indeed, sitting on the carriage seat, with one of her forelegs braced against the squabs, doing her best to peer out the window like any fellow traveler.

"Pig, I'm warning you, get down there where you belong, or we'll be having pork dinner tomorrow!" Patrick threatened in as hushed a voice as he could assume, given the urgency of the situation, not to mention the state of his temper.

"Patrick!" said Megan in an outraged whisper, even as she tried to dislocate the adamant, nonbudging pig.

But it was Suzanne who saved the moment from becoming the abortive catastrophe Patrick was beginning to envision. Reaching into the portmanteau full of clothes they'd brought for Ashleigh—for Higgins had been forced to explain, abashedly, the state of affairs, with regard to dress, that kept the duke satisfied his duchess would not attempt an escape— Suzanne produced a fashionable bonnet with large blue feathers adorning it and proceeded to tie it about Lady Dimple's human-size head.

"Voilà!" exclaimed Suzanne. "Now she may seet by ze weendow!"

At this, Lady Dimples immediately calmed down. In fact, she almost preened under the shadow of the gently waving ostrich feathers.

Patrick took one look at the animal and burst into semisubdued guffaws of laughter. Megan looked from him to the pig and did the same, and it was only Abner Thornton's puzzled voice outside Patrick's window that brought them back to the seriousness of the situation at hand.

"Begging your pardon, sir, but are we going through with this or not?" the first mate asked.

Instantly sobered, Patrick nodded. "We are, Thornton. To your post." He gave each of the women a pointed look, bestowed a final, admonishing glance on the seated pig, and then opened the door on his side. "This is it, then," he whispered, "and may we be in Heaven an hour before the divil knows we're dead!"

Inside the town house's drawing room, Lady Margaret was pouring Lady Bunbury her third cup of tea.

"Thank you, my dear," said Lady Bunbury, "and I'll have another of those scrumptious tea cakes, too, if you don't mind."

Margaret watched her guest reach for the last of the dozen or so rich little cakes that had filled the silver tea platter only an hour before, suppressing a shudder of disgust at the greedy appetite of the corpulent woman who sat beside her on the settee. Looking down at her own half-tasted tea cake, she realized Lady Bunbury had consumed nearly the entire batch and wondered at her own fortitude in enduring this gluttonous old gossip's visit. If it weren't necessary to make use of the creature's dependably loose tongue to ensure the proper cast to the inevitable gossip that would attend the divorce, she would never have considered inviting the woman.

"Mmm," murmured Lady Bunbury around a mouthful of the confection, "delicious . . . absolutely delicious. My compliments to your pastry chef, Lady Margaret."

Again, Margaret stifled a grimace, recalling the scene in which her nearly insubordinate abigail had wailed incorrigibly at being forced into kitchen duty to bake the cakes, owing to the absence of the duke's staff. Ah, well, a few more well-calculated tidbits in the old creature's ear and it would all be worth it.

"Yes, my dear," said Margaret, "it is fortunate that His Grace was able to find the man and reengage him after this new bride of his let him go. And the pastry chef wasn't the only member of the staff the poor, uneducated girl dismissed. Why, she had it in her head to replace them all—servants who'd been in our family's service for years—just to demonstrate the power of her own newly acquired position!" Margaret shook her head in sympathy. "Poor Brett . . . I mean, I realize he was acting nobly in honoring that twenty-year-old betrothal contract the brother located, but, my dear! The circumstances had changed since her parents and my dear brother agreed to the alliance when the girl was born!"

"Yes," murmured Lady Bunbury sympathetically, "I'd heard. Orphaned, they say, and raised in some sort of institution...hardly the proper place for the training of a future duchess! Tsk, tsk," she added, shaking her head, "and do you mean to say His Grace took her to wife, knowing how ill fit she was?"

"Precisely," Margaret nodded, "and now feels duty bound to put up with the results, regardless of the consequences. I've tried to reason with him, of course—especially in light of the latest development..." She allowed her voice to trail off suggestively.

"The latest *development*?" questioned Lady Bunbury, setting down her teacup with an avid look.

"Well..." mused Margaret, "I'm really not certain I should be repeating this, but...dear Lady Bunbury, if you promise not to—"

"Oh, not a *word*, my dear! I shan't breathe a syllable!" Lady Bunbury exclaimed as she leaned forward eagerly.

"Well," said her hostess, lowering her voice to a whisper, "the worst news of all, and I have it straight from an old, devoted servant, the chambermaid who tended to their marriage chamber. It seems Brett's new duchess was not a..." Margaret's hushed whisper imported the damning tidbit into the old lady's ear, causing her guest to recoil with a predictable show of shock.

"No!" exclaimed the matron in a loud whisper. "And your poor grandnephew had no idea?"

"None," murmured Margaret, shaking her head with distress.

"Oh, my dear," muttered her guest, "how terrible for him! But now what can he do?"

Margaret eyed her assessingly, trying to gauge the precise manner in which the reply must be uttered, then proceeded to speak in careful tones. "I'm afraid it's an ugly situation, my dear Lady Bunbury, but I think, after a while, His Grace will come to see there is no help for it. *Divorce* is so *distasteful* a subject, I know you'll agree, but as I have already told him, what else can he do? It's beginning to look as if the girl is, ah, breeding, and, of course, the child cannot be his... and the dukedom must be protected at all costs, mustn't it?"

Lady Bunbury's ears fairly twitched with this latest news. Oh, it was all too delectable! She glanced at the mahogany tall clock that stood in an alcove across the room. Slightly past five—too late for another afternoon visit—but if she hurried, she'd be able to rest and still change in time for dinner at Lord and Lady Mowbry's. Thank heaven they had returned from Brighton and had the grace to be entertaining, even in this heat! August was such a difficult time to be full up with news to tell! There was hardly anyone about worth telling it to!

"Well, my dear," said Lady Bunbury as she reached for her reticule, "I am ever so distressed at your family's unfortunate situation. You have my complete sympathy, I can assure you. But I really must be on my way, I'm afraid. I had no idea it was so—"

A soft knock at the door cut her short.

"Yes?" called Margaret.

The drawing room's doors parted, and Higgins stepped between them. "Another caller, your ladyship... Sir Patrick St. Clare."

A brief, perplexed frown crossed Margaret's brow before she responded. "Thank you, Higgins. Lady Bunbury was just leaving. Show her out before you show Sir Patrick in, please." She bestowed a meaningful look upon Brett's manservant. It would never serve for the chit's brother to be allowed to exchange words with Bunbury, and having caught the look of interest on the old gossip's fat face at the mention of who the caller was, Margaret was taking no chances that she would change her mind and decide to prolong her visit.

"Yes, your ladyship," murmured Higgins; he deftly propelled the departing guest into the entry foyer and past the huge man who stood studying a priceless Renaissance sculpture on the calling-card table nearby, nodding briefly to Patrick only after he'd ushered Lady Bunbury to the outer door.

Having been informed of the manservant's impressment into majordomo duty owing to the sad state of affairs where the duke's servants were concerned, Lady Bunbury did her best to accept graciously Higgins's unseemly hurry to rush her past the new caller, especially as it related to the gossip she'd just gleaned, suppressing her regret that she wasn't being allowed to exchange a few words with the unfortunate duke's new brother-in-law. Instead, she contented herself with a thorough inspection of the large carriage that stood directly behind hers, viewing, with a gossip's eye for details, the profile of the beautiful redhead at its window.

Then, just as Higgins was propelling her in the direction of her own vehicle, Lady Bunbury was treated to a most curious sight. As the redhead's profile withdrew into the recesses of the closed carriage, another bonneted head came into view. It had a face that looked for all the world like a—

"*Good Heavens!*" exclaimed Lady Bunbury. She turned to Higgins. "My good fellow, what—I mean, who—? That is, do you see . . . ?" The words came out in a sputter.

Higgins glanced in the direction of Lady Bunbury's line of vision, and nearly collapsed. It was that *pig*, with a lady's bonnet on her head, no less!

"Ahem, ah, yes, your ladyship," he murmured, deftly steering the ogling matron away from the larger carriage. "Right this way, your ladyship. Your carriage awaits."

Craning her neck over her shoulder, she could still glimpse the porcine face gazing serenely at her from beneath a profusion of waving blue ostrich feathers. Lady Bunbury continued to sputter. "B-but, my good man, that woman looks *exactly* like a—"

"Shh!" murmured Higgins, raising a finger to his lips. Then, in lowered tones, "I beg your pardon, your ladyship, but it's such a delicate situation, you see."

"Delicate?" Lady Bunbury lowered her tone to match Higgins's, but her eyebrows were arched almost to her hairline, the look of astonishment on her face absolute.

"Yes," murmured Higgins with a sad shake of the head. "You see," he continued as he engineered the path of the large matron toward her own vehicle, "Ah, that's Sir Patrick's carriage, and the young lady inside—the one with the red hair, that is—is his fiancée."

Lady Bunbury shook her head, disbelief still etched on her features. "Not that one! I meant—"

"Indeed, your ladyship," Higgins nodded patiently, "I was just coming to, ah, *that one*."

Lingering shock warred with impatience on Lady Bunbury's rounded features. "Yes...? Well, my good man, speak up, *speak up*!"

Having finally stalled for enough time to concoct his story—and with a last, assessing glance at the matron's well-fed figure—Higgins plunged ahead. "As I was saying, Lady Bunbury, Sir Patrick is engaged to wed that *other* younger lady in the carriage, but, into the bargain, the poor man's had to accept the, ah, companionship of the lady's ... mother."

Rounded eyes in an astounded face questioned him. "Good Heavens, do you mean—?" Lady Bunbury glanced again at Patrick's carriage.

"Exactly." Higgins nodded solemnly. "And needless to say, your ladyship, the poor woman is not the least bit handsome like her daughter."

Lady Bunbury's eyes widened further at this understatement, but Higgins continued, seemingly nonplussed.

"But the poor dear wasn't always, ah, that way, you see. They say it was from eating too much rich food—" Higgins eyed the horror-stricken countenance of his victim for a full five seconds "—tea cakes, as I recall...they were her favorite food. Always stuffing herself at teatime, she was, and—oh, I say, your ladyship! Don't be in too great a hurry, now. Wouldn't want you to trip, entering your own carriage, would we? There you go, now, your ladyship, safe home, ma'am."

The apoplectic look on the large woman's face was so intense as she signaled her driver, Higgins nearly choked on the tongue he'd been biting to keep from laughing. *Oh, well done, old boy*, he congratulated himself. *Edmund Kean himself couldn't have done it better! You'd best take care, or they'll be signing you up at the Drury Lane!*

And in the carriage that was traveling down King Street at a steady pace, Lady Bunbury briskly fanned her perspiring face as she made a mental note to inform her cook about some forthcoming and immediate changes in her diet.

Meanwhile, inside the town house Lady Margaret eyed Patrick speculatively as she prepared to answer the question he'd posed as to her knowledge of the whereabouts of his sister. There was something about the man, or, more particularly, his behavior right now, which didn't sit well with her. He seemed…confident, that was it, even overconfident, for a man who ought to be frantic to locate a sibling who'd been kidnapped several days before. What was he up to?

Hearing the sounds of a carriage leaving the drive, Margaret moved with an apparent casualness toward one of the long windows. Heaven knew, she would be only too happy to see the sister spirited away, but she could ill afford Brett's nasty temper if it occurred while she was in charge. What was it he'd said? Something about *never* securing the divorce if that happened! Well, if there was an escape being executed at the moment, she'd be damned if she were going to allow it to occur beneath her nose!

But when Margaret moved the heavy velvet drapery aside and gazed out at the courtyard, the only thing she saw was Patrick's carriage with the lovely profile of a familiar-looking redhead at its window. Satisfied for the moment, she turned to the big man standing across the room from her. "Why, no, Sir Patrick. I've no idea where Her Grace might be. As a matter of fact, the last I heard from the duke was that he suspected she'd gone off with *you*! But I do wish someone would inform me as to what is going on."

"Very well, Lady Margaret," said Patrick, more than glad for the opportunity to extend his visit, "why don't you pour me some tea while I explain…."

Twenty minutes later, Patrick bent gallantly over Margaret's hand as he prepared to follow Higgins to the door. "Farewell, m'lady, and thank you for the tea. You have the address of my lodgings if you should hear anything. Please do not hesitate to send word."

Nodding, Margaret watched him leave, a faint note of suspicion in her eyes. *I wonder . . .* she mused. She stood in the drawing room, engrossed in thought for several long moments, while Higgins returned from the foyer and began clearing away the tea service.

Higgins was not blind to the pondering look on Iron Skirts's face, especially when he caught her glancing upward in what was clearly the direction of Ashleigh's chamber. Then, when he saw her nod decisively, as if having reached some conclusion, and turn to leave the room, he knew he had to act quickly.

Balancing the heavily laden tray in one hand, he rushed for the double doors, saying, "Oh, allow me, your ladyship!"

A second later, at the precise moment when Margaret would have charged through the doors and up to Ashleigh's chamber to determine whether she was still there, the entire tea service, slops bowl and all, came crashing to the floor in front of Margaret, thoroughly soiling her skirts in the process.

"You clumsy fool!" she shrieked, drowning out the hastily murmured apologies of the duke's manservant. "Look what you've done! Oh, you *oaf!*"

But as Higgins scraped and bowed, vowing to have the damage—and her ladyship—repaired in no more than ten or fifteen minutes, Patrick's crowded brougham was already speeding across town, its interior filled with the relieved sounds of Ashleigh's laughter as she hugged the two redheads and her brother while Finn licked her face in welcome and Lady Dimples grunted happily as she gazed again out the carriage window.

It was late when Brett let himself into the house on King Street. He'd stabled his horse and phaeton himself, in the absence of any servants, and found no fault in the fact that Higgins had not waited up for him. They'd long ago dispensed with his grandfather's Old Guard requirements that a manservant stay awake for his master, no matter how late the hour. Too many years had passed with nights in which Brett never came home at all.

After doffing his jacket in the front hall, the first thing Brett noticed was a folded piece of parchment with his name on it, lying on the calling-card table. He'd ordinarily have ignored any correspondence until morning, but he recognized Margaret's tight script, and it prompted his curiosity. Unfolding the note, he read:

Your Grace—
I am returning this evening to Ravensford Hall. When you enter your wife's chamber, I suppose you will quickly guess why.

Margaret

Brett's brows drew together in a frown, and he murmured, "What puzzle does that old witch set me now?" even as he bounded up the stairs for his wife's chamber. Reaching the door in the darkened hallway, he paused for a moment, not sure he wanted to greet what awaited him there.

He'd kept thoughts of Ashleigh purposefully at bay all day and into the night, welcoming the unusually late meeting at Whitehall that lasted well past midnight. He'd known that, if he allowed it, his confusion at the conflicting emotions that had driven him out of the house shortly after dawn would have given him no peace.

Indeed, during the short drive home, despite his weariness and the lateness of the hour, he'd been prey to the most damnable set of torturous images, and they all had to do with his wife... well, almost all. There'd been thoughts of Ashleigh in a sunny meadow, laughing helplessly amid the wildflowers at a pig and her dog; then, quickly supplanting this, he saw Ashleigh on Ranleagh's arm, bestowing her most winning smile on the blackguard; but the next image was of her lying in his arms on their wedding night, murmuring, "Brett, oh Brett." Yet still another picture came to goad him: of a young footman handing him a cursed farewell letter....

Finally there was that last image, the most hellish of all, where his boyhood nightmare returned, as it had last night; servants carrying a woman's portrait from the Hall as he, a small boy, cried for them to stop. But this time the vision was different. They did stop, and when they turned the portrait toward him, he saw the woman in the portrait was Ashleigh!

Shutting his eyes to blot out the image, Brett reached into his waistcoat pocket and extracted his key, but when he went to insert it, he found the door already unlocked. Steeling himself against a flood of new emotions, he opened the door slowly, already knowing what he'd find on the other side.

Except for the lambent ruffling of the curtains at the open window, the chamber was still. His gaze drifted toward the large tester bed, which, even in the shadows, he could see was neatly made. Slowly, like a figure in a dream, Slowly, Brett walked across the silent chamber, finding his way amid the shadows of the furniture by the moonlight filtering through the windows. Wearily, he ran a hand through his hair, his head slumped in a gesture of defeat.

He knew that she was truly gone this time; he dismissed all notions of a late-night ride to search her out and bring her back. Even if that were possible, she clearly wished herself rid of him, so much so that, despite the obstacles he'd set forth, she'd found a way to escape. Well, it was what he'd wanted, wasn't it? For days he'd longed for some way to make a decision about her, and tonight she'd saved him the trouble; she'd made it for him.

*But then why did he feel so hollow inside?*

Heaving a tired sigh, he braced an outstretched arm against the mantel of the fireplace, lowering his chin to his chest as he studied his boots in a contemplative gesture. Then he saw it— a tiny gleam of metal catching the moonbeam that reached the corner of the cold hearth. Bending forward, he retrieved the object, then straightened before transferring it to his open palm. Her wedding ring.

The palm of his hand trembled slightly before it met his fingers to become a clenched fist that squeezed the ornate band so tightly, its sharper edges cut into his skin. Slowly Brett walked to the window and stared into the night, and then the fury began....

# Chapter Twenty-Eight

The Ligurian Sea's blue-green waters sparkled in the early-October sunshine, and gentle waves curled and foamed about the random scattering of rocks that laced Livorno's surf. Here and there a gull cried as it floated effortlessly under the blue dome of sky covering northern Italy's coastline, and the only clouds in view were puffy white mounds that formed a friendly backdrop for the little village that rose upward on the hills above the beach.

From the open carriage that stood on the unpaved road well above the water's edge, Ashleigh had a commanding view of the beach, but it was not the beauty of the day or the picturesque coastline that had her attention as she sat, fanning herself, in the sun. For the past half hour or so, as she waited with their driver for Megan and Patrick to return, she'd been fascinated by a group of a dozen children playing in the surf under the watchful eye of a tall, slender woman.

What fascinated her, firstly, was that each of the children, who appeared to range in age from about three to perhaps ten or eleven, was in some way infirm. Several of them limped when they walked, and two or three had even arrived on crutches when she first spied their little band coming along the road, which was a short while after Patrick had taken Megan to the village to ask directions, leaving her here because she was feeling fatigued again and in need of a rest after their trip from the *Ashleigh Anne*. Now, as she watched the youngsters frolicking happily in the waves, she saw that one small boy had a deformed foot but managed to enter the surf bravely on the arm of a larger boy whose other arm ended at the elbow. Both, she noted, were grinning happily as they jumped a wave together.

And then there was the woman. Wearing a light summer dress she had hiked above her knees, she held by the hands two small twin girls, who walked with no visible infirmity, but smiled at their companion with continually closed eyes, for they were blind. The woman was not young, although she had appeared so at a distance; she carried her straight yet willowy frame with youthful ease and moved agilely among her young charges. But Ashleigh could see prominent streaks of gray in the hair that escaped the straw bonnet she wore, and her voice, as she called to the children in lilting Italian, or laughed with them at their play, had a mature quality to it.

But what struck Ashleigh as the most intriguing thing of all, was a strange, unshakable sense that this woman was familiar to her, and she wondered at this, for there was no one thing in particular that signaled this should be so. It wasn't the woman's features, for they were hardly visible beneath the shadow of the bonnet's brim; it couldn't be her speech, for it was in a tongue Ashleigh couldn't understand. But there was something about the way the woman moved, and her rich, vibrant laughter as it spilled across the sounds of the surf....

Wryly reminding herself that she was probably growing fanciful in the heat, Ashleigh fanned herself more vigorously and forced her thoughts back to her own circumstances. It was slightly more than two months since the evening she'd escaped from the house on King Street in that ridiculously crowded brougham. Two long months in which Patrick's every effort to take them to his home in America had been thwarted by the British sea patrols along England's coastline. Such vigilance against the upstart Americans threatening war had been vastly increased especially since the patrols no longer needed to contend with Bonaparte. Even though Patrick had known the reasons for England's impressment of American seamen, largely responsible for the United States's declaration of war on Britain in 1812, were no longer valid—the end of the European conflict relieved the Royal Navy of their desperate need for men to populate their fighting ships—he nevertheless feared an encounter with the English at sea. The *Ashleigh Anne* was still an American ship and, as such, would certainly be seized by the Royal Navy, most likely for spying, or possibly for smuggling, by the revenue cutters.

So for many weeks their little party had waited aboard Patrick's schooner as it remained anchored in one hidden cove or another along the English coast, even then traveling only at night from one clandestine port to the next when threats of discovery forced them to move.

But a little less than a fortnight ago, when Ashleigh's recurring queasiness upon awakening each morning, coupled with her admission, under Megan's gentle questioning, that she'd missed her monthly flux for the second time, made it clear she was pregnant, Patrick had determined they could wait for safe passage to America no longer. After learning of her condition he had at first tried to convince her to return to her husband, but when this proved fruitless, he'd devised a second alternative to that of sailing to his home in Virginia.

"We'll fly a false flag," he'd said. "Dutch or Belgian, I should think, and then make our way carefully south, keeping to the coastline once we've crossed to France. It's risky, but not as dangerous as braving the open sea."

And when Ashleigh and Megan questioned him on their ultimate destination, he'd shown them a letter he'd received from the little seacoast town of Livorno, off the coast of Tuscany—a place the English referred to as the Leghorn—and told them the incredible story of the woman who'd sent it, a woman named Maria, Contessa di Montefiori—the former Mary Westmont and Brett Westmont's mother!

Now, as she sat in the carriage awaiting word as to whether they would, indeed, find a welcome at the contessa's villa, as the letter had said, Ashleigh felt a curious mixture of emotions disturb her calm, though she'd hardly been calm very often these past weeks. Oh, she'd long since ceased weeping as she had in the cabin she shared with Megan aboard the *Ashleigh Anne* during those first depressing days away from London. In fact, if she concentrated very hard, she could even assume a cheerful mien most days.

But the nights were a different matter. Even after she reached the point where she felt she could cry no more, there was a deep and abiding melancholy that would come to her late at night when everything was still and she would lie in the darkness, listening to the gentle lapping of the waves against the hull of the ship that bore her name. It was during those times that she would fight sleep, knowing it could only bring dreams of a pair of turquoise eyes and visions of warm, enfolding arms that faded and mocked her when she awoke alone in her narrow bunk.

And then there was the mingling joy and pain she'd felt at learning she carried a child—*his* child! She felt joy just thinking of the tiny life growing inside her, and joy, too, together with a humble sense of participation in sharing in the wonderful, mysterious process of bringing a brand-new human into the world.

But knowing the child would forever be a link between her and the father she'd never see again was a joy steeped in pain. And she knew this would always leave her less than whole in the years to come; a part of her would be forever tied to Brett—the part that was her heart.

The wind changed, and a brisk breeze from the water allowed Ashleigh to put aside her fan. Leaning around the nodding form of the carriage's driver, she peered down the pebbled road in hopes of spying Megan and Patrick returning. *Now there,* she thought, *is something else to be joyful about.* No one could have been more delightfully surprised than she, to learn of the love that had sprung up between her brother and her closest friend. Megan and Patrick planned to marry soon, and it was the joy she felt in their happiness that had made her determined to bury her own sadness, at least when they were about.

Finding the road ahead still empty, Ashleigh sighed and leaned back on the carriage's seat while her thoughts returned to Brett. *He must truly hate me now,* she thought sadly. *But what choice did I have, other than to leave? His mind was made up on the matter of the divorce, and even if it weren't, there were still the doubts about his ability to be faithful . . . or care for me, as I have come to care for him. . . .*

Uneasily, her thoughts swung to her own feelings for him. She wondered how it was that she'd grown to love Brett Westmont. After all, they had known each other only under the most trying of circumstances, and not for all that long a time. And for a great part of that time he'd made himself known to be arrogant, ill-tempered, unreasonable, and, when angered, fierce and ruthless as well. But he'd also shown himself to be generous beyond measure when others in his position might not have been, and he was honorable, too. Moreover, he wasn't afraid of admitting he'd made a mistake. Despite her and Megan's doubts at the time, he'd truly been willing to make amends when he came to Hampton House and offered her honorable employment and a chance for a better life.

And he could be gentle and kind. Spontaneously, Ashleigh's lips curled into a wistful smile as she recalled the day he'd come upon her in the meadow and the happy hours they'd shared with the animals there. He'd been a different person then, full of laughter and the capacity to enjoy life without the rancor and bitterness she knew lurked beneath that suave surface.

Also, Patrick had told her things about him that verified other characteristics she'd sensed but hadn't actually observed outright. During the week before the wedding, her brother had spoken of the time they'd been youths together, telling her of Brett's limitless capacity for hard work, of his incisive intelligence and ability to think quickly and act upon it when the situation called for it, and of his unflinching attention to duty. And he was fiercely loyal to those he deemed worthy of such loyalty, frequently going out of his way to support his friends, even if their station in life was far beneath his. There was the time he'd cut short a potentially profitable trading voyage to appear before the bench to testify on behalf of a former second mate who'd been accused of murder, Brett bearing witness to the fact that the man had been with him in another port when the deed was done. And the time he'd visited the widow of one of his sailors who'd died at sea and, learning the woman was destitute, had set up a lifetime trust for the support of her and her three children.

Yes, despite his faults, Brett was all of these things—generous, honorable, kind, diligent, loyal—and in his arms she had found a heaven she hadn't dreamed—

Abruptly, Ashleigh cut her summation short as she felt tears threaten her eyes. *No,* she told herself firmly. *You're not going to cry again—you're not! It can't help you, and it won't help the child.... There, focus on that. It's the child who's important now... you must think of the child....*

Finding some measure of peace with these thoughts, she turned her eyes again toward the beach and noticed the tall woman was collecting her charges, helping them dry their well-browned little bodies with some toweling she'd brought along, and urging them cheerily up the path to the road. A few moments later their small band was marching happily in the direction from which they'd come while the woman led them in a brisk, melodic little song.

As they passed, not too far from where the carriage stood, the woman waved at Ashleigh and gave her a warm, sunny smile, while continuing her song. Several of the children followed suit, and Ashleigh smiled happily as she waved back at them.

When they had gone, she found herself humming to herself the gay little tune they'd sung, and she suddenly realized she hadn't felt this lighthearted in weeks. Then, a short time later, when Megan and Patrick returned to tell her they'd spoken with the contessa's steward—for the lady was out for the afternoon—and Maria had left word she was anxious, after receiving the note they'd sent ahead, to welcome them to her home, Ashleigh began to truly relax for the first time since she'd left London, or perhaps even before that. Italy, with its blue skies and sunny coastline, even this late in the year, might not prove such a bad place in which to spend some time... time in which to set her life aright and gain a foothold in the future, whatever that might bring.

\* \* \*

Ashleigh's first impression of the cool white stucco Villa Montefiori was that it seemed to exist chiefly as a backdrop for a profusion of flowers. There were colorful blossoms everywhere she looked—along the drive of crushed, sun-bleached seashells, in a riot of color among the terraced gardens, dripping lavishly over low stone walls, nestled against the open verandas attached to the lower levels of the house. Her eye was filled with a palette of lush florals, and the air was heavy with their scent. The house itself was a testament to airiness and simplicity despite its large size. In addition to the open verandas, there were galleries—or loggia, as she later learned to call them—on the second level, roofed with flat, bracketed eaves and partly enclosed. The asymmetrical arrangement of numerous large, rounded windows and doorways seemed designed to let in the maximum of sunlight and air. Flat-roofed, except for a soaring, off-center tower, the structure appeared to nestle snugly into the hillside on which it was built, and the overall effect was one of inviting coziness, light, grace and charm.

The steward met them at the double-arched doors that faced a large, flower-surrounded courtyard; he quickly ascertained from Patrick when he might be expecting the arrival of their baggage from the ship, and led them inside. The cool marble-floored entry hall was richly decorated in the Italian Renaissance style, from its ornate blue and gilt ceiling to its beautifully muraled walls. Several doorways led off either side of it, and they were shown through the first on their right.

"*Signore Santa Clara,*" the staid, white-haired steward announced, "*e Signorina Santa Clara, e Signorina O'Briani.*"

A warm, throaty chuckle emanated from across the large drawing room as a tall, slender, and beautifully gowned woman stepped toward them. "Enrico and I must really work on his English one of these days," she said, laughing, then held out her arms in welcome. "Patrick, my dear, how wonderful!"

Patrick rushed forward and without so much as a second's hesitation, swept the immaculately groomed woman into a smothering bear hug. "Maria!" he shouted. "My God, but you're a sight to make these sore eyes smile!"

Ashleigh and Megan exchanged horrified glances at this obvious breach of protocol on Patrick's part; after all, the woman *was* a *contessa*! But Maria's response of delighted laughter—muffled as it was by the smothering embrace—quickly wiped the alarm from their faces.

"But, here, let me look at you," said Maria, at last freed from the hug and holding Patrick at arm's length. "Merciful Heavens! You've grown even bigger than you were!" she laughed.

"And you've changed not a bit—" Patrick grinned "—except, perhaps, you've grown more beautiful than I remember."

"*Adulatore!*" the *contessa* chastised playfully. She lightly touched gracefully slender, beringed fingers to a wing of silver hair that swept away from her temple. "Here alone is a change to remind us of how much time has passed in this woman's life."

"Still, I'm not the flatterer you called me," returned Patrick as he turned and led her toward where Ashleigh and Megan waited. "Some women simply age well, improving with it, like a fine wine. But come, I want you to meet my ladies before I'm accused of lacking manners as well as honesty." He winked down at his hostess as he said this.

But, as they drew nearer, the *contessa* paused as her turquoise-flecked hazel eyes found Ashleigh's. She was silent for a long moment, then smiled and said softly, "Ashleigh, my dear, welcome. I would know you by those wonderful eyes, if nothing else. Had I been close enough to see them out there this afternoon, I'd have recognized you then, you know."

Ashleigh's lips parted silently with belated recognition. The woman on the beach! The *contessa* was the woman with those children on the beach this afternoon! Why, she'd scarcely have believed the transformation! In place of the barefoot, casually dressed country woman was this elegantly coiffured and be-gowned lady looking every inch the noblewoman she was.

Blushing with her astonishment, Ashleigh made a brief curtsy, murmuring, "How kind of you to welcome us into your home, *contessa*. Thank you."

"Nonsense, my dear," said Maria. "It is I who should be thanking you for coming at last, to visit your old friend after all these years. And please don't be embarrassed because you failed to place me. I've more than once been taken for one of the peasant women when I've gone on an outing with my children."

"*Your* children?" questioned Ashleigh.

"In a way, yes," said Maria, her voice grown a shade more serious, "but more about that later. For now, I wish to meet this stunning redhead my steward called Signorina O'Briani. Judging by your breathtaking coloring, my dear," she said, looking up at Megan, "I'll wager the name's really O'Brien, is it not?"

Megan grinned and nodded while Patrick completed the introductions. At Ashleigh's request, he'd made no mention in his brief note to their hostess of her marriage or relationship to Brett, agreeing that the proper time for imparting that information must be carefully thought out and done only in person; therefore she was for now, as the steward's announcement had indicated, merely Ashleigh Sinclair. He did at this time, however, include the information that Megan was his fiancée, and when she heard this, Maria reached up to give the young Irishwoman a delighted hug.

"Oh, what wonderful news!" she cried. "I cannot wait to hear all the details." Then she turned again to Ashleigh, her expression more serious. "And the specifics of your situation, too, *cara*. I realize Patrick's note had to be brief, but if you think I shall last much longer wondering what has been happening in your life all these years, think again!

"But come, you must all be quite travel weary by now. I'll have Enrico show you to your chambers where you can rest and freshen up. We'll meet before dinner on the west veranda, and I warn you," she added, brandishing a wagging finger goodnaturedly at them, "I shan't be content until I've heard every detail."

\* \* \*

A few hours later the *contessa* and her three guests were sitting in comfortable chairs on a spacious veranda that gave them a breathtaking view of the darkening sea. They sipped a light, refreshing wine from heavy, jewel-encrusted silver goblets that, Maria had just finished explaining, were part of a wealth of Montefiori family heirlooms she'd inherited, along with three villas and hundreds of acres of vineyards, from her husband, who had died five years earlier.

Patrick nodded thoughtfully. "That explains it, then. I was wondering why the villagers we spoke to made reference only to *la villa della contessa*. My Italian may be poor, but I knew I'd caught no mention of *il conte*. I'm so sorry, Maria. How did it happen?"

Maria shrugged, but there was a sad, faraway look in her eyes as she replied. "The war. Gregorio was not a young man, but, as you know, Napoleon's rape of Europe included an obsession to populate the thrones of the Italian peninsula with his relatives. My husband's family owned extensive properties all over Italy, not just here in the north, and when he tried to come to the aid of one of his mother's cousins who was about to lose his lands to the French . . ." She shrugged again, as if unwilling to go into details that were painful to her.

"But we had a number of good years together, Gregorio and I. Our only regret was that they were childless." All at once a sparkle heightened the turquoise flecks in her eyes. "Of course, in the years since Gregorio passed on, I've done something to fill that emptiness . . . but look," she added more briskly, "enough talk about me for now. It is you I wish to hear about. Start from the beginning, my children, and tell me, won't you?"

And so, with Patrick initially doing most of the talking, they told her of the odd quirks of fate that had kept brother and sister separated for so many years, beginning with the events following the fire and proceeding through his years in America and his recent arrival in England.

Maria made appropriate murmurs of regret and surprise as she listened attentively, but when the tale wound down to include the account of Patrick and Ashleigh's incredible reunion, her astonishment rendered her speechless for several long moments.

When at last she could speak, Maria's face was white with shock. "*Brett* did such a thing?" Her eyes closed, and the slender white hand that held her wine goblet began to tremble so violently, she had to set it down.

The three across from her exchanged serious glances before Ashleigh reached across the little tea table separating them and took Maria's hand.

"Please, *contessa*," she said softly, "you must not judge him too harshly. You see—" Ashleigh paused, searching for the right words "—Brett has been living under a great burden these many years. It—it has to do, I think, with the old duke...with the way his grandfather raised him...."

Not really intending to do so, but somehow feeling she must, Ashleigh proceeded to open up completely to this warm woman before her, for she knew that the former Mary Westmont and she shared a great burden of their own, a burden that came of loving the man they spoke of while he shunned that love because of things Ashleigh could only guess at, but which she knew might come to clearer light now that the two of them could talk.

Slowly, reluctant to omit a nuance of detail that might help to explain how it came to be, she told her of her first meeting with Brett, then of the strange arrangement she and Megan had entered into with him, of her months at Ravensford Hall, and finally, their bizarre marriage and its bitter aftermath. Through it all, Maria's eyes never left her face, and at times, Ashleigh could swear the emotions she read there were her own.

And when Ashleigh at last finished, with a hesitant explanation of her discovery that she was with child, tears ran freely down Maria's cheeks. "Oh, my dear child," she whispered hoarsely, "to think that the poisoning that began to infect us all so long ago has now come to touch you, too! And my beloved Brett..." Wearily, she shook her head, then accepted the linen handkerchief Patrick handed her with a sad, grateful little smile. When she had blotted her wet cheeks, her eyes again found Ashleigh's.

"You love him, don't you, child?"

Choking back a sob, Ashleigh merely nodded, but Patrick's incredulous voice broke the silence.

"Then, Ashleigh, why, in the name of Heaven, if you love him, wouldn't you let me—"

"*Caro*, dear Patrick," Maria interrupted gently, "do you really need to ask? Certainly you never questioned me as to why I left without trying harder to reach Brett's father."

"But that was different!"

"No, my dear, it was not," Maria said softly. "Oh, I may not have been carrying my husband's child, but the one I was forced to leave behind was every bit as great a tie."

Ashleigh's heart twisted with pain at the brief, haunted look she caught in Maria's eyes.

"But," Maria continued, "we were both unable to remain with a husband we loved in the face of the irrational anger, and perhaps, even hatred, that each felt as a result of—" here the *contessa*'s eyes hardened, and her lips became a grim line that reminded Ashleigh of Brett in a similar emotional state "—of an evil poison that insinuated itself into the lives of the occupants of Ravensford Hall."

Patrick leaned forward to speak, but Megan's voice came more quickly. "Ye've spoken o' this poison more than once, now, m'lady. Would it be the grandfather's doin's ye're meanin'?"

Maria's look was still grim. "Him, of course I can blame, the poor, twisted fool, but I must tell you that I have always felt there was something more pernicious at work ... or some ... *one*." She glanced at Patrick. "I recall you met the old man a couple of times. Whatever you may have thought of him, did he ever strike you as one who was underhanded or would operate by stealth and deceit?"

Patrick shook his head, his answer a flat "No."

Maria nodded. "For all his narrow-mindedness and other failings, John Westmont was open and direct in his dealings. He may have been intolerant of my foreign heritage and liberated ideas that he termed 'bluestocking nonsense,' but the duke would never have stooped to planting those letters among my possessions, letters that couldn't fail to be discovered by his son—*letters pointing to my nonexistent infidelities!*''

Megan lowered the wine goblet she'd raised to her lips, her eyes narrowed. ''Then who—?''

''A good question,'' Maria replied. ''I've gone over it a thousand times in my mind. Who would stand to benefit if—''

At that moment there was a clattering noise, followed by the sounds of several pairs of light, running feet coming from the chamber that opened onto the veranda, and as the four turned to look, several small figures appeared near the arched doorway.

''*Scusa, Signora Contessa,*'' said a small boy whose face was framed by a wealth of glossy black curls. Then the child's huge brown eyes fell on the guests; he turned silent with a look of shy embarrassment.

''Antonio.'' Maria smiled; then, glancing beyond the boy, who looked to be about five or six, she grinned, saying, ''Very well, Anna, Vittorio, the rest of you . . . I see you, and you may come forth. My guests won't bite, but I warn you, to avoid seeming rude, you must speak to us in English.''

Slowly, the boy Antonio edged forward onto the veranda, followed carefully by five other children of similar age or younger, until all six were standing in a neat row in front of Maria and her guests.

Out of the corner of her eye Ashleigh noted the faint looks of curiosity on Megan's and Patrick's faces as they beheld the crutches and limping movements of a few of the youngsters, but she, of course, was not surprised at what they saw; these were some of the children she had already seen on the beach. She did glance at her hostess with a look of anticipation, however, for she was eager for an explanation as to the identities of the children and how they fit into Maria's life.

''Your Grace,'' said Maria, turning to Ashleigh as she rose from her seat; then, to Megan and Patrick, ''Sir Patrick, Miss O'Brien, allow me to present to you some of my children: Antonio, Anna, Salvatore, Gina, Vittorio and Palmina.''

The three adults rose and smiled at the children when their own titled names were mentioned, and as Maria pronounced each child's name, the youngster bowed or curtsied formally with solemn eyes fixed on the *contessa*'s guests.

"Children," Maria continued in slow, carefully articulated English, "This is Her Grace, the duchess of Westmont—" Maria gestured at Ashleigh "—her good friend, Miss Megan O'Brien—" she smiled at Megan "—and Her Grace's brother, Sir Patrick St. Clare." She gave Patrick a smile.

Ashleigh and Megan continued smiling at the children, utterly charmed by their serious little faces and wondering eyes, but when he was formally introduced by name, Patrick stepped forward and graciously shook the hand of each boy while bestowing a courtly kiss on the shyly offered hands of the three young girls. The last, an auburn-haired waif of about six, blushed furiously when her turn came, and this produced muffled giggles from her two female companions.

"So," said Maria with a twinkle in her eye, "the six of you couldn't wait to meet our guests, unlike your more patient brothers and sisters, eh? Very well, my darlings, I forgive you. To be very honest, I must admit, had I been in your place, I should have found it difficult to wait also."

At this, all six youngsters grinned at Maria with unabashed relief, if not delight.

"But now," Maria continued, "I must ask you to go upstairs with the others, to dine and prepare for bed. Then, when our guests and I have finished our dinner, you may come down, along with the others, to say good-night in the drawing room. *Capite?*"

Nodding and still grinning, the children turned, and with Vittorio and Gina grasping their crutches, began to file out.

When they had gone, Maria turned to her guests. "I can tell by your faces you are anxious to learn about my children. It should make for a good beginning to our dinner conversation, I think, and since dinner is about to be served . . ." She glanced at the doorway where a white-jacketed Enrico had silently appeared. "I suggest we proceed."

With a warm smile, she took Ashleigh's arm, leaving Patrick to escort Megan, as she followed her steward into the house.

In the large and sumptuous dining room with its rich, Renaissance furnishings that fed the eye as well as the appetite, Maria told them about "my children," as she called them. But the youngsters were neither naturally nor legally hers; they were orphans, largely foundlings who had been in the care of a local orphanage run by sisters of the church. But the nuns had encountered difficulties in caring for the increasing numbers of homeless children created by the war in Europe in recent years—something Maria and the *conte* had been aware of even before he died, owing to their philanthropic support of various charitable institutions across the Italian boot.

When Gregorio died, Maria went to the Convent of the Little Flower's orphanage, thinking to offer her time as well as her money to help care for the children. But when she arrived, her shock at the crowded conditions and paucity of helping hands was matched only by the pity she felt for the children there, especially those who were handicapped because of the war's atrocities, or who had been born handicapped—and frequently dumped on the sisters' doorstep because, as such, they were unwanted. These were the little ones, she was told, who would never appeal to the rare couple seeking to adopt a child; these were the ones destined, for certain, to spend the rest of their childhood days in an institution—the ones nobody wanted.

But Maria had wanted them. Within hours of her first visit to the orphanage, she was meeting with the mother superior of the convent and the local priest, a lifelong friend, to arrange to become a foster mother for the then eleven children who constituted "the unplaceables." These she took into her home, turning part of the upper floor into a suite of children's bedchambers, a playroom, a schoolroom and a nursery. She hired an additional separate staff of eight to help her in this endeavor: two nurses—for four of the children were then infants—a tutor, two governesses, a pair of chambermaids, and the children's own private footman—although this last, a wizened old man named Giovanni who adored children and had sadly outlived his own grandchildren through the devastation of war, was really far more than a servant; he was a surrogate grandfather who regaled his young charges with jokes and funny stories and spent hours carrying the little ones about on his shoulders or carving toys for them out of discarded pieces of wood and the like.

Maria herself spent the bulk of her time with the youngsters, taking an active part in such things as instructing them in French and English, introducing them to good music and art, escorting them on outings and teaching them to ride on the half-dozen gentle ponies she had added to her stables. In the five years since she'd begun doing this, the initial group of eleven had grown until it numbered twenty, which was just last year. But this year she was down to nineteen, she told them proudly, because of her first "graduate." A boy named Alonzo who had lost a leg to a cannonball, and who had been almost fourteen when he and the others in that first group arrived, had succeeded in gaining entry into the University of Bologna and was, with Maria's financial support, successfully studying law there.

As Maria talked of her life with these children, Ashleigh watched her face light up with an inner joy that spoke volumes beyond her words. Deeply moved, she saw how this beautiful, kind woman who had lost so much when she was torn from the child she loved, had filled the void in her life by enriching the lives of these little ones with hope and joy; she had taken the brutal blow fate had dealt her and turned it into an opportunity to perform an act of love, and Ashleigh found herself humbled in her presence.

Moreover, she found herself basking in the calm air of serenity that marked the older woman's every movement, longing for a taste of it herself, as a thirsting man longs for water. It was instructive. If Brett's mother could attain such a profound state of inner peace after all she'd been through, why, then, couldn't she? It was something to think about, and Ashleigh resolved to do so, gathering her thoughts for a time when she could be alone. But she already half knew what she wanted; it just depended on the right moment to put it into action.

And so it was that the following morning, when Ashleigh arose early and came downstairs to learn Maria was breakfasting alone, she eagerly sought her out and accepted the *contessa*'s invitation to join her.

"So, *cara*," said Maria, "what is it that has you up and about so early, and in your condition, too? I thought I was the only one who kept such outrageous hours." She nodded a dismissal to the hovering footman and poured Ashleigh's tea herself.

"Well, m'lady, I've always been an early riser, and now that the morning sickness appears to have left me, I really do not feel comfortable lying about in bed. What's more, I—"

"Please, my dear, call me Maria," said the *contessa* as she handed Ashleigh her tea with a smile. "Now, what was it you wished to say?"

Returning the smile, Ashleigh hesitated, wanting to be sure she phrased properly the idea that had been running about her brain ever since dinner last night. She prolonged the moment by taking a sip of the expertly brewed tea, then continued. "Well, Maria, it—it's about the children. It seems I could hardly sleep for thinking about them." Her mouth curved in a soft, radiant smile as she recalled the moments in the drawing room when all nineteen youngsters had been presented, even the littlest ones, a pair of infants in their nurses' arms. "And I was just thinking, wondering, actually, if—that is—"

"You were thinking how you might like to share some time with them, were you not?" questioned Maria with a soft smile.

*"How did you know?"*

The smile broadened as Maria reached out to pat her hand. "Ah, my dear, I was not in your presence more than a few minutes before I sensed a certain ... kinship between us. Call it something that comes of loving the same man—my son, your husband—or call it just a natural affinity certain people occasionally have for each other, but this closeness exists. I have felt it."

Slowly, Ashleigh nodded, her eyes fixed on Maria's. "I have too."

"Then how can you wonder that I have read what is in your heart, darling Ashleigh?"

Again a nod.

"And you are right to look to the children as a means of finding your own path. Oh, I'm not for a minute suggesting this is something for everyone who may be feeling he or she has . . . lost her way." The hazel eyes were intense as they held Ashleigh's gaze. "But for you . . . yes, I think it might be just the thing."

"Oh!" exclaimed Ashleigh with a grateful look in her eyes. "Thank you, Maria! You cannot know how—" She paused and thought better of what she'd been about to say. "But of course you can," she added quietly.

"But you must promise me you won't tax yourself, *carissima*. Children can be ever so, ah, energetic, and I shan't have you endangering your health at a time when you should be taking extra pains to maintain it." Maria rose from her place at the table and came around to where Ashleigh sat. "Plenty of rest, good food—my chef, Roberto, and I shall see to that!—and a moderate amount of exercise," she added, wagging her finger in the good-natured way Ashleigh had seen her use with the children.

"Oh, yes, I promise!" cried Ashleigh, her face alight with enthusiasm. "When can we begin?" She began to rise from her chair.

Gentle hands settled on her shoulders, urging her back into her seat. "Just as soon as you've eaten a healthy breakfast," Maria laughed. "I'm off to the church, for I must see Father Umberto about posting the banns for Megan and your brother's wedding."

Ashleigh grinned, recalling the moment last night when Megan and Patrick had whispered briefly together and then surprised them both by announcing their desire to be wed in Livorno.

"Of course," Maria was saying, "dear old Father Umberto is a bit long-winded, bless his heart. He'll want to chat about the latest news from the villa, asking about each and every child, and then he'll want to arrange to meet the prospective bride and groom...and you, too, of course, and then we'll have a spot of tea, and..." She gave Ashleigh an apologetic smile. "I think before I leave I'd better ask Giovanni to meet with you. I could be gone for hours!"

"Perhaps days!" Ashleigh grinned.

"Aha! See how quickly you attune yourself to life in Livorno? Well, I'm off, my dear. Enjoy your breakfast, and I'll have Giovanni join you in about an hour. I think he's planning some kind of picnic on the beach before this last spell of warm weather we're enjoying disappears...I shall see you later." With a whisper of silken skirts, Maria left the room.

In the days that followed, Ashleigh spent as much time with the children as Maria would allow, for her mother-in-law had summoned her own personal physician to examine the mother-to-be, and the two of them had devised a set schedule of rest periods Ashleigh had to promise to adhere to; and she did, though often reluctantly, for she quickly found her time with the youngsters a thing of joy. From picnics on the beach to romps in the garden with Finn and Lady Dimples—each of whom immediately exhibited a love of children equal to that of their mistress—she plunged headlong into activities she could share with the youngsters, activities that quickly became the mainstay of her life in Livorno. While dinner was always a formal affair for the adults, in the *contessa*'s dining room, Ashleigh almost always shared other mealtimes with the children, frequently joining them in their upstairs dining room for an easy, relaxed meal accompanied by much laughter as the youngsters attempted to teach her bits and pieces of Italian. And not a night passed wherein Ashleigh couldn't be found in the playroom, sitting on the floor in a circle of little ones, reading them a bedtime story in slow, carefully articulated English.

Sometimes they were joined by Megan and Patrick, as in their excursions to the stables, where the children laughed to see the tall lady and her even taller gentleman towering over the stout little ponies they helped saddle and lead about, and Patrick quickly became a favorite, especially with the older boys, to whom he told stories of America and its Indians, or tales of the sea.

At other times it was Maria and Ashleigh who shared with the youngsters the pleasures of outings in town or of leading the children in little Italian *canti*—the melodies of some of these surprising Ashleigh by their familiarity until Maria reminded her *she* had once been a child to whom a woman then named Mary had sung the songs,

The "old grandfather," as he was lovingly called in Italian by the children—Giovanni—grew especially fond of Ashleigh, often treating her as just one more of the children he adored. He took to calling her *la duchessa piccola*, the little duchess, and with Ashleigh's laughing consent, the children soon followed suit.

And so the days and weeks passed, October giving way to a chilly November, and that, to an even colder December. Patrick and Megan were married three weeks before Christmas, for Patrick, much to Father Umberto's delight, had decided to take instruction in the Roman faith, and he and Megan wanted to wait until his conversion was a fact before stating their vows at the high altar.

It was a candlelight ceremony, with two of Maria's children officiating as altar boys, and when the children's choir, made up of a dozen more of Maria's band, began singing the "Ave Maria," Ashleigh found herself weeping softly as she stood behind Megan and Patrick at the rail, her heart nearly full to bursting.

During these months the relationship between Maria and Ashleigh grew ever closer, and a day rarely passed without the two of them spending some time together apart from the others. Sometimes it was a quiet breakfast shared downstairs before a toasty fire, before the rest of the household was awake; often it was a peaceful walk through the gardens on afternoons when the sun was strong enough to offset the chilly breezes from the sea; occasionally they sipped a mug of hot, mulled wine together before the fireplace in Maria's private sitting room after the children were in bed and Patrick and Megan were off somewhere spending time together as lovers are wont to do.

It was during one of these late-night talks in mid-December, when Megan and Patrick were away on their honeymoon—at the *contessa*'s villa on the isle of Capri—that their conversation at last touched on the one topic they'd somehow been avoiding until now. It began when Maria noticed Ashleigh staring silently into the fire, a sad, pensive look on her face.

"You are thinking of him, aren't you, *cara*?" the older woman said gently.

Nodding, Ashleigh slowly turned to look at Maria, in the chair beside her. "You always seem to know what I'm thinking," she said.

Maria smiled. "In this case it didn't take too much intuition to determine what could change your expression from one of gay exuberance—when we were discussing our Christmas presents for the children a few moments ago—to the one I saw just now. Tell me, you think of him often, no?"

Ashleigh's smile was tinged with sadness. "A day doesn't go by that I don't think of him. Oh, don't take me wrongly, Maria. You and the children and my life here at the villa have been wonderful, and there are many hours when I am totally immersed in this—" she gestured to the walls around them "—but..."

"But your heart longs for him," Maria said quietly. "I know...for so it has been with me, every day, if you can believe it, for all these long years. Child, adolescent, or man fully grown, he has never been far from my thoughts."

Maria paused and reached her hand suddenly into the neckline of her dressing gown where she withdrew a delicate gold chain with a locket attached to it. Cradling the locket in the palm of her hand, she tilted it forward to reveal a miniature of a small boy with chestnut curls and vivid turquoise eyes.

"Oh!" gasped Ashleigh, recognizing at once whose portrait it was, and recalling where she had seen its mate. "*You* placed the miniature of Brett's father on his pillow!"

Maria nodded. "It took some daring and not a little courage, too, I can tell you. Giovanni helped me sneak into the garden at Ravensford Hall that night—he was among the men Gregorio sent with me when I made my clandestine visits to Kent—but it was I, dressed in seaman's trousers, who scaled the ivy-covered wall beneath my son's window and placed his father's portrait where he'd find it. I know it was crazy. I only knew I wanted him to have something . . . some memento of the . . . happier past. . . ."

She sighed. "Ah, it was the hardest thing to bear, I think, losing Brett . . . harder, even, than the loss I felt with Edward, or with Gregorio's death. Death, after a while, brings an acceptance of a kind. One comes to terms with it. But to fully accept the loss of a living child—or in your case, a husband you love—knowing he is still . . . somewhere, living, laughing, feeling pain, perhaps healthy, perhaps not . . ." She shrugged, giving Ashleigh a look that was meant to be resigned, but succeeded more in appearing helpless—and infinitely sad.

Ashleigh nodded thoughtfully and took a sip from the mug she held between her hands. "Have you given up hope of ever seeing him again, then?"

"Oh, no." Maria smiled. "One can always hope! Miracles do happen, you know. Look at my children. They were thought to be among the hopeless once. But here they are, aren't they? Loved, cared for . . . and happy, I think."

"Oh, how can you doubt it?" cried Ashleigh. "Maria, when they found you—or, rather, when you found them—they became the most fortunate, happiest children alive!" She paused in thought for a moment, and her hand moved absently to her belly, which had grown quite rounded by now, visible even beneath the Empire cut of her gowns. "I can only wish this little one I carry to be as fortunate as they, after . . . after she arrives."

"Ah, so it is to be a young lady, is it?"

Ashleigh's smile was wistful. "I have prayed that it will be a girl, yes. For if it were to be a boy, I . . ." She looked into Maria's eyes, her expression troubled. "Oh, Maria, I cannot think but that a boy needs a father by his side when he is growing up!

And this wee babe will have none!'' As if ashamed of this emotional outburst, Ashleigh dropped her eyes and stared into the contents of her mug, then added softly, ''Yes, I want it to be a girl.''

The *contessa* was silent for a moment, then reached to place a gentle hand on Ashleigh's arm. ''He may try to find you, you know...just as he did once—no, twice—before, as I recall. We, Gregorio and I, had word through my husband's war connections, that Brett is highly placed in certain... official functions of the Foreign Office—naval reconnaissance, I think, was the term Gregorio used. As such, not to mention the many private means at his disposal through his vast personal wealth and connections, he could probably trace you here if he chose—especially now that peace has come.'' Maria shifted slightly. ''Tell me, Ashleigh, what will you do if he comes for you?''

Ashleigh raised startled blue eyes to her. ''Why, I—I don't really know! I hadn't thought about it, actually. Indeed, most of my thoughts since leaving London have been bent on resigning myself to the idea that I shall never see Brett again.''

''Hmm,'' said Maria. ''Yes, I can understand that. But I will tell you something, my dearest. Even as a small boy, my son was a determined fellow, knowing, from the time he could express it, exactly what he wanted and rarely veering from a course that would obtain it for him. And, over the years, the reports I've had of him seem to have borne that characteristic out, being true of the man he has become as well.

''Knowing this, I suggest, darling, that you begin thinking on the possibility he might turn up. I suggest it very strongly, and urge you, with all the love a mother could have for a daughter—for I do love you, Ashleigh, as much as if you were my own—to decide what you will do when he does.''

# Chapter Twenty-Nine

It was the coldest winter in memory. Late in 1814 and continuing on into January of the New Year, a monumental deep freeze had settled over the face of England, blanketing the land in snow and ice. London was no exception, and for the first time anyone could recall, the Thames was frozen solid, immobilizing river traffic and the commerce it affected.

But Londoners were hardy souls and made the best of the situation. Soon, a number of fairs and temporary marketplaces appeared directly on the ice, with vendors erecting booths that offered everything from roasted chestnuts to hot cider and sausage rolls. Children and adults alike skated across the ice in a holiday mood, playing games of tag, gossiping with their neighbors, dancing about the great bonfires set right on the surface of the ice that had frozen thick enough to withstand their blaze.

It was early evening on the second Saturday of the New Year. A pair of enterprising fishermen's sons had managed to cut a hole in the ice and were now busy casting their baited hooks into the freezing, dark water below.

"'Ats it Jamie, play 'er out right careful like, and mind yer 'ands! They'd freeze right ter yer mittens if yer wuz ter get 'em wet!"

"I know whut I'm about 'Arry," said his companion as he carefully lowered his line into the swirling waters at the bottom of the hole. "'Ere, bring 'at lantern closer, would yer?"

Jamie waited as Harry complied, and when the fish line was sufficiently lowered to meet with the acceptance of both, the two boys, who looked to be about fourteen or fifteen, settled back on their haunches to await their first catch. While they waited, they looked about them, taking in the busy scene on the river.

Several dozen yards away, a string of children were playing "snap the whip" as they skated along on crudely fashioned, homemade wooden skates resembling clogs, in contrast to the more sophisticated variety some of the wealthy had purchased from the Dutch merchants who were able to make it through before the river froze over in December. On the far bank a horse-drawn sleigh skidded merrily by, lit by the glow of several small bonfires along the bank. The air was filled with the sounds of merchants hawking their wares, people calling to one another, and laughing lovers, strolling two by two under the dark, frozen sky.

Not too far from where the young fishermen squatted, there was the booth of a bookseller who, quick to size up the situation, had closed up his shop on Fleet Street, which was too cold these days to be heated by its single iron stove anyway, and moved his wares out here on the ice.

Suddenly the boy named Jamie whistled softly. "Blimey, if it ain't 'at toff all London's buzzin' about, 'Arry! Whut's 'is name, now? You know, the devilish 'andsome one whut just got wed, an' now they say 'is wife left 'im an' 'e's always in a black, killin' mood."

Harry, too intent on his fishing line to glance in the direction of the bookseller's booth, merely mumbled, "The 'andsome one? Oh, 'at'd be Lord...Lord Somethin'-or-Other...um...ah, I've got it! Lord Byron! Wed just last week, 'e wuz."

"No, no," muttered Jamie, "not 'im! 'At one's got a crippled foot, I 'eard, an' this bloke's tall an' fit, by the looks of 'im. 'Ere, 'Arry, give a look. 'E's standin' right over there...an' bloomin' broodin', too, by 'is dark looks."

Harry finally deigned to cast a glance in the direction pointed out by his companion, and when he did, he saw the dark silhouette of a tall, broad-shouldered man, bareheaded and wearing a greatcoat, as he stood beside the bookseller's booth, outlined from behind by the light of yet another bonfire.

"Oh, *'im*!" muttered Harry. "*'E* ain't just no lord—'e's a *duke*! Raven-Somethin'-or-Other. Oh, I'd mind me own business if I wuz you, Jamie! 'E's a mean one these days. They say 'e's killed two men in duels just fer lookin' at 'im crosswise!"

Jamie's mouth gaped wide at this revelation, and when the tall man laid aside the book he'd been holding and took a few steps closer to where they were squatting, both boys busily involved themselves in their ice fishing.

Brett jammed his hands into the pockets of his greatcoat and gave the scene of revelry and merrymaking around him a final, scornful glance. It was no use. No matter how he tried to distract himself from the images that haunted him these days, nothing worked. Tonight he'd forsaken the feverish rounds of partying, gambling, drinking and, yes, even fighting—though the rumors of duels were just that: exaggerations growing out of the city's appetite for gossip fed by its lively imagination. But he'd certainly thrown himself into all kinds of wild activity every night for the past several months; only tonight, he'd thought to immerse himself in the gay crowds of common folk out here on the river, hoping it would be different from the distractions he'd tried to summon among the *ton*. But there was no difference. No matter where he went, even in the thickest of crowds, he was alone. Completely and utterly alone.

Where was she now? Was she safely ensconced in Patrick's home in America, beginning at last the decent, new life she'd longed for while a menial at the brothel? Or was she hiding out somewhere on the Continent with her brother, awaiting the end of the conflict with America before chancing it across the Atlantic?

Inside the pocket of the greatcoat, Brett's fingers closed around a folded letter he'd received a few days ago from Simon Allerton, an agent who sometimes acted as a messenger for those involved in the more clandestine dealings of the Foreign Office. The letter said a schooner had been spotted off the Leghorn . . . a schooner flying a Dutch flag, but bearing the inscription *Ashleigh Anne*. Was it Patrick's ship? And if so, what were they doing in Italy where there were still too many of Napoleon's brothers and other sympathizers about? Didn't Patrick realize that area of the world could become a powder keg if some of the whisperings about Elba were true?

Brett shook his head and smiled grimly to himself. But, of course, Patrick couldn't know that. Few in the Foreign Office believed the rumors themselves. And it was highly unlikely, after all. Where would Napoleon gather an army on that remote little island?

Still, Carlton House was interested, as were Whitehall and the Admiralty, and as soon as this damnable deep freeze was over, certain reconnaissance ships would be leaving the London Hole to do a bit of "unofficial" investigating. It was Brett's choice as to whether he wished to be on one of them. On the other hand, he could simply head south as a private citizen. It would certainly leave him more autonomy in dealing with his private situation if this *Ashleigh Anne* did prove to be Patrick's ship.

Did he *want* to find her? That was the question that had plagued him ever since he received Allerton's letter. *Damn!* He should have been quit of her by now! Why couldn't he keep her out of his mind?

And if he found her again, what did he plan to do with her? It had been months since he'd been awakened by those dreams of some fitting revenge. Lately, the nightly images had been of a different sort—of Ashleigh laughing as she bent her slender frame over Irish Night's neck and raced her across the flats...of Ashleigh looking incomparably lovely in a wedding gown of silk and old lace...of Ashleigh raising solemn, wide blue eyes to his and saying, "It meant everything to me."

Somewhere there was an answer to the riddle she presented. Somehow he knew he had to discover why he hated her and longed for her in the same breath, why he couldn't seem to think of her as a she-devil without simultaneously, in his heart, if he was honest with himself, believing she was an angel, the epitome of the kind of woman he wanted by his side, to bear him children, to grow old with....

But she had *left* him, dammit! Just when he'd begun to think there was a chance—that perhaps he'd been wrong about things. . . .

A few soft flakes of snow began to fall, and Brett left off his ruminations and turned toward the near bank of the river where his carriage waited. His tall form melted into the darkness as he walked, a solitary figure in the night.

Wearing a midnight-blue velvet, hooded cloak lined with ermine, Ashleigh snuggled against the cold in a deep wing chair Giovanni had set out for her on the southern veranda. From around the corner of the east wing she could hear the children breaking into fits of giggles as they readied their "surprise." Smiling, she shoved her small, gloved hands more deeply into her ermine muff—like the velvet cloak, a Christmas present from Patrick and Megan. Her smile broadened as she recalled the newlyweds' note accompanying the gift when it arrived on Christmas Eve: "Blue velvet to match your eyes, ermine to match your soul—for it was once a fur forbidden to all except royalty, and you are such to us. Happy Christmas, princess—we love you!"

Now her smile grew wistful as she thought about those two. She hadn't seen them in over a month, for they were still honeymooning in the south, and she missed them terribly. Nevertheless she'd kept her letters to them bright and gay, for theirs to her had bubbled with happiness, and she was determined not to dampen their joy. And besides, her life here with Maria and the children held a joy of its own. Every day was filled with an abundance of things to do, things deeply satisfying because they involved sharing her time with those who truly needed it; indeed, the more she gave of herself with these little ones, the more she found her own life enriched.

It was a time of reflection for her, too, of spiritual growth, enhanced by the building of a certain kind of inner peace. And if it lacked the soaring rapture she'd experienced once, for a brief euphoric time in her life, well, that too was something she had come to accept during these recent weeks and months. Such emotional heights, she'd concluded, brought with them valleys of despair—emotional lows that could well destroy a person. It was better to seek the middle ground; there, one could be safe.

Suddenly, from around the corner of the veranda came the sound of a trumpet's fanfare, and Ashleigh turned her head in anticipation. That would be Antonio, she thought with a smile. The seven-year-old was the most musically gifted of the youngsters, already able to play several instruments by ear—not entirely delighting the music tutor Maria had hired to come weekly from Pisa, for Maestro Vivianni, as he called himself, adamantly insisted Antonio learn to read music while the boy, equally adamant, insisted he didn't need to; he could play without it, couldn't he?

As Ashleigh watched, a parade of children emerged from the far wall, each of them dressed in a bright red cape and matching cap—surely stitched by Francesca and Alessandra, Ashleigh mused, for the two older girls were deft with needle and thread. Each child now also played a musical instrument of sorts—blocks of wood banged together, cymbals fashioned out of pot lids, a couple of horseshoes suspended from string handles and clanged with metal spoons—each grinning at her as they marched to the tune of Antonio's lively trumpet and Aldo's flute—still somewhere "offstage."

Ashleigh grinned and clapped briefly in encouragement before drawing her cloak more closely about her and preparing to settle back to enjoy the show. She was very proud of these little pageants the youngsters staged; their first had been performed at her suggestion when, after taking a group of them into Pisa to see a performance of the commedia del l'arte in October, she had caught Antonio and Aldo staring wistfully at the stage on their way out of the theater. That evening she had gone to the two boys and proposed they make use of their own talents, as well as those of the other children, to put on performances here at the villa. Excited by the idea, twelve-year-old Aldo, a natural organizer as well as a fairly able flutist, had taken it from there and mounted, with Ashleigh's help, a delightful production of songs and dances to celebrate All Saint's Day at the beginning of November. This was performed in the villa's large drawing room, with Maria, Patrick, Megan and all of the staff a delighted audience. In December, there were no less than three more pageants: one to celebrate Megan and Patrick's wedding, with Salvatore and Anna costumed to resemble a miniature bride and groom; another to celebrate the Nativity; and a third as a surprise Christmas present for Maria, its songs telling the story of a great queen who became the savior of all the homeless children of the world, rescuing them from a wicked monster named La Guerra—Madame War—played indulgently by Giovanni in a superbly ugly costume designed by Alessandra and Francesca.

Ashleigh settled back into the wing chair, wondering what had prompted the children to stage a surprise for her this afternoon—she'd been told very little about it, and for the past fortnight had been politely asked to keep away from the playroom, which, she knew, served as a rehearsal hall these days; moreover, when she'd chanced upon some of the children from time to time lately, there'd been much buzzing and whispering that fell to silence as she drew near.

Suddenly Ashleigh leaned forward, her jaw agape as the full ensemble came into view. There, in a pony cart being drawn, ever so stoically, by a red-harnessed Finn—who wore an expression that asked: How do I get myself into these things?—sat Lady Dimples, once again decked out in human finery. On her head she wore a huge red hat covered with paper roses of the same hue; draped over her shoulders was a scarlet cape that resembled those the children wore, except hers was festooned with ropes of more red paper roses; clamped firmly in her mouth was a real rose, obviously plucked from the small conservatory Maria kept at the back of the villa. And as the children began to sing a song about "the beautiful lady of the roses," the pig's jaws spread slightly, and Ashleigh could have sworn she was grinning! Moreover the song was a highly lyrical one, with a strong, rhythmical beat, and as the youngsters threw themselves into the refrain with no small amount of gusto, the porker's bonneted head began to sway back and forth to the music.

Ashleigh could stand it no longer; bending over as far as her distended stomach would allow, she broke into howls of laughter, tears streaming down her cheeks. It was all too, too much!—the children grinning openly as they sang the laudatory lyrics, the giant dog standing before the cart in a long-suffering pose, the preening pig with a rose between her teeth, gazing about with a dignified air as she moved her head to and fro.

Soon shrieks of laughter joined Ashleigh's as Maria emerged from the end of the veranda, her tall frame bent nearly double with mirth. Behind her came old Giovanni, trying hard to appear serious, but failing as his white mustache twitched with half-contained amusement, then curved above lips that gave way to hoots of delight.

The song ended, but the laughter continued to reverberate from the rafters as giggling youngsters joined the adults. Three or four house servants came running to discover the cause of all this commotion, and when they saw the little tableau with the costumed pet in its center, their laughter drowned out that of the others until all, adults and children alike, were propping themselves up on one another's shoulders, howling with merriment.

When at last the laughter died down, Ashleigh ran forward and bestowed a hug on each child, murmuring, *"Grazie, grazie!* Oh, you were wonderful—just wonderful!" She gave Finn a hug, too, after that, and for the first time the big dog looked as if he were enjoying himself. Finally she approached the cart, reaching out to give Lady Dimples an approving pat, but when she did this, the pig forestalled the action by dropping the rose at her feet with a happy grunt. Then, as everyone cheered, Lady Dimples turned and accepted a sweetmeat from Aldo before the entire troop of children broke into a chorus of "God Save the Queen" and led the cart away.

"Oh," said Ashleigh to Maria as they watched the others depart, "I don't know when I've laughed so hard!"

*"You!"* Maria chuckled. "I was invited to a dress rehearsal the other day and nearly fell out of my chair! It's a good thing we sent you into town to select those hair ribbons for the girls,

or you'd have heard me shrieking and the whole surprise would have been ruined."

"How did they ever succeed in getting Lady D. to hold that rose and then drop it at the right moment?"

"Oh, that part was easy!" laughed Maria. "The pork chop is a natural-born thespian, or so Giovanni claims. The hard part was getting your dog to pull the cart. He kept looking at Aldo as if he'd been sentenced to a fate worse than death."

"Poor Finn." Ashleigh smiled. "He's put up with an awful lot because of me." Her mind flew back to an image of the hound squeezed onto the floor of a carriage as it made its escape from a house on King Street.

"I hardly think he minds, *cara*," said Maria, sobering. "From what Megan told me, you saved his life, and from the way he adores you, I'd guess he's never forgotten it." She paused for a moment, her hazel eyes meeting Ashleigh's quietly. "You have a way with those who are weaker than the rest of us, Ashleigh. Helpless animals, the children—who have taken to you like a duck to water, I might add."

Ashleigh shrugged, picking up the muff she'd left on her chair before joining Maria, who began to walk toward the door leading into the house. "I don't do anything special, really. I—I've always had a fondness for animals, and now, I realize, for children as well."

"But you are wrong, *cara*—you do a great deal that is special, beginning with showing an open and sincere heart that pours itself out to these little ones, and they can see it, so they blossom under its care."

Again Ashleigh shrugged. "I . . . I just love them, I guess."

Pausing at the door to the villa, Maria gave her a long, compassionate look. "So much love to give, and my insufferable son sits in London and—ah, forgive me, *cara*. Sometimes I talk too much." There was another pause, then Maria reached out to give Ashleigh an embrace. "You are going to make a wonderful mother, my darling."

Ashleigh hugged her back. "That's mainly because I'm taking daily lessons—from you."

Maria's warm laughter spilled about their shoulders. *"Adulatrice!"* she scolded. "But come, if there is any decent mothering instinct in me, I'd best get you inside, out of the cold. We must think of your health—and that of your *bambina*!"

Arm in arm, the two women entered the house.

# Chapter Thirty

Maria's stweard knocked on the door to her study, entering when the *contessa* called out for him to do so.

"Yes, Enrico?"

"*Contessa*, he is here," the steward told her, "the gentleman who sent the letter this morning. Shall I show him in?"

Maria froze for an instant, then forced herself to appear at ease as she nodded. "Give me a few minutes, Enrico. Then admit him to the small drawing room. I shall be there."

Maria watched the steward withdraw, then rose slowly from her desk. So it had finally come. The moment she had dreamed of, all these years. She would see her son again.

But the meeting would not be as she had imagined it countless times in the past; far from it. For one thing, she was certain Brett had no idea who she was. "Dear Contessa di Montefiori," the formal letter had read, "I have reason to believe you entertain as a guest in your home someone I have been searching for, for some time. I should like your leave to call upon you this afternoon to discuss the matter. If this will not cause you any undue inconvenience, please send word to my ship...."

Of course, it was not as if she hadn't been expecting it. She had as much as warned Ashleigh to be prepared in case Brett showed up. But that was months ago, when the possibility seemed to loom only in the distant future; now here it was, nearly the end of February; the situation was at hand, and she was not at all sure she was prepared for it herself.

After the letter—which was signed, "Your servant, Brett Westmont, Duke of Ravensford"—arrived this morning, delivered by a seaman from Brett's vessel, which was docked in the harbor, she had taken immediate steps to protect Ashleigh's privacy by sending her on an outing with the children; it being a lovely, warm day, this had posed no problem, and then she had alerted Megan and Patrick, who accompanied her.

So she was free to face him alone; she could gauge his mood and weigh his reasons, even test his intentions before deciding whether a confrontation between him and his wife might take place. And, she had to be honest, it would also allow her a few precious moments to view her son in terms of her own emotional attachment.

Looking down at her hand as it rested on her desk, she saw that it was trembling. Summoning her will, she thrust it into the folds of her amber silk skirt and moved toward the door. As she left the study and walked toward the drawing room, Maria only hoped she had sufficient strength—and the wisdom—to carry it all off.

He came through the door Enrico held open for him and paused for a moment as Maria turned from the window where she'd been standing, nodded to dismiss her steward and then met his gaze.

*Oh, how much like Edward he looks!* she thought. *Despite the chestnut hair he has from me, and, of course, those wonderful turquoise eyes! But his mouth, too, is more like mine than Edward's, which was weak and never bore such a determined line.* Oh, Brett, my son! How beautiful and manly you have grown! *And how I long to run to you and—*

Maria schooled her features to reflect none of these thoughts, firmly clamping down the emotions that, just for a second, threatened to rage; she smiled, saying, "Your Grace, do come in. I have been expecting you."

During the pause before she spoke, Brett had time to assess the beautiful woman before him. She was younger than he'd assumed her to be, this wealthy widow of a highly placed Italian nobleman, although, as he looked more closely, he realized she appeared of an indeterminate age. Her face, with its excellent bone structure, was the sort that would age well; unlined and with a beautiful complexion, it could have been the visage of a woman close to his own age, and only the dramatic wings of silver in her otherwise dark chestnut hair indicated she was probably somewhat older.

And then, as she moved forward to greet him, he noticed her eyes. Of a most unusual hazel hue, flecked with gold and turquoise, they were eyes that had seen a great deal, he knew. These were the eyes of a woman who had experienced a gamut of human emotions; their serene depths reflected a familiarity with pain, and the kind of wisdom the more enlightened of the human race are able to draw from it; but they reflected a knowledge of joy, too, and of their owner's ability to store its bounty, and Brett found himself strangely heartened by this discovery, although he wondered why this should be; he'd hardly met the woman.

Meeting her halfway across the warm, richly furnished room, Brett took her outstretched hand and raised it to his lips. "My pleasure, *contessa*," he murmured. "Thank you for agreeing to see me, especially on such short notice."

"Won't you be seated, Your Grace? I've just sent for tea, and I hope you'll join me in the ritual your countrymen are so fond of, and whose custom I adopted when I lived in England as a young woman." She sat on a damask-covered sofa and indicated he might take the green velvet chair it faced over a small tea table.

"I noticed your flawless English, m'lady," Brett returned, "and was wondering how you came by it. Did you live there long?"

"A number of years, yes," answered Maria. Then, wanting to direct the conversation away from her, she added, "But tell me, what is it that brings you away from England yourself?"

Brett lowered his large frame into the comfortable chair, but kept his posture more formal than relaxed. He had yet to determine whether this woman would prove friendly regarding his quest, if indeed she was harboring Ashleigh in her home. And if she was, just how had she come to do so? What was her relationship to Ashleigh?—or to Patrick, whose schooner it surely must be in the harbor; the Dutch-flagged vessel, as some of his officers had already determined, was manned by a crew that spoke American-accented English. No, despite the charming demeanor she presented, it was best not to let his guard down where this woman was concerned.

"You read my letter, of course," he said.

"Yes," said Maria, "but I fear it was somewhat, ah, unen-lightening . . . as to specifics, I mean." She paused as Enrico appeared in the doorway carrying a tea service on a silver tray. "Ah, I see our tea has arrived. You may set it down here, Enrico," she added in Italian, then nodded her dismissal after the steward had complied.

"Specifics?" asked Brett as he watched her pour the tea from a heavy silver pot.

"Yes, Your Grace. You see, I am in the fortunate position of being able to care for a number of children who needed fostering, and I have taken them into my home to live with me over the years. Your letter spoke of someone you've searched for, and—" She paused, teacup in hand. "Do you take cream . . . sugar?"

"Neither, thank you." He accepted the tea as Maria continued.

"So you can imagine my wondering just which one of these children it might be that—"

*"Contessa,"* Brett broke in, "the person I seek is not a child. She is a fully grown young woman who left England some time last summer."

"I see," said Maria, taking a sip of her tea. "And her, ah, identity . . . ?"

The turquoise eyes fastened on the gold and turquoise flecks in hers, and, as he was about to satisfy her query, Brett had an arresting intuition: *He had met this woman before!* As to when, or where, he had not the faintest notion, but he was absolutely certain—without knowing how he was certain—that the Contessa di Montefiori was familiar to him. Checking the urge to question her about it immediately, he forced the impression to the back of his mind—for now—and resumed the conversation.

"Her name is Ashleigh Sinclair Westmont . . . and she is my wife."

The hazel eyes shuttered at his statement, and Brett could detect no hint of recognition in her response, so he pressed further. "Of course, she may be traveling under an assumed name. I—"

"You are telling me it is possible this woman, your wife, does not wish to be found. Is that not so, Your Grace?" The hazel eyes that again met his were cool and reserved.

An exasperated sigh broke from Brett's lips, and he nodded. "That is correct."

Maria was silent for a moment as she appeared to digest this information. *Now it comes,* she thought, *the critical moment wherein I must determine what is to be done. Sweet Mary,* she prayed, *let my choice be the right one!*

"Tell me, Your Grace, what is it you truly seek? This lady who is your wife . . . suppose she were here. What are your intentions, should you find her?"

Brett ran a careless hand through his well-groomed curls. "M'lady, I've asked myself that same question hundreds of times since she . . . disappeared." He shook his head in a weary gesture. "I suppose there's no help for it, but to tell you some of the sorry details, so that—"

Just then, a resounding bark echoed from the hallway outside the drawing room, and a second later, Finn's shaggy form bounded through the partially open door, followed by a pair of curly-headed toddlers.

"*Via, via,* Finn!" one of them cried, then, raising startled eyes to Maria and her guest, grabbed his red-cheeked companion's arm and stopped short in his tracks, lowering abashed eyes to the floor. "*Scusa, Signora Contessa,*" he mumbled.

The second boy, a four-year-old named Carlo, lowered the red harness he'd been thrusting at the wolfhound and smiled apologetically at Maria before lowering his eyes too, but Finn rushed up to Brett and gave him a welcoming bark, his tail wagging furiously.

Brett patted the dog on the head, then turned to Maria. "So she *is* here."

Maria sighed. "She is here," she answered resignedly, then glanced at the two toddlers near the door and spoke gently to them in Italian.

The small boys raised their eyes and brightened, sending her glad smiles, then walked quietly over to Finn and led him out of the room.

Brett watched them go, a gentle half smile on his lips as he observed their chubby little legs endeavor to keep up with the wolfhound's gigantic strides, but when he turned back to Maria, his expression was stern. "Just what is your relationship to my wife, *contessa*?"

Maria faced him for a moment, then gave him the answer she had prepared. "I am an old friend of her family's. I knew her and Sir Patrick years ago."

"When you lived in England."

A pause. "Yes."

"Then I assume you are privy to the circumstances that brought them here."

"I am."

"Then may I also assume you see me as the villain in this situation?" Brett's eyes grew hard with this question.

Maria met them with a resolute look. "That depends, Your Grace."

"On...?"

"On what your intentions are, now that you have located Ashleigh."

"I see," said Brett, rising from his chair. "And if I refuse to explain them to you?"

"That could prove t' be very unwise," said a female voice from the doorway.

"Megan!" Maria exclaimed. "When did you get back?"

Megan stepped into the drawing room. She wore a leaf-green cloak of soft wool; her glorious hair was tousled and wind-blown, and her cheeks bore the rosy hue of someone who has been out-of-doors. "Just a few minutes ago, m'lady, but, not t' fash yerself—the colleen's not with us. We left her—" she glanced at Brett "—ah, somewhere in the village. Hello, Yer Grace. I had an idea ye'd turn up...like a bad penny!"

Brett's face reflected his irritation at the remark. "I see these few months have done nothing to soften your sharp tongue, Miss O'Brien."

"That would be *Lady St. Clare* now," said a voice from the doorway as Patrick's huge form filled it. "Megan and I were wed in December."

Brett watched the big man come to stand beside his wife and then saw the two exchange a look that spoke worlds to each other; their eyes communicated mutual adoration, trust, respect . . . in short, total love of the sort he had come to believe could never exist between a man and a woman, and he felt a momentary stab of regret at the discovery.

Schooling his features to reflect none of this, he replied stiffly, "My congratulations to you both. I wish you every happiness."

Patrick accepted this with a cool nod. "Why have you come, Brett?"

Brett's reply was tight, even defensive. "I should think that would be fairly obvious. I've come to see Ashleigh."

"I find it less than obvious that a man should seek out a wife he's thrust aside," said Patrick.

Brett's control began to slip as he met the grim determination of Megan and Patrick's protectiveness. Hell, it had been difficult enough, coming here to face the question mark Ashleigh represented, without having to undergo an interrogation from these two! He wanted to see his wife, dammit—not undergo a bloody inquisition! Struggling to keep his temper in check, he questioned softly, perhaps too softly, "Are you going to let me see her or not?"

Megan's green eyes met his with a cool, resolute look. "I think, Yer Grace, that will be up t' the wee colleen t' decide. She's free t' do as she pleases here, ye know." Then, insinuatingly, "She comes and goes wearin' a full set o' *clothes* these days."

Maria thought she saw her son wince at this remark and felt her heart go out to him. Not that she blamed Megan and Patrick for their protectiveness; there was considerable justification for it. But she also realized how Brett must be feeling at the moment. He was clearly a proud man, one who didn't find it easy to admit he'd been wrong—at least, she *thought* he was trying to admit he'd been wrong—but how to know for sure? Well, it was certain they weren't going to uncover his feelings by backing him into a corner like a fox at the mercy of a pack of hounds. Someone had to steer things in a different direction—and quickly!

Stepping forward, Maria placed a gentle hand on Brett's arm, forestalling his response to Megan's remark. "Pardon me, Your Grace," she said, "but I believe I have a suggestion that might be of some help." She glanced at the ornate gold clock on the mantel. "It is growing late, and I promised some of the children I'd hear their lessons. It seems we can accomplish little more at this time—that is, not until we have consulted Ashleigh herself on the matter of when—and if—she wishes to meet with you. Why don't you allow us time to talk with her and then come back—shall we say tomorrow? For luncheon? You will have your answer then." She looked questioningly at her son, then at Megan and Patrick.

Patrick sighed, then sought Brett's eyes. "I can agree to that if, Brett, you'll answer just one question."

Brett nodded for him to continue.

"Did you divorce her?"

"No," said Brett, "nor, if I can help it, do I intend to."

Brett sat at a table that was laden with an abundance of perfectly prepared delicacies and smiled at the woman across from him. He was deciding he'd never met a more gracious, charming woman in his life. He discounted those he'd pursued with a sexual liaison in mind, for Maria di Montefiori was definitely in a separate category. She was a delight—this witty, graceful and serene Italian noblewoman, a pleasure to be with in a host of ways that were totally divorced from the usual male-female game of chase, charm and conquer.

In the brief hour they'd spent dining at her table they'd discoursed on a variety of topics—art, music, even politics—and he'd found her highly intelligent, cultured and well-read—in short, able to converse on almost any subject. And when the talk had turned to what was clearly the center of her life—the children she'd taken into her home—he saw yet more admirable qualities, and a nurturing quality rarely seen in women of the upper classes, women who usually left child rearing to those they'd hired to do it.

Before he'd been with her even an hour, he'd come to appreciate how very rare she was. Special. In this short while she'd put him completely at ease—no small feat considering the circumstances under which he'd arrived. Even now, when he should be champing at the bit, to be done with the meal so that she might lead him to Ashleigh—for she'd greeted him with the news that his wife was amenable to a meeting—he found himself so intrigued and relaxed by her company, that it left him quite willing to defer to Maria's lead in timing the meeting, which was to follow their luncheon.

"So the result of that particular pageant," Maria was saying, "was that the pig is not content to let a day go by without being given a rose to clamp between her teeth and drop at your wife's feet the moment they meet in the garden or wherever!"

Brett laughed heartily as she finished her anecdote, one of several she'd amused him with in the hour. "A delightful story, *Contessa*, and not the last you'll have to tell about that pig, I'll warrant! The animal's a living conversation piece!"

Maria smiled, warmed by the cheerful good humor she saw in her son's eyes. It had been her intent, of course, to bring him to such an easy state while they dined. She'd been worried by the way things had gone yesterday, distressed to find Brett so sharply on the defensive. It had been impossible to get to know him under such circumstances, to gauge what he was really like, and to help him, as well as dear Ashleigh. And that was what Maria wanted above all else—to bring these two together.

But this afternoon, how different he was! Here, in this relaxed young man, she caught glimpses of the sunny, happy child he'd once been. Here at last was the living proof that her hopes for him over the years had not been futile. Brett Westmont, at his best, was a charming, warm, sensitive man who, at the same time, exhibited keen intelligence and a sense of the ability to guide his own life in a positive, meaningful direction. No shallow, spoiled scion of the aristocracy, he! Oh, no, her son had depth of character that was carved out of qualities that represented the best the human race had to offer. She was proud of him. And she ached to tell him so.

Yet she put aside her own inclinations—at least for the moment. Warm and wonderful he might be, but her son was also still living under a heavy burden. And she knew the key to unlocking the chains that kept it there lay largely in the person of his wife. If Brett could be brought to come to terms with Ashleigh—or, more to the point, Ashleigh's love—then perhaps Maria would be free to unlock the past where mother and son were concerned. At least that was how she saw it. She hoped she was right.

"I suppose you've had a busy time of it," Brett was saying. "Not only do you live with all these children, now you find yourself hostess to a menagerie as well."

"It has not been dull." Maria smiled.

*There it was again!* For the third or fourth time since he'd met her, Brett was seized with the feeling that he'd met this woman before... known her... in some distant time, perhaps in the past. It was especially apparent when she smiled, as she had just now, or when she gestured in that particular way she had... those graceful hands seeming to smooth the very air through which they moved....

"No," said Brett, "I don't suppose it has been dull." Suddenly he grew thoughtful, his expression sober. "It...it's been good to hear that Ashleigh's stay with you has been a pleasant one. That is, your stories seem to suggest as much." He paused, as if uncertain whether to continue. "She... has been happy here, then?"

Seeing the hint of pain and confusion in his eyes—as if he hoped for his wife's happiness and at the same time dreaded to hear it came because she was free of him—Maria was convinced there was a chance for him. If he could show concern for his wife's happiness even while being aware it could cost him his own, then Brett had the capacity to love her. It was a start.

"Why don't you endeavor to find that out for yourself?" she asked softly as she indicated that luncheon was finished. "I think it's time."

As they began to leave the dining chamber, Maria paused and looked up at him. "There is one thing I must tell you, Your Grace, before we go to your wife."

"Of course," he smiled, "but only if you promise to call me Brett from now on."

Maria's answering smile was radiant. How she had longed to address him by the name she herself had chosen! It had been her maternal great-grandfather's name, and she'd succeeded in giving it to her son with great difficulty; Edward and his father had fought her on it, even though the old man it commemorated had been an adored favorite of hers as a tiny girl, and she'd vowed, when he died, to name her firstborn after him.

"Brett," she said warmly, "as I was saying, there is one thing you should be prepared for. Ashleigh is...changed...in at least one very important way—a way that will be apparent to you the moment you see her."

"Oh?" he questioned, then added with some concern, "She isn't ill, is she? Or—"

"Oh, no. It's nothing to be alarmed about. It's..." Maria examined his face carefully. "It's something I think you should discover for yourself. But, Brett?"

"Yes?"

"I...would like you to give me your word, as a gentleman, that you will be kind to her. She has been through a great deal, and—"

"Madam, what do you take me for? Some kind of blackguard?" he questioned, showing the first trace of annoyance since yesterday. "She is my wife, and I would not be here if I thought I couldn't approach her as a gentleman."

Again, Maria searched his face. "Yes..." she said, nodding, "I think you mean that. But, Brett, if I may, I'd like to suggest you go even a step further...."

"Meaning?"

"Meaning that if your hope on this visit is to reconcile with your wife—and I think it is—I believe you will stand a better chance of doing so if you proceed slowly and carefully with her...almost as if you were courting her, as if you were not yet wed. I've come to know Ashleigh quite well in these past months, and I must tell you, she is a gentle creature, more often given to running and hiding than facing a battle she's afraid she cannot win." Maria hid a smile at his grim nod. "Yet I've also found your wife has a certain...quiet strength, Brett. A wellspring of inner fortitude few suspect because it is hidden under that delicate exterior. Seek out that strength, if you can. By traveling a softer path, you may find it."

Brett looked into the unusual hazel eyes and knew they mirrored a kind of hidden strength as well...and wisdom. He was briefly taken aback. When, if ever, had he encountered wisdom in a woman? It was a sobering thought.

"Very well, *contessa*." He grinned. "Ah, may I call you, Maria?"

"You may," she smiled.

"Well, Maria, I find myself liking the sound of your advice, and I intend to take it. God knows, it's better than anything I've been able to come up with. I only hope I can see it through."

"You may surprise yourself, Brett," she said softly; then, placing her hand on his arm, she added, "Very well, sir, let us find your wife."

# Chapter Thirty-One

The late February sunshine warmed the bricks of the veranda where Ashleigh stood, surrounded by a dozen children. They were playing a game of tag, but not the ordinary version of that game. The little twins, Allegra and Alissa, who were blind, had come to her several days ago with downcast faces: they had been sad not to be able to join in a game some of the others were playing, a game barred to them because they could not see. That was when Ashleigh had gotten the idea to devise a series of new twists to a variety of children's games with the idea of making them viable for children whose handicaps might otherwise prevent them from participating.

On that first day she'd called the whole group of children to her and suggested they all pretend to be blind—like Allegra and Alissa—by tying blindfolds over their eyes and then proceeding to "hide and go seek." It had worked beautifully. Oh, at first there had been a few bumps and bruises, but soon all the youngsters, the twins included, were giggling and laughing as they moved around the garden, using their senses of touch and hearing to locate the one who had hidden.

Encouraged by their enthusiasm, Ashleigh had gone on to design a race where all who joined in had to bind up one leg and use crutches, like the ones who really did need them. Soon the children themselves were thinking up new versions of old sports, each with the idea of making the activity accessible to those who'd had to sit it out in the past. Ashleigh was thrilled, for she began to see how these experiments imparted a new sense of tolerance and compassion among the youngsters. They were now eager to view the world through the eyes of those who were different. They were learning a valuable lesson.

Ashleigh laughed as she saw Francesca, who was deaf, signal to Antonio that his "baby" was slipping. The "baby" was a bulky pillow, additionally weighted with some large stones, that was tied about each child's middle, for today was *"Il giorno della duchessa piccola,"* or "the little duchess's day": everyone pretended to be heavily pregnant—like Ashleigh.

A girlish giggle erupted behind her and, turning, Ashleigh saw Alessandra point to Antonio, who was trying furiously to adjust his overly large pillow while running from Aldo. "Poor Antonio," said the girl, "I think he has given himself twins!"

Ashleigh laughed as she returned her gaze to the seven-year-old, and then froze. There, in the arched doorway behind Antonio, stood Maria, and at her side was Brett.

As Maria called to the children, promising them some lemonade if they came with her, Ashleigh kept her gaze focused on her husband. Tall and erect in the sunlight, he was the essence of male beauty in all the ways she'd fought to forget, and which had haunted her nightly in her dreams. He wore a formal coat of deep blue, its expert cut emphasizing the breadth of his shoulders. Against it, the white of his stock was dazzling in the sunlight and played dramatic counterpoint to his handsome, chiseled face, which was deeply tanned. Dove-gray breeches hugged his long, muscular thighs before they met high boots of shiny black, and there was an aura of power in his stance that did not pass Ashleigh by.

Children rushed past her in the sunlight, calling out their goodbyes, but Ashleigh remained, unmoving, where she stood. Just seeing him again brought back a flood of memories, and she was helpless to fend them off...memories of Brett bending over her hand in his drawing room, saying, "You're lovelier each time I see you," of Brett towering over her in a small Norman church, speaking holy vows, of Brett telling her on their wedding night, "Oh sweet, merciful God, I cannot think for wanting you!" and, again, of Brett, saying, "Just stay with me...be with me...."

Oh, she loved him so much! She had never stopped loving him, but now that he had come, that love became a searing ache that threatened to shut out all else but the fact that he was here, and he was real, and maybe, just maybe . . .

Brett, too, was unable to move as his head spun with the implications of what he saw. *She was with child!* And not too far from her time by the looks of her. Stunned, he heard Maria's voice coming as if from a great distance.

"Your heir will be born in the spring, Brett. Late April or the beginning of May, my physician thinks, although Ashleigh appears as if she may deliver sooner. It is because she is so tiny. Well, I shall leave you now. I wish you well."

Nodding as he felt the touch of her hand leave his arm, Brett could only stare at his wife, unable to speak.

A child. *She was carrying a child . . . his child—no . . .* their *child!*

His eyes traveled over her small form, still fragile looking despite the burden she carried, and he was aware of how heart-stoppingly, achingly lovely she was. *Like a Madonna,* he thought as his eyes devoured the contours of her face, *a delicate, fragile Madonna*.

The last echoes of children's footsteps faded, and they were alone. A gull cried overhead, and in the distance Ashleigh could hear the faint crashing of the surf against Livorno's rocks.

"Hello, Ashleigh."

"Hello . . . Brett."

He took several of those long, graceful strides she remembered so well, until he stood a few feet in front of her. She looked up to meet the intense gaze of his turquoise eyes.

"I had no idea you were . . . with child." His voice was low, careful, while his eyes searched hers.

"I am well aware of that," she said, a bit more abruptly than she had intended. "How could you have known when I did not know it myself? Until I was well away from . . . London."

Put off by her tone and annoyed to be reminded of her flight, he fired back, "But you could have sent word, once you found out!"

She glanced away. "To what end, Your Grace? To force you to abandon your pursuit of a divorce merely because I carried your heir?" The words, as they came out, were bitter, for she was remembering Margaret's face when she had told Ashleigh she'd come to help him implement the divorce, and before that, Elizabeth's, when *she'd* mocked Ashleigh for being so naive as to think he wanted anything out of marriage but an heir.

Her tone fired his anger. "Dammit, Ashleigh, I've sought no divorce! Not once, not in all these months!"

She paused, confused. Patrick had told her he'd questioned Brett on the status of their marriage, and if Patrick believed him, it must be true, yet . . . Nervously, she twisted the fingers of her hands together. "Then . . . then why did you bring Lady Margaret to London? She said you required her help in—in effecting your di—"

"Lady Margaret!" he thundered. "You accepted the word of that bitter old crone? *Knowing* how she felt about our marriage?" He ran a hand distractedly through his hair, wondering if he were going mad. Here he was, defending himself of charges that he'd sought a divorce, when he'd intended to question *her* along the same lines!

Then he looked down at her face and saw her confusion and chagrin. Dammit, he hadn't *meant* to lose his temper! Maria had been right. If he were to make any progress here at all, it had to be through gentleness and a sensitivity to Ashleigh's feelings.

But it was so blasted hard! He'd never had to deal with a woman in such a manner before.

Slowly, tentatively, as if testing his ability to do so, he formed an apology. "Ashleigh, I . . . Forgive me. I . . . hadn't meant to storm at you over this." His eyes lifted to the gardens beyond the veranda, still bare of their foliage, but showing hints of spring in red-budded expectancy. "It is a warm day. Will you walk with me in the gardens awhile?"

The corners of Ashleigh's mouth quirked in a half smile. She'd seen the difficulty he had in apologizing but was surprised and warmed by it.

"I think spring will be early this year—or perhaps it's just that we're this far south. The gardens are full of . . . promise. Yes, Brett, I'd like to walk with you."

He smiled and took her hand, about to place it on his arm, when suddenly he paused, a look of concern on his face. "Um, will it tax you overly to do so? I mean—" he glanced at the rounded form of her belly under the yellow velvet of her empire-cut walking dress "—perhaps we ought to sit somewhere instead. We can—"

Her light laughter intervened. "Walking will be fine, Brett. I am with child, not ill or doddering!"

He gave her rounded shape a last, skeptical glance. "Well, if you're sure . . ."

"I am quite sure, Your Grace." She dimpled.

"If you insist on 'Your Gracing' me, I shall 'Your Grace' you back," he teased.

Finding the turquoise eyes meeting hers in open warmth, Ashleigh felt a delicious shiver run up her spine. At the same time, she realized he had not released her hand and now held it warmly in his own. Flushing slightly, she smiled, saying, "Then I am quite sure, *Brett*."

He laughed softly and began walking with her, their clasped hands between them.

As they wandered through the gardens in the warm sunshine, they talked. He asked her when she'd arrived in Italy and what she thought of her hostess—to which she replied with abundant enthusiasm, convincing him that her impressions of Maria were aligned with his. Then he asked her how she'd been spending her days at the villa, at which Ashleigh waxed enthusiastically about the children, telling him in great detail what each one was like until he began to feel he knew each child as intimately as she.

"Maria's children," he said as they rounded a bend in the walk, "they mean a great deal to you, don't they?"

She paused and looked up at him. "They have given my life a sense of purpose, Brett. I mean, before I came here, what was I? I was someone who had always been passive, who allowed myself to act, or *react*, I should say, to things that happened *to* me." She gazed off into the distance where a small sailboat could be seen in a wedge of ocean framed by two evergreens. "There was the tragedy that took my parents lives and took *me* to London...to Hampton House.... There was the education I received there while I remained precariously suspended between Madame's threatening grasp and—thank God!—the benevolent watchfulness of Dorcas and Megan.... And finally—" She glanced back at him, as if trying to gauge his mood. "Oh, please do not take this the wrong way! I only mean it as an example. Finally, there was the strange twist of fate that brought me to—to Ravensford Hall—hardly something of my own choosing.

"Oh, I know there are those who might marvel at my transformation from serving menial to duchess and ask what I have to be dissatisfied about, but don't you see? It was nothing I had actually achieved by myself."

Brett frowned. "Are you trying to tell me it was living the life of a member of the upper classes that made you—"

"Oh, no!" she cried. "No, that is not what I meant...." She gave him a little smile. "You must remember I was born into that class to begin with, and had been quite happy in it as a little girl. But, on the other hand, I've found myself thinking more and more about your friend, Mr. Shelley, and his egalitarian views lately. There is something almost...parasitic about the lives some of those in our class lead.

"But I was speaking more of my own lack of choices, rather than the nature of the *non*-choices forced on me."

Brett nodded. "Yes, I think I understand. There are in most lives, I believe, choices that are not of one's own making." It was Brett's turn to gaze off into the distance; he continued. "I loved my grandfather extremely, but I am well aware, as I stand here now, that the life I live has been almost totally shaped by him." He gazed back at her. "It is not a notion I am entirely comfortable having."

Ashleigh nodded, then smiled. "Then you do understand!"

"I think so. When you landed in Italy—another circumstance that came of fate acting *upon* you—you could have chosen to lie about here, in this gracious home owned by its even more gracious mistress, doing nothing more than—" another glance at her belly "—waiting for yet something else to happen. Instead, you *chose* to become actively involved in helping others." He smiled at her. "Unselfishly involved, I might add."

"Oh," murmured Ashleigh, blushing, "I don't know about that. The pleasure I receive from working with those little ones—it's difficult to conceive of it as selfless. And there are those who do far more than I...the *contessa*, for instance, and Father Umberto."

"Do not take yourself lightly. From what I have seen and heard, you can be proud of what you've chosen to do."

Looking into his eyes, she saw that he'd meant what he said, and suddenly she felt lighter than air. There was a welling buoyancy inside her that belied the extra stone or so she carried these days and the smile she threw him was dazzling.

Seeing the smile that had haunted his days and kept him awake nights, it was all Brett could do not to crush her to him, extra girth and all, but Maria's advice fixed in his mind, and he cautioned, *Patience, old boy, patience.*

Looking down, he saw her hand had become disengaged from his while they were talking, and he took it up again before they resumed their walk.

They had gone but a little way when Ashleigh cried out, "Oh, Brett, look!" She pointed at a brightly colored object high in an old oleander tree. "It's the kite Antonio lost yesterday. He thought it had blown away after its string snapped."

Gazing at the kite, Brett told her, "Strings on kites don't snap, Ashleigh. They become hopelessly entangled, yes, but take it from an old kite-flier, they never snap."

She grinned at him. "They do when one of the babies has used your ball of string as a teething toy."

He quirked an eyebrow at her. "I see what you mean."

Ashleigh's attention was back on the kite. "It looks of a piece. Do you think we can rescue it?"

"We?" The eyebrow again.

She looked at him with bright expectancy. "Why, yes—you and I! The tree isn't very high, and—"

"*You*, madam, are hardly in any condition to be climbing trees!" He tapped her lightly on the nose. "You will remain here. *I* shall fetch the ruddy kite."

She took the jacket he'd removed and watched him roll up his sleeves. "I hope Antonio appreciates this," he grumbled.

"Oh, he will!" she assured him. "He made it himself."

"An admirable occupation. I once did the same—when I could be sure Grandfather wasn't about." He found a toehold in the tree and began to climb.

The tree was large for an oleander, about twenty feet high, and the kite rested against some of its leathery, evergreen leaves, near the top. It took a few moments for Brett to reach it.

As he climbed, Ashleigh watched him and thought of the small boy he had been—a boy who'd found precious little time in his arduous schedule for flying kites or climbing trees, and had probably grown up too early and too fast. And she realized they were kindred spirits in a way, each of them surviving, over the years, through circumstances that were not of their own choosing.

"Here you are, m'lady." He executed a lavish bow and held out the brightly colored kite to her.

"Thank you, kind sir," she said, accepting it. Then, "You are an expert climber of trees, you know." There was a twinkle in her eyes. "I couldn't have done it better myself, and believe me, I was once quite adept at it."

"Cheeky wench!" he chided playfully as he captured her free hand and resumed walking. "Not only does she rate me on an ability I acquired from the time I was out of the cradle—she presumes to be an expert herself!"

Ashleigh grinned. "Just you wait a few months—" she tapped her belly with the kite "—until I'm myself again. I'll show you a few things I know about the so-called boys' sports!"

"I don't doubt it. I still recall your abilities at horse training—*and pig training*!"

They shared a laugh, but privately Brett was thinking of what she'd said about waiting a few months. It was the first allusion she'd made to sharing a future together, and he was keenly aware of the flush of pleasure this gave him. So far, things seemed to be going uncommonly well; perhaps, just perhaps, there was a chance for this marriage after all.

Walking a little farther, they came to a low stone wall, and before she knew what was happening, he bent to lift her up in his arms and carried her over it.

Managing to hold on to the kite, Ashleigh's arms went around his neck as she cried, "Oh, Brett, don't! I'm entirely too heavy these days!"

"Hah! You're still as light as a feather!" He gave her a grin when they'd cleared the wall, but continued to hold her in his arms.

"Well?" she demanded. "Aren't you going to put me down?"

But Brett was thinking how he'd like to hold her like this for a long, long time. It had been months since he'd had a woman. In those dark winter days in London he'd quickly given up his frenzied pursuit of other females; they'd all paled in comparison to Ashleigh, and after a while he'd found he preferred celibacy to anything less than the perfection she'd brought to his bed.

But another glance at the rounded protrusion of her belly reminded him this was hardly the time to be thinking of how much he wanted her. And besides, other things were at stake...much more important and enduring things. With a sigh, he summoned his patience and lowered her slowly to the ground.

But as he did so, Ashleigh was pressed against the front of him, her belly in contact with his middle, and suddenly he felt a sharp thrust against his abdomen.

"What the—?"

She laughed—a clear, musical sound in the still garden. "Don't look so surprised," she told him. "It's the babe. She kicks mightily these days."

Brett gave her belly a suspicious glance. *"She...?"*

Ashleigh nodded. "I fully intend to have a daughter." Suddenly her smile faded. Perhaps she oughtn't to have said that. After all, how could she tell him about her hopes for a female child so that she would be able to be a better single parent? Now that he was here, it didn't seem to be the thing to say.

Carefully, she formed her next words. "Brett...would—would you be terribly upset if—if it were a girl?"

He warmed at the thought that she would consider his feelings in the matter, reminding himself that this was the second time in less than an hour that she had alluded to a shared future between them.

"No," he answered, the turquoise eyes brilliant as they fastened on hers, "not if she's the image of her mother." Then, "You're even more beautiful than before, Ashleigh, if that's possible. I find it difficult to take my eyes off you."

He was standing very close to her now, his tall frame looming over hers as his eyes traveled over her face, at last fixing on her lips, which were softly parted...and faintly trembling.

Slowly, as if she were in a dream, she saw his hands come up to rest lightly on her shoulders, and then she felt them slide higher, under her heavy curls, which she wore loose, until they cupped her wondering face.

Then, again slowly—ever so slowly—his dark chestnut head lowered until his lips brushed hers in a kiss as light as down.

Ashleigh closed her eyes as she felt their touch. She felt herself floating, far away, to another time and place, when she had felt their touch before, and all at once she was consumed by a longing so great, she could scarce contain it. *Oh, Brett!* her heart cried out, *Brett, my love...my only love!*

Brett closed his eyes, gripped by an ache so fierce, he had to suck in his breath to withstand its force. Merciful God, how he'd missed her! He opened his eyes to find her looking at him with an unreadable expression on her face. Then his arms lowered and he drew her to him, and his mouth closed over hers in a kiss that was warm, sensual and fraught with longing.

Suddenly a sharp bark rent the air, forcing them apart abruptly, as Finn came bounding into sight. Behind him ran Lady Dimples, a red rose clamped firmly in her jaws.

"I don't believe it," Brett groaned.

"Fourth rose this week," said Ashleigh as she bent to retrieve the bud the pig had just deposited at her feet. "Thank you, Lady Dimples—'' she glanced at her scowling husband "—I think.''

Finn was busy tugging, gently but firmly, on Brett's sleeve.

"What does *he* want?'' he growled.

"I believe we're being summoned for tea, Your Grace,'' said Ashleigh.

Mentally pocketing his inclinations, Brett gave her a good-natured laugh. "Yes, Your Grace, by all means. Let us have some tea!''

# Chapter Thirty-Two

Ashleigh withdrew a burgundy velvet cloak from her wardrobe. Slowly, with a dreamy expression on her face, she moved to the cheval glass in her chamber, the cloak over her arm. Here she paused, her mind not really on donning it. All she could think of was Brett.

She had just left him in the playroom where the two of them had spent time with the children after dinner. Ashleigh had read them their customary bedtime story while Brett stood by and quietly watched. But when she'd finished the story and gone to join Maria in tucking the littlest ones into bed, Brett remained to talk to a few of the older boys. They'd had some questions for this English duke who had appeared suddenly on the scene two days ago. A duke who captained his own ship? *Fantastico!*

After she and Maria had said good-night to the last toddler, Brett suggested she fetch a wrap and wait for him downstairs, saying he wished to walk with her in the gardens as soon as he finished talking to Aldo and his companions.

Now, as she stood before the mirror, her reflection blurred before her eyes while her thoughts turned inward.

What was on his mind? When she'd learned, the day before yesterday, that her husband had arrived in Livorno, she'd been filled with all sorts of apprehensions regarding his intentions. And it had required a great amount of fortitude to agree to see him the next day—yesterday.

Was it only yesterday that they'd met again? Strolled in the gardens like lovers who had no barriers between them? Held hands and kissed?

He was being so gentle—and *kind*! Except for that one brief exchange regarding the divorce that had never materialized, there'd been no harsh words between them. It was as if the nightmare following their wedding had never happened.

But of course it had happened. And that's what worried her. There were still some major problems between the two of them, and sooner or later, they'd have to be faced. Was that what he'd had in mind when he invited her for this walk tonight? Surely he couldn't mean to avoid their differences forever, nor could she. Perhaps he was waiting for her to broach the subject.

But with this new, accommodating mood she found him in, how could she? How did she dare risk upsetting the newfound peace between them?

A smile turned the corners of her mouth upward as she recalled Brett's appearance at the villa late this afternoon. He'd been invited for dinner but arrived early, laden with an armful of toys and other gifts purchased in town that morning. Oh, the shrieks of delight and bubbling laughter that had erupted as he'd met with the youngsters and handed out dolls, toy sailboats, tin soldiers and the like! The children had immediately adored him, not only for his generosity, but for the special way he seemed to take an interest in each of them, asking questions about what they liked to do, telling funny stories of similar activities from his own childhood. It was almost as if—

"Ah, there you are!" said her husband from the open doorway.

"Oh," murmured Ashleigh, stirred from her reverie. "I—I hadn't realized I was taking so long." Hastily, she shook out the cloak and swirled it about her shoulders, then draped the full hood over her hair and attempted to secure the neck closure with fumbling fingers.

"Here, allow me." Brett smiled as he came behind her and gently turned her to face him.

As his fingers closed over the silver braided frog under her chin, Ashleigh chanced to look up. Intent on his task, Brett didn't realize she was watching him, and she took the opportunity to study him at close range. She loved the way his mouth was set in a determined line as he concentrated on the mechanism of the fastener; she adored the way a lock of his chestnut hair brushed his forehead as he worked; she noted the way his height made him tower above her in such an overpowering way. Suddenly she felt nearly undone by the turn her thoughts were taking and began to squirm and fidget with the realization.

"Hold still, you moppet," he chastised with an indulgent smile, "or I shall never have this done. Ah, there we are!" His eyes left the fastening and moved upward. There was a long moment of silence.

"You're beautiful," he breathed.

Caught off-guard, Ashleigh murmured the first thing to come into her head. "S-so are you."

His mouth quirked in an odd smile, and she had the feeling he was remembering something in another time, another place. "I am content to know you find me so," he murmured. "But come, sweet, there's a beautiful night awasting in the gardens."

He led her outside and they began to walk, talking desultorily as moonlight silvered the branches of the trees and shrubs, turning the garden into an oasis of soft shadows and lambent quietude. It was a warm night for early March, and the soft, rich scent of the sun-warmed earth beneath the awakening foliage hinted at the coming of spring.

"The children love you, you know," said Brett. "I can see it in their faces when you look at them or read them a story."

"Oh, but look who's talking!" Ashleigh exclaimed. "Only two days in their presence, and they absolutely adore you!"

Brett chuckled. "I suspect I'm just a novelty right now. Something like the rich uncle who visits once every few years, bringing gifts from his trips abroad . . . that sort of thing. But the feelings they so obviously have for you, and for Maria, well—" he shook his head "—I've never seen such a manifestation of love."

"Maria's really the one responsible for it all," said Ashleigh. "She's an extraordinary woman, isn't she?"

"Remarkable," he agreed. "And I wonder about her. Here she is, with all the wealth and comfort anyone could want, a life of ease, and yet she selflessly gives of herself, day after day, in ways that might seem totally alien to others of our class. Oh, there are those with wealth who do their share with charitable contributions and the like, but this woman actually rolls up her sleeves and plunges into the heart of it! I wonder what it was in her background that made her what she is."

Ashleigh's response was cautious. "You . . . suspect something, ah, out of the ordinary?"

He nodded. "I'm sure of it. It's in her eyes. I've seen things there that—" He shook his head. "Yet, every time I've tried to question her about it, she's steered the conversation deftly in another direction." He laughed. "In the most charming manner, of course!"

Ashleigh began to wish she had some of Maria's skill now, for the conversation was hovering dangerously about a subject she'd sworn not to reveal. "You, ah, find her mysterious, then?"

"Quite. It's nothing I can put my finger on, but I have this unshakable feeling Maria's not all she appears to be . . . or perhaps that she's something more." He glanced at Ashleigh. "I don't suppose you'd be able to shed any light on the subject? I mean, she did say she was an old friend of your family's."

Shifting her glance from his face, Ashleigh hoped the shadows hid her flush as she responded. "Oh, I know, but Brett, you must remember that I was such a tiny girl in those days. There isn't much I can recall."

"Hmm. Yes, I suppose you're right. Perhaps Patrick's the one I ought to be asking."

They walked a while in silence, and then he said, "She doesn't seem to have any children of her own, natural children, that is, yet she's as nurturing and maternal as any mother I've ever seen. And then there's this other feeling I have. . . ."

"Other feeling?"

He nodded. "That I've seen her somewhere before . . . known her. I realize it doesn't make sense." He shrugged.

Determined to steer the conversation elsewhere now, Ashleigh dug the toe of her slipper into a crack in the walk and pretended to stumble.

Instantly, Brett's arm shot out to steady her, and when the other arm joined in, she found herself encircled in his embrace.

"Careful, little one," he murmured. "You carry a precious burden these days."

Casual as they sounded, his words reminded her that she did indeed carry a precious burden—his heir—and suddenly she remembered other words spoken about an heir of Brett's. She had a swift recollection of Elizabeth's hurting words that morning, and all at once she felt pain so real it was almost palpable.

"Brett, why did you marry me?" she whispered.

Brett paused, his arms still about her as he saw the anguish in her eyes. She'd caught him off guard with this sudden question, and he wasn't sure he could give her a ready answer. Slowly, as if he half expected her to vanish if he misstepped, he groped for the right words.

"The immediate reasons, the awkward circumstances, we are both well acquainted with, Ashleigh. But beyond that, I think—I believe—there was something more, something deeper...." His hands moved from about her girth and settled gently, but firmly, on her shoulders. "You were—*are*—different from any woman I've ever known, Ashleigh. And if I didn't consciously realize it when I married you, I've come to realize it more and more during these months we've been apart. Beyond that, I'm not sure." He sighed, then moved a hand to touch her cheek gently with his knuckles. "Ashleigh, why did you flee from me that morning?"

The blue eyes darkened as she focused again on the scene with Elizabeth the morning after their wedding. "She said the only reason you—you had for wedding me was that—that—" Ashleigh bit her lip and glanced down at her belly "—you wanted me to bear you heirs."

A sharp frown creased Brett's brow. "*Who* told you that, Ashleigh? Who?"

A sob cut him off as Ashleigh dropped her eyes and turned her head away. "It was Elizabeth! She rowed across the lake after you left to see about the—"

*"Elizabeth!"* he stormed. *"Elizabeth* came to see you that morning?"

"Yes, and she said you could never be faithful to one woman, that marriage would make no dif—"

"That cold bitch!" he snarled. "She's so consumed with jealousy and self-love, she—" He ran a hand distractedly through his hair, then caught her chin with the other, forcing her to look at him. "And you *believed* her?"

The pain in Ashleigh's eyes deepened, then changed to anger. "There were good reasons! Hadn't I just seen the way you—you cast Pamela Marlowe aside so casually? Because your appetite required new conquests?"

Tears were streaming down her cheeks, but Ashleigh dashed them aside with an angry hand as she plunged onward; it was as if a dam had been opened, and all the pent-up anger and pain of the past months was suddenly let loose. "And later, in London after we quarreled, can you deny that you went to other—"

At that moment, there was a confusion of screaming and shouting at the end of the garden nearest the house. Ashleigh turned and saw Giovanni moving toward them as swiftly as his aged legs would allow.

*"Duchessa, Signore Duca,* coma queek! *Incendio! La villa!* She's-a-burn! The leetle ones! Hurry!"

Behind him were several of the servants, all waving their arms and shouting, and then Patrick.

"Brett, Ashleigh!" Patrick yelled. "It's the children's wing! It's afire! Come quickly!"

Ashleigh threw Brett a horrified look. "Oh, my God!" she gasped, then began to run toward the house.

But Brett was already far ahead of her, pausing only to shout over his shoulder, "Be careful, Ashleigh! Mind your steps in the darkness!"

As she neared the house, Ashleigh could see smoke pouring out of a couple of the upstairs windows, while, in the courtyard below, a number of people, children and adults alike, were rushing about, crying and shouting. She saw Patrick dash into the house, only to emerge helping Megan make her way down the walk as she clasped two infants in her arms.

Brett met them first, shouting, "Who else is up there?"

But Megan just shook her head at him, appearing dazed.

One of the children's nurses came dashing out, coughing and gasping for air. Patrick took the blanket-covered toddler she carried while Brett helped the stricken woman to a seat on a nearby stone wall.

"Water!" he called to one of the servants he spied carrying a bucket.

Several of the children standing about in their nightclothes were crying, and Ashleigh hurried over to them, speaking quietly in reassuring tones. Then she withdrew her cloak and, gathering them close, wrapped it about them.

The nurse drank the water Brett had given her from a wooden dipper, then pointed agitatedly to the upper reaches of the house. *"La contessa,"* she gasped, *"la contessa!"*

*"Contessa?* Maria's in there?" Brett questioned.

*"Si!"* The nurse nodded, then began coughing some more.

Brett whirled toward Patrick, taking off his coat as he moved. "I'm going up there. Is there any count as to—"

"Enrico just took a nose count," Patrick told him as he watched Brett soak his coat in the bucket of water. "Only Maria and the twins are missing. He thinks she went in after them after she brought the first group out."

As Ashleigh watched Brett run into the burning villa, flames began to shoot out of one of the lower windows.

*Oh, my God!* she thought. *It's burned through to the lower floor!*

Several of the servants must have noted the same thing, for there was a mad scramble for the well while others, their buckets already full, began running toward this new source of flames.

Meanwhile Ashleigh saw more servants coming from the direction of the stables; they were pulling a small wagon loaded with several huge barrels, and she recalled that ironically, these were water barrels kept on hand in case of fire in the stables— *while no one thought to keep a single such barrel on hand near the house itself,* she thought.

Then, as she watched the chaos about her, she had a flash of another fire long ago. She became, for a moment, a tiny child again, and Mary Westmont was wrapping her in a blanket and carrying her to safety.

A shout brought her back to the present. The gallery outside the children's wing had collapsed in flames, nearly missing Enrico and a group of stable men below.

She saw Patrick moving toward them with an entire water barrel on his shoulder, saw Megan wrapping her robe about two of the older girls, saw Giovanni standing near a tree with his arm about Lady Dimples, gazing about, shaking his head.

But Ashleigh's thoughts were on the burning building. Maria was in there—Maria who had saved her life from just such a fire ... and Brett! He'd been gone for several minutes, now. Where was he? And there were the twins, poor blind babies! And Finn! Where was Finn?

Suddenly Ashleigh knew she couldn't just stand by and do nothing; she had to act! Moving quickly through the chaotic throng of people, barrels and buckets, she approached the door Brett had entered. As she neared it, she heard a whimper, and then saw Finn emerge from the smoke; clinging to his back was Allegra, one of the twins!

"Oh, thank God, Finn!" she exclaimed.

Allegra was sobbing, but appeared to be unharmed. Ashleigh rushed up to her and pulled her into her arms.

"Oh, the poor darlin'," said Megan from behind them. "Here, come t' Megan, *macushla*." She took the child from Ashleigh adding, "Ye oughtn't t' be carryin' her, darlin'. She's a might too heavy fer ye in yer condition. And, fer Heaven's sake, get some rest while ye're at it!"

Rest? How could she rest when Maria and Brett and a little blind girl were still in that inferno? Without another moment's hesitation, Ashleigh withdrew a handkerchief from her sleeve, dipped it in a passing bucket of water, and, tying it about her face like a highwayman's mask, slipped into the burning building.

Upstairs, in the children's wing, Brett was frantic. He'd checked almost all of the rooms, those nearest the fire first, but still no Maria. And now the smoke was growing so thick, even at this end, he was forced to go down on all fours, close to the floor where the air was less noxious. And even here, he kept his sodden jacket over his head to protect himself.

"Maria!" he called. "Maria, where are you?"

No answer. And there was only one chamber left.

Brett crawled to the door up ahead of him. He could barely make out the shape of it in the hazy, smoke-filled hallway. Feeling his way, he reached the aperture he knew was the doorframe and gave the door a shove.

Raising the jacket slightly, he called, *"Maria!"*

A childish whimper met his ears, and his eyes followed the sound. Then he saw them. A tiny girl was huddled near the window. Beside her, on the floor, lay Maria's prone form.

"Sweetheart," Brett called. "Alissa, isn't it?" He moved toward the whimpering child. Reaching out to touch her, he said, "It's *il duca*, sweetheart. Put your arms around my neck and try to climb onto my back. I'm going to take you and the *contessa* out of here."

Surprisingly, the girl ceased her whimpering and complied, as Brett removed his wet jacket and wrapped it over her.

"Hold onto this, too, *cara*," he told her and forced the lapels of the jacket between her clutching fingers.

Then, summoning all his strength and whispering a dimly remembered prayer, he took Maria's prone body in his arms and rose, sucking in a great gulp of relatively clear air before he did so. Then he raced out the door and for the stairs at the end of the hallway as fast as his double burden would allow.

Down below, Patrick was soaking his own jacket in a bucket of water, preparing to go after Brett, who'd disappeared into the building a frightening number of minutes ago.

"Patrick," said his wife as she came rushing up to him, "have ye seen Ashleigh? Nobody's seen her fer some time!"

Alarm on his face, Patrick looked about him in panic. "God, no, Megan! I haven't, and I was just about to go after—"

Suddenly a shout met his ears, and he and Megan turned in the direction of the door to the villa where two of the stable men, buckets in hand, were urging someone to do something in rapid Italian.

Then they saw what they were shouting about. An apparition that appeared to be a headless giant carrying something, came lunging through the door.

"It's Brett!" Patrick shouted, "and he's got Maria and Alissa!"

"Saints be praised!" Megan cried.

Rushing forward, the two of them relieved Brett of his burdens, Patrick taking Maria, who was beginning to cough and sputter, while Megan clasped the sobbing Alissa to her breast.

Brett was gulping in huge breaths of clean air, but he managed to get out, "I...think...that...does it. How's...Maria?"

Bending over Maria, whom he'd laid on a coat one of the men had spread on the ground, Patrick said, "She's taken some smoke, but I think she'll be all right. But Brett," he said, grimly facing his friend, "no one's seen Ashleigh for some time!"

The blood drained from Brett's face as Patrick's words registered. Then he whirled and ran toward the villa, pausing only to pick up Patrick's wet jacket.

"Brett, wait!" Patrick shouted. "You're too done in! Let me go!"

"Stay here and see to Maria!" came the reply.

"But—"

"I've *got* to find her, man! Don't you know that?"

These words were hardly out of Brett's mouth when, from the interior of the villa, he heard a faint bark.

"Finn!" he shouted as he entered the smoke-filled doorway, "Finn, where are you, boy? Where's Ashleigh?"

Another bark met his ears when he reached the foot of the stairs, louder and clearer this time, coming from just above him.

Shielding himself with Patrick's coat, he began to crawl up the stairs. When he was nearly to the top, he could make out the wolfhound's shaggy form on the landing.

"Finn! Where—?"

Then he saw her. She was lying very still under Finn's standing body. The dog was pulling at her gown, as if trying to nudge her over the top step.

"Ashleigh!" Brett cried. "Dear God, Ashleigh!" As gently as he could, Brett retrieved her still form, clutched it to him, turned and flew down the stairs, Finn at his heels.

Outside, a worried Megan was ministering to Maria while Patrick stood by, his eyes on the door to the house. Although he knew the fire was largely extinguished now, he realized there was still a heavy amount of killing smoke. Where were they? The dog's last bark had been several minutes ago.

Then he saw a movement at the door and a second later, Brett stumbled out, Ashleigh clutched in his arms.

"Megan, he's got her! Thank Heaven!" He raced forward to meet the faltering Brett, just as he heard Finn's excited bark.

"Here, man, I'll take her," Patrick said.

Brett shook his head wearily, then sank to the ground, Ashleigh still safely in his embrace. *"No!"* Then, "No, I—I'll keep her," he managed to get out.

He cradled his wife's head in his lap and gazed anxiously down into her face. "Ashleigh?" he whispered, and when there was no response, the whisper became a frantic cry. *"Ashleigh!"*

Patrick knelt beside his sister's swollen form and took her wrist, throwing Brett a worried look as he felt for a pulse.

"The dog...Finn...saved her," Brett was gasping between gulps of air. "Please God let him have saved her!"

"She's alive," Patrick announced, "but her pulse feels irregular. She's in a state of shock, I think. I'm going for a blanket."

As Patrick left, Brett heard Ashleigh moan and bent anxiously over her.

"Ashleigh?"

"Brett..." he heard her whisper faintly, "Brett... where...Maria?"

"She's fine, love," he said to her. "Now, hush. Don't try to talk anymore. Just—"

"H-had to...find her," Ashleigh continued, "had to... help...."

Brett was shaking his head. "You silly little fool... Sweetheart, you could have been killed!"

Ashleigh began to cough and choke as she shook her head at him. "H-had to...Brett," she gasped. "Sh-she's your *mother*...."

At that moment, Patrick came rushing up to them, a blanket in hand. He was in time to catch his sister's words before she sighed and lost consciousness. He was in time to catch Brett's incredulous stare.

# Chapter Thirty-Three

"So now you know the whole story, Brett," Patrick was saying, "or at least as much as I know of it. For the rest, you'll have to talk to Mar—to your mother."

They were sitting in Abner Thornton's cabin aboard the *Ashleigh Anne* while nearby, in the captain's cabin, Signore Capetti, the *contessa*'s physician, was examining her for damage from smoke inhalation and a few minor burns. Following last night's fire, Brett and Patrick had decided to take everyone to their two ships in the harbor, for, though the fire was out, there was extensive damage to most of the villa and Maria's home was deemed uninhabitable for the time being.

"I see," said Brett, a bitter twist to his lips. "All this time you knew who she was, *where* she was, and yet you never said a word!"

"Oh, have off, Brett!" Patrick's tone was sharp, tinged with weariness. They'd been up all night fighting the fire and performing the rescue work, and now he was fighting exhaustion. "Maria made me promise—made us all promise—not to reveal who she was. *I gave my word!* Can't you understand that?"

Brett nodded, but the cynical expression did not leave his face. "I understand that there was a massive effort at concealing from me some information that was central *to my life*! And in your case, and hers—" he nodded his head in the direction of Patrick's cabin "—it went on for years!"

Patrick leaned forward, his blue eyes boring into Brett's. "For God's sake, man, what would you have had us do? Storm the gates of Ravensford Hall and demand to be taken to you so that you might learn the truth? Oh, your grandfather would have loved that! He'd have welcomed her with open arms, this woman he'd exiled, wouldn't he?"

Brett was silent at this, and Patrick thought he saw a flicker of doubt in his eyes. But at that moment there was a knock on the door, and further discussion cut off.

"Yes?"

"Signore Capetti and the priest to see you, Your Grace," said the first mate's voice.

"Show him in, Mr. Thornton," said Patrick.

The door opened, and in walked the small, bearded physician whom Enrico and one of the grooms had fetched and driven to the *Ashleigh Anne* earlier. Behind him stood Father Umberto, who was functioning as a translator.

"Come in, please," said Patrick, rising from his chair. "Ah, you know His Grace, the duke of Ravensford?" He gestured from them to Brett, who had also risen.

"*Si, si, buon giorno, Signore Duca,*" said the priest, bowing.

Brett nodded impatiently, then addressed them both. "How is she?"

Father Umberto turned toward the doctor, but the little man began speaking in rapid Italian, as if he'd already understood the question. When he was finished, the priest smiled at both Brett and Patrick.

"He says *la contessa*, she's-a rest-a comfortably, *signores*. She's-a, how you say? Out of danger."

There was another rapid burst of Italian from Signore Capetti, and the priest translated. "He says he's-a geeve-a her someteeng to make-a her sleep. Please-a, not to ask-a her questions unteel she's-a wake up."

A smile of relief broke over Patrick's face. "Well, that's good news, I should say! Now, what about the children? Shall we—"

Another barrage of Italian cut him off.

"Signore Capetti says he's-a weesh to-a see *la duchessa piccola* and-a da *bambini* on-a da beeg-a sheep. He's-a say he's-a alraddy examine da bambini on-a dees-a sheep, and-a dey varry good."

Brett nodded. "We'll board the *Ravenscrest* immediately." He strode to the door of the cabin and opened it, then turned to Patrick. "Patrick, I'd appreciate it if you'd stay here...with *her*. And send me word when she awakens?"

Patrick nodded.

"Very well, then, *signori*," he said to the other two, "if you'll follow me?"

They boarded Brett's ship, which he'd moved to lie at anchor beside Patrick's during the early hours of the morning. Brett's first mate, Geordie Scott, met them as they came on board.

"Is my wife still in my cabin, Mr. Scott?" Brett asked.

"Aye, Your Grace," said Scott. "I looked in on her not fifteen minutes ago. Sleepin' like a babe, she was."

"And the children on board, what of them?"

Mr. Scott's weather-beaten face crinkled as a wide grin spread across it. "Livelier 'n a barrel o' eels, Cap'n. Isn't one o' them tykes looks the worse for what they've been through. Cook's feedin' 'em breakfast right now."

"Very good, Mr. Scott. Sounds like you've got things well in hand. Carry on while I escort these gentlemen to my cabin."

"Aye, Your Grace."

Scott left them, and Brett motioned to the priest and the doctor to follow him as he strode briskly to his cabin.

As he walked, his thoughts were jumbled and disjointed. *Maria, his mother? It didn't yet seem possible! She was* nothing *like what he'd come to—God! The fire! They had* both *nearly died in the fire! They'd both lied to him, too.... Deceit...wasn't it the one thing you could rely on where women were con— But Patrick had lied, too, and he was an honorable ma— Oh, God, Mother! Why did you keep silent all these years? I thought you were dead—or as good as dead. I believed you didn't care....*

Suddenly the door to his cabin loomed up before him, and Brett's thoughts switched to the moment at hand. He turned to the two men behind him.

"Here we are, gentlemen, but I ask you to give me a moment with my wife before you join us."

The priest nodded and spoke briefly in Italian to Signore Capetti in low tones; Brett opened the door.

When he entered, his first thought was that she'd fled his cabin because the huge bed at one end of it was unoccupied. But then his gaze flew across the room to his desk. There, her hands braced on the back of the chair in front of it, stood Ashleigh, dressed in one of his shirts, its ample folds nearly dwarfing her.

She looked up at him, a bewildered expression on her face, then glanced at the floor near her feet. "Oh, Brett, I— *Help me, please!*"

Following her gaze, he saw that the hem of his shirt was clinging wetly to her thighs and she was standing in a puddle of water.

"Oh my God, Ashleigh!" he cried as he rushed over to her. "It's the baby! Your water's broken!"

Lifting her up into his arms, he shouted over his shoulder, "Signore Capetti, come quickly! The baby's coming!"

But as the door behind him opened and he carried her toward the bed, he thought, *but the baby isn't supposed to come for two more months yet!*

"If ye don't stop that pacin', ye're liable t' wear a hole in the floor, Yer Grace," said Megan. "Relax. This isn't the first babe t' enter the world, ye know, and of all those that did, I niver heard o' one 'twas helped along by the father's pacin'."

Brett turned sharply to look at her. "But most of those that arrive safely come after nine months—not seven!"

Megan smiled. "Perhaps, but ye're lookin' at one that did come at seven!"

He frowned. *"You?"*

She nodded. "Aye, *me*. And a good thing 'twas, too, fer me poor ma! Full size, I was, at seven months. I weighed *half a stone*! Can ye imagine what might have happened if I'd gone t' nine? 'Twas God's way o' intervenin', the midwife told me ma. Said if I'd been in there much longer, I'd have split her asunder.''

Brett winced at this, and Megan felt instantly sorry for him. He was nervous as the proverbial cat in a roomful of rocking chairs, poor man, and exhausted, too, by the looks of him.

"Look, Yer Grace," she began, "why don't ye—"

"Megan, if you 'Yer Grace' me one more time, I swear, I'll—" He stopped, forced a smile to his weary features and softened his tone. "That is, don't you think you might call me Brett now? After all, you are my best friend's wife as well as my wife's best friend—and Lady St. Clare, to boot. How'd you like it if I suddenly took to calling you m'lady all the time?"

Megan hid a smile. "Why, I wouldn't fancy it at all, at all ... Brett."

"There." He attempted a smile. "That didn't hurt a bit, did it?"

"No." The redhead sighed. "But, Brett?"

He raised an eyebrow.

*"Yer bloody pacin's drivin' me t' Bedlam!"*

Brett paused, then broke into a hearty laugh, and Megan joined him.

"That's the trouble with the Irish," he scolded good-naturedly. "Give them an inch and they stretch it to a furlong!"

"No, no, you've got it all wrong." She laughed. "'Tis our Irish horses'll take the furlongs—we folk'll settle fer acres—as many acres o' good Irish soil as we can take back from—"

Just then, a knock sounded at the door. Brett whirled around, tensed, then forced himself to relax. It was probably just Abner Thornton again, coming to retrieve something from his cabin.

"Come in," he called.

The door opened, and Maria stood there, leaning shakily on Patrick's arm. She wore a beautiful day gown of peach silk with dark green trim, and her hair was neatly braided in a high chignon, but her face appeared pale as she attempted a weak smile.

"I . . . thought it was time we . . . talked," she said quietly.

Brett gave her a long, searching look, then nodded.

"I'll be lookin' in on Ashleigh," Megan said softly, then left with Patrick, but not before lightly touching Brett's sleeve and sending Maria an encouraging smile.

When they were alone, Brett offered Maria a chair, saying, "I hope it won't prove unwise for you to leave your bed this soon. How . . . how are you feeling?"

Accepting the chair, Maria attempted a laugh. "I've felt better." Then she looked up at him. "But I think you'll agree that . . . that this couldn't wait."

"If, by 'this,' you mean a long overdue conversation, I suppose not." His eyes met hers and held. "*Years* overdue, Maria."

Again an attempt at laughter, but it came out forced and broken. "I suppose I should be glad you've addressed me as Maria! It could have been *'contessa'* or 'my lady,' couldn't it?"

The cynicism was back in Brett's eyes. "What did you expect, Maria? Surely you didn't think I would address as 'Mother' a woman I haven't seen for *twenty-seven years*! Twenty-seven years, Maria!"

His mother's eyes closed for a moment, as if to shut out some remembered pain. She breathed deeply, then opened them to look at him. "And not a day, an hour, really, in all of them that I didn't yearn to be with you . . . didn't hold you in my heart."

Brett's eyes were expressionless as he raised them to a point above her head. "I wish I could believe that."

"But it's true! And the only reason I'm here is because I've made myself hope that I can convince you to believe it! Oh, Brett, you cannot know what it was like at the time they forced me to—" She caught the rising emotion in her voice and took a moment to compose herself, then continued.

"I want you to know that I loved your father. And, if you will let yourself believe it, that I went on loving him, even after, after he—they—obtained the divorce. Oh, I was hurt, deeply hurt, that he should have given in so easily to . . . to those forces that opposed my presence in his life; that he should have so readily believed the lies in those forgeries—I understand Patrick explained the details?''

''He did.'' Brett's eyes flew back to hers. ''But why didn't you fight them? I've seen you here in Livorno. You're a strong woman. It's evident in everything you do, Maria. So how can you expect me to believe you meekly stood by and let them vilify you, drive you out of my life, and my father's, when—''

''But you are wrong, Brett! The young woman I was then bore no resemblance to the woman I am now! Mary Westmont was a bewildered, frightened young woman who suddenly found herself in an untenable position in a country that was not even her own. I was alone—without family or friends, except for the Sinclairs, and believe me, they were no match for the powerful duke of Ravensford! Maria di Montefiori is the product of years of—of pain and finding the strength, somehow, to endure in spite of it—that, and a little luck.

''Did you know that I only remarried after I received word of your father's death?'' She watched him register surprise. ''It's true. For even though he divorced me, shut me out of his life, I continued to consider myself his wife until . . . until he died. Then, and only then, did I accept Gregorio's offer of marriage—an offer that was made years earlier!''

''Then . . . how did you survive? I thought—''

''You thought I walked right out of one rich marriage and into another?'' Wearily, she shook her head. ''Hardly. Oh, I knew Gregorio and his family, and for a while after I first arrived, they gave me a roof over my head and wanted me to remain with them, but I told them I couldn't. After the initial pain and shock wore away, I went to see Father Umberto with an idea. My mother—your grandmother—was a successful opera singer. Although I hadn't inherited her talent—or, more important, her drive to sing, to train my voice in the rigorous way that the profession demands, I had received some early training and had a reasonably good voice, and some basics of a musical background.

''So, with Father Umberto's help, I set myself up as a music teacher. I gave lessons in voice and on the pianoforte. For seven years, Brett, until your father's death, and I felt myself free . . . to marry.''

Brett looked astounded. "It—it couldn't have been much of a living. I've seen what they pay music masters in England, and I doubt it could have been different here. My God, Maria, you might have starved!''

She laughed, and this time it wasn't forced. "Oh, there were a few times, I daresay, when it was close—when I went fishing to put food on the table. But, truly, Brett, it wasn't that bad.

"You see, for the first time in my life, I was forced to rely on myself, and—I know this will sound odd, but it's true—there was a kind of exhilaration about it, to know I was able to do it, despite the odds!''

She smiled softly to herself, her eyes looking as if they saw something far away. "Those were wonderful years, really. During that time I truly came to know myself, what my strengths were . . . and my weaknesses.''

Her gaze returned to Brett. "The only thing that kept them from . . . from being truly satisfying or—or fulfilling was a great gaping hole I had inside me . . . the void left by you.

"And whether you choose to believe me or not, Brett, I tell you, I loved you—have continued to love you, every moment since the day I bore you thirty years ago. And it was that love, and the unquenchable hope that I would one day see you again, that really allowed me to survive those years.''

She reached into the square neckline of her gown and withdrew the chain with half a locket on it; with trembling hands, she unfastened it and handed it to him.

"Here, my son," she whispered as tears began to form in her eyes, "I think it is time you had this.''

Brett took the locket into his palm and stared at it, stunned, for several long seconds. At last he raised his head and met her shining eyes.

*"It was you?''* he whispered.

Nodding her head, her eyes on his, his mother smiled through her tears. "It was. This is the first time, in twenty-seven years, I have taken it off. And I only do so now because I have you here with me, in the flesh.''

Brett stood very still, trying to assimilate everything her words implied. It was not an easy moment for him. In just a few minutes, with a few simple words, she had begun to demolish some very basic notions he had lived with nearly all his life. And actually, if he were honest, the demolition had begun even before this; it had started the moment he'd come to Livorno and met her, when he'd seen the reality that was Mary Westmont, unhampered by the blinding prejudices he'd been raised with.

This was no woman who could have deserted a child! Her very life centered around children, children she'd taken to her heart and loved because—

"Your...children," he questioned in a voice hoarse with emotion, "were they—that is, did you—?" He stopped, finding it difficult to continue.

She smiled. "They were never really a substitute for you, no...but they did need love, and having them to love...well, it helped to ease the pain, the emptiness. I think I—"

"Oh, God, *stop!*" he cried. "No more, I beg you!" A host of swirling emotions was seizing him, throwing him off balance. Guilt, terrible and real, surged through him. He'd been wrong about this woman who was his mother, and if that were true, then what did it say about others in his life? What of the grandfather who'd raised him? What did it say about him? And his perceptions of women? What of them? And Ashleigh! Dear God, *what about Ashleigh?*

Maria saw his doubt and her heart ached for him. But she also sensed he needed to be alone, to have time to sort out his feelings and come to terms with what had suddenly turned his emotional world upside down.

Rising, she was about to tell him she was leaving, when there came a sudden pounding on the cabin door.

"Your Grace!" It was Geordie Scott's voice. "I've critical news!"

"Come in, then, Mr. Scott," said Brett, his private thoughts pushed aside as he responded to the alarm in the first mate's voice.

The door opened and Geordie Scott entered, his face flushed, excited. "Your Grace, terrible news! We just received word from a messenger. Bonaparte's escaped from Elba! He landed at Cannes two days ago with fifteen hundred men!"

# Chapter Thirty-Four

Brett made an entry in his ship's log, but his mind wasn't on what he'd written. Within hours after receiving the news about Napoleon, he'd convinced Patrick to join him in setting a course for England. Patrick had been reluctant at first, but the argument that Italy bore too many powers friendly to the Corsican had finally persuaded him; that, and the fact that his sister was in enough danger from what was proving to be a long and difficult labor, and would hardly benefit from having their ships boarded and possibly detained by enemy sympathizers.

For the third time in as many minutes, his thoughts focused on Ashleigh. Had he made a mistake in giving the order to set sail? It was true, the weather was mild, with calm seas, but what if that changed? Could she withstand a rough voyage while she labored to bring a child into the world?

Suddenly a muffled scream met his ears. Brett thrust his quill into its holder and slammed shut the logbook. What in hell were they doing to her? What, if anything, were they doing *for* her?

Maria had succeeded in convincing Signore Capetti to remain aboard with his patient—the matter had required little more than a promise of a handsome fee and that he would be returned home on the first available ship. Father Umberto had remained as well, and so had the children. The alternative to their sailing to England was a return—at least for a while—to the orphanage, and Maria would not have it. Moreover, she implied—through Patrick, for Brett had not seen her since the news broke—that she had a desire to see England again.

The scream came again, and Brett's face paled. An hour ago, at the doctor's request, a tired Megan had been roused from the catnap she'd taken amid hours of bedside attendance to her friend, and she'd been asked to bring the priest along as well. Brett tried to force himself not to think of the implications of that.

Suddenly the door to the cabin burst open, and a haggard-looking Megan stepped inside.

"I'm sorry I didn't knock, Brett, but—"

"What is it? What's wrong?"

"'Tis—'tis the birthin'. Ah, she's so tired, Brett, and the babe... There are... difficulties."

Brett froze. "What difficulties?"

Megan wrung her hands. "I wish Maria were here and not on Patrick's ship. I know she's still recoverin', but—"

*"What difficulties, Megan?"*

Megan shook her head. "As I said, she's tired...up all night with the fire.... Brett, the babe may not make it through unless... 'Tis likely 'twill come t' a matter o' choosin' betwixt the babe and the mother, and—"

"That's no choice!" he shouted, then started for the door. "Dammit, they shouldn't be letting her suffer this way! I'll tell them! There can be other babes. For now—"

"Wait!" Megan clutched at his sleeve. "I think ye ought t' know somethin'. This is a Catholic doctor, and a priest with him t' boot. I cannot be sure 'twas true, but I heard o' such a case in Ireland when I was a lass. The midwife summoned the priest and he—he ..."

"Go on!"

"He said if it came t' choosin' betwixt an innocent life and that o'... anither, the Church would have the innocent be the one 'twas saved." Megan closed her eyes and looked away, then back at Brett. "Brett, 'twas said *they sacrificed the mother!*"

Brett went white, then froze as another scream rent the air. He grabbed Megan's arm, shouting, "Let's go!" and stormed out the door.

Seconds later, Megan in tow, he ripped through the door to his cabin. Ashleigh lay in his bed, moaning, the doctor at the foot of it, the priest beside him.

*"Out!"* Brett thundered.

*"Mi scusi?"* Signore Capetti questioned.

"I said *out*, and take this chanting beadsman with you!"

"But Signore Duca, we—"

"You heard me! No one's touching my wife, but me and those I trust. The two of you will leave . . . *now!*"

Shrugging, Father Umberto exchanged a few words in Italian with the physician, and the two of them hurried from the cabin.

When they were gone, Brett motioned Megan forward, and the two of them approached the bed. As they reached it, Ashleigh moaned again, then cried out.

"Oh, the pain! Megan, the pain! I—"

Suddenly, she bit her lip and reached for a twisted strip of sheeting that had been tied across the head of the bed, from post to post, wrenching it downward with both hands as another contraction seized her.

Brett saw her teeth draw blood and more sweat break out on her already dripping forehead. He reached for a cloth lying in a nearby basin of water, wrung it out and gently wiped her brow while out of the corner of his eye, he saw Megan move to the foot of the bed.

Ashleigh felt the contraction subside and opened her eyes. "Megan, I— *Brett* . . . ? Is that you?"

"Shh, love," he told her. "Save your strength. Megan and I are here. We're not going to let anything happen to you."

"Ashleigh," said Megan, as she bent to examine her. "Listen to us. We're goin' t' help ye."

"So tired . . ." Ashleigh whispered. "So— Oh, God! I can't— I—"

"Ashleigh!" Brett clasped her hands in each of his. "Here, hold on to me. I'll help you, love. We'll do this together. . . . That's right, squeeze. Squeeze my hands, and don't let go . . . I won't let you let go, love."

"I see the head!" Megan cried. "Glory be, I see—" Suddenly she turned and sprang toward a bowl of water with soap nearby. Feverishly, she scrubbed her hands, calling over her shoulder to Ashleigh, who was squeezing Brett's hands and panting.

"Good lass! Keep pantin' the way I showed ye." She glanced at Brett, who was eyeing her ablutions. "'Tis a good idea. I once saw a midwife with dirty hands deliver a babe and..." She shuddered, then finished drying her hands and hurriedly resumed her position at the foot of the bed.

"That's it, *macushla*," she encouraged. "Just a wee bit more now—there! Now, when I say push..."

The minutes passed, with Ashleigh alternately pushing and panting as Brett urged her on, willing her his own strength, coaxing her forward, while Megan muttered Hail Marys between imprecations to half-forgotten Gaelic spirits, and did her best to recall all she'd once seen watching her mother give birth to child after child, long ago.

Then, as Ashleigh dug her nails into Brett's hands and screamed, giving a final agonizing push, a wet and darkly matted tiny head slipped into Megan's waiting hands, and then a shoulder, and then a small, slippery and squirming body, and in a few seconds it was over.

"Saints be praised!" Megan cried. "'Tis a lovely wee lass! She's tiny but healthy. Listen t' her howl!"

Ashleigh heard her and let out a sound that was half laugh, half sob. A daughter. She'd borne a daughter!

Brett gazed at the glistening, wriggling creature in Megan's hands for a moment, in total awe. Then he looked down at his wife. "You got your little girl," he whispered, and blinked rapidly several times before bending to kiss Ashleigh on the brow.

Ashleigh raised weary eyes to meet his. "You're not angry, are you? I mean a girl is—"

Brett gently touched his forefinger to her lips. "Angry? Ashleigh, darling, I'm so proud of you, I can't begin to tell you! Thank you for our daughter, love. She's beautiful."

Ashleigh searched his face for a moment, then slowly smiled as her eyelids lowered.

"And thank you for you," he told her.

But his wife was already asleep.

Brett gazed quietly for a long time at the tiny, swaddled creature lying beside Ashleigh in his bed. Slowly, almost reverently, his eyes fell on each minuscule feature of the small pink face framed by a feathering of dark, downy hair... the dark-lashed wide-set eyes, closed now in slumber... the perfectly shaped little nose... the sweet rosebud mouth, barely parted with quiet breathing.

His gaze shifted to the face of his wife. She appeared to him more beautiful than he'd ever seen her, despite the faint mauve shadows under her eyes, the increased hollows beneath her finely sculpted cheekbones. He was brought to mind of another time he had studied her while she lay sleeping, and an amazed smile crossed his face. How could he have ever thought this sweet, gentle creature capable of the things he'd been ready to imbue her with then? Had he, indeed, been that blind?

He studied the sleeping pair a moment longer, as if committing the scene to memory. Then he turned and stole softly from the cabin and made his way on deck.

The helmsman on duty gave him a salute and Brett returned it, then walked past the mizzenmast to a place on the railing where he could be alone.

It was a beautiful night—the dark, cloudless sky brilliant with stars. Bracing his hands on the railing, Brett gazed up into the star-spattered universe and felt the most profound feeling of peace he'd ever known. He was overwhelmed by a sense of something timeless and eternal and felt he was somehow a part of it, and the feeling was good.

He glanced down to see the shaggy form of Finn emerge out of the darkness and come to stand quietly beside him. He reached down to scratch the big dog affectionately behind the ears, then drew his gaze back to the sky.

What was different now? He'd gazed at these same heavens a hundred times before in his life, during dozens of half-remembered sailings. Why had he never seen them this way before?

But he knew the answer before his mind formed the question. Always, before, he'd gazed at them as a being apart, separated, somehow, from their vast mystery and beauty, from the miracle of creation their presence implied. But now he was no longer a man apart from the miracle; he was part of it.

He'd just seen a brand-new life brought into the world, and that, too, was a miracle. And they seemed connected, these miracles—the vast, infinite mystery of the stars; the sweet, tiny mystery of new life; and coursing through them was yet a third miracle that connected it all, and him as well: love.

His brain tripped on the word as soon as he thought it, and Brett caught his breath at the impact. Images of Ashleigh swept through his mind as they had dozens of times before, but this time there was no pain in them, no anger, only...*love*! He loved her, loved her with an intensity he'd not thought himself capable of—this sweet, winsome creature he'd never meant to care about, except in ways associated with duty...obligation...maybe honor—but never *love*!

How had it happened? How had he gone beyond seeing her as a potentially threatening female, to regarding her as a separate human being with a host of traits he'd come to admire and respect and cherish?

She'd borne him a child and he was grateful for it, but that wasn't it; he'd expected any wife he took to bear him heirs. He'd been frightened beyond belief when he thought he might lose her; but no, that had been a step in the process of coming to realize what she meant to him, but it wasn't the whole of it. He'd come to Italy expecting the near child he'd married and found a stronger person, someone who'd begun to find her own identity in the world and act within its framework. That was part of it, too, yes, but—

His mind suddenly switched to a picture of Maria and the last time they'd seen each other, and he felt he was getting closer to the truth. Maria, Mary, was his mother, and she *loved* him, had never stopped loving him. But how did his discoveries about her relate to the way he now felt about Ashleigh? How did—

And then suddenly he knew. It wasn't the changes in these women in his life that allowed him to love—it was the change in *him*!

He, by admitting this love, by coming to terms with his own blindness, had made the difference!

Suddenly Brett threw back his head and laughed, a deep, joyful laughter from the heart, from his soul; and as it echoed across the deck and across the water, he knew that a great, aching hole that had been at his center all his life had been filled and would never be empty again.

"Oh, Grandfather!" he said as he looked once more at the stars. "I loved you, too, and I'll always carry part of you with me. But the hatred you taught me was wrong. As long as I lived by it, I could never really live. But now I'm done with it. Now, watch me live, Grandfather. *Watch me live!*"

The next morning the *Ashleigh Anne* pulled near the *Ravenscrest*, and a dinghy was used to transfer Patrick and Maria to Brett's ship. Geordie Scott met them on deck.

"What is it?" asked Patrick. "We received your signal to board and—"

"Nothing to trouble yourself about, Sir Patrick," the first mate told him. "But for the details, I've only my orders, which are to take you below. If you'll follow me, please, your ladyship...sir...?"

Casting Maria a worried look, Patrick allowed the mate to guide them below deck. He felt it had to be news of Ashleigh and the child, but he half feared to speculate on what the developments were; it had already been an overly long labor.

"Here we are, sir, your ladyship." Scott knocked on the door to Brett's cabin. "Party boarded and ready to see you, Your Grace."

The door opened, and Brett stood before them, smiling. "Come in, both of you!"

As he stepped aside, they saw Ashleigh propped up against several pillows in the center of the large captain's bed. Her hair had been combed and brushed until it shone, and she wore a blue ribbon in it that matched the blue of her night rail. At her breast she suckled her infant. She looked tired, Maria thought, but also radiant...happy.

"Hello, you two," Ashleigh smiled. "Do come closer. There's someone we'd like you to meet."

"Someone brand-new and beautifully female," added Brett as he came by his wife's side.

Maria noticed him touch Ashleigh's hair ever so softly, then gaze at her warmly as her eyes met his and held for a moment, until a soft blush forced her to glance away.

"Sir Patrick, henceforth also to be known as Uncle Patrick," Brett grinned, "we'd like you to meet Marileigh Megan Westmont, Viscountess Westmont, if you please."

"Marileigh Megan?" Patrick questioned softly as he looked down at his new niece with wonder in his eyes.

"We named her after three important women in her life," said Ashleigh, lifting the contented infant to her shoulder.

"Here, let me," said Brett. He took his daughter gently from her, then turned toward Maria.

"Yes, the three most important women in her life—and in mine," he added. "Her mother, her aunt and future godmother, and her grandmother." His eyes looked solemnly into Maria's. "Would you like to hold your granddaughter... Mother?"

Hot tears stung Maria's eyes as she realized what he'd said, but she blinked them away and reached for her grandchild.

"Yes, yes, I would...Son."

# Chapter Thirty-Five

They took a leisurely twelve days to make the voyage to England. The seas remained calm, the weather friendly, and neither Brett nor Patrick wished to take any chances with their precious cargoes by pushing for speed. They'd determined that, after Trafalgar, French naval power was largely nonexistent, as was that of the Spanish, leaving Britain supreme on the high seas. If Bonaparte were making any headway at all with a comeback, it could only be by land; Brett's and Patrick's ships, both flying the Union Jack now, were very likely safe.

Ashleigh spent most of this time in bed, recovering slowly, but steadily, from the birth of Marileigh. Maria and Brett were in constant attendance, for her mother-in-law had traded places with Megan in deference to Patrick's grumbling that he'd been missing his wife lately. One by one, Maria brought the children into the cabin to see the now thriving Marileigh and to visit with the new mother.

Brett continued sleeping in a hammock in Geordie Scott's cabin, but took all his meals with his wife and daughter, and when he saw, after a few days, that Ashleigh grew restless with her confinement, he made it his business to free himself from enough of his duties to spend additional time with her.

He sometimes read to her from the array of books he kept in his cabin—the poetry of Shelley and Byron quickly became her favorites as well as his. Often they merely talked, but Ashleigh noted that Brett seemed to direct their conversation to impersonal subjects: the politics of Shelley, the implications of Napoleon's escape, the problems they might encounter in arranging things at the house on King Street to accommodate all the children and extra servants.

She wondered at this, for, just as she had back at the villa, she felt a need for them to talk about the past—*and* the future—and she couldn't understand why Brett seemed in no hurry to do the same.

On the other hand, he was, in every way, at his kindest and most considerate, and she had no wish to alter that! Was it the birth of their child that had made the difference? The reconciliation with his mother? These things had undoubtedly lightened his spirits, but...

But though it was tied into those other fortunate events, it was something more—something she couldn't put her finger on, something that went deeper.

He laughed a lot these days. And patience no longer seemed alien to his nature; he had an abundance of it, which he lavishly expended with ready smiles and thoughtful acts. It was as if he looked at the world in a new way... with an acceptance, a contentment, even a touch of the thing the French call joie de vivre, and none of this had been there before.

Also, when at certain times she caught him looking at her, she sensed there was some unspoken question on his mind. What was it? Was he, too, hoping for a way to open up the past and sort it out between them without upsetting this suddenly peaceful, domestic apple cart? Was he waiting for her to make a move?

These and similar thoughts were on her mind one evening when she was sitting alone in the cabin. She had just finished nursing Marleigh, and Marla had offered to take the infant to nap with her so that Ashleigh might have some undisturbed rest.

But rest was the furthest thing from Ashleigh's mind. She'd had enough bed rest to last her until doomsday, thank you! And suddenly a thought struck her. She had told Brett in the garden in Livorno that she had come to a turning point in her life when she decided to stop being a passive being, waiting for things to happen to her, when she had begun to exert a more active control over her own life. *So, what,* she asked herself now, *am I doing, sitting here in this cabin, waiting for my husband to come to me to discuss the things I have on my mind concerning the situation between us? Falling into my old, unwanted pattern, that's what! And that, Ashleigh, my girl, will never do!*

All at once she was a figure in rapid motion as she flung back the covers and slid out of bed. There was a moment of feeling wobbly at the knees from having lain abed for so long, but she forced herself to take a few careful steps toward the stand that held the pitcher and wash basin, and it passed.

She flew through her ablutions and then went to a trunk they had brought aboard from the villa before sailing; it contained some clothes Patrick had had made by Madame Gautier and sent to the *Ashleigh·Anne* before they left London.

Soon she was dressed in a rose velvet gown trimmed with cream-colored lace at its square-cut neckline and at the wrists of its long, tight-fitting sleeves. A glance in the glass above the washstand told her she'd do well to don the matching velvet pelisse, and not just for its added warmth; her breasts, since the birth of Marileigh, had grown much fuller, and the twin mounds pushing upward above the low neckline were somewhat beyond what decency would allow for an appearance above deck.

And, of course, going topside was exactly what she had in mind. Brett was up there, and it was time she took the proverbial bull by the horns!

She found him at the wheel, the brisk breeze that was causing the sails to flutter and snap ruffling his hair as he stood with his back to her. It was a stance that accentuated the breadth of his shoulders under his seaman's coat, the strength of the muscular thighs of his long legs that were slightly spread and braced to maintain an easy balance.

A young crewman appeared as she made her way toward the bridge. He smiled shyly and doffed his cap, then glanced at the bridge and back at her with a question in his eyes.

Ashleigh smiled and raised a finger to her lips, indicating she would surprise her husband. After another quick glance at his captain, the seaman gave her a tentative smile, bowed and disappeared from sight.

The sea was fairly calm, nevertheless Ashleigh had a bit of trouble resurrecting her "sea legs," as Patrick had called them when they sailed from England, and it took some doing to keep her balance as she made her way to the bridge, but at last she reached it.

Brett caught a movement in the semidarkness—for there was a half-moon and myriad stars to augment the light from the lantern that swung nearby.

"Mr. Carter, I thought I told you to— Ashleigh! How—"

"Oh, please, Brett! Do not be angry. I just had to get out of that cabin tonight! I was beginning to feel I'd become permanently attached to the bed."

"But your health! The doctor said—"

"Oh, piffle!" she exclaimed with a small gesture of annoyance. "I feel fine. And the air up here is so lovely, I'm sure it can do me no harm." She finished with a wide smile and blue eyes focused directly on his.

Brett met her look and couldn't help smiling back. She looked so incredibly beautiful with the wind ruffling her long curls about her face and shoulders, her huge eyes bright and shining as she faced him with a look of expectancy.

"Very well," he said as his eyes swept over her diminutive form. "You have escaped from the beastly confinement I've been well aware you were beginning to abhor, and you don't appear any the worse for it. But it would be foolish to overdo it, Ashleigh. You'll stay for a few minutes, and then I'll take you back. Agreed?"

"But, Brett—"

"I won't have you endangering your health, Ashleigh." Brett's expression grew somber. "My God; when I think that we nearly lost you *twice* in—"

Moved by the concern in his eyes, Ashleigh reached out to touch his arm. "I understand," she told him, "and a few minutes it will be." *And I'd better use them profitably,* she added to herself.

He smiled his gratitude for her show of good sense, then asked, "Ever handle a ship's wheel?"

Her eyes widened, then smiled their delight. "Oh, Brett, may I?"

"Of course." He grinned, then motioned for her to slip in front of him.

She stepped into place, then felt his arms come around her from behind as he positioned her hands at the wheel. It was the closest bodily contact they'd had since before the baby's birth, and she suddenly found herself overwhelmed by his nearness. Sensory memories flooded her brain—memories of other times when they had touched, when she'd breathed in the clean male scent of him as she was now, when—

"Hold her steady," he murmured from somewhere above her right ear. "That's it, steady now."

As he spoke, Brett had to force himself to concentrate on the dark sea ahead of them, for he, too, was well aware of their closeness. As she'd moved into position before him, he caught the faint scent of violets from the perfume she wore, and his senses danced with the memories it evoked. Several silken strands of her long hair, whipped by the wind, passed across his chin and mouth, and it suddenly became all he could do not to press his lips against her temple and savor her more fully. He perceived her body's return to its former slenderness as the wind molded her clothes to her, and he was a man in frustrated agony.

What in hell was he to do? He stood grinding his teeth as he reminded himself it was out of the realm of possibility to take a woman this soon after childbirth, and this wasn't just some woman—this was Ashleigh, his wife!

He loved her, and was presently bent on a course to make her care for him if he could. He realized she had every reason to hate him, after the way he'd behaved in the past. But his mother had given him good advice that day: to be gentle with her and court her, much as if they were not yet even wed. And since he'd taken that advice and begun to see it bear fruit, he'd made up his mind to do more than court her to win him her good opinion; he began to hope he could make her love him, if not as much as he loved her, then at least a little, and perhaps, in time, even more than a little.

But now, as he clamped his jaws rigidly together, he was beginning to see that the process would not be as easy as he'd imagined. Going slowly, biding his time... Merciful God, how was he to do it when the slightest closeness, the merest touch, as now, set him afire?

Gritting his teeth, he forced himself to release slowly the breath he'd been holding and stepped back, away from her slightly, at the same time wondering what was taking Carter so long to return to the bridge following the errand he'd sent him on.

Ashleigh felt the loss of his body heat as he moved away and with it, a return of her spinning senses. She breathed deeply to hasten this sense of release, then glanced upward.

The star-studded brilliance of the sky was quite unexpected, for her thoughts had been turned inward. It was the heavens such as she had never seen them before, and their beauty nearly stole her breath away. In a canopy of midnight-blue velvet, the stars seemed to hang so low, she felt if she reached up, she could almost touch them. And yet, at the same time, she felt the vastness of it all and felt herself, Brett, and even the sturdy ship they were sailing on, to be nothing more than tiny ripples in the ageless, eternal beyond that surrounded them.

"Oh, Brett," she breathed, "isn't it just...perfect? Isn't it a *miracle*?"

Taking the wheel with one hand, Brett turned her to him and found himself gazing down into her wondering, upturned face. "Yes, love," he whispered hoarsely, "a miracle."

Ashleigh's lips parted expectantly, for suddenly she wanted nothing more than the touch of his mouth on hers. Oh, she loved him so much! And she suddenly found herself screaming inwardly with the longing to tell him so.

But, as his eyes held hers, she caught the look of restraint in them, little guessing at what an effort it took for him to maintain that restraint. Forcing her emotional inclinations aside, she made herself focus on her initial reason for coming out here.

"Brett," she heard herself say in a quivery voice, "I—I want to talk to you about my reasons for running off, for leaving you in—in England." There! It was out. Now all she had to do was follow it through carefully.

"But you've already told me," he said easily.

"I . . . I *have?*"

He smiled. "Back at the villa, remember? You told me how Lady Margaret insinuated that she was in London to—"

"*Oh, that!* Oh, yes, I recall our clearing up that misunderstanding, but it was the—the other I was referring to. The morning after our wedding when—"

"When Elizabeth came to do her dirty work. Yes," he added, "you told me about that, too. Apparently she quite convinced you that you had just wed the greatest cad that a woman could ever take as husband."

Wide-eyed and somber, Ashleigh nodded.

"I imagine Elizabeth could have been quite convincing on that score. You see, in a way, she was right."

Seeing the dismay on Ashleigh's face, he leaned down and kissed her lightly on the lips. "If it had been she I'd wed, silly goose, but not you! Never," he added softly as he bent to brush her lips with his again, "never you."

Ashleigh felt her lips tingle with his kiss and a tremor ripple through her body. "I—I don't understand," she managed to say.

Brett smiled down at her. "I'm afraid what Elizabeth suspected of me at one time was true. I was prepared to marry merely to provide myself with heirs while at the same time pleasing myself with mistresses and whatever other, ah, pursuits I chose to indulge in, on the side. Indeed, if it had been she whom I'd wed, I would have done exactly that."

"But—"

He reached to place a pair of fingers gently against her lips. "But I did not wed Elizabeth. I wed you, and suddenly found myself with a wife so different from anything I'd imagined, I'd have had to be mad to be taking my . . . inclinations elsewhere."

Ashleigh's mouth gaped in astonishment. "You mean—?"

"I mean, my very perfect, womanly little idiot, that you were all I, or any man, I'm sure, could ever wish for in bed! Does that answer your question?"

As she glanced downward, he saw her deepening blush even in the moonlight that silvered her features. Gently, he curled his fingers under her chin and raised it until she met his gaze again. "But it goes beyond that," he told her. "For I must admit I've had mistresses in the past who were . . . pleasing in bed, and yet I was never faithful to any of them."

*"Oh."* The look of dismay again. "I see."

"No, little one, you don't see." *Not yet,* he added to himself. "I told you, with you, it goes beyond anything that went before. Ashleigh . . ." He paused, searching for the right words. Finally he decided a direct approach was best until such time as he might chance confronting her with his deeper feelings. "Ashleigh, I want to tell you, here and now, that I never had any intention of being unfaithful to you, and I have no such intentions now. I shall always remain faithful, I swear it."

He saw several expressions cross her face as she took this in. Astonishment, pleasure, doubt—each left its mark.

"You're not certain you believe me," he said.

"Oh, Brett!" she exclaimed. "I simply don't know!" Her eyes grew remote and subtly filled with pain. "Those nights in London . . . after—after we quarreled, you came to bed smelling of—of perfume that was not mine. You . . . cannot tell me there weren't other . . . females then."

He sighed, then ran his hand impatiently through his hair. "You're right, of course. But that was when I was under the impression that you were different. That was when I was cut to the quick by the knowledge that you had left me, just as I was beginning to think—"

The wind shifted and the wheel pulled from the loose hold he had on it as the ship veered sharply to starboard. Catching Ashleigh firmly with one arm, he grabbed hold of the wheel with his free hand and worked to steady it.

From below them a voice called out, "I'll be there in a moment, Your Grace! I'm sorry I took so long!"

Ashleigh looked to see the young seaman she'd run into when coming topside.

"Looks like the wind's changed, Your Grace. Had I better summon Mr. Scott and—"

"I'll take care of it, Mr. Carter," said Brett as he handed the wheel over to his newly promoted second mate. He gazed up at the sky. "It doesn't look too serious yet, but if it continues, we're liable to have a bad time of it crossing the Channel. Hold her steady, Mr. Carter. I'll rouse the hands."

He turned to Ashleigh. "Let's get you below before some weather hits."

"Did you say, 'The Channel'?" she asked as he escorted her from the bridge.

"I did." He grinned. "By this time tomorrow, we should be home."

# Chapter Thirty-Six

Ashleigh paced the length of the beautiful Aubusson carpet in the drawing room of the house on King Street, waving a sheet of paper in her hand.

"I simply cannot believe it!" she exclaimed as she cast a look of outrage at Maria who was standing near the marble fireplace. "*Arrested!* How dare they arrest them!"

"Ashleigh, *cara*, calm yourself, please!" Maria told her. "You'll sour your milk if you go on this way. Think of the *bambina*! Why, if Megan weren't crooning her that Irish lullaby right now, she'd be as fussy as she was for hours after the first shock you received at the dock."

"But how can I be calm when my husband and my brother have been arrested for *spying*?" She whirled as she reached the end of the carpet and began to pace again.

"Now, the letter doesn't say that!" Maria admonished. "You read it yourself, in Brett's own words. It says, 'under suspicion of spying,' and there is quite a difference."

"Yes, but when those men met us at the dock they merely said Brett and Patrick were being 'detained for questioning'! *Now* it seems *detaining* is not sufficient! *Now*, they are under *arrest*!"

"Merely a terrible formality, darling, I'm sure of it. Why, what do they have for evidence? Of anything?"

"They have evidence of Brett's ship passing suspiciously near the escaped enemy's landing site after an unexplained visit to a land crawling with his sympathizers, and in the company of an

American flying a false British flag on his ship! Oh, it is all too dreadful!''

"Yes—" Maria sighed "—it is.'' She tried to force a smile. "But I still wish you wouldn't work yourself up over it so. Try to trust Brett's judgment that it is all just a tempest in a teapot, my dear. After all, he does have connections in the Foreign Office and at the Admiralty—not to mention at Carlton House. Just you wait. They'll have him and Patrick cleared of these ridiculous charges in no time. Before we know it, the two of them will be standing right here, sharing a laugh with us over it, and these past two days will seem like a bad joke, no more.''

But Maria was mistaken about the ease with which their men would be released. As Brett explained in the letters he was allowed to write to his wife, the problem was twofold. First, Bonaparte's escape from Elba had resulted in his attracting thousands to his cause, enabling him to march on Paris and force Louis XVIII to flee. As a result, the entire nation was in a state of panic, and men in high places who would normally have listened to Brett's story with reason and good judgment, were now behaving as if they were afraid of their own shadows and trusting no one. Secondly, although the Treaty of Ghent had been signed in December, thus officially ending the War of 1812, Patrick's position was by no means secure. One of the oddities of the conflict with the Americans was that the Battle of New Orleans was fought—and won by the Americans—a full two weeks after the treaty was signed, because of poor communications. How were the British officials to know that Patrick's illegal behavior wasn't another piece of post-treaty hostility? The fact that Patrick was now also a peer of the realm and had thereby attempted to justify his flying of the Union Jack on his ship held little weight; letters would have to be sent to Washington and ambassadors contacted, and until satisfactory answers arrived, His Grace and Sir Patrick would remain as unwilling guests of His Majesty's government—with official apologies to Her Grace, the duchess, of course.

After the first week passed with no resolution to these difficulties, Ashleigh grimly determined to settle down and await their outcome, for she realized Maria was right; it would do her and her daughter little good to sit around and weep over the situation. She therefore joined Maria and Megan in setting up as normal a household as they could in the large King Street house, doing everything possible to maintain an aura of outward calm for the sake of the children. Menus were planned and meals served, lessons were given in one of the upstairs chambers hastily converted into a schoolroom, and clothes were ordered from Madame Gautier, who was delighted to see Ashleigh again and totally charmed by the *contessa*, her beautiful mother-in-law. Brett had immediately sent word to his solicitors that his wife was to have any necessary funds at her disposal so that she might run their household effectively until this sorry mess could be straightened out.

One of the side effects of the visits to Madame Gautier was that news of their situation quickly found its way into the *ton*'s grapevine, and Ashleigh and Maria began to have callers. At first there were just the curious—the gossips who came to see if all they'd heard were true, and whether they might learn something new to embellish their own telling of tales as they sallied forth from one afternoon tea to another.

But then a curious thing happened: as word got out as to who Maria was—or Mary, as she now called herself in an attempt at being supportive of Brett's patriotism—a steady stream of well-wishers appeared at their doorstep. There were, it seemed, a number of people who remembered Mary Westmont from before the time of her so-called disgrace—remembered her and liked her well enough to call her a friend. These were members of the upper crust who, they confided, had always thought she'd been unfairly treated by the Westmonts, and now that they'd learned she was reconciled with that family, went out of their way to welcome her back into their society.

Soon invitations to tea, dinner parties and balls began to arrive for both Mary and Ashleigh—for Mary let it be known that she would socialize with no one who did not accept the present duchess as well, no matter what the state of the duke's situation. At first Ashleigh was disinclined to accept any of these, but at Mary's urging—that she must, to present a bold and confident picture of support for her husband—she began to venture out.

Before long the young duchess and her mother-in-law began to be seen about the city. Most of these forays into society took place during the day, for Ashleigh had no wish to attend, unescorted, balls and soirées where the majority of those attending were couples; but luncheons and afternoon teas often saw the two women in attendance. And the rains of March gave way to a warm and surprisingly sunny April, allowing them to join the throngs of riders and carriages in Hyde Park.

On one particularly balmy, blue-skied day, they were joined by Megan and Marileigh—with Miss Simms, her nurse—as they rode in their open carriage along the thoroughfare.

"It's really amazing, Maria—uh, Mary," said Ashleigh as she saw the older woman smile and nod to greeters in a passing carriage, "how many people have come to accept you since our return. Why, wasn't that the haughty Lady Castlereagh herself who waved to you a moment ago?"

"It was." Mary smiled. "I ran into her at Lady Bessborough's luncheon the other day—the one you were too tired to attend because Marileigh had been fussing with the colic all night." She peered at the blanketed bundle currently being held by Megan. "By the way, how is our little viscountess doing, Megan?"

"The picture o' contentment, Mary. Wide-awake she is, with her da's turquoise eyes lookin' back at me."

Mary smiled as she peered at her granddaughter's delicate face. *Raven-haired and with her father's eyes!* she thought. *Already showing every promise of becoming a great beauty!*

"I just thank God the colic's gone!" said Ashleigh. She turned back to Mary. "But you were saying...about Castlereagh, I mean?"

"Oh, yes, that one! Well, it seems she remembers me from when I was a girl. Her mother knew my mother—that sort of thing. And it seems the late Caroline Westmont, Edward's second wife, once snubbed her at a garden party. She now greets me as if we've been bosom friends all our lives, if you can fancy that. She even let it be known that I would have no trouble finding entrée at Almack's!"

"Really!" Ashleigh exclaimed. "But I thought, that is, with all the trouble over Brett and—"

"Oh, you are quite right on that account," said Mary, smiling. "She hinted that while *I* might gain entrance at Almack's, *you*, my darling duchess, might have to wait until, ah, 'the winds blow more favorably,' I believe was the expression she used."

"I see," said Ashleigh.

"Humph!" said Megan.

Mary grinned. "Think not a jot more about it! I immediately informed that august patroness, you see, that such an arrangement was out of the question! That, where I go, my son's little duchess goes, or I do not go at all."

"You did not!" Ashleigh exclaimed.

"Of course I did. And do you know what she said? She said we really ought to appear at the establishment in question on Wednesday night, next; that scandalous dance, the waltz, was making curious headway there, and she would value our opinions on it—our being lately so well traveled on the Continent and all!"

Ashleigh chuckled. "Mary, I fear you've already taken London by storm!"

"Hmm, perhaps—perhaps not. But give me some time, my dear, and I think I shall. I'll do whatever is necessary to help Brett and Patrick, you see."

"Oh-oh," said Megan, "speakin' o' seein', here comes that old gossip, Lady Bunbury, and she sees us well enough. She's headin' straight toward us!"

Lady Bunbury's carriage drew up alongside theirs, and Ashleigh signaled their driver to halt.

"Good day, Your Grace," the plump matron called. "Countess, Lady St. Clare." She nodded amiably in their direction. "It's so good to find such pleasant weather in April, is it not? I see it even prompted you to take your little one out."

"Indeed," said Mary, "our little viscountess seems to thrive in this air." Privately, she was detesting the appearance of this woman. Unbeknownst to Ashleigh, whom she had no intention of worrying with it, she had recently learned that Bunbury was the carrier of a scurrilous piece of gossip about Brett's wife. Where she'd gotten the idea, Mary had no inkling, but this fat gossip had begun putting it about last summer, after Ashleigh left London, that the duke's young wife had been wildly promiscuous prior to their marriage and that, indeed, the duke was divorcing her because she even carried another man's child!

Fortunately, the couple's arrival in London *together*, as well as the obviously satisfactory status of their marriage, had helped Mary in her efforts to put the lie to that rumor since she'd caught wind of it. But now, as she peered distastefully at the corpulent Bunbury, she got an idea that she felt might deal the whole gossipy business a final deathblow.

"You really ought to see this healthy child," she said to Lady Bunbury. "Here, Megan, dear, hold our sweet Marileigh up so dear Lady Bunbury can see her."

Megan gave her a look that indicated she thought she'd gone daft, but carried out her wishes. Propping the gurgling infant up, she held her aloft so the old matron could clearly see her face.

Ashleigh, too, appeared puzzled as she looked on. Had Mary had too much sun? What was so particular about Bunbury that she should be treated to this private viewing of the baby?

"I think you will agree," Mary was saying, "that the viscountess will be a beauty of the first water, Lady Bunbury. She favors her beautiful mother, of course, but look at those eyes! Are they not the very replica of her father's? His Grace, of course, has not seen them since they changed color from their former baby blue, but we have informed him of their present hue, and, I must say, he is ever so proud!"

Lady Bunbury, faced head-on with evidence that her choicest piece of gossip in years simply wasn't true, had the good grace to blush. And one look at the grandmother's face assured her that her little speech and demonstration just now had been done with a calculated purpose. Moreover, this countess was quickly becoming the darling of the *ton*, and if she, Amelia Bunbury, weren't careful, she'd find herself on the outside looking in!

Looking about distractedly for a way to change the topic of conversation, her eyes fell on Megan. "Ah, Lady St. Clare, how nice to see you again. It isn't often we see you about, or at least not as frequently as Her Grace and the countess. Tell me—" she peered curiously at the redhead "—how is your mother?"

"Me—*me mother*?" questioned Megan, perplexed. What did this old gossip know of Pegeen O'Brien, now comfortably warm and well-fed in Ireland, thanks to the generosity of Patrick?

"Ahem—ah, yes... her *health*, that is. I... was wondering if she was still, ah, enjoying her food these days."

"Oh, more than ever!" Megan assured her. "She sends word that she and all my brothers and sisters have grown plump as eels!"

*Eels!* thought Lady Bunbury with a horrified expression. Quickly she forced herself to make her farewells and, after signaling her driver, took off in her carriage at a brisk pace. *Eels!* she thought again as she cast one last, over-the-shoulder glance at Lady St. Clare. But, instead of eels, there was another kind of animal that loomed in her thoughts as she sped away in her carriage, looking quite aghast.

Ashleigh sat across from Mary in Brett's brougham as it traveled along Pall Mall. They were on their way to her first cotillion at Almack's, and yet she felt no thrill over it. It was now over a month since they'd arrived in London, and there was still no word as to when—or *if*—Brett and Patrick might be released.

Somehow, it simply didn't seem right that she should be attending a fancy-dress ball while her husband and brother languished in prison. Of course, she quickly corrected herself, perhaps "languished" wasn't exactly the right word. Brett's letters assured her that their well-furbished rooms at the Admiralty were actually quite comfortable and, except for their inability to leave, they were enjoying all the comforts they were accustomed to, and were in no way ill-treated.

Nevertheless, she thought, here she was, dressed in a gown that was all the crack—or "all ze crek," as Suzanne had so charmingly put it—and on her way to Almack's! Oh, if Brett hadn't written to add his urgings to his mother's, she'd never have considered it!

"Nervous, *cara*?" asked Mary. The countess was sitting across from her, dressed in a cream-colored satin gown trimmed sparingly—elegantly—with bits of gold embroidery and clusters of seed pearls on its empire bodice and again on its slightly flared hemline. She wore a matching floor-length evening cape, and at her throat was a magnificent triple-strand choker of perfectly matched pearls.

"Not really," said Ashleigh. "My head is too full of the unfairness of Brett and Patrick's situation for me to worry about this frivolous cotillion, I'm afraid."

Mary nodded. "We are both of the same mind, I fear." She smiled and leaned forward to smooth the skirt of Ashleigh's gown, which showed between the parted folds of her cloth-of-silver evening cape. The gown itself was constructed of layers of sheer, midnight-blue silk shot with silver threads, and wearing it, Mary thought, together with the diamond necklace, earrings and tiara she had lent her, Ashleigh looked every inch a duchess.

"But it is just as well that you haven't the inclination to be nervous, darling. That way, you'll walk into Almack's looking as if this is very much an everyday affair, and that can only add to your status among the *ton*. They very much admire a coolness of aspect, you know."

"Oh, I know," said Ashleigh wearily, "but if you think I care a fig about those snobbish—"

"Now, now, *carissima*, contain yourself, please. You and I both know that what those people think is not ultimately crucial to us. But we must think of Brett . . . and your brother. Winning a favorable opinion among the *ton* can only help them. And think of the future while you're at it, my dear."

"The future?"

"A debutante ball may not mean very much to you now, but how will you feel when Marileigh is of an age to be presented? Will their acceptance mean as little to you then?"

Ashleigh smiled and shook her head, thoughts of her sweet little daughter filling her head. She was growing by leaps and bounds. Already she recognized the faces of most of those she saw every day, including all the children. And just the other day she had smiled her first truly genuine smile—not one of her mechanical little newborn smiles—and her entire face had lit up when Ashleigh bent over her cradle to see if she was awake.

Oh, how she wished Brett could be here to see her grow, to play with her and watch her smile! *It wasn't fair.* It just wasn't! Something had to give, and soon, or she wasn't sure what she was going to do. This waiting was beginning to drive her mad!

The carriage came to a halt outside of Almack's, and one of Brett's grooms sprang down to open the door for them. As they stepped down, another carriage pulled up behind theirs and Mary exclaimed, "Good Heavens, it's Agatha! I'd know her family crest anywhere. Why, I haven't seen her since . . ."

But as Mary stepped toward the other coach to greet her old friend, Ashleigh's eyes were drawn to another scene taking place on the street in front of the building.

"Take your bloody paws off me!" snarled a filthy, garishly dressed blonde who had all the earmarks of a woman of the streets. She was protesting violently against being urged, physically, away from the area in front of Almack's by two footmen whose livery matched that of the one standing near the entrance.

"Here, now, Miss Doxy," said one who had her by the arm, "we can't have the likes of you plyin' your trade near this fine establishment. There's a good girl . . . on your way, now."

"I tell you, I must see Baron Mumford!" screeched the whore. "He doesn't know about how his wife and daughters threw me out, and I *must* tell him—*I must!*"

Suddenly Ashleigh froze. *That voice!* She'd know that voice *anywhere.* It was *Monica*, dressed in that embarrassingly low-cut, dirty red satin dress! Monica, who'd made Ashleigh's life miserable at Hampton House!

Then, all at once, Ashleigh saw Monica break loose from the two footmen and run toward where she was standing. She pulled up short, however, when she saw Ashleigh in her path. The footmen were right behind her, but as they went to grab her, Ashleigh held out her hand to indicate they should desist.

"Just a moment, gentlemen," Ashleigh said. Then she looked at the heavily made-up face she barely recognized from a year ago, so had it changed, showing signs of age and other ravages. "Monica?" she questioned. "Don't you know me? It's Ashleigh."

A frown of confusion, and then dawning horror crossed the blonde's features. She froze for a moment, and then murmured, "No...no, it couldn't be!" She began to back away from Ashleigh, the look of horror on her face increasing. *"It couldn't be!"* she repeated, then, after a brief downward glance at her ragged dress, followed by a quickly assessing look at Ashleigh's finery, she whirled and began to run. "No!" they heard her cry as she disappeared into the darkness. *"No!"*

"Ashleigh, is something amiss?"

It was Mary's voice.

"I'm dreadfully sorry to have left you like that, but I thought I'd seen an old friend. As it turns out, it's not she, but her daughter-in-law. Ashleigh...? Are you feeling quite well? You look as though you've seen a ghost."

Ashleigh managed a small smile as she turned to join Mary in walking toward Almack's doors. "Perhaps I have," she stated quietly. "Perhaps I have."

Mary gave her a perplexed look.

"Oh, it was nothing, really. I—I suppose I'm just nervous about tonight, after all."

"Well, don't worry, *cara*," said Mary. "I'm certain you'll do just fine."

She gave Ashleigh a wink as they walked toward the front doors of the gaily lit building. "For St. George and old England," she whispered, and then, in an even softer voice, "and for Brett and Patrick!"

The footman inside examined their vouchers and announced them; then another escorted them a short distance to the Great Room, as it was called, and they were announced.

"Her Grace, the duchess of Ravensford, and the Countess di Montefiori."

A great many heads turned as they made their entrance, but Ashleigh barely noticed as she kept her head regally aloft and her eyes focused on one of the many glittering chandeliers while she and Mary descended the short flight of stairs to the ballroom. Out of the corner of her eye she saw the small orchestra that was playing in the balcony; the music was light and energetic, and she was reminded of the accompaniment for the French contredanse she had learned as a child.

"That would be a quadrille they're executing," Mary whispered to her from behind an exquisite ivory-and-gold fan. "I understand Lady Jersey brought the dance back from her visit to Paris."

Ashleigh smiled and raised her own fan, a beautiful piece of workmanship in silver and jet. "She may thank her stars that she returned well before the twentieth of March!"

Both women smiled grimly at her reminder of the date Bonaparte reentered Paris.

They were quickly surrounded by a number of smiling faces, and after several people greeted Mary, she proceeded to introduce Ashleigh to those she was unacquainted with. There was Lady Susan Ryder, Lady Harriet Butler, Miss Montgomery, the Count St. Aldegonde, Mr. Montagu, Mr. Montgomery and Mr. Standish.

But then the patroness of the evening, Mrs. Drummond Burrell, arrived and with her, someone Ashleigh knew only too well.

"Ah," said Elizabeth Hastings as she raked Ashleigh's form with cold, silver eyes, "the little duchess has returned. But, tell me, Your Grace, do you not find it, ah, rather awkward to be here without the escort of your husband?"

Ashleigh bristled inwardly, but to Elizabeth and the others—whose conversation had suddenly grown hushed—she presented a cool, unruffled exterior as she replied, "Why, no Lady Elizabeth, I should never call what I feel *awkward*. Regretful, perhaps, and sad, certainly, that His Grace could not join me, but also hopeful."

"'Hopeful'?" queried Elizabeth, clearly put out that her nasty little arrow had failed to make its mark.

"Yes, hopeful," said Ashleigh with a cool smile, "for I am every day more hopeful that His Grace will soon be free to join us."

"Well spoken!" said Charles Standish who, it was clear, had quickly become an ardent fan of this beautiful duchess of Ravensford.

The orchestra, which had taken a pause, started up again, and the Count St. Aldegonde requested the pleasure of Her Grace's company in the dance.

Ashleigh hadn't actually given it prior thought, but now she wondered if it was proper to be dancing while things were the way they were with Brett and Patrick. A quick glance at Mary, however, caught her mother-in-law's approving nod, and she accepted.

As she danced the quadrille with Aldegonde, she recognized various people on the floor, among them Lord and Lady Holland, who were known for their hospitality at Holland House, their home in the city; the duke of Devonshire, who was over six feet tall and, her partner whispered, being unmarried, was considered the most eligible "catch" in England, now that Brett Westmont was married; Christopher Edwards, the earl of Ranleagh—who winked at her as she passed by him—and Lady Pamela Marlowe.

Brett's former mistress was resplendent in a gown of jade-green silk trimmed with fine gold braid. Ashleigh didn't expect Lady Pamela to be exceptionally friendly to her and was astonished when she left off talking to Christopher, who was her partner, to throw her a bright smile.

*Why,* thought Ashleigh, *she looks positively radiant! What a transformation from the sour-faced woman I met at Ravens-*

*ford Hall! I wonder what could have caused the transformation.*

Her thoughts were interrupted by the sudden cessation of the music. At the same time, a stilled hush came over the room, and Ashleigh saw every head turn toward the entry steps. She turned. And then gasped.

There, standing proudly erect in formal evening clothes and looking heartbreakingly handsome, stood *Brett!*

His eyes swept the room as the footman announced him, then came to rest on Ashleigh. A slow smile broke over his handsome face, and he descended the steps, never once removing his gaze from her.

Ashleigh felt her knees grow weak and threaten to buckle. She felt the blood begin to throb in her veins and her heart pound so loudly, she was sure the entire room could hear it.

Frozen to the floor, she knew she couldn't have moved if her life depended on it. All she saw was her husband's face as he moved directly toward her, his turquoise eyes locked with hers.

Dimly, she was aware the music had resumed playing; out of the edges of her consciousness she saw Aldegonde bow and retreat. But it didn't matter. None of it mattered, except that Brett was free, and he was *here*!

Then he was standing in front of her, his turquoise eyes blazing into her blue ones. His smile was heart-stoppingly, achingly wonderful in his handsome, chiseled face as he continued to gaze down at her without words.

Then she heard him whisper, "Come," in a hoarse voice while he took her hand and led her toward a door to one of the small antechambers that led off the great room.

Half dazed, as if she were walking in a dream, Ashleigh followed until he drew her around a corner, and they were alone. He turned to her, but Ashleigh could only stare up at him. It was as if he weren't quite real, and soon she would awaken and all the loneliness and yearnings of the past days and weeks would come crashing down on her.

He stood quietly looking at her for a moment as his eyes drank in her face. Then his arms went about her and his head lowered as he crushed her to him.

With a small cry, she threw her arms about his neck even before his mouth found hers. Then she was returning his hungry kiss as fiercely as he gave it, and the room, the ball, the night itself disappeared as they melded into a single being.

Again and again his mouth slashed across hers. It was as if he couldn't get enough of her, as if he were starving for her, and she, for him. And when they finally needed to break for air, he buried his face in her hair, pulling her even closer, if that were possible, pulling her up, off the floor, from the tiptoes she'd been standing on, and murmuring her name into her ear, her brow, her hair.

*"Ashleigh, Ashleigh,* oh, God, how I've missed you!"

She gave a breathless little laugh that was half a sob and began to plant little kisses wherever she found her lips touching his face. "Oh, Brett!" she cried, and then laughed again, a bright, musical sound. "Oh, I missed you, too!"

At last he found her lips again, and giving them a quick, light kiss, managed to pull himself away slightly to look at her.

"My God," he whispered, shaking his head in wonder, "is it possible that you've grown even more beautiful?" He eyed the delicate contours of her face and then her figure, evident beneath the gossamer folds of her gown, and noted that childbirth had changed her, and for the better. There was an increased roundness to her lithe curves, a fullness of a kind that hadn't been there before. Her breasts had a lush ripeness to them that he hadn't noticed aboard ship, even though he'd been present when she'd nursed their daughter. But here he wasn't viewing her so much as the mother of his child, as the woman he loved.

"Do...do I please you, Brett?" she whispered worriedly. She was aware, if only from alterations Madame Gautier had had to make in her measurements, that her figure had altered since childbirth, and she was suddenly afraid he would find her less attractive.

*"Please me?"* he breathed. "Just let me take you home, and I'll show you how much you please me!"

There was no mistaking his grin and the desire that flashed in his eyes as he said this, and Ashleigh found herself blushing furiously.

He laughed softly, then drew her to him in a warm hug. "But the truth is, sweetheart, I fear we'll have to wait a while before I can do that. There are people here tonight whom courtesy demands I at least speak to. Ranleagh, for one, and Lord Castlereagh. They were two of several who worked tirelessly to have me and Patrick released, and I must thank them."

"Patrick!" she exclaimed. "Where—"

"Gone home to his apartments—after stopping at King Street for Megan, of course." He grinned. Then he cast a roguish eye over her hair, mussed somewhat from their embraces. "You look delectable, Your Grace, and if you don't want me to disgrace us both, right here at Almack's, you'd best hasten to the ladies' withdrawing room and repair your coiffure while I make my obligatory rounds."

"Oh," she murmured, her hand going to a tendril that had worked its way loose from the pile of Grecian-style curls on her head. "Oh, yes, of course." The blush was back.

"Meet me in the cloakroom when you're finished," he said huskily as his eyes continued to roam over her. "I'll tell Mother to make your farewells for you." He reached out to lightly touch the dimple in her cheek, then turned back toward the Great Room.

Ashleigh was pleased to learn she could gain entry to the room reserved for ladies who wished to withdraw, without going back into the ballroom. She was tingling in a dozen places from their encounter, as well as from the anticipation she'd read in his eyes, and the last thing she wanted was to be seen publicly in such a state—especially since everyone out there had seen them disappear together and would realize at once what was afoot.

The alcove led to another chamber where footmen directed her to her destination. The room she entered was beautifully decorated in shades of powder blue and ivory. Several Sheraton mirrors were on the walls, and in one corner there was a washstand with basin and pitcher, as well as soap and a pile of fine linen hand towels. In the opposite corner stood a large folding screen, and a blue velvet upholstered settee faced a pair of matching chairs near one wall. No one was about.

Ashleigh was in the process of tucking the errant curl in place before one of the mirrors when she heard the door open. She looked up to see Elizabeth Hastings's snidely smiling face in the mirror.

"Well, well, well," sneered Elizabeth, "if it isn't *Her Grace*, hiding away in here after making a complete fool of herself!"

Ashleigh whirled to face her old tormentor. "Lady Elizabeth, I don't think—"

"You really shouldn't allow yourself to be so completely obvious where your husband is concerned, my dear," Elizabeth continued. "It will only make him more sure of himself with you, you know."

"Wh-what do you mean?" Ashleigh asked slowly.

"Why, only what I've already warned you about in the past, little Ashleigh. A woman who falls all over Brett, as you obviously just did, can only expect to bore him and drive him into, ah, other waiting arms."

Ashleigh's winged brows drew together in a frown. "I have no intention of listening to any more of your viperish lies, Elizabeth. Now, if you will excuse me..." She turned to leave.

"Lies, are they?" spat Elizabeth from behind her. "Well, *my fine duchess*, I just dare you to go out there right now and see for yourself! Go ahead, take a look at your randy duke. At this moment he stands in a corner making an assignation with his old mistress. And Pamela! Why, she fairly drooled when she saw him approaching!"

Ashleigh hesitated, old fears trickling to the surface as she digested Elizabeth's words. Then she took a deep breath and walked resolutely to the door. She would not believe these lies—she *wouldn't*!

But as she left, she heard Elizabeth's ugly laughter behind her. "I told you he'd never be faithful. His kind never is!"

Ashleigh approached the door to the Great Room with cautious steps. She realized she shouldn't even be walking in this direction, for the way to the cloakroom circumvented the ball-room; the footman had told her so.

But, much as she wanted to disbelieve Elizabeth's hurtful remarks, something wouldn't allow her to pass without check-ing the ballroom for herself—if only to prove Elizabeth had lied.

She entered the ballroom and stood just inside the door. A waltz was in progress, but a quick check told her Brett wasn't on the dance floor. Then, suddenly, she saw him, for his height made him stand out easily among the crowd.

And he was with Lady Pamela! In an intimate stance, his head was bent toward her, and Ashleigh saw him laugh at something the honey blonde whispered behind her fan.

All at once Ashleigh felt nausea well up inside, and she bit her lip to keep from crying aloud as a sharp pain tore through her.

Blindly, for tears were blurring her sight, she groped for the door frame to steady herself. Then she turned and stumbled from the room.

## Chapter Thirty-Seven

It took her several minutes to find the cloakroom. A footman handed her her wrap and she threw it about her with trembling hands.

Then, as she was wondering how she could gracefully summon the brougham without conferring with Mary, she stopped.

*What are you doing?* she asked herself. *Is this the way a woman in love behaves when confronted with slander against her man?* For, as she stood there assessing the situation, she became more and more convinced that Elizabeth's words were probably just that—a vicious slander!

Hadn't Brett just made her see how that woman had operated in exactly the same manner before? What if he *was* talking to Lady Pamela? It proved nothing. They were old acquaintances, after all, and it was only Elizabeth's words that insinuated it was something more.

Well, the callow girl she'd once been may have been taken in by such deception, but not she! She was now a woman grown, mature, and far more sure of herself . . . and of her love for her man. She was Brett's wife, the mother of his child, and he had missed her. He'd told her so in no uncertain terms. What's more, he *desired her*! Of that she was fairly certain.

"Ah, there you are, sweet!" Brett came up behind her and planted a kiss on her ear. "I'm sorry if you had to wait," he added as he ushered her toward the door. "I got caught up in a conversation with Pamela Marlowe. She's a changed woman, and you'll never guess why."

Ashleigh glanced up at him, hardly daring to breathe. "Why?" she whispered.

"She and Ranleagh are engaged to be wed! She's in love with the rogue!"

Suddenly he stopped, his face a mask of concern as his hand went to her cheek. "Ashleigh, have you been crying? Sweetheart, what's wrong?"

"Oh, nothing, Brett." She smiled as she felt her heart start beating again. "Nothing in this whole wide world!"

A while later, as Brett drove them home in his phaeton, Ashleigh refrained from saying a word, even if he did seem to urge his blooded bay a bit too fast. And if he seemed uncharacteristically hasty as he threw the reins at the stable boy at home, it caused her no concern. Her own pulse was racing so, she couldn't speak.

Brett, too, was silent as he led her up the stairs toward his chamber. But as they neared it, they heard the awakening cries of their daughter coming from the room across the hall.

"Marileigh!" exclaimed Ashleigh. She glanced at Brett. "I've been keeping her with me down here." She didn't add that she'd been reluctant to sleep in the master bedroom when she returned because it housed too many disconcerting memories she wasn't ready to deal with at the time. "I guess she's hungry." She gave him an apologetic look. "It won't take me long to feed her."

"I'll come with you," he said warmly. "One of the things I dreamed of in my confinement was watching you nurse our daughter. I wouldn't miss this for the world!"

They dismissed Miss Simms, who had just finished changing the infant's nappies, and amid Brett's wondering exclamations over how much she'd grown and what a beauty she already was, Ashleigh settled down in a comfortably upholstered chair to nurse their daughter.

But it was only after she'd seated herself that she realized her ball gown fastened down the back and thus hardly lent itself to the task at hand.

Seeing her awkwardness and then her helpless blush, Brett chuckled and came behind the chair. "Here, let me," he whispered, and began to unfasten her gown.

A minute later the bodice dropped and Ashleigh moved the fussing infant to her breast. Marileigh rooted frantically for a moment, then seized the proffered nipple and settled down at once.

Brett laughed. "It doesn't take her long to get down to business! She's a young lady who seems to know what she wants. A Westmont, if I ever saw one!" Privately he was thinking that there was a male Westmont in the room who knew exactly what he wanted as well. He wanted Ashleigh. And not only in the physical sense, although the sight of her ripe breasts, exposed as she nursed the babe, was enough to set him on fire.

But beyond this, he wanted her in a far more enduring way. This was a woman he would love forever, a woman to bear his children, to laugh and cry with over the years, to grow old with. And as he saw her now, stealing an abashed glance at him from time to time as she nursed their child, he was seized with the terrible need to tell her how much he loved her, to share with her his heart and his soul.

But then he smiled ruefully to himself. He had waited this long; he could wait longer. Because what he wanted was not just for now—it was for a lifetime.

Ashleigh felt his eyes on her as she fed their child and was suddenly caught up in a maelstrom of love and longing so overpowering she could hardly breathe. Oh, she had loved him for so long now! How much longer could she go on loving him this way—in silence—when her soul cried with her need to tell him! If only she could believe he might come to love her too!

But she forced her hopes away from that impossible dream, telling herself it was enough that he had begun to treat her tenderly. Better to accept the bounty fate had already sent her, than to be greedy and ask for more. It would have to do.

She glanced down and saw that Marileigh had fallen asleep. Gently, she removed the infant from her breast, then raised her to her shoulder and began to massage the tiny back.

A soft burst of air from his daughter's mouth caused Brett to chuckle. "Even her belches are delicate and ladylike," he said as he took the still-sleeping babe from Ashleigh and laid her in her cradle. He bent and placed a soft kiss on the tiny head, then straightened and came toward his wife.

"Come, sweetheart," he said quietly and held out his hand.

Ashleigh let him pull her from the chair, then paused awkwardly as her eyes dropped to her bared breasts.

Brett laughed softly, then removed his jacket and draped it over her before leading her across the hall and into the master bedroom.

Someone had lit several candles whose light bathed them in a soft glow as Brett shut the door. He took Ashleigh by the shoulders and gently turned her to face him. "Now," he said, looking solemnly into her eyes, "you're going to tell me why you'd been crying at Almack's."

Startled, she tried to look away, but found she couldn't. The turquoise gaze was far too riveting. "I—I'd had an encounter with Elizabeth Hastings in the room where I went to repair my hair."

Brett's face darkened grimly, but he kept his voice soft. "Go on."

"She—she taunted me with the fact that you were...with Pamela Marlowe. Sh-she—" Ashleigh faltered, the sting of tears assaulting her eyes as her words conjured up the pain she'd felt. Feeling foolish that even the memory could reduce her to tears, she wiped at them impatiently with her hand and continued. "She said you were making an assignation with Pam—"

"Bloody hell!" Brett exclaimed. "That poisonous *bitch*! I'll—"

"Oh, but, Brett! You cannot think she succeeded! For she did not—not this time," she added in a softer voice. "That's why you found me in the cloakroom, why you didn't find me...gone." Ashleigh began to speak more rapidly now, as if it were important to tell him all that had happened before he misunderstood. Her next words came out in a rush.

"You see, I did spy you in the Great Room with Pamela. And my first impulse was to run from there and never look back. That was when I succumbed to tears. But when I reached the outer room, my...good sense, I suppose you'd call it, took over. I remembered what you'd said about Elizabeth's perniciousness before and—" her voice dwindled down to a low whisper "—I decided to stay and hear what you had to say about it."

Brett released the breath he hadn't realized he'd been holding as he was seized with uncontainable joy. *She had trusted him!* And where there was trust, there was the hope of something more!

"Ashleigh," he said in a shaky voice, "I'm so proud of you!"

"Proud?"

"Yes. Because you came to me after what you'd heard and seen, even though you were hurting. Don't you see? You found the strength to face the evil Elizabeth was spewing, instead of running away. You trusted me, even though you were in pain...enough pain to bring you to tears before you faced me...enough to bring these tears now."

She nodded mutely, the tears streaming down her cheeks. But through the tears she met his eyes and was struck by the notion that he could see what she was feeling...that he could see into her very soul.

"Ashleigh," he murmured as he took his fingers and gently wiped the moisture from her cheeks, "I'm so in love with you, I can't see straight!"

"Wha-what?" she stammered. Disbelief warred with dawning joy as she digested his words. Then she met his eyes and knew it was true.

"I said I love you, Ashleigh." He hadn't meant to blurt it out that way. Somehow, the words had just tumbled out by themselves. But now that he'd told her, he felt an overwhelming sense of relief and only hoped his admission was something she could handle, that it wouldn't send her scurrying from him in confusion or guilt because she couldn't return his feelings. "I realize," he added with a queer, tender smile on his face, "that you have every reason not to care for me in the same way. I know I've given you reasons in the past, not to—''

A sharp, inarticulate cry cut him off as Ashleigh threw herself into his arms. "Oh, Brett!" she cried, her voice somewhere between laughter and tears, *"I love you so much, I could die!"* Her arms tightened about him, and she was trembling. "And now that you've told me you—oh, I think I *have died*! I think I'm in heaven!"

Brett forced her gently from him and held her by the shoulders as he searched her face for the truth. And he saw it, mingled with shadows of the pain and longing she'd tried to deny during those terrible months of separation and which now gave way to the love and joy shining in her eyes.

"My love..." he whispered as he cupped her face with his hands and lowered his head for a kiss that was full of tenderness, and joy and love—the sweet miracle that had touched his soul.

As Ashleigh parted her lips for his kiss, she knew she would never forget this moment, and she drew into her memory, her heart, the essence of it, hugging it to her as a talisman for a lifetime, for the life and love they would share.

Brett released her lips and let his hands trail down until they were resting lightly on her shoulders while his gaze locked with hers.

She saw his eyes darken with passion, and her breathing increased with this awareness. A pulse throbbed at the juncture of her neck and shoulder; Brett felt it under his hand and his own blood pounded in his veins. He held her gaze, then saw her eyes become two deep blue shimmering pools, and he felt he could lose himself in them forever. Closing his eyes, he smelled her soft perfume, along with the musky woman-scent he remembered well, and his head reeled with it.

Ashleigh was unprepared for the sensations that were rapidly assaulting her body. He'd barely touched her, and she was on fire!

"Brett," she breathed. "I...I..."

But he knew what she wanted. His own hunger was thrumming his pulses, and when he read the need in her eyes, he shuddered as a shock of desire rocked him.

Then he was sweeping her up into his arms, the jacket he'd wrapped her in falling to the floor as he carried her to the bed. There he laid her down quickly, and then his hands flew to his cravat, which he tore away with deft fingers.

"Beautiful," he murmured as his eyes lingered on her face a moment, then fell to her lush breasts, "so beautiful."

His shirt joined the cravat on the floor, and as she drank in the stark male beauty of him—the broad shoulders, the muscular chest covered with whorls of dark chestnut hair—Ashleigh could wait no longer. Reaching up her arms to him, she cried, "Brett, please! I . . . I need you!"

He made a sound like a low growl in his throat and instantly joined her on the bed. Pulling her to him, he exulted in the feel of her bare breasts against his skin, their nipples already hard with desire. "So anxious, my love?" he murmured huskily into her hair. "But we shouldn't rush it, you know," he added as he raised his head to capture her eyes. "We—" he brushed her lips lightly, teasingly, with his "—have," he added as his mouth trailed down her throat, " . . . a lifetime. . . ." The word barely left his lips before they found the aching peak of one rosy-tipped breast and drew it into his mouth.

Ashleigh felt a jolt of pleasure sluice through her, moving from where he held her with his mouth to the juncture of her thighs. With a moan, she drove her fingers into his curls, while at the same time she began to twist and writhe under the sensations that were assaulting her body. "Brett," she gasped, "oh, Brett, hurry!"

Brett heard her, felt her response, and was enflamed by it. He wanted to go slowly, to savor what they'd waited for for so long, but it seemed she would have none of it.

With a shaky laugh, he raised his head to look at her again. "So it's to be love in a hurry, is it? Faith, but you're a delicious wanton, my darling," he teased, "but I think we ought to take . . . our . . . time. . . ." His thumbs were teasing too, as they brushed her nipples, and Ashleigh moaned again, deep in her throat.

Then his mouth came down on hers in a kiss that didn't stop. His tongue found the seam between her lips and slipped between as she parted them for him, hungrily, her own tongue darting to meet his. Tongue meeting tongue, they tasted of each other, withdrew, then tasted again.

His hand moved to her bodice and he rolled with her, pulling her against him with the other while he finished the work he'd begun earlier and removed her gown. Her petticoats soon followed, and then he was kneeling beside her on the bed as he slipped off her kid dancing slippers. His fingers went to the top of a silk stocking and he began to bare her leg, bending to plant feather-light kisses along the exposed flesh until the silk fell away and he was tasting the delicious curves of her toes, sucking on them, slipping between them with his tongue.

The sensation was unlike any she'd ever felt. Her body tingled in a thousand places, but all joined to drive a burning message to the core of her femininity where she felt moisture gathering, making her ready for him.

But Brett took his time, sharply quelling his own need, to give her pleasure. Murmuring her name and his love for her again and again, he repeated the process with the other stocking, raising her toes to his mouth once again.

He stroked her calves with his hands, and then her thighs. One hand trailed across her flat abdomen before coming to rest on the nest of raven curls below.

Ashleigh sucked in her breath at this touch and heard him laugh lightly. Then she saw him above her again, and his eyes found hers while a hand cupped her breast and the one below gently parted her thighs, and then his finger slid between, entering her slippery warmth.

"Oh!" she gasped and saw him smile.

"Oh, what, love?" he whispered. His eyes were hard with desire and focused relentlessly on her face as he withdrew his finger and passed it over the tiny bud above. "Tell me," he persisted as he stroked the pulsing nub once, twice, a third time.... "Tell me what pleasures you, Ashleigh, and I'll—"

"*Brett!*" she cried, and then she was beyond words. Intense spirals of pleasure began emanating from deep within her, flinging her into a world where there was only Brett and his touch. She felt her whole body shake with it, her thighs eagerly parting yet farther for him, her hands reaching about his neck to pull him closer. Ah, she had to have him closer!

And finally Brett could wait no longer. Satisfied that he had brought her to the brink of fulfillment, he now prepared to join her in the ultimate pleasure. He pulled away only long enough to remove the rest of his clothes, then wrapped her in an embrace that was fierce, his need shuddering through him as he murmured into her hair, "Oh, God, Ashleigh! I cannot get enough of you! Sweet, sweet wife of my heart, my life, how I need you... God, how I love you!"

And with this he raised himself above her trembling frame and pushed her thighs apart with his own, his turgid, throbbing maleness seeking entry. And then he drove it home.

A renewed surge of desire came on the heels of Ashleigh's pleasure of moments before, and just when she thought she couldn't bear it, she felt him enter her, and the feeling was so intense, she cried his name aloud.

But Brett captured her cry with his mouth as he thrust, then thrust again, then harder, still, as he felt her body arc up to meet his in perfect rhythm.

Again and again, their bodies pulsed together, man joined to woman, she, sheathed around him, he, deep inside her in the age-old movements that, for the two of them, were also fresh and new and wondrous.

Finally Ashleigh felt herself spinning, spiraling in a vortex of pleasure so intense, she could do naught but give herself up to it. She heard Brett hoarsely call her name, urging her on with him, and all the while she felt she was getting closer...closer....

And then it happened. A white-hot shaft of pleasure drew her mind from her body, her sense from her feeling, and all about her the universe danced at her feet while time itself stood still. Brett cried her name and she felt him convulse, felt his seed pumping into her, seeking a home, and then she was sobbing her pleasure, her love for him, until she thought she would never stop.

Minutes passed, and the ticking of the clock on the mantel began to make itself heard over their ragged breathing. Sated and replete, they lay on their sides, facing each other with their thighs entwined, their bodies still locked together as one.

Ashleigh's face was buried in his shoulder, her swirling hair, long since loosed from its pins, tangled about their shoulders and arms. He took her hand and raised her fingers to his lips, where he began to kiss each one with exquisite tenderness.

"I love you," he whispered as his lips brushed each delicate tip, "I love you . . . love you . . . love you. . . ."

Ashleigh opened her lips against his shoulder, uttering a soft, ecstatic cry. "Oh, Brett!" she managed. "*My* Brett!" Then, wonderingly, "Are you really mine, my darling?"

He raised his head and braced himself on one elbow to look at her. "For as long as you want me, love," he breathed.

"Forever," came the hushed reply.

Brett closed his eyes, drinking in the scent of her, then the warm, musky scent of their lovemaking. He swallowed past the lump of emotion that lodged in his throat when he thought of all they'd suddenly found together, and of how close they'd come to missing it.

He opened his eyes to find Ashleigh gazing at him, a look of total adoration on her face, and he smiled into her eyes, then kissed each one tenderly.

"Never," he told her solemnly, "if I live to be a hundred and ten, will I ever forget this night . . . this night of miracles, with you at its center. In some ways, this is the beginning of my life, love. Whatever went before has little meaning, compared to now."

He pulled away from her then, and feeling him slipping from her encasing warmth, Ashleigh nearly cried out. But he quickly drew her attention as he smiled and ran his fingers along the chain that encircled his neck.

When he'd removed it, she saw that a whole locket replaced the half that had once been there. He smiled and parted it to show her the miniature portrait of the child he'd been.

"My mother thought I should have the other half," he murmured.

But then she saw him slip another object from the chain, and, before she knew it, he was taking her left hand, grasping its third finger, and slipping it on. It was her wedding ring—the one she'd dashed into a corner of this very room in anger!

The ring in place, he slowly, almost reverently, bent his head and kissed her finger. Then his head came up and his eyes locked with hers.

"With this ring, I thee wed," he whispered huskily.

"And I, thee," she answered, tears of joy brimming in her eyes.

"And know this, my love," he murmured softly. "From now until I draw my final breath, you are my life . . . you, and the child brought forth from this strange and wondrous love at last gone right . . . and the children God, in his infinite wisdom, might see fit to bless us with in the future. Nothing else matters. . . . Can you believe that?"

Ashleigh's answer was a kiss that stole his breath away. "Nothing else matters," she echoed in a breathless whisper, "nothing. . . ."

And then speech ceased as they found themselves in each other's arms again, and words became unnecessary, and nothing else mattered.

## Chapter Thirty-Eight

Ashleigh relaxed against the plush squabs lining the seats of Brett's brougham while it sped along the road leading to Kent. She smiled as she observed the handsome profile of her husband, who was sitting across from her and gazing out the window; she was remembering another time she'd sat in this carriage and studied him thusly, and she couldn't help thinking of the differences in their positions then and now.

Was it really almost a year since they'd met? So much had happened in that time, and yet it scarcely seemed possible. And sometimes it still didn't seem possible that the beloved profile she viewed once belonged to a man as brooding and remote as a distant star. Today that face seemed ever at ease and given to ready laughter. His wonderful turquoise eyes, once so mocking and cold, now danced with good humor and smiled their perpetual warmth at the whole world.

*Love,* she thought as she hugged his adored presence to her, in her mind, *it can make all things possible.*

She closed her eyes for a moment, savoring a recollection of their last hours alone together. He had awakened her in the predawn this morning, with a delicious nuzzling of her ear and then that susceptible area where her neck and shoulder joined; at the same time his hands had been most industrious, one playing with the peaks of her breasts while the other had slipped between her thighs to seek softer flesh.

Thus she had been awakened, barely finding consciousness before realizing she was already hot and moist between her thighs for him, prompting a sleepy demand, to Brett's grinning delight, that he take her immediately—which, of course, he obliged. Later, she'd found herself blushing at her wanton antics, but Brett had merely laughed and held her close, saying it was time she ceased to be disturbed by a part of her nature he cherished. And she was forced to admit he was right; she should hardly be surprised by it, when such had been a regular occurrence with them during the month they'd remained in London, the month since that wonderful night after the cotillion at Almack's.

The pages of her mind flipped back over the days that had passed since then. After spending the first week largely closeted together in their private rooms—*almost* satisfying their hunger for each other after the separations that had gone before, she mused with a smile—they had ventured out to attend the various balls and parties at which their presence was eagerly requested. To Ashleigh's astonishment, the duke and duchess of Ravensford had suddenly become the darlings of the *ton*! Their romantic and, some thought, glamorous story both intrigued and fascinated that closed society that detested the mundane and was always ready to be amused and charmed by the lives of its more interesting members.

A frown marred her brow as she reminded herself that sometimes this interest did not extend to amusement or being charmed; sometimes it brought harsh censure and disdain. To wit, many of their acquaintances were shocked and horrified by the news that the poet Shelley had abandoned his pregnant wife, Harriet, to elope with his mistress, Mary Godwin—*who was also carrying his child!* Though Shelley had never exactly been one of the *haut ton*, he was born of the upper classes, and if his behavior had been eyebrow-raising before, he was a social pariah now.

And then there were the dark rumors about one of English society's former darlings: Lord Byron, who had wed Sir Ralph Milbanke's daughter in January, was known to be having marital difficulties. This in itself was no cause for scandal, but if the ugly gossip was to be believed, a major source of their troubles could be traced to Byron's involvement with a houseguest of theirs at Piccadilly Terrace, and the woman was none other than Mrs. Augusta Leigh, the poet's *half sister*! And although the rumors hadn't reached the proportions of a full-blown scandal yet, Brett, who was acquainted with Byron and some of his intimates, said he feared it was just a matter of time until they would.

Even the prince regent wasn't immune to gossip. Most of the country was scandalized by the shocking manner in which he treated his wife, poor woman. Prinny had always made no bones about the fact that he hated her, but lately he had taken to forbidding her to appear at any number of public and private places—not to mention most official functions. Yes, Prinny was quite beastly to Princess Caroline, and Ashleigh felt deeply sorry for her. Fortunately the common folk pitied her, too, and had begun to protest against George's treatment of the princess, and Ashleigh suspected it was only the country's current panic over the renewed war with Napoleon that kept Prinny safe from outright public displays against his behavior.

As for the war, all anyone could do was remember that Boney had been defeated once before, and hope for the best. Under the command of the duke of Wellington, Britain had joined with her allies, Austria, Prussia and Russia, to raise a million men, who were moving toward the Little Corporal's armies— somewhere near the Belgian border, Brett thought—and many felt there would soon be a major confrontation.

*Thank God the conflict with America is over!* she thought, and her mind drifted to Patrick and Megan. Those two lovebirds were currently on their way to Ireland to visit with Megan's family. They'd promised to return to England briefly for Ashleigh's birthday next month, but their ultimate destination was America, where they planned to live permanently, on Patrick's plantation in Virginia. Ashleigh and Brett missed them terribly already, and plans were afoot to visit them there in a year or so.

*And Mary will probably be the next to leave us,* she thought sadly, *and with her, the children.* But for the moment, at least, Brett's mother and her little ones were accompanying them to Kent. Ashleigh glanced out the window as she felt the carriage negotiate a sharp bend in the road and spotted the three additional carriages that comprised the entourage that was traveling to Ravensford Hall. Neither Brett nor Mary felt it was safe for her and the others to return to Italy these days, and even though word had come from Father Umberto—who *had* returned—that the villa was almost completely restored, the decision had been made for Mary and the children to remain in England until peace came again.

Moreover, Mary had referred cryptically to some unfinished business she had in this country, though try as she might, Ashleigh had been unable to coax any more out of her on the subject. It was as if—

"Penny for your thoughts, love."

Ashleigh looked up to find Brett smiling at her; his heavy-lidded gaze was lazily seductive, and Ashleigh suddenly felt tingles along her spine.

"Oh, I, um—" she flushed "—I forget what they were!"

Low laughter and a look that left no doubt as to his thoughts made her blush bright pink.

"I'll wager your current thoughts are worth much more than a penny, sweet," he teased.

"Brett!" she chastised, then blushed even harder as she saw his eyes drop to her breasts, whose nipples, in her suddenly aroused state, had peaked and thrust outward under the thin fabric of her summer gown. "You know you . . . you only have to look at me a certain way and—and—"

"Come here," he ordered softly, and patted the seat beside him.

"Brett, not in the carriage!"

He grinned, and the turquoise gaze was mesmerizing. "Ashleigh, either you come here or I'll come there, though at present, I admit, these tight breeches make it difficult for me to move."

Glancing down at the apparel in question, she found herself going from pink to scarlet.

He laughed again, his eyes teasing and utterly seductive as they held hers. "Now," he said quietly, "are you going to come over here or do I come and get you?"

Ashleigh felt her breathing go shallow as she nodded. Then she pulled herself up by one of the carriage straps and made the transfer. Or almost.

Brett's arm reached out, and before she knew it, she was sitting on his lap, and then his arms were around her, and then . . . *oh, then!*

His mouth went unerringly to one of the peaks that thrust impudently outward while a hand found its way under her skirts and upward, between her thighs.

"Brett!" she exclaimed, and then she moaned. He drew her nipple into his mouth, right through the damp material, while his hand found her woman's place and slowly, inexorably, made it magic.

"I've been wanting to do this ever since we left London," he murmured against her breast. "Oh, God, you're sweet, my Ashleigh . . . so damned sweet!"

Ashleigh's self-consciousness, which had been fading fast, fell away completely with these intimate caresses. She became aware of Brett's hardness beneath her buttocks and, deciding two could play his game, began to wriggle enticingly on his lap.

His mouth came away from her with a gasp. Then he looked up, and a bold grin slashed across his face. "You little minx! You're asking for trouble, you know."

"Am I?" She grinned back at him as she took a forefinger and slowly traced the curve of his lower lip.

Sucking in his breath, Brett closed his eyes for a moment and leaned his head back against the seat. Then both arms came around her and drew her against his chest.

"You know," he breathed, "I only thought to play a while and not go any further, but the way you have me feeling now, I swear, I'm ready to take you right here, on the floor of the carriage."

Ashleigh giggled and maneuvered onto the seat next to him. "It was only a matter of what's good for the goose being good for the gander, Your Grace."

One chestnut eyebrow quirked as he threw her a mock glare. "I think I've taught you too much for your own good, you imp!"

"Mmm, perhaps," she mused, "but then again, perhaps not." She reached out and began playing with the hair that curled around his ear and at the nape of his neck.

Brett growled and turned to pull her into his arms. "Meaning?" he queried, his mouth hovering inches above hers.

"Meaning," she whispered with a smile suddenly gone shy, "that my husband has spent these past weeks showing me the thousand-and-one ways he knows to please me . . . but what he hasn't done is show me ways I might please *him*."

"Little innocent," he breathed, "and, yes, I can still call you that, though you've shared my bed all these weeks and borne me a child, so don't look so surprised. But don't you know that you have ways to pleasure me that have nothing so much to do with what you *do*, as with what you *are*? My God, Ashleigh, all I need do is watch you come into a room or walk across a floor and I find myself unable to *think clearly*! To begin with, your natural, unpracticed beauty alone is a potent aphrodisiac for me. Beyond that, however, are the myriad things you do unconsciously every day that have me trembling like a schoolboy for you. There's the unconscious grace of your walk, the musical lilt of your laughter, the way you sometimes turn your head . . . and *your smile*!" He closed his eyes and drew in a ragged breath. "Sweet merciful Heaven, there have been times when your smile alone could drive me mad with longing!"

Ashleigh watched his face through all of this with a growing look of rapt wonder. "Do I do all *that*?" she questioned softly.

He let out his breath and shook his head. "That and more, you angelic, enticing, tempting little witch!" And then his head lowered, and his mouth captured hers in a kiss that was achingly sweet, plying the honey from her lips as he moved his own over them in lazy, unhurried circles, touching his tongue to the corners of her mouth, grazing her teeth with it, sipping at the nectar between.

Ashleigh felt the familiar curling in the pit of her stomach, the sweet lassitude invading her limbs; her arms stole unthinkingly around his neck as she kissed him back with all the burgeoning eagerness of love awakened and fulfilled. He was her first love and her last; he was all things to her, and she knew she could never get enough of him; he was her present, her past and her future, and she loved him with every fiber in her body...and in her soul.

"Brett," she whispered breathlessly, when their lips at last parted, "oh, Brett, it's the same with me! I...I find I want you almost all the time, because I love you all the time, and more and more each day! It's all mixed up together—loving you, wanting you. Is it that way for you, too?"

He withdrew slightly, but kept her in the circle of his arms as he looked down into her flushed, upturned face. The turquoise eyes were very serious as he answered her. "It is," he said solemnly. "And there are those about us—men, I'm speaking of, specifically—who would say this cannot be so, that for a woman it is natural that love should govern and intertwine with everything she thinks and feels and does, but that for a man, love is separate from the rest of him, his sexuality included. My friend, Byron, is such a man. He once told me...let's see, how did it go? 'Man's love is of man's life a thing apart, 'tis a woman's whole existence.'"

Ashleigh pondered the quoted lines a moment. "He wrote that somewhere?"

"Or was planning to," Brett told her. "I could never be sure with George as to whether he was quoting from things he'd already written or merely trying out on me some tidbits he was storing for future use."

"But...oh, Brett, how sad...that he should feel that way, I mean."

He nodded. "Yes, but not only feel that way himself—he believed what he felt to be true of all men!" He chuckled, then bent to place a soft kiss on her nose. "And I, poor, misguided fool that I was, readily concurred with him at the time!"

Ashleigh sent him a soft, radiant smile. "But not now."

"No," he said, smiling tenderly back at her. "Not since the moment I began to fall in love with you. And when I took you to my bed and suddenly found myself enjoying your untutored, innocent body in a thousand ways better than anything I'd tasted before, at first I couldn't fathom what was happening to me."

He gave her a brief, apologetic smile. "There'd been scores of women in my life before, all of them worldly wise and, ah, well practiced in the arts of love. And yet they'd failed to bring a fraction of the satisfaction you've brought to my bed, sweet, darling wife." Another kiss on the nose.

"For the longest time it puzzled me, for you see, I'd begun to love you—I realize now—long before I knew it consciously."

"You thought you hated me," she said soberly.

A brief look of pain crossed the turquoise eyes. "And put you through hell until I got it all sorted out. Ah, Ashleigh, can you ever forgive me?"

"I forgave you long ago, my darling," she whispered as her fingers came up to still his lips.

Brett closed his eyes and put his hand over hers, pressing her fingertips to his lips. "I'll never hurt you again, Ashleigh, I swear it. God, I love you!"

This time, when he pulled her to him, the kiss was fervent and passionate, his mouth and body telling her what he felt, where words left off. His mouth slashed across hers again and again while his arms crushed her to him fiercely, and Ashleigh responded in kind. They fell along the carriage's seat, molded to each other, their hunger building, building into a white-hot heat that wiped all else from their minds.

And then the carriage stopped.

"Brett! Ashleigh! Are you two asleep in there?"

"It's your mother!" Ashleigh managed to exclaim in a shaky voice.

Brett muttered an expletive under his breath and pulled them into a sitting position.

"Ashleigh, I say, are you awake? Miss Simms says Marileigh's hungry. She wants feeding," Mary's voice told them.

"I—I'll be right with you, Mary," Ashleigh called as she did what she could to rearrange her disheveled appearance. She glanced at Brett, who was leaning back against the seat, attempting to control his ragged breathing. "I suppose I'd better join them." She smiled ruefully.

"Indeed," he murmured, cocking an eyebrow at her as he managed a grin. "Our daughter will have her due now, the unmannered little vixen, but, lest my wife misunderstand, I want her to know I intend to have *mine* not more than ten minutes after we reach the Hall. Is that clear, Your Grace?"

Ashleigh grinned, then blushed as she caught sight of the bulge that had not yet subsided beneath his fawn-colored breeches. "Perfectly, Your Grace. My husband will have his due."

And an hour later, amid the bustle and excitement of baggage being unloaded, greetings from the staff, and delighted chatter from the children, the duke and his duchess disappeared to their rooms, and he did.

Their presence at Ravensford Hall was greeted with hearty good cheer on the part of the staff; from the Busbys to the stable help, the servants at the duke's country seat had grown exceedingly fond of Ashleigh, and during the time of the duke and duchess's estrangement—well-known to them through the servants' ubiquitous and well functioning grapevine—most had privately hoped the marriage might be repaired. Moreover, members of the older staff, such as the Busbys and a few others who had been around when Brett was a small boy, were both astounded and delighted to see that Mary, the former viscountess, had returned with the obvious blessings of her son. She, like Ashleigh, had been a favorite of theirs before she left, and to a person, they had always believed her innocent of the charges the senior Westmonts had levied against her.

Little Marileigh quickly became the adored darling of all, and while there were some initially raised eyebrows at the horde of foreign-accented children who descended on them with this visit, the near-perfect manners and discipline with which the contessa had imbued her charges soon manifested itself, relieving the servants' fears and bringing smiles to their faces as the old house echoed with childish laughter and youthful energies.

And finally there were the changes in the master; there was no containing their gasps of dawning delight as they quickly became aware that His Grace had become a different person. And when they saw the soft looks of love exchanged between the duke and his radiant little duchess, the unspoken but patently visible chords of mutual adoration between them, they readily guessed at the source.

"I knew that sweet little thing was someone special the first day she came, Henry," said Hettie Busby to her husband the day after the entourage had arrived, "but I never guessed she had it in her to tame the likes of His Grace. Beyond hope, I thought he was. But she just went on being herself, Lord love her, and even that hard case was forced to come 'round."

And Henry had grinned at her, saying, "Oh, 'Is Grace 'as tumbled 'ard, 'e 'as, Lor' love 'im. An' a more deservin' man I've never known. Near thirty years since I seen 'im 'appy like 'e is now!''

But there was one person at Ravensford Hall who was far from happy over these latest events. Less than a day after they arrived, Lady Margaret appropriated a handful of servants and made an exit; bag and baggage, and in tight-lipped silence, she withdrew from the Hall to live in the dowager's cottage by the lake, sending only the briefest note to her grandnephew on the matter, wherein she curtly informed him that she would be sending her lady's maid to deal with Mr. Jameson regarding any of her future needs.

Ashleigh expressed dismay at the unbending attitude of Lady Margaret, and Brett shrugged, saying it was to have been expected, but Mary viewed the retreating back of her old antagonist in thoughtful silence, a pondering look in her eyes.

# Chapter Thirty-Nine

Weeks passed, the warming weather and soft rains of spring melding into the sunshine of early summer. Crocuses and daffodils bloomed, leading the way for the thousands of roses that grew in the gardens at Ravensford Hall.

Life among the estate's inhabitants settled into a comfortable routine. Mary busied herself with the children, as did Ashleigh, although, since Marileigh spent more of her time awake and was not sleeping as much during the days as she had when she was younger, most of Ashleigh's daytime hours were devoted to her own child.

The nights, however, were reserved for Brett. The duke found his days consumed by the demands of his estates—neglected to some extent during the time of his confinement—so Ashleigh and he, to their chagrin, had found themselves spending most of their days apart. This had quickly elicited a pact between them: No matter what the business at hand, no matter how pressing the domestic scene around them, once the dinner hour passed, they would repair to their private chamber and see no one but each other—until well after breakfast. And if Her Grace seemed a bit eager to get through the evening feeding of their daughter, or if His Grace appeared to rush his consumption of the evening meal, no one remarked upon it; indeed, there was little reaction, save for an occasional shared wink or a smile as members of their household watched those two hold hands and ascend the stairs together, their eyes only on each other.

One morning in early June was to see an exception to all this. Ashleigh was about to send for the maid to remove the breakfast tray from the master bedchamber—she and Brett took of that repast in private, since breakfast, for them, was usually a sharing of far more than mere food—when Brett emerged from their dressing room with a grin on his face.

"How soon can you feed Marileigh and be dressed—in riding clothes?" he asked.

Ashleigh put down the hairbrush she'd been wielding, hoping to put some order into the tangled mass of curls that hung down her back before summoning the maid. "Oh, I should think—*riding clothes*?"

"Yes. I'm off to the stables now, and I'd like you to meet me there in an hour...that is, unless you've something better to do than accompany me on a ride—and then a picnic."

"A...*picnic*! Oh, Brett, do you really *mean* it?" She whirled sharply to face him, the brush flying out of her hand.

"Yes, I mean it," he chuckled, then opened his arms wide to catch her as she threw herself into them with a cry of delight.

"Oh, I cannot believe it!" she enthused as she clung to his neck and placed little kisses all over his laughing face. "We're to have some hours together today, then?"

Laughing and swooping her up off the floor as he swung her around, Brett answered, "The entire day, love, if you like."

"Ohhh, *I like!*"

He released his hold enough to let her slide down the front of him until she reached the floor; then he sucked in his breath. All she wore was a semitransparent chemise, and he'd just felt enough of the ripe curves beneath it, seen enough of the twin, rose-tipped peaks and a triangular shadow below, to become distracted.

"But if you don't hurry into something...more decorous," he breathed, his hands spanning her tiny waist and itching to travel, "the picnic will be postponed...*indefinitely*!"

Ashleigh felt a familiar hardness pressing against her belly, and her breathing diminished almost to nothing. She looked up, and the message in his eyes made her knees go weak. "I...a picnic could be used to accomplish more than...the partaking of food, Your Grace . . . if its site were to be completely private, that is."

A moment of silence followed, and then a deep rumble of laughter from her husband's chest. "In that case, Your Grace, I accept. A picnic it shall be, in the most private of places. I know just the spot!"

An hour later, a groom led Raven and Irish Night to where the duke and duchess waited outside the stables. As it was a warm morning, Brett wore only a white lawn shirt, minus any jabot or stock, with dove-gray breeches fitted into his shiny black riding boots. Ashleigh had donned a light blue linen riding habit, but shunned the small, feathered hat Madame Gautier had made to go with it, opting to tie her curls at the nape of her neck with a narrow blue ribbon instead.

After they were mounted, Brett dismissed the groom, then turned in his saddle to Ashleigh. "Irish Night's well behaved over fences now. I tested her yesterday afternoon, just to confirm what Old Henry told me. He completed her training himself while we were away, you know. The old curmudgeon had the impudence to wink at me, if you can imagine it, and calmly inform me he'd thought it would be only a matter of time before I brought 'Er Grace' back home, at which time he'd assumed you'd be needing a safe mount to ride."

Ashleigh laughed. "Why, that old rascal! I had no idea he was such a romantic! But Hettie tells me he, is a bit superstitious. *Her* version of the story is that he was merely *hopeful* I'd return and, not wishing to give the, ah, 'spirits of safe returns,' I believe she called them, any wrong ideas, he insisted on behaving as if I *were* coming back any day. She says if there was any hope of dissuading him of his 'un-Christian, heathen notions' before, it's lost now."

Brett laughed too, then headed Raven out of the stable's courtyard with Ashleigh following. It warmed him to think of how fond the servants here at the Hall had grown of Ashleigh—and those in London, too. He reflected back to an evening a year ago when he'd struck a "bargain" over a tiny, blue-eyed waif he'd later made a duchess, and found himself grinning.

The woman riding beside him, he mused as he looked at the perfect, delicate profile of his wife, had proven more of a bargain than any of them had ever suspected. She was a born lady, dignified and regal in her bearing, and able to pass the true test of her station: she commanded the love and respect of those beneath her as well as those of her own class, effortlessly putting at ease all those around her. Why, even that old harridan, Margaret, was beginning to come around. She'd shocked them all just the other day by inviting Ashleigh to tea, whereupon she'd presented the new mother with a beautiful silver cup she'd had engraved for Marileigh, saying the birth of a new Westmont was worthy of a healing of their differences. And by the time the tea was over, she was clearly trying to become Ashleigh's friend. Such was the power to charm, of his lady wife!

Brett laughed at himself with a sudden realization. He hadn't made her a duchess! She had come to him already formed in that mold; he'd only set to rights what fate had seen misplaced. And thank God he had, he reminded himself soberly. Thank God he had!

"I'll race you to that copse of trees over there," said Ashleigh, breaking his reverie.

"You think you have a prayer of winning, do you?"

She eyed the picnic hamper he had fastened to Raven's saddle, then saucily ran her gaze over his form. "Raven may be the more powerful horse, but he's carrying more weight. I refer not only to our victuals, but to a certain... ah, good-sized.. muscular male body. I may win, Your Grace."

Brett drew his mount even with hers. "Oh, and what will Her Grace have as a prize if she wins?"

A slow grin emerged on Ashleigh's face. "She would have you agree to... an experiment I have in mind."

A chestnut eyebrow shot upward. "Without knowing its nature in advance?"

She shrugged, the grin still in place. "'Tis only if she wins, Your Grace."

It was Brett's turn to grin. "And if *I* win?"

"You've only to name your prize now."

He shook his head, his eyes meeting hers with a look of amused mischief. "I think I'll name it later."

A frown and then a pout.

"'Tis only if I win," he mimicked, grinning at her again. 'Now, shall we race? Begin on the count of three. One...two..."

They took off in unison, their superbly bred horses eager to flex their muscles, each game for the win. Out of the corner of her eye Ashleigh saw Raven beside her, but beginning to nose ahead, and she leaned forward, bending low over Irish Night's neck to urge her on. The little filly responded with an additional burst of speed and began to draw ahead of the stallion.

"That's it," Ashleigh crooned to the filly. "Good girl, we can do it!" She crouched even lower, a tricky thing on a sidesaddle, but she wished to provide as little wind resistance as possible, for Brett had just asked the stallion for more speed and was getting it, the powerful horse closing the gap between them.

Continuing to murmur words of encouragement to the filly, Ashleigh let her have her head. It was just what the game little horse wanted. She shot out ahead of Raven by more than a length, and a quick glance over her shoulder told Ashleigh this came as a total surprise to Brett. But then she saw her husband hunch forward and ask the stallion for more, and she had no time to do anything but see to her mount; Irish Night, who had somehow understood Raven's challenge, was lengthening her strides even more in an all-out effort to win.

And then it happened. The sidesaddle swung crazily downward, around the filly's girth, and at that instant Ashleigh was certain she was about to hit the ground and die. But her instincts saved her. Preventing what could easily have been a fatal fall, she grabbed the racing filly about the neck and held on.

Behind her she could hear Brett shouting, but couldn't focus on what he said as she concentrated on holding on and not thinking about the ground flying by under the filly's pounding hooves. The loose saddle was bumping against her belly and thighs, and the muscles of her shoulders began to burn with a searing pain, her arms feeling as if they were about to be torn from their sockets, but still, she managed to cling to the filly's neck, and to life itself.

She thought she sensed, on her left, her husband drawing alongside her on the stallion, thought she heard him shouting some instructions, but before she could assimilate this, the sidesaddle gave way completely, dropping to the ground that reverberated with beating hooves. She felt Irish Night's powerful neck pull sharply to the right and heard the filly's shriek of fright as she veered to escape the falling saddle. Ashleigh screamed as her arms were wrenched loose from the lathered neck, and then, suddenly, there was nothing at all as blackness wiped out the day.

Ashleigh floated aimlessly in a black void, unable to comprehend where she was, or why she was there, but all around her she sensed imminent danger. Then a flood of moonlight pushed the shadows away, and she was on the little balcony at the dowager's cottage. Something seemed to be pushing her toward the railing, and as she moved toward it, it broke away, leaving a gaping hole. She screamed and drew backward, only to find herself thrown onto the saddle of a racing horse. Knowing she must somehow not trust the safety of her perch, she leaned over her mount's neck, intent upon grasping it, but suddenly the horse dissolved beneath her, saddle and all, leaving her once again in the black void, and this time she was falling, falling. . . .

"*Ashleigh, don't!*" Brett's voice came to her out of the darkness, and she struggled to open her eyes.

"Dear God, sweetheart, please don't scream! It's all right. You're here, with me, my darling, and you're *safe*! I have you, and you're *safe*!"

Ashleigh opened her eyes to find Brett bending over her with an anxious look on his face. Behind him, above his head, she saw leafy green branches interspersed with small patches of blue sky and the air about them was filled with the friendly chirping of birds.

"Brett . . . ?"

She saw him close his eyes briefly, as if to shut out some unbearable image, and then open them again as he smiled down at her.

"Thank God you're back," he whispered.

"Back?"

"You blacked out just as I was able to pull you to safety when that damned saddle fell." Brett forced his words past grimly tightened lips and paled visibly before continuing. "You've been unconscious for a good ten minutes or so. Oh God, Ashleigh, I've been so worried!" Turquoise eyes searched her face. "How do you feel, love?"

Ashleigh managed to summon a smile. She was here, and she was alive, and Brett's strong, comforting presence chased the ghosts of her nightmare away. "I—I feel surprisingly fine, actually...now." Her eyes darkened as she recalled the images in her dream, and she realized it was these, more than the narrow escape she'd had, that had the power to frighten her. "Did...did I really scream before, Brett? I mean, if I did, I'm terribly sorry. I know it must have sounded aw—"

Strong arms lifted her upward as Brett drew her to him in a tight embrace. "Hush!" he whispered hoarsely. "And don't ever apologize for showing me your emotions, sweetheart," he murmured into her hair, "no matter what form they take! You were unspeakably frightened and had every reason in the world to *be* frightened. I won't have you denying your right to voice such feelings—not now, not ever!"

Ashleigh closed her eyes and tightened her arms about Brett's waist, basking in the utter comfort and security she felt in his arms. There was a time when, despite the presence of friends such as Dorcas and Megan, she'd forced herself to hide her fears, dragging them out to face alone when she was able, burying them in forgotten places when she was not. But now, because of the presence of this man she loved, she realized she'd never have to do that again. Oh, life was such a miracle when it was shared!

She proceeded to tell him, then, of the dream she'd had before regaining consciousness; her voice was steady as she spoke, reflecting none of the terror of her first recollection. When she finished, Brett loosened his embrace, holding her gently in the circle of his arms as he looked down at her.

"Brett, what is it?" she questioned, for there was a clouded look in his eyes that hadn't been there before.

Brett wrestled with himself, debating whether to tell her what he'd learned—and what was foremost on his mind now that she'd underscored it with the story of her dream.

After he'd miraculously been able to pull her off Irish Night, and once he'd pulled both horses to a halt, he'd circled back to inspect the sidesaddle as it lay on the ground. Even at the distance afforded by his perch on horseback, he clearly saw the evidence he'd feared: the saddle's cinch belt had been tampered with! Someone had sawed at its underside with a sharp instrument, not enough to sever it completely, just enough to weaken it so that it would give way at a critical moment—in all probability, when the filly was being ridden hard!

What Brett had suspected the morning after Ashleigh's close call on the balcony was now confirmed: *Someone was trying to kill his wife!* And whoever it was, wasn't even being very subtle about it at this point—it would have stood to reason that any saddle accident would have warranted an inspection of the tack of Ashleigh's mount. The would-be killer hadn't even cared!

But now, in the split second that all these thoughts replayed themselves in Brett's mind, he focused on an additional problem: How much should he tell Ashleigh? Would warning her of the danger she was in help make her safer? Would it really offset the hazard of instilling her with the worst kind of fear—a fear for her life—that she'd be forced to live with until the villain was found out? Praying he was right, and vowing to catch the would-be murderer before he could strike again, Brett made his choice.

"It's nothing, love," he told her. "I merely took a moment to reflect on what happened—on what *might* have happened if I hadn't been in time to—"

"*Shh!*" Ashleigh interrupted as she threw her arms about his neck and hugged him fiercely. "You *were* in time! That's all that matters!"

Brett held her close, and prayed she was right—that he'd be there to protect her until the evildoer was caught. His brain tripped with ideas on how to go about catching whoever the scum was, while he silently vowed not to let Ashleigh out of his sight—or that of some discreet guards he would appoint—until this happened.

Ashleigh again succumbed to his soothing embrace, her fears truly behind her now. She opened her eyes and noted for the first time that they were in a small clearing in a heavily wooded glen of sorts, and she reflected that he must have carried her into the wooded area she'd spotted in the distance as they'd raced. Nearby, Irish Night and Raven cropped calmly at some lush grasses that lined a half-hidden brook of bright, clear water.

Withdrawing a bit, she smiled brightly at her husband. "Oh, Brett, what a lovely place this is! How did you ever find it?"

Glad to see her acting more herself, Brett smiled. "I used to come here often when I was a lad. Sometimes it was because I needed a respite from the strictures of my daily schedule." He reached out to finger a shining lock of the raven hair that had come undone from its ribbon. "Sometimes, because I needed to think." He bent to brush his lips tantalizingly across hers. "And sometimes it was to have a picnic—by myself, of course, on food coaxed out of cook or Mrs. Busby—I've never brought anyone else here—until now." His eyes met hers and held.

A delicious shiver rippled the length of Ashleigh's frame as she allowed him to press her gently down upon the soft green grass. "This place has meant something special to you over the years, hasn't it?" she whispered. "This beautiful little glen in the woods. I feel honored that you're sharing it with me."

Brett shook his head slowly as his fingers undid the buttons of her bodice, his gaze never leaving her face. "Oh, no, my love," he whispered throatily, "the honor is mine . . . but the pleasure, ah, the pleasure shall be yours. . . ."

A mischievous twinkle danced in Ashleigh's sapphire eyes as his hands cupped the fullness of her breasts. *Not "yours alone," my lusty husband,* she thought as she felt herself capitulate to the magic of his knowing hands, *for this time I mean to pleasure* you *as much as you do* me!

Brett caught the look in her eyes and wondered at it, then bent to give one saucy nipple a playful nip through the fine cambric of her shift.

"All right, wench!" he laughed as his attention drifted to her parted, half-smiling lips, "What are you up to, hmm?" Bracing himself above her with his hands on the grass on each side of her head, he gave her a wicked grin, then rolled to the side, pulling her on top of him and drawing her hips against his with hands that clasped the rounded curves of her buttocks.

"*Oh!*" Ashleigh gasped, feeling the bold stirring of his passion against the juncture of her thighs, even through the linen of her riding skirt.

But she had little time to say more, for Brett's hands moved upward, stroking the length of her before gently cupping her head and bringing her mouth to his for a kiss that robbed her of breath.

It was an utterly sensual kiss, beginning with his warm lips moving over hers from side to side, lazily, deliberately, his tongue gliding temptingly along the seam between. His thumbs underscored this rhythm, tracing lazy circles along her temples while his fingers laced through the thick hair behind her ears.

Then his tongue gently sought and gained entrance, advancing ever so carefully between her teeth, grazing them, then tempting the tip of her own with its touch.

At this, Ashleigh shuddered, feeling the rush of something familiarly warm and moist at her core. Brett guessed at her reaction, his soft, knowing laughter eclipsing her rapid intake of breath while his mouth moved to her ear and a hand once again stroked and cupped her buttocks.

"Ah, little one . . . sweet, beloved wife," he murmured as he turned them so they were facing each other on their sides, and his free hand moved back to her half-exposed breasts. "You're always so ready for me, darling. Here . . . see?" he murmured as he undid the lacing of her shift and a pair of hard-tipped, thrusting breasts spilled free. "See how you peak for me here, love?'' he questioned. "See how your lovely body tells me you want me?''

Ashleigh felt his questing fingers graze the thrusting peaks he spoke of and softly moaned her passion against his lips, lips that nibbled and played with her own, teasing, tantalizing even as his fingers did the same below.

But then she forced herself to pause a moment while she pondered his words. *Yes, my darling,* she thought, *you know how to tell when I want you, but I, too, can read the signs of passion.*

Carefully, cautiously, not wanting to err in the execution of her plan, she trailed her hands lightly down his muscled back and then around and between their two bodies until at last she found her courage and placed one small palm over Brett's hard, throbbing shaft.

"Wha—?'' her husband questioned, then groaned as nimble fingers traced the bulging length of his maleness through the cloth of the riding breeches. *"Ashleigh,"* he rasped, "for God's sake, *Ashleigh*!''

But his wife only smiled deliciously, looking at him through half-closed lids as she continued her experiment.

"You little vixen!'' Brett gasped, but as he would have said more, he felt her fingers undoing the fastenings of his breeches, and with a groan more desperate than before, he rolled with her until she lay beneath him.

"Witch!'' he murmured as he buried his face in her hair.

Ashleigh twisted until she could see his face. "But Brett, I was only trying to see if I could do to you, what you do to me,'' she explained, innocence evident in her wide-eyed gaze.

Brett managed a chuckle. "Oh, little one,'' he breathed, "if you only knew what you do to me without even *trying*!''

"But if I don't experiment with something more, how will I ever keep you when I grow old, when my beauty fades?''

With gentle laughter, he cupped her face between his hands and bent to place on her parted lips a kiss that was fraught with tenderness.

"Oh, little love,'' he murmured as he raised his head and gazed deeply into her eyes, "don't you know the way I feel about you has more to do with who you *are* than with how you *appear*? Always, even when I am an old, old man, and you, a little snowy-haired angel, I shall want you ... because it isn't your perfect beauty I fell in love with—although, I'll admit, it did much to open the door at first.

"But Ashleigh, my darling, it's the *you* that's *inside* that draws me far more than all your lovely physical charms. It's your heart and soul that draw me to you, sweetheart. It's like you're the other half of me ... of my heart, my own soul ... and that will always be, with no amount of infirm flesh or silvered hair to change it."

He shifted his weight and reached down to take both her hands in his. Turning them over, he bent to place a kiss, almost reverently, in the palm of each before gently folding her fingers and then drawing her closed fists to his heart.

"Love took almost half a lifetime to reach me, Ashleigh," he continued softly. "Do you think that something as superficial as physical beauty—or its loss—would ever cause me to cast it aside? Ah, no, my love. I shall love you beyond time ... I shall love you forever."

The blue of Ashleigh's eyes deepened, yet they sparkled, becoming two midnight prisms where light and shadow mixed, and he thought their brilliance put the stars to shame. "And that's how I love you, my darling," she whispered.

But then a glint of mischief shone from beneath her thick, dusky lashes. "Brett ... ?" She grinned as her audacious hands began to slide under his shirt.

"Aye, minx?" he answered, catching his breath as she began to remove the shirt.

"What if I weren't to, um, experiment in order to learn ways to hold your love ... ?" The shirt was pushed down, off his shoulders. "But, instead, for the sake of ..." The shirt found its way to the grass beside them. "Of giving you pleasure? Would that be so wrong?" Her slender fingers wound through the matted chestnut hair on his chest, then found the flat male nipples and began to stroke and entice them.

With a shudder, Brett fell back and threw one arm across his forehead, then took a deep breath before answering her.

"That would be like carrying coals to Newcastle, love. Just *being* with you, *touching* you, already affords me so much pleasure, I—" He gasped as Ashleigh's delicate fingers completed the undoing of his britches.

"Ashleigh, love, I beg of you!" he rasped. "Do you want this loving to be over before it's begun?" With a fierce growl, he wrapped his arms about her small frame and rolled with her until she was trapped beneath him.

"I—I don't understand!" she stammered. "These are the things you do to me!"

"Little innocent," he said softly, looking adoringly into her eyes. "No, I suppose you don't understand...yet...but I think I can demonstrate better than tell you."

"Demonstr—?"

But her words got no further as his hands began to move over her body, gliding over all the treasured parts of her as lightly as a butterfly's touch, sliding over, slipping between her heated flesh until she began to writhe and twist in his arms, begging him to take her.

But Brett only shook his head and smiled, taking his time, and further arousing her passion with caresses that were deliberate and slow.

One by one, the pieces of clothing she wore joined his shirt on the ground, until she lay moaning on the lush grass, wearing only her delicate shift, which had been deftly raised from below, until it bunched about her waist—it was long since lowered from above—so that her aching breasts spilled free for his touch.

By now Ashleigh was a frenzied, twisting, wild thing, crying out to him, pleading sharply with him, begging to be taken. But Brett continued at a measured, studied pace, gently pressing her hands to the grass on either side of her while his mouth took over what his practiced hands had begun.

Each rosy-tipped breast succumbed to the magic as he traced circles about her nipples, languidly, magically, before finally taking them, first one, and then the other, into his mouth to suckle.

"*Brett!*" she cried, driven half out of her mind with an aching, pulsing longing at her core.

"No, love," he murmured as his mouth and tongue began to work their way lower, to her tiny waist, her flat abdomen, her navel, her twisting hips and trembling thighs, "for I mean to show you how it is when pleasure is heaped upon pleasure...."

Then she felt his lips brush the soft triangle of hair that covered her woman's mound. Startled, she would have stopped him, but he held her hands firmly at her sides. Frantically she tried to twist away. *This was so intimate! This was so—!*

But then she could no longer think at all. Her husband's tongue found the delicate bud above the entrance to her throbbing femininity and began to stroke... and stroke again....

Suddenly Ashleigh was mindless with pleasure as wave after wave of it washed over her and through her, making her shudder and convulse with each deft pass of his tongue. She became a delirious mass of sensation, sobbing out her pleasure, crying out her love for him as she came, again, and again, and again.

At last he heeded her cries and released her hands as his head returned to hover over her ecstatic face, watching her, loving her, glorying in the pleasure he could bring her.

Ashleigh opened her eyes and sanity returned for one full heartbeat as her gaze locked with his. Then, with a cry, she moved her hand downward and found him, and her fingers closed over him.

Brett shuddered and shifted his weight, taking her fiercely, carrying her swiftly with him into a maelstrom of frenzied, thrashing ecstasy that finally burst and showered about them, making them one as they'd never been before.

It was a long time later, a *very* long time later, before the two of them could even move, or feel, or think.

Ashleigh was the first to break the spell. "Brett?" she whispered.

Brett blinked twice before opening his eyes to gaze lovingly down into hers—oh, so blue, and heavy-lidded now with sated passion. "Aye, love?"

"I...I never knew pleasure could be...almost too much," she sighed.

He chuckled, then raised Ashleigh's limp, delicate hand to his lips and planted a kiss on the fingertips. "That was part of my...lesson, yes," he said, "but I doubt if a woman could ever really have too much pleasure. But sweetheart—" He raised himself up on his elbows, but Ashleigh noted he made no move to disengage their lower bodies, which were still intimately joined. "Ashleigh, with a *man*, it *could* be too much."

"It *could*?" she whispered, her blue eyes as round as saucers.

Brett nodded, then smiled. "Do you remember how it felt when my tongue made you shudder with pleasure, love?"

A blush suffused her already glowing face. "I...I remember," she whispered shyly.

Brett smiled, then reached to claim her lips for a soft kiss. "Well, love," he explained, "what happened to you then is exactly what happens to me when...I spill my seed. Are you aware of that?"

"I...I never thought of it that way, but I suppose it's true because, in the past it's happened to me when we've made love, and I've felt you giving me your seed at about the same time."

Brett laughed softly, delighted by her innocence despite the fact that she'd already borne him a child, delighted further to be her teacher in the ways of how it is between a man and a woman.

"But Brett!" Ashleigh suddenly withdrew the fingertips he'd been playfully nibbling and touched them to her own lips in a gesture of wonder. "This time it wasn't—" She paused, blushing. "That is, this time, when it happened to me, *you* weren't *inside* me yet...and it—it didn't happen to you until later, when—when you *were*!" She finished with a lowering of her lashes, embarrassed to be speaking of such intimacy.

Brett tipped her small chin gently upward until she was forced to look at him.

"That's true," he smiled, "but you had your pleasure anyway, again and again."

Mutely she nodded, wondering what he was getting at.

"Such is the advantage of the female body over the male, love," he explained, a tender smile on his face. "I pleasured you again and again, and still you were ready to repeat your pleasure when at last we joined—all in a matter of minutes, I might add.

"But how would it have been if *you* had pleasured *me* in, ah, similar fashion?" Noting her wide-eyed questioning look, he couldn't help grinning and planting a soft kiss on the tip of her straight little nose. "It would have been over in an instant, my sweet. I'd have had my pleasure—not to be repeated for some passage of time—and you'd have been left to have yours alone."

Ashleigh's eyes widened with dawning comprehension. "Ohh," she breathed, "you mean that a man—"

"Exactly, my sweet innocent," he nodded.

There were several seconds of silence as Ashleigh digested this fact. Then a tenuous smile played across her lips. "But, Brett . . ." she ventured thoughtfully.

"Mmm?" he murmured, his gaze intent upon her ripe, love-bruised lips.

"It must be possible for a woman to learn, somehow, how to be . . . er . . . *active* in pleasuring her man without going too far, don't you think? I mean—"

A burst of delighted laughter met her ears. But then Brett quickly sobered at her look of chagrin. "Forgive me, love," he told her. "It wasn't you I was laughing at. It was the delight I found at your quick, ever-discerning mind!" He bent and kissed her with some passion, fully on the mouth.

"Yes, my love," he whispered happily when he'd released her eager lips, "there *are* ways to learn how to . . . pace yourself in your . . . attentions . . ."

"Ohh," she breathed, fully cognizant of the growing hunger in his gaze, feeling his manhood stir as it lay still buried within her. "Then will you teach me how?"

A slow, tantalizing nod was her answer as her husband's eyes locked with hers. And then all talking ceased.

# Chapter Forty

'H appy birthday, love," Brett whispered as he bent over the drowsy form of his wife in the bed. He watched her stir and murmur something unintelligible as she sought to burrow deeper into the bedclothes. He smiled. His wife was one of those rare women who looked just as beautiful in the morning as she did during the rest of the day—perhaps more so. She lay there with her magnificent ebony tresses charmingly tousled, her rosy lips barely parted with quiet breathing, her creamy skin lightly flushed, looking for all the world like an elfin princess sent to show mortals how short of beauty's mark they fell.

"I say, sweet slugabed, how does it feel to be quit of your teen years?" he persisted, then grinned as he put his lips to one perfect, shell-like ear. "Or were our ardors of last night too much for one of such a vast, advanced age!"

*"Advanced age!"* came the reply as Ashleigh's blue eyes snapped open and flashed her disbelief that he could have said such a thing.

Brett chuckled and bent to kiss her parted lips. "I love to tease you, I'm afraid." He grinned. "Your eyes turn the most incredible shade of blue when you're vexed."

Ashleigh affected a mock pout. "Nevertheless, Your Grace, twas an ungentlemanly thing to say, even if it was in jest." Her lips curved into a small smile. "Besides, you say the same thing about the color of my eyes when I'm . . . when we've . . ." She blushed, lowering her lashes against his amused gaze.

"When we've just finished making love and you're de
ciously sated?"

The blush deepened and she nodded, making her husba
laugh lightly as he sat on the bed and drew her into his arm
"Ah, but, little one, *that* is a different shade of blue entirel
Trust me, and you must, for it is one that only I have seen." H
hands moved deliciously over her bare shoulders, for her th
night rail lay on the carpet where he'd discarded it last night.

Responding instantly to his knowing touch, Ashleigh felt
shiver course through her; she threw her arms about his necl
seeking his mouth.

A long minute later, when the kiss finally ended, Brett mu
mured huskily into her ear, "If you kiss me like that agaii
love, we're going to spend your entire birthday in bed."

Suddenly Ashleigh withdrew, turning her head to glance :
the clock on the mantelpiece. "Good Heavens, it's after ten!'
she exclaimed. "I promised Lady Margaret I'd meet her at th
cottage before noon! And I haven't even selected my dress fc
the luncheon!"

The invitation to the luncheon she spoke of had come as
startling surprise. A note delivered the day before yesterday b
a footman from Cloverhill Manor, invited her and the duke t
the Hastings estate for a luncheon in honor of her birthday, an
it had been personally penned by *Elizabeth Hastings*! She'
been hard-pressed to fathom this about-face attitude in her ol
nemesis, for the note had been full of cordiality and languag
that strongly implied Lady Elizabeth wished to let bygones b
bygones and was using Ashleigh's birthday as an occasion t
begin healing their differences.

Always willing to make friendships where none had existe
before, however, Ashleigh had decided to accept Elizabeth'
offer at face value and attend. She had, of course, discussed th
matter with Brett and Mary, both of whom conceded that sh
was probably right in her decision, but urged her to maintaii
caution regarding what ultimately transpired between her an
their blond neighbor.

Margaret, however, had been enthusiastic and encouragin;
when she'd joined her for tea later that afternoon, saying, "M;

ear, of course you must accept Elizabeth's olive branch! Af-
r all, if you and I could mend our fences and become friends,
hy shouldn't you be able to do the same with my dear god-
aughter? I thoroughly wish for the two of you to become fast
iends, and I just know you will—I just *know* it!'' Then she
ad gone on to invite Ashleigh to join her in traveling to Clo-
erhill Manor on the day of the luncheon, saying that if the
eather was fair, she would be going there in the skiff and she'd
ver so much appreciate Ashleigh's company when she rowed—
lso implying, subtly, that Ashleigh ought to regard this as an
onor; she only invited those nearest and dearest to her for a
emonstration of her rowing skills, ''a sport I excelled in as a
oung woman and can still accomplish with pride, my dear, I
ssure you!''

A delicious nuzzling at her ear brought Ashleigh back to the
resent, and it was only then she noticed the coverlet had
ropped to her lap and Brett's hands were cupping her breasts,
is thumbs brushing their suddenly hardened peaks.

''Ohh,'' she moaned, feeling the familiar tightening in the pit
f her belly, ''but Brett . . . the luncheon . . .''

''Damn the luncheon!'' he growled, a hand moving to her
are, rounded, little buttocks and then testing the gathering
noisture in the juncture below as he joined her on the bed. . . .

The tall-case clock at the foot of the stairs was striking eleven
vhen the two of them were finally able to remember what day
t was, and that they had obligations that wouldn't wait.

For Brett's part, he knew the afternoon was destined to hold
nuch more than a luncheon. He'd been sworn to secrecy by
Elizabeth and Margaret, who were actually holding a surprise
party for Ashleigh, involving all-day festivities, including a
panquet and, later tonight, a ball. The two had come to him
several days ago with their plan, saying they were genuinely
contrite over their past behavior toward his bride and wished
o stage this celebration as a means of making amends. Most of
he *ton* was to be in attendance, they'd told him, and since the
duchess was fast becoming a darling of that set, how could he
refuse to help them?

Weighing their words carefully, Brett had at last agreed. H
still wasn't sure he trusted this turnabout on Elizabeth's par
she was a patently rigid person, too molded by the narrowne:
of her upbringing to make major reversals. Moreover, he hadn
entirely dismissed her as a candidate for whoever it was that ha
made the vicious attacks on Ashleigh's life, although he kne
that if his former fiancée was behind them, she had most ce
tainly hired some blackguard to do the actual dirty work; Eliz
abeth was too daintily squeamish to soil her own hands.

Thoughts of the danger Ashleigh was in caused Brett to dra
his wife more tightly into his arms, fitting her replete bod
closely against his, while his mouth formed a grim line and th
turquoise eyes grew hard.

It had been several days since the harrowing accident on Iris
Night, and during the interim he'd taken several steps towar
ensuring Ashleigh's safety, and one significant step towar
catching the culprit. Ashleigh didn't know it, but from the tim
she left their rooms in the morning until the minute he es
corted her back upstairs each evening, a pair of Old Henry':
most trusted grooms discreetly watched her every movement
Moreover, her ladies' maid, Annie, a young woman whose
honesty Jameson and Mrs. Busby swore to—and whom he
doubly trusted for the way she had always seemed to adore he:
mistress—had been set to guard their chambers when he and
Ashleigh weren't there, to make sure no one tampered with
anything that might result in harm to the duchess. And
guards—footmen handpicked by the Busbys—were stationed
in the kitchens, to watch carefully the preparation of He:
Grace's food and drink, while yet others kept round-the-clock
watch over the stables, paying particular attention to all the
carriages Her Grace might use, as well as to Irish Night and he:
tack.

Then there was the matter of flushing the villain out. On their
way to Ravensford Hall at this very moment were Lieutenant
George Hodges and his sister-in-law, Mildred Hodges. The
lieutenant was a specialist in naval intelligence, a highly trained
spy. He was also one of Brett's closest associates in the Admiralty. His younger brother had been, too, but Mildred Hodges's

usband had been killed five years ago in Belgium, on an as-
ignment for the Crown. Three months later the diminutive
brunette had arrived at the Admiralty on the arm of her
brother-in-law, asking to be trained as a spy; there had been a
vengeful look in her eyes, but the overall impression had been
one of intelligence and cool control before her late husband's
superiors, and her request was granted. A year later she com-
menced a four-year career that saw her become one of His
Majesty's most valued agents.

Brett relaxed his grip on Ashleigh somewhat as he considered Mildred's expertise. Through a few carefully staged ma-
neuvers in which the petite woman would dress in Ashleigh's
clothes and masquerade as his wife, the three of them, he felt
sure, would flush the bloody bastard out!

Feeling him relax against her, Ashleigh turned in his arms
and smiled languidly. "You really oughtn't become too comfortable, darling. You promised to drive Mary to the luncheon
in your phaeton, and I'm due at Lady Margaret's in less than
an hour."

Brett was reaching for his jacket and, more specifically, for
the small package in its pocket—a package that had been delivered yesterday through a special order he'd placed in London weeks ago. At the mention of Lady Margaret, he hesitated,
examining his feelings about his grandfather's twin. He'd been
greatly heartened by her overtures to Ashleigh in the past few
weeks. God knew, no one wished, more than he, for the entire
world to love and accept his wife, and it had been a relief to see
that old harridan's heart warm to her.

But he was also skeptical of this sudden change in the
woman. New baby or no, it just wasn't like Margaret to resign
herself to something she'd been opposed to for so long, much
less embrace it. He sighed. Margaret, too, was not entirely
above suspicion.

Nothing, he reminded himself, could lull him into taking any
chances when his precious wife's safety was at stake. That was
why young Jonathan Busby and Tom Blecker, the master carpenter who'd repaired the broken railings at the dowager's
cottage, were stationed there right now—in pretense of mend-

ing a garden fence; in actuality, they were to protect Ashleigh at all costs.

"What's wrong, darling?" Ashleigh questioned as she saw him hesitate.

Brett forced himself to appear relaxed and smiled at her. "Not a thing in the world, love—except that I haven't given you your birthday gift yet." He picked up his jacket and withdrew the package from its pocket. "Here," he said softly as he placed it in her hand. "Happy birthday, love."

Ashleigh's eyes sparkled as she examined the small bundle. Then she peered at it more closely, curious. "Why, it's wrapped in—" her fingers carefully pried the outer wrapping loose "—some kind of document!"

"Oh, that...yes," Brett acknowledged. "Actually—"

"*Oh, Brett!*" Ashleigh squealed excitedly. "Oh, it's a certificate of ownership—of Irish Night?" She looked up at him, incredulous. "I—I cannot believe... *It has my name on it!*"

"Of course it has, goose," he chuckled. "Don't they usually place the owner's name on the space where—"

An embrace that, from any larger person, would have been a bone-crusher, cut him short. "Oh, Brett!" Ashleigh cried, "I've never had a better gift!"

Brett held her close, delighting in her exuberance, marveling at how easy she was to please. "She's been yours all along, Ashleigh," he murmured against her hair, noting for the dozenth time that morning how it smelled like fresh rainwater and violets. "I wanted to give you this paper when we got married."

At this, Ashleigh sobered and withdrew to look at him. "And I spoiled everything by being frightened off like a scared rabbit, by not trusting you and—"

Gentle fingers closed her lips. "Hush, love," he murmured. "We both made mistakes in those days. But we love each other, and the past is behind us. And I'll not have you troubling yourself about any of it—especially on your birthday!"

Ashleigh kissed the strong, tanned fingers at her lips and smiled tremulously while tears misted her eyes. "Oh, Brett, I love you so very much!"

"And I you, Ashleigh...forever." Suddenly he grinned. "Now, aren't you going to open the box the paper was wrapped around?"

Ashleigh blinked. She'd been so caught up in the perfect moment between them, she'd forgotten about it! Hastily she flipped up the lid of the small black box. Then she gasped.

There, lying against a bed of deep blue velvet, lay a huge oval sapphire pendant, surrounded by diamonds. It was a piece of jewelry fit for a queen.

"Oh, Brett," she breathed, her hands trembling as she only half dared to touch the delicate gold chain attached to the pendant, "it—it takes my breath away!"

"And the woman who'll wear it robs me of mine," he told her quietly. "Here, love," he added, helping her extract the neck piece from the box, "let's see you with it on."

He rose and helped her from the bed, then guided her toward the large cheval glass near the door to the dressing room. Once there, he faced her toward it and, positioning himself behind her, fastened the chain about her throat.

They were both silent for a long moment as Brett stepped back a pace and viewed her image.

She stood there wearing nothing at all, save his gift. Her shiny black hair tumbled down her slim back and over slender, creamy shoulders that appeared even fairer in contrast, and her sweetly curving lips were tinted the color of wine from his kisses. The stones of the pendant, as it nestled in the crevice between her lush breasts, sparkled and winked reflections of sunlight, yet he found these poor rivals for the light shining in her eyes. Slowly the words of Byron's poem took shape in his mind, and he whispered:

"She walks in beauty like the night
Of cloudless climes and starry skies;
And all that's best of dark and bright
Meet in her aspect and her eyes."

Ashleigh barely breathed as she heard him murmur the

words, then watched as he bent to place a kiss at her neck where the delicate chain touched it.

"Thank you," she whispered when he'd raised his head and found her gaze in the mirror.

The mantel clock chimed the quarter hour and broke the spell.

"*Damn!*" Brett swore, glancing at the time. "I'd better leave you to your toilette, sweet," he told her with a rueful grin. "If you hurry, you might just be in time for the old witch's rowing exhibition."

"Brett!" she chided as he kissed her cheek and turned to leave. "I'll admit Lady Margaret may have warranted such epithets in the past, but she's been so thoughtful and sweet lately. The least we can do is respond in kind. She's really just a poor, lonely old woman deserving of some kindness, you know."

"Sorry, love." He grinned. "I'll try to mind my tongue in the future. Well, I'm off. See you at the Manor. Hurry, or you'll miss the boat." He gave her an affectionate swat on the buttocks and left.

A few minutes later he found his mother in the library.

"Brett, dear," she said after accepting his kiss on her cheek, "I realize I'd asked you to drive me to the party, but the children are planning a pageant to present at Cloverhill Manor before the ball—in honor of our birthday lady—and Aldo asked if I couldn't remain to supervise a final rehearsal before leaving. I can have one of the grooms drive me over in the barouche in a short while. Do you mind?"

"No, of course not." Brett grinned. "Those little ones certainly adore Ashleigh, don't they?"

"We all do," she said.

*Not quite all,* was the ominous thought that crossed his mind, but he pushed it away as he glanced at Mary who was looking beautiful in a turquoise voile Empire day gown that brought out the turquoise flecks in her eyes. "You look lovely, Mother," he murmured appreciatively.

"Thank you, *caro*." She smiled. "Now, run along, and do not worry about me. I shall make the festivities in plenty of time, and, from what I understand, Elizabeth needs you."

Brett reflected on the note that had arrived yesterday, begging him to arrive early and help Elizabeth keep her father sober so that he wouldn't "spoil our fun." His mouth straightened into a grim line as he pondered the task that lay ahead of him. Perhaps he'd just assign a couple of footmen to lock the blighter in his room and keep him there until the festivities were over!

When Brett had gone, Mary rushed up to the schoolroom on the third floor and witnessed a perfectly executed pageant in which Alessandra and Georgio were decked out as the king and queen of the fairies, Oberon and Titania—Aldo had just finished reading Shakespeare's *A Midsummer Night's Dream*. The two were meant to represent Ashleigh and Brett. Alessandra had black hair and blue eyes and wore a replica of one of the duchess's gowns while Georgio, the only one of the boys with chestnut-colored hair, did his best to emulate the duke as he postured with a bold, masculine stride he hoped all would recognize.

Praising them for their work, Mary told them she would see them all at seven that evening, when Old Henry and one of the grooms would drive them to Cloverhill Manor. Then she hurried downstairs to summon the barouche.

But as she arrived at the foot of the staircase leading to the front hall, she spied a solitary, gray-clad figure standing there. At first glance, she didn't recognize the woman, but then the footman on duty came forward from his post—where he'd been hidden by one of a pair of tall Jacobean chests that flanked the entryway.

"Lady Jane Hastings to see Her Grace, mum. I told her Her Grace was not at home, but—"

"Why, Lady Jane! Of course!" exclaimed Mary. "How do you do, my dear?"

Jane Hastings looked frightened for a moment. She stood there in the richly appointed hallway, wearing a somber gray frock that appeared to have been made for a fashion that had passed out of date thirty years earlier. In her hands she clutched a carved ivory casket that was about the size of a breadbox.

"Lady Jane?" Mary questioned. "I'm Mary...ah, Westmont. Don't you know me?"

Hazel eyes met hers, but whereas Mary's were bright and gaily flecked with shards that matched her dress, Jane's were somber and apprehensive.

Finally the drably dressed little woman spoke. "Mary... yes...I remember...you were kind to me once...." Suddenly her eyes flashed a hint of emotion. "But *they* weren't kind to *you*! *They* weren't kind to you...either."

"You wished to see my daughter-in-law, did you?" Mary questioned. She smiled at the woman she had pitied many years ago, hoping to dispel the fear that still lurked in her eyes. "I'm afraid Ashleigh has gone on ahead...ah, to the party. You'll see her back at the Manor if you hurry." She glanced over Jane's shoulder, to the windows beside the door, and thought she saw a carriage waiting in the drive.

"Oh, dear!" said Jane. "Oh, no! Oh, that might be too late!" She glanced down at the ivory box she now clutched to her ample bosom, then back at Mary. "I...have this gift for her, you see." She glanced furtively in the direction of the footman who had returned to his post, then added in a whisper, *"It could save her life!"*

Mary made an effort to quell the grip of terror that clutched at her heart. Brett had taken her into his confidence regarding the attempts on Ashleigh's life after the riding accident, but made her promise not to tell Ashleigh, stating his well-pondered reasons, and Mary had reluctantly agreed. She'd privately felt her daughter-in-law was more than up to dealing with such information; she had watched her grow in strength and maturity herself, after all, and she was not inclined to underestimate Ashleigh's fortitude. But Brett had insisted, and she'd been forced to agree. The last thing she wanted to be was a meddling mother-in-law!

But now, as she heard Lady Jane's fearfully whispered words, she wondered if she might help in another way.

"Lady Jane, is there something in that box that the duchess should be aware of?" she ventured cautiously.

The hazel eyes searched her own for a long moment. Then Jane nodded, before thrusting the casket toward the woman she remembered as one who'd befriended her years ago. "Here," she stated emphatically. "You might know how to help her...you...were a lot like her in those days."

Mary accepted the box, then watched Jane spin about and scurry toward the door. When she reached it, she glanced back at her over her shoulder. "Read them," she said fearfully. "Read them, *quickly*!"

Mary watched her go, then glanced at the ivory casket. Deciding time was of importance here, she hurried into the nearby drawing room, satisfied herself that no one was about, and sat down on a sofa to open the box.

The hinges on the box creaked, indicating it had probably seen little recent use. Inside, she spied a pile of what appeared to be some very old letters, their stale-smelling musty pages indicating years of disuse9. She took the first in her hand and began to read....

Brett stood on the terrace behind the Hastings's E-shaped Elizabethan manor house and watched as an elegantly coiffed and begowned Elizabeth fussed with an arrangement of summer flowers in a vase on one of the nearby tables. Yes, Elizabeth certainly was beautiful, he mused, as his eyes ran over her ice-blue gown fashioned in the latest mode, but cold... haughtily and distantly cold. He stifled a shudder as he thanked Heaven for the turn of events that had brought Ashleigh into his life and saved him from a life shared with this winter.

"It's not like you to be nervous over hostessing some simple country celebrations, Elizabeth," he said. "Even something as elaborate as what I'm sure you've planned for today." He gestured at the array of perfectly decorated outdoor tables on the terrace, each of them covered by a snow-white damask tablecloth and set up for luncheon with matching, paper-thin china, ornate silverware and sparkling Waterford crystal.

Elizabeth frowned at the bouquet she'd rearranged a dozen times, then pulled her hands away and forced a smile. She chastised herself for forgetting that her former fiancé was a man who rarely missed anything that went on about him. She'd have to be more careful. Auntie Meg had been very particular about the necessity of keeping Brett busy here at the Manor, and she had no wish to foil her godmother in carrying out those instructions.

Of course, as to *why* she was to do this, Elizabeth had no idea. Margaret had simply stated that it was imperative that Brett be kept away from his own estate, and the dowager's cottage in particular, today. But she'd hinted at the fact that, once the day was over, the duke might yet again become free to marry in the future, and that was enough for Elizabeth; despite his betrayal, she still longed to be Brett's duchess. Indeed, hardly a night went by when she didn't dream of it, though the dreams more closely resembled nightmares since he'd returned to England with that little usurper!

But it had also been part of some secret plan of Margaret's that they pretend to befriend the little black-haired bitch, and Elizabeth had gone along with this. If Auntie Meg had a need to keep secrets, there was likely good reason for it. Auntie Meg was clever; in fact, they didn't come any more clever than her godmother. If she had a plan to deliver Brett into her hands again, Elizabeth had no doubt that it would work and she would obey her unquestioningly, even blindly, to see it effected.

Now, as she smiled at Brett, her mind fastened on the need to keep him from suspecting anything. "Oh, Brett, darling, it's just like you to read me like a book. But I have every reason to be a trifle nervous. I've never given a fête for a duchess before. And besides, you know why you're here. I'd simply *die* if father were to imbibe too many spirits and pass out in the middle of things!"

Brett grimaced in distaste. "Yes, well, speaking of his rum-loving lordship, where is he?"

"Ah, upstairs in the library," she answered quickly. "Shall I take you to him?"

\* \* \*

Ashleigh thanked the groom who'd driven her to the dowager's cottage and watched him turn the team of matched grays and head back to the Hall. She saw Jonathan Busby and Tom Blecker working on the picket fence that enclosed the front garden.

"Good morning to you, Mr. Blecker, Jonathan!" she called.

Both men paused in their work, old Tom pulling on his forelock in the old fashioned gesture of respect while young Jonathan merely gave a slight bow, then grinned and waved.

At that moment the cottage's front door opened, and Lady Margaret came out. She was followed by her abigail, who carried a tray in her hands; the tray bore a pair of tankards.

"Good morning, my dear," said Margaret. "I see you're on time, as usual. Promptness is a virtue I applaud, you know. I'm so pleased to note your adherence to it. So many of your generation seem to have forgotten the old standards."

"Well—" Ashleigh smiled "—it's really just a matter of common courtesy, as I see it. I wouldn't dream of making someone wait for me." She bit her bottom lip to keep from smiling at her recollection of what had almost made her late this morning, for after her morning lovemaking with her husband, she'd had to race through her toilette to be here on time!

Margaret was mumbling something about there being nothing common about the thing called courtesy as she gestured with a loftily pointed finger for her abigail to carry the tray with the tankards to the men working on the fence. "A cooling drink of my special chilled herb tea for you, gentlemen," she called to the perspiring workmen. "Do pause a moment and refresh yourselves."

Tom and Jonathan each pulled on their forelocks this time, Ashleigh noted, then set down their tools to accept the drinks.

"Dora," Margaret continued to her abigail, "collect the tankards immediately they're finished and scrub them thoroughly before you go out to the rear garden to cut those flowers. I want a fresh bouquet in each room before you leave for your half day, is that clear?"

Dora bobbed a curtsy, murmured, "Yes, m'lady," and stood attentively beside the fence, watching young Jonathan and old Tom quench their thirst.

Margaret chuckled to heself as she joined Ashleigh and nodded in the direction of the lake where the skiff awaited them. "She'll grab those tankards the second they're empty, if I know her! And the flowers will be cut and arranged in record time, too! The lazy slut never fails to do her work in half the time it usually takes her when it precedes her time off. I guarantee she'll reap herself an extra hour today. Ah, servants! They're such a trial!"

Ashleigh refrained from commenting, for her private assessment of Dora's lot was that she was one of the hardest working servants at Ravensford Hall—and the unhappiest. The poor girl ran and fetched for Margaret day and night, and Ashleigh had never once seen her smile.

But, as they neared the little skiff and she was forced to pay heed to Margaret's instructions for entering it, Ashleigh thrust these thoughts aside. After all, Margaret was making every effort to be kind to her, and she felt it was hardly right for her own thoughts to wax ungenerous toward the woman in return.

Mary sat in disbelieving silence as she allowed her eyes to scan once more the letter she'd just read. *It wasn't possible!* It just *wasn't possible!*

But even as her mind attempted to deny what she'd read, she knew it was the truth. The letter was signed by Margaret Westmont and had been penned to "My dearest love, Andrew," in the year 1766. Mary held it in her trembling hands as she digested the words:

My dearest love, Andrew,
We were fortunate, indeed, that my brother's extended stay at his estate in Surrey helped us keep my pregnancy a secret. But your news that Jane bore you a stillborn daughter, though unfortunate, must also be seen as welcome. Of course, I share your grief at the loss of the child, but take heart, my dearest! In a matter of hours—for, yes, I have

egun to labor, even as I write you this letter—I shall be
earing you a child which it will now be infinitely easier to
place in your home as your *legitimate* offspring! I pray it
will be a son, and if what you've been telling me is true, we
should have little trouble placing it in your befuddled,
grief-stricken wife's empty cradle and convincing her it is
hers.

The letter had left off here, then began anew:

Wonderful news, my love! Between the hours of seven and
eight last evening *I bore you twins!* The elder is a boy, and
I have named him David as we agreed on, for a male child;
the second twin, a girl, I've named Caroline, our choice of
a feminine name. As we also agreed, I've arranged for the
midwife we brought down from Glasgow to be driven
home; she leaves just as soon as that deaf-mute girl from
the village is brought to attend me. *No one* must discover
what we've done. . . .

Mary dropped the letter onto her lap, almost too stunned to
ink. David...Caroline...why, those were the Hastings twins
ho— *Caroline!* Caroline had married *Edward* after the di-
orce! But—but that meant that Margaret had stood by and
atched—no, *encouraged*—Edward to wed his own *first
ousin!*

In an unbelievable web of plotting, she and her lover, Lord
ndrew Hastings, had substituted their illegitimate offspring
or Lady Jane's stillborn child and kept it a secret all these
ears!

A secret from all except Jane Hastings, that is. The poor,
retched woman had been kept befuddled through the use of
ertain drugs—for the letter went on to caution Andrew not to
op administering these to his wife for a while yet—"our
erbal brews," Margaret called them. They'd thought her wits
louded sufficiently that she'd not notice what they did. But
omewhere along the line, Jane did discover the truth, the proof
vident in her possession of these letters. Had she come across

them after her husband's death? Hastily, Mary thrust the l
ter aside and went on to read the next....

Brett uttered a sigh of disgust as he viewed the unconsci
figure of Lord Hastings sprawled in an easy chair in the
brary, an empty decanter of spirits on the floor near his feet

"Well, Elizabeth, it seems your father won't be requiring
chaperonage after all. I'd say he's tucked himself neatly aw
and out of your hair for the day."

"Oh, Brett, why must you be so flippant over what is clea
a disaster?" Elizabeth's perfect pink lips twisted in distas
"Oh, why did he have to go and do this?" A cool rage settl
into her gray eyes, turning them into silver slits. "The Ha
ings men have ever been weak! My *father*—" she spoke t'
word as if it were a curse "—my grandfather before him.
Auntie Meg always said it would be up to the *women* in o
family to—" She gave a mirthless laugh. "Ah, but I do ra
ble! And if I'm not mistaken, that's a carriage I hear on tl
drive. Guests are arriving."

"I suggest you see to your guests, then, Elizabeth. I'll su
mon a couple of footmen to carry m'lord to his bed." Bre
threw a final disgusted glance at his host and turned toward tl
door. "After that, I think I'll go down to the lake and watch f
Ashleigh and your godmother. You certainly won't be needin
me around here for—"

"Oh, but you cannot!" Elizabeth exclaimed, clutching h
sleeve. Auntie Meg had been adamant about the need to kee
the duke busy here, to keep him away from his wife at all cost
and the thought of failing Margaret in so simple a task mc
mentarily filled Elizabeth with dread. It had shown in her ton
of voice and, too late, she sought to cover her error. "Ah, it
just that I'm so apprehensive about the day being a success
Brett," she said, recovering herself. "I really need you here t
give me moral support."

Brett studied her face intently for a moment, wondering wha
had given rise to the alarm in her voice. Elizabeth, in need c
moral support for a social gathering? *Not bloody likely!* But i
it wasn't the festivities she was worried about, what was it?

decided to test her. "I'm sure that's my mother's car-
coming up the drive. She assured me she'd be arriving
ly after me. I'm sure she'd be more than happy to lend you
ah, moral support you need, Elizabeth. I'll ask her for you,
u like."

izabeth had sensed his doubts and fought the panic that
atened as she sought to allay them. They had left the li-
y now, and she hurried to keep up with his long strides,
ag, "But Brett, my chief worry is that Ashleigh will arrive
soon—before we've had a chance to settle everyone suffi-
ly, to make our surprise effective. If she spies you waiting
ier across the lake, she may wish to hurry across, and that
ld spoil our timing. We really ought to leave her in Lady
garet's capable hands, don't you think?"

rett paused a moment. He turned and looked at her. *Mar-
t's capable hands?* Why did that phrase cause chills to run
is spine? Suddenly he realized that it was imperative, for
nore than a satisfaction of his curiosity, that he discover
t Elizabeth was up to. Or perhaps what *Elizabeth and
garet were up to!*

Elizabeth," he said in a tone that brooked no argument,
mmon those footmen to remove your father to his cham-
and then follow me to your small drawing room—now. You
I are going to have a little chat."

lary's hands clenched the yellowed letter so hard, the
chment began to crumble. *God in Heaven!* she thought.
v could I have been so blind?

ler eyes focused on a passage that leaped up at her from the
e.

)o you not think, my darling, that this backhand I've de-
eloped for these secret missives is terribly clever? Since I
o longer sign my name, it should be impossible for any-
ne to connect them with me in the event they are inter-
epted. I urge you to do the same when you write to me,
or secrecy is imperative.

The backhand the unsigned letter spoke of was identi
that of the forged notes that had falsely implicated Mary
adulterous affair more than twenty-seven years ago! And
of the characters resembled the forehanded script of the
lier, signed letter. *Margaret Westmont* had been the one
engineered her disgrace and exile! She'd long ago susp
Margaret as the culprit but after arriving back here at the
and noticing Margaret's penmanship was in a *forehand*, s
the matter drop and reluctantly dismissed her suspicions—
that she'd been!

But even that old injury to her had not been the wor
Margaret's scheming. The rest of this letter, and several
came after it, were apparently written in response to her
er's pleas that she cease her scheming "to place one of my
direct line in the ducal seat. The dukedom ought to have
the firstborn's," the backhand went on to say, "and I inte
rectify the injustice of an accident of gender by placing
correct heirs in the Hall."

A bitter smile found its way to Mary's lips. *So much for
guising your identity through use of a backhand, Margaret,*
thought. *Any schoolchild could put two and two together
discern who wrote this by its dire contents!*

But suddenly the smile gave way to a look of horror as
eyes dropped to the page of the final letter. It was writte
response to the news that Lord Andrew was dying. He had
parently penned a deathbed plea that his inamorata cease
quest to unseat the present duke's line, and she had answe

I reject your assessment that God punished us by killin
Edward and our Caroline and dear little Linley in th
carriage intended for Brett. And of course I join with yo
in grieving for them, but now we must consider the fu
ture, or their deaths will have been in vain.

Installing D. is out of the question. He is far too *weak*
But his daughter, our young E., shows promise, and I in
tend to place our hopes in her—by making sure she *wea
the current heir*! So you see, my darling, you need n
longer fear over my plans for B. as something too mon

ous to contemplate. The boy will live now, for we must
n his line to ours. The only danger will come to those
o might stand in the way of that union....

ry's hands began to tremble so badly, she dropped the
and clenched them into fists to still the tremors. The D.
e letter was, of course, the drunken Lord David. Like-
E. referred to Lady Elizabeth—and B.! B. was Brett—*for
n the carriage that accidentally killed Margaret's daugh-
nd grandson had been intended! The heinous bitch had
to murder Brett when he was but an innocent child!*
fling the bile that rose to her throat when she was truly
to digest this, Mary glanced down at the letter one more
and forced her benumbed brain to focus on its contents
. The words, "those who might stand in the way," flew up
, and she froze for one terrible instant, then jumped to her

hleigh! The one who stood in the way now was *Ashleigh*,
Brett's wife was at this very moment alone with— *"Oh, my
!"* Mary choked, running for the door. *I've got to get to the*

hleigh tied the periwinkle-blue silk ribbons of her bonnet
rely under her chin. She was glad now she'd brought the
net along, for the sun's rays were strong, casting a blind-
glare on the water, and she'd been squinting as she endeav-
to watch Margaret's expert rowing.
e marveled at the older woman's strength as she wielded
oars. They were halfway across the lake now, with the
tings dock just coming into view, and it had taken Mar-
t almost no time at all to get them there.
uddenly the motion of the oars ceased, and Ashleigh
ced up from the periwinkle folds of her lap where she'd
smoothing a wrinkle in the silk fabric.
er eyes found Margaret's face, and for a moment, what she
ght she saw made her shiver. The smile on Margaret's lips
ked positively feral!

But now Margaret was smiling pleasantly at her—v
she?—as she paused in her rowing.

"I'm awfully sorry, my dear, but my hands, I fear, ar
ribly unconditioned for this sport these days. They pai
terribly right now, and I believe I've begun to blister."

"Oh..." said Ashleigh, "oh, dear! Is there anything
do? I—"

"As a matter of fact you can, Ashleigh, child. It really
very difficult to get the gist of rowing. If I instruct you, I'm
you can get us to the other side."

"Well... I don't know... I—"

"Of course you can, my dear! You're far younger tha
and stronger, I'm certain, despite your diminutive size!
you *are* wearing gloves!"

Ashleigh glanced down at the delicate kid gloves she
and had her doubts about their effectiveness, but forced
self to shove these aside. If Lady Margaret had been able to
them this far and was now troubled by blisters, who was sl
be selfish and refuse to pitch in?

"Very well, Lady Margaret—" she smiled "—I'll give
try."

"Good girl," said Margaret. "Now, all we need do i
change seats carefully...."


Brett raced out the front door of Cloverhill Manor just a:
Earl of Ranleagh's carriage was pulling to a halt on the dr

"Christopher!" he cried. "Take me on down the far sid
the drive, to the lake!" He pulled open the carriage door
entered quickly, to the astonishment of the earl and his c
panion, Lady Pamela. Ignoring their bewilderment, Brett s
his head out and called to the driver, "Take this carriage
past the house and follow it to the left at the fork. And hurr

To Christopher and Pamela he added, "I'll explain as we
but I have every reason to believe Ashleigh's in danger! We
got to reach the lake—*fast!*"


Mary held on to Finn's shaggy neck as the barouche vee
sharply around the final curve on the drive leading to the d

s cottage. She'd spied the dog basking in the sun near the
ache as it waited outside the Hall, its driver prepared to
her to Cloverhill Manor, and she'd decided to take the
ound along. She feared Margaret might have Ashleigh
out onto the lake by now—*if, indeed, she's even allowed
o live this long,* she thought with a shudder—and Finn's
y as a swimmer might be needed.

Oh, I pray I'm right!" she whispered to the big dog. *"I pray
 not too late!"*

hleigh felt the small skiff wobble as she maneuvered to
ange seats with Margaret. She stooped to clutch the sides
e boat to steady herself. As she did so, there was a shadow
ovement before her, and then she felt herself shoved, hard,
all at once, she was toppling into the cold waters of the

shriek of triumph, and then a burst of mad laughter met
ears as she hit the water just as an impossible realization
ded her brain: *Oh my God! Margaret pushed me in!* But
she felt herself sinking and all coherent thought fled as her
ncts took over, and she resurfaced and began to tread wa-
trying desperately to acclimatize herself under the sodden
s of her bonnet.

Ah!" Margaret's voice rang out. "So the poor fish can
n, can she? Well, 'twill do you no good, you little gutter-
e! I mean to finish you this time, and then the dukedom will
to mine! *Mine*, do you hear?" And with a vicious shriek,
pulled one of the oars from its lock and raised it with two
ds over her head, like a club.

shleigh dove beneath the surface, narrowly avoiding the oar
 crashed onto the water's surface near her head, her mind
ing with a single, sickening thought: *Margaret's trying to
me!* She wondered how long she could manage to dodge the
ally aimed weapon. The heavy, sodden folds of her gown
e tangled about her legs, dragging her down, making
nming nearly impossible. Out of her blurred vision she saw
oar wielded aloft again.

Then, suddenly, she heard a familiar bark, and spied
shaggy head in the water, a few yards away.

A shriek from Margaret told her her assailant had also
the dog, who was fast approaching the boat. The oar cr
a second time, and this was met by Finn's sharp yelp of p

"*Oh, God, Finn—no!*" Ashleigh gasped. She swam
sily in the dog's direction and saw her beloved hound
gling in the water, a bloody gash on the side of his head
the tip of the oar had slashed him. And the oar was now
thrust at him, like a battering ram!

But Finn was not finished yet. With a menacing grov
lunged through the water, straight for the advancing oar.
next instant Finn's giant jaws had hold of the oar's blade,
giving it a sharp yank, he pulled Margaret with it into the

Margaret screamed as she hit the water, then began to t
about in desperation when she felt herself sinking. "Help!"
choked. "Help me! *I cannot swim!*"

Even as the awareness of what Margaret had been atte
ing throbbed in her brain, Ashleigh would have swum to
her, but her skirts were badly twisted about her legs now
she could barely move. Water seemed to be everywhere—a
her, around her, everywhere. She felt herself being sucke
exorably downward; the last thing that appeared to her fa
consciousness was a blurry, dark-gray shadow, and then
that faded and there was nothing.

# *Epilogue*

Brett watched his eighteen-month-old son toddle over to his older sister and hand her a bunch of violets he'd picked, minus their stems, of course. Marileigh, now almost four, smiled sweetly at the sibling she adored—and who adored her in return.

"Why, thank you, John," she murmured. "And I shall help you pick a bouquet for Mama. She loves violets, too, you know."

Brett's contented gaze fell on his wife. Ashleigh . . . how he loved her! She sat on the grass, several yards away, surrounded by a group of youngsters who were listening attentively to a story she told them. Her eyes raised, caught her husband's gaze and she smiled at him. Brett returned the smile with a look that promised more, once they were alone.

But he really didn't mind sharing his wife with the children, both their own offspring and the eight they'd adopted in a process that began almost four years ago—a process that came out of a joint decision to follow the example of his mother, and take into their home orphans whom no one else wanted.

His mind drifted back over the four years, savoring the happiness they'd shared. Theirs was a blissful marriage, their home a happy one, filled with children's laughter as well as their own.

He allowed his thoughts to wander further as his eyes fell on the lake in the distance. The lake. Where it had all almost ended.

He shivered, recalling that terrible day when he'd almost not been in time—when he'd barely reached his unconscious wife in the water and then managed to swim with her to the shore, just as Christopher had done with the failing Finn.

Christopher's driver had been able to pull Margaret ashore as well, but the evil madwoman—for such was the only way he could allow himself to think of her—had already drowned. And a blessing it had been, he mused—not for the first time these past years. For Margaret would surely have been forced to face justice before the bar, had she lived, and even he would have been hard-pressed to see her hang. And hang she would have, for the murders of her own child and grandchild years ago, not to mention Edward, Brett's father.

His mind passed quickly over the remaining events of that day in June, nearly four years ago... the shocked staff and arriving guests at Cloverhill Manor, the hysterical weeping of Elizabeth who cried over and over, "I didn't *know* ... *I didn't know*...."

And then there had been his mother, her face white with concern, as she flew into the upstairs chamber where they'd taken the dazed, but otherwise unharmed, Ashleigh and bandaged the cut on Finn's head. Mary had arrived at the lake too late to stop Margaret, but she'd found Tom Blecker and young Jonathan heavily drugged from the tea they'd been served, and hastily sent Finn into the water to "Fetch Ashleigh!" By the time she managed to hurry to the Manor in the barouche, Mary was nearly hysterical with fear—until she at last assured herself that Ashleigh was unharmed, and then, with Lady Jane Hastings's help, Mary had explained what she'd learned from the letters, and the ghastly puzzle of Margaret Westmont's crimes had been pieced together for them all.

Brett's grandfather's sister, it seemed, had never gotten over the fact that she, the firstborn twin, had been denied the dukedom by virtue of having been born female. And her twisted mind had spewed and plotted evil from the time she'd been old enough, apparently, to think she could install one of her own in place of John Westmont's line.

Lady Jane was now a contented dowager, happy to play fond auntie to Elizabeth's twins—for Elizabeth had been taken under Mary's wing following the tragedy and had at last found contentment herself by wedding an Italian duke. But Jane Hastings had astounded them during the inquest by swearing that, before he died, her husband had confessed everything to her, including the fact that Margaret had deliberately gotten herself with child by him, seducing him with the intent of bearing an heir she could somehow insinuate into her brother's dukedom.

But when Jane would have gone to the authorities to tell what she knew, Margaret, whom she had foolishly confronted with the truth, had threatened to end Jane's life if she dared to speak to anyone of it again. But Jane had prudently saved Andrew's letters and not told Margaret she had them. Then, finally, after all her years of silence, Jane had dared to bring them to light in the face of some encouragement—encouragement in the form of the kindnesses of a small slip of a girl named Ashleigh.

Ashleigh . . . Brett's mind savored the syllables of her name as his turquoise eyes again found her laughing face amidst the children's in the grass. How he loved her—today, it seemed, more than ever.

Next week they'd be welcoming Megan and Patrick back to England, and their two small sons as well. It was the first trip abroad for the St. Clares since they'd left to live in America, although he and Ashleigh had sailed to Virginia to visit them a little over two years ago. Brett grinned to himself. Young John had even been conceived there!

Brett's expression was grim as thoughts of the St. Clares forced him into the unpleasant past again. After the constables arrived to investigate the circumstances surrounding Margaret's death, a thorough search of Ravensford Hall turned up a diary written in the now infamous backhand. Hidden in a secret compartment in a desk Margaret used in the dowager's cottage, it not only confirmed the substance of the letters to Lord Andrew, but revealed that it had also been Lady Margaret who'd set the fire that killed the parents of Ashleigh and

Patrick. She'd learned of Mary's clandestine visits to Kent through an informant who'd had loose free-trading connections with the St. Clares, and fearing Mary's abduction of Brett—who was then essential to her crazed plans—she'd coolly plotted to kill Mary!

Suddenly a voice from the present shut out the disturbing memories.

"Father, Father!" Marileigh called as she came running up to him. At her side was Brett, a ten-year-old rescued from the slums of London where he'd been forced by poverty to work as a chimney sweep. The lad was bright—sharp as a tack, Brett thought—and his handsome young face glowed with health— a far cry from the emaciated, haunted look it had held three years ago, when they'd found him.

"Father," Marileigh continued, "Brett made a bargain with me that I could ride his pony if I managed to keep my dress clean when I played with Finn and Lady Dimples, and I *have*," she indicated, holding out the skirts of her sprigged muslin frock, "and now he says he's not so sure he's going to keep to his end of it!"

Brett bestowed a fatherly frown on young Brett, then glanced over the two children's heads at the advancing figure of his wife before returning his attention to the boy.

"Brett, did you strike such a bargain?" he questioned.

Brett squirmed uncomfortably, then stared at his toes. "I did, sir," he murmured.

"Well, then, you know you'll have to honor it," Brett told him. "And take heart, lad, for it might turn out to be a very good thing." Brett's eyes met Ashleigh's as she stood behind the children. "You just might, when you've made a bargain, receive far more from it than you ever dreamed of.... You might just find a miracle."

\* \* \* \* \*

# *Harlequin*® *Historical*

## HARLEQUIN HISTORICALS
## ARE GETTING BIGGER!

This fall, Harlequin Historicals will bring you bigger books. Along with our traditional high-quality historicals, we will be including selected reissues of favorite titles, as well as longer originals.

Reissues from popular authors like Elizabeth Lowell, Veronica Sattler and Marianne Willman.

Originals like ACROSS TIME—an historical time-travel by Nina Beaumont, UNICORN BRIDE—a medieval tale by Claire Delacroix, and SUSPICION—a title by Judith McWilliams set during Regency times.

Leave it to Harlequin Historicals to deliver enduring love stories, larger-than-life characters, and history as you've never before experienced it.

And now, leave it to Harlequin Historicals, to deliver even more!

**Look for *The Bargain* by Veronica Sattler in October, *Pieces of Sky* by Marianne Willman in November, and *Reckless Love* by Elizabeth Lowell in December.**

**When the only time you have for yourself is...**

Christmas is such a busy time—with shopping, decorating, writing cards, trimming trees, wrapping gifts....

When you do have a few *stolen moments* to call your own, treat yourself to a brand-new *short* novel. Relax with one of our Stocking Stuffers— or with all six!

Each STOLEN MOMENTS title is a complete and original contemporary romance that's the perfect length for the busy woman of the nineties! Especially at Christmas...

And they make perfect **stocking stuffers**, too! (For your mother, grandmother, daughters, friends, co-workers, neighbors, aunts, cousins—all the other women in your life!)

Look for the STOLEN MOMENTS display in December

STOCKING STUFFERS:

**HIS MISTRESS** Carrie Alexander
**DANIEL'S DECEPTION** Marie DeWitt
**SNOW ANGEL** Isolde Evans
**THE FAMILY MAN** Danielle Kelly
**THE LONE WOLF** Ellen Rogers
**MONTANA CHRISTMAS** Lynn Russell

HSM2

**WORLDWIDE LIBRARY**

# *Harlequin® Historical*

Nora O'Shea had fled to Arizona seeking freedom,
but could she ever find love as a mail-order bride?

## MARIANNE WILLMAN

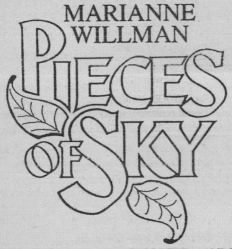

From the author of THE CYGNET and ROSE RED,
ROSE WHITE comes a haunting love story full of
passion and power, set against the backdrop of the
new frontier.

Coming in November 1993 from Harlequin

Don't miss it! Wherever Harlequin books are sold.

# *Harlequin® Historical*

From *New York Times* bestselling author

**Elizabeth Lowell**

**Reckless Love**

The powerful story of two people as brave and free as
the elusive wild mustang which both had sworn to
capture.

A Harlequin Historicals Release
December 1993